THE
LIES OF
MORTALS

MALARIE
WEBER

First edition 2025

Paperback ISBN: 979-8-9923264-0-6

Ebook ISBN: 979-8-9923264-1-3

Cover design by Franziska Stern @coverdungeonrabbit

Map design and scene break artwork by Malarie Weber

Prologue artwork and chapter header artwork by Alice Cao @alicecaoillustration

Character Art by Eirlysa Lawrence @winterofherdiscontent

Edited by Caitlin Lengerich @chronicledbycait

This is a work of fiction. All characters, names, places, events, and incidents in this publication are the product of the author's imagination or are used fictitiously, and any resemblance to real persons, living or dead, or events, or locales is entirely coincidental.

For a list of content warnings, please see the Author's Note.

AUTHOR'S NOTE

THANK YOU from the bottom of my heart for choosing to read The Lies of Mortals. I was craving a particular type of fantasy book—one that was both magical and romantic, yet complex and gripping, so I decided to write it. The Lies of Mortals is just the beginning of my passion project, and I hope you enjoy every word of it.

This book is for mature readers who love high fantasy, intricate world building and multi-faceted plots, delicious banter, slow burn romance, meddling gods and fates, he falls first, fated mates, prophecy, chosen one, darkness and light, good vs. evil, hidden identities, enemies to lovers, one bed, found family, and books that are part of a series (hint hint).

Content warning: This book contains descriptions of death and the death of loved ones (on-page), wartime death, blood and gore, violence, sexually explicit content (on-page), attempted sexual assault (on-page), explicit language.

You are encouraged to look for the many instances of foreshadowing and "easter eggs" in this book.

Happy reading!

GLOSSARY

THE FIVE FAE COURTS AND TERRITORIES

ELANDREW *(ELL-AN-DREW)*
High Lord Killian's Territory, home of the Woodland Court.

CALLEDAN *(CAL-LUH-DAN)*
High Lord Niall's Territory, home of the Mountain Court.

VAHRENHALL *(VAH-REN-HALL)*
High Lord Vanir's territory, home of the Highland Court.

BENMOOR *(BIN-MOORE)*
High Lord Ramil's territory, home of the Desert Court.

DRASTIA *(DRAW-STEE-UH)*
High Lord Laurent's territory, home of the Arctic Court.

AGE / TIME

1 Human year = approx. 15 fae years (ex: 30 HY = 450 FY)
Time is linear.

GLOSSARY

PLACES

GAIA *(GUY-UH)* - The world inhabited by humans, and the fae, of which the god-king Karios reigns supreme.

ANBRYA *(AN-BREE-UH)* - The fae realm.

BELTHRIA *(BELL-THREE-UH)* - The human realm.

GALENAGH *(GAL-EN-AW)* - Capital city of the human realm.

SALTERRA *(SAL-TERR-UH)* - Region in the north that is desolate and dry, known as "The Wastelands."

THE NEVESHIR ISLES *(NEH-VEH-SHEER)* - Located off the coast of Vahrenhall and Calledan. Home to the Witches and The Dionachs.

THE GREAT WOOD - Human forest bordering The Veil on the west side of Belthria.

THE ELDERWOOD - Located at the base of the mountains in Calledan, where the territory meets Vahrenhall. The area is home to the oldest temple, built by the Ancient Fae, and was the place where a foreign goddess descended long ago.

THE VEIL - The dividing line between the human realm and the fae realm, created by the fae for separation and protection.

THE SPRINGS OF SEPHTA - Sacred springs of the Ancient Fae. There is a spring in every fae territory.

GLOSSARY

IMPORTANT TERMS

THE ADORNERS - Members of each fae court who oversee archives, records, and historical documentation, and are the only beings granted the power to "shroud" individuals.

THE ALATYR *(AL-UH-TAIR)* - The stones given to the Elders of the Ancient Fae by the fates. Five stones, five Elders.

BATTLE OF PARRADIOM *(PUH-RAD-EE-UM)* - The first battle fought between Lyceius, the fae, and the humans. During this battle, Lyceius's talisman is taken from him at the hands of Karios. *Parradiom* means "betrayer/traitor."

BATTLE OF OLETHROS *(OH-LEH-THROWS)* - The second battle fought between Lyceius and the fae. During this battle, the High Lord Evander unleashes his power, wiping out a majority of the enemy, as well as his own forces, and himself. *Olethros* means "destruction."

BATTLE OF GABBATH *(GAH-BATH)* - The third battle fought between Lyceius and the fae. *Gabbath* means "stepping stones," as this battle took place near the step-stone-like area at the base of the mountains of Calledan.

THE SEIDR *(SAY-DER)* - The record of the Ancient Fae, written and bound in book form. There is a copy in each fae territory. The Seidr teaches the purpose of everything the fae believe in, and the practices with which to hone their magic. Designated Elders take responsibility for each book and carry on the knowledge.

THE SHROUD *(SHH-R-OW-D)* - An adornment in the form of inked markings, given to elite fae warriors who perform a selfless act for the greater good. Each shroud is unique to the fae upon whom it is marked. It circles one's neck across the collarbones and upper chest, out to each shoulder, and circling back down across the shoulder blades. To be shrouded is to wear a distinction above all others and is a great honor.

GLOSSARY

THE TALISMANS - A god's talisman is what allows them to focus their power in a more precise and potent state.

EURYPHAESSA *(YUR-EE-FAY-SUH)* - The Ancient name given to the Bringer of Light. It means white light of a star, divine and wide-shining. A cold, deadly, kinetic energy.

LUMERI *(LOO-MARE-EE)* - The fae Festival of Light, celebrated by all courts in late March/early April, when spring dawns on the territories. Each court celebrates on different days due to the sun's positioning. The Woodland Court celebrates on March 24th, The Highland Court celebrates on March 27th, The Mountain Court celebrates on March 29th, The Arctic Court celebrates on March 30th, and The Desert Court celebrates on April 1st. "Laetus Lumeri" means *Happy Lumeri/Happy celebration of light.*

BEINGS & CREATURES

HUMANS - Beings who have no magic capability.

THE FAE - Beings who are gifted with magic and varying levels of power. They can have life spans lasting upwards of two thousand years if they are not harmed or compromised. But eventually, their bodies will grow weary, their power will fade with time, and death will claim them. They are descendants of the Ancient Fae.

THE ANCIENT FAE - The Ancient Fae lived and inhabited the world long before the first High Lords ever existed, and were the first form of fae on Gaia. Their magic was wild and untamed, being drawn straight from the earth itself (Old Magic). Eventually, they drained the earth of its power, and Karios had to intervene, changing their physical form so that they no longer required the earth for a magic supply. Very few of the Ancient line remain, but their lifespans surpass even that of the more modern fae.

THE GODS - A primordial assembly of god-kings and the panel of gods that rule under each of them. They work harmoniously with the fates to oversee their creations and the course of life.

GLOSSARY

THE FATES - Three primordial sisters, Delyth, Kaina, and Sephta, who weave the destinies of all living beings across the universe.

THE CHESHM ZADAN *(CHEH-SHUM ZUH-DON)* - Very rare beings that carry a special gift. Time and space appear to pulse around them. This distortion —referred to as "The Aura"—is like a second set of eyes and ears, capable of seeing and hearing things that even the most gifted beings can not. Because of this, they are highly coveted by all courts.

THE DREKI *(DREH-KEY)* - Huge, winged beasts, that are five times the size of a horse. They have four legs with deadly sharp claws, and scales covering their entire body down to their long tails—which are covered in spikes. They can breathe fire. The species hails from Vahrenhall, in the highland hills.

THE WITCHES - Born of the witch goddess, who came to Gaia from another distant world. They can sense glamours and enchantments, and they thrive in the darkness.

THE DIONACHS
- DIONACH: *(DIE-UN-OCH)*: Means guardian/defender. They are descendants of witches. Dionachs are beings that are bred solely for protecting others. They can protect anyone at will, but their true purpose lies in finding their Dionam and ensuring they are protected. Dionachs are born with markings along the temples of their face that glow red like fiery embers during battle, or when they are pulling from their well of power. They are susceptible to death only by a blade/arrow through the heart, or decapitation. They do not bleed, and have instant healing abilities. They have heightened sensory receptors, giving them hyperawareness.
- DIONAM: *(DIE-UN-OM)*: The being who is fated to each Dionach.

THE KERES *(KEY-REES)* - Mutated creatures created by Lyceius; the first of his experiments. Abominations, made from the product of his mingling with humans. They feed on power and are drawn to it.

GLOSSARY

MAGIC / POWER

THE MAGIC / POWER SYSTEM - All magic requires payment in the form of power. There must be a balance. A fae can use magic, but only until their power is depleted, at which point they will need to rest to replenish their power reserve.

FAE MAGIC VS. FAE POWER - Magic is a particular set of skills that the fae are born with. Their power is the level at which it is used / the extent that it can be used—or its effectiveness.

GLAMOURS / GLAMOURING - A glamour is a way to mask or cover up one's appearance.

OLD MAGIC - Old Magic is what was woven into the world from its creation. It is no longer common practice, nor is it common knowledge. Spells can be cast using Old Magic, by reciting the ancient words.

GLOSSARY

CHARACTER GUIDE

ALERIS *(UH-LAIR-ISS)* - One of the founding brothers of Calledan (deceased).

AMARNA *(UH-MAR-NUH)* - The Ancient Fae Elder of Calledan.

AREMIS *(AIR-UH-MISS)* - One of Niall's Trium. Second in command in the Mountain Court.

ARRDUINA *(ARE-DUE-EE-NUH)* - The goddess of the forest and the hunt.

AUREN EVERTON *(ARE-EN EVER-TON)* - The female main character. This book is written from her point of view/perspective.

PRINCE ALSTON *(ALL-STUN)* - The human realm's current prince.

BRECK *(BR-ECK)* - Emissary and cousin to the High Lord Killian.

KING BRODERICK *(BRAH-DER-ICK)* - The human realm's current king.

CARINA *(CUH-REE-NUH)* - The goddess of patience and grace.

QUEEN CORRINE *(CORE-INN)* - The human realm's current queen.

DELYTH *(DELL-ITH)* - One of the three fates.

EATHRIL *(EE-THRILL)* - An ancient entity who serves the Mountain Court as an interrogator—of sorts.

ELSPETH *(ELL-SPETH)* - The Ancient Fae Elder of Elandrew.

KING EMMERIC *(EM-MER-ICK)* - Ancient human king (deceased).

ERIK *(ERR-ICK)* - King's Guard competitor.

ERYX *(ERR-ICKS)* - The god of the sky and night.

EVANDER *(EE-VAN-DER)* - Niall's great grandfather. Known as The Dark One. A previous High Lord of Calledan (deceased).

FALLON *(FAL-LON)* - Son of Ramil, and rightful heir to Benmoor. Brother to Morah.

FARELO NEMAR *(FAR-EL-LOW NEH-MAR)* - King's Guard competitor.

FERHAN *(FAIR-HAAN)* - Ramil's advisor.

FOLQUIN *(FOL-QUINN)* - Niall's trusted spy. A shifter.

GARETH *(GARE-ETH)* - The Woodland Court's tailor.

GAVRIN *(GAV-REN)* - Evander's father. A previous High Lord of Calledan (deceased).

KAINA *(KAIN-UH)* - One of the three fates.

KARIOS *(CARE-EE-OHS)* - The god of creation. Primordial god-king of Gaia.

KILLIAN *(KILL-EE-EN)* - The High Lord of Elandrew.

LAURENT *(LAW-RENT)* - The High Lord of Drastia.

LEONORA *(LEN-OR-UH)* - Ladies maid in the king's castle.

LIAM EVERTON *(LEE-UM EVER-TON)* - Auren's brother.

LYCEIUS *(LIE-SAY-US)* - The (fallen) god of light, who rebelled against Karios.

MAESON *(MAY-SUN)* - A fae friend of Auren, Niall, and the Trium.

GLOSSARY

MARIS *(MARE-IS)* - Auren's mother (deceased).

MORAH *(MORE-UH)* - Ramil's daughter.

NIALL *(NYE-ALL)* - The High Lord of Calledan.

RAMIL *(RAH-MIL)* - The High Lord of Benmoor.

REMIC *(REM-ICK)* - A Dionach, and one of Niall's Trium.

ROIRDAN *(ROAR-DEN)* - One of Niall's Trium. Commander of the Mountain Court's armies.

SENNA *(SIN-UH)* - The Lady of Drastia. Laurent's mate.

SEPHTA *(SEFF-TUH)* - One of the three fates.

SILAS BELSPEAR *(SIGH-LAS BELL-SPEAR)* - King's Guard competitor.

SORSCHA *(SORE-SHH-UH)* - An Ancient Fae under the employ of the Woodland House.

SYROS *(SIGH-ROSE)* - Also known as Syros The Adorner, keeper of the archives.

THIAGO *(THEE-AH-GO)* - Auren's father (deceased).

VANIR *(VAN-EAR)* - The High Lord of Vahrenhall.

VERDI *(VER-DEE)* - The Ancient Fae who was loyal to Evander and oversaw efforts to help him in his struggle with his power (deceased).

WESTON *(WEST-IN)* - A high ranking guard at the castle in Galenagh.

THE
HUMAN
REALM

BELTHRIA

THE
GREAT
WOOD

GALENAGH

◇ TERRITORY GATE

⫼ THE VEIL

For my husband, who has shown me what true love is.

And for all those out there who know they are destined for more . . .

Rise.

PROLOGUE
The beginnings

AT THE DAWN OF TIME, the primordial assembly of god-kings emerged from the midst of chaos alongside the three fates, and together, they brought order to the tumultuous expanse that is the universe.

Under their divine, uncontested rule, the god-kings created what they desired, each on a world of their own, stringing the universe upon a cord of order and stability. Each world boasted its own laws, its own gods, and its own unique beings that thrived under a variety of different conditions.

Karios, one of the great primordial god-kings, was given charge of the world of Gaia.

He breathed his life's-breath unto its barren expanse, and where it rolled over desolate plains, glittering springs surged. Mountains broke forth from the earth, splitting the air, reaching up with wild, jagged faces toward the sky above. Trees and vegetation in every variety sprang into existence throughout a multitude of climates.

His breath burst through the sky, dotting it with creatures that took to the currents with wings of all shapes and sizes, screeching and singing their vivacious cries. It rippled through the waters, and life swirled within, making homes in the salty shallows, and in the great deep.

And finally, Karios's breath tumbled over the dirt, drawing forth one life form. Then another.

Two species were given dominion over Gaia—the fae, and the humans.

The fae, born to harness and wield magic, drew it from the ground they were given, while the humans cultivated their ground with crops and brought forth its bounty. They were gifted with free-will, and existed harmoniously, each inhabiting their respective realms, interacting when needed, when wanted, or when the fates saw to it that they should.

Karios manifested a panel of gods to reign under him—brothers and sisters that he could rule with, who answered to him, and to whom he bestowed the command over certain aspects of his world.

Creation thrived throughout the universe. The three fates—ever in harmony with the god-kings—stood watch over it all, weaving their will and orchestrating a balance throughout all of existence.

But as time stretched on, the seeds of discord took root and began to show their faces in many corners of the cosmos.

One god within Karios's panel grew restless in his eternal divinity. Lyceius, the god of light, became covetous, wanting more than what he'd been given. He rebelled against Karios, and his actions sent a rift of chaos through the fae and human realms.

In the midst of the unrest, war was waged, but Karios and the fates could only intervene so much without negating free-will. So, a prophecy was placed upon Gaia. A chosen one would rise, to right the wrongs and bring stability and balance back to the realms.

But threads were unraveling across multiple worlds, and this was just one of many frayed edges in what was once a perfectly woven tapestry of existence.

The prophecy, as recorded in the *Seidr*, reads:

> *With the coming of the dawn,*
> *the fate of all to the fate of one.*
> *A flame of light, a flame of dark,*
> *a golden shroud brought from a spark.*
> *A piece is lost, and then it's worn,*
> *stars and ash bring forth the storm.*
> *Two great powers to bring the change,*
> *the gods will rise upon a new age.*

PART ONE
THE LIES OF MORTALS

1

THE INVITATION

I REMEMBERED THE MOMENT THE SWORD'S TIP SLICED INTO THE SIDE OF my ribs and how the pain burned like fire.

I had fallen to my knees in my stupor, grasping at my shirt and pulling away my hand to witness the bright red blood that clung to my shaking palm. And before I knew it, the man I was defending myself against had raised his sword to land—what would have been—a killing blow. But my hand moved, and I snatched the dagger from his waistband and shoved the blade up into his diaphragm.

I could still see his lifeless body lying in front of me alongside the bodies of my parents. He had no right to be amongst them. Not even in death. I should have made his death last longer—made him writhe in agony for what he had done.

We had been ambushed in our own home. Raiders from another village had come on one of their pillaging runs that were becoming more frequent as the years went by. And that time, they had found our small cottage, on a day when none of us were ready.

It had been my mother's birthday. She and I were preparing a cake while my father and brother tended to chores outside and prepped the meat for dinner. None of us expected the men to come rushing in from the tree line armed and intent on taking what little possessions of value we had. Thankfully, my father always kept a sword on him, and he had taught me to as well.

My brother fought alongside our father, taking on as many of the men outside as they could, while I defended my mother inside our home. But we were swarmed from every angle, and no matter how good you are at wielding a sword, death comes for everyone eventually.

My father had taken a blade to his chest and staggered through the door, clutching his fatal wound. Distracted by my emotions, I barely heard my mother's cry as she was next to taste the sword.

And then that same blade had come for me.

Whether it was by the protection of the gods or the will of the fates, my brother and I survived, and I recovered from my wound.

That was a little over two years ago.

But for a moment, I was back in the aftermath, kneeling in my parents' blood as it flooded the weathered wood floorboards.

I remembered how I'd sat in a daze, staring at the lifeless bodies and overturned furniture, and the look of heartbreak on my brother's face as he burst through the door and beheld the grim scene.

Those painful moments now served as aching reminders. Little shards of shattered memories that stuck with me; spurred my reasoning for training and fighting as more than just a pastime. I would never again be caught off guard. I would never again let the ones I loved be slaughtered around me.

My father had a knack for swordsmanship. A skill he'd been born with, but never pursued as an occupation. He introduced my younger brother and I to the art out of his own love for it, training us to be proficient with both our fists and feet, as well as with a blade of any kind, just as he was. He argued that there might come a time when we would need to use one skill or the other, and he wanted us to be able to hold our own.

From the moment he placed a blade in my hands, I never looked back. I took to sparring and sword fighting like I was born to do so. My father frequently joked that I must have known the techniques in a previous life.

Blessed by the gods, he'd always said.

My brother Liam was decent with a blade, but was too analytical for his own good. He often spent his free time helping me train, despite his constant teasing that I was too pretty to be throwing a punch or swinging a sword.

A woman wasn't supposed to be a fighter. Especially not a petite, attractive young woman like myself. But society's warped concepts were no deterrent to me. As soon as I could, I put my skills to the real test, earning a name for myself during small duels and sparring contests, saving my winnings in hopes of someday traveling the rest of the realm and seeing more than just the same landscape and the same people day in and day out. But those winnings had been plundered during the attack on my family, and Liam and I were left with next to nothing.

After our parents' deaths, Liam dove into his work to keep himself busy and help take his mind off the new reality we lived in. But a carpenter's wages only went so far. My skills quickly became a necessity for us to get by.

While I was thankful for my talent, I always felt that there was more in store for me than just swinging my fists or sword at an opponent for a mere handful of coins in a market-side duel. Like I was meant for more than the dusty makeshift arenas and the split knuckles and occasional busted lip.

But bloodied and bruised helped keep food on the table.

The city of Galenagh held the most paid opportunities each year, seeing as it was the capital city of Belthria and home to the king and queen. Our little village sat on the outskirts of Galenagh, far enough away to live a quiet lifestyle, but close enough to still attend the city's events whenever we pleased.

Galenagh was pleasant. The streets were clean, the stone buildings were still holding strong, and the people were—for the most part—cordial.

The city and castle grounds were nestled up against the beautiful backdrop of The Great Wood, a wooded forest that skirted the entire western and northern edge of our realm. Those woods were also home to The Veil.

The Veil was our boundary line; the territorial divide between the human realm and that of the fae. All humans grew up hearing stories of the fae realm of Anbrya—which bordered ours to the west. Tales of the fae —of their ruthlessness and tricky magic—were ingrained in our memory. Spoken around the dinner table and whispered under candlelight, widening sleepy eyes and filling us with dread. We were warned from a young age to never go seeking The Veil.

Not that we could cross it anyway. Only the fae could. Humans were bound to one side, thanks to our non-magical status. Though, there was a time when The Veil didn't exist and humans and fae occupied their respective realms without quarrel. But that was long ago, in a time before a fallen god waged war against the realms.

The Veil went up at the hands of the fae; a result of the growing tensions between our realms following the war. The generations of humans that came afterward had kept their distance from it out of fear and spite, and their sentiments lingered, passed down in stories that told of the harsh and careless fae.

Then there was the other threat that we humans feared—that which loomed in the north. The god who had rebelled still sulked in the shadows of the land he'd claimed as his own. In his ancient conquest, he'd stolen away dozens of human women, and tainted their wombs to bear him his creatures—soldiers for his army.

The Veil had once kept those creatures at bay, but as time passed, they found ways to breach it. Such occurrences had been more prevalent as of late, and the northern parts of our land suffered their terrors. Whispers of the disturbing scenes that were left behind always set everyone on edge. No one could say for certain what their motive was, or how they'd broken through The Veil, and rumors became muddled amongst an already hapless history of speculation.

One thing was certain: humans always did have a way of formulating stories to best suit their needs.

Despite our fallacies and fears, it was known that the fae had a prophecy. It foretold that one day the lingering darkness in the north would be defeated, and as a result, the realms would be united once more and ushered into a new age—or something along those lines. We humans cared little for a prophecy that was foretold by beings as foreign to us as the fae, and had no hope of seeing that fateful day anytime soon.

I often wondered if at one point, long ago, we would have shared similar beliefs when we dwelled alongside them, instead of the current ideology of fear and mistrust.

The few who did care about the fae's prophecy nowadays weren't enough to entice the rest of us to take interest. Most of those people made up the groups of insurgents, who lived in irrational fear, proclaiming a great change was coming to both realms. They were the ones who had attacked my home and killed my parents.

When they weren't being hunted down by the king, they often conducted raids on smaller villages, pillaging weapons and valuables, killing those who got in their way. They believed that when whatever enemy came calling on us—fae or monster—they could either fight their way out, or bargain for their freedom. Common sense told most of us that if the fae ever did venture back on this side of The Veil, that we—being without power or magic—would stand little to no chance against them, regardless of our valuables.

Thankfully, it was my talent with a sword that held value to me. I knew that skill would get me a lot further than coin or jewels—should I ever encounter another true threat.

Being a woman, I was often regarded as weak or incapable, and most onlookers would laugh when I entered a fight. But by the end of every match they were no longer laughing.

My sword was a part of me. Blood, and even death, no longer fazed me. I'd fought too many times to count, and successfully faced a variety of opponents. Yes, I'd certainly made a name for myself over the past couple of years.

And today, I sharpened my sword, and let the thoughts of that fateful day two years ago wash over me, as I prepared for an entirely new type of fight.

A letter had come two weeks ago, delivered by a messenger wearing the king's royal colors, who shoved the folded paper in my face and hurried off to his next destination.

I'd sat and stared at the bubbly, blood-red seal that puckered the seam of the letter, knowing it could only be one thing.

An invitation.

For the past six years, the king and queen had hosted a tournament at the castle, pitting Belthria's most impressive sword fighters against each other for a chance to earn a prestigious spot amongst the King's Guard. The elite group had been a royal staple since the dawn of the kingdom, with positions only coming available when a member had aged past their prime, or died in the line of duty. But in recent years, the king had begun making efforts to grow the force at an exponential rate, adding multiple new recruits each year.

Those who secured a place within the formidable ranks would leave their former lives behind and be afforded the rights and reputation of a life in the castle, while receiving a healthy pension befitting their duties. The champion who was the most impressive would also get the chance to duel with Prince Alston, an elite swordsman in his own right—having never been bested in a fight.

The offer also boasted an additional incentive: every competitor who accepted the invitation, and competed to the best of their abilities, would receive a handsome bonus—whether they won or lost.

Participation in the tournament was by invitation only, which required that the king had heard of the swordsman's name through their accomplishments and talents. And the fact that I'd received an invitation meant that my skills were paying off.

This invitation, this tournament, could be what I was searching for: the opportunity to become something greater. A chance to be named into a line of swordsmen who were held above the rest. Not to mention the income would be sufficient enough to help my brother live comfortably, and maintain our family home and property. And the bonus it offered would replace what I'd lost in the raid, and then some. I would be a fool not to compete.

I glanced down at the letter bathed in sunlight on the windowsill, the paper now crinkled and soft from the excessive folding and re-opening I'd been doing the past few hours.

Today was the day the king's men were expected to collect me. My stomach danced in anticipation as I sat beside the window near the front door of our cottage, watching down the road, waiting for their arrival.

I was instructed to bring only my sword and the clothes on my back, so I fiddled with the worn leather strap on the scabbard at my hip—the only other thing my anxious hands could find.

The champions would be provided everything they'd need for their new life within the castle walls. Those who did not succeed in their efforts would return home upon their defeat. But I had no plans of failing, so I drank in my surroundings as if it were my last time to see them.

I glanced around the cozy space, marking the bits that I loved so much

—the fireplace mantle that always held a bundle of wildflowers in a small vase during the warmer months, the butcher block table where my mother and I had spent countless hours laughing and baking, and the coat rack that sat by the weathered door, where my father's overcoat still hung like he was going to sweep back through the entry and snatch it saying, *can't forget this,* with a winning smile.

I prepared myself to not see those things again for a long time, maybe ever. I was determined to win, and that meant this might be my last glimpse around the place I'd called home for my entire life. But like usual, the moments that require the most time are always cut short.

Dust stirred down the road, and six of the king's men rounded the bend on their towering horses, adorned in the royal colors of crimson and gold, with an empty-saddled mare in tow.

I said goodbye to my brother Liam, giving him a long hug and taking an earful of "good luck" and his famous tactical—yet sentimental—advice. He always poured his critical thinking into everything he did, even if it was just wishing someone good luck. I quite loved that about him.

Ever since our parents died, we were all each other had. I was doing this as much for him as I was for myself. After all, he was a handful of years younger than me, and I always felt the need to watch over him, even as we got older.

I ruffled his mousy-brown hair—the color of our mother's—one last time, and he grinned as he waved me off.

"Give 'em hell!" he called after me.

"I will!" I yelled back, waving a hand over my head, and earning a grunt from the guard who rode just slightly ahead, glancing over his shoulder at me.

The horses kept a casual, staggered procession through the countryside until the path began to narrow closer to town, where we fell into a single line as we approached the streets of Galenagh proper. Villagers stopped to gaze at the finery of our entourage, and to gape at the sight of *me* amongst it. I stood out like a sore thumb—a commonly dressed young woman, amidst a group of armor-encrusted guards.

I held my head high nonetheless.

The streets cleared in a hurry, people shuffling aside to allow us passage. Dogs barked and nipped at the heels of the horses, earning a few harsh shouts from the king's men. Ahead, the stone spires rose up from behind the castle's battlements, stretching for the fluffy clouds above, and my heartbeat kicked against my chest in anticipation.

King Broderick's castle was a vast and stoic beast of a building, tucked behind its protective stone wall. Built from bleached white limestone, it stood alone on the edge of The Great Wood, a stark contrast against the lush green foliage.

We passed through the impressive iron gates and the horses halted just inside the stone courtyard. I followed the guard's lead and dismounted, handing my horse off to the nearest stable boy, who led them away through an arched corridor.

I proudly adjusted my sword at my side.

I'd never been inside the castle's walls; it felt like walking into a whole new city. If I won, the grounds would be my new home. Perhaps the position would even take me places I hadn't seen before. If I were to be stationed on guard duty when the king was traveling that would mean new towns, new faces, new—

Relax. One step at a time.

I was escorted into a long, narrow corridor that opened up into another considerable courtyard. Swordsmen were standing throughout, busy preparing their weapons, or stretching their muscles. I was the only lady, which came as no surprise to me.

I straightened my shoulders as every man's attention turned my way. Their stares were hard and calculating, each one trying their best to get a read on me and see what made me worthy of earning an invitation.

Even though I was almost twenty-nine years of age, I could often pass for several years younger. I didn't have an excessive amount of muscle to visibly unnerve an opponent, but years of training had ensured I was lean and toned. Most men were at least a head taller than me, but what I lacked in height, I made up for in speed and agility. My long, thick, golden-brown hair and heart-shaped face made me look demure and delicate, but my small fists packed a nasty punch.

I used my appearance to my advantage.

Let them think of me as weak.

Let them underestimate me until the knots in their throats are brushing against the point of my blade.

A squire approached on my right. I barely registered what he said, my mind too busy assessing which man would be the biggest threat in the competition. It wasn't until he cleared his throat loudly and repeated himself that I realized he was asking for my sword.

I stared at him, blinking, heart lurching. My sword was of particular sentimental value to me, and the thought of handing it over to some stranger was gravely distressing.

The young man shifted his weight on his feet and frowned, suddenly looking more nervous than before, like if I didn't comply, he would have to answer to someone for it.

I pushed a harsh breath out of my nostrils and unfastened the scabbard from my hip, handing it over with a pointed look that said *don't lose it.* His head bobbed urgently, answering my silent command, but his frown suddenly returned. He looked down at his arms, then back up to me. A reaction to the weight of the sword, no doubt. He must have thought it unexpectedly heavy for someone petite like me.

I grinned to myself. By all means, it was. My father had it made that way to ensure that my muscles stayed toned, and so that I would be capable of wielding any *other* man's blade with ease—should I ever need to.

The blade was made of iron, with a beautiful tapered edge and a leather wrapped wooden pommel. The hilt was rounded and hammered in texture—perfect for knocking someone in the jaw with.

The young squire scurried off across the courtyard with my weapon, and I watched the other competitors relinquish theirs as well, until at last, we were all left empty-handed.

No one seemed to say much.

I continued glancing around discreetly, trying to get a read on the others. Most of the men had gone back to securing their belts and baldrics or stretching.

All except for one.

A tall, toned man with broad shoulders and chin length golden hair stood across the way, stretching out his muscular arms, and watching me like a hawk. I checked behind and around me to ensure I wasn't mistaking his stare, but there was no one else nearby.

I'd never seen this man before, but something about him seemed oddly familiar, and he appeared as if he was fighting the urge to walk over to me.

I shook off his stare and continued raking my eyes across the courtyard before stopping on a pale man with thick black locks of hair that curled around his ears. He leaned against the far wall with his arms crossed over his chest and one boot flush against the stone behind him. The smirk on his face remained as he stared directly across the courtyard at me.

What is with these men and staring?

He appeared around my age, wearing a loose white tunic that was untied at the neck and tucked into black pants that hugged his slender legs. Even though his eyes cut like daggers across the space between us, the rest of him didn't reflect much of a fighting man. He lacked the muscle-tone and build that the rest of the competitors had.

An easy opponent then, I thought.

As if he could hear my thoughts his smirk fell into a scowl, and he pushed off the wall and disappeared around the corner.

I scanned the courtyard again, marking potential threats, and noting their various outfit choices. Looking down at what I had chosen to wear, I felt pretty confident that I was off to a good start. My leggings were breathable and allowed me to move freely, while my tunic cut in close to my waist and arms, leaving no spare fabric that could be snagged on someone's hand, foot, or blade. The less surface area my opponent could grab onto, the better.

I didn't have the busty chest that most men seemed to find attractive, and I was thankful for that when it came to fighting. My petite size allowed for just the right amount of muscle tone and agility, while remaining a small target.

I combed my long hair back with my fingers and began weaving it into a thick braid down my back, tying it off with a leather strap that I always kept in my pocket. The shorter pieces of hair that framed my face and forehead blew gently in the light breeze.

Just as I finished, a horn sounded from the mezzanine above us, bringing everyone to attention, and a man in full armor stepped up to the railing to make an announcement. "Competitors, please make your way to the south entrance and form a line. The tournament's procession will begin momentarily." His voice was stern and a bit unnerving.

The men formed a line of stoic faces, but beneath their flat expressions, I knew they were all itching to put their skills to the test.

I waited, before slowly walking up to take the final spot behind a man who was about the same height as me. He leaned out of line to catch a glimpse of what was going on at the front, and when he turned around and beheld me, he frowned.

"How does a lady find herself in this tournament?" he asked, looking me up and down with distaste.

I weathered his harsh perusal and pushed my shoulders back. "I was invited by the king."

"We all were, *girl.*"

I paused at his remark. He clearly didn't see me as anything special. Or perhaps he thought I was incapable? I didn't like being thought of as incapable.

I lifted a brow, dishing him a dose of his own skepticism. "And how did *you* find yourself here?"

The man narrowed his eyes, and just when his mouth opened to retort, the voice from the mezzanine bellowed, "Move along."

I tossed the brooding man a mocking smile as he turned and stalked away, catching up to the line that was now filing one by one into the dark hall through the doorway ahead.

As I stepped up behind him once more, he leaned back over his shoulder and sneered, "Take my advice, girl. Bow out gracefully now, and save yourself the humiliation, or you'll have your ass handed to you in front of the entire royal court."

I grumbled to myself at what he thought was "advice."

When I elected to ignore him, he scoffed and shook his head, mumbling a few choice words under his breath.

The door slammed shut, echoing behind me as the last of us entered the building. Everyone kept silent as we filed down a dim, narrow corridor. Up ahead, the tall man with the golden hair peered back down the line until his eyes found mine. A quick look, marking me, then he turned back around.

So strange.

A faint applause grew louder as we approached an entryway, which

13

opened up into a grand ballroom that had been outfitted for the tournament.

The royal court and other finely dressed nobles lined both sides of the room, applauding our entry, eyes wide with excitement.

The king's banners hung from the white stone walls; bold swaths of crimson and gold fabric, embroidered with a crossed sword and shield in the center. In between the pennants, the walls were lit with dozens of ornate candle sconces, casting the room in a bright golden glow. From the vast ceiling, extravagant chandeliers dangled, their crystals dripping down toward us, glittering as we passed underneath.

The centermost section of the room was lined with a deep purple padded carpet that broke up the solidarity of the pristine white marble floors. The area had been roped off into twelve separate fighting sectors, all poised to offer the best view from the royal dais that sat perched upon the marble steps at the far end of the carpeted arena. There, King Broderick and his wife, Queen Corinne, stood in front of their thrones, hands held high in applause along with the rest of the court.

I didn't see the prince, but that didn't mean he wasn't in attendance.

We fell into a line across the room, opposite the dais, which was surrounded by guards wearing crimson capes.

The King's Guard.

The king himself stepped forward and lifted his hands up, motioning for everyone to take their seats. As the applause died down, he bellowed, "Competitors, welcome!"

His brown hair reached to the nape of his neck and was heavily laden with silver. Atop his head sat a crown of gold spikes adorned with rubies at the base. His facial hair was trimmed neatly, and despite the gray that gave away his age, he looked like he could still hold his own in battle.

However, the queen seated next to him looked as if she had never once set foot outdoors or held a blade in her life. Her pale skin was a stark contrast to the deep blue gown that hugged her thin, lithe body. Her long, straight, black hair hung gracefully down her back, tucked beneath a golden crown that matched the king's. Her face was soft and gentle. She looked primped and poised, as any royal queen should be.

I scanned the rest of the great room, taking in everything that I saw, while the king began his spiel about the great competitors of the past six years, and the importance of the still-new tradition of this tournament.

Since the tournament's inception, twenty-nine men had earned spots in the King's Guard, but none of those chosen to duel against Prince Alston had been able to defeat him. That final act was mainly for show, and no killing was allowed. It served to prove that, year after year, Prince Alston was still the best and strongest hope this kingdom had for a future.

But no one had forgotten the near tragedy that occurred six years ago. The reason that the king was inducting multiple members into his guard every year on a continual basis . . .

The prince had been attacked.

Reports said it was a pack of soulless creatures that had torn him from his horse while out hunting the section of The Great Wood to the north.

After the attack, the prince had fallen into a deep sleep, and the realm's finest physicians worked tirelessly to try and nurse him back to consciousness. The kingdom waited in suspense for several months to see if their heir would live.

Then, one day, his eyes opened.

But something had changed in him. Ever since he woke from his near tragic death, it was said that his skills had sharpened to perfect precision. He'd become an insanely adept fighter, more capable with a sword than any man in the King's Guard. No one could best him. The court marveled at his sudden expertise and his resolve to never again be brought to his knees.

Despite his impressive skills, he had also become known throughout Belthria for his temper and impulsive behavior. Although I'd never seen or met the prince, the talk in the town was that he was an arrogant lush, always avoiding court duties and disappearing with no explanation for days on end. Then there was gossip of his infamous drunken escapades and the lavish parties that he seemed particularly fond of.

For a young man nearing his thirties, he sounded more like an immature, spoiled brat. And for him to not be present to welcome his competition? Well, that spoke volumes to me.

I tuned back in to the king's speech just as the crowd's laughter died down from a joke I'd apparently missed.

"This year, we have twenty-four skilled competitors. For the first round, we have paired each fighter with another—twelve pairs in total—in hand-to-hand combat. The winners will move on to fight in the second round, which will allow the use of weaponry. Those subsequent winners will be the contenders for the following round, and so forth. At the end of the final round, the court will elect the strongest amongst the winners and he or she will receive a chance to duel with the prince. And good luck to them."

The crowd snickered at the king's words.

Ready to be sorted into dueling pairs, the men around me began shifting anxiously on their feet. A pulse of my own eagerness fluttered in my stomach.

The fully armored man from the courtyard mezzanine stepped in front of the fighting area and began calling out names, pointing to each roped off section as he moved down the line.

My eyes continued to survey the dais until I locked eyes with the queen. She was staring directly at me with an intensity that I didn't understand. I tried not to feel unnerved under her watchful eye, but I couldn't help it. She looked as if she had seen a ghost . . .

"Auren Everton," the stern voice called out my name, snapping me back to attention. I turned as the man pointed to the left side in the middle of the fighting sectors where my opponent was already waiting.

I ducked under the ropes and stepped up onto the padded carpet of our small, square arena, where the man I was to fight squatted low, resting his elbows on his knees. His head was shaved clean, and his full beard covered the bottom half of his face. He let out a deep growl as I approached.

I cut him a snarky smile and watched as he smirked back.

Then, he rose to his full height, and my smile faltered as I stared up at a very unfairly matched opponent.

2
ROUND ONE

THE STOCKY MAN I WAS TO FIGHT WAS AT LEAST EIGHT INCHES TALLER than me and built of heavy muscle. A bulging brute. But I had brawled with men big and small. The larger men tended to tire more quickly, and were less precise with their movements.

I hoped that would be the case this time.

In the section to my right, the man who had spoken to me in line met his opponent. They were quite unfairly matched as well. Clearly whoever paired the competitors had no knowledge of our physical stature.

Or they just simply didn't care.

But I wouldn't let that deter me. I had won plenty of duels and brawls with men who could easily overpower me. The key was to stay focused.

My father always taught me that nothing else mattered during a fight except your breathing and your blade. I recalled his words like a prayer.

Your mind must be blank and focused. Always.

I'd learned the hard way what losing my focus could cost.

I would not make that mistake again.

My attention snapped back to my opponent. He narrowed his eyes at me and began stretching out his arms, alternating pulling one across his chest with the other.

I rolled my neck and shoulders several times to keep the tension from settling in. It was always in the moments leading up to the fight that I was the most nervous. Once the match began, I would find my rhythm and reconcile my confidence.

Up on the dais, King Broderick surveyed the room, while the queen still glanced over at me, repeatedly. She was most likely just nervous that a female was in this competition to begin with. All she probably saw when she looked at me was a young woman who appeared out of place amongst these men.

The room grew quiet as the king called out, "Competitors, your body is your weapon in this round. Members of the King's Guard need to be able to fight without a blade if necessary. If at any point you decide you no longer wish to continue the fight, simply kneel and raise your arms above your head. If both you and your opponent are still standing at the end of the round, the crowd will choose who will move forward. The round will last seven minutes."

Seven minutes? My eyes went wide.

I looked around at the men nearby to see their reactions. Seven minutes was a long time to keep up your guard *and* actively pursue someone. It was also a long time to fight knowing there were potentially several other rounds to follow. The men around me seemed to be thinking the same thing, as they too cast uneasy glances at each other.

"A single blow of the horn will signal the start, two quick blows will signal the halfway mark, and the final long blow will be the end." The king paused, smiling. "Ready yourselves, and may the gods be with each of you. Let the tournament begin!"

The audience roared in approval, desperate for the first spectacle—one that promised black eyes and bloody knuckles, at the very least.

I bent my knees and took a low, L-shaped stance. My arms hung loosely at my sides, steadying myself, ready to maneuver in any direction, depending on my opponent's first move.

I toed back and forth, grateful for the padding we stood on. It would help to break any falls or takedowns. Otherwise the marble floor underneath could be deadly.

My opponent faced me fully, his knees slightly bent, chest pitched forward. His hands flexed open and closed at his sides.

He looked like he intended to launch himself on me from the start, so I planned to deflect immediately to my right as soon as the horn blew.

Several tense moments of silence stretched by, and I inhaled a deep breath before our dance of fists and feet began.

The horn sounded—a wild burst of a trumpet—and my opponent launched himself forward, just as I'd predicted. I wasted no time leaping to my right, keeping low as his arms grabbed at empty air behind me. He whipped his head toward me with a maddened snarl.

I began circling him slowly, trying to get a feel for his technique, watching his heavy feet.

He lurched forward again, this time grabbing for my arm, and I jumped out of his reach, finding the rope against my back. I pushed off of it and continued to my right, bringing my hands up in front of my face, ready to throw the first punch.

The man lunged a third time, hands wide open. Clearly, he had no technique other than to try and take me to the ground and overpower me. He probably won all of his fights that way.

So, as he neared and bent forward yet again, I deflected with my left forearm and landed a punch to his face with my right hand. His nose cracked harder against my knuckles than it should have—thanks to his momentum. The sound was a pleasant reward, and the sting of the contact made my fingers itch for more.

The brute stumbled past me, catching himself on the rope and grasping his nose in one hand as blood began dribbling down his chin and into his palm. When his eyes met mine again, I smiled, and his face contorted into rage.

He hurled a vengeful punch in my direction, a sloppy execution—all weight and no form. I dodged it with ease and spun around his left side this time, catching him off guard with a combination of punches to his ribs. He let out a hard breath as he took each hit.

As he briefly hung over himself, I seized the opportunity to land a kick to his midsection, sending him staggering back.

The spectators nearest to our area began to clap and yell, "Again! Hit him again!"

I glanced to the arena next to us and saw the only man I had spoken with, locked in a brutal fist-fight with his opponent. He didn't look like he was faring too well.

Blood and spittle landed on the carpet in front of me, as my opponent spat loudly, drawing my attention back to him as he composed himself.

"All right you little bitch," he growled. "You've had your fun."

He devoured the space between us in three long strides, and I waited until he was nearly upon me before I dropped to my knees and kicked out with my right leg, taking him down with my heel in one hard swoop. He landed on his back with a heavy thud and a grunt.

I turned to stand, but he thrust out his hands and grabbed onto my ankles, ripping them right out from under me. The world tilted, and I hit the ground, rolling away onto my stomach to try to get out of his long reach, but he recovered all too quickly and seized me by my shoulders, yanking me on top of him as if I was a rag doll. My back collided against his chest and his right arm snaked around my neck, but not before I slid my forearm in-between.

My breaths came in short gasps as I tried to grapple at his arm with my free hand. But it was no use. He only tightened his grip further, cinching my own wrist against my pounding carotid.

I forced myself to slow my breathing, steadily inhaling through my nose and sinking back into my training.

My brother Liam had pulled this same move on me in one of our sparring matches, and when he did, my father had stepped in and showed me that if I could protect my air supply, I could give myself a chance to get out of the hold, instead of being choked out into darkness.

I was also taught to never let an opponent have my open back in the first place, but . . . too late for that.

Focusing back on the task at hand, I balled my restrained fingers into a fist between my opponent's forearm and my neck.

The spectators' voices grew louder behind me. I didn't know if they were yelling for me, or for the other fighters, but they were getting invested in the spectacle.

I had to get out of his hold.

Two blows of the horn sounded, and my opponent flinched, his grip loosening slightly. Using that to my advantage, I rose up from his hold, just enough to drive my elbow back into the side of his temple. Bone met bone, and he cried out and his arm fell away from my neck, freeing me. I scrambled to my feet and quickly backed away, rubbing at my wrist where the pressure of his arm had been.

A few people cheered, while others gasped in surprise. I tuned them out so I could focus. I had three and a half minutes to make the winning blow. I refused to let this come down to a measly vote.

My opponent grunted even louder in frustration as he stood and wiped at his brow, his expression now fuming.

We set into stalking circles around each other. But time was ticking away, and I didn't want to dance around the ropes for the remainder of the fight, so I shuffled toward him to try and land a few punches.

I jabbed out combos.

One-two.

One-two-three.

He blocked each one with irritating ease.

I threw a kick toward his thigh, but he dodged it, and my frustration began building.

I dipped in to try and land a low punch, but he side-stepped me and drove a swift jab into my ribs, knocking the breath from me.

The crowd gasped as I buckled over, lungs emptying.

I staggered across the carpet, waiting several agonizingly long seconds for my diaphragm to decompress and allow precious air to fill the space between my rattled ribs. When I straightened, I was instantly met with a fist to my cheek. Pain exploded through my skull and my eyes watered, blurring the world.

"Where's that smile now?" he taunted.

I blinked away the tears, bringing my opponent's vague silhouette back into focus just as he landed a strong kick to my outer thigh. The blow forced me down on my knees in front of him.

Time seemed to momentarily slow as he began circling me like I was wounded prey.

Next to me, the man I had spoken with fell to one knee and raised his arms above his head—surrendering his win.

Throughout the room, the slaps and cracks of fists and feet echoed, followed by cheers and applause.

I looked up at the dais across the room and locked eyes with the

Queen. She shifted uneasily in her seat, fists white-knuckling the rounded ends of her throne's armrests, but she didn't break my stare.

Diagonal from my arena, the tall, golden-haired man was looking at me too. Like he wanted to run to my rescue, seeming more invested in my well-being than in his own.

The man above me muttered something, mocking me as he moved. I took a deep breath waiting for the arrogant bastard to circle back around once more.

Then, out of nowhere, a stern, commanding voice sounded in my head, *Get up. Get up and fight.*

I startled.

I often recalled my father's lessons and my brother's advice, especially in moments like this. But this voice was different from theirs. Richer.

Almost . . . *primal.*

A strange calm washed over me.

Liam taught me to use any means necessary if cornered. And, well, this situation called for a cheap shot.

My opponent stopped in front of me—just where I wanted him—and I didn't hesitate. I drove my fist up between his legs with as much force as I could. He buckled over and roared in pain.

I reached up and grasped his upper body, leveraging myself up as I swung my legs around his shoulders, catching his neck between my thighs. With a grunt, I twisted my body, throwing all of my weight as a counter to my leg's grip, taking us both down to the carpet. He broke the fall for us, his lungs deflating with the impact.

I squeezed my thighs together around his neck as tightly as I could, arching myself off the ground. The thigh muscle that had taken the brunt of his kick shook under the strain, but I held it in place.

Torn between the pain between his legs, and the lack of air to his lungs, my opponent writhed on the ground beneath me, his arms flailing wildly. He grasped at the air on either side of him, but I didn't let up. I held on and waited patiently for the horn to sound.

I had him.

The people behind me rose to their feet to get a better look. I heard some of them holler praise at my efforts, their voices rising louder the longer I held the man down.

The brute made one last attempt to push back, but I slammed his shoulders to the floor with a final squeeze of my legs.

I grunted through clenched teeth, angling my hips to press harder against his neck with my good thigh, feeling his pulse pound. Slower, slower . . .

Come on. Come on.

He went completely limp just as the horn sounded.

3

ROUND TWO

The horn was a long-awaited reprieve.

The ballroom flooded with the roar of the crowd as they rose to their feet.

Releasing my grip on my unconscious opponent's neck, I rolled away, onto my hands and knees, panting, and assessing the state my body was in. My ribs ached, and my thighs shook like a newborn fawn fresh out of her mother's womb.

I touched my throbbing cheek, hissing at the sting. A bruise was sprouting—if it hadn't fully bloomed already—the exact angry shade of the midnight violets that thrived outside my cottage.

After a moment of allowing my legs to recover from the strain, I stood and looked around the room at the other competitors. Some were lying unconscious. Others were rolling on the ground clutching various body parts. Blood dripped from noses and knuckles onto the purple carpet. Bruises and broken wrists were already starting to swell. In the arena directly in front of the king, a man had fallen outside of the ropes. His body was lying prone, blood seeping from his cracked skull where it had collided with the marble floor.

The king assessed the dead man with a look of distaste, then raised his eyes to the rest of us. "Well done, well done. A much-deserved win for the lot of you. Now, take a few minutes to prepare yourselves for the next round."

THE LIES OF MORTALS

I was gathered up, along with the five other men that won their match —all of whom had fared well. One man was rubbing his wrist—which was most likely sprained or strained. Another had a slight limp—probably a rolled ankle, or a kick that landed wrong. A few bloody knuckles and a laceration along an eyebrow presented amongst the rest of them. All injuries that would heal.

The tall man, with the chin-length golden hair who seemed overly concerned about me, stood amongst us. He wiped the blood off his knuckles, which—judging by the battered and bloodied man still lying in his fighting ring—was all his opponent's, and none of his own.

He would be the one to watch out for.

Six others were still standing, but each had suffered a serious beating and barely prevailed. They were pulled aside and tended to by a physician who assessed each one of them. The men who remained on the ground, either unconscious, too injured to get up, or dead—in that one man's case —were slowly hauled off.

Squires approached our small group of victors and released our weapons back into our possession. Along with our swords, we were also given a new, smaller blade. It was about twice the length of my palm, with a deadly sharp tip. I tested the grip of it before fitting it into the backside of my leather belt. Then, I strapped on my sword, content to feel its familiar weight at my hip once again.

Attendants began passing out cups of water to each of us. I gulped mine down while I watched as more of the king's men filed into the room and collected the ropes, rolled up the flooring, and mopped blood from the base of the dais until unblemished marble shone once more.

The physician finally returned wearing a frown. She climbed the dais to discreetly give the king her report. I watched as he stroked his beard, nodding every few words, and then rose to speak to the room. "Unfortunately, the other half of the winners from round one are in no condition to move forward."

The crowd let out a collective sigh of disappointment, while our small winning group stood in shocked silence.

"Now, now," the king consoled. "This is known to happen when the competition is fierce." He looked out over the six of us who remained. "As it is, I would prefer to take all of you on as part of the guard . . ."

He paused, and the crowd murmured with unease, tension bracketing the room, until a few spectators finally voiced their displeasure.

"Let them fight!" someone yelled.

"One more round!" another chanted, earning an echo from multiple others, who repeated the three words over and over until the king held up his hand.

With the inclination of his head, he announced, "Those of you who stand before me will face one last match." He steepled his fingers, considering the task he was about to deal out. "But let's not make this too easy. For this final round, you will be separated into two groups of three."

The audience whispered amongst themselves.

"You will each face two opponents. You may use your given weapons, and any other means necessary to secure your win. If at any point you wish to bow out of the fight, simply walk away and surrender your weapons to any one of my guardsmen. You will be disqualified, but no judgment will fall upon you."

The six of us looked around at each other, wondering who we would be paired up against. I could see the same question in all the men's eyes: who would be fighting against *the girl?*

The same man who called our names before stepped up near the dais and announced the first group. "Would these competitors please approach the dais: Farelo Nemar, Silas Belspear, and Auren Everton."

I held the king's stare as I stepped out of line and slowly made my way across the room alongside the two other men.

As we approached, the announcer instructed, "Do introduce yourselves to your king."

The smaller of my two new opponents stepped forward without hesitation, arms held straight at his sides and feet stomping together as he came to a halt. His skin was a rich, dark brown and his ebony hair was shorn to his scalp. He had a thin, neatly trimmed mustache and stood with complete confidence. With a curt bow at the waist, he introduced himself, "Farelo Nemar, My King."

My second opponent stepped forward. It was the man with the golden hair who had been keeping an eerily watchful eye on me throughout the tournament.

What a coincidence.

"Silas Belspear, My King." His voice sounded strangely familiar. As he dipped at the waist, he glanced back at me.

I didn't know why he insisted on keeping tabs on where I was, but it was starting to set my nerves on edge.

With what was surely a bothered look on my face, I stepped forward and introduced myself. "Auren Everton, My King."

I almost forgot to curtsy and the movement came out more erratic than I would have liked, thanks to my thigh muscles, which were now quivering with the bending of my knees—bloated with blood from the earlier strain during that grapple.

King Broderick chuckled and took in the three of us, standing at attention before him like prized soldiers. "I look forward to witnessing more of your talents," he said, dismissing us and motioning for the next group to approach.

We stepped aside and watched as the remaining three men made their way forward.

They could have been brothers—or at least cousins. Each of them was easily over six feet tall, with muscles that entered the space before they did. The only difference between them was their varying hair styles.

My attention strayed back to the throne where I noticed Queen Corinne glancing nervously between me and my opponents. Perhaps she just didn't favor this portion of the tournament. After all, when swords and daggers came into play, the outcome usually didn't end well—for one person, or the other.

As the second group backed away from the dais, the king held up a hand to the room. "I almost forgot to mention that the fight is to be full contact, just as the last match. No need for this to be a training session. It will last until it's clear who the winners from each group are. May the gods bless your endeavors, and if you die, may they greet you with open arms."

The crowd fell into a frenzy, and a buzz of names and bets began taking place as the king sat back on his throne. Farelo sighed like this was just another day at work. Silas, on the other hand, looked torn between fighting or fleeing as his eyes met mine.

The announcer guided our two separate groups to our sections. The group of burly men was stationed directly in front of the dais, while my group was granted the other half of the room. Each of us was instructed to only fight amongst our designated opponents. If any move was made against a member of the other group—intentional or accidental—the person who made the move would be automatically disqualified.

So, the rules were simple: keep to our half of the room, and don't die.

I found solace in the thought that it could be worse. *I could be fighting against those hulking men in the other group.*

My odds seemed better here.

I bent over and stretched my legs, then shook them out one at a time, trying to stabilize them. Once the adrenaline began pumping through me again, they would straighten themselves out, but the effort helped me focus.

The court members were now chanting names and waving their hands —their surplus of wine adding fuel to their enthusiasm.

King Broderick called out, "Ready yourselves!"

As one, we unsheathed our swords and some withdrew their daggers. I left the latter tucked where it was.

My mind began to race. *What if Farelo and Silas decided to come at me first, thinking I was the weakest?*

I paced nervously back and forth as I eyed them both.

Farelo swung his sword in figure eights in front of him, while Silas steadied his blade in his grip, taking a neutral fighting stance. He narrowed his eyes at Farelo. The moment I saw the move, I noted it and fixed my sights on Farelo as well—deciding that if Silas went for him first, so would I.

Better to rid myself of one opponent quickly, then concentrate on the other.

Sword in hand, I readied to move at the sound of the horn. Seconds ticked by and the crowd's roar climbed again, setting us all on edge. At last, the horn blared its permission to begin, and our feet moved.

Silas immediately advanced on Farelo without giving me a second thought. Their blades clashed with a deep and resounding clang, and I trailed each movement with my eyes, marking the perfect moment to insert myself into the fray.

As Farelo defended himself, I struck from the other side, but he was quick, and his blade met mine without pause. I stepped back again, reassessing, and in a split-second he was back to hounding Silas, parrying with all his might.

Silas held his sword vertically, using the slight movement of his wrist to angle his blade at each strike, his movements appearing frustratingly effortless. For the gods' sakes, he wasn't even breaking a sweat. If his tactic was to appear as if he could do this all day and not tire, he was certainly succeeding at it.

I circled behind Farelo, keeping to the original plan of taking him out first, but he spun with deadly precision and brought his blade down on mine.

And then, his focus was solely on me.

My heart began racing as he advanced a series of steps, tactfully slashing his blade right and left. I backed away, countering each swing, our blades clanging out in a repetitive chorus.

Silas quickened his step to catch up to us and jabbed his sword towards Farelo's right side. As quick as a viper Farelo spun away, swatting at Silas's sword with his. My jaw fell in disbelief. He was a very skilled fighter indeed. I guess we all were—to have lasted this long against each other already.

I glanced over to the other group.

One man was already on the ground, clutching his right flank. A flesh wound, but one that would take a moment to recover from.

The closer clang of swords brought my attention back to my own predicament. Silas and Farelo parried in a series of blows that almost looked rehearsed.

Their sword arms moved so quickly, I almost didn't see it as it happened. Silas brought his blade down upon Farelo's, while unsheathing his small dagger with his other hand. He flipped it in his grip and sliced upward, catching the edge of the blade along the inside of Farelo's bicep —severing a main artery. Blood instantly gushed and Farelo dropped to his knees. His sword clanged to the ground as he clutched his flayed arm, a rush of red spilling out from between his fingers. Within seconds the color drained from his face and he fell over onto the blood-slickened marble.

The crowd *roared.*

I watched as Silas wiped his blade along the edge of his tunic and examined it for a moment, as if there wasn't still an opponent waiting to take him down.

A cheer rose up again, but not for us. We both looked toward the dais to where another competitor had fallen. The man standing over him made a show of slowly removing the blade from his chest, painting the floor beneath him as crimson as the king's banners.

I whipped my head back to Silas, expecting him to make an advance on me, but he had gone back to examining his blade.

He'd taken out my other opponent—which was lucky for me—but it also made him my only threat. The only thing standing between me and a chance at the tournament's victory.

And there he stood, more concerned with his damn *sword* than with me.

Was this a joke to him?

If he would rather stand there and be mesmerized by his blade, then I would make the first move. I lunged at him and cut upward with my weapon. It caught him completely off guard and nicked the skin on his left forearm. His eyes went wide as surprise and shock stretched across his face.

I looked down at where my blade should have split his skin, but no blood welled up or flowed. There wasn't even a mark.

My brows knitted together. I had felt my blade catch on him.

It was a significant feeling—when a blade was dragged across flesh. Like cutting slightly chilled butter.

But his skin was unmarred. Tauntingly so.

To my surprise, he didn't look mad. In fact, he looked a bit *amused,* and I didn't know what to make of that other than to take it as a challenge.

I dropped down low and kicked out with my leg, but he skipped right over it, so I rolled away—out of reach. Without hesitation, I advanced on him again. He met my blade over and over until I had him backed up dangerously close to the spectators, who shrieked and pushed at each other to move out of the way as we neared.

At the last minute, he spun to the right—so quickly that I briefly lost my view of him. I whipped around to find him standing behind me, arms and sword extended out to his sides as if to say, *come and get me.*

I stormed toward him and swung high, but he caught my sword arm by the wrist and twirled me around to his chest, quick as a blink.

No, no, no. Not this position. I panicked.

He leaned into my ear and whispered for only me to hear, "Let's give them a show, shall we?" He pushed me away in a dramatic movement that might have appeared rough, but was actually very gentle. "Give me all you've got, little one."

I tried to not let my confusion show on my face.

Was this all a show for him?

And *little one?* The term grated on me. I ground my teeth together so loud I could hear it over the cheers and chants that rang in my ears.

A competitor went down across the room, the same man who'd taken a slice to his ribs, except this time, he was coughing and spluttering as he bled out from his neck, choking on his own blood.

The crowd cheered. But I kept my eyes narrowed on Silas.

We advanced the length of the room, meeting each other strike for strike, and I began to swing harder until I was grunting out of frustration.

Then, he suddenly became sloppy, like he was faltering on purpose to make me look like the better fighter.

I blew a harsh breath out of my nose. I didn't need handouts. Nor did I need to do this the hard way.

I spun mid-step and withdrew my dagger with my free hand. When I faced him again, I jabbed low with the small blade, catching him in the thigh with the tip.

He stumbled a step, but recovered quickly.

Again, no blood.

I was alarmed to say the least, but I pressed on in my rage—quicker with my blades. I twisted and spun, parried and thrust with both sword and dagger, slicing several pieces of his shirt open.

His eyes flicked to mine, and I could have sworn I saw him give me a slight nod. My brows pinched together in question, but suddenly his guard was wide open.

I seized the moment, not caring if it was an easy invitation. I flipped the blade in my hand—just as he had done—and brought it right up to his throat. As I pressed the edge against his pulse, he backed himself up until his heels hit the foot of the dais, and he fell backward onto the steps with his hands in the air.

With a slight grin, he yelled, "I yield!"

4
KING'S GUARD

THE ENTIRE ROOM BURST WITH CHEERS AND APPLAUSE AS PEOPLE CAME out of their seats with enthusiasm. The king and queen even stood from their thrones above me and joined in.

My chest rose and fell as I stared down at Silas. When he simply looked up at me with reverence in his eyes, I staggered back, lowering my weapon. I was certain the pressure of my blade had cut into his skin just enough, but there wasn't even the faintest mark left on his neck.

It was an effort to pull my eyes away from his unmarred neck, but I managed, turning to survey the space around us. We had cut a line that spanned the length of the entire room, a trail of crimson footprints left in our wake from the pools of blood surrounding the three dead men sprawled across the marble.

I was in a daze.

So much red on the white floors . . .

Not enough on Silas's skin where there should have been.

The winner from the other group stood in silence as well, examining the aftermath.

I barely noticed when someone came up and gently took my blades from my hands before bowing back off to the side of the room.

Men hurried out to remove the bodies while others mopped vigorously behind them until our reflections, once again, shone on the freshly polished floor. Not a single indication was left of the blood and death that muddied it just minutes ago.

The crowd still clamored over themselves and their winnings, as if three men hadn't just lost their lives.

Three good fighting men, who would have been absolute assets to the King's Guard, had the king not pushed for one more round just for entertainment purposes.

I scowled at the spectators, a sour taste lining my mouth.

The king stepped down from the dais and motioned for the other winner to join Silas and I, gathering us into a line before him. "A truly impressive spectacle." He smiled, before looking out over the crowd. "The royal guard has gained three new swords today!"

A heavy, formal applause cracked the air, the crowd's earlier blood lust seeming to have been satiated.

"And now," the king continued, "who deserves a chance to duel with my son?" He gestured toward the strong man to his right. "Will it be Erik?"

Claps and a few hoots and hollers sounded.

I hadn't seen much of Erik's fight, but he'd slit two men open, and it didn't look like he even had to try very hard.

Clearly, he'd impressed the crowd.

The king moved along. "What about Silas?"

Even though he'd yielded, Silas's fighting skills were some of the best I'd seen. The applause, however, didn't seem to pick up.

"Or, will it be . . . Auren?" Amusement laced his voice.

The tempo rose exponentially and everyone began chanting my name. My mouth fell open slightly as I looked across the room, a swirl of conflicting emotions wrapping me up from within and stealing my breath.

Several moments passed, then the king reached for my hand and hoisted it skyward.

My head became a whirlwind.

King's Guard. And, *I* had been chosen to duel with the prince. The gods must have been in my favor. *Or* they had a wicked sense of humor.

I looked over at Erik, whose baffled expression mirrored mine. Next to him, Silas was clapping contentedly. He nodded at me as he smiled.

As the applause carried on, I couldn't help but let a small smile of my own spread upon my lips.

Then, a loud boom sounded at the back of the room as the doors flew open and slammed into the walls. Everyone hushed and turned as a tall, pale man with black hair strutted through at a leisurely pace.

I recognized him from the courtyard. He still wore the same smirk on his face. A royal cloak of solid gold flowed behind him as he stalked directly toward me.

The prince.

5
THE DUEL

Prince Alston had stared me down upon my arrival here, and I hadn't known who he was then.

Now, he made his way across the room, spinning around and flinging his arms out in a grand motion like *he* had just won some sort of victory.

"You cleaned it all up without me." He clicked his tongue. "You know I always like to see the aftermath of these things."

These things.

Like those men's lives were nothing more than materials to be discarded. The insult had me clenching my fists, cheeks heating with indignance at his lack of empathy.

As the prince approached, Erik and Silas took several steps back from where I stood, leaving me alone, on display, alongside the king.

Upon seeing who now stood next to his father, Prince Alston's smirk fell into a scowl, realizing that *I* was the champion chosen for the final duel. "Oh, please tell me this is a joke?" He laughed as he looked me up and down. "*This* is who I have to duel with?"

I lifted my chin in defiance, meeting his stare, taking in his bright blue eyes that I hadn't been able to see the color of from across the courtyard earlier. They reminded me of topaz stone—a burst of color against his pale skin and midnight hair.

King Broderick stepped forward until he was nearly upon his son and leaned in closely to speak into his ear, his voice low, menacing. "That is correct. If you would have been present for this tournament, you would have seen that Lady Auren has proven herself a worthy opponent. You'd do well to acknowledge that fact." He lingered a moment longer before straightening to look at his son.

Prince Alston's face was tight. He despised being talked down to—that much was clear.

As the king stalked off, the prince circled me. "Such a delicate thing," he sneered. "Are you sure she's the one?"

Several people in the crowd chuckled, and the king looked back over his shoulder at his son in warning.

With a long sigh, the prince stared down his nose at me. "Well, let's get on with it then." He snapped his fingers and turned toward a squire who quickly jogged up to him, taking his cloak and handing him his blades in return.

My eyes flared in disbelief and my throat suddenly dried up. The weight of fighting two rounds in quick succession with no time to recover in between sank onto my bones like a water-logged cloak. I whirled on the king, mouth opened to protest—or at least ask for a short reprieve—but the words dried up on my tongue under his challenging stare.

He smiled, but it didn't reach his eyes. "Gather your blades and your wits, Auren Everton. Not many men get this opportunity. Certainly, no *woman* has ever earned the chance." With that, he took his seat again on his throne and waved a hand.

A squire rushed out to me in haste, handing me my sword and small blade. I'd forgotten they had been collected during my stupor after Silas yielded the fight to me.

I slid the freshly shined dagger into my waistband and turned my sword over in my palm. The familiar weight grounded me and reminded me to breathe.

"Oh, *Auren?*" Prince Alston cooed. He tapped his blades together, taunting me. "Tick tock."

And there it was. The incentive I needed to get my head in this fight. Prince Alston needed a rude awakening. Or, at the very least, to be taught what respect was.

I faced him fully and watched him twirl his twin blades simultaneously. He sunk into a low stance with his legs spread wide as he continued twisting the weapons in front of him like he was some depraved jester showcasing his sadistic talents. The crowd raved with amusement—feeding his undeniable ego.

As I continued to watch him, it dawned on me that he had *two* swords, whereas I had only my sword and small dagger. I looked around, but no one else seemed to notice. Nor did they care.

I knew I wouldn't be given another full-sized blade even if I asked, so I took a deep breath and steadied myself.

Without warning, the prince leapt into the air, bringing both swords down, *hard*. They collided with my iron blade, and my arm shook as the clash reverberated down my body.

He was significantly stronger than anyone I'd fought, which was at odds with his relatively unremarkable build.

I gritted my teeth and readjusted my grip on my sword as he swept back and began circling me, dragging his blades against each other in slow, taunting movements.

A fresh and spritely fighter against his worn-out opponent.

I turned with him, following his movements, searching for tells of his weaknesses—other than the fact that he looked more like he spent all his time studying in a dark library than training for battle. He may be able to swing a sword with gusto, but surely this wasn't the famed "undefeated fighter" everyone claimed him to be.

"You've been awarded a great honor, you know," he said, pointing a blade directly at me before lunging forward using the same outstretched arm.

I skirted his attack and spun with my momentum, switching sword hands and bringing my blade around to his right side. He turned into it from behind and met my blade with his.

We were suddenly face to face, and he leaned forward, his breath mingling with mine as he snarled, "But you'll go down just as easily as all the others."

I reached behind me, pulling the dagger free and sweeping in low with it, but he anticipated the move and swatted it away with his other blade.

Damn.

"Cheap shots won't get you very far Auren," he tutted.

I let out a grunt of irritation as I spun the opposite way, bringing my sword arm upward, cutting to the right, but he blocked it with ease and brought his second blade up to point at me as he pushed me away.

He turned his back to me as if I wasn't a threat, and began gesturing to the crowd. They praised his antics, forgetting about me entirely as they cheered him on, feeding his haughty ego.

I used the moment to catch my breath, glancing up at the king who was the picture of boredom, smoothing the pads of his thumb and forefinger together while he rested his elbow on his armrest. He had probably seen this same spectacle dozens of times—where his son would taunt his opponent, belittling them, preying on their spent energy and tired muscles, until the right moment presented itself. Then, the prince would land a pathetic strike that wouldn't even be that impressive, but the hype would ensure that it appeared the opposite.

My goal was to change that narrative.

The prince turned back around and faced me with a wicked smile as he held his arms out to his sides, giving me his open chest. I envisioned my blade driving right into it; the bright red blood that would trickle to the ground as he choked on his words and bled out.

I knew that to actually kill the prince in this duel was forbidden, but there was no rule against drawing some sort of blood.

And I wanted to see him bleed.

My feet leapt into motion, and I lashed out in a combination of strikes. Each, unfortunately, found his blade and not his body. As he twisted, I brought my sword down, aiming between his shoulder blades, but his right arm swung behind him and he blocked it.

I let out a snarl.

There's no way he's really this good.

The prince pushed my blade away from his back and used the leverage as momentum, spinning, and bringing one sword across in a vicious slash aimed for my chest. I jumped backwards to avoid the tip, which came dangerously close to my tunic.

"Might I suggest you try something I haven't seen before?" he sneered.

Though the words grated against my ears, the corner of my lips lifted just a fraction at the undertone with which he spoke.

He was frustrated that he hadn't bested me yet.

I reminded myself that my spot in the King's Guard had been secured. I had nothing left to prove to the royal court. This duel was just for show.

And yet . . .

The longer he smirked at me, the quicker the fight was becoming a stage for my spiteful musings. If I couldn't beat him, I would at least make him work for his win.

He moved before I did, his lips peeling back from his teeth as he lunged, stabbing one sword straight at my chest, followed by the downward swing of the second. I deflected the first, then crossed my blades, catching the second in a bind and thrusting it back at him with a yell.

I countered his advances, resorting to a series of steps that my father had taught me. They were simple, but usually effective, and would hopefully allow me to catch the prince with an unexpected open guard. He parried with no major struggle, but for a moment I thought I saw a hint of surprise cross his face when I manipulated the angulation of my blade to go around his guard.

"Old party tricks," he scoffed. But as he attempted to counter, I dropped to my knee and spun hard, grunting as I lashed out with my sword and sliced clean and deep across his left thigh.

A streak of bright red blood coated my blade like a prize.

He staggered back in disbelief, dropping to his good knee and losing grip on one of his swords. Blood soaked his pant leg as he scrambled to staunch the wound with his free hand. His face was aghast with shock, as if he'd truly never been sliced with a blade, or seen his own blood.

The crowd gasped at the sight of their kneeling, wounded prince, as I took a defensive stance, pointing *my* blade at *him* now.

His eyes flared wide at the mocking gesture. He tried to stand, tried to lunge, but my sword's thick, iron blade had sliced through too much muscle. His leg gave out under his weight, and he went down onto his knee again, letting out a yelp that rang through the vaulted room.

He snapped his head up, flinging the hair from his face as he snarled. "How *dare* you?"

I circled him while the audience hung on bated breath, anxious eyes darting back and forth between their prince, their king, and me.

After I made one full rotation around the fallen prince, he spun on his good knee—a sad attempt at the same move I had just used to best him. He whipped his remaining sword in my direction, but I dodged it and slapped him across the back with the flat end of my blade. The crowd launched into a frenzy of gasps and laughter, further fueling his rage.

In his final attempt to reach me, he lost his balance altogether and fell onto his side. His injured leg lay stretched out before him as he pressed a hand to the wound. He was panting hard through his teeth, and something strange flickered in his bright blue eyes amid his pain.

Although there wasn't nearly as much blood as I'd expected for how deep I gouged his thigh, it was enough of a win just to see him in pain, tormented by the seeds he'd sown.

I wiped my blade on the hem of my tunic and laced my words with sweet venom as I said, "It seems, My Prince, that you are unable to finish this duel."

At that moment I looked up and saw Silas across the room, arms folded across his chest and grinning with approval.

I had to suppress my own smile. Needed to restrain myself before the king decided what I'd just done was unacceptable. So, I turned toward the dais and looked up at him, awaiting my orders.

"You will pay for what you've done," the prince spat from behind me.

Ignoring his threat, I held my head high and continued my silent inquiry to the king, whose fingers had stilled, brows narrowed on the scene, contemplating the predicament that lay before him. I supposed he had never encountered this before—seeing that Prince Alston had never been bested.

The silence hovered around me like it was awaiting a command to sink its teeth in. But I stood patiently, content to let the prince marinate in his defeat while his father debated with himself.

A few moments later, the king stood abruptly and began clapping. The crowd—along with the queen—followed suit, and a few people even dared to whistle.

The prince hissed at the approval, cursing the crowd with his glare.

King Broderick descended the steps and walked over to me in haste. I yielded a step backward—unsure of his intentions, even though he'd just appeared to give his approval.

His broad hands landed on both of my shoulders, and he pinched his face into what looked like a forced smile. Then, he announced to the room, "This is a rare day indeed. Lady Auren has bested my son." He spun me around toward the audience. "Our champion," he proclaimed, and the crowd rushed forward with applause.

I should have felt victorious, but strangely, I felt used.

6

GUEST OF HONOR

THE REST OF THE AFTERNOON WAS A BLUR.

Lords and ladies of the king's court came in droves to shake the hands of the newest members of the King's Guard, and inquire as to how we learned such skills. I stood alongside Silas and Erik and shook each stranger's hand, smiling politely as I wrestled with my own thoughts.

I still found it strange that Silas would concede the win to me when he was so close to taking it for himself. We had both secured our places as champions, but I somehow felt like I hadn't properly earned my spot.

Not with his *yielding.*

A frown twisted my features. Glancing over at him, all I could see was his golden hair shifting forward with each bow he gave as he extended his hand out to yet another babbling court member.

After what seemed like a lifetime of mingling, I was finally led to my guest chambers across the vast castle. A customary celebratory dinner was soon to take place, in honor of our new positions. King Broderick informed us that our temporary rooms were being prepared with everything that we would need, and that we would be outfitted with something appropriate for the evening. Our permanent quarters would be ready in a few days' time, in the Guard's Wing. We had until then to learn the layout of the castle.

The hallways were wide enough for multiple people to walk side by side, but the guard that escorted me kept oddly close. He looked over his shoulder, then slowed his pace until he matched my stride. "I have to ask," he inquired quietly, "how did it feel to best the prince?"

I tried my best to catalog the turns we made while formulating my answer.

Earlier, I'd offered anything but the truth, telling the lords and ladies that, "It was just a stroke of luck," and, "I would never truly think of *seriously* harming the prince."

What I really wanted to say was, "Prince Alston is an insolent, arrogant piece of work, and I'm thrilled with the outcome."

I should never voice those thoughts aloud, unless I wanted to lose my title—or my tongue. But something came over me and I found myself letting a hint of my true feelings show. "It felt . . . empowering," I replied quietly.

The guard grinned at me. "I've been waiting years for someone to give him a taste of what it's like."

"Of what, *what* is like?"

He leaned in closer. "Of what it's like to bleed."

I turned to him, surprised by the equally treasonous words that came from his mouth.

His thick, cocoa brown hair looked a bit windblown and mussed, and his dark brown eyes were soft at the edges—friendly and sincere. He couldn't have been much older than I was, but his face was covered in small scars—like he'd seen a lifetime of battle. One particular scar cut from the top of his forehead straight down through his brow on his right side. Another stretched in a long horizontal mark across his left cheekbone.

He cleared his throat. "What I mean to say is that Prince Alston is a talented swordsman indeed." He threw me a cheeky grin.

Right.

Loyalties.

I smothered my own grin and nodded, changing the subject. "Have you seen many battles then, Sir . . ."

"Weston, my lady," he replied politely. "No need for *sir*."

"Weston, then." I nodded. "And please, just call me Auren."

"As you wish, Auren."

We rounded a corner, and he checked back over his shoulder. "To answer your question, yes, and no. Lately, the king has received reports of more creatures stalking The Great Wood to the north. They've been terrorizing some small towns as of late. Units get dispatched and usually neutralize the threat fairly quickly, but the events are becoming more frequent. I wouldn't consider them battles—yet. But they're a challenge."

I had heard of these creatures and their attacks. Things that look like they crawled out of the darkness, stalking villagers, catching them alone just after twilight, and leaving mutilated husks in their wake. It was said that one of these beasts was responsible for the prince's near-tragic accident.

"Do you know where they're coming from? Are they from the fae realm?"

"No," Weston replied.

I looked over to him, waiting for him to elaborate further, or at least indicate which question he'd answered, but his mouth remained shut and he continued walking.

"Ah, here we are," he said as we came to a stop at an arched door. He opened it, gesturing for me to enter first. "After you."

The room was quaint, nothing extraordinary—a plush bed, centered on the wall directly across from the doorway, framed by windows that opened to view the gardens below, an armoire next to a door leading into the bathing chamber, and a petite writing desk next to a small fireplace.

I turned in a circle and was just about to say something when a small, brassy-haired woman came out of the adjacent chamber with a gasp. "Oh, gracious gods," she said as she clutched at her chest. "I was not expecting you so soon, my lady."

Weston put a gentle hand on my shoulder. "Auren, this is Leonora. She will make sure you have everything you need for the evening."

Leonora patted out her skirt. "I will, indeed. You are one of the king's new champions after all. I hear it was quite the escapade."

I looked down at her as she gave me a pleasant smile. Her face was gracefully wrinkled at the corners of her mouth, and her eyes looked a little grayer than they probably should, but she seemed to be in good spirits.

"Yes, I guess that's a good way to put it." I sounded a bit ashamed, but the truth was that I still didn't know whether or not the king was truly happy with me. After all, I did publicly embarrass his only son and heir. I would imagine some part of him might resent me for it. "And please, just call me Auren."

Leonora hesitated and pursed her lips like she wasn't sure whether or not she felt right addressing me without a proper title.

Weston straightened the sword at his hip. "I will be back at half past seven to escort you to dinner," he said, before bowing toward me and pulling the door closed behind him.

Leonora wasted no time tugging me into the bathing chamber.

I beheld my reflection in the mirror as I passed by it and sighed. The sweat had begun to stiffen my shirt, and my boots were caked with dried blood. My hair had matted to my forehead with sweat, and the apple of my cheek was swollen, a flaming splotch of red and purple and blue skin that stretched beneath my eye.

I looked *rough.*

"Yes, my dear, you are in desperate need of a bath. And that bruise needs tending to."

She opened a small cabinet and began stacking clean linens and rags alongside the already filled clawfoot tub, while dishing out instructions. "The water is hot, so don't dilly-dally. Here are your linens for washing and drying. Soaps and scrubs are by the tub. Don't use the one in the brown jar unless you want to smell like a bundle of roses all night long. I will have your outfit laid out for you when you're done. Any other items you need can be found in that drawer." She pointed to the top drawer of the cabinet.

I nodded as I watched her check the temperature of the bath water. Her mannerisms reminded me of my mother's. Always particular. Always keen on specifics.

With a smile and a nod, she left the room, and at last, I was alone.

I didn't hesitate to strip off my clothes and submerge myself under the steaming water. It instantly soothed my aching muscles, and I melted into it with a breath of relief.

Staying away from the soap in the brown jar, I opted for the clear jar with white soap that smelled like lavender. Not my favorite scent, but anything was better than smelling like roses.

After a good, long soak, I rustled through the cabinet drawer and found a wide-toothed comb. I sat in front of the mirror, staring at myself, picking through my tangled locks as my mind began wandering.

All at once, the reality of it hit me. I had won, and starting now, I would be living in the castle.

The thought should have excited me.

I'm just in my own head, I tried to convince myself. *This is what I wanted.*

Wasn't it?

I should feel honored, or like I was on the right track, but this . . . this didn't feel quite right.

A knock at the door shook me from my thoughts. Leonora chimed on the other side, "My lady, you'd do well to hurry. Dinner is in twenty minutes." Clearly, she didn't feel it was appropriate to drop the formalities.

I rolled my eyes.

Out in the bedchamber, the fire had been lit, and a crimson red dress with golden leaves stitched along the neckline was laying on the edge of the bed. Matching embroidered slippers sat on the ground below it. I caught the implication immediately. I guess it was only fitting that I would be dressed in the king's colors, as I'd soon be donning armor with a crimson cloak at my back.

Leonora was nowhere to be seen, so I slipped off my towel and slid into the dress. The fabric hung a little loose near my waist and the shoulders were a bit ill-fitted for my frame, but it would do. Just as I fastened it up, the lady's maid bustled through the door with a couple of jars in her hands and waved me back into the bathing chamber.

There wasn't much that could be done for my hairstyle in the little time we had left, so she towel-dried it as best as she could and loosely pulled back the top half, securing it with a long velvet ribbon.

The jars that she brought were for the bruise and the rest of my face.

She tsked as she turned my head by my chin to examine the discoloration on my cheek. "That must have hurt." She scooped a dollop from the jar and dabbed the clear paste over the tender skin. It smelled faintly of lemon. "This is witch-hazel," she stated. "It will help heal this right up."

Wiping her fingers on her skirts, she moved on to the next jar. The creamy liquid was refreshingly cold as she spread it gently over the bruised area and blended it around the rest of my face. She then plucked a small, puffed paintbrush and dabbed it into a dish containing a loose, rose-colored powder, clinking it against the side of the glass a couple of times before patting it delicately over my cheekbones, careful to not aggravate the swelling.

As she stepped back to examine her work, I turned toward the mirror. To my surprise, the bruise had disappeared under the cream, which had also evened out the faint red blotches that naturally adorned my cheeks, smoothing my skin and lending it a soft glow. A rosy color kissed my cheekbones, making my caramel brown eyes stand out.

I smiled at the transformation. I hadn't felt lady-like in quite some time.

"That'll have to do. No time for anything else my dear. Get those slippers on."

As I did, she swatted at the skirts of my dress and smoothed out the neckline so that it laid flat along my collarbone. Then, she smiled.

"You look—"

"Lovely," a gentle voice cut in from the doorway where Weston now stood.

He had changed out of his tunic and breastplate from earlier, and now wore his full armor and sword. A floor-length crimson cloak hung down his back from his left shoulder, the edges trimmed with a delicate gold embroidery—something I hadn't seen on any other cloak.

I blushed, not realizing he had been standing there. "Thank you," I said as I walked over to him and took his arm.

Leonora waved us out the door with her arms, and I drew in a deep breath as Weston escorted me to my first royal dinner.

7
THE DINNER PARTY

WESTON AND I WALKED DOWN THE LONG HALLWAY OF CLOSED DOORS, AND I wondered if perhaps Silas and Erik were staying behind any of them.

I hoped I would get time to speak with Silas about his strange behavior. There had to be a reason for his actions. It was too strange. He was a perfectly capable fighter—

"I can practically hear you thinking," Weston said, startling me. "Whatever it is, it must really be bothering you."

"It's nothing."

He glanced sidelong at me.

"I'm just hungry."

He wasn't buying it.

I was starving, actually. And I was in dire need of water. Lots of water.

I sighed. "I really am hungry."

Weston suppressed a grin and simply nodded.

I chewed on my lip for a moment before speaking again. "I was also thinking about the tournament."

He let out a small laugh. "I knew you weren't just thinking about food."

"I was wondering about the man who yielded—"

"Best not spoken of here."

His eyes scanned the hallway ahead, and I looked around as well, searching for the phantom he sought. But we were alone.

The halls were quiet, the thud of Weston's boots and the whispering of my skirts the only sounds filling the space. Candles flickered their warm flames against the limestone walls, and twilight poured in through the keyhole windows that offered a view of a grassy courtyard below.

"Try to keep a low profile this evening—even if you are a guest of honor," he said, speaking low. "I've been assigned to look after you throughout the night. If you need anything, simply signal me and I will come. I won't be far."

I wondered why I even needed a guard to escort me, considering the title I'd just won. But on second thought, it would be difficult for a newcomer to find their way around the castle alone, so I accepted him for what he was: my escort.

We passed a series of several small doors that were grouped together on one side, and a woman wearing a freshly pressed apron hurried out of one, carrying a basket of freshly rolled linens.

"Staff's corridors," Weston explained. "Laundry, kitchens, and other areas that only certain people access."

I nodded, watching the attendant disappear down the next hall without so much as a sound.

The chatter of the court echoed toward us as we rounded another corner, and I could see the grand dining room ahead, bracketed by large, open double doors.

The prince was leaning against the wall outside, with a wooden crutch situated under his left armpit, speaking low with two of the guards.

All of them fell quiet and glowered at me as I approached.

Weston adjusted his sword and scabbard at his side as he led me steadily past the brooding men and into the dining room, where I shook off their stares and took in the new space.

With my dress, I blended right in. From the walls, to the ceiling, to the ornate rugs—everything was bathed in red and gilded in gold.

The guests turned their attention to us, nodding their welcome as we strolled past, and I suddenly wished I had taken less time submerging in the bathtub and more time preparing my hair. Everyone looked perfectly primped and styled, and I didn't miss the puzzled looks they began to throw my way, noting my half-soaked locks, tied back in a bow that felt like more of a mockery under their scrutiny, than an adornment.

I fought back the itch in my fingertips to rip the sliver of red velvet out and toss it onto the matching rugs.

The king and queen were standing near a pair of oversized, tufted chairs, situated along the back wall under a giant tapestry depicting a wild hunt. The small group of noblemen with whom they were chatting excused themselves as we approached.

"My King. My Queen," Weston greeted them. "May I present Lady Auren."

"Lady Auren, so good to see you. You wear the colors well," King Broderick said, taking in my ill-fitting dress.

"Thank you, My King," I replied, offering up a curtsy.

Weston kept his elbow casually linked with mine as he turned to scan the room over my head.

"Always on duty, Sir Weston," the king observed. "Take the evening to enjoy yourself. And see to it that Lady Auren is well fed and enjoys her time tonight. We are gracious hosts, are we not?" He turned to the queen, directing the question to her.

She cleared her throat gently and nodded her head toward her husband. "Yes dear, without a doubt." She smiled politely, her eyes staying on me as if in awe.

We took our leave, and Weston plucked a couple glasses of sparkling wine off a passing tray as he led me across the room to a large table with a spread of hors d'oeuvres. When he handed me a glass, I took it with gratitude, but looked at him warily.

"Do you think I could have some water instead?"

He laughed as he removed the glass from my hand and held up a finger in its place before he disappeared into the crowd.

I perused the table of delicious looking food before settling on some plump purple grapes. I popped a couple in my mouth just as my stomach rumbled.

A gentle hand touched my shoulder and I turned, ready to thank Weston for the water, but instead, Silas stood in front of me—wine in hand. I almost didn't recognize him with his slicked back hair and his red and gold dress jacket, courtesy of the king.

He smiled down at me and raised his glass. "Congratulations, little one."

My face fell into a frown, and I rolled my eyes at the pet name he used yet again. "Why do you call me that?"

His green eyes sparkled as he tilted his head to the side and took an irritatingly long sip of his wine. "You're rather small, compared to me."

I scowled, moving onto the next question as I went back to picking grapes. "Then why yield to me? I saw you fight. You're a perfectly capable fighter. Why let me win?"

He lowered his glass slowly, watching my hands drift over the fruit before I made my choice and plucked it from the stem. "I've won plenty of good fights in my day."

"And you don't think I have?" I popped the small globe in my mouth.

"I have no doubt that you have. But—" His words ended abruptly as his eyes flicked up to something behind me.

I turned to see what had snagged his attention and saw Weston approaching with a glass of water. The guard extended the glass to me without breaking eye contact with Silas.

"Silas." He nodded. A short, clipped acknowledgement.

"Weston . . ." Silas said warily, brows pinching in question.

The awkwardness settled in as I stood there between the two silent men, while they stared at each other, sipping their drinks.

What the—

A chime sounded somewhere in the room, snapping everyone to attention.

Weston gripped my elbow firmly. "Come along, Auren, it's time to be seated."

I was officially, thoroughly confused.

I looked to Weston for answers, but he just guided me through the crowd to the long, elegant table that had been prepared for a feast.

We were seated a few chairs down from the king and queen, who took up the head of the table. Silas strolled up on the opposite side and sat directly across from me.

Wonderful.

Erik—clad in the same color red as Silas and I but in a different cut of a jacket—took the seat next to Silas, across from Weston. He inclined his head toward me with a respectful smile, and I did the same.

As if the gods wanted this evening to be even more of a headache, the prince appeared, along with the two guards from the hallway helping him to the table.

Watching his painfully slow trek, I imagined his leg stitched up and wrapped in bandages underneath his black dress pants and grinned to myself.

He seethed as he eased his way into his chair—a seat with a direct line of sight to me.

Well, this just keeps getting better and better.

Not willing to give him any attention, I averted my eyes and began observing all the fine details at the table. Fresh, plump fruits and sugar dusted pastries were arranged delicately on golden platters, and intricately folded crimson napkins adorned each place setting.

Back at our small cottage, we had the basics and the necessities. We were lucky if we ever had enough to fill our plates to the heaping servings the king would probably provide. Dessert? That was a rare delicacy. I wasn't used to all this food and finery, and it showed.

Glancing down to my own plate, I frowned even further. Three of each type of cutlery lay on either side, as if they were there to mock me. I had no idea which one to begin with.

"A toast . . ." the king announced, raising his glass as the rest of the guests found their seats. "To our newest guards."

Everyone raised their glasses to the center of the table and toasted us, taking dainty sips.

I opted for a large gulp of my water, wishing I had just kept the sparkling wine.

A man served our plates from over our shoulders while I watched those around me, waiting for someone to reach for their damned cutlery so I could follow suit with the correct one.

Weston leaned over to me. "Start with the fork on the outside and work your way in."

My face reddened. "Was it that obvious?"

He laughed quietly and plucked up his own outermost fork. "After dinner, there will be some music and dancing. You're welcome to stay, or I can escort you back to your chambers. I'm sure the king and his guests won't take offense. You had a long day and deserve to get some good rest. They'll understand."

I gave him a polite smile, thrilled that I had the option to call it an early evening. I was very tired. And I knew that once I filled my stomach with hot food, I'd be battling my eyelids for consciousness.

"Thank you. I would very much like to retire after this."

He nodded.

Across the table, Silas was watching us as he cut into his roasted meat. Weston shifted in his seat beside me as he caught onto Silas's stare.

The two men entered into a sequence of squints and pursing lips, eyes flicking to a few other people at the table, and more uneasy shifting. My mouth fell open a bit at the weird, coded interaction I swore they were having.

Then I felt eyes boring into me from down the table, from where Prince Alston reclined in his chair with one elbow thrown over the headrest and the other splayed out across the table.

He hadn't touched his food.

His blue eyes pinned me to the spot with a menacing glare, and I knew he hadn't taken them off of me since he'd sat.

It was my turn to shift uncomfortably in my seat.

A bit unnerved, I quickly ate all that I could and tried to enjoy it. And just as it looked like everyone else had come close to finishing as well, music flared to life from the corner alcove and several couples vacated their seats to dance.

I leaned into Weston and attempted to inquire about us leaving soon, but Silas suddenly stood and extended his open palm toward me. "A dance, Lady Auren." It was a statement, not a question, which made me more annoyed that I would have to put off sleep a little while longer.

I couldn't say no. Not in front of the entire court. So, I stood and inclined my head toward him as he came around to my side of the table. This time, he didn't look at Weston as he took my hand and led me out into the open area of the room. With a steady lead, he brought me into his arms and began the dance.

"Before you question me again, little one, I must tell you, I was very proud to see what you made of the prince today."

That damned nickname again.

I leaned back in his arms to look up at him. "Do you know me from somewhere? Is there something I'm missing? Do you and Weston know each other or something?"

He smiled as he continued moving us across the dance floor. "So many questions."

"And you seem to have no answers whatsoever," I snapped.

A grin tugged at the corner of his mouth as he pushed me out for a gentle spin.

I caught a few bystanders watching us as I twisted my way back to him under the twirling guide of his fingers.

Amused by our matching outfits, I thought to myself, nearly sputtering a laugh as I examined the gods-awful pattern of Silas's dress jacket in front of me.

He tugged me closer, pulling my attention back up to his face, which had dropped back into seriousness. "You need to be careful," he warned.

Weston had told me to keep a low profile. Dancing surely wasn't helping. And now this warning from Silas?

"Weston told me something similar. What are you two talking about?"

Silas leaned in closer, his voice pitched low. "How about you just pretend to enjoy this dance with me."

I had no idea what to make of that and my frustration grew.

Sensing I was about to ask another question, he spun me again, and I grunted in frustration. His grin returned as he reeled me back in.

He looked so different from earlier—when he was covered in sweat and his hair had been untamed from fighting. There was something about him that felt familiar, but I couldn't place it. He didn't look like anyone I knew. I would remember someone with his stature and build.

Most men in my village were dark haired and a bit pale, and not quite so tall and broad. Silas's skin was sun-kissed and his body looked toned from many years of training.

I decided to see if I could get answers from a different sort of question. "So, have you always been a fighter then? I mean, were you trained when you were young, or is it a newfound talent?"

He lifted a brow, but answered. "I've always been the fighting kind. Where I'm from, fighting is a life skill we acquire when we're young. In all honesty, I haven't done much of it until recently. I've just been . . .

searching for the right reasons to fight." He looked away. "It's hard to explain."

My curiosity piqued. "Where are you from that would train everyone to fight? Certainly not Galenagh?"

He scanned the crowd over my head before answering. "South of here."

I leaned back in his arms. "South of here? There's not much south of here."

"Mmm." The sound rumbled in his throat.

"Care to be specific?"

He simply offered me a polite grin and leaned forward, gently dipping me and straightening again as the song ended.

Across the room, the prince shoved his chair back with his free arm, garnering our attention, and that of a few bystanders. He stood with as much grace as he could—given his wounded leg and pride—and took his leave.

Men began wandering the room again in search of their next dance partner, and I had no plans to be one of their options, so I dropped Silas's hand and tossed him an irritated smile.

"Well, *Silas from south of here*, perhaps you'll be more forthcoming in the future, seeing as how we're to work together." It was the only logical thing I could think of to say.

But before I could turn away, he reached for both of my hands and brought them up between us, regarding me with a look that I had only seen once before. It was the same look my father had given me when he watched me walk away for the first time to spar in a local tournament. I had been eighteen at the time, and I was only going down to the main square, but one would have thought my father was watching me walk away forever, given the conflicting mixture of pride and worry that swelled in his eyes.

The expression on his face that day had stuck with me. And somehow, as I looked at Silas, his face was an exact mirror of that.

Pride and worry.

"I plan on it, little one." He gave my hands a squeeze and gently kissed the backside of them before turning to walk away.

My hands lingered in the air after he departed, my feet rooted in place by some strange sense of loss. The entire moment left me perplexed.

The feeling didn't add up. It didn't belong.

So I shook it off.

A couple light taps on my shoulder had me readying to decline the man who I assumed was about to ask for a dance, but I turned and beheld Weston instead. He motioned toward the door with his head, and I sighed with relief.

"Unless you'd like to grant me a dance?" he asked, throwing me a lopsided smile.

I gently reached out and touched his arm. "I would love to, but if I don't go get some rest, I might just sleep through my duties tomorrow, and the king would surely strip me of my new title."

He gave a hearty laugh and offered me the crook of his elbow. "Next time then."

"Of course."

I glanced over the room to find the king laughing in conversation with several other men. Wine was being poured and passed in abundance, and he and the rest of the room looked to be guzzling it. Reassured that it was indeed acceptable to excuse myself, I turned alongside Weston and strode to the door.

No one gave us a second look as we walked out.

8

THE RESTLESS NIGHT

THE STRAIN FROM FIGHTING WAS FINALLY CATCHING UP WITH MY LEGS, and I was beginning to struggle to keep up as we made our way back through the castle.

"Do you mind if we slow down a bit? I desperately want to get to bed, but if I have to walk any faster you'll end up having to carry me."

Weston slowed his pace drastically. "I can get you something for the muscle aches—"

"Oh no, thank you though. I prefer to tough it out."

He nodded, glancing back behind us for what seemed like the fifth time.

"If you have some other place to be, I'm more than capable of finding my own way—"

"No, no other place to be," he said. "I'm stationed outside your chambers tonight."

I lifted a skeptical brow at him and laughed. "Outside *my* chambers? I think I proved today that I don't need protection."

He dipped his head offering a kind smile in repentance. "I didn't mean any offense. But until you're sworn in under oath, I'm to look after you and make sure you have everything you need."

I wanted to question him further, but I wasn't in the mood for more vague answers, so I nodded and let him lead the way.

He checked my chambers when we arrived. Then, he went a step further and stoked the fire, before ensuring the windows were closed to keep out the evening chill. Finding everything satisfactory, he said, "You can lock this door from the inside. I'll knock in the morning when it's time to wake. If you need anything, I'll be right outside. Get some rest."

Before he pulled the door closed behind him I called out, "Thank you for getting me out of there without anyone noticing."

He bowed his head. "The wine was already weighing heavy on them. They don't tend to notice much after that. Goodnight, Auren."

"Goodnight."

When the door clicked shut, I walked over to it and quietly slid the lock into place, then immediately kicked off my slippers and stripped off my dress.

My bruised cheek stared back at me in the mirror after I washed off the concealing cream Leonora had slathered over it. I frowned as I poked at it, deciding I would ask her for more tomorrow, before I had to make any more public appearances.

A set of night clothes had been left folded for me at the edge of the bed, and the sheets were neatly turned down. On the small tufted chair next to the bedside table, I spotted my leggings and tunic—freshly washed by the looks of them—folded over my boots, which appeared to no longer be caked in blood.

My sword and scabbard hung on the chairback.

I sighed as I stared at the only items I had to my name, thanks to the fact that I had accepted this invitation on the premise of leaving everything else behind. I supposed I would get a new wardrobe along with my permanent residence in the Guard's Wing.

I crawled under the sheets and laid there, mentally unpacking the day and all its strangeness.

I had so many questions . . .

What comes after this?

Will I be sworn in tomorrow?

Will Liam be invited to witness it?

Would the crown even notify the winners' families?

Surely they would. Or perhaps I could write a letter?

The crackling of the fire was about to lull me to sleep, when the silence was broken by men's voices outside the door. I recognized one of them to be Weston's and strained my ears to listen.

He was arguing with someone.

A man with a nasally voice was saying something about being summoned by the king for a matter involving one of the guests from dinner. I heard Weston tell the man that he was ordered not to leave his post, but the man insisted and mumbled something that I couldn't make out.

There was a long pause, then I heard boots stomp away from the door.

All fell quiet again.

I wondered what had occurred after we left the party, but my brain finally lost to lethargy, and my eyelids drifted closed.

In my dream, there was a steady, beating drum.

I tossed and turned trying to make the beat stop, but over and over it pounded, louder, heavier.

Then my eyes flew open and panic set in.

It was no drum.

It was the door to my chambers.

I knew it couldn't have been Weston because he said he would *knock*. And whoever this was wasn't knocking. They were trying to break down the door . . .

Alarms went off in my mind, and I threw back the covers, snatching my clothes from the chair. I dressed as quickly as I could, and not a second after I shoved my feet into my boots the door busted open and swung aside, hanging jagged off its hinges.

Three men, dressed as guards, stood in the doorway, and they had already pinpointed me. There was nowhere for me to go except through them. All I could do was reach for my sword.

They entered the room one by one and my stomach hollowed out. Two of them were the men I'd seen the prince talking with outside the dining room earlier. Judging by the utter contempt on their faces, they must have been planning something. And I had a sinking feeling that *something* was about to come to fruition.

"What is this?" I shouted. I looked toward the door for Weston, but he wasn't there.

I unsheathed my sword and tossed the scabbard aside.

"Do you really think that sword is going to win you any battles this time around?" the first man jeered. He didn't have a weapon . . . that I could see. In fact, only one of them did. "Bring her to me," he commanded.

The man with his sword drawn stepped in my direction, and I didn't hesitate. I struck first, swinging my blade down as hard as I could, but my arms wobbled with fatigue. He met my swing with a counter, rotating my blade down and around with such force that it flung from my hands and clattered against the wall.

I backed up into the bedside table as two of them descended upon me. I lashed out, kicking my legs in all directions, trying to keep them from lifting me off my feet. But I failed. My body was sluggish and weak, still trying to wake up.

I was hauled to the foot of the bed and held against it as the first man made his approach, shirt untucked, eyes bloodshot and glazed. The look he gave me told me this wasn't going to end well.

"What are you doing?" I yelled.

The man ran his drunken gaze up and down my body slowly, and the corner of his lips raised in a wickedly vile grin that promised nothing but retribution. "The prince sends his regards."

I bowed off the bed, but was slammed back onto it.

"He was undefeated, until you came along," the man taunted. He reeked of stale wine, and contempt oozed off of him as he came to stand at the foot of the bed and began unbuckling his belt. "You made a mess of his leg, and now, he's sent us to deal out your punishment." He inched closer, eyes pinned on where my legs were being held open by the other two men.

They snickered as I struggled against their painful grips. With their weight on my shoulders and thighs, I couldn't get any leverage.

I cried out for help and one man shifted his hand to cover my mouth, leaving my right leg unrestricted. With it freed, I brought it across my body and drove it into the man on my left, cracking his nose. Blood sprayed, and he spluttered a gravelly "fuck" and released me.

I twisted out from underneath the other man's grip and crawled toward the headboard.

"Oh, try as you might, but you're not going anywhere you little bitch." The first man laughed. "You're going to learn your place in this castle, and how to respect your superiors."

He snapped his fingers and the other men moved around the bed to apprehend me once more. I heard him yank his belt free just as one of the men grabbed me by my hair and yanked me down onto my stomach. Tears welled up in my eyes, and I yelped at the stinging pain as he dragged me down the mattress.

My legs were spun toward the foot of the bed, to where the first man stood ready and waiting to humiliate me in the worst way.

To take what was not freely given.

My heart pounded harder as tears streamed down my face. I couldn't get a deep breath in with the man holding my neck back by my hair. I tried to scream, but all I could do was clench my jaw as a bleating groan tore through my throat.

I grasped desperately at the sheets and pillows around me, praying to the gods for help. Praying to Karios for mercy, and to the fates for a way out of this . . .

"If you don't hurry up and take her, I will," the man to my right said.

I jolted, wrestling against their grips, but another pair of hands landed on my pants and began tugging.

My heart lurched.

No. No. No—

I would not let this happen.

I bottled up all of my panic and fear and desperation and willed it all into a ball of fury in my core, preparing my muscles to use every ounce of force that I could muster to get the men off of me before it was too late.

Something stirred deep within my chest, like a torrent of anxiety and wild energy as I gathered my strength to break free.

The walls suddenly began to rattle and the floor trembled. The man between my legs stumbled backwards, tripping over his pants and catching himself on the door while the others careened forward on top of me. As their weight smothered me, I pushed back against them with all the energy that I could gather.

I let out a powerful yell as I made to heave them off of me, and as I moved, a sudden burst of white light exploded out from under me, throwing the men into opposite walls.

A wave of dizziness rolled through me, and once it ebbed, I scrambled back up to the headboard and surveyed the room, ears ringing at a deafening pitch.

The two men who had restrained me were now face down on the floor, unconscious. Maybe even dead. The other was groaning in pain in the hallway outside the door. When his eyes met mine, they were wide with terror.

I looked down at myself and the bed. The sheets were shredded and splattered with blood that wasn't mine, and I was shaking uncontrollably.

The fire in the fireplace had gone out, and the temperature in the room had noticeably dropped. But the newly chilled air was already much too cold for it to be from a lack of fire—which had only gone out seconds ago.

I shivered as a strange sensation washed over me, like a crackling in my veins. Then, I heard a scuffling sound.

When I looked over to the hallway, the man was gone.

9
A LIGHT AWAKENS

I TOOK SEVERAL DEEP BREATHS TO TRY AND CALM THE TREMORS THAT rocketed through me.

Everything had happened so fast. Then that powerful light exploded.

It felt like rage. Like raw power.

Like *magic*.

But that was impossible. Humans didn't have magic, and neither did our realm.

I searched my brain for an explanation, but my mind was still in shock and too tired to make sense of it. All I knew was that I had to get out before the remaining men woke up—if they were even still alive.

Footsteps sounded down the hall—running toward my room. That was the motivation I needed. I scrambled off the bed and grabbed my sword from where it lay just as Weston slid into the doorway, panting.

He beheld the scene, then ran to me, gathering me in his grasp. "Gods, what happened, Auren? What happened here?"

My body shook anew as I wilted in his arms. "They broke through the door and held me down. They tried to . . ." I trailed off.

He surveyed the men . . . the bed and the ruined sheets, indicating the struggle that occurred. Realization hit him, and he frantically held me out at arms-length, inspecting me up and down.

"They didn't . . . It's not my blood. I-I'm okay," I assured him, though my voice shook.

Confirming that I was unharmed, he gathered me into his arms again. "I must get you out of here."

I nodded and wiped my eyes.

With our swords drawn we stepped out into the hall. To our right, there were only a few more doors until the hallway came to a dead end. To our left, the corridor was dark and quiet. The whole castle seemed eerily silent. Surely someone heard what had just happened? Or felt it? I didn't really remember there being any sound, but I was pretty sure the entire castle shook.

Weston whispered through the dark as he gripped my hand and led the way "What exactly happened back there Auren?"

"The prince's men—"

"The *prince* was there?"

"N-No. He wasn't. He sent his guards." I shook again at the words—not from fear this time, but from rage. Rage that Prince Alston would send those men to violate me.

Weston paused at the end of the hall and peered around the corner. "And how exactly did the men end up unconscious?"

"I don't know. One minute I was being pinned to the bed, and the next, everything started to shake. Then there was this blinding light that exploded and threw them off of me."

Saying it out loud made it sound stupidly unrealistic.

Weston whipped around, eyes wide. "A light? *What light*, Auren?"

"I-I don't know! I was lying on my stomach, and the light seemed like it came from underneath me. I know it doesn't make sense—"

"Was it just the two men?"

"No. There was another, but he fled afterward."

Panic washed over his face. His mouth opened to speak, but a door squeaked open somewhere down the next hall, startling us.

He leaned around the corner again, checking for anyone nearby, then turned back and whispered, "I felt the entire castle shake beneath my feet. Was that when the light appeared?"

"No, the castle shook just before it happened. And it didn't just appear Weston, it *exploded*."

He breathed out with a new determination. "Listen to me, Auren. That man is probably informing the king as we speak. There will be guards sent out with direct orders to apprehend you. I must get you out of the castle."

He tightened his grip on my hand and pulled me down the adjacent hall.

"Weston!" I called out in a whisper. "Wait! I didn't do anything wrong! The prince's men—"

"I know, Auren," he cut me off. "But when word of what the guard witnessed reaches the king, he'll want to interrogate you. He's already on edge after all the attacks. And when he hears of what just happened . . . he'll see you as a threat."

We made a left, then a right, then Weston jerked us to an abrupt halt. Seconds later, two men rounded the corner ahead and approached us with swords drawn.

They had definitely been sent by the king.

Weston pushed me behind him. "Stay back," he commanded me.

The men drew close enough that I could see their faces in the candlelight. When their eyes locked on me, I knew Weston was right.

One of them spoke. "Stand down. By order of the king—"

The man's words were cut short as Weston struck. He moved lightning fast, his blade cutting through the darkness with precision. His movements were so quick and forceful that the candle flames on the walls shuddered as the air rippled down the hallway, and a flash of red momentarily lit the space.

In two moves both of the guards were painting the floor with their blood.

We launched into a run as additional footsteps echoed down the hall toward us.

This time, there were many.

We veered left into a hallway that I recognized. A series of small doors stretched along one side.

The staff's corridors.

Weston slid to the last door, flinging it open and frantically waving me inside. Without hesitation, I obeyed. He followed right behind me, snicking the door shut silently.

The corridor opened up into a small room full of tables and shelves. Weston made straight for a bookshelf and tugged hard on the corner. It cracked away from the stone and mortar, releasing a puff of dust that bled into the air before it was quickly sucked into the sliver of darkness. With another pull, the shelving swung away from the wall on its hinge, revealing a hidden passage that smelled of damp dirt.

He lifted two lit torches off the wall, handing one to me and motioning for me to enter first. "Quickly!"

Inside, the floor descended into a set of steep, winding steps, and I lowered the light in front of me to find my footing.

Weston pressed a hand against my back to steady me as we launched down the stairs, but not even ten steps down, my legs buckled, and I stumbled forward, catching myself against the stone wall with my free hand.

I was *so* tired.

"Steady, Auren. We don't have much time."

Normally, I could have descended the steps in twos, but with exhaustion weighing on me, I wasn't sure my legs would allow it.

Between my breaths I asked, "What happened to you? I heard a man talking with you before I woke up to them beating on my door."

"That guard must have been sent by the prince to remove me and keep me distracted. I was told there was a disturbance at the party; some belligerent guest who'd had too much wine and was causing trouble. I knew it didn't sound right. There were plenty of other guards who could have handled it. But if I had disobeyed, the king would've heard of it.

"When I arrived, a man was causing a scene, but he'd more than likely been antagonized into acting out. I was dealing with him when I felt the castle shake. That's when I knew something else was wrong. I ran back to your chamber as everyone dispersed."

I looked back at him, panting as I said, "Thank you for coming back for me."

"I should've never abandoned my post—regardless of the command." Shame echoed in his voice.

"You were just doing your job."

When he didn't respond, I glanced back over my shoulder at him. In the flickering torchlight, I could see him offer me a small close-lipped smile, but it didn't mask the guilt that haunted his scar-marked face.

"We need to keep moving," he said quietly, ushering me along.

The stairs continued unfolding before me.

My thighs burned.

And just when I thought my muscles couldn't handle another step, the ground leveled out into a dirt floor.

The air was colder here, and there was a draft, carrying the scent of the forest.

"The tunnel system," Weston said, looking down the dark corridors in both directions.

"Tunnel system?"

"Runs east to west under the castle. The stairs intercept it at its westernmost point. From here, it lets out in a clearing at the edge of The Great Wood." He pointed toward the left. "That way."

I stared into the darkness, stretching my torch out toward it.

Nothing.

"Don't worry, we're the only ones down here." His strong hand remained on my back, guiding me forward alongside him. "Trust me."

I forced my thigh muscles to cooperate and form steady strides to match his brisk pace. "How do you know for sure?"

"I just know. And there's not much further to go before the opening. It's just up here around this bend."

My brows pinched. How could he even see beyond the four feet of flame-light around us?

Regardless, I was thankful for his efforts.

Perhaps the fates had willed it that Weston was assigned to be my guard. Perhaps Karios decided to intervene on my behalf. That *would* explain what happened back in my bedchambers. And it did seem like some other force had a hand in the entirety of yesterday's events—given how strange they were.

A swirl of cool, fresh air stirred around us, chilling the sweat that had gathered on my forehead and neck, and bringing me out of my thoughts just as Weston brought us to a halt.

"You only have to go about twenty yards until the opening. It's almost dawn, so the light should guide you. Drop your torch behind as soon as you see it. You don't want to give the king's men a beacon to find you."

I nodded, then registered the fact that he'd said "you" not "us".

"Wait . . . You're not coming with me?"

"If I don't get back to my post, they'll know I helped you out of the castle. I'll try to keep them off your trail as long as I can. The last place they'd expect you to run to is The Great Wood. We frequent the area for training and patrols, but other than that it's rare that anyone ventures into them—for obvious reasons. But they *will* come looking eventually, and I want you to be far away from here when they do."

He placed his hands on my shoulders and held my stare with an intense seriousness. "Auren, I need you to run toward The Veil, and don't stop."

I froze.

What he told me went against everything I had ever been taught.

The Great Wood was beautiful, but the fae could be lurking just beyond The Veil, and nothing was stopping them from being tempted to cross.

"But the fae—"

"Don't worry about the fae or The Veil, Auren—those are the least of your worries. You need to focus on staying away from the guards. Do *not* let them catch you. That is paramount."

My mind whirled.

How are the king's men a threat, but the fae aren't?

"But why? What safety could I possibly find at The Veil? What if—"

Weston cut me off, shaking me by my shoulders. "Auren, I would never betray you. Please, just do as I say."

I heard the plea in his voice.

In the short time that he had been in charge of me, he had reverently watched over me, and some part of me knew I could trust him. And right now, I had no other choice *but* to trust him.

I nodded, biting at my bottom lip.

"You'll know the marker when you see it," he said.

There was only one marker for The Veil. Our parents had warned us of the shimmering colors that skirted the boundary like an iridescent cape. The colors were the telltale sign that you had wandered too close. From there, it was said that the fae would be lurking nearby, watching.

Waiting.

A shiver went down my spine. "How much time do I have?"

"We were lucky enough to get a decent head start, but it won't be long until they've figured out you're no longer on the castle grounds."

My heart slowly sank.

I needed to prepare myself to run as far as I could, as fast as I could. That was going to be dreadful. And I didn't want to part ways with Weston. Especially when I had no idea what was going to happen.

Thankfully, I had my sword. I clutched its pommel with my free hand, the familiar leather-wrapped hilt bringing me a sliver of reassurance.

"When you enter the trees, don't stop running. Run until you can't any longer, and then run further."

"But where am I supposed to go? Once I get to The Veil, I'll have nowhere else to run to."

He gave me a soft smile. "Trust in the gods, Auren. But for now, please, run."

Reluctantly, I nodded. "Thank you for getting me here."

"It has been an honor." He stepped back and nodded sternly this time before turning to leave.

"Wait!" I called after him. "I'm not going to see you again, am I?"

He was already jogging in the opposite direction, but he turned toward me, slowing to a backwards walk and giving me a casual shrug. "The fates work in mysterious ways." He winked, then faced away once more and charged down the tunnel.

I lingered a moment longer and watched his torch flame fade down the corridor as the distance between us stretched further, before I turned and started toward the opening. After a couple of slight bends, it appeared just up ahead.

Weston was right, dawn was creeping in.

I did as he instructed and set my torch down, scuffing dirt over it to snuff out the flame. Then I approached the opening, to greet the dawn . . . and whatever came with it.

10

THE GREAT WOOD

GRAY LIGHT CLUNG TO THE ATMOSPHERE IN THE FINAL MOMENTS JUST before the sun peeked above the earth's edge. By the time I'd crept out of the tunnel's opening and climbed the small ravine in the clearing, the silvery sky had bloomed pale orange and lavender.

I crouched low as I approached the top of the incline and scanned my surroundings. The Great Wood stood in front of me, silent and still. Lying in wait, as if it knew something I didn't.

It was still early into spring, but the forest was already green and regaining its foliage. I took in the tall trees above me; elms and oaks that mingled and tangled amongst each other in a crowded canopy. The ground was covered with dew and moss. Small plants clung to the tree trunks and their roots. It truly looked like a lovely place—if one didn't know better.

As I surveyed the remaining world around me, my eyes snagged on movement not too far off in the distance.

Men on horses. Men with swords.

The king's men.

I froze as a knot formed in my stomach.

They were steadily patrolling, with no urgent speed to their pace, so they must not have seen me yet. There were no tracks for them to trace— thanks to using the tunnel system. But their arrival was too soon. I thought I'd have more time.

Quietly, I backed down the ravine and moved further along the path, putting some distance between me and them before climbing up again and braving the true depths of the forest. The castle was behind me, so that meant The Veil was straight ahead. But as I emerged this time, another set of guards descended on me from my left.

The king must have dispatched multiple patrols.

"There! She's there!" a guard shouted as he maneuvered his horse around the trees.

I had no other choice. The urgency of Weston's instructions to not get captured hit me in full force, and I sprinted off into the heart of The Great Wood. I ran blindly, dodging trees and jumping over roots that tangled themselves above the ground like snares. I focused on lifting my feet higher so I didn't trip. Thankfully the horses and men fell behind as the terrain grew considerably denser.

I was so very tired, but I had to keep pushing forward—even if my pace was slowing tremendously. I'd fought hard yesterday, but this level of exhaustion was new to me. Come to think of it, I'd never felt this tired in my life. My body was wracked. My emotions were frazzled. And as I pressed on, my fatigue intensified, my sword suddenly feeling as heavy as a sack of grain.

Why was my energy waning? I'd trained every day leading up to this. I had years of experience wielding weapons and using my fists and feet to fight. My body should have been plenty prepared. So why did I feel like I was about to keel over?

I just needed to make it to The Veil and hope that Weston was right, or that he had something planned.

Up ahead was a small incline littered with ferns and gray stones poking out of the wild brush. I grabbed onto the low-lying tree limbs to help haul myself up the berm.

I wasn't sure just how far I'd run. No one ever ventured here, so there were no recent accounts of how deep The Great Wood actually went. Worry crept into my gut. I estimated that I should be getting awfully close to the boundary, but I'd seen no markings thus far.

In the midst of my pausing and contemplating I heard horse hooves in the distance and the clang of swords against branches.

My pursuers were gaining back their ground.

I gritted my teeth and prepared my aching body to move. My lungs and legs barked in protest as I pushed away from the trees and set myself into another fleeting pace.

My eyes darted frantically as I began flitting from tree to tree, pausing briefly to listen for any sound—to pinpoint which direction the men were coming from. But as quickly as it came, the sound of the chase ceased. Only the pounding of my heartbeat echoed in my ears as I reined in my breathing.

Maybe I'm close enough to The Veil now.

Perhaps they turned back?

I crept forward around a large tree trunk and peered back down an all too quiet, hollowed-out deer path. The silence seemed strained, and the stillness was full of so much tension that it felt wrong.

Then, out of the shadows, thundering hooves and towering guards with drawn swords came rounding the corner, barreling right toward me. I stumbled back, tripping over gnarled tree roots, nearly losing my sword amongst the mishap. I regained my footing and skirted a nearby tree, launching into a sprint. But they were gaining on me. I could hear the horses huffing as they closed the distance.

My ears began ringing. Whether it was from the blood racing through my veins, or the exhaustion weighing down on me, I didn't know, but something deep inside me stirred and became aware.

A pit formed in my stomach.

I frantically scanned the trees ahead, looking for any sign that I was close to The Veil. It was out here somewhere, and blindly running for my life with no sense of direction meant that I was probably closer to it than I thought.

My breath turned ragged, lungs screaming with protest, burning with each inhale. I searched for the colors, the distortions, anything to signal that I was out of bounds. But none of those things stood out to me.

My vision tunneled. I could feel the utter finality of my exhaustion creeping up over me, ready to pull me under.

No. No—

Nothing warned me that I should go no further until it was too late. I was suddenly upon The Veil. And I was wholly swallowed by it.

It was a trap.

A perfectly laid trap.

11
THE VEIL

THE WORLD AROUND ME WENT WHITE.

The air was suddenly thick with a dense fog. But there was a wrongness that hung heavy within it. It was as if all time had stopped.

I wasn't at The Veil . . . I was *in* The Veil. I knew I needed to either keep pushing forward, or turn back, but instead, I just stood there—caught in the solid space of it, holding my breath as if I was waiting for my death. And maybe I *was* waiting for it. Waiting for a wretched fae to run me through with a sword, or string me up with their magic. It was only a matter of time before something came and stole the breath away from my lungs—I was sure of it.

I waved at the fog, desperately trying to clear it so that I could gather any sense of direction. It felt like the atmosphere was an entity in and of itself, and it wanted to keep me prisoner in this void. It began calling to me, coaxing me. Many voices—both male and female—faded in and out, all at once, as if they were swarming in erratic circles.

Then, it *pulled* at me. Not a physical pull at my body, but a greedy tugging at something deep inside me.

At my *soul.*

The feeling prickled every nerve in my body, and I descended into a panic. Whoever, or whatever was near, it wanted me. And I feared it wanted me *dead.*

Suddenly, a muffle fell upon the voices, and the tugging was replaced by a tender presence that enveloped me and guided my body away from the hungry entity. I broke out of the white fog, falling to my hands and knees in the forest once again. When I looked back behind me, The Veil was gone. I saw only the continuation of the trees, the vivid colors dancing their way between them. The slight distortion shimmered around every tree, leaf, and blade of grass, and ran down a line of foliage in both directions as far as I could see. In all of my panic and exhaustion, I must have missed it before.

The air was now damp, and a mist danced heavily through the dense tree cover—where it had just been dry moments ago. The morning light was filtered by the tree canopy which stretched out above me like a dark blanket, forcing a gloomy quiet upon everything beneath it. It was eerily beautiful, but vastly different from my side—my realm.

Dread crept up my spine and my body spasmed with it.

There had been a time when there was no Veil, only open territory. But even then, humans and fae tended to stay away from each other. The fae had magic which grew stronger with the passing of time. And the fae lived on, seeing human lives pass by like a blink. They were seemingly immortal to us, living for thousands of years, whereas we were lucky to see the age of sixty.

Humans had fought beside the fae in the first war against Lyceius, but didn't fare well. After the war, the human king at the time—King Emmeric—demanded access to the fae lands for refuge and protection of his people, but the fae High Lords refused. And when Lyceius launched another war against our realms, the fae erected The Veil. It was warded with magic to keep Lyceius confined to his own territory, cutting off his access to our lands. But it also locked us on our side, indefinitely. Woven to the fae's advantage. Putting an end to our efforts for a treaty between their kind and ours.

Centuries passed with continued strain, and tensions didn't ease. Kings came and went, and more talks and treaties were attempted with the fae. But none prevailed. Ever since then, all we knew of them was what we had been told from past generations. Because from the moment The Veil split our realms, no human had been able to cross it.

Except me.

I kept still, not knowing what to do, but when none of my pursuers followed me across, I knew that this had to have been a fluke. A trap of some kind. As I scanned my surroundings, a new awareness settled over me. One that reminded me of just what might be lurking nearby . . .

The fae.

That rich, stern voice crept into my head—the same as before in the tournament—commanding me. *Run.*

I blinked upon hearing it.

Run!

A sense of urgency washed over me. I knew it was best to never stay in one place for long during, or after a fight—and this qualified as such a time. I needed to move.

I grabbed my sword and stood on wobbly legs, stumbling across the moss-covered ground. I caught myself on a nearby tree for balance just as a crack sounded in the distance.

My heartbeat kicked into a frenzy. I shook away the unsteadiness and began a sad attempt at running once again. I tried to avoid breaking too many twigs under my feet, but my legs were so heavy that I was failing miserably at keeping quiet.

If I crossed back to my realm, the king's men would capture me. If I stayed . . . who knows what would find me. I couldn't stay put, but I had no idea which way to run. Common sense told me I needed to put as much distance between myself and The Veil as possible, and hide for a while.

After several minutes of stumbling more than running, my chest was rising and falling in a ragged rhythm, and my heart was pounding uncontrollably. Sweat, and the accumulating mist, mixed together and trickled down my face and neck, soaking my chest.

I paused and tried to tame my breathing. My eyes flicked across the mossy forest floor in front of me, up the sopping trees, and further strained to survey the impossibly dense canopy.

There was no sign of any other life thus far, but that didn't mean it wasn't out there.

Did Weston have a plan to keep me safe? He told me to run to The Veil. What if I ruined his plan by actually crossing it? My head spun with thoughts and doubts as I tried to figure out what to do.

I pressed my back into a nearby oak tree. I could feel my body straining to stay upright. My feet throbbed, my calves ached.

Everything felt heavy. But I couldn't relax—*wouldn't* relax. Not yet. I swallowed hard and blinked away the moisture on my lashes. If I let my guard down for more than a second, that's when the opponent always struck. I'd learned that more times than I could count in combat.

I tried to push off my crutch of a tree, when another heavy wave of exhaustion swept over me. My legs trembled uncontrollably, and I collapsed against the roots, drawing in long, labored pulls of air. I didn't want to linger in the open, but my body begged for rest.

As I sat sprawled out against the tree's roots, my vision began blurring in and out.

No, please.

I blinked rapidly in hopes of warding it off. The last thing I wanted was to be unconscious in a foreign realm.

I didn't fear much, but I did fear the unknown. I only knew of the fae from the stories and lore that we grew up on. We were taught that the fae reveled in their power, and humans were like a prize to them. Mortal flesh to be toyed with at their leisure. The stories said that the fae didn't feel emotions the way humans felt them. With no regard for sentiments or morals, they did as they pleased and wielded deadly power and untamed magic.

I certainly had no intention of running into any of their kind, but being on their side of The Veil now made that a very real possibility.

Blinking to regain some clarity, I dug my palms against the soft, wet bark, and slowly made to push myself up when a wall of air slammed into my body, forbidding me to move. The force pressed against me from all angles, holding me in place against the mangled roots.

My mind began reeling. Maybe something was wrong with me after passing through The Veil. Perhaps that eerie presence had followed me, and was taking this moment of weakness to strike. Maybe this was some tricky tree magic—planted by those ruthless fae.

I realized none of those scenarios were correct when a tall male stepped into my peripheral, hands clasped behind his back.

My breath caught in my throat as my heart sank.

A fae had caught me.

The wall of air pinned me in place, like a fish under a weighted net.

There was nothing I could do, and no move I could make that would resist fae magic.

The male stepped into full view and tilted his head to the side. His eyes narrowed as they met mine. Piercing orbs of golden honey that had a faint glow to them stared back at me with uncertainty and a bit of mischief. He was, without a doubt, the most handsome male I had ever seen.

The clothes he wore seemed out-of-place for someone out in the middle of the forest. His fine black pants and tunic were like a second skin, clinging to his broad shoulders and muscular legs—leaving nothing to the imagination. And he wasn't sopping wet from the mist. He stood perfectly polished and dry.

Some sort of magic, I thought.

He reached up to slick his fingers back through his dark hair, but a few of the longer strands on top fell back over his forehead as he looked down at me.

My eyes snagged on the tell-tale tips of his pointed ears.

Positively fae.

His power radiated off of him like a dark, pulsing essence, and I began to shake under the restraint as he stepped closer, closing the distance between us. He halted only a few feet away and continued to stare at me like he was reading my soul.

I felt a natural urge to fight or flee, but it was washed over entirely by a strange thrumming that flared to life within my chest. Every fiber in my body became attuned to it, my senses scrambling—trying desperately to decipher what was happening. It was as if a rhythmic humming had taken root and threaded itself between my ribs.

There appeared to be no other magic at work, other than the force rooting me in place. But *something* was there—sliding under my radar. It was as if my soul was being summoned. My heart lurched, hands straining against the invisible net, as if freeing them would allow me to cling to whatever aspect of myself he was pulling into his orbit.

Is he trying to steal my soul?

It was said that the fae could influence your thoughts and emotions with a few simple words, or the flick of their wrist. How they could compel a human to do their bidding on a whim—as easily as breathing.

But this male had neither spoken nor flicked his wrist at me in the brief moments that I had my eyes on him.

Although there wasn't a weapon on him to be seen, I had no doubt that my captor was lethal.

I also couldn't deny that he was gorgeous.

I decided right then that I must have lost my mind when I crossed The Veil.

He started to turn his head, parting his lips as if he was going to whisper something to someone over his shoulder. But no one else was there. It was just the two of us. Then, as if in sudden realization, he slowly turned his face back towards me, and the corner of his mouth lifted.

With a voice as deep and smooth as rolling thunder, he said, "It's *you*."

12

CAPTOR

THE HANDSOME MALE STOOD UNNATURALLY STILL, EYES WIDE WITH AWE and fear, as if he recognized me but wasn't supposed to.

What he had to fear, I didn't know. He was fae. I was just a human. And my mortality became a very real concern as I strained against the pressure he held me down with.

I opened my mouth to speak, and to my surprise, the strange force lessened just enough to allow me to.

My voice had become terribly hoarse and raspy from running, and when I finally pushed words past my lips, they were a shredded whisper. "Please, don't hurt me. I can explain why I'm here."

He took a step forward. "I don't think you quite know . . ." His voice trailed off, and he halted mid-step at the same moment the strange thrumming in my chest spiked. He angled his head at me again, as if he was working out an impossible puzzle.

Time seemed to stop around us for a brief second, and I found myself unable to look away from the glow in his golden eyes. Something about them felt like they were calling to me.

Magic, I thought. *This has to be his magic.*

I was about to speak again, when I heard the crisp snap of a branch somewhere behind me.

The handsome fae jerked his head up to scan the forest beyond, and his face hardened when he spotted something in the distance. He quickly looked back down to me, and those golden eyes sparked with something I couldn't quite place as he said, "I'll see you soon." Whether it was a threat or not, it sent chills down my spine. If anything, it was most definitely a promise.

All at once he vanished from sight, and the force pressing down on me lifted away, the vibration within my chest ceasing along with it. I exhaled with relief—not realizing I'd been holding my breath—and my body sank down into the sopping wet tree roots.

I could hear footsteps growing closer. Several, then two.

Leaves and twigs crunched just on the other side of the tree I was lying helpless against. I strained to turn my body, wanting desperately to confront whatever creature was surely about to make its kill. When I managed to move enough to see, I was shocked to find another fae male crouching down on the ridge above the root system.

This male looked far different from the one I'd just seen. His bronze hair fell in waves over his pointed ears, brushing his temples and the nape of his neck. He was outfitted like a hunter, wearing brown pants the shade of the earth, tall leather boots, and a green tunic that matched the leaves on the trees above. A well-worn leather baldric of knives was strapped tightly across his chest, and a quiver of arrows was slung over his back. A bow rested across his knees, and he gripped it as he leaned further and looked down at me.

The mist had begun to come down like rain, yet he was untouched by the moisture—just as the other male had been. When I met his deep forest green eyes, something like pity showed there.

I wanted to tell him not to hurt me, to say that I was there by mistake —to say *anything*—but my vision faded as a new wave of weakness washed over me.

This one seemed final.

I slumped back against the roots, too drained to hold my body up any longer. As I sipped shallow breaths and drifted in and out of consciousness, my hand twitched, and I shakily reached out towards him. A plea for help.

I could have sworn he reached out and took it with a faint smile.

13
CAMP

I WOKE TO A LUSCIOUS WARMTH THAT SETTLED ALONG MY ACHING BONES.

My entire body hurt. My muscles were weak, and it felt as if my mind had been weakened as well. My only explanation was The Veil. Or perhaps this realm was the cause?

The warmth was a welcomed reprieve, but I suddenly held my breath, my stomach hollowing out. I was under a blanket and I was dry when, last I remembered, I'd been soaking wet.

Without opening my eyes, I listened to my surroundings so as not to alert anyone that I'd awoken. I heard the crackling of a fire, and the stirring of a metal pot. Somewhere nearby a few male voices were speaking low. Behind me, a few others chuckled softly. I was still outdoors; I could hear an owl in the distance and the ticking chorus of insects.

It must be night.

I briefly recalled the events leading up to me going unconscious: *crossing The Veil, running, resting, being held against that tree by the magic of that devastatingly handsome fae male wearing all black, the other fae male—the hunter that crouched over me and took my hand—*

The *hunter.* My stomach gave another slight drop at the memory that someone *else* had found me. But he had smiled—faintly—with what looked like pity on his face when I reached out for him.

Oh gods! I'd reached out for him!

I reeled my spiraling thoughts back in. I was wrapped in a blanket and still fully clothed. Those had to be signs of someone with a decent amount of respect.

And I was still alive.

Whoever he was, he, and those with him, could have killed me if they wanted to. And judging by the dryness of my hair and clothes, plenty of time had passed for them to have done so.

How long was I unconscious?

I decided to take a look at where I was. I shimmied my face out from under the thick blanket to find that I had been laid in front of a generous fire. Beyond that, there were four tents set up facing the flames, and several fae males were sitting around a large, flat tree stump with mugs in their hands.

My foot twitched, and a shadow was immediately towering over me. I turned my head up toward the figure and blinked. It was the fae from before. The second one, who had taken my hand as I fell into oblivion.

"She finally wakes," he mused. His voice was warm and welcoming as he came and sat in front of me on a tree stump.

I stared at him, not really knowing what I should say or do.

He looked . . . oddly human—aside from the pointed ears that peeked out from under the tousled bronze waves of his hair. His sleeves were casually rolled, and he sat in an oddly vulnerable position, watching me like I was about to perform a trick.

I didn't know what I expected the fae to look or act like, but this wasn't it.

When I didn't say anything, he spoke again. "How does a human come to cross The Veil?"

"How do you know I'm human?" My throat was raw, but my voice had slightly recovered, pitching low in more of a rasp than my normal smooth, lively timbre.

He eyed me for a moment, then pointed to his ears. "It's rather obvious."

I scowled at him, and he laughed lightly to himself.

My attention went back to the fire and the other fae in the vicinity. By the looks of it, the mist had ceased some time ago, and everything had decently dried-out.

"What happened?" I asked.

"You passed out after I found you. I don't know what you got yourself into, but you were exhausted. It felt like you were on the verge of death. It felt like how it feels when one of *us* has drained most of our power."

He could sense *things like that?*

I eyed him for a long moment, then snorted through my nose. He was mistaken. "I don't have power. I'm clearly human." I tucked my face back into the woolen blanket.

He must have felt the power from that other fae. The dark haired one with features I could only dream of . . .

Stop that, I silently scolded myself.

The fae male remained quiet.

When the silence got too awkward, I pulled the blanket back down so I could look at him.

He was still staring at me.

"*What?*"

"What happened to you?" he asked curiously.

I reminded myself that if he wanted me dead, I wouldn't have woken up. I sighed deeply, shifting my gaze over to the flames again. "I was running, and I accidentally crossed The Veil."

He slowly leaned over into my line of sight and gave me a pointed look.

"I'm serious. I was running, and then I just ended up here. I don't know how it happened." I was just as confused with the entire event as he was.

"You just *happened* to enter our realm, and you had no intention of doing so?"

"My goal was to run toward The Veil. Not cross it. It had to have been a trap." I began to get worked up again at the thought of it.

He shifted on the stump and leaned forward, over his knees. "There are no traps at The Veil. No human crosses it. It has been that way since its existence."

"Well I don't know what you think occurred, but I know that I went through that horrible place and was spat out on your side, completely exhausted. And now I'm here." I lifted my head to look around the space again. "Where exactly are we anyway?"

He straightened himself. "Camp."

There were a few empty cages near one of the tents, and bundles of rope hanging from a nearby branch, coated with what looked like dried blood.

"Is it a prison camp or something?"

He let out a short chuckle and shook his head. "Hunting camp."

I sat up on my elbows.

Hunting camp. Of course.

He was dressed like he had been out scouting—or something along those lines. Hunting made sense. I glanced around the campsite again, looking harder this time, and recognized the truth to his claim; the cache of weapons piled outside the tents, the cookware set next to the fire, the pair of deer strung up by their bound hooves in the trees near the horses. And further off, another cage with what looked like a lifeless, wild boar inside, dripping blood onto the forest floor from a wound to its belly.

He followed my stare and explained. "It's a typical scouting detail. We go out every few nights to patrol the borders of The Veil, and while we're out we hunt this area—if we're able to. It's full of deer." He motioned towards, what I assumed, were their latest kills.

"Are they *special fae deer?*" I asked, half joking, half serious. I couldn't even believe I was having this conversation with a fae.

He tossed his head back and laughed, the sound surprisingly light-hearted. "I suppose so. They taste delicious, and we never seem to have trouble finding them."

My cheeks heated at how stupid I'd sounded.

I watched as he reached over to snatch a leather flask off the nearby bedroll. "Here, drink. It's just water," he said, handing me the small tankard.

I hesitated before taking it.

Was it poisoned?

I sniffed at it suspiciously.

He had plenty of chances to kill me earlier, why poison me now?

At this point, I would probably die just as well from *not* drinking water. So, I sipped. My eyes widened at the taste of it on my tongue. I had never tasted fresher water. I drank deeply, letting the coolness of it soothe my dry throat. All the while, the fae male just sat and watched me, as if I was a wild animal he was only just discovering.

I took one last gulp, wiped my mouth with the back of my hand, and handed the flask back to him. In our brief moment of eye contact, I willed my face to convey my gratitude.

He nodded in understanding. "Would you like some food?"

Maybe it was the concern in his eyes that made him feel less like a threat and more like an inconvenience. Despite his kindness, I couldn't continue making niceties with fae hunters in the woods. I needed to formulate a plan and get home. I had lucked out this far by coming across someone with his temperament, instead of one with crueler intentions.

And if I learned anything from past experiences, it's that luck runs out eventually.

"I appreciate your kindness and hospitality, but I need to get back to The Veil. It was just after dawn when I crossed, and I have no idea how long I've been here, but I'm already certain it's been too long."

"Back to The Veil? That's not possible," he said matter-of-factly, completely ignoring my thanks.

"What do you mean?" Panic surfaced in my voice. "Surely, it's back the same way we came from. This is your land isn't it? You should know its layout—being a scout or a hunter or *whatever* you are."

He lifted his deep green eyes to mine, but his expression was almost sorrowful. "I am both those things. But first and foremost, I'm a dignitary in my High Lord's court. His is the land you crossed onto, and it is to him that I must deliver you. The law of the land says that any trespasser must be taken before him."

"I am no trespasser!" My voice rang out—finally gaining back some of its gusto. The other fae shifted around the camp, turning their heads to me, but I continued speaking to the male in front of me. "I assure you I came here against my will. If you would just show me the way back, you can pretend you never even saw me."

He stood abruptly, as if summoned to a call. "It won't matter. He can already sense your presence. He'll know you're here. We'll ride out shortly after first light and should make it there by mid-day." He let out a deep sigh. "I apologize for the abruptness. I'm bound by the law. But I assure you that while you're with me, you're safe."

86

I'd been told that before. That I would be safe. I was a bit wary to trust it this time. Though, I was still alive, so technically, Weston's words had held true thus far.

"My name is Breck," the fae said. "And you are?"

I opened my mouth slightly, then closed it as I narrowed my eyes at him. I threw the blanket back over my head, deciding to ignore him instead.

Breck let out an amused laugh and crossed the camp to join the others.

14
A QUESTION FOR A QUESTION

I SLEPT LIKE I HADN'T IN WEEKS. AND AS I SLEPT, I DREAMED WILD dreams, full of magic and fae. And amidst it all, one thing stood out. A fae male—tall and powerful, with dark hair and golden eyes.

He kept his distance, but his presence was palpable. His stare lingered on me as he watched me from afar throughout the dream.

When I grew too curious and approached him, he vanished into thin air, leaving a wisp of smoke where he'd stood.

When I woke, the sun's buttery light was shining overhead through the tree canopy. I squinted as my eyes adjusted to it.

As I regained my full consciousness, I became aware that I was moving, and there was a presence around me—like an invisible brace against my body, holding me upright. It promptly melted away the moment I lifted my head to look down at myself.

I was atop a horse.

I reeled back, bumping into whatever I had previously been resting my head against. Twisting, I beheld the same fae from the hunting camp, boasting a smile as warm as his body felt.

Breck, I recalled his name.

The filtered sunlight rippled over his face, highlighting the golden-brown tones in his bronze hair. His verdant green eyes reflected the surrounding foliage.

"Good afternoon, sunshine," he said in a mockingly chipper tone.

I rolled my eyes at him and didn't reply.

How did I get on this horse anyway?

I surveyed the line of horses we were in. There were five other mounts with riders atop them. Two additional mares brought up the rear of our unit, carrying the lifeless deer, the caged boar, and the supplies from the camp.

"You slept all night, and through the morning as we packed up camp. I was starting to think you weren't going to wake up." When I didn't reply, he continued. "And in case you were wondering, you were perfectly secure up here without me having to lay a hand on you."

I looked down to where his hand was casually holding the reins in front of me. His other rested on his thigh.

"I felt it—whatever was holding me up."

He reached around me and took the reins with both hands. "*That* was my magic. It would have stayed there as long as you required it."

I knotted my brows. "Your magic? But I couldn't see it . . ."

"Not all magic can be seen. In fact, most of it is hidden to the eye. Many fae can produce a shield to protect themselves, or others. Some fae can even manipulate those shields and form them into something a little more useful, like a barrier or a brace. Or even a net of sorts. In this case, it acted as a brace, because I willed it to."

My mind immediately went to the dark-haired fae male who'd first found me in the forest, and the weight that had fallen on me like a net. I started to open my mouth to speak of it, but decided it was probably best to feel things out, before mentioning I'd been seen by anyone else. Evidently, I was already trespassing, and one particular High Lord wasn't too happy about it.

Instead I asked, "So, you're one of those special fae?"

"I'm glad you think so."

I didn't have to turn and look at him to know he was grinning, but I did anyway. "That was a question, not a statement," I replied, dryly.

"Whatever you say, sunshine."

"Stop calling me that," I said in a low, clipped voice. His grin widened, and it irritated me even more that he found me amusing.

He chuckled as he steered our horse around a fallen tree. "Shielding isn't the most impressive thing we can do, but it's convenient. In fact, The Veil is a type of shield in its own right—as I'm sure you know. Which is why I'm more than curious as to how you crossed it."

"Perhaps someone manipulated The Veil when I crossed."

"No. Our magic allows us to move across it without pause, so there's no need. Not to mention, there was no one else on this side of The Veil when I found you. We'd already patrolled that area before you appeared."

But there was . . .

I wanted to tell him about the other male, but something told me to wait.

I shifted in the saddle, my lower back already beginning to strain and grow stiff as I continued to sit forward away from his chest.

"You can relax, you know. I'm not going to hurt you."

A name and an ability to shield was all I knew of this male, and that wasn't enough for me to feel comfortable settling back into him for a cozy horse ride through a foreign forest. So, I remained as I was—straight as a rod—as the horse continued down the path.

He sighed. "You're incredibly stubborn."

"What does it matter to you if I'm comfortable or not?" Maybe I *was* being more difficult than was necessary.

"We're decent beings. We care for others and know how to be hospitable. We're not beasts."

A twinge of guilt nipped at me.

Breck had been nothing but kind so far—aside from refusing to take me back to The Veil. He'd taken care of me. And I was neither dead nor dying. The least I could do was be cordial and go with him to see his High Lord before returning home. Who knows, maybe I would get more answers as to how this all happened. A High Lord must have some insight into matters like this . . .

"I'm sorry, you've been very kind. I shouldn't have said that." I sighed deeply. "You're only doing your job. I'm just a bit irritated."

Breck nodded his head in understanding.

We rode in silence for a while, and I took the time to study my surroundings. I hadn't really paid close attention when I crossed; my focus had been on running and not passing out—both of which I'd failed miserably at. And everything had been sopping wet and gloomy at the time.

Now, the forest had dried out under the sun's gentle touch, and the scenery was enchanting. Everything was richer, lusher. There were so many vivid shades of green that my eyes felt tricked. The trees loomed high above and seemed to stretch out to greet one another, the bark appearing like soft, brown velvet, the leaves dancing and shimmying as we passed by.

Every sense was heightened. The smells were stronger, the air was cleaner, even the sun was more golden—a stark contrast to the dull and drab land on my side of The Veil.

"The land here has a magic of its own," Breck said, noticing where my attention had gone.

I breathed in, long and deep, filling my lungs with the fragrant air as I turned my head up towards the sunlight. I could feel Breck staring down at my face from behind me.

"What happened there?" he asked, a hint of concern flaring in his voice.

I opened my eyes to find him fixated on my cheek—the one that harbored the gruesome bruise. "I got it while I was fighting." There was no sense in lying to him. What good was the information to him anyway?

"Like, fighting on purpose?" he asked.

"*Yes,* like fighting on purpose. I can handle a sword just as any other man can—better, even." I lifted my chin. "There was a tournament at the castle. The king invited me to participate—which I did—and I won. I was awarded a spot in the King's Guard." I reached up and touched the tender flesh. "This is just a souvenir."

While it was still slightly swollen, it didn't hurt as much as before. *Strange.* Usually when I bruised, it would take at least a week before the splash of purples and blues faded to muddied greens and browns, and another few days for it to lose its tenderness before it disappeared.

"I uh . . . I just wouldn't have pegged you for a fighter," he said, surprised.

"You don't know me."

"No. I do not." A long, awkward moment passed between us until he said, "Let's remedy that shall we? There's still another hour left to ride. How about a question for a question?"

I sighed.

At least he's being pleasant. At least I'm not being dragged behind the horse in chains, or locked in one of those cages, I reminded myself.

But another hour? How far was this place? I wanted to start the game by blurting out *that* question, but he beat me to asking.

"When did you start learning how to fight?"

I wiggled in the seat a bit and sighed. An hour of the damn question game, I could do that. "My father trained my brother and I when we were children. My turn." I knew my answer could have been more detailed, but I didn't feel like elaborating.

Breck's shoulders shook a little as he laughed to himself. "Ask away, sunshine."

I glared back at him. "Where exactly are we going?"

"Well, the forest is a vast expanse." He flourished his hand out in front of me with obvious sarcasm. "We were at the easternmost edge of it, and the main dwelling lands of our court lie near the center. That's where we're headed." I waited for him to be a little more informative, but he was dishing out what I had served him: minimal details. He leaned his head around into my peripheral. "*My turn,*" he said sarcastically.

I blinked at his mockery.

All right, I'll play this game.

"Ask away. I don't have to answer you."

He threw his head back and laughed loudly—the sound like a welcoming drum—and I bristled. I hadn't intended for my words to be funny. The other fae males in front of us turned in their saddles to see what the commotion was all about.

Breck blew out a breath as he reined in his laughter. "Such a fiery little human. A word of caution though: be careful with who you speak to in that manner. Not all fae are as forgiving as me." I could tell he was smiling by the tone of his voice, and I rolled my eyes. "Now, for my question," he continued. "You say you're good with a blade. How are you with a bow?"

I hesitated. "I-I've never shot a bow before."

My father and brother had always handled the hunting, so I never bothered with it.

Breck leaned over my shoulder to look at my face, reading the hesitation there. "Are you afraid to?"

"No! Why would I be afraid to shoot a bow? I was just never taught how."

"Well, you're in luck. I just happen to be an excellent shot."

"Oh really?" I scoffed. "Show me then."

I expected him to make up some excuse like, "Now isn't the proper time or place," but instead, he snatched his bow from his shoulder and knocked an arrow so fast that I hardly saw the movement. He leaned back against the horse's hind end, so as to have room to fully draw the string with the complete span of his long arms. Aiming skyward, he pulled the bowstring taut and loosed an arrow straight up into the air.

I whipped my head around, looking above us to find what he shot at. When I saw nothing but the tree canopy I looked back at him. "Anyone can do that."

Suddenly, the arrow came down with a thud—tip first into the dirt beside us. Our horse startled and let out an exasperated snort.

But there, skewered on the end of the metal tipped wooden shaft was a bright yellow bird. Its wings twitched wildly before finally stilling, its chest ceasing to rise.

I snapped my eyes back to Breck who had a smug grin on his lips. "Impressive," I conceded. It was more than just impressive, but I didn't want to give him something else to gloat on.

I turned back around and thought for a moment. It would be very beneficial to learn how to shoot a bow, and I was a quick learner. Maybe he could show me the basics, and I could practice with my brother when I got home . . .

As if he could read my mind, he said, "I could teach you."

"Really? I mean, just the basics, as I'm sure we won't have much time."

His grin turned a little south at the edges. "We will have more time than you think. Anyway, it's a great skill to have. I'm sure if you're as good with a sword as you say you are, you should pick up archery in no time."

I internally agreed with him. Part of me wished I could whip my sword out and demonstrate my skills just as he did with his bow. Carve up one of those limp deer that were strapped to the dapple mare and show him my talent of precision.

My heartbeat sped up. *Where is my sword?*

I felt my hips for my belt and scabbard. Both were missing.

"Don't worry, it's strapped under our pack." He patted the back end of the horse we rode on.

I let out a breath of relief.

"Is it important to you?"

"My father gave it to me. He had it made for me as a twenty-fifth birthday present. That was a little over three years ago now." And it hadn't left my side since. "It's all I have left of him. I'd be devastated if something happened to it."

"You lost your father?" he asked quietly.

I nodded. "Both of my parents, actually. I don't really talk about it much."

"I'm sorry for your loss."

"Thank you. They were good people."

I hoped he wouldn't press the subject further, and thankfully, he didn't. His arms tightened around me slightly, tugging the reins to the right.

A stilted silence stretched between us as we continued riding down the cleared path, until I decided to break it with another question. "Would you really teach me to use a bow?"

"That counts as one of your questions," he said, trying to make light of the situation. I appreciated the effort. "And yes, I would teach you," he added.

"I have another question," I said, smiling, knowing it was breaking the rule of our back and forth game.

He let go of the reins with one hand and waved it in front of me as if to say, *go on then.*

"Who is the High Lord you're taking me to see?"

"His name is Killian. He's the High Lord of Elandrew—which is the territory we're in. Each territory has its own High Lord."

I'd heard of the fae having multiple ruling lords, but I knew nothing of the territories of which he spoke. "In my land, there is only one territory, but many cities lie within it. King Broderick rules them all. It's not like that here then?"

"Not quite," he said. "Where your realm has one king and queen, ours has several ruling High Lords, and it is in their bloodlines that true power resides and shows its full extent. In ancient times, there was a power struggle between the elite fae houses. The separate territories we have today—along with their own ruling High Lords—became established as a result."

"And how many territories does your realm have?"

"We have five territories here in the realm of Anbrya and each has its court and High Lord. The courts are named after their varying topographies. Take here, for example"—he gestured to the landscape around us—"this is the Woodland Court. The territory itself is named Elandrew. Think of it like one of your cities. People live all throughout Elandrew and answer to Killian."

It was surprisingly easy to understand, and I couldn't deny my curiosity, which tapped playfully at the forefront of my mind. "What are the other territories?"

Breck huffed a laugh. "How did I know that was going to trigger a million other questions?"

I couldn't help the grin that surfaced, but I dipped my chin in an effort to keep it to myself.

"There's Vahrenhall, home of the Highland Court, which borders us to our west. They have a vast and beautiful land that's as rocky as it is lush and green. Then there's Calledan, home of the Mountain Court. Their mountain range is something to marvel at. Dangerous, but defyingly beautiful. Benmoor is home of the Desert Court. That's a harsh and arid land, but stunning in its own right. And Drastia—the Arctic Court—is covered in an endless snow-pack. I honestly don't know how they're not miserable most of the time."

Each territory sounded like something wondrous. And Breck seemed to have knowledge of them all.

"Have you seen any of them in person?" I asked, all rules to our question game officially abandoned.

He gave me a slight laugh. "All of them."

I was instantly envious. I always dreamed of traveling and seeing new places. I'd heard stories about what merchants saw when they came back from their travels. But all I'd ever known before this was my tiny cottage on the outskirts of town, and the immediate area that surrounded it. Not many people back home ever got the chance to see new places.

"And you?" he inquired. "Are you well-traveled in your realm?"

A wave of disappointment crested and washed over me. "No. Almost twenty-nine years behind me and nothing to show for it." My voice was tainted with enough self-pity that Breck didn't press on.

"Once we get this business with Killian taken care of, I promise to show you some of this territory. I think you'll like it," he said softly.

"Thank you. I'd like that—and a quick round of bow practice."

Breck's warm laugh danced through the trees. "Thought you weren't planning to stay long?"

"I'm not," I confirmed. "I do have another question though."

"Of course you do," he said playfully.

"Why do you call him 'Killian' and not 'High Lord'?"

"Ah, that." He shrugged a nonchalant shoulder. "Here, nobility is recognized by power and magic. Addressing a High Lord with formalities each time isn't all that necessary. Everyone knows what title they hold, and what power they wield. Why run through the motions every time?"

"That's refreshing. Our kingdom is so caught up in the formalities of titles and status that it gets tiresome. If someone were to call the king by only his surname, he'd probably order their house to be burned down."

Breck's face turned sour. "That's ridiculously cruel."

I shrugged. "I'm exaggerating a bit, but you get the idea."

He nodded, but his expression told me he was still skeptical.

Our horses crossed over a stream of water that sparkled in the beams of light coming through the tree canopy, and Breck steered us around the others toward the front of the line.

"We're getting close now," he informed me.

The others nodded to us as we passed by, then they peeled off to head down a separate path. None of them had given me grief or made me feel the least bit fearful while in their company. And Breck had been a rather pleasant captor—if that's what he was. Maybe humans had misjudged the fae after all.

"Are they going somewhere different?" I asked, following them with my eyes before they disappeared into the trees.

"They're headed to the stables, then to the hunter's cabin to drop off supplies and prepare the meat."

"And where are *we* heading?"

Breck leaned forward against me as our horse climbed a grassy knoll, his breath brushing against my ear as he answered, "To The Woodland House."

15
THE WOODLAND
COURT

THE WOODLAND COURT WAS SITUATED DEEP WITHIN THE HEART OF Elandrew's dense forest. The narrow pathway we were on wound through a glen alongside another sparkling stream. The whimsically entangled trees seemed to watch us as we strode underneath them. Now and then I would catch a whiff of something sweet—like sugared berries—over the constant woody scent of spongy moss and swirling oak leaves.

We crossed through a thicket, tucking our heads forward to narrowly miss the branches that stretched down as if to greet us.

As I lifted my head, my eyes landed on the most beautiful double-doors I had ever seen. They were encrusted in a pointed arch of stone and easily stood twice the height of an average man. They looked as old as time itself—the wood pitted and worn with age. Under the various marks and scars were the most delicate carvings of vines and leaves, weaving and winding their way across the structure. Large, scrolling, iron hinges anchored them to the stone, and two massive oak trees encased them on either side.

Each tree bore their giant root systems above the ground like a badge of honor. Delicate vines crept up the tree trunks, and moss encrusted the stone walls that stretched out from either side of the entrance, winding off through the woods.

As we approached, our horse slowed to a halt a few feet from the doors, and Breck shifted in the saddle.

"Do we need to knock?" I asked sarcastically, but I was honestly just curious.

As if I'd said the magic word, a breeze swirled around us. Leaves rattled and lifted off the path as the doors slowly opened inward, creaking as they moved, boasting their age.

The horse started forward on its own.

I wasn't sure what I expected to see on the other side, but to my surprise, there was no structure immediately lying in wait—just more of the vast forest . . .

And magic.

Orbs of golden light floated along the pathways, while tiny clusters of small, glowing specs bobbed and danced on a phantom wind, scattering off behind the trees as we passed by. Even in the daylight they shone like beacons, beckoning and inviting us down each curving pathway.

What had been a dirt and moss-covered path outside the doors was now paved with smooth, rounded stones, winding around tree trunks and down into glens.

The ground rose and fell around us. Stone stairways lined with gilded railings climbed up berms and disappeared into enormous trees, where ethereal, arched structures sat suspended amongst the branches.

Bright red and blue berries, spindly mushrooms, and other flowering plants grew wild and untamed along the giant root systems that sprawled out above the earth. A few carved wooden doors were tucked deep into the roots as well, and I wondered where they led to, and who lived beneath them. Wreaths of both fresh and dried florals were hung on them, a tell-tale sign of civilized beings. Of something humans would do.

"A lot of our healers dwell out here," Breck said, noting my gaze as it snagged on each door. "Our court specializes in healing herbs and tonics and such. Elandrew contains many plants that the other courts do not have, therefore, we supply medicines and herbs to the other territories, as well as our own."

My eyes continued drifting along the path, drinking in the streams of gleaming water that flowed between trees, under roots, and over smoothed stepping stones. A few small, red foxes gave chase through the ferns, cackling at each other and not bothering to notice us at all.

After we'd traveled a bit further, Breck let out a low whistle to draw my attention forward as he pointed. "Welcome to The Woodland House."

My eyes widened at the sight of the towering, cream colored, stone structure which stood covered with moss, bound up within the trees' grasp. Pointed archways framed the many open corridors, and numerous levels were built atop the rising and falling hills, wrapping around trees, and spiraling along bent limbs. Vines and roots crawled up every corner, staking partial claim to the beautiful dwelling. Even the stone pillars were carved with intricate swirling patterns. The higher levels boasted open, arched bridges, linking separate parts of the structure that spanned off into the trees, further than I could see.

It was ethereal.

"*This,* is what you call a *house?*" I asked, completely aghast by the size of the dwelling. It was like a palace—beautiful and romantic; unlike anything I had ever seen with its openness to the outdoors and oneness with nature.

Breck patted my shoulder. "Oh, just wait."

We came to a stop at the foot of a large set of steps that led up to an archway draping with vines. Breck swung off the horse in one smooth movement then reached back up for me. I slid down into his arms, and he gently slowed my landing, lingering a moment to make sure I had my footing.

Satisfied that I could stand on my own, he stepped back and began unstrapping our swords from the horse's pack. He fastened his around his waist, and slung mine over his shoulder with his bow. The horse received a gentle pat on its backside, which sent it trotting off down another pathway that disappeared into the trees.

"Shall we?" Breck gestured toward the steps.

"Wait." As easy as Breck made it seem to just follow him up into this massive structure, I had no idea what I was walking into.

This place looked lovely, but I was still an outsider. A *trespasser,* as some might believe.

I wished I could at least have my sword strapped to my own damn hip.

"It's all right. I'm taking you to Killian. I always report directly to him when I return from any scouting or hunting detail. He'll already be aware of your presence though, since you breached The Veil in his territory."

"Does he know I'm . . . human?"

Will he be as welcoming as you? was the real question I wanted to ask.

"He might have sensed that you weren't fae, and that's enough to cause alarm. All the High Lords have the ability to sense when a guest arrives at their gates. But you kind of barged right into the territory without invitation."

"That's not making it any better." I scowled.

He tossed me a half-hearted smile. "You'll be fine. On my honor."

I weighed his words, finding them somewhat satisfactory, and nodded.

We started up the steps, and I kept one eye on my surroundings and stayed within arm's length of my sword.

I would pry it from Breck's hands if I had to.

Surprisingly my legs were steady, and my knees didn't feel weak. The only thing that ached were my thighs and backside from riding all morning long. I prayed I wouldn't need to run for my life again, but it was good to know that if I needed to, my legs felt fairly reliable.

A gentle breeze ushered us into the open entry, where the sunlight slid around the pillars and through the pointed arches, painting the large cream floor tiles a rich, golden hue. The smell of lemon and rosemary mixed with sugared berries and wooded moss filled my nose. But for all the loveliness that these halls invoked, I didn't see a single fae. Nor had I seen one during the entire trek here . . .

"Is it normally this quiet?" I asked Breck in a near whisper.

"No . . ." He hesitated as he looked around suspiciously. "It isn't." He stepped a bit closer to me.

We walked down the open hallway, until we came to another set of double doors similar to the ones at the gate. Huge boughs of gathered greenery hung in the center, ornamented with colorful ribbons that swayed gently in the breeze. They groaned open on our approach, revealing a vast gathering hall that was exposed to the open air on one of its longest sides. The ceiling was vaulted, with pillars of delicately carved stone standing throughout, wrapped in swaths of climbing vines. Set into the ground in the center of the room was an elongated rectangular pool of the deepest blue water, strewn with lily pads of every shade of green.

And along either side of the room, stood the fae. They ceased all conversation and swung their heads in our direction as we entered.

My heart started racing. I was suddenly wholly aware and concerned with my appearance. I felt filthy and probably looked like a ragdoll. And I was sure my cheek was still an ugly shade of purple.

Breck placed his hand on the small of my back and gently guided me forward as my jaw clenched repeatedly.

I had so many questions I wanted to ask him.

Why is everyone here? Why are there no walls in this place? Why did you bring me here looking like a piece of filth?

We skirted around the pool, and my eyes lifted to a dais, where a pair of piercing crystal blue eyes met mine.

There, lounging on a throne of carved wood with his legs kicked up over one arm, the High Lord of the Woodland Court stared me down.

16
INTRODUCTIONS

THE HIGH LORD WAS NOT WHAT I EXPECTED.

I should have known by the look of this place that my vision of what its lord looked like was probably very incorrect. I'd assumed that a High Lord—like our human king—would be older. But shockingly, the male that sat on the throne in front of me looked to be around my age.

I quickly reminded myself that it didn't mean he wasn't hundreds of years old—given that the fae could live thousands of years in their lifetime.

As he swung his legs down to sit upright, I took him in.

His white-blonde hair was slicked back, feathering along the nape of his neck, with darker roots showing along his scalp. His squared jawline and smooth, creamy complexion were accented by his thick, dark brows. He wore a loose, white tunic, which he'd left casually unbuttoned at the top and belted at the waist, silver embroidering twisting up the length of both arms. His black pants were tucked neatly into his polished knee-high boots.

He was tall and lean. Toned, but not as intimidating as I expected. It was his eyes that gave me pause—the pure, bright blue of a gemstone. I found that I couldn't look away as we neared the foot of the dais.

Those blue eyes ran up and down my body in a greedy perusal, and a quick pin-pricking sensation pulsed over my skin, as if an invisible presence was testing my physical existence, making sure I was real. Then, he tilted his head ever so slightly, and his eyes narrowed, briefly flashing with something like bewilderment—there and then gone before I had time to linger on it. I gave my head a slight shake to right my senses and shed the strange sensation.

He shifted in his seat and looked at Breck. "Back from your prowl so soon?" he said by way of greeting. His voice was suave, but it dripped with haughtiness.

Breck dipped his head deeply in reply.

The High Lord flicked his eyes back to me, but continued speaking to the male at my side. "How do the woods fare to the east?"

"They were quite eventful," Breck said plainly as he laid a hand on my shoulder.

"I see that they were." The High Lord's tone was curious and suspicious as he assessed me. "Aren't you going to introduce us, *Cousin?*"

I glanced over at Breck as my jaw fell open a little.

Cousin? He failed to inform me that he was the High Lord's *cousin.*

Breck gave a closed-lipped smile in response. "May I introduce Killian, High Lord of the Woodland Court. Killian, this is . . . *the human.*"

I harrumphed at the title. *The human?*

Breck's voice rose and carried for all to hear. "She refused to give me her name when I found her."

Whispers and giggles skittered amongst the court, and I ground my teeth together under the weight of their derision.

Killian surveyed me, the skepticism in his eyes slicing through my skin like a thousand little paper cuts. "And what, pray tell, is a *human* doing on this side of The Veil?"

"I didn't mean to cross it—nor did I do so willingly. It was a trap," I explained. It was the only reasonable explanation I had at the moment.

More murmurs floated throughout the room.

Killian smirked. "A trap you say? Well, *human*—"

"I have a name," I cut him off.

A hush fell over the room. In the silence, Killian leaned forward over his knees and raised a brow at me.

"My name is Auren."

Killian let my name linger in the hall for a moment. "Auren?" He narrowed his eyes as if he didn't believe me.

I looked around then lifted my chin higher. "Auren Everton."

The High Lord studied me for a long moment before giving me a smile that didn't meet his eyes. "Is that your *real* name?"

The court snickered amongst themselves again.

"I—yes," I stammered.

"You look so . . . delicate. A tell-tale quality of most humans, wouldn't you all agree?"

Murmurs of agreement circulated. I could feel every eye in the room as it fixated on me. On my *humanness.* I could also feel Breck side-eyeing me from where he stood, silently begging me not to retort.

Killian brought the attention of the room back to him. "What I was going to say before I was interrupted, was that—as you all know—no human can cross The Veil."

The room quieted.

"So," he said loudly as he stood up from his throne, "what am I to do with you?" He made a show of taking the stairs slowly, then began circling me. "Want to know what I think? I think either your story is a lovely little lie, or you're not who you say you are." He paused his prowl and came unnervingly close to my ear as he whispered my name, "*Auren.*"

I flinched.

Breck stepped in. "When I found her, she was exhausted from the ordeal. She passed out just as I approached her. I've noticed nothing strange or gifted about her—besides her constant need to ask questions. I'm afraid she truly is just a human."

I swung my head over to Breck and gave him a look of contempt. He would get an earful for calling me "*the human*" later. The corner of his mouth twitched up, as if he expected no less.

Killian stepped into my view once more, his eyes cutting into me like shards of diamond, flaying me layer by layer, as if there was something deep within me that he needed to see for himself. His expression toed the line between uncertainty and intrigue. "If you're lying to me, I *will* find out."

My mouth opened, then closed, not knowing what to say.

"Do you know what happens to someone when I discover they've lied to me?"

Once again, Breck stepped in. "Killian, perhaps . . ." His voice trailed off as he glanced around at the court.

"Ah yes, *that*." Killian rolled his eyes. He leaned down to my ear again. "You can tell me all about your little trespassing adventure tonight," he bit out.

I drew back upon hearing his words.

Then he spoke louder for the entire court to hear. "Auren will be my honored guest tonight at our feast and merriment, as we celebrate Lumeri." The court seemed apprehensive, but they gave a gentle clap, and the High Lord mustered up a flat smile in return. "Now, go. Make your preparations. Evening is quickly approaching."

As everyone dispersed, I noticed a fae female with long dark hair and eyes lined with kohl lingering by one of the pillars. Her gaze pierced the room, pinning a spot between Killian's shoulders. Then she narrowed her eyes at me for a long moment before turning to leave.

When it was just the three of us, Breck spoke plainly. "Killian, tonight is—"

"The perfect time for storytelling and wine," the High Lord interjected, perusing over me again. "The first human to set foot in Anbrya in over thirteen hundred years . . . I would be a fool to not entertain her company and hear her story." Sarcasm laced his every word.

Breck stiffened at my side.

I decided that I was past due to speak for myself in this conversation. "I'm honored that you would have me as your guest, but as I insisted to your *cousin* several times, I really must get back home. I told you that this was an accident, and now that you've seen with your own eyes that I am not a threat, I—"

"Not a threat?" Killian raised his brows. "I've only just met you. I was alerted yesterday morning that something had breached The Veil. I had the entire estate keep to their quarters until I knew what to make of the intrusion."

That would explain the lack of people moving about.

He glanced at Breck—who stood closer to me than was necessary—and scoffed. "It seems you've convinced my cousin of your innocence. But you've failed to convince me." He looked at me as if I was an animal that might turn on him. Someone he didn't trust. "And I don't take kindly to trespassers."

Breck shifted uneasily.

I kept my hand loose at my side, ready to whirl around the High Lord's cousin and snatch my sword from where it hung on his shoulder. I may not be able to resist magic, but I was quick, and Killian didn't know of my skill with a blade.

"I will hear your story tonight and decide where we go from there. In the meantime, a room will be prepared and outfitted to suit your whims and needs. Breck, I'll leave you in charge of her." His gaze dropped to my filthy clothes, and he grimaced. "And see to it that she sees the tailor. He'll have to whip up something for her for tonight's festivities."

Breck agreed without argument.

I, however, tried to protest, but Killian simply turned his back on us and vanished into nothing.

17
COMMON GROUND

I STUMBLED BACK AND GASPED, STARING AT THE SPOT WHERE KILLIAN HAD just stood.

Breck let his head loll to the side as he blew out a breath. "Right. About that . . . It's called porting. Anyone with a certain degree of magic can do it."

I blinked back at him. I knew the fae were capable of magic—everyone did—but no one had ever told me that they could simply *vanish* into thin air.

After seeing my lack of understanding, Breck continued. "It's like seeing a point in space and then telling your body to deconstruct itself and materialize at the other destination. It's as easy as visualizing a tether between here and that door." He pointed to where we had entered. I turned to where he was pointing, but when I looked back at him he was gone.

His voice suddenly echoed behind me where the door was. "I can send myself down that tether and appear at the other end of it."

My mouth hung open in stunned silence. "Can you go *anywhere?*"

"As long as I've seen the destination. But each trip pulls from my power. The longer the distance the greater the power usage. It's just like running. If you run a short distance it's an easy feat and requires no long recovery time. If you ran for a full day you'd need to rest and regenerate your strength. Of course, there are some places where spells or wards are put in place to prohibit spontaneous porting."

My mind began spiraling down a hundred different paths with just as many questions about the types of magic these fae were capable of.

Breck pulled me out of my thoughts with my name, barely a whisper on his lips. "Auren?"

He was back in front of me again, and the way he said my name made me really look at him. He was a little rough from the road, but he wore it well. The scruff along his jawline, his wind-mussed hair, the flecks of dirt along his neckline and across his tunic, and even the faint smell of firewood that clung to him seemed to only compliment him. He looked as if he was spun from the woods themselves.

It suddenly dawned on me that he hadn't known my name until now. Maybe that was why he had spoken it as if more to himself than to pull me out of my rabbit hole.

I realized then that I'd been staring.

And so had he.

We broke our eye contact at the same time, and his hands went to rest on his sword belt, while mine fiddled nervously in front of me.

He cleared his throat. "We should get you to your chambers. The evening will come quickly, and you'll need some time to get ready."

I scoffed as I gestured to myself. "Clearly. I'm on the verge of being hideous right now. And you just paraded me in here to your High Lord like this."

His expression turned serious. "You are far from hideous, Auren."

The response caught me off-guard, and my mouth opened, but no words came out.

Is that all he heard in that sentence?

The room seemed to become entirely too small for the two of us, and I dipped my head to hide the flush of color that threatened to creep across my cheeks. Thankfully, he turned, and I followed him as he led us back through the doors we'd entered.

Several long corridors later, we came to an open courtyard where a beautiful stone statue of a goddess stood. At her feet, water bubbled up and cascaded gently down over a bed of rounded stones.

Breck paused in her shadow. "Arrduina," he said, pointing to the figure, "goddess of the forest and the hunt."

She was strong and agile—yet feminine and graceful. I noted her flowing hair and billowing robes, her bare feet and strung bow directed with purpose, forever frozen in a state of pursuit.

"I've never seen a depiction of her."

Not a single statue of any god stood in Galenagh—that I knew of. I'd never thought about it before, but the lack of tributes to them suddenly seemed a bit strange. The king always spoke of the gods and their continued blessings, but the few temples that we did have were never coveted, nor did we have an abundance of them. They were only frequented when someone desperately needed something, or when certain calamities fell upon the people, and they had nowhere else to turn.

My parents had always taught my brother and I to fear the gods—that theirs were the hands that steadied the realms, and they were the divine presence behind every action. Yet, I had never stood in front of a physical depiction of one.

"It seems humans are lacking when it comes to our faith and devotional practices," I thought aloud.

"Mmm." Breck nodded. "The fae have always been close to the gods. The ancient temples and statues are an important aspect of our culture. Some were damaged long ago, or were simply lost to time, but many still exist."

We lingered a moment, staring at Arrduina's stone figure and listening to the soft falling water. Then a thought entered my mind, trailing off his last comment. *Time.* Another thing that was vastly different for humans and fae.

"Just how old are you?" I asked.

He grinned, but didn't answer me right away. His eyes were fixed on Arrduina's stone bow and arrow. "How old do you think I am?"

I snapped my head to him. That had to have meant he was *old.*

"A ridiculous amount of years old?" I guessed.

He let out a small chuckle. "To you? Yes. I'm nearing my four hundred and fiftieth year." He seemed at ease with the revelation, but all I heard was a number nearly eight times what I hoped to live to in my lifetime.

My jaw fell open. "I can't even fathom living that long."

I circled the stone goddess, admiring her form, wondering how old the gods were—if time mattered for them in any way. Arrduina was carved from one solid piece of alabaster, worn smooth as glass over time, and yet remained free of any blemishes or algae from the years of flowing water. I ran my fingers through the stream, finding it cool and soft.

Breck watched me and began trailing my orbiting path. "You said you were nearing thirty years of age . . . In my realm, fae can live thousands of years, so, given that I'm only just nearing the half millennium mark, I would say you and I are roughly about the same—give or take a few years."

I looked past Arrduina's stone face, to his.

A common-ground.

He was trying to find some kind of common-ground between us, which I decided was rather nice. The fact that he had cared to take note of the passing mention of my age took me by surprise.

"Well then, I guess that's somewhat of a relief. Now, just give me some of your magic, and we might just be equal."

His brows rose, and he let out a small laugh. "Is that so?"

"I'll take it easy on you if we ever cross swords." I grinned.

He grinned back. "Whatever you say, sunshine."

I thought about calling him out for the use of that pet name again, but this time it fell a little lighter on me than it had before.

"We'd better get you to Gareth before it gets too late."

I shook the water droplets off my hands. "Who is Gareth?"

"He's the master tailor behind our celebratory attire."

"For this 'Lumeri' event that Killian spoke of?"

He nodded and gestured for me to walk with him. "Lumeri is our festival of light. The fae celebrate it every spring. It's when we usher in the sun after the winter months. Superstitions have long since turned it into one part celebration of light, and the other part warding off evil spirits. It's celebrated differently in each court. Even the Desert Court celebrates it, despite them not really having a change in climate. Here, everyone dresses in flamboyant outfits and drinks until they're practically unconscious."

"Sounds riveting," I said.

We made our way deeper through the open-air halls of the Woodland House, where all around us, fae had begun rushing about, carrying wreaths and garlands and swaths of fabrics, and pushing carts full of candles and colorful baubles.

My eyes widened as a small, fae-like creature darted by us, carrying baskets of flowers. A pair of petite wings sat above her shoulder blades, though she wasn't using them to propel herself.

I gasped, noting her pointed ears framing eyes of solid black.

As children, our bedtime stories often consisted of the mischievous fae across The Veil who dwelled in the forests and had wings and tricky magic —an entertaining bit of fun before we fell off into our dreams. But as we aged, the stories matured and changed with us. What were once bedtime tales gradually became everyday warnings. The fae were no longer tricksters with wings. They'd become ruthless, cunning foes, who had powers we couldn't begin to fathom. Everyone would say, "Humans would do well to keep away from The Veil and the fae." And so, we did.

"Are those . . . There are stories of fae with wings . . ."

Breck nodded. "They are the Ancient Fae. They were the first form of fae to exist here. We descend from them. Their ancient line has been slowly dwindling down for centuries now, and very few are left compared to what was. The ones who are in service to The Woodland House are called house-fae."

"They're so small," I noted, watching the house-fae scurry off. "House-fae . . . does that mean they're . . . *servants?*"

"In a sense," Breck replied. "It gives them purpose."

I didn't know what to make of that.

"They're not slaves, if that's what you're thinking," he quickly added.

"Oh. Good."

If Killian didn't keep slaves, that meant I was less likely to be made into one if he decided not to let me leave. Though a *servant* was no better.

Breck continued on, and I shook myself free of my spiraling thoughts to listen. "The Woodland Court has always specialized in its elaborate celebrations. But ever since Killian took his seat as High Lord, things in the court have . . . changed. He was very young when the power passed to him, and with his youth came his naivety. He revels in parties and the pomp that comes with them. He could care less about the responsibilities of running a court." His voice became laced with disdain. "For the past several years, he's spent a suspicious amount of time away—which is becoming a concern. But that's beside the point. Tonight, *everyone* will be as careless as the wind, and drunk on an excessive amount of wine."

And I would be the High Lord's muse.

The thought didn't sit well with me. The last thing I wanted was to be ogled at by an entire court of fae—let alone be attending this event anyway. If I had my way, I'd be back at The Veil by now, not on my way to get fitted for a dress.

My eyes lowered to the floor, watching the creamy stones pass by under my soiled boots. "I never thought I'd find myself attending a fae celebration."

Breck eyed me for a moment before replying. "I would have never imagined a human attending one either. This will be interesting indeed."

18

THE TAILOR

I EYED EVERY DETAIL ALONG OUR TREK, BUT I HAD LOST TRACK OF WHERE we were amongst the vast pillars, patios, and archways.

Every bit of the estate was embraced by the woodlands that enveloped it. Creeping vines and moss-peppered branches twined up pillars and crept around corners, spreading out across the arched ceilings. Even the sconces and artwork on the walls were gently wrapped in soft, green, climbing plants with tiny white flowers that seemed to sprout from within the walls themselves.

We came to an arched door at the end of the hall that swung open on a phantom wind—err, *magic*. My human mind still hadn't recognized that magic was the most likely cause.

A fae male—who I assumed was Gareth—looked up from his stack of papers and fabrics across the room and grinned. "You must be Auren."

His neatly combed hair was dark brown along the top, while the sides were symmetrically streaked with gray. The shadow of a mustache and finely trimmed facial hair complimented the angular features of his face, and a rather small ink quill was tucked behind one of his pointed ears. His long blue robes dusted the ground behind him, the perfect contrast to his crisp, ivory tunic and pants.

Several small orbs of light scurried out the open, arched window above his desk, disappearing into the trees.

His space was organized and well-kept. I half expected a whirlwind of clothes and textiles and sewing needles scattered across every surface. Instead, fabric swatches of every texture and color were hung neatly from wooden dowels and set into looms. Rolls of silk and chiffon were packed neatly in giant urns. Papers were laid out across a work table on the right side of the room where several larger lighted orbs floated in place above.

"Please, come forward." He urged me with the gesture of his hand, then met me in the center of the space. "A human in our realm again. I never thought I'd see the day—and yet, here you are." He unspooled a measuring tape and studied my form as he spoke. "I've been instructed to create something for you for this evening, which means you must be of particular importance."

Without hesitation, he went to work taking my measurements and reaching out to write on the air with his quill as he went.

I looked over to Breck, who was now leaning against the wall with his arms crossed, eyes gleaming with amusement. He gestured with his head toward Gareth's work table, and I turned to see what he indicated. As the tailor scribbled numbers and notes in the air, the writing appeared on the paper across the room. I smiled to myself at the ease of a magic as simple as that.

Gareth brought my arm up and slid the measuring tape along the underside, from my wrist to my armpit, then the other arm, then the precise length of each of my shoulder blades. I'd never had this many detailed measurements taken of my body in my life.

"What I have in mind for you came to me in a dream," he said, squatting to stretch the tape across the span of my hips. "It requires someone bold and beautiful to wear it."

I stiffened at his words. I knew that I was bold, but I was always a bit more modest when it came to calling myself beautiful, regardless of the compliment. My mother had told me many times of how the boys would always look at me with longing in their eyes. But when they saw me wielding a sword or swinging my fists, they simply turned away.

All except for one.

When I was sixteen, a curious, brown-haired boy had worked up his courage and approached me in the market. I was enthralled by him.

One hour of conversation quickly turned to four, and we became friends.

We would meet at our usual spot in the market to spend time together. And one day when a storm took us by surprise, we huddled under and empty trader's tent nearby to avoid the deluge.

He'd kissed me that day. My first kiss. And as the storm raged on, and the market cleared of people, we found ourselves tangled up together inside that canvas tent.

That boy was my first for a lot of things.

The following months held more of the same. I skipped my training and other things I enjoyed, just so I could spend time with him. We'd stroll down the streets browsing the vendors, sharing freshly baked bread and talking about everything under the sun. Every now and then we would dip into an empty alley or wander off to the glens just outside of town and explore each other. We had become something more and it was invigorating.

But we were young. The real world had not yet fallen into our laps with its trials and lessons, and a day came when he wasn't at our usual spot. I'd waited and waited, and finally, he rounded the street corner—smiling as he always did—but he was not alone. My heart fell at the sight of another girl on his arm. I'd briefly sulked in the shadows, watching them, before running away in tears.

He'd looked at me and told me all the sweet things I wanted to hear, but apparently, I wasn't enough. And despite the hurt, my heart had wanted to give him another chance—to ignore what had happened, or write it off as a misunderstanding. I always saw the best in everyone, and even if there wasn't much good, I convinced myself there was.

I had let myself become so open and vulnerable—only to be abandoned. He'd drawn my attention from what I'd enjoyed so much before, and I lost a bit of myself in the process. That was my first mistake. And I was left alone with a crack in my heart.

So, I went back to my training and the one person I knew was consistent and reliable: myself. I fell back into my rhythm of solitude and went through life oblivious to how men looked at me. And everyone around me kept their distance like they'd done before. There had been a few other men who expressed interest over the years—all of them fleeting. Late nights with fast, heated passions that went nowhere upon the dawning of a new day.

Having this attention on me now—even though it was just Gareth fussing over my measurements, and Breck looking far too amused in the corner with a smug smile on his face—I felt awkward. Hearing someone refer to me as beautiful was hard for me to believe.

Breck pushed off the wall and came to stand in front of me, drawing me out of my thoughts and memories.

"So, what do you have in mind for her?" he asked Gareth.

The tailor grunted. "If you think I'm going to spoil the design, you're mistaken." He rose to his full height and gently rubbed his hands on my upper arms. He started to say something but stopped short, looking back and forth between his hands as they halted on my shoulders. When his eyes met mine, something like suspicion flashed across his face—there and then gone. "Mmm, you are a rare thing indeed," he murmured.

With his brows in a pinch, he spun and went to his work table, mumbling to himself as he read the notes that he'd written into the air. Then, he scribbled a few more.

After a few more moments of paper shuffling and amending his notes he turned and clasped his hands together. His broad smile was back on display as he dipped his head. "Auren, you will be a sight to see."

He turned to Breck next, clearing his throat. "It's rumored that *all* the High Lords are attending this year . . ."

Breck simply shrugged. "That's the talk of the court. If it's true, it will be the first time in several hundred years that all five will be attending the same event."

Gareth twirled the quill in his fingers. "Schedules do align every now and then, but perhaps the fates are up to something. A human in the fae realm for the first time in over thirteen hundred years? *And* all the High Lords gathering? Seems fortuitous." His gaze went distant again.

The confusion must have shone on my face because Breck tossed me an apologetic smile and offered a bit of context. "Lumeri is observed across a stretch of several days due to the sun's arc. Each territory's celebration falls on a different day during that time frame. That also allows for each High Lord to attend the other court's celebrations if they so choose. The invitation is always extended to them."

I sensed there was an exception. "But . . ."

"But . . . It's been quite some time since all the High Lords have *willingly* made the effort to attend the same one. Usually one or two might make the trip for another court's celebration, but all five at one event?"

His question hung over us in the room.

"Do they all get along?" I asked.

"They're cordial. But thousands of years of history between them and their predecessors inevitably puts strains on some relationships in one way or another. Some fare better than others."

Gareth began gathering fabrics and examining the bolts of cloth before either chucking them to the side or adding them to the growing pile in his arms.

He glanced up at us. "I've heard whispers that a certain, unexpected High Lord arrived only hours ago." Breck stiffened, and the tailor noted it. "If so, I'd say it will make this evening very interesting indeed."

Breck frowned. "Mhmm. You do always seem to know the whispers before they make it to every other ear, don't you?"

Gareth's mouth curled up into a grin. "A talent of mine, to be sure." He eyed Breck as he spoke, and then reached out to scribble something in the air as he smiled. "You two had best be off. I will have to work down to the wire on this, but I will deliver it myself when it's ready. And Auren, I recommend having your hair styled down. It will complete the look." With that, he took a bow and turned his back, dismissing us.

"Shall we head to your chambers then?" Breck asked, leading me out into the hallway.

"Or The Veil. That would be even better," I suggested, half hoping he would start to feel bad for me and agree. Instead, he gave me a pointed look which told me that wasn't an option. I sighed. "It was worth a try."

He chuckled, then swerved to the side as a few small specs of light whizzed past us and darted into Gareth's chamber just before the door snicked shut.

We walked a little ways before Breck spoke again. "I should probably warn you about the other High Lords before this evening commences."

"Should I be concerned?" I asked.

"You should be vigilant. Once they get wine in their systems their true natures all tend to come pouring out, and as you will come to know, magic is always at play here."

19
WARNINGS

My biggest concern was figuring out how to get back home, not which High Lord was capable of what. Nevertheless, Breck proceeded to tell me about each of them. He didn't bother with their names, so as to not overload me with information. His focus was to warn me of what they were capable of.

Benmoor was home to the Desert Court, and its High Lord was older —around eight hundred years of age—which Breck assured me was "not *that* old." But that lifespan was unfathomably long to me. He reminded me that fae do not age like humans do, so someone of that age might look as my father had looked in his early fifties.

"This realm is permeated with magic—in the earth, in the air, in every living thing," Breck explained. "We can harness that magic and bend it to our will. If one wants to light a candle, all they'd have to do is will the wick to spark into flame."

"Isn't that the same as wielding fire itself?"

"No. They're not commanding the fire. They're manipulating oxygen into a flame that has gone out, reigniting it. To make the candle go out, simply remove the air from it. Those with fire magic can command it directly, and that's far deadlier."

"Oh."

"There are also what we call Weavers, beings who possess the power to harness the magic that this realm exudes and form it into their *own* making—apart from what it does naturally. The High Lord of the Desert Court is a Weaver. He can spin his own versions of reality right before your eyes. A dead loved one can appear as a vision before you, and you'd think their soul had returned to a mortal form, all because of his ability to weave the strands of reality into his own twisted lie. He could transform this entire hall into a vision of a cavern, and you'd believe you were miles underground.

"It can be dangerous, especially if you're his enemy. He has the ability to make you see what he wants, and if caught off guard, a vision could lure you into a trap, or make you agree to something you would otherwise stand against. I've never trusted the male, and knowing his skill makes me all the more wary. And, his court has dabbled in the forgotten ways of Old Magic, which sets me on edge. You shouldn't mingle longer than a few minutes with him."

I nodded, committing the information to memory.

The High Lord of the Highland Court in Vahrenhall was around five hundred and fifty years old. I was shocked at the age revelation as it came a second time. Breck noted that Vahrenhall's High Lord was more of a loner, preferring to keep to himself and his people. He was skilled in shielding and had a certain degree of foresight, and was a great asset to have as a friend. I didn't need to avoid him, but Breck did warn me to not get on his bad side. "He holds onto grudges like a snake constricts its prey —to the death," he said.

Drastia was home to the Arctic Court, and Breck had no particular warnings pertaining to its High Lord. Slightly younger than Breck—at around four hundred and ten years—he was said to be a lively but observant male, who was well respected and practical. His ability was influencing the elements. "It's always an entertaining magic to see," Breck assured me.

I was sure it would be, considering I had never seen magic of any sort. Except for Killian disappearing before my eyes.

As if my thoughts conjured up words on Breck's tongue, he said, "Then, of course, there's Killian. He's younger than the rest—only three hundred and forty years. He assumed the throne after his family's untimely death, but wasn't ready to lead by any means. The Woodland Court fought amongst themselves for a brief time to try and find a placeholder until he was ready for the responsibility. Obviously, that didn't happen."

"And what of his power?" I asked.

"Growing up, he started to show signs of having shapeshifting abilities, often changing his face so his mother wouldn't spot him venturing out after bedtime, or changing into an animal while hunting so as to sneak up on his kill. But for some odd reason, that ability faded with time until he claimed he no longer had full access to it. He can still do small things, aesthetic changes like hair and eye color—which he often does. He's become exceedingly adept at enchantments and compulsion, which I'm afraid he doesn't always use in the best way. And, he's a fierce hunter. We grew up together, hunting these forests and learning from the wilder Woodland fae how to track any animal, though he's never been as good at hunting or tracking as I have."

"None of that sounds very dangerous."

"Compulsion magic can be very dangerous, Auren. There are different levels of it, all of which involve influencing your mind."

"And, how does one do that?" I asked—equal parts curious and worried of what it would entail.

"It's done using a process called mind-walking. Many fae can do it if they're gifted enough, and their power allows for it. The harmless level of mind-walking is when someone bridges a pathway of communication in your mind, allowing them to speak so that only you can hear them, and for you to respond. The Ancient Fae still communicate this way most of the time. Then, there's the compulsion aspect of mind-walking, which is rarely used for good. It can be done by simply lacing words with a magical edge to affect your mind—to make you obey, or be inclined to do as you're told. Or worse yet, if someone's essence gets into your mind, they can read your thoughts and sift through your memories."

"Oh."

No thank you.

"What makes Killian dangerous is that he has a temper and is easily triggered. He can also be possessive and doesn't like being denied what he wants, which makes him inclined to use his ability for more harm than good."

We rounded a corner and Breck's face turned even more serious.

"There is one other High Lord whose presence is . . . concerning, to say the least."

"Someone worse than Killian?" I joked, but Breck's seriousness didn't lessen.

"The High Lord of Calledan. The Mountain Court. He's just older than me, at four hundred and sixty years."

Which puts him at only a few years older than me too—in terms of a human lifespan, I thought.

"Auren," Breck said, drawing my attention back to him. "This male is one you do not want to linger around. He's deadly. The court that he keeps is a band of traitors to their own territories, and that alone is enough to set anyone on edge. He has a reputation of killing anyone for the thrill of it, and his power is, well . . . You don't want to cross him."

"And what exactly makes him so dangerous?"

Breck hesitated to explain further but relented. "It's called shadowfire. It's rare, and hasn't been seen amongst the fae for fourteen hundred years. The last—and only other—time a fae possessed that ability, the High Lord that wielded it was unstable and nearly wiped out much of Anbrya in a brutal war that ended up costing him his own life. That fae was this High Lord's ancestor. With the company he keeps, the realm is already uncertain about his rule and what will come of it. I've seen him slaughter an entire room full of Woodland fae without even lifting a finger. Killian has only just become somewhat amiable with him in recent years. They still don't get along.

"Out of all the High Lords, I'm surprised the most by *his* acceptance of the invitation tonight. It would have been all too normal for him to ignore it, keep to the mountains, and wait for his own court's celebration." He paused, seeming perplexed for a brief moment before continuing. "And I'm more than certain he can mind-walk, which poses even more of a threat to you. He's not someone to mess around with. Most fae in the Woodland Court are terrified of him. It's best that you avoid him at all costs." He bit at the inside of his cheek as he watched me for a reaction.

I simply nodded in return.

I could tell when he looked at me that all he could see was a lowly human with only the measly title of a skilled sword fighter. Apparently, being skilled with a weapon wasn't enough to get him to stop worrying about me.

I made note of everything he was telling me. I also reminded myself that I needed to set aside time to discuss my return to the human realm with Killian—preferably when he had a glass or two of wine in him and would be easily pliant. Fae wine was rumored to have twice the effect on the consumer as human wine. Maybe after a night of celebration, he would be a bit more understanding.

"I appreciate the information, but I'm sure the High Lords are not going to care who I am. Killian didn't even take it upon himself to assume care over me. He assigned *you* to me."

"Hey," Breck scolded me playfully. "I was not *assigned* to you."

"Killian's exact words were 'Breck, I'm leaving you in charge of her.' So yes, you were."

"Hmm," he grunted. "That also means I have the right to lock you up if you don't behave and heed my warnings."

I raised my brows and gave him a sharp look, drawing a playful grin from him.

We approached a beautifully arched door and Breck gestured toward it. "Here we are." A small wreath with light pink flowers hung slightly off-center. Green ribbons dangled from it, dancing in the breeze.

Breck waved his hand and the door opened to reveal my chambers. As I entered I was thankful that it was an actual room with four solid walls and not an open-air veranda.

The space was pleasant. A large, light-colored stone hearth and fireplace greeted us from across the room. Two wing-backed chairs were placed in front of it, and situated between them was a small table, displaying two crystalline glasses and a pitcher of what I assumed was water. A lovely bed with sheer ivory drapes hanging from the golden bed posts sat against the wall to my left, next to an arched window with a small bedside table underneath. On the wall behind me was an oversized wooden armoire, and to the right side of the room another stone archway led to a bathing chamber, which, from what I could see, housed a quaint clawfoot tub, a vanity, and a private area for more discrete matters.

I turned in place, noticing the floors. A stunningly delicate mosaic of fireflies and curling ferns laid beneath me—the centerpiece to the room.

Breck smiled. "I'm assuming this is to your liking?"

I gave him a soft smile and nodded as I walked toward the bed and ran my fingers down the sheer cloth flowing from the posts. The finery was exquisite. Far grander than anything the king had provided me in his royal castle.

"Gareth will be bringing your dress, and I'll return when it's time to leave. A house-fae should be along soon to tend to you." He walked over to the bedside table, sliding my sword and scabbard off his shoulder and leaning it against the wood before turning back toward the door.

"What if I need something?" I started after him with a million questions lining up at the forefront of my mind like they always did.

"Good news is, if you need me, I'm just a few doors down the hall."

I followed him out the door, and he turned to gather me back up inside the threshold. "Auren, you'll be fine. I promise. Just bathe and wait for your dress. I'll come to collect you soon."

With that, I watched him stroll down the hall and dip into a room four doors down from mine, on the opposite side.

I let out a breath. At least he wasn't far.

I was like a child in the market square who had lost her parents. Everything was new and uncertain, and I needed explanations, instructions —someone to guide me. Breck was that someone in this strange fae realm. I reminded myself to be thankful that he had been so pleasant and forthcoming. He could have taken me hostage and seen to it that I had been thrown in a dungeon. But he had spoken for me in front of Killian and warned me about the High Lords when it was seemingly of no benefit to him.

And oddly enough, I trusted him.

I stepped back inside my chambers and made my way straight to the bathtub.

20
A MASTERPIECE

AFTER A BATH, AND A VERY EVENTFUL MOMENT OF A HOUSE-FAE appearing out of nowhere while I was naked as the day I was born—scaring me out of my wits—Gareth arrived with my dress.

He hung the garment bag in the armoire, and when he opened it, the material that cascaded out onto the mosaic floors took my breath away. He had chosen a brilliant white fabric—the color of the brightest full moon on a cloudless night. I'd expected a vibrant mix of oranges or blues, or perhaps greens like the forest. White was a complete surprise.

I admired the dress as I stood awkwardly in front of the tailor in my underclothes, trying to cover myself as best I could.

He tossed me a look over his shoulder. "Modesty will do you no good my dear. The brassiere has to go, I'm afraid." My eyes widened, and he let out a clipped laugh. "Relax, I won't look." He kept his back turned and snapped twice into the air to hurry me along. "Time is of the essence."

I unclasped the back of the garment that held my breasts in place and tossed it onto the bed, covering myself with my arms.

"Arms out," Gareth instructed.

I balked, but he snapped his fingers again, and the dress floated toward me, forcing me to expose my chest.

Before my eyes, the fabric magically separated into two at the seams. I didn't have time to gasp before it encompassed me like a second skin, knitting itself back together, leaving no trace of separation.

How I would get out of the dress, I was entirely unsure.

The fabric was smooth as a pearl and clung to my body from my shoulders to my knees like it had been charged with static. The neckline plunged down to my navel, leaving my cleavage exposed. It felt scandalous at first, and the modest part of me wanted to dip my shoulders inward in an attempt to hide my half-exposed assets. Thankfully, the long sleeves helped to offset the openness. They clung tightly to my arms and came to points just above my wrists.

The shoulders of the dress were drizzled with gold starbursts, and clear crystals cascaded down over the tops of my arms and breasts. The entirety of my back was exposed, scooping down to just above my backside, where the silk gathered and cinched just under my rear, lending the perfect accentuation to the curve of my hips. From there it cascaded into a waterfall of wide, petal-like pieces of fabric that fluttered in a train behind me. Gold swaths of gossamer peeked in and out of the flowing white silk.

I couldn't keep my jaw off the floor. It was the most beautiful piece of clothing I had ever seen or worn.

Gareth spun and beheld me, beaming as he boasted, "The finest silk in the realm."

He ushered me to the mirror that hung inside the giant armoire, and when I saw my reflection, I sucked in a breath.

I looked like a *goddess*.

He motioned for me to spin, and as I did, the dress fluttered and danced around my feet. The small house-fae who watched from the corner let out a shrill of wonder, just as transfixed on the garment as I was.

"Oh, and we mustn't forget this," Gareth said, striding back over to the leather bag he'd set on the floor upon entering. From it, he retrieved a small wooden box. Inside was a dazzling headpiece of pure gold, encrusted with crystals that matched my dress. He plucked it from the box and placed it gently atop my head, smiling proudly.

The arched band fit snug from ear to ear, and it held in place a series of small pointed arches that sat suspended above my head like a delicately spiked, vertical halo. I reached up to touch the metalwork in admiration. To be able to fabricate such intricate and beautiful items in such a short time was baffling.

Gareth began fiddling with my hair. "The dress will detach at the end of the night when you are in your quarters and wish for it to be removed."

"What if I never wish for it to be removed?" I grinned as I spoke the words, but part of me was absolutely serious. It was the most beautiful thing I would probably ever wear, and I didn't think one night would be long enough to admire it.

He chuckled. "I'm afraid the dress is a one-time show-stopper. When you are ready, simply wish it away, and it will be done. Just be sure you're in your chambers when you do so. We don't want you baring yourself to the entire court by accident." He laughed. "You'd have all the High Lords beating down your door after that—I'm sure of it."

Like that would actually happen.

I rolled my eyes in dismissal of his statement.

Gareth saw the motion and clicked his tongue. "You do not give yourself enough credit. You are a true beauty—with or without that dress."

A warm familiar voice floated across the room from the doorway. "We are in agreement on that."

I turned to see Breck, frozen on the threshold, his deep green eyes staring in awe.

How long has he been standing there?

Gareth bowed out of the way, allowing Breck to approach.

"What do you think?" I toed back and forth, from left to right, giving the dress a slight swish. The fabric kissed its way along the stones with a gentle whisper.

Breck's eyes were bright as they roved over me, surveying every inch. It seemed like he was observing more than just the fabric.

The room suddenly felt too small once again.

"You are a vision," he said.

I looked back toward the talented tailor, giving him a genuine curtsy. "All thanks to Gareth."

The tailor sketched a proud bow. "Do enjoy your evening, Auren. It will be a pleasure to create for you any time." He slipped out of the room wearing a full smile.

The house-fae suddenly appeared in my peripheral, her small wings twitching nervously behind her. I jumped in surprise for a second time and fisted my hands at my sides. "Please quit doing that!"

Her solid black eyes simply blinked at me.

Breck looked between me and the house-fae—trying to read the situation.

"I stepped out of the bath for a towel, and she just *appeared* out of nowhere, and I slipped and fell back into the tub. I'm pretty sure I have another bruise on my hip now thanks to her," I explained, pointing at the small creature.

Breck threw his head back and laughed. It was the most genuine laugh I'd heard from him yet, and it tugged a corner of my lips upward.

"It's not funny," I said. "I'm fine by the way, thanks for asking. If you're done cackling would you please tell her to not do that anymore? I don't think she understands what I'm saying."

The house-fae extended her arms to me, offering me a pair of golden slippers and then popped back out of existence as soon as I took them. I swiveled my head to locate where she had gone, but there was no trace of her.

Breck regained his breath. "She understands. Her name is Sorscha, by the way."

As if summoned by her name, Sorscha materialized—in the doorway this time—and peered into the room cautiously.

"Simply ask and it will be done." Breck motioned for Sorscha to come over once again. She obeyed.

I looked at her, this time studying what I saw.

She was much smaller than me, and her wings were delicate. They obviously didn't serve the purpose of flight, but they leant her a truly otherworldly presence—twitching nervously behind her as she stared at me. Her skin was light and pale, as if she had spent too much time under the trees and in the shadows. Her pointed chin was accented by her cropped hair, the color of pitch. And even though she moved in quick, startling movements that unnerved me, her face was calm and her expression was soft.

I bowed my head to her. "My apologies. I was not aware of how your station works, and I didn't mean to offend you. Thank you for your help earlier with my hair and the cosmetics."

I was truly grateful. Before my dress arrived, Sorscha had curled my hair quicker than I'd ever seen done, leaving it down—just as Gareth had asked—so that it fell in soft, golden-brown curls down my back. Then she'd applied a smooth cream to my face and kohl around my eyes with the flick of her wrist.

Her black eyes blinked slowly at me, and her head tilted to one side as if contemplating why I would apologize to her, or thank her. After a moment of silence, she reached for my hand, turning me back to the mirror. She flicked her wrist again, and I felt a small tingling across my cheeks where a natural blush appeared and a rich, rose-tinted balm stained its way across my lips.

When I looked at her reflection, she seemed to be trying to form a smile but quickly abandoned it and dipped her chin before turning away into nothing again.

I tried to follow her whereabouts but failed. "What just happened?" I asked Breck.

"It's not often that a house-fae receives thanks and praise from anyone above her station. Sadly, they're not normally treated with such respect."

"That's a shame," I said. Irritation bloomed at the thought of anyone being treated with such a lack of decency.

"I think she likes you," Breck added as he took Sorscha's place, standing next to me in front of the mirror.

We admired our reflections.

He was wearing a forest green jacket that matched his eyes. It fastened all the way up the center, embroidered with golden vines and leaves that wound from his collar down across his chest. His dark tan pants clung to his legs and tucked neatly into his tall brown leather boots. His soft, bronze curls were a bit tamer than before and fell freely over one side of his forehead.

"Your bruise is gone," he noted as he turned and reached out, gently brushing his knuckle against my cheek.

I'd noticed the same thing earlier while Sorscha prepared my hair. The dark discoloration, the swelling, the pain, all of it had completely vanished.

"Maybe it was something the lady's maid back at the castle put on my cheek. She said it would help speed the healing."

"Hmm," was all Breck said as he studied me.

A long moment passed between us. Then, in the same hand he'd touched my cheek with, he summoned a simple gold mask and held it up to his eyes. When he brought his hands down it stayed in place across the bridge of his nose.

"Unfortunately, this is as festive as I get," he informed me, turning back toward the mirror.

I raised a brow at his reflection. "I'm wearing this work of art, and you're escorting me with a simple mask?"

He bit his lip, then waved his hand above his head. A golden wreath of vines and brambles appeared and settled into his hair. "Better?" he asked playfully.

I snorted at his effort. "It'll do."

He held out an elbow for me. "Shall we?"

As I took his arm, and we walked out into the hallway, I could have sworn I heard Sorscha's tiny giggle echo after us.

21

LUMERI IN THE WOODLANDS

BRECK LED ME, ARM IN ARM, THROUGH THE HALLS, UNTIL WE CAME TO AN arched portico with a set of grand steps leading down into the forest.

The sun had finally sunk far below the tree canopy, and the forest had come to life.

Out past the steps, the ground was paved with small fitted stones, forming paths that wound through the trees—all leading to a large clearing. Golden lanterns full of colorful lights were strung throughout low-lying branches, and hundreds of fae orbs bobbed and weaved along the pathways.

Out amongst the clearing was a sizable pavilion, where the fae were congregating and socializing in all their finery. Flower arrangements, wreaths, and garlands decorated every surface—on tables, along branches, strung over the pathways—some so full and heavy that attendees had to duck their heads as they passed underneath them. Colorful ribbons in shades of yellow, pink, and orange waved in the breeze from every bough and lantern. Tables were piled high with sweet and savory delicacies, and golden goblets were being passed freely to the crowd.

Breck watched me as I took everything in. Behind his mask, his green eyes glinted under the lights of the orbs as they floated up to encircle us, ready to guide us down the stairs and into the evening's festivities. The crystals of my dress sparkled, casting flickers of the entire color spectrum onto his jacket as he stepped closer to me.

The fae nearest to the steps gasped when they noticed us, and every head turned as we made our way into the forest.

Breck leaned into my ear and murmured, "There is no denying that every eye is on you."

I blushed at his words. But indeed, every fae we passed stared in awe and wonder. I'd expected them to turn their noses up and shun me for being a human. Instead, they looked enraptured by my presence. Or perhaps they were just entranced by Gareth's work.

I tucked my arm tighter into Breck's elbow, and he squeezed back, keeping a steady step as we made our way through the gathering groups.

My eyes scanned the crowd, then fell on a tall male standing at the edge of the pavilion. I was confused by his appearance, because I had only just met him a few hours ago, yet his hair had changed to a metallic gold—tinted down to its roots. Striking topaz blue eyes pinned me on the spot.

Killian. He was waiting for me like a chaperone at a child's dance.

As we approached, I noted his outfit. He was in a fine jacket of solid spun gold, his black pants and polished black boots a stark contrast. Around his neck was a garland of green leaves and yellow evening primroses. And atop his now shining gold hair was a band of glowing fae lights, bound together like a luminous crown.

He certainly liked to stand out.

His eyes meandered over my dress, my hair, my crown, while his lips spread into an impressed smile. He stretched out a hand toward me, and I reluctantly slid my arm from Breck to offer my hand.

"Thank you, Cousin," Killian said, not taking his eyes off of me. "I'll take her from here."

Breck stiffened enough for me to notice, then brushed off the lapels of his jacket to compensate for the move as Killian proceeded to lead me out across the floor where the majority of fae had gathered.

Whispers floated past us as we crossed the space, and I noticed many fae moving closer to the edges to get a better look.

I glanced back at Breck, who nodded at me in reassurance, then gestured in the direction he was headed, indicating that he would be keeping a watchful eye on me from the far side of the pavilion.

Killian's voice called me back to him. "It seems you've outdone me,

Auren. I find it quite odd that fae culture suits you so well." His voice . . . something about it was off.

Whatever words he spoke seemed to fall on my ears like sugar onto freshly cut fruit, melting into me, drawing my attention to their sweetness. But in reality, they weren't sweet at all. He hadn't even offered me a compliment. He only said that I looked better than him. As if it was a crime to steal the attention from him. And even though I knew those words sounded as if they should be tainted with jealousy, they drenched me like sweet wine.

He threw me a sidelong glance. "What do you make of my tailor's work? Must be the nicest thing you've ever worn."

Again, I knew I should feel offended by his statement, but instead, I somehow found myself wanting to thank him. To *please* him.

Wait, this isn't right.

"I'm very pleased with it," I said, trying to fight the urge to say anything more.

He said nothing in reply as we approached the center of the room where a series of grand, golden basins were freely suspended in the air. Inside each one was a burning bath of fire, casting shadows upon those standing underneath, making the guests look as if they were fading in and out of existence.

After we took our places underneath the burning vessels, he held his arm out and walked me around him in a circle to show me off to the crowd like a prize. As I turned, my dress fluttered along the polished stone floors, and breaths of wonderment from the bystanders flitted around the space. When I'd completed a full circle, he tightened his grip on my hand and reined me back in.

"Laetus Lumeri," he proclaimed to the crowd. They repeated the words with an applause, and thin sticks adorned with colored ribbons rose above the sea of faces and waved through the air. "Another year has come and gone, and now we celebrate the return of our brightest light to the realms." Another applause. "My guest of honor this evening is Auren." He paused, moving his hands to my shoulders. "She is from the human realm."

The crowd broke into a frenzy of hushed whispers and gasps. Many seemed to lean in intently, waiting on bated breath for more information.

But there was no outrage. No taunting or wickedness of any kind. Only curiosity and intrigue.

I was *shocked.*

I scanned the crowd and caught sight of Breck's golden mask. He was standing exactly where he'd indicated, arms crossed, looking thoroughly unimpressed and anxious.

As I continued scanning faces, I thought I caught a glimpse of a tall male with chin length golden hair looking directly at me from the far side of the pavilion. But in a blink, he was just another face.

Killian continued his announcements. "Other honorable guests have graced us with their presence as well—as I'm sure most of you have figured out." He placed a hand on his chest and waved his other out toward the crowd. "All five High Lords are in attendance."

The chatter picked up as more claps sounded. I was glad that I wouldn't be the only one receiving attention tonight. Perhaps I could even sneak out early if Breck escorted me back to my chambers. I still had no idea how to find my way back to them on my own, but if he'd lead me, maybe I could begin planning an escape.

Killian raised his hand and a golden glass appeared in it—filled to the brim with fae wine. "The night is young. Eat to your heart's content, and let the wine flow heavily. We will usher in this new season properly."

Everyone who had a glass raised theirs in response, and cheers went up as one. "Laetus Lumeri!"

The crowd dispersed, and a low tempo drum and several fiddles bloomed into a pleasant chorus. Younglings began running across the open floor, laughing and trailing their ribbons on sticks behind them.

A second golden glass appeared in Killian's other hand, and he passed it to me with a smile.

I hesitated, before reaching out to take it. "Isn't fae wine twice as potent as human wine?"

He frowned. "Who told you that?"

"It's common knowledge in our realm." I eyed the deep red liquid, even dared to bring it to my nose to sniff it.

He laughed and took a gulp. "Have a taste. You'd be surprised," he said over the rim. He didn't confirm or deny my suspicions, so I didn't try it.

Instead, I asked, "What does Laetus Lumeri mean?"

He instantly seemed annoyed. "It means happy light." His focus remained on the rest of the room until the tempo of the drums changed to a quicker pace that invited dancers onto the floor. With it, he thrust his hand back out at me, more of a command than an offer. "Come."

I immediately wanted to open my mouth to protest, but one look at his eyes, and I was placing my hand into his. Their blue depths commanded, and I answered.

How was this going to work? Was the dance a waltz? A step? There's no place to set my wine—

He pulled me out onto the floor and set us into a series of steps, walking forward toward each other and backward away from each other, all the while keeping our free hands out to touch. At least it was a dance that I could do while holding a heavy pour of fae wine. I watched the other couples as they mirrored the same sequence. Inward, outward, then touching hands and gently skipping around them like they were circling a maypole.

Simple enough.

As I turned in step, I caught sight of Breck in conversation with another male by a table piled high with all sorts of foods. He glanced over at me—keeping tabs. A part of me was grateful; should I get into something I wasn't comfortable with, he would probably step in on my behalf and remedy the situation.

Killian's voice cut through my thoughts. "Is my cousin seeing to it that you have everything you need?"

I fumbled for words. "Uh, yes—I mean, of course. He's been very helpful and even explained some fae history to me before we arrived." Breck had warned me that Killian was possessive and that his magic was untried, so, I would try to keep my answers as vague as possible and keep my distance if I could.

Killian let his eyes roam over me almost as if in suspicion. "Gareth is a true wonder with his work. Years ago, he crafted this crown." He gestured to his head. "It hasn't dimmed a bit since." He scanned the crowd. "You could pass for a fae if not for your rounded ears." Again, his words chimed sweeter than they should have.

Enchantments, I told myself. *He enchants anything he can.*

Breck had spoken of this.

I forced a dry smile.

As the song came to an end, he pulled me into him. So close that his scent flooded my nose with a blend of lemon, tart berries, and the forest.

"It's quite enthralling," he murmured into my ear.

"*What* is enthralling?" I breathed out, looking ahead into the crowd as they watched our interaction.

"*You,*" he said through a sly smile. "You, sweetheart, have me very curious."

The words sent a thrill through me, but I knew it was all wrong. They shouldn't have. Not when I looked closer at what they meant. Something inside me fought to decipher the way he spoke. It was as if his words wore a magical mask.

And my mind didn't like it.

In a blink, he dismissed me for someone across the pavilion that caught his attention, and I was left standing there hanging on his words like a lost puppy as the dancers maneuvered around me.

What. Just. Happened?

"Auren?" Breck's voice cut through the noise. He walked over to me, his head dipping into my view. "You look confused and angry at the same time."

"You were right about Killian. He's . . . different." I didn't know what else to call it. "It's like I can't think straight when he speaks. Like his words are messing with my mind. Like even if he were to tell me I was the most disgusting person in the realms, I would plant a kiss on his cheek for having said it." I shuddered at the thought.

Breck nodded and escorted me off the dance floor. "I couldn't have described it better myself."

Without thinking, I took a sip from the glass in my hand. As soon as it hit my tongue I knew what I'd done. It washed over my senses and brought life to the sugared-berry smell that I'd picked up on earlier. Against my better judgment, I took another small sip and savored the taste on my lips.

Breck noticed and immediately cautioned me against it. "You may want to rethink that."

I giggled. "I have no intention of finishing even half this glass. I just thought I would taste it." I swished the liquid around in the goblet, watching what looked like flecks of stardust swirl within it. Then, to my horror, my stomach let out a raucous growl that I was sure everyone nearby heard.

Breck's brows lifted, and he proceeded to push me through the crowd right up to the grazing table.

A decadent spread of charcuterie meats and cheeses, fruits and vegetables, and delicious looking dessert breads covered in swirls of sugars and jams lay before me. My mouth watered and hung agape at the sight of such rich foods piled high in abundance. I plucked a strawberry that was dusted in sugar crystals and bit into it. The sweet juice ignited my taste-buds, and I closed my eyes. I'd never tasted a strawberry with that much flavor.

I immediately reached for another.

A fae male approached us just as I popped another berry into my mouth. But he was not there for me. I overheard him asking Breck if he could have a word in private. Breck hesitated and looked back at me.

"I'm fine, go," I said through a mouthful of sweetness and gestured to the table before me. He smiled and gave me a single nod as he wandered off to speak with the male.

I selected a piece of sweet bread next, then began observing the fae. They all looked so ethereal. The females were a vision of vibrant colors. Some wore dresses that flowed and flounced around them in trains of elegant gossamer. Others wore shimmering tops and billowing skirts that looked like giant flower petals and moved like cascading waterfalls. Gilded adornments sat upon heads, and delicate garlands of greenery draped around necks. The style was unlike anything I'd ever seen in the human realm. Come to think of it, everyone here was so finely dressed, I wouldn't know a high born from a low born. The males all seemed to prefer tailored jackets or fine tunics that varied from every shade of the green forest, to the deepest red of fae wine. Many donned masks in all different styles.

What surprised me most was how *human* they appeared at first glance. They had the same range of human skin tones, from pale white to the darkest brown. I half-expected gangly green limbs and sharpened incisors. Something other than . . . normalcy.

It was only when I looked deeper, lingered on their exteriors, that I noticed how their features were somewhat sharper. There was an innate beauty in each figure, upon each face. Other than that, the only thing that was notably different—aside from their clothing style—was the tell-tale pointed tips of their ears.

Oh, how our stories were wrong.

I sipped from my glass, when all of a sudden it shook in my hand as a thrumming flared to life in my chest—the same strange thrumming that I'd felt after I crossed The Veil.

The scent of vanilla and chestnut hit me next. Then *he* stepped into my view.

It was the same dark-haired fae male from the forest.

I'll see you soon, he had told me. And as promised, there he stood, a few paces away, hands tucked into his pockets. A vision of darkness embodied in fae form. He stared at me with a predator's gaze, his eyes glittering like pools of gold in the firelight.

His voice was just as I remembered, deep and smooth like rolling thunder, a purr of darkness and allure as he said, "We meet again."

22
THE DANCE

I BECAME A NERVOUS WRECK. MY HANDS WERE TREMBLING—CLUTCHING fae wine in one and sweet bread in the other. My chest thrummed. My heart palpitated.

What is happening to me?

The male's eyes flicked to my quivering hand, and the corner of his mouth lifted.

I set the bread and wine on the table behind me—before they wiggled free from my grasp—and tried to compose myself. The thrumming in my chest was so pronounced that I considered finding a quick exit.

Despite the thought, something anchored me in place. I couldn't have fled even if I tried. The thrumming wasn't a warning. It was a directive. And I found myself obeying its command and turning back to the beautiful stranger.

He stepped up next to me, casually perusing over the display of food— which I was pretty sure he had no real interest in.

I remained awkwardly frozen, caught up in my thoughts.

Staring.

His fine, black, dress jacket was the color of fresh ink that shimmered slightly in the firelight. It hugged his chest and waist like a glove and was cinched up to just beneath his collarbone. His pants and boots were of the same color, and though he wore no festive adornments of any kind, he stood out from the crowd.

A blackened thorn in a rosebush of color.

His deep brunette hair was so dark it was almost black. Longer pieces were loosely combed back on top, though a few strands feathered forward over his forehead, and the sides were a bit shorter—but swept back all the same. The stubbly shadow along his chin and cheeks accented his strong jawline. He was even more devastating than I remembered. Strikingly handsome in a wicked way that was all sharp lines and rough edges. His golden eyes begged to be lost in, and the planes of his tanned face promised to keep me staring forever.

His perusal paused above the sweet bread, then his eyes slid over to me. He raised a brow. "It's rude to stare, you know." His voice was like velvet on my eardrums.

I hadn't realized that my mouth was slightly hanging open. I quickly closed it and tore my gaze away, only managing to avert my eyes for a moment before they were pulled right back to him.

He looked back down at the food, making no attempt to hide his smirk.

My voice wobbled, but I managed to say, "You were in the forest."

"I was. And just what were *you* doing there?"

I fell into a silent debate of whether or not to give him any information. He'd seen me struggling after I had crossed The Veil and then he'd simply *vanished.* I wasn't sure if I could trust him, but something deep inside my thrumming chest pressed at me—a silent plea that I *could.*

"I'm sorry, I don't even know who you are," I stated, opting to withhold all information for now.

He turned to face me—bowing slightly—and raised a sun-kissed open hand between us. I hesitated, but found myself gently placing mine in his.

"Niall," he introduced himself as he wrapped his fingers around mine, "High Lord of Calledan."

My eyes widened at his title. *Calledan. The Mountain Court.* Breck had warned me specifically about this male.

He stood back to his full height—towering over me—and with my hand still firmly in his grasp, said, "Dance with me." The request was a gentle one. Nothing like the demand Killian had made.

Strangely, I felt drawn to him. Like a primal instinct had suddenly surfaced from the recesses of my existence, urging me toward him.

The moment I yielded a step, he whisked me into the open. The fae gave us a generous berth as he brought me around in a wide arc and into his arms.

More string instruments joined in the melody, setting the pace for a waltz and inviting more dancers to fill the floor.

His leading hand held mine gently while his other pressed firmly against my waist as he steered us across the room. I tried not to grip onto his shoulder too tightly, but this dance was slightly different from what I was used to in the human realm, and I needed his guidance.

As if reading my thoughts, he said, "I've got you, just relax."

He was taller than Breck by an inch or two, which made me feel even more petite. His broad shoulders were solid as stone beneath my hand. I could tell even through his dark jacket that he was a mass of muscle beneath the fabrics he wore.

"A human in the realm of Anbrya," he said, keeping his head up to steer us across the dance floor. "Is the world ending?"

His attempt at light humor didn't rally a laugh out of me.

I cleared my throat. "I'm just as struck by it as you are, I assure you. I never meant to cross The Veil. I don't have a death wish."

"I would hope not. Surely you knew that humans cannot cross The Veil." He raised a brow. "Yet, somehow, here you are." He angled his head to try and meet my eyes, but I looked away. I wasn't feeling in the mood to have this conversation again—least of all with him.

"Auren? Is it?" His deep voice, and the sound of my name falling off his lips, drew me right back to him in an instant. Pools of molten honey stared back at me, aflame from the basins of firelight as we passed underneath them.

He didn't wait for confirmation. "How are you here?"

I thought about his question for a moment, then sighed. I still had no answers, only my own explanation, and it didn't make much sense. "I was participating in the king's tournament to win a place in his guard. And after I won, I bested the prince in a sword match and wounded him pretty badly—"

"You bested the prince?" Niall cut me off.

I scoffed. "It was a flesh wound really. It hurt his pride more than it did his leg." Niall stared at me silently, waiting for me to continue. "That night . . ." I hadn't truly stopped to think about what had almost occurred.

Too much had happened since then, and I was still processing it all. But I found my voice again, along with a rush of anger as I recalled the memory. "The prince's men came for revenge."

I glanced out into the crowd again, then back to Niall. His jaw was a hard line, and his pupils had flared, as if he didn't like the thought of anyone enacting revenge on me.

I shook my head, trying to shake the memory away with it. "A friend in the castle helped me escape into the forest. I ran just as he told me to, but the king's men caught up to me. They pushed me right across The Veil. I had no idea I was even near it. I mean, I knew it was out there somewhere, but I just kept running, and then—"

"You crossed," he finished my sentence. "When I found you—"

"You *left* me."

He hesitated, thinking over his next words. "I had no choice," he bit out. "It seems your savior has taken good care of you ever since." He looked over to where Breck was standing in deep conversation with the fae male that had pulled him away. They were tucked into an alcove of trees, almost completely hidden by shadows.

He must not be aware that I was dancing with the High Lord of Calledan. If he was, he would certainly lose it on me.

Niall brought me back to our conversation. "If he'd seen me there it would've caused a bigger mess than it already was."

"I felt like I was dying! Maybe I should be thankful you didn't stay. You probably would've let me die there." The words stung as they left my lips, and I remembered what Breck had told me: *he's deadly.*

I nearly winced, hoping I hadn't offended him, but instead I straightened my shoulders and kept my head high.

He only tightened his grip around my waist, cinching me closer to his chest as his mouth settled back into a hard line. The scent of vanilla and chestnut caressed my nose—his scent, I realized. It was a cozy aroma that reminded me of the warmth of fireside hearths and cold evenings spent under thick blankets and stormy skies.

The heat from him seeped into my exposed skin, and my chest thrummed even deeper.

Can he not feel that?

I shivered at the sensation, suddenly aware that I was entirely too close to his body. There was absolutely no free space between my exposed chest, and his. I tried to lean back, but he held fast.

"I wasn't aware that the fae had no regard for personal space while dancing," I said, frowning.

He lifted a brow at me. "Are you complaining about dancing with a High Lord?"

"I'm just pointing out that you've practically been on top of me this whole time."

He laughed, and the sound was as smooth as warm whiskey. "Darling, if I was truly on top of you, I guarantee you wouldn't feel disappointed about it."

"I—you—" I fumbled over my words, trying to come up with a retort, but failing miserably. I opted to just shut my mouth. His responding grin was laced with amusement.

He continued guiding us, commanding the room with his presence. Couples peeled away as we swept through the space. He spun us into a quick turn, and I did my best to follow his steps.

"You've danced a fae waltz before?" he asked.

"Never. We have a waltz back home that's similar to this—without so many quick-paced turns."

"Could have fooled me."

I didn't reply this time.

He straightened his face into seriousness again. "What do you make of the Woodland Court?"

I looked around the pavilion. All manner of fae were enjoying themselves, and joyful smiles were everywhere to be seen. "Honestly, it's not what I expected," I answered.

"And what did you expect?"

I pressed my lips together and stared directly at his chest. Beneath the banded collar of his jacket, I caught sight of the edges of raised black markings that etched their way across his collarbone.

"Auren?" The way my name rolled off his tongue drew my eyes back up to his.

Right. Stop staring. Quit getting distracted.

"I expected a land full of cruel and ruthless fae. Not . . . this." I nodded to our surroundings.

"Yes, this is surprising I'm sure."

"Are you one of the High Lords that doesn't get along with Killian?" I asked.

He looked out over my head and focused on a point somewhere off in the distance behind me. "Breck talks too much."

I found myself feeling defensive of the only fae male that had put stock in my well-being thus far. "He gave me basic information because he was looking out for me."

"Mmm. If that's what you want to call it."

"He's been the only decent male I've met in this realm."

Niall pressed closer and purred into my ear, "Come spend some time with me in the mountains. I can assure you there are many more decent males in *my* court than you will ever find in this one."

Before I could retort, he pushed me out into a small twirl and brought me back to him.

"Unfortunately, I've been told that you are the worst of all the High Lords, and that I should stay far away from you," I said, narrowing my eyes at him.

"I hate to inform you, but you're doing a terrible job with that." He tightened his grip on my waist, and my chest gave another jolting thrum. I gasped, and he leaned back slightly to get a better look at me. "Does my touch amuse you?"

I made a sound of disgust. "Of course not. You're just holding me awfully tight."

My thoughts narrowed to the feel of his palm, pressed against the dip of my back . . . where my dress swept dangerously low just below his fingertips . . .

The corner of his lips lifted. "Is that a problem?"

I gritted my teeth. "Yes." But I didn't try to put distance between us this time. Instead, I dissected the positioning of his strong hand, how it fit exactly to the slope of my spine. The heat of it against my exposed skin.

"Your thoughts and your words say two different things."

I looked up at him incredulously. "Are you reading my thoughts?"

He smirked, eyes full of amusement. "First you claim that I'm on top of you, now you think I'm in your mind? If you want one or the other darling, all you have to do is ask."

I let out a repulsive sound and looked away, even as his words sent a jolt through me. "How do I know you haven't been in my head this whole time?"

His soft, smooth laugh rumbled from his throat, but he didn't answer.

"Breck told me your magic is . . ."

"Unprecedented?" He finished my sentence. "He's right. Though, I hope you haven't come to a conclusion about me so soon."

Our eyes met and his expression softened. I quickly looked away—waiting a moment before replying, so as to make a show of my indecision. "I don't have much to go on."

He certainly looked lethal, in the way that a war helm was meant to both evoke awe, and instill fear. His presence alone induced intimidation, and yet . . . it elicited allure.

But despite all the sleek darkness that he embodied, I found myself feeling safe in his arms. I felt a pull somewhere within me that I couldn't justify or rationalize to myself. And I wasn't sure if it unsettled me or not.

A sexy smirk spread across his face, and I realized I had been staring again.

Damn his good looks.

The music began to intensify, and Niall's steps quickened with them, commanding our path. His hand splayed a little wider on my back, sending shivers up my spine.

"Tell me something, Auren . . ."

"Yes?" I said more softly than I wanted to.

"Do you believe in the fates?"

Out of everything he could have asked, I was not expecting that question. "I believe in both the gods and the fates, yes." He remained quiet, his eyes searching mine as if they were combing through my soul. "Why do you ask?"

"I'm curious."

"Let me guess, you think the fates are responsible for this fluke? That I'm here by the grace of their divine plan?"

He cocked his head slightly. "Are you saying you don't believe that?"

I hadn't thought that far—yet—but now, I *was* thinking about it. "Haven't given it much thought. I've been too busy being whisked around by you fae and not allowed to return home."

"But you only just arrived here. Have we made that bad of an impression on you already?"

I wished I could make light of the situation like he was, but I couldn't. Instead, I looked at our hands. His was so much larger, wrapping almost completely around mine—

His voice cut through my spiraling thoughts. "You're a good dancer by the way."

"I'm just going where you lead."

It was the truth. I had only attended a handful of festivals and one ball in my years. None of them had been enthralling enough to make me long for more.

"When was the last time you danced?"

I slowly lifted my eyes to meet his again. "Are you making small talk?"

A grin lifted the side of his mouth. "Would you prefer if we didn't talk while we—"

"Yes." I quickly cut him off. "I would prefer that."

Why is this dance lasting an entire lifetime?

A smirk tugged at the corner of his mouth. "I can think of a few other things we could do that don't require talking."

I leaned back from him, aghast at his words. Yet, at the same time, something flitted around inside my stomach upon hearing them, and I internally cursed at myself.

"You're insufferable," I clipped.

He held me against him as a deep-rooted laugh rumbled through his chest. "Then why haven't you asked me to release you from this dance?"

I looked up at him from under my brows. "I can do that?"

"You can do anything you'd like," he purred.

I hesitated. I couldn't tell if he was tricking me.

Sounding more skeptical than sure, I pushed my shoulders back and said, "I'd like to end this dance."

He spun us around the edge of the dance floor, his eyes not leaving mine. The corner of his mouth lifted again. "No."

I bristled. "And why not?"

"It's bad etiquette to end a dance midway through," he replied, taking us into another quick step.

"You said I could do whatever I want."

"I did."

"Well, I *want* to end this dance."

"Are you sure that's what you *really* want?"

His fingers slowly slid across the exposed skin on my back, and I sucked in a small breath. Truth was, something inside me didn't really want the dance to end at all. And what bothered me more was that I didn't know why.

I shook my hair back over my shoulders, lifting my chin in an attempt to appear more certain. "Aren't you supposed to be the High Lord everyone here fears? Not the High Lord who worries about etiquette?"

"I *am* feared, by many more than just those in this court. Why does that mean I can't also be proper and considerate?"

"Because those things don't go together," I said wryly.

"You don't sound so sure of that either," he pointed out.

Gods, he's frustrating.

"Why dance with me at all? I'm sure you have better things you could be doing."

He tilted his head down at me. "Because you looked so lonely over by that table."

I rolled my eyes. "Don't tell me you're a romantic beneath this dark, ominous façade?"

"Perhaps you shouldn't be so quick to draw conclusions."

"You're wearing all black at a celebration of light. I'd say that's pretty dark and ominous, wouldn't you?"

He grinned like he relished every ounce of frustration that bubbled up from me, and that was enough of a reply. I let out a deep sigh through my nose and looked away before I started staring again.

No one should look that handsome. Certainly, no human man ever could. But he was no human. He was fae. With a face spun from dreams, and a body hewn from stone.

I forced myself to avoid his gaze, settling my eyes on the crowd that had gathered around the edges of the pavilion.

He followed my stare and nudged his chin out toward them. "They don't like me, remember? That's all for you."

"I wouldn't be so sure about that," I said, eyeing the fae, trying to read their expressions—awe, curiosity, apprehension, intrigue, admiration. The last one stunned me. "I've only ever drawn a crowd for sword fighting. Not for dancing."

"I don't think it's because of your dancing, Auren." He was now staring at me the way that I'd looked at him. "Have you seen the way you look tonight?" His voice dipped low and soft, like a lover's caress, and he looked at me like I was the most stunning creature that had ever walked the realms.

A flush of pink washed across my cheeks. Not only because of his tone and awe-struck gaze, but because I knew what he meant. I *had* seen myself. Breck even noted it.

I had to admit, I did feel beautiful. And I hadn't felt that way in a very long time. Most of my time was spent swinging a sword, wrapping my split knuckles, or scrubbing the sweat off my brow. It definitely wasn't spent in a dress fit for a queen, twirling in the arms of fae High Lords.

But this was a crazy happenstance.

Half of me was desperate to return home, while the other half was delighting in the literal magic of everything. I wanted to feel at odds with this entire situation, but instead, a strange sense of empowerment had overcome me the moment Gareth wrapped me in this dress.

The tempo of the song picked up. The final summit, ready to be conquered. A culmination of every graceful and elegant musical note.

Niall pushed me out into a spin along with it.

My dress spun out in all directions, illuminated by the golden fae lights that had somehow maneuvered to hover above where we were. A spotlight upon us. Upon me.

I spun, and spun again, as long as his hand continued to lead me, letting his steps direct my path. I felt weightless and graceful. I knew all eyes were on me, and I didn't care. I lost myself in the moment.

I could hear awes of amazement and wonder that came and went by as I whirled.

The music crested beautifully on the note of a single violin, and as it drifted down into a lull, Niall smoothly reeled me back into his arms. Our breaths mingled between us as we faced each other once again—closer this time. *Much* closer.

The thrumming had now encompassed my entire being, and I was sure the entire room could feel it.

Niall's head was bowed down to mine, and his eyes burned like pure gold, glowing brightly as he gazed at me. They weren't lit by any reflection or light from above us. This time, it was from within—from his magic.

As I lowered myself down from the tip of my toes, I noticed another, more startling glow. I looked down at myself to see that a faint white light had settled around me like a second skin. Where it had come from, I had no idea. My immediate thought was that it was from the dress. Niall seemed to think the same thing, his lips parting as he surveyed me. But the light faded out as quickly as it came, and the crowd burst into applause around us.

Then, Niall was bringing my hand up to his lips, pressing a kiss against my knuckles.

Time seemed to slow. And as I watched him hover over my hand, I began to feel like Breck had been mistaken about this High Lord. Perhaps only conveyed rumors had everyone thinking all the wrong things. From what I'd gathered, Niall was not what those rumors spoke of. He might have been a bit arrogant, but there was nothing about him that I felt the need to fear.

As he lowered my hand from his lips, I caught sight of movement in my peripheral.

A figure was quickly approaching us on our right.

It was Killian. And he did not seem pleased.

23
THE HIGH LORDS OF
ANBRYA

ALL THE JOY FROM THE PREVIOUS MOMENTS WASHED AWAY WITH Killian's irritated glare.

"Seems we have dinner *and* entertainment this evening," he announced, glowering at me upon his approach.

I narrowed my eyes at him as Niall finally released my hand and slowly turned to face him as well.

Across the pavilion Breck was pushing through the crowd, urgently trying to get to us.

Killian sized Niall up from a few steps away. "I should've known that your first time back in my court in over half a century would be a spectacle of sorts."

The High Lord of Calledan straightened his jacket and leveled a stare at Killian. "I seem to recall you being one to enjoy a good spectacle." He looked back at me. "Besides, I haven't danced in quite some time, and Auren is delightful." His eyes glimmered with his words, and he donned a heartbreaking smile that made my insides flutter.

It wasn't hard to see that the two males were at odds in every way. Where Killian was a pretty face full of cleverness and cunning, Niall's was carved from mountain stone. Threatening. Devastating.

I wasn't sure who to look at as Breck slid up next to me, his hand coming to rest protectively against my back.

"Setting a lovely standard for the evening," he observed, his voice a little unsteady as he attempted to diffuse the tension. "Killian, would you like to join—"

"No, Cousin, I would not." Killian reached his hand out for mine. When I didn't move, irritation flared in his eyes. "Come, Auren. There are others who are interested in an introduction."

I hesitated and glanced at Breck—the only one in this group of fae males that I had any real trust in at the moment. But there wasn't much he could do when Killian was a steaming pot of frustration that was about to boil over.

Suddenly, there was a pinching twinge in my head, like a chord had been plucked in my mind. My hand moved, obeying a silent command, reaching out to accept Killian's. All I could do was steal a look at Niall as I was pulled past him. With that one glance, I swore I saw him take a step after me, and Breck thrust an arm out to stop him, but the High Lord of the Woodland Court hauled me into the crowd, obscuring my view.

Several females smiled and dipped their heads toward me as I was pulled past them. A fae youngling watched me with wide eyes, then waved her hand at me. I raised mine in return, and she grinned sheepishly and burst into a fit of blushing giggles as she raced off into the trees.

"You're making quite an impression with both the high and low born," Killian informed me. "And just what made you take up a dance with the High Lord of Calledan? Did he compel you?"

Did he compel me?

Breck had mentioned compulsion being one of Killian's tricks of choice. Niall had *asked* me to dance. He didn't force me. It was no trick.

"No. He didn't compel me."

Killian scoffed and looked back at me. "Do you even know what compelling magic is?"

That set my jaw off-kilter. His belittling mannerisms were really starting to annoy me. "In a sense," was all I replied.

He stopped short and turned on me quicker than my eyes could follow. His face slid right up into mine, and I breathed in his rushing scent of tart lemon. "You look absolutely *breathtaking* tonight, have I told you?" His voice was sensual now, his eyes full of mischief. All at once I felt myself longing to swim in their blue depths and taste his skin as he pulled me closer. His finger slowly traced along the side of my jawline and moved over my lips.

I began to lean into his touch, my breath hitching. He was so close, I could practically taste him. He made me *want* to taste him. But I fought the urge because it wasn't really *me* thinking those things.

It was *him*.

He pressed his finger down on my bottom lip, then swiped it away. When he abruptly pulled himself back, I stumbled forward a step, choking on a breath. The wicked smile on his face was dripping with arrogance as he turned and sauntered off toward the tree line, leaving me swaying in a mental fog.

When my head suddenly cleared, I felt . . . *violated.*

He had *compelled* me.

And when he'd forced my hand into his . . . that too had been a compulsion.

A form of mind-walking, I recalled Breck's warning.

I knew then that Niall had done no such thing before or during our dance.

Against my better judgment, I followed Killian, wiping furiously at my bottom lip, like my palm could scrub away the tainted feel of his touch.

"How dare you!" I called after him.

He clicked his tongue and glanced back over his shoulder. "Come now, sweetheart, don't tell me you didn't like that." He flashed a smirk. "Seemed to me like you did."

I caught up to him as quickly as my dress would allow me to. "What I *like* is being treated with respect, not being worked over with magic!"

Before I had the chance to truly lay into him with my words, a fae male approached us with another in tow.

"Ah, there you are," Killian said to the stranger, clasping him on the shoulder and earning himself an annoyed glance. "Auren, meet the High Lord of Benmoor, Ramil."

Breck's words sprang forward in my memory: *Benmoor. Desert Court. The eldest of the High Lords. Weaver of false realities. Old Magic— whatever that was.*

I gave him a small curtsy out of respect, and he offered a strained smile in return.

His dark brown hair was styled back from his face, ending in loose waves that fell behind his ears, leaving his full, neatly trimmed beard on display. His skin was lightly tanned, his eyes a cool hazel. Breck had been right, he didn't look as old as his age implied. He appeared as perhaps my father would have. The creases between his brows had just started to set in, and a faint line cut across his forehead.

His clothes—I assumed—were more traditional to his court. A long, burnt orange tunic reached to just above his knees, embellished with intricate gold threading. His pants were a matching shade, and his pointed brown leather boots were cropped low beneath his ankles. A gold-plated belt with yellow jewels embellished his slim waist, contrasting his square shoulders, and a long golden chain clutching a deep amber colored stone hung around his neck.

Killian toyed with a strand of my hair that had come forward over my shoulder. "Lovely, isn't she?"

His words grated against me.

"And a talented dancer it seems," Ramil said, lifting a brow as he observed me.

I raised my chin. "You should see me with a sword."

Killian stiffened.

Ramil held my stare for several long moments before a slow smile spread across his face. "I am curious, how does a human sword-wielder come to find herself on this side of The Veil?"

Killian's face fell into a frown. "I myself have yet to gain this information from her. Perhaps she will be more forthcoming this time." He crossed his arms, leveling a look at me.

Ignoring him completely, I told Ramil the same story that I'd told Breck: that I had no intention of being here and no explanation as to what happened.

The High Lord of Benmoor tutted a hiss of dismissal at the male who stood next to him, and with a bow the male quickly made himself busy elsewhere. It was then that Ramil leaned in and spoke low to Killian. I strained my ears to listen, but the only words that I thought I could make out were "prophecy" and "intentions."

"I don't mean to interrupt," I cut in, "but please, if you have any insight or information that might help me understand, I would welcome it."

Ramil contemplated my request for a moment, sipping on his glass of wine, while Killian watched him out of the corner of his eye, seeming equally as eager to gain any insight into what he might know. Finally, he said, "Unfortunately, I do not have the answers you seek."

"No one does," Killian tacked on. He summoned more wine from nothing and drank.

The High Lord of Benmoor took the stone around his neck in his grasp, turning it in his palm as he pondered. "She certainly looks human."

Killian swirled the drink in his cup. "Easier to compel than a youngling is."

I cut him a glare.

Ramil studied me harder. Closer. He lingered on my rounded ears—the obvious marker of my lineage. "I do not sense a glamour on her. But I do sense . . . something." His voice was steeped with curiosity. "Very interesting," he murmured.

Killian's attention perked up. "What? What's interesting?"

Ramil ignored his questions. "I will do some consulting. Perhaps we can uncover the true reason why you are here." Something rang differently about his statement. Like he was implying that I was an intruder or a spy.

"I have no ill will," I practically pleaded. "I would go home right this instant if only someone could take me—"

"I'm afraid that is not possible." Ramil leveled his eyes with mine.

My brows pinched together. "Not possible?" I looked between him and Killian.

"This occurrence is not to be taken lightly. No human has been able to cross into our realm since before The Veil, yet you are here." Ramil gestured to our surroundings. "You've even been embraced by our magic."

Confusion spread across Killian's face as well as mine.

"My eyes did not deceive me when you lit up like a star in the night sky."

The dance with Niall. Ramil had seen me glowing. But that wasn't me. That was . . .

I had no explanation.

"You cannot simply return. Not until we know by what means you are here."

Unease slithered along my insides. I could tell there was more that he wasn't saying, and it was making me anxious.

What if I'm never able to get back home?

Killian drained what was left in his cup and summoned both a refill and an additional glass—handing it to me. I took it and sipped, if only to ease the emotions that were bubbling up. I felt as if my realm was growing further from my reach by the second.

I sipped from the glass again. Killian monitored the movement.

A deeper drumbeat began throbbing through the trees, shifting into a more primal sound, and Ramil excused himself, feigning a summons elsewhere.

I watched him disappear back into the crowd as numerous lanterns and orbs of light began to pulse, keeping time with the beat. All manner of fae had gravitated to the dance floor now, and some were even dancing along the paths between the trees. They swayed and let their bodies flow as freely as the wind, while the giant bowls of fire flickered above.

To our left, two males and a female approached.

I took another sip from my glass and straightened my shoulders, pushing my emotions down and bracing for more introductions and scrutiny.

The shorter of the two males was holding the hand of the female next to him. They both inclined their heads toward us. The other male, did not. Killian greeted them all with what seemed like a forced smile.

The coupled male spoke first. "I'm glad that all five High Lords were able to come together for this occasion, for once." His voice was pleasant, and when he shifted his attention over to me, he smiled politely.

His light brown hair fell in thick waves that swept across his forehead and down around his pointed ears, curling out just underneath them. His eyes were such a cool blue they appeared almost gray, set against fair skin. He had a neat and thin dusting of facial hair that circled around his mouth and faded up his cheeks, reminding me of the younger men in our village.

The dark blue, fitted doublet that he wore was adorned with five gold fasteners and clasps down the center, and his black pants and boots looked pristinely kept.

He extended his hand out to me in a warm greeting, and when I took it, he hoisted it slightly higher and dipped his head. "It's a pleasure to meet you, Auren. I'm Laurent." As he lowered and let go of my hand, he indicated to the female next to him. "And this is Senna."

Enchanting sea-foam green eyes held mine as she dipped her head toward me. Her small, square face boasted delicate features and pouty lips, which she pulled into a genuine smile. Her light golden hair was tied back in a simple bun at her neck, and her clothes were a mirror to Laurent's in color, but styled as a straight, floor-length dress that hugged her small frame.

She was lovely.

"Laurent is High Lord of Drastia, the Arctic Court," Killian informed me with no real enthusiasm.

Drastia. Arctic Court. Influencing the elements. Friendly.

I recited Breck's brief history lesson to myself, and nodded.

The tall man standing to the other side of Laurent shifted on his feet as he eyed me.

"And *this* is Vanir," Laurent said, clapping a friendly hand on the brute's shoulder, which rose well above his own. "He is High Lord of the Highland Court of Vahrenhall."

Vahrenhall. The Highland Court. Shielding and foresight. Keeps to himself. Holds grudges.

"What makes you think I can't introduce myself?" Vanir said, his voice like churning gravel.

"I just thought you'd probably scare her off," Laurent joked lightly. Senna smiled and shook her head at the two males.

Vanir had still not smiled, or made any type of facial expression for that matter. "She doesn't look like the type to be scared easily," he observed.

A sly grin spread across my face at his observation. "You would be correct."

Vahrenhall's High Lord was tall and built like a mountain. His head was shaved on both sides, but his hair was grown out past his shoulders down the center, which he wore woven back into a thick, dark-blond braid that fell to between his shoulder blades. He had strong cheekbones to offset his light blue eyes, and donned a thicker beard than any other male I had met in this realm thus far. If I were to guess, he was a few years older than me—in human years—even though he looked like a well-seasoned warlord.

A tunic the color of darkened ash stretched over his burly shoulders and chest, and a black leather vest with an intricate, interweaving pattern stitched on the hem, was layered on top. His pants and boots were simple, no pleats or polished clasps anywhere to be seen. He wasn't dressed as finely as the other High Lords, but he didn't look like he cared much for appearances anyway—unless it was to intimidate someone.

His hand was perched on the pommel of his sword which hung at his side in a worn, leather scabbard. He tilted it forward slightly, as if allowing his arm to relax a bit. As I noted the motion, I also realized that he was the only one carrying a weapon.

Laurent saw where my eyes had landed and spoke for Vanir again. "This brute doesn't trust a damn soul. Don't be alarmed. He just wears it to make a statement."

Vanir turned and cocked his head at Drastia's High Lord. "There has been more than one occasion where I was glad to be the only one with a weapon."

Laurent puffed out his cheeks with a breath and rolled his eyes playfully.

I cleared my throat quietly and smiled at them all. "It's nice to meet you, Vanir. And you, Laurent, and your wife."

Laurent and Senna exchanged a light-hearted glance, and Killian snorted.

Did I say something wrong?

Senna gave me a merciful smile. "We have a slightly different take on what humans would call husband and wife," she said with a gentle voice. "Laurent is my *mate*. We are married, just as humans would be, our oaths taken before the realm and the gods. But to be someone's mate means that you are destined for each other by the fates. To find your mate is to find the other half of your soul." Her eyes moved tenderly over her mate's face, and he gazed back in adoration.

"That sounds lovely," I said as I admired them.

"Mates have a life bond," she continued. "It is given to us upon birth. A blessing from the fates and the gods. As we age, the bond strengthens and becomes woven into the fabric of our being. We are able to feel its presence if our mate is near. It can be a startling thing if you are young and do not know what it is that you're feeling." She giggled softly to herself. "Both will feel it though. It's an undeniable sensation."

Her face fell into a frown as she took Laurent's hand in hers. "Sadly, some never find their mate, or circumstances cause one to be taken from the other earlier in life than expected. We all pray those things never happen."

Laurent gave her a sweet smile.

It sounded beautiful, and I could see the love between the two of them. I didn't think I had ever been in love. Not even with that boy from years ago. I never looked at him the way Senna looked at Laurent. And he'd certainly never looked at *me* that way.

Killian picked that moment to inconveniently and rudely intervene. "That's enough of the romance, Senna. Not everyone is as blessed by the gods as you and your dear mate." Senna dipped her chin and leaned into Laurent. "Auren has no need of that information anyway, as it doesn't apply to her, does it?" He directed the question to me.

I shot him a look. "No, I guess it doesn't. But I do find it beautiful." I looked at Senna apologetically, and she gave me a graceful smile in return.

Next to her, Laurent straightened his already seamless doublet, his face pinched with irritation as he glared at Killian. "Well Auren, have you witnessed any good magic yet?" he asked, pulling the conversation back out of the hole Killian had tossed it into.

I shook my head. "None." I wasn't going to admit that Killian had briefly, but successfully, compelled me.

Laurent grinned. "Well, allow me." He brought a hand up in front of him, palm facing the sky, and moved his other hand over it in a circular motion. A small swirl of water appeared in between his palms and he spun it with the guidance of his upper hand. It twirled and wound on itself like a miniature water-spout—not a drop spilling where he didn't want it.

He leaned forward and sent a swift breath from his mouth, between his hands, and the water evaporated, forming into a funnel of air instead. It twisted all the same, except faster, and on a smaller axis point. He glanced up at me and his grin broadened. Then, he spun around and with the push of his palms, he released the whirling wind out into the world, where it grew, and barreled down the path toward a couple of younglings who let out startled, yet excited screams. It chased them between a few nearby trees before dying out completely.

"That's amazing," I said in awe.

Laurent sketched a bow and smiled.

All of a sudden, a chill snaked up my spine and a presence pushed into my head like an unwelcome thought. Every nerve ending stood on edge as my senses balked and scrambled to piece together what was happening.

A swath of red mist gathered on the horizon of my minds-eye, quickly spilling forth, drawing closer. Just as it reached for my thoughts, a pulse of energy rippled through the atmosphere around us, shaking the goblet in my hand.

The presence vacated my head in an instant, and I gasped, stumbling back a step as I glanced around.

Laurent and the others scanned the crowd with concern, but when I did the same, I immediately noticed someone staring back at me. Ramil's glare cut across the pavilion, his expression perturbed. The longer I held his stare, the more unsettled he became. He gave a nervous glance to those nearest him before turning on his heel and slinking back into the throng.

I watched as he disappeared, debating if it was him that had tried to get into my mind, when suddenly, back by the pavilion, a loud crack split the air. We all turned to look as the centermost of the suspended basins split in half, sending burning coals and flames pouring onto the ground below. Several guests shrieked and others scrambled to get out of the way.

As I assessed the situation, a figure lingering in the shadows caught my eye. There, behind the burning coals and frantic flames that littered the floor, stood Niall, hands casually tucked in his pockets. Shadows writhed around him, blending in with the smoke.

His golden eyes burned brightly, and he held my gaze for a moment until two figures moved in front of me and broke my line of sight.

Killian made his way to the flaming mess with Laurent on his heel, already summoning a wave of water.

I watched as the High Lord of Drastia quickly put out the remaining fire with the gentle wave of his wrist, the flames hissing as they were doused. The ash was cleaned up with a few more quick movements of his hands, a controlled whirl of wind sweeping up every last cinder. Then, the music resumed, coaxing the guests onto the pavilion once again.

Tensions eased and the ambiance returned, along with the crowd. But when I searched the shadows again for Niall, he was gone.

24
A LATE-NIGHT VISITOR

A GOOD DEAL OF FAE HAD UNWILLINGLY SOBERED UP—THANKS TO THE incident. But it wasn't long before they dove into their wine again, chasing that feeling of carelessness. Many opted to take their revelries deeper into the forest. I could hear them laughing and singing throughout the trees beyond The Woodland House as Breck escorted me back through the halls.

The house was bustling as well. Courtly fae, house-fae, all likes of them romped about. Some cackled in conversation, sloshing goblets of their wine, while others snuck off behind closed doors with each other. Some made their grabs and stole their kisses in plain sight, oblivious—or too drunk—to care if anyone saw.

We passed a shadowed alcove, and a fae male gluttonously reached for me as he pulled away from his female companion. Breck tugged me out of the stranger's reach and growled low at him in warning. The male simply snickered and went back to indulging the antler-crowned female who was busy hiking her leg up around his waist.

"Well that was an interesting Lumeri," Breck said, sounding less than pleased.

"Something I'll definitely never forget," I replied, watching more intoxicated guests drag each other through the shadows.

"You danced. With him," Breck said, the words snapping my attention. *Did he mean Killian? Or . . .*

Niall. That's undoubtedly who Breck was referring to.

I scoffed. "It was one dance, Breck, and it wasn't even my choice."

He stopped us in the middle of the hallway, suddenly concerned. "Did he compel you?" His voice was accusing, on the cusp of threatening.

"No. He asked me. Kindly, actually."

I thought back on the High Lord of Calledan's words.

Dance with me.

A sweet request.

I knew that I'd willingly accepted because not long after, Killian used compulsion on me and nearly had me falling on my knees against my will at his touch. The feelings were night and day.

My expression turned sour and Breck noticed. "What's wrong?"

"*Killian* compelled me earlier."

Breck practically stumbled. "When? When did this happen? H-How do you know?"

"It was after I danced with Niall. Killian made a comment about me not knowing what it meant to be compelled, and then he just . . . did it. I don't know the logistics of it, but he made me long for him—or something along the lines of that. Then he acted like it was nothing."

"My *cousin* is partial to all manner of compulsion, especially to get his way. But to use it on you . . ." Breck worked his jaw in irritation. "He should not have disrespected you like that."

We turned down the long, familiar hallway where my chambers sat, but we were no longer alone. Standing sentry outside my door was a tall male in silver armor, a sword hanging at his side. Breck thrust a hand out in front of him, commanding the doors to my chambers to open with his magic, and breezed past the guard without so much as acknowledging him.

He glanced around the space. The candles and fireplace were already lit, and a couple of orbs bobbed in the center of the room, lending their warm white light.

He swept the bathing chamber for threats next, while I made straight for the wooden box that had been left on my bed, and took off the heavy headpiece. My scalp practically sang with relief—free of the weight. I gave the crown one last thorough admiring before returning it to the box.

"Auren, I'm sorry for what happened this evening with Killian," Breck said as he re-entered the bedchamber. "I'd like to say that he doesn't know better, but I'm afraid he gives in to his cruel delights more often than he should."

"I don't hold you accountable for your cousin's actions, Breck. I will say though, that I'll probably give him a piece of my mind, sooner rather than later."

"You do that, and you'll definitely need to be shielded." He snorted, then looked up at me from under his brows. "Just . . . promise me you'll do it when I'm around, so I can shield you. And so I can see his reaction."

I grinned at the same time he did. "Certainly."

We stood in awkward silence for a moment, and just when I thought I'd better say something, he spoke. "Tomorrow, there will be a lot of cleaning up around the House, and probably a good-way into the forest—judging from the sounds of everything tonight. It's best that we stay out of the way. I was thinking an archery lesson might do the trick."

Excitement raced through me. "I'd like that very much," I said with a smile.

He smiled back, warm and . . . attractive.

I didn't think much of his looks before, but Breck was a handsome male. I'd just been too busy being hauled off to his High Lord to pay enough attention. I'd also been too skeptical of his kindness at the start. But now, I noted that he might be one of the more decent males in this realm. Everything he had done so far seemed genuine, and that comforted me.

It also helped that he was nice to look at.

"I'll be back in the morning, then. We'll grab breakfast before we head out. I'll see to it that Sorscha finds some appropriate clothes for you."

"Please, no fluffy dresses or skirts!" I called out to him as he opened the door. "I prefer fitted pants and a tunic."

He inclined his head before reaching back to grab the handle. "Don't forget, I'm only a few doors down if you need anything."

I nodded, and the guard outside my door grunted, his armor rustling as he shifted his weight to remind Breck he was there.

The door snicked shut, and I stood in the stillness, assessing. The crackling pops of the fire punctuated my thoughts as they began spilling forth in my mind.

The guard at the door would be a problem if I decided to try and make a grand escape back to The Veil. But strangely, the thought of Breck watching out for me all night, only to find me gone the next morning, made me reconsider. The least I could do was stay the night. Take advantage of the archery lesson in the morning. Perhaps then I might find a path back through the forest.

Then I recalled the celebration, and how I'd seen happiness, love, joy, desire, fear, surprise—all emotions that were so *human*. I didn't expect those notions to even exist on this side of The Veil.

And, for someone who was considered a trespasser, my fate seemed a bit . . . odd. Instead of being interrogated in some cell, as one would expect, I'd been dressed in finery and paraded around. Something I hadn't expected from what was supposed to be a brutal, conniving species.

I wasn't being held captive—not yet at least. Though, I could argue that the guard outside my door meant otherwise.

I let out a long breath and peered around the room. A folded set of nightclothes sat on one of the wingback chairs in front of the fire, collecting warmth. And in-between the chairs, on the small side table, a fresh half-loaf of bread and a slab of butter sat next to a full pitcher of water.

Sorscha must have known I didn't have a whole lot to eat at the event.

I made my way toward the table, my stomach giving a confirming grumble as I poured myself a tall glass and tore off a strip of bread. It was delicious; slightly sweet, with a sponge-like texture. I turned it over in my hand, considering how everything in this realm seemed to be a better version of my own. The thought made me recall how Niall had asked me for my opinion of this place. I swiped the bread across the pad of butter and took another bite as I considered what I'd amend my answer to if he were to ask me again.

But what did it matter? I would be gone soon, either by my own escape or a coaxed release, and there would be no more parading around in dresses or mingling with fae High Lords. Especially with one who looked like sweet temptation and destruction all at once.

I swallowed and glanced over at my sword, which—if I remembered correctly—Breck had left leaning against the bedside table . . . Except now, it was propped against the fireplace a few feet to the right.

Before I had time to think any further about it, a shadow materialized in the center of the room, and tendrils of black flame gave way to a tall male form.

I stumbled back at the sight of Niall emerging from the darkness, and my chest thrummed from the inside out.

A faint grin rested on his lips as his eyes met mine.

"Doesn't anyone knock or use a door?" I scolded him.

I briefly contemplated throwing my half-eaten bread at him for startling me. Instead, I set my glass on the table and the bread back on the plate like a civilized person.

He stood with his hands clasped behind his back and looked around the space. "I prefer porting," he said, shrugging.

"What are you doing in my bedchamber?"

"I wanted to check on you," he replied, finding my eyes once more. "Are you all right?"

"Why wouldn't I be?"

He studied me, like he was trying to glean something deeper . . . as if I was hiding something. "You seemed flustered when I last saw you."

That's because someone had tried to meddle with my mind—

I shook the thought from my head.

"I'm fine. Now, if you'll excuse me . . ." I walked to the armoire and opened the doors to reveal the mirror. I wanted to see myself in the dress once more before I willed it off of me. Niall followed, coming to stand behind me.

"Stunning," he said, studying my reflection.

I scoffed, but he continued to linger. From the looks of it he wasn't about to leave, so I reached down and worked the shoes off my feet. When I rose again, he was still standing there, waiting.

"What?" I asked.

He grinned playfully and nudged his chin toward me. "Now the dress." I gave him an incredulous look, and he chuckled. "Relax, darling. I'm only joking."

"You know, they say behind every joke is a half-truth," I stated flatly.

He raised a brow. "Is that so?"

I got the feeling that some part of him *was* waiting for my dress to come off next. Perhaps he knew that if I simply willed it off me with a thought, it would obey. I quickly and carefully wiped the notion from my mind, not wanting to risk thinking it while he was in my presence.

He took a step toward me, and when he spoke again, it was softer, his voice deep and smooth. "You looked lovely tonight. I just wanted to come and tell you that."

"I thought you said you were here to check on me?"

"That too."

He watched my every move like he was committing it to memory, tilting his head as I set each shoe neatly at the foot of the armoire. Maybe I was just as foreign to him as he was to me, and this was his weird way of observation.

I sighed. "If you're trying to figure out how the dress glowed earlier, I don't have answers for you. You'd need to talk to Gareth for that. Now would you please leave?"

His eyes sparkled in the warm light, and amusement settled into his features. "I'm not entirely sure it was the dress that glowed."

There it was. That same look. The one from before, where he looked at me like I was the most stunning creature to walk the realms. "Would you stop looking at me like that?" Not only was it making me nervous, but strangely, it was making me want him to *continue.*

"Can a male not admire something he finds fascinating?"

I pinched my lips together.

No.

Yes.

Finally, I found words. "Perhaps it was you and your magic trying to make a fool of a poor human who ended up here."

"If it was magic, it didn't come from me. And I would never make a fool of you. You must have confused me with Killian."

"But that *was you*—when the basin fell apart onto the pavilion floor?" I assumed based on his proximity that he was most likely responsible. *And* he'd winked at me. That alone screamed *guilty.*

"I don't know what you're talking about," he said as he made a show of looking at the mosaics on the floor around us.

"You wanted to show off your power, make people tremble in your presence and remind them of who you are. Breck filled me in."

"I think you're drawing conclusions about me too quickly again,

Auren. And your source isn't as reliable as you think. My power is not something I play with." He scuffed his perfectly polished black boot along the mosaic dragonfly's delicate wings.

"Oh, yes. I forgot. It's *rare* and *deadly,*" I mocked as I side-stepped him to retrieve my glass of water again. An amused sound rumbled from him, and he watched me curiously as I finished my drink. "I need to clean up and rest. Humans sleep too, you know. Should I expect you to stand here all night and monitor my movements?"

A sly smirk spread across his face, his eyes gleaming as if I'd extended him some sort of invitation.

"That wasn't an offer," I said dryly.

Despite my words, some part of me didn't quite want him to leave just yet. Even if it was an intrusion in the first place.

What is wrong with me?

His smirk remained as he sauntered toward me, completely ignoring my previous question. He stepped intimately close, forcing me to press up against one of the chairs. I held my breath as he reached up to run the back of his finger along my jawline in a slow, smooth movement. Where Killian's touch was brash and greedy, Niall's caress was intentional. Meaningful.

His eyes began to glow a molten gold like they had earlier when we danced. "Curious little thing. You say you're human, but you don't feel human to me."

I focused on his touch, his fingers on my skin. "What do I feel like?" I asked, my words coming out low and breathy.

"Like something I've never come across in all of my existence," he murmured.

All at once, a dozen questions floated into my mind, but I didn't have the will to ask any of them. I just stared into his eyes. He was mistaken if he thought I was anything but human.

"I don't know what else to tell you," I said.

The thrumming in my chest continued, a steady anchor for my body and soul. I contemplated asking him if he could feel it radiating through me . . .

His finger halted under my chin and lifted it gently. "Our wine doesn't affect you like it should, and you set yourself aglow. Tell me, do either of those things sound human?" It wasn't an accusation, just an observance.

And my thoughts went right to the wine.

I had finished almost a full glass, and then sipped on another. Niall was right, that should have been more than enough to either make me do ridiculous things in public, or knock me out if I wasn't seasoned to it.

But I couldn't get my mind to focus on asking questions when he was looking at me like that. He was sweet temptation and destruction all wrapped up in a sleek black jacket, and his mere presence stamped out all my remaining resolve.

I breathed out, "I think perhaps *you* have had too much wine, and now you're thinking too hard on what does or does not make me human."

The corner of his lips lifted in a grin. "I would joke with you about that, but I'm afraid you would sniff out the half-truth."

Turning my earlier words against me. Clever.

He withdrew his finger from my chin and took hold of my hand instead, bringing it up to his lips and planting a kiss against my knuckles. Butterflies took flight in my stomach at the feeling of his warm breath across my skin.

"I'll leave you to your thoughts then, Auren. Until tomorrow." He turned and walked to the door.

Amidst my stupor, the word *tomorrow* rang in my mind. "What do you mean, *tomorrow?*"

He grinned over his shoulder as he turned the handle. "I'm staying for a few days. It seems I'm due for a small vacation of sorts. The mountains can get quite stuffy after a while, and Killian has an abundance of unused guest chambers." He shrugged casually. "Right along this hallway, actually," he added, patting his hand on the door frame.

A strange mix of feelings danced around inside my chest. Then, my eyes widened, and I lurched forward, words gathering on the tip of my tongue to warn him that the guard was just outside. But when the door swung open, the hall was empty.

"Sleep well," he said as he vanished into black smoke on the threshold.

I hurried across the room and leaned out into the hall to see which room he had gone to, but there was no sign of him. No trace of smoke. He had ported right into his chamber—somewhere close to mine. I cursed at myself for even wanting to know which one it was.

There was no trace of the guard either.

Strange—

Another door creaked open.

My heart picked up a beat, then fell flat inside my chest when Breck stepped out.

"Everything all right?" he asked, still sounding wide awake. "I thought I heard some—where's your guard?" He looked both ways down the long corridor.

"Oh, uhh, I thought I heard something too. Maybe it was just the guard leaving."

The look on Breck's face told me that the guard was under strict orders not to leave his post.

"Goodnight." I quickly closed my door and leaned back against it.

The guard's whereabouts wasn't my problem.

The entire interaction with Niall however . . .

I was confused. Enthralled. I'd never been so conflicted with feelings in my life.

Why is Niall so interested in my well-being?

Why was anyone, *really?*

There were so many things calling my attention. Things that weren't adding up. Not to mention the gods damned thrumming in my chest. It had calmed to a dull hum that was hardly noticeable now, but I could still feel it.

The entirety of the day suddenly caught up with me, and sleep beckoned. I strolled over to the edge of the bed, testing the mattress and plush blankets, before flopping down on them and releasing a deep sigh.

I began running through the last few hours in my head, but the longer I strained to remember every detail, the further I slipped toward a much-needed sleep. My eyelids drooped and then fluttered open a couple of times, until the last thing I remembered before tumbling into my dreams was my dress, and how I should have probably changed into my night clothes.

25
A STRANGE MORNING

I WOKE TO A SHRILL GASP FROM SOMEWHERE ACROSS THE ROOM.

I jerked my head up from where I'd been face down in my pillows. Warm sunlight was streaming in through the window. There were towels scattered across the floor, and Sorscha was covering her eyes with her small hands as she backed away towards the bathing chamber.

I came to my wits and looked down at myself. Other than the undergarment around my hips, I was completely naked. I grasped for the blankets, but I'd slept on top of them, and they were pinned underneath me, so I yanked up the corner from the side of the bed and wrapped it over myself.

What in the blessed fates happened?

Somehow the dress had vanished from my body, leaving me utterly bare. I remembered briefly waking in the night, thinking that the room seemed particularly warm . . . I glanced over to the chair by the fireplace, where my night clothes sat untouched. I must have fallen asleep before I could get changed, then wished the garment off myself when I got too warm.

Taking the bedding with me, I climbed out of bed and knocked on the bathing chamber door.

"Sorscha? You can come out now."

Slowly, she emerged, avoiding my eyes until she was sure I was covered. Once she saw the bedding wrapped around my body like

170

swaddling on a child, she disappeared, then reappeared in the same place with fresh clothes.

I smiled, reaching out to take them. "Thank you for these. And, I'm sorry about that . . ." I motioned over my shoulder and laughed as the sound she'd made echoed again in my mind. She dipped her head toward her shoulder, as if she considered laughing too.

Before I had the chance to say more, she popped out of sight, the pile of towels disappearing along with her.

I huffed a small laugh, shaking my head as I entered the bathing chamber. "Busy body," I muttered.

She reappeared, peeking around the doorway, and flashing another one of those sad attempts at a smile that came off as a bit more creepy than happy.

I chuckled. "We'll need to work on your smile a bit."

She disappeared again.

I slipped into the fitted, suede pants, and the long ivory blouse she'd brought me. The blouse was a tad big, but it would do just fine. I tucked the front into the waist of the pants and slid into the boots that I was wearing when I arrived. A quick braid of my hair and I felt good as new.

What now?

I began to pace the room. That sleep must have done wonders because a new sense of energy coursed through my body. I needed an outlet for it and was glad that Breck would be teaching me archery today.

I wondered when he would come to collect me.

"Sorscha?" I called out quietly. She appeared near the fireplace this time, taking note to emerge at a further distance rather than up close.

"Do you think you could bring me a book for later? I might like to have something to pass the time while I'm here."

She bowed her head and tried to smile again, but abandoned it and vanished before she managed to form one properly.

A knock sounded at the door.

When I opened it, Breck was leaning his shoulder against the doorframe, donning a friendly smile.

"Good morning, sunshine. You look like you slept well."

He wore a loose, pale green shirt with a pair of fitted brown pants that showed off his long, toned legs. His tall leather boots looked like they were made for gallivanting out in the forest.

"I slept . . . unconventionally," I replied, stepping out to meet him. "But yes, all was well."

"Good. I hope you have an appetite. Breakfast here is quite a treat."

As we walked down the hall, I took note of each door, wondering which one Niall might be behind. Wondering if he could feel my presence, or if he could hear Breck rambling about breakfast foods.

I quickly shook some sense back into my head.

Why do I even care?

I also took note that there were now guards standing at every corner. Their silver-plated armor was dappled in the morning light that shone through the tree canopy into The Woodland House. Details of golden vines decorated each breastplate, and dark green cloaks draped over their shoulders, spilling onto the floor behind them, ruffling in the slight breeze. Their helmets folded inward around their cheeks, leaving their eyes on full display. At their sides, intricate scabbards and silver longswords hung at the ready.

The guards might as well have been carved from the stone walls, seeing as they didn't shift or make a sound as we passed them. Only their eyes moved, tracking everyone's comings and goings.

Our day-breaking meal was served under the morning sun on an outdoor patio. The spread of food tasted divine—just like Breck raved it would. I ate a full plate of fruits and sweet breads and watched each new face that entered and left the area.

But there was no sign of Niall.

A jitteriness settled in my limbs, so I went back for seconds, thinking more food would fix it. When it didn't, I began bouncing my knee repeatedly underneath the table.

Breck took note of the movement. "You seem a bit anxious this morning." He waved his fork in my view to call my attention.

I cleared my throat. "I woke up with a lot of energy."

Energy that spawned overnight.

Breck shucked a finger over his shoulder at the two bows and the quivers of arrows that leaned against the patio railing behind him. "We'll fix that energy issue soon enough."

He sat back in his chair, sipping on his drink as he ran a hand through his hair, which shined more golden than bronze in the bright morning sun. "Want to fill me in on your introductions with the High Lords?"

No.

I chewed on my last piece of raspberry jam filled pastry. "They seemed just as you said they would be," I said.

"And what of the High Lord of Calledan? You two seemed to be having a moment last night."

I froze. *Did he know Niall had shown up in my chambers?*

"The dance?" Breck clarified.

Oh. Yes. That. Why is he still pressing me about that?

I studied the pastry in my hand and didn't answer.

What else do I say? Niall seemed . . . decent? He won't leave my mind? Did we have a moment?

I wouldn't call it a moment, but something . . . yes.

I opted for, "The High Lord of Calledan was respectful. They all were. Except for your cousin."

Breck frowned into his drink as he took another sip.

I sampled my own glass of lemon-flavored water. "Where *is* Killian this morning anyway?"

"Apparently in a very important meeting. He called all the other High Lords to it as well."

"The other High Lords . . . they *all* stayed last night?"

"Yes. Though a couple of them normally wouldn't have."

"So, why did they?" I pressed, trying not to sound too curious.

Breck leaned forward across the small table. "Auren, last night, something was stolen from Killian's trove. A . . . relic of sorts." He opened his mouth, but then closed it again on second thought, flicking his eyes up as someone walked past. He lowered his voice. "It's best not spoken of here."

I nodded, noting the fae who were strolling in at a steady pace.

"But if you're finished eating . . ."

I drained my glass. "Where are we off to?"

"Your first bow lesson."

26
THE LESSON

THE FOREST WAS QUIET AS WE MADE OUR WAY THROUGH THE TREES toward what Breck claimed was his favorite meadow for training.

As I followed him, I couldn't help but notice how he blended in and traversed the terrain seamlessly, almost silently. I noted where he placed his feet, how his gait was smooth and light, how he maneuvered around the trees—careful not to snag his bow and quiver on the lower branches. The weapons barely shifted along his shoulders. I studied his movements, committing them to memory, learning more than just the skills of archery that he'd planned to teach me.

We walked for a bit, until he was sure no others were nearby, then he picked up our conversation from breakfast. "Last night, an ancient relic that has been kept in this court for centuries was removed without consent. Killian's ancestral line was charged with protecting it."

"What sort of relic?"

"We think it's what's directly referred to in the prophecy given by Karios," he clarified, but I still stared at him blankly. "The prophecy?" he repeated. "You're not familiar with it?"

"I've heard of a fae prophecy, but I don't know it well enough to recite it to you. Humans aren't really the type to dwell on those things."

He frowned. "Do humans have such little regard for history or the future? It's a prophecy for both realms."

"Well, when a human's lifespan is so short, what are the chances that a prophecy is going to come to fruition in our lifetime?" I replied dryly.

He considered that for a moment.

"But go ahead, indulge me," I said.

He recited it smoothly:

> *"With the coming of the dawn,*
> *the fate of all to the fate of one.*
> *A flame of light, a flame of dark,*
> *a golden shroud brought from a spark.*
> *A piece is lost, and then it's worn,*
> *stars and ash bring forth the storm.*
> *Two great powers to bring the change,*
> *the gods will rise upon a new age."*

I twisted my mouth to the side. "I didn't hear any mention of a relic."

"The 'piece that is lost' is believed to be the reference. It's the talisman that belonged to Lyceius—the god of light," Breck explained. "It was his crown, of sorts—a thin, golden band which he wore across his forehead, imbued with his magic. Ring any bells?"

I winced and shook my head.

"Gracious fates, Auren."

"What? Half of our realm lost its devotion and respect for the gods when Lyceius rebelled." I harrumphed at how terrible that made humans sound, but it was true.

The fact that Karios and the other gods even allowed such horrible things to happen to humans was enough to make people turn their backs. Some managed to retain enough respect toward them, but it wasn't enough to hold onto belief in prophecies.

"And which of those humans do you fall under?" he asked.

"The latter." My ancestors must have truly been devout, seeing as how my parents raised us to still pray and give thanks. "But I think, for most humans, the way we often struggle through life makes it difficult to keep our faith, and asking for help and guidance when it often goes unanswered . . . you get where I'm going with this, don't you?"

The fae were much more in-tune with the gods than we ever cared to be. They had magic, and magic was like being a step closer to the divine. Why wouldn't they be more attuned to them? After all, their kind weren't the ones that had been taken advantage of in the past.

Breck blew out a long breath. "Perhaps humans just have a lack of understanding of how the gods operate. The gods can't always intervene when things go awry. If they did, there would be no free-will, and the fates would have no destinies to weave."

I thought about that for a moment. "You may be right about the lack of understanding."

Breck looked over at me. "Want to tell me what you *do* know, and I can help you fill in the blanks?"

"Are you some type of scholar on the topic, or something?"

"Something like that." He grinned. "I always wanted to be an Adorner. They oversee the archives, records, and historical documents of our kind. We have an ancient text that details the history of the gods, fates, and magic. I've studied it in depth."

"Well then, it seems the fates have smiled upon me by sending you to be my teacher," I said, lacing my words with sweet sarcasm.

He snorted a laugh.

"You might as well just refresh my memory of it all. I'm afraid the specifics aren't really common knowledge in my realm anymore."

"What would you like to know first?"

"Start with talismans," I said.

"Well, a god's talisman is what allows them to focus their power in a more precise and potent state. Without it, they don't have complete control. Lyceius—the god of light—lost his talisman after the first war he brought upon the realms. It was hidden away, here, in the fae lands, to prevent him from regaining his full strength . . . Until it was stolen last night. Now, to get to *how* he lost his talisman in the first place . . . it's a bit long-winded."

I made a show of gesturing to the forest. "How far is our walk?"

"Far enough." Breck grinned, catching my implication.

"Plenty of time, then."

He chuckled lightly. "I'm sure you know, Karios, the king of the gods of Gaia, created humans and the fae, and all other gods of this world answer to him—Lyceius being one of them."

I nodded, listening closely.

"Over time, Lyceius became restless and desired a greater degree of power for himself. He'd also grown close to one of the fates, Sephta. In his first attempt to gain more power, he tried to sway Sephta to help him change his fate. But she would not risk the balance of the god-kings."

"She refused him?"

"Yes. And in his rage, Lyceius turned his own power of light on itself and created something corrupted, something that consumed him. With his new dark power, he rebelled against the divine order. He thought that if he could wreak enough havoc on Karios's creatures, perhaps the fates would intervene and give him what he desired. So, he glamoured himself as a human being, and came down upon the human realm. He tricked and seduced many women, whisking them off to a stretch of land north of our realms, in Salterra, where he bred with them, creating abominations—each possessing a small kernel of his power that would make them loyal cohorts to his cause.

"It was the ultimate disrespect against Karios—taking his creations and using them to make sinister beings. And as his own evil intentions spread within his offspring, so too did a rot spread throughout the land, turning the once thriving space into a wasteland. The power he'd corrupted within himself gave life to all sorts of wicked creatures, and the humans and fae who had once dwelled in the territory fled south, in fear of the dying land, and what came with it."

I shook my head in contemplation. "I never understood why Lyceius chose humans and not fae."

Humans had lost their faith in the gods for that very reason. It was why faith as a whole still teetered on a delicate pedestal. For who would allow such a thing to befall their creation? How could Karios watch and do nothing?

"He chose humans because they were unable to sense glamours or compulsion. Not to mention they're powerless and—"

I playfully shoved Breck in his shoulder. "I get the gist. We're lowly beings."

He gave me a wry smile and a laugh.

"Go on, continue," I urged.

"Well, as time passed, dozens of beings turned into hundreds, and hundreds became thousands, and soon Lyceius had amassed an army to take on the realms. When Karios and the fates still did not grant Lyceius what he desired, the rebellious god unleashed his creatures on our lands in what is known as the Battle of Parradiom. Humans and fae battled side by side against Lyceius's forces at the northern border, driving them back enough to allow your kind to move further south, to safety. But after days of fighting, nearly all humans who'd gone into battle perished, or were taken hostage into the Wastelands, never to be seen again.

"We were losing terribly, until Karios intervened. In his divine authority, he stripped Lyceius of his talisman, cutting off his access to fully hone and use his power, and bound his existence to the lands he'd turned to ruin. Karios gave the golden band to the fae for safekeeping, out of the hands of the gods, somewhere Lyceius wouldn't find it."

"And that's why it was here?" I asked.

"That's correct."

"I didn't know about the talisman," I said. "Karios tried to help us?"

"Yes. He never wished ill upon humans, and neither did we."

"But didn't your kind deny us when we asked for help?"

From what I *did* know of our history, when the threat of a second war with Lyceius loomed, the human king at the time—King Emmeric— begged for access to the fae lands for refuge and protection of his people, but the fae refused.

Breck looked over at me. "Yes, but that is only half of the truth—"

"Your High Lords didn't value our lives enough to care?"

"Is that what you've been taught?" he asked, sounding a bit shocked. When I didn't reply, his face soured. "Fae lands hold a wealth of magic, Auren, and that is something we will not give up easily. Not then, or now. But your king didn't understand that. And when he became desperate, he violated our agreements. He *invaded* our lands."

"To beg for help—"

"To slaughter us," he hissed over his shoulder.

I stopped in my tracks and stared at him.

He halted too and sighed, turning around. "Your king butchered our kind in an ambush."

My brows pinched in confusion. "What do you mean?"

"After centuries of coexisting harmoniously, humans took advantage of the knowledge they'd gained from us—knowledge of our weaknesses." He paused, eyeing me, realizing from my expression that I had no prior knowledge of this. "The king equipped his soldiers with iron, knowing it was deadly to us."

My face fell. I hadn't known. That was something our histories neglected to teach us—maybe it was left out for a reason.

Breck lowered his eyes. "Our lords were outraged at the betrayal, and they didn't hesitate to use their power and magic to put humans back in their place."

I flinched. Perhaps that was why stories had warped over time about the "ruthless fae." They wanted everyone to believe that the fae were the ones who had been wrong—were evil in their intentions. But no one wanted to admit that it was really *us* who had driven them to it.

"I didn't know," I said quietly. "Our history teaches that the king fell ill soon after the second war, and the royal court blamed the fae, claiming your kind had placed a curse on him."

"That's not true. His illness was not of our doing. As I've told you before, the fae aren't a vengeful race. We didn't seek the destruction of humans, nor did we wish ill upon them. But we would not yield our lands, and we would not see our own kind be subject to a war on both fronts. So, we erected The Veil."

"To keep us away from you . . ." I trailed off.

I started walking, and Breck followed, watching as I slowly pieced together all the misinformation we'd been fed over the generations.

Centuries had passed with continued strain between the humans and the fae, stemming from that fateful turning point, and the generations after were raised to fear the fae.

It all made sense.

"*We* were the problem. *We* were the reason The Veil went up," I concluded.

"In a sense," Breck said. "It ensured that humans would stay out of our realm, so that we could focus on the threat to the north. Our kind were the only ones capable of standing a chance against Lyceius's armies. We could still cross The Veil—if need be—to be in communication with the human king."

"But on *your* terms," I added.

"Yes. We also stretched The Veil along both our realms' border with Salterra, in hopes that it would keep Lyceius's creatures out of our lands and give your realm some sort of reprieve. A small mercy the humans were never thankful for." He held a branch out of my way, allowing me to cross a small stream before he continued. "Humans never trusted us again, and your king refused to send his armies to our front lines during the second war against Lyceius. So the fae were left to fight alone. The Veil bought us time, and kept the second battle contained to The Wastelands, preventing it from spreading south into our realms, but that war was still brutal. Lyceius had spent his time wisely, evolving his creatures into terrifying beasts, stronger and more vicious than before. Without his talisman, he was vulnerable, and he knew it. And after that battle ended in a cataclysmic event, Karios stepped in once again."

I wanted to ask what cataclysmic event he was referring to, but he continued on without pause.

"Which brings us to the prophecy. Karios couldn't deal away with Lyceius himself because a god cannot expel another god—not directly. It would cause too much of an imbalance of power. And he couldn't banish the evil that was imbued into Lyceius's offspring. Not while the fallen god was still in power. He would need to imbue some of his own power to someone else for the task."

"But they're gods. Can't they just do whatever they want?"

Breck huffed a laugh. "There is such a thing as 'divine law,' Auren. Think about it . . . if the gods could do away with each other on a whim, one small quarrel could turn into something with chaotic consequences very quickly."

"Well, that seems to have happened regardless," I said dryly.

"That is why Karios did what he did next. He knew it would take a massive amount of power to undo everything that Lyceius had achieved, and to rid the realms of his existence entirely. So, he formulated a plan to create a bloodline of his own that would one day produce the being that would usher in the prophecy. The one who would have Karios's power in their blood—but was not a god. A force that would be enough to defeat Lyceius and still abide by divine law. The tricky part is, whoever deals the final blow will have to ascend to take his place as the new god of light so that there's no imbalance of power. Therefore, the one to *eliminate* Lyceius must also be *descended* from him."

I frowned. "That's not possible."

Breck lifted a brow at me, grinning. "Are you so sure?"

My own brows pinched in confusion. "That would mean it would have to be done by one of Lyceius's own offspring. But, didn't he take them all away with him?"

Breck's grin spread. "Not all."

We rounded a bend and crossed a small creek before he continued. "The fates were intent on rebalancing the realms. They laid an opportunity before Karios. Call it *divine intervention,* if you will. A human woman managed to hide her baby—a daughter who'd been born of Lyceius. And though the child carried Lyceius's kernel of power, the fates played their hand, and she remained pure of heart and was never taken by his forces.

"When she came of age, Karios made his move. He came down, and upon lying with her he bestowed a particular kernel of his own magic into the child they created; a power of uncorrupted goodness—to stifle the kernel of darkness that was passed down. Something that would alter the gift of light that came from Lyceius, and provide what was needed to overcome him when the time was right. The woman took a vow of silence, never speaking of their mingling, and she carried on living a normal, unsuspecting life with her child.

"The power would continue to remain concealed and undetected in her human bloodline, passed down through the generations without materialization—just as the fates willed it. It would surface in the right individual, at a point when many timelines would align, and the prophecy would fall into place. The descendent of both gods—the one wielding both their powers—would be the key to Lyceius's undoing. This is what the prophecy speaks of."

We stepped into an open meadow, and Breck swung the bows and arrows off his back and leaned them against a nearby stone, while I found a spot to sit so I could process the information.

I'd known some parts of the story, but there was so much I *hadn't* known. I shook my head in disbelief. We blamed the gods, believing they never intervened, when in reality, they did. All this time, we'd been taught that they allowed the hardships of war and devastation to fall upon Belthria, and that the fae were just as responsible.

Over the course of time, faith had become increasingly scarce. Hearts hardened, and temples and worship became all but abandoned. Which now led me to believe that this was why our society knew half truths about our history, and was oblivious to the rest. We had rewritten our wrongs to be someone else's. We had purposefully plucked what portions of our history made it to the generations that came after, and we'd placed the blame on the gods and the fae, when in reality, neither had ill intent at all.

And on top of all that, the prophecy continued to fall on deaf ears in Belthria. Perhaps that's the way our kind wanted it. After centuries of believing the fae had wronged us, why would we ever put stock in one of their prophecies that boasts of a savior for both our kind? Humans would sooner run straight to Lyceius's den than put their faith in a savior acclaimed by the fae.

But what no one knew was that this realm was nothing like what we had been taught. The fae lived normal lives—they weren't brutes or beasts as we believed them to be. They weren't ill-willed or evil. Yes, they had placed The Veil between our realms to keep us out, but that was because of our own actions. By extending The Veil northward, the fae had actually given us a reprieve. They had been the ones to keep Lyceius at bay all this time.

The stories were wrong. Warped. History had been whispered on the tongues of the naïve and the ignorant.

It was built on the lies of mortals.

"I know it's a lot to digest all at once," Breck said, cutting through my rampant, spiraling thoughts as he assessed his bow.

"There's something you said earlier that doesn't quite make sense."

"And what's that?" he asked curiously.

"I thought the gods were eternal? If one can be killed, then that would mean they're not truly immortal. Right?"

Breck's mouth twisted to the side in contemplation before he said, "Technically they are, because they don't ever really die; they just cease to exist as they were—stripped of all power. Think of it as their energy being transferred to another form. They would no longer have the power of a god, nor would they be capable of ever returning to that form. It's a transfer of power from one source to the next. Where their physical form goes, no one knows. Perhaps some plane of existence that we cannot see or comprehend."

I lifted a skeptical brow. "And how do you know all of this?"

Breck chuckled and gave a shrug. "Just a genuine interest I've always had. There are several Ancient Fae here in the woodlands who have studied our ancient text in depths far beyond what I have. I've taken it upon myself to read some of their personal notes. The Highland Court's text has an entire section about the gods that none of the others have. Some scholars say it was written by the hand of someone who witnessed an ancient goddess fall to this world, and that the being recorded all they'd learned from the goddess while she dwelled among the fae. But no one really knows for sure. It's what I like to believe though."

"Hmm." More questions piled up on my tongue. "You said the fae created The Veil, right?"

Breck stopped fiddling with his bow string and looked at me. "Yes. Why?"

"When I crossed it, I felt this awful presence. I remember thinking it wanted my soul. It pulled on something deep inside me. Then, something pushed me past everything that felt wrong—like it wanted to help me. It *did* help me." I stared at the ground. "Do you think that could have been the fates?"

Breck was quiet for a moment. "I don't know. But, Auren, you're human, you should have never been able to cross in the first place. The Veil is spelled with very strong magic." He came and crouched before me, searching my eyes as if he was looking for something he hadn't found, but that he knew existed. "When I found you, I felt some sort of power lingering around you. But it wasn't the power of The Veil."

My brows bunched up. "What do you mean?"

"I'm still trying to figure that out. I've thought about it a lot. It's possible that you were being shielded. From who—I don't know. You're sure you didn't come across another fae before me?"

"Yes. I'm sure," I lied.

I began picking at the grass beneath me.

Breck worried his lip as he watched me pluck the green blades from the earth one by one. "Well, between your arrival and the talisman being stolen, I'm concerned many will start to ask questions."

"Why would someone steal the talisman though? What could anyone do with it anyway if it's linked to Lyceius's power? Wouldn't it only answer to him?"

"I'm not sure. Unless they know something that we don't and it was taken out of fear. And technically, yes, it's linked to him. But anyone that carries his power in their blood might be able to wield it."

I stopped picking the grass and looked up. "That could be any number of beings . . ." All those who Lyceius had created when he laid with human women . . .

Breck ran his finger along the bow's string, contemplating the scenario. "If the talisman were to fall into any of their hands, it could spell catastrophe. For everyone else, it could be used as a bargaining chip, and that doesn't bode well either."

"There are bands of humans that live in fear of what lurks beyond The Veil. Perhaps one of them—"

"They're *human,* Auren. None would have been able to cross The Veil in the first place, remember?"

I kept forgetting that part.

"Auren," Breck drew out my name and raised a playful brow. "Did *you* steal the talisman?"

I gave him a pointed look. "Yes, amidst the constant company of either you, or a High Lord, I somehow found time to steal the talisman. It's tucked into my boot. Want to see?"

Breck chuckled and went on fiddling with his bow.

A piece is lost and then it's worn, stars and ash bring forth the storm.

I spread the churned-up grass around while churning over the prophecy's words in my head. "So, let me get this straight. The talisman is needed to fulfill the prophecy, because whoever the prophecy is about will need to wear it to channel their power?"

"We assume so. It's said that when the prophecy has been set into motion, and the descendant—chosen and blessed by Karios—had arrived and was coming into their power, there will be signs and indications. It's also said that the earth will quake, and that the fae will witness a reemergence of things of old."

"What are *things of old?*"

"Could be anything. The resurfacing of the talisman could be one. And there are a lot of Ancient Fae traditions that have long since fallen by the wayside, either by fate or by choice. There are things that used to happen frequently that are now very scarcely seen or done. For instance, a human crossing into our realm."

I rolled my eyes again. "I highly doubt my crossing was a sign of anything."

Even if a human crossing The Veil could be considered a *reemergence of things of old,* there's no way that I would be part of ushering in a prophecy.

"What would another sign be?" I asked.

A deep, sensual voice cut across the air, answering my question, and startling both Breck and I. "More fae would become shrouded."

We turned and beheld Niall, his voice echoing from across the meadow where he leaned against a crooked tree.

He pushed off and crossed the distance to us, casually tucking his hands into his pockets. "Meaning more elite warriors would come into their power for the great battle that is to come."

Breck's jaw muscle ticked with annoyance at the High Lord's presence. "What are you doing here Niall?" he growled.

"Eavesdropping. Obviously," Niall said dryly.

I looked down to hide my grin, my chest now humming from within.

"This was a private conversation," Breck ground out as he stood and brushed off his pants.

Niall cocked his head. "Really? I wouldn't have known. Didn't sense a shield or anything." His eyes flared with a golden brilliance as they found mine. "Hi there, darling."

He was dressed more casually today in a fitted black shirt with an unbuttoned collar that hugged the base of his neck. His black pants pulled against his strong leg muscles, and his tall black boots hit him just under his knees.

I gave him an uneasy smile.

Breck had wanted this conversation to be private, and I could feel the frustration radiating off of him as he stared Niall down. Still, I made no move to get up from the grass.

"So, why are the two of you out here whining about the gods?" Niall drawled.

I watched Breck's grip tighten around his bow as I answered, "He was filling me in about the relic that was stolen last night."

"Ah, the relic." Niall swung his head over in Breck's direction. "Yes. The one that was first given to *my* ancestors long ago."

I dropped the uprooted pieces of grass and stood.

Breck had left that part of his recounting out completely.

"It was given to *your* ancestors first?"

"Seems he forgot to mention that part," Niall tutted.

Breck's jaw clenched as Niall took it upon himself to explain. "After the Battle of Parradiom, it was stripped from Lyceius and taken deep into the mountains, hidden within my court where it wouldn't be found—"

"Until your ancestor lost control over his power and nearly wiped out both realms!" Breck spat, not a hint of remorse in his tone.

Niall turned to him slowly, his voice darkening. "I'd watch your tone if I were you."

Breck stiffened.

A long, silent moment stretched between us all before Niall finally spoke again. "Shall I continue?"

"By all means." Breck flourished his hand sarcastically at us before he stormed off across the meadow with our archery equipment.

I gave Niall a look and crossed my arms. "What else did he leave out?"

"He was only slight on that one part. I practically heard your entire conversation." He pointed to his ears. "Excellent fae hearing."

How convenient.

"Why would he leave that part out?" I asked.

Niall looked off into the trees. "Perhaps he didn't want it known that my court was chosen for safekeeping above all others."

I tried to get a read on his face, but he looked down.

"My ancestor was born with a rare form of magic that terrified everyone. And worse yet, he didn't know how to wield or control it. It was new to him and to the realm, and everyone on the outside saw it as a curse. As we age, our power eventually wanes, but as *he* aged, his power strengthened. It took no time at all for our court to move the relic as far away from Calledan as possible once his demeanor started to . . . change. Of course, Killian's greedy family had no issues taking it in."

He briefly paused, as if to calm himself. "When Lyceius amassed another sizable legion, he didn't expect to be met with this particular force of power. During the second battle against Lyceius—the Battle of Olethros—my ancestor unleashed his power as a last resort, and that alone brought Lyceius's forces to their knees. It was a pivotal moment in history."

The cataclysmic event Breck had referred to . . .

Niall's voice lowered. "Unfortunately, it also wiped out a large portion of our own forces in the battle, and it ended up costing him his own life. And ever since then, our court—*my family*—has been labeled a sinister kind of fae with no restraint on our *'dangerous, dark power.'*"

He sighed deeply and lifted his head up to survey the canopy above. "My ancestor's power died with him and was not seen in another descendant . . . until me."

I knew what it was—this power he spoke of. Breck had told me. But I wanted to hear Niall confirm it.

"What was this power your ancestor possessed?"

He stared directly at me and answered, "Shadowfire."

My heart skipped a beat.

"Four generations passed and not an inkling of that power showed its face in any of my family members. Yet the realm still didn't trust us—didn't trust the High Lords who came before me. They thought that my family's bloodline was just hiding their power, waiting to unleash their wrath upon the other territories on a whim.

"When I was born my mother knew something was different about me the moment I opened my eyes. She said she felt it—the power. It leaked off of me like tendrils of smoke."

He raised his hand between us, palm facing the sky, and thin black wisps wafted to life, bleeding into the air. I took in a startled breath, but I didn't back away. I didn't even flinch.

It was mesmerizing—the way the smoke danced like the flames of a fire would.

When I looked back up at him, his face had hardened.

"These shadows will light into black flame if I will them to. It burns so cold that it feels like the hottest fire. It can permeate and penetrate anything. And it took many, many years to learn to control."

"But you *can* control it, right?"

He dipped his chin once, then turned his hand over, and I watched the wisps of shadowfire continue streaming upward from the backside of his palm.

"You're not afraid?" he asked, watching me with awe.

I shook my head. I wasn't afraid at all. I was intrigued. Mesmerized. And most of all I was sympathetic, because what I had seen from Niall last night and in the last few minutes was not the malicious High Lord that Breck seemed to paint him as. "I see only power, and someone who seems to have a leash on it."

He gave me a soft smile and closed his fist.

As I followed the fading tendrils of smoke with my eyes, I caught sight of something beyond. I focused on the figure—which I realized was Breck—holding a bow. He stood completely still across the meadow with an arrow knocked and drawn.

And it was pointed directly at Niall's back.

27
REVELATIONS

"Breck! No!" I shouted, moving around Niall and waving my arms. "Put it down. He's not going to hurt me."

When he didn't move to lower his bow, I tried again. "He was just showing me his power—explaining where it came from."

Seconds ticked by like minutes and finally, Breck let slack into the string and lowered it.

I exhaled the breath I was holding and turned back to Niall. "Are you all *that* untrusting of each other?"

"It's a bit complicated." He chuckled softly, clearly not worried that an arrow was just pointed at him.

"I would say *tell me about it,* but I'm seeing it firsthand," I said sarcastically, tucking my shirt back in where it had come loose from my waistband.

Niall flicked a hand in Breck's general direction. "You don't need to worry. Unless the arrow is tipped with iron, it won't do much."

Right. Fae were notorious for being affected by iron. That was something humans definitely knew. It would stifle their power and healing abilities and could be deadly if left in a wound.

I wasn't sure if Breck's arrows were tipped in iron or not, but the thought quickly faded as I was reminded of the powerful male who stood before me.

"That's not the only power you're capable of, is it?"

Niall's mouth lifted on one side. "No, it's not."

"It's mind-walking, isn't it—your other power?"

He folded his arms across his chest and raised a brow. "Someone seems to have filled you in on quite a lot about me. I'm also wickedly good in bed. Maybe you should be aware of that too."

I blushed from head to toe. "Excuse me?"

"You heard me," he said, his voice dropping into a deep, sultry tone.

I had no idea what to say to that, so I laughed.

He stepped in closer to me. "You wouldn't be laughing if you knew just how truthful I'm being. I could show you . . ." His fingertips grazed my shoulder with the slightest touch, lifting my hair and letting it slip slowly through his fingers.

I stood my ground and took in a breath. "You'd have to compel me."

His flirtatious smirk widened. "I can do that too."

"You wouldn't dare."

We stared at each other, neither of us willing to break first.

Finally, I narrowed my eyes to slits as I said, "You compelled my guard last night didn't you? That's why he was missing."

Niall took another small step forward, nearly breathing down my neck. "And what if I did?"

Breck cleared his throat loudly behind us, and we turned to see that he was now standing a few feet away. "If you two are done romanticizing dark powers," he said, entirely annoyed, "Auren and I have a lesson to begin."

I straightened. I'd forgotten what we came out to the meadow for in the first place. As I side-stepped Niall, I apologized to Breck for our rudeness. "We're here for an archery lesson, are we not? Show me how it's done."

I took Breck's arm in mine and strolled off to the far side of the meadow where he had set up both bows and quivers on a fallen, moss-covered tree trunk.

Niall bit the inside of his cheek and followed.

Once Breck had gone through a series of explanations and demonstrations about how the bow operated, his annoyance tempered down a bit and he loosened up.

Niall kept his distance, staking out his own viewing area nearby where he sat reclining against a fallen tree, legs crossed at his ankles on the grassy floor.

Breck handed me a bow and an arrow, then stood behind me positioning my hands with his. "The fletching goes here." He slid my fingers up the string to nock the arrow in the correct place, and his other hand moved to gently lift mine a half inch higher along the bow's designated grip. "And your front hand steadies the tip."

He leaned his head toward mine to get a better view of my line of sight, his soft, wavy hair brushing against my temple. Then, his entire body pressed firmly against mine as he helped me pull back the arrow.

Niall shifted behind us and cleared his throat louder than was necessary, but Breck ignored him.

I fought back a childish grin.

"Remember your anchor point as you aim," Breck instructed. He lifted my hand that was holding back the arrow and situated it against my cheek. "Here."

His fingers lingered a moment along mine before moving to adjust my elbow in line with my forearm. Then he placed his hands on my hips, angling them slightly. I could sense Niall nearly coming out of his skin at the sight.

"Now, steady yourself and release," he whispered.

I exhaled, long and slow, and loosed the fletching from my fingertips, keeping my front arm straight, but not locked. The arrow soared across the meadow and planted its tip just shy of the center of the target.

Niall quickly stood.

I smiled proudly as I stared at the arrow protruding from the round, wooden target.

"You're a natural!" Breck clapped.

"Of course she's a natural." Niall scoffed from behind us. "She's part of the King's Guard."

I winced. "I wouldn't be so sure of that—after what I did."

I hadn't thought about how the king's men were probably still searching for me, to bring me to the king to answer for whatever the prince's men told him they'd witnessed.

"What, exactly, did you do?" Breck asked.

I looked back at him. He appeared confused, and behind him, Niall was glancing between us both, realizing that I hadn't told Breck as much info as I'd told him.

Shit.

I hoped he wouldn't try to be coy and hold it over Breck.

Thankfully, he remained silent.

I still hadn't told either of them about the light that had burst from me. I wasn't ready to tell that to *any* of the fae just yet. Not after how Weston made it seem like there would be a price on my head for it.

I sighed, opting to keep the information to a minimum. "I bested the prince. No one has ever done that."

When I didn't elaborate further, Breck studied me. "I see," he said. He seemed to want to ask for more details, like he knew I was keeping information from him, but he didn't pry further.

I picked up another arrow and breathed in as I nocked it in place against the bow. I aimed, exhaled slowly, and released it. It found its mark, nearly on top of the first one.

"Impressive," Breck stated. He elbowed my arm as he walked by me to retrieve the spent arrows, and I quickly recalled how I'd made the same one-worded statement when he shot the yellow bird out of the sky.

"I'll be shooting birds out of the sky in no time," I called after him. His shoulders shook as he laughed.

Niall walked up to my side holding a fresh arrow and brushed the feathered fletching between his forefinger and thumb. "You told me, but you didn't tell him," he murmured.

I gave him a look of warning to not say a word about it. He nodded and handed me the arrow, grazing my fingers with his as he released his grip.

Breck walked back to us, examining the tips of the two arrows that I had shot, and suddenly I thought of another question from our earlier discussion.

"You mentioned a shroud earlier. What exactly is that?"

Niall huffed a laugh. "You don't miss a thing, do you?"

Breck offered the explanation. "A shroud is an adornment in the form of inked markings. It's bestowed to elite warriors or those with immense power—someone who performs an impressive and selfless deed. It's a great honor. To be shrouded is to wear a distinction above all others."

"Like this," Niall cut in, pulling the lapels of his shirt apart to reveal a swath of black markings. "Each shroud is different and unique to the fae upon whom it's marked. It circles one's neck, across the collarbones and upper chest out to each shoulder, dipping down the top of each arm and circling back and down between the shoulder blades." He traced his fingers over his body to mark the places as he spoke.

From what I could see, the shroud sat slightly raised atop his skin, reaching out across his collarbones like ink in water. It had been the tip of those markings that I'd caught a glimpse of last night during our dance.

Breck was staring too, not in anger, but in surprise.

Niall straightened his shirt collar, then turned to Breck as if waiting on him to add to the story or say something else.

Breck just folded his arms and cleared his throat. "I wasn't aware that you'd been shrouded."

"It was during the Battle of Gabbath."

"Gabbath?" I asked.

"It means 'Stepping Stones,'" Niall answered. "It's the name given to the northernmost section of Calledan, where the mountain range meets Salterra. Lyceius chose that particular spot to bring his forces to our doorstep for that battle."

"And what did you do to earn the shroud?" I asked quietly.

He stared straight ahead across the meadow at a fixed point, taking his time answering. "Word of the prophecy had reached Lyceius, and he was becoming desperate to retrieve his talisman. His forces were stronger than we'd anticipated, and some were even able to break through The Veil. The fighting had only just begun, and we were already losing too many." The battle was playing out again right before his eyes as he spoke. "I watched some of our best warriors go down at the hands of Lyceius's creatures—my father was nearly one of them. And so, for the first time since learning how to fully control it, I plunged so deep into my power that I exhausted it all in one bout. I wiped out nearly half their army. Obliterated them."

Breck watched him for a moment before sudden realization flooded his face. "I heard about the majority of Lyceius's army being turned to ash in an instant. I never knew what the true cause of it was . . ." He searched Niall's face for some sort of confirmation. "We always just thought it was a favor from the gods, or that perhaps they had sent one of their own to our aid. There was even a name given to the mysterious being . . ."

Niall's stare was still fixed across the clearing as he offered the name. "The Asher." His eyes became shadowed, recalling the memory. "The Adorner appeared to me on the battlefield seconds after it happened. *Seconds.* I knew that what I'd done hadn't been seen since my ancestor lost control on the battlefield long ago. But Syros adorned me right there in the midst of the chaos. I knelt in the mud and received the damned blessing of the gods as wounded warriors took their last breath. As those that I'd fought alongside lay dead in the fucking dirt."

The memories ate at him. I could see it in his face. The fact that he was deemed worthy, while others were not. Worthy of a power that he saw as a curse more than a blessing. It clearly riddled him with guilt.

Breck shifted on his feet as the reality of who truly stood before him sank in. When he finally spoke, his voice was merely a murmur. "*You're The Asher?*"

Niall didn't answer. He only flicked his eyes down to a lower spot amongst the grass, his jaw tightening.

"All this time I thought The Asher was a being sent by the gods. I didn't know that it was *you.*"

"Not many do," Niall said. "When Syros appeared to adorn me, I glamoured us. I didn't want everyone making the connection or knowing it was me. And I've worked hard to keep it that way." He looked pointedly at Breck, who dipped his chin in a nod. "Most know of the name and think it was the work of another entity. No one can say for certain, and I prefer it that way. I've never acknowledged it publicly. The territories and courts already fear me because of what my ancestor brought upon this realm. Imagine if they knew it was me on that battlefield that turned thousands to ash—enemies or not. They'd see me as the embodiment of him, and what little trust they do have in me would be squandered." He looked at me, eyes alight with their mesmerizing molten glow.

I stared back. "Niall, your eyes . . ."

"They change and glow when my emotions get a little . . . strong." He closed them and stretched his neck out to each side, rolling his shoulders as if to ease some built up tension. When he opened them again, they were their normal golden tone. "It's similar to the way you . . ." His voice trailed off and he angled his head as if he'd just realized something.

"The way I *what?*"

"When we danced, you were glowing."

Breck straightened, seeming to immediately know where Niall was going with his statement. "You think she has powers?"

Niall slowly walked over to me and studied me like a piece of intricate artwork on an easel. "There are more than a few curious things about you, aren't there?"

I frowned at his words.

Breck moved in closer and began his assessment as well. "When I found her in the forest after she'd crossed, I felt something odd. Like a remnant of a power signature. But it was weak—similar to when one of us exhausts our power."

"*She* was exhausted," Niall said more to himself than to Breck.

I felt like a flea under a magnifying glass the way the two of them picked me apart with their eyes.

"What did you feel in the forest after you crossed The Veil?" Niall asked.

"What does this—"

"Auren?" he pressed, cutting me off.

"I-I was stressed and worried and . . . I'd never felt so exhausted." Just thinking about it made me a little nauseous. I didn't want to feel that weak or fragile ever again.

"And what about when you were dancing?" Breck asked.

I paused, recalling the memory. How a thrill had coursed through me that I still hadn't been able to decipher.

"Alive," I answered. "Alive and beautiful."

Niall and Breck exchanged a look.

"Would you two please speak out loud? I can't read minds."

"I think what Niall and I are getting at is that we've both been suspecting there was something different about you. Whether anyone else suspects the same is uncertain."

"Different? How?" I began to get antsy at where this conversation was going.

Niall held my concerned stare. "Auren, when we say no human crosses

The Veil, it's not some joke or idle thing. The fact that you crossed and are here is significant."

"That's why Killian is so interested in keeping you here, under his watch," Breck added.

The pit in my stomach that I'd slowly filled up with reasons not to be anxious suddenly spat back out all my progress. "What? He can't keep me here!"

"He mentioned it at the High Lords meeting," Breck explained. "With your arrival and the relic going missing all in the same day . . ." He turned to Niall. "He might suspect that she has something to do with it. And any chance he has at gaining a leg up on someone . . . you know he'll take it."

"Mhmm." Niall crossed his arms across his chest and spread his legs wider in a contemplative stance.

I began to feel as if the trees were closing in around me like a cage. "Killian can't just keep me here. I need to go home. To *my* home. I don't belong here. Whatever this silly backstory you two seem to have drummed up about me isn't real, and I'm not going to sit hostage in Killian's stupid house while everyone tries to figure out where a relic went—something that has nothing to do with me!" I turned on my heel and stormed off toward the tree line.

I could hear the two males speaking behind me, their voices rising and falling briefly. Then a set of footsteps started after me.

I didn't bother running. Where would I go anyway?

Maybe I would just stomp my way back to The Veil. I'd rather try to find it on my own than be subject to Killian's whims and held against my will.

I will not be kept as a prisoner.

Soon, Niall caught up to me. "Careful, Auren. There are other things in this forest that I'm not sure you want to learn about the hard way."

His fingers touched my wrist, but I yanked away from his near-grasp and kept trudging on. I heard him sigh deeply behind me, but he followed.

My pace picked up as my frustration grew. "I don't know what you and Breck think you know about me, but you're wrong. And I'm not going to just sit around and wait for all you High Lords to find your lost treasure, when I have a brother to get back home to."

The truth of it was, when I got back, my brother and I would have to run. I knew the king would probably never stop looking for me, but that didn't matter. There were plenty of other places in Belthria that we could flee to. I could go by another name. Maybe cut my hair and take up baking, even though the thought of cutting my long hair made me cringe, and baking had been my mother's strong suit, not mine.

What would my brother think of all this? Would he be proud of me, or would he scold me for running? Panic set in further, and a cold sweat broke out across my shoulders. What if the king went looking for him . . . looking for answers? What if he—

"Auren?" Niall called from behind me.

I ignored him and pressed on, too busy tumbling through my own thoughts and matching my footsteps to my racing heart.

"Auren!" It was not a question this time, but a command.

And then his firm grip on my forearm was too much to shake off. He pulled me back to him, and his arms closed around me from behind, holding me close to his chest. Half a thought crossed my mind to panic because my back was to his chest—the same position I was taught not to let happen to me in a fight. But this was not a fight, and somehow, I knew he wouldn't harm me.

Still, I shook, trying to break free, but he held fast.

"Auren, would you just stop? Look down."

I grunted, but I did as he said, and suddenly jolted back into his body. I was glowing again. The same faint white light radiated from my skin, just like it had at Lumeri.

All at once, the pieces began falling into place, and I stiffened as everything Niall had just said began to sound terrifyingly right.

My heart slammed into my ribcage in a panic.

"Relax. Take deep breaths," he instructed. His chest rose and fell behind me, as if showing me how.

I inhaled deeply and closed my eyes, matching my breathing with his, willing myself to calm. When I opened my eyes again and looked down, the glowing had ceased.

Niall slowly released his arms from around me, but he didn't move away. For a moment I didn't want to move away either. Something about him grounded me, steadied me.

"Want to hear my theory?" he murmured into my ear.

His voice was like a gentle caress, and the feeling of his breath against my skin made my heart flutter slightly—a stark contrast to the raging panic it had just come down from. But despite the feeling he seemed to elicit from me with that voice of his, I couldn't help but feel frustrated that he had a *theory* about me at all.

"By all means, *Asher.*" The words fell off my lips harsher than I'd planned.

Faster than I could comprehend, he spun me around to face him and pushed me up against the nearest tree trunk. His face leveled with mine as he snarled, "That is *not* my name."

His firm body pressed up against mine as he stared me down. This close, his vanilla and chestnut scent drowned out the smell of the forest—a pleasant contrast to the leaves and mustiness.

I edged my nose toward his. "If you have the right to theorize about me, I have the right to call you whatever I want."

He tightened his grip on my arms, not enough to hurt, but enough to imply that he didn't like my reasoning.

My chest thrummed wildly as I gave him a sarcastic smile. "I'm not scared of you."

"You should be," he rasped.

"Just take me back home."

"As you wish, the mountains are just a quick port away."

It was my turn to snarl. "I meant *my* home. In *Belthria.* You know— where humans live."

"Ah, that brings me to my theory. See, I don't think Belthria is where you truly belong."

I drew back what little distance I could, pressing into the tree. "What are you talking about? It's where I was born—" I stopped myself. "You know what, I'm not having this discussion with you!"

"First of all, don't start glowing again. You'll attract unwanted guests. Second, I'm drawing conclusions based on the information you gave me, so if you're leaving something out, I recommend that you remedy that."

I tried to cross my arms, but he pinned me against the tree with a bit more force. I let out a grunt of frustration. "I'm not going to run off. You can let me go."

He smirked. "Despite you being rude, I find that I like holding you."

I rolled my eyes and looked away from him, settling my stare on an unremarkable tree with mushrooms climbing up its bark. Though, if I was being honest, a sliver of me was starting to like the feeling of being this close to him.

The thought was startling.

"It seems you don't mind it as much as you claim to," he murmured.

"Get out of my head!" I kicked my feet back against the tree to try and leverage myself away from him.

"I will when you stop acting like a heathen and listen to me." He pinned me back with a thud and raised his brows at me.

"I told you, I won a competition, fled for my life, and got trapped in this . . . place. And you've decided that I suddenly belong here?"

Niall exhaled through his nose. "Auren, you're overlooking the bigger picture here. In our lands, we live by traditions and the will of the fates. The prophecy Breck spoke of earlier is—"

"That prophecy has nothing to do with me! Please just take me home and go about your own business and whatever the fates have in store for you."

He gave me a calculated stare while he ran his tongue along his bottom lip. The motion did something to my insides.

"As I was saying," he tried again, while I glared up at him with obvious ire, "the prophecy is something ingrained into us from birth. We're all aware of what's happened and what's to come and are watchful of the signs. I don't expect you to understand it all in a day. But I need you to understand that you coming here was no mere accident. It was destined by the fates. It's a sign."

I thought about making another judgmental remark, but he was probably content to hold me against the tree, so long as it meant he was holding me—like he'd said. A sarcastic remark would do me no good.

"If you were *just* a human, you would've never been able to cross. But you're here. That can only mean one thing: you're not fully human. I don't know what your past consisted of, or who your parents were, but I don't think your lineage is a normal one. All I know is that you're here when you shouldn't be, and you glow when your emotions get the best of you— just like I do. It's like wearing your damn heart on your sleeve. It's a sign of immense power. Something no *human* is capable of."

I wanted to protest again, but something inside me reasoned that he was starting to make sense.

"Auren, if there's anything else that you need to tell me, please do so. Not just for my sake, but for yours. With the talisman going missing and these anomalies occurring with you, I don't want to see anything bad happen to you. Let me help you."

I settled on staring a hole through his broad, muscled chest. The hint of his shroud was peeking out from between the top two loosened buttons.

Finally, I let my shoulders sink. Not having answers was going to be worse for me in the long run anyway. I'd drive myself mad trying to make sense of all the information he and Breck had just given me. Maybe telling him everything would warrant an immediate return to my own realm after all.

I could only hope.

So, I let out a relenting sigh and began to tell him everything.

28

SECRETS AND BLOOD

"AFTER THE KING'S COMPETITION, I BESTED PRINCE ALSTON. HE'S NEVER lost a sword match, and I ended up slicing his leg open. Cut right through the muscle." I couldn't help the grin that formed as I spoke, recalling the surprise in the prince's bright blue eyes. "He came to dinner that night on a wooden crutch."

I could tell that Niall was picturing me slicing up the prince by the curious expression on his face, which he didn't bother hiding.

"That night, I was asleep in my bedchamber at the castle when three of his men tricked and relieved my guard. They broke down my door and . . . they tried to take me for their own pleasure, on the prince's orders."

I felt Niall go unnaturally still. When I looked up, his eyes burned like the sun set ablaze, as if the incident disturbed him.

I refocused on the inked points beneath his shirt collar and continued. "They overpowered me and held me down—"

Niall instantly released my arms and stepped back. He turned around and began pacing as he ran a hand through his dark hair.

Something about seeing him so affected by what almost happened to me, softened my heart. I hadn't even told him that the men weren't successful in their endeavors, yet he acted as if he was planning out how he would force shadowfire down their throats.

"I panicked when I couldn't get free, and then I willed all of my strength into making a single move to get out from underneath their grips.

Then, the whole castle shook, and the next thing I knew, a blinding light exploded from underneath me in all directions, and the men were thrown across the room by it. Two were either unconscious, or dead. The other one got away and went straight to the king.

"When my real guard returned, I told him what happened, and he helped me escape through a hidden passage that led to The Great Wood. He told me to run to The Veil, so I did. I ran until the king's men caught up to me, and then I just . . . crossed. I didn't even see it coming. I knew it was out there, but there was no warning that I'd gotten so close."

Niall stopped his pacing, and paled.

"I'm sure you heard what I told Breck about my experience inside The Veil. It felt like something wanted me dead. And then something pushed me through. After I crossed, my exhaustion took over. When I told you I almost died, I really thought I nearly did. I've never been that weak in my life, and I've been in a lot of sword fights." I let out a small laugh, trying to lighten the mood.

"The Veil aided you." He nearly whispered the words, like he was afraid someone else would hear.

And given that he'd managed to hear my entire conversation with Breck, who's to say someone else wasn't out there listening?

"But why? Why not lock me out like every other human?"

He became unnaturally still as he spoke, his eyes intently focused on me. "It recognizes power. You've never been that tired before because you'd never used that much power before, Auren."

I squeezed my own eyes shut in frustration, but tried to keep my voice down. "I don't have power, Niall. I told you—"

"That light that burst forth from you in the castle when you were under immense stress? That's raw power. There's no other explanation. Magic doesn't exist in the human realm. That means it didn't just happen on a whim, and that also confirms that you're not just a human."

I wanted him to stop right there. I wanted to take back everything I'd just told him, because I knew that whatever he was about to say next would change my entire existence and make me question my whole life.

But the moment came nonetheless.

"It means that you could be a descendant of the gods."

The next few seconds were a blur.

I could hear Niall in the background saying my name, but I was in a daze. What he said couldn't be possible. I was human. My mother and father were as human as a human could be. Not a single person in my family had ever shown signs of anything extraordinary aside from impressive swordplay. Then again, I wouldn't have known to look for anything before gaining the information I just did.

Deep inside, a part of me seemed to stir and crack open an eye at this revelation, and I wasn't sure if I liked the feeling.

Niall brought me back from my stupor the moment he touched my arm again. "Auren, look at me. This is a theory, all right? I may be getting ahead of myself, but based on what you've told me . . ."

I swallowed hard and shook my head as I looked away.

"There are ways we can get answers," he went on. He stepped closer, and his hand began moving up and down my arm in a smooth, soothing motion. "I have a friend who might be able to help."

I didn't know what to say, but I found myself leaning into his touch, letting it soothe the raw edges of this new reality I was struggling to digest.

Somewhere behind us a large branch snapped.

Niall instinctively pulled me into his chest, and I spun in his arms to scan the area.

I couldn't see anything except the trees and the forest. I couldn't even see the meadow or Breck.

Did we venture that far?

I instantly cursed myself for storming off and letting my emotions get the best of me.

A sudden hiss slithered through the trees and seemed to scatter around us in all directions.

Niall tensed and leaned down to whisper in my ear. "I hate to inform you, but we have company."

I searched the trees, but nothing moved.

"Remember when I said there are things in this forest?"

Another branch snapped, closer this time. A hiss gave way to a wailing screech that grated against my eardrums and made me recoil.

"Move! Now!" Niall commanded. He grabbed my hand and pulled me into a run.

I willed my legs to move, lifting them higher over the tangled brush beneath our feet. This part of the forest was less groomed, and fallen trees rested at every other turn, creating more obstacles.

We leapt over a massive root system, rounded a sharp bend, and plunged down into a shallow creek. It was unexpectedly cold, and I whooshed out a breath as the water splashed up onto my pants.

Niall let go of my hand and thrust his arm out across my chest, instructing me to wait. With his other hand, he held a finger to his mouth, and we stilled as everything went eerily silent.

The babbling of the water was the only sound, until a crack split the air from the berm above us. In an instant, Niall was pulling me across the knee-deep water. There was no way to cross it quietly. It splashed and sloshed with the heavy thunks of our feet as we trudged across it.

He quickly scaled the outcropping of rocks on the other side and reached down to pull me up, hoisting me onto the ledge like I weighed nothing at all. But I had no time to marvel at his strength when something that sounded like the soul of death was chasing us.

The screeching sounded again, this time just around the bend.

"Fuck," Niall cursed. He pushed me back into the shallow cave we stood in front of. It certainly wasn't deep enough for us to disappear into and hide. The slab that hung above was the only thing that justified it as a cave and not a rocky alcove.

His body shifted in front of me to shield me from whatever was going to come crawling around those rocks.

"Why can't you just port us out of here?" I whispered.

"They're drawn to power. Porting would give them a direct line to us. Not to mention it would be a beacon for more of them."

"What are they?" I asked, half afraid to know the answer.

"Keres."

A cascade of small stones and leaves rolled off the ledge above, pelting the ground in front of us, and an ominous hissing sound echoed around the shallow space.

A pulse of power rippled off of Niall and settled around me. It felt like the same presence that held me down against the roots of the tree when I'd first seen him near The Veil. But instead of trapping *me* this time, it was meant to keep something *else* out.

A shield.

He was shielding me from whatever was closing in.

All sound ceased as spindly, gray fingers wrapped inward around the ledge above, talons clicking against the ceiling.

My breathing seized as the keres lowered itself into the opening in a slow, tantalizing movement. As more of its unnatural body was revealed, I pressed further back against the wall, praying the stone would give way into a deeper cave, or that I could just go through it altogether . . .

No such luck.

The creature had a bony, hunched frame that was contorted along its spine. Its sickly skin was so grossly dehydrated that it clung to each knobby bone. Its arms were long and lanky, ending in sharp black talons, and the pair of legs looked somewhat lupine with crooked, fused joints that knocked out backwards.

It lowered itself completely to the ground, and two enlarged black pits where eyes should be, stared out at us from a face that looked like it was once human but had been sucked dry of all life and blood. Nothing more than a skull with withered shreds of gray skin, its bald head a host to a bony ridge that ran the length of it. It was the most repulsive creature I'd ever seen. I didn't think I could dream it up if I tried.

Thankfully, there only seemed to be one.

What was left of its lips stretched apart, revealing black teeth, a black tongue, and a very foul stench. It tilted its head to the side as it surveyed us, and then a groaning wail crept from its vile, inky mouth, the sound like the howling wind carrying a dozen tortured voices, both male and female, lilting into one mangled cry. I wanted to cover my ears to block it out, but I was stunned into stillness.

In front of me, Niall was the portrait of calm, hands in his pockets, staring down the creature as if it were a disobedient child.

When their stares met, the keres attempted to stand to its full height, meeting the challenge. With its unnaturally bent legs it could only rise up so far, yet still, the creature towered over Niall.

Not a hint of fear was reflected in Niall's demeanor as he tilted his head back and said, "You've rudely interrupted the little heart-to-heart we were having."

The keres hissed, blackened spittle dripping from its chin, and then, those many voices blended into one terrible chorus as it spoke. "Which of you called forth your power?" Its hollowed-out eye sockets moved from Niall to me, and a terrifying smile spread across its face.

It opened its mouth to speak again, but Niall beat the creature to it. "You do not speak to her. You will address your questions to me."

The keres snarled and snapped its head back to Niall. It took a hulking step forward and sniffed deeply.

Still, my protector stood perfectly at ease.

His earlier fear—I realized—had been for *me*.

"Dark One, we do not want trouble. Just a taste of the one who harbors the *light*."

As much as I wanted to deny it, I knew it spoke of me. It must have sensed that glowing light when I let my emotions go untethered.

I silently cursed at myself.

Niall smirked. "I'm afraid, she's not yours to taste."

I wanted to smack him on his shoulder or elbow him in his back for making such a snide comment to the deadly creature.

The keres huffed in rage and began an unsettling pace back and forth along the rocky ledge. "If you do not give us what we seek, you will pay with your life," it threatened.

When Niall didn't reply, the creature launched itself toward us, but within an instant, it shrank back on itself, wailing and furiously clawing at its throat, talons shredding its own skin to ribbons. It collapsed to the ground and lay motionless as black liquid spilled from its wounds and the smoke of Niall's shadowfire wafted out from its gaping mouth and mangled throat.

I coughed at the stench as I stared down at the lifeless creature.

My father had taught me to fight and to swing a sword with purpose and skill, so that I'd never have to rely on another person to protect me. So that I could always protect *myself*. But without my sword, I could have done nothing against a creature like the keres, and that was a sobering fact.

Niall hadn't given a second thought to shielding me. And that was true concern I'd seen in his eyes. But I didn't like feeling like a liability.

The shield disappeared as Niall turned toward me. "Are you all right?" He pulled his hands from his pockets and brushed my hair back from my face.

"I'm fine. Thank you for that." I nodded toward the dead pile of filth, then stole another glance at Niall's hands.

His touch was so tender when just seconds ago, he was burning the keres from the inside out without lifting a finger.

"I'm afraid we must keep moving. There's—"

Another screeching wail sounded. Close.

Too close.

"The keres said 'we' . . ." I choked out.

Niall and I looked at each other, and he threw his shield up once more just as a figure in a dark green cloak dropped into the entrance where the dead keres lay.

Seeing the bow in its hand and a quiver of arrows on its back made me think of Breck, but whoever this was looked much too small to be him. In fact, whoever it was looked to be almost the same size as me.

A light-skinned hand reached toward us and motioned to us hurriedly.

Niall wasted no time debating as he grabbed me. We leapt over the fallen keres and followed the hooded figure around the rocky ledge and up into the trees once more.

The hissing faded away as the three of us set out deeper into the forest.

Niall hadn't hesitated, so I assumed he trusted whoever the mysterious figure was. And I had decided that I trusted his judgment. After all, my well-being seemed to be his greatest concern.

We ran in silence, careful to place our feet on the softest parts of the ground so as to not draw attention to ourselves. And when we had run for a good distance, the figure in front of us suddenly disappeared behind a tree. I dug my feet into the ground thinking it was a trap, but Niall hauled me around the tree with him.

On the other side, a door carved straight from the tree's trunk was wide open, baring the hollowed depths of a corridor that sunk deep into the earth.

I hesitated, my body protesting the thought of being pulled down under the earth, but Niall tugged me through the opening, and everything went dark.

29
UNDERGROUND

THE WORLD AROUND ME SMELLED OF DAMP EARTH AND WET BARK.

I couldn't see a thing as Niall hauled me further down into the chilled darkness.

We were in a narrow, descending corridor, and it took everything in me to not begin panicking at my lack of sight.

Then, a faint light drew closer just up ahead. A fae orb was floating toward us, illuminating the small space. As soon as it met us, it whirled, and began guiding us deeper into the earth.

"Niall, where are we going?" I breathed out.

"You'll see," was all he said as we continued forward.

His hand was still clutching mine, with no sign of letting go. So, I held on too.

After rounding a couple of turns, the corridor opened up into a larger area with several more orbs lighting the space. The dirt floor was packed and smooth, and above us, a tangled mass of roots yawned across the ceiling. To our left and right, several hallways led off through the underground in each direction.

The cloaked figure turned around to face us and pulled back its hood, revealing a young female with thick red hair—the color of a red fox's mane. The points of her ears peeked through her tousled locks, and her moss green eyes blinked brightly under the fae orb's light.

"Cutting it close this time." Niall grinned at the red-headed female.

"Everything that I do is precisely planned and executed. You know this, High Lord." Her voice was a silvery song, clear and pleasant, and carrying an air of authority.

Niall chuckled deeply. "None of the formalities. We're all friends here."

Strangely, my heart stuttered a little at his use of the term "friends." Perhaps I'd had a minuscule hope that all his little jabs and innuendos had meant something else.

I quickly reminded myself that I shouldn't be feeling that way in the first place.

But he *had* made a few passing comments that someone who was just a "friend" wouldn't normally say. And just a while ago, with the keres, he implied that *he* was the only one allowed to taste me.

Now, I wondered if I was just reading too far into things.

The female bowed her head toward me, the motion sending her hair tumbling forward. "My name is Maeson."

I offered her a slight smile in return. "I'm Auren."

"Maeson is the friend I was telling you about," Niall informed me. "We go back a few centuries. She's the only one I fully trust in this territory."

"Plus, I've saved him a time or two, so he's forever in my debt," she chimed.

Niall let out a short laugh. "It was *one* time. She also has a slight memory issue. Too much time spent meddling with herbs and mushrooms."

She poked him in his shoulder. "You'd better watch it. Those herbs and mushrooms have been critical parts of our work."

He finally let go of my hand and reached out to pull her in for an embrace. "It's good to see that you're well."

Their embrace was quick and light, but I still scrutinized it.

Maeson let go first and smiled again. "So, this is the female you spoke of in your summons?"

Summons?

Niall grinned down at me. "Yes. I meant to come to you without the mess of dealing with the keres, but she let a little bit of her power slip."

I gave him a sharp look.

Is he just going to blab about my power to anyone? And, wait—am I really acknowledging that I have power?

As if reading my thoughts, he assured me, "I trust Maeson with my life. She will not betray me, or you."

Maeson pressed her hands together in thanks and bowed her head. "I'm always here to help. When you said you needed answers, I sent for the Elder. Come." She turned and strode toward the hallway behind her.

Niall touched the small of my back to guide me after her, then leaned in and murmured in my ear, "I know you have a thousand questions swirling inside that head of yours." I could hear him grin as he spoke. "To answer them, quickly, these tunnel systems were built by the Ancient Fae. They run beneath this entire forest, spanning the length and width of Elandrew. There are many entry points, all of them spelled with wards and protective enchantments. Only the Ancient Fae—or anyone that they give permission to—can access them."

"Maeson has permission?" I knew it was a dumb question, but she didn't look like an Ancient Fae. She looked . . . normal.

"Yes. She's . . . different. She was born in this forest and is the embodiment of it. Her upbringing is the reason she's so close to the Ancient Fae. They practically raised her. She's as much an Ancient Fae as the rest of them—accepted and known in their culture as one of their own."

The hallway that we entered shrunk in size, forcing us to walk in a hunched manner. It was clearly made for the Ancient Fae's small bodies. Poor Niall was practically walking on all fours.

Maeson moved from one corridor to the next without a second thought, and we followed without question. Several winding passages came and went, then she was pointing ahead as she held back an errant root that dangled into our path near another entrance. "Last one."

The hallway gradually widened. I welcomed the ability to stand up straight as we emerged into a very large room.

The space smelled of wet earth, dark berries, and dried herbs. Colored lanterns and orbs bobbed along the walls, casting a warm glow. All sorts of cushions were situated along the now moss-covered floors, and several small wooden tables sat amongst them. In the center of the space, the roots of a giant tree twisted along the earthen ceiling and punched into the world above.

Maeson slipped the bow and arrows off her shoulder and leaned them up against the nearest wall, then led us to a small table where a kettle looked to be brewing itself, and four cups were neatly set. She went right to pouring tea, handing cups to Niall and I as we took up seats on the surrounding cushions. "It's just herbal tea to warm your bones. It can get quite chilly down here when you're not moving around much."

After seeing Niall sip from his mug, I lifted mine to my lips, breathing in the aroma—lemon, with a subtle hint of honey.

"This is one of the common rooms, used for meetings and discussions," Maeson informed me, gesturing out to the room around us.

But before she could say anything else, a tinkling bell sounded down one of the corridors opposite from where we sat.

All three of us looked up as a small Ancient Fae appeared in the entry and slowly hobbled over to our table.

Her pale green wings looked as frail as she did, and she was barefoot —save for a thin silver chain around her ankle where a tiny silver bell dangled. It tinkled softly with each shuffle forward that she took.

Her delicate green robes hung in various lengths, embroidered with silver along the hems, and her graying hair was wrapped up in a matching cloth that tied at the base of her head. Around her neck hung an oddly familiar silver necklace, which held an emerald stone.

Her skin was much paler than Sorscha's—probably from spending so much time underground. Heavy wrinkles had settled in around her neckline—a token of her age. But her solid black eyes were lively, aware, and curiously honed in on me.

As she approached, she flicked one of her fingers, and the fourth cup filled itself from the bottom, up.

The tea kettle hadn't even moved.

She shuffled around the table, touching Maeson's shoulder in recognition as she passed by. Her stare lingered on me in an inspection of sorts as she continued her approach.

"Welcome, High Lord," she said with a soft, slightly raspy voice, barely looking in Niall's direction.

He dipped his chin, as he watched her move.

She began sniffing the air around me as she drew closer, and when her eyes widened, I swore I could see black pupils dilate amongst the dark void they were set in.

She cocked her head slightly, then whispered three words that made the hair on my neck stand on end . . .

"Bringer of Light."

30
THE ELDER

"I'm sorry, what did you call me?"

The Ancient Fae blinked back at me, but didn't answer.

Maeson cleared her throat. "Elspeth is the Elder of the Ancient Fae in this territory. She can sense power and determine lineage quite easily. She's also a skilled seer of the mind—all Elders are. If you would offer her your hand, she can glimpse into your past. It might help answer your questions."

I was uncertain about allowing anyone access to my memories, and I found myself looking at Niall, as if his instinct was the one I should trust. He nodded his head to me, so I extended my hand to Elspeth.

Her tiny, unexpectedly warm fingers clasped around mine. "Do not be afraid. Let me see how you got here." Her accent was odd, and her solid black eyes seemed to peer into my soul as she stepped closer.

I tried to hold her stare, but closed my eyes instead, replaying the events that brought me here: *The moment I received the letter inviting me to the king's competition. The ride there, and the faces I'd seen in the courtyard. The pain of the punch that landed across my face. Silas keeping tabs on me—yielding the fight to me. The lack of blood when I cut him. The bright red blood that spilled when I cut the prince. Weston, and dancing, and my hideous red dress that matched the king's dining room . . .*

My memories turned dark. *The door breaking inward, and the men holding me down. Their horrible words, the feeling of hopelessness, then the trembling. The blast of light. The sight of the men lying across the chamber, and the one who fled the scene. Weston's horrified face when he found me. Stairs and secret passages; being told to run to The Veil. How the dawning light greeted me as I broke out into The Great Wood. Hoofs, swords, men chasing me . . .*

My heartbeat kick up as my eyes darted underneath my lowered eyelids. *The sudden intense whiteness of The Veil. The feeling of death approaching—reaching out to collect me. Those otherworldly voices calling to me, and the presence pulling at my soul. Then the other presence—helping me through, allowing me safe passage . . .*

The mist that hit my face on this side of The Veil. The complete exhaustion as I pushed myself as far as I could. The beautiful fae male, Niall, who had thrown out a shield to hold me in place—unsure about what he had stumbled upon. His glowing eyes like liquid gold. The thrumming in my chest that had begun so suddenly and stayed with me ever since . . .

Elspeth sucked in a small, quick breath.

. . . Breck crouching over me, taking my hand as I blacked out. Waking up in the hunting camp. The trek to The Woodland House. Breck shooting a yellow bird out of the sky with an arrow. The beautiful doors. Meeting Killian. Meeting Gareth. Falling into the bathtub when Sorscha scared the life out of me. The dress. The lessons about the High Lords. Lumeri—the decorations, the sweet bread, the fae wine. My dance with Niall. How my chest thrummed when I was near him. How I'd glowed. How he'd said my name and held me. Killian's annoyance. Breck's jealousy. The other High Lords and our introductions. The amulet that Ramil wore around his neck.

Elspeth's hand tightened at that image.

Niall porting into my chambers without asking. His scent, his eyes, his passing sensual jokes, his lips on my hand as he kissed it for the second time that night . . .

Then, I thought about today: *The intention of an archery lesson with Breck that turned into an intense history lesson—that somehow included Niall. The learning of Niall's other name. The way he'd snarled at me when I'd used it. The keres—how it looked like walking death, and how it told Niall that it wanted a taste of my light. The stench of its rotting flesh when Niall burnt it from the inside out with shadowfire.*

The last thought I recalled was of Maeson dropping down from above and leading us to the door in the tree.

I opened my eyes and loosened my grip, but Elspeth only clutched my hand tighter. Her eyes were now darting back and forth under her fluttering eyelids, brows pinched in concentration, scouring my memories.

A few seconds later, she let go and stumbled back slightly.

I didn't expect her to look firstly at Niall, and apparently, neither did he. He straightened his shoulders as his brows bunched up at her in question. "Surely that look is meant for her?" He pointed at me.

"You and I will have words later. Privately," Elspeth said rather sternly to him.

She turned to Maeson next, and they shared a long moment in what appeared to be a silent conversation.

"Are you communicating with her some other way?" I asked Maeson, whose lips were now pursed together to suppress a grin.

"Yes. Apologies. The Ancient Fae have used mind communication between one another since the dawn of time."

"Mind-walking," I stated.

"Exactly. They can speak using the mind as easily as they can read thoughts and feelings. Niall can bridge a path of communication in the mind that works both ways as well. Though"—she turned toward the High Lord—"he's never confirmed if his capability extends to any other levels."

Niall lifted his mug and sipped his tea, shrugging a shoulder.

"Well that's convenient," I muttered.

Elspeth's voice suddenly echoed in my head, clear as day. *You can hear me, can you not?*

I nodded back in astonishment.

"The Ancient Fae usually reserve the mind for more private conversations. Otherwise, they speak normally," Maeson explained.

My thoughts went to Sorscha. "The house-fae that attends to me hasn't spoken at all. Is that normal?"

Elspeth's face fell slightly. "Sorscha is one of the unfortunate few affected by an illness at a young age—a magical blight that fell over our kind long ago. It caused an impediment of her communication skills, both vocally, and in the mind. But she understands you."

My heart sank knowing that Sorscha couldn't voice her own thoughts. But it was good to know that she could understand me.

Elspeth took a seat and folded her hands in front of her. "As an Elder, I hold the near entirety of this realm's history. There are Elders in each territory, and they are all privy to the same knowledge. There is not much that we do not know."

"They are like our kind's living memory—from the beginning of time," Maeson tacked on.

"We lived and inhabited this realm long before the first High Lords ever existed. When the world was young, and there had not yet been a full moon, we dwelled here. There were no humans either. Not yet. Magic was wild and untamed then." She reached for the amulet around her neck and held it in her shaky hand, marking my gaze as it landed on the emerald stone. "The Alatyr," she said, bringing it closer for me to see.

Maeson offered the explanation. "The Alatyr stone is a time capsule of sorts. It allows the Elder to glean information, both past and present. The stones were given to the first Elders by the fates at the dawn of our civilization. Five stones, five Elders. Each stone offers protective properties to the one who wears it, and enhances their natural abilities using Old Magic. When the Elder comes to the end of their lifespan, they pass the stone and their knowledge on to the one who will take their place."

"What exactly is Old Magic?" I asked.

Elspeth answered. "Old Magic is what was woven into this world from its creation. Thousands of years ago, we drew off of that magic as our own, siphoning what was needed. But some of our kind grew power hungry, and began pulling greedily on it, draining it to its dregs. Over time, as it dwindled down, so did we, in size, in stature, and in numbers. That was the price to be paid for taking so much. There is always a give and a take. But Karios is a merciful god. He intervened and bestowed new life unto us.

"The fae thereafter were changed. The generations that followed evolved to have greater height and stature, were wingless, and no longer required the earth as a source of power. Magic began to evolve in each being, manifesting in the different abilities you see today. Old Magic has since replenished itself and can be drawn upon once again, but only the

Ancients know the ways. Very few of us remain, but our lifespans surpass even that of these fae." She gestured to Niall and Maeson for reference.

I nodded as I stared at the stone around her neck—the color as deep a green as the depths of the forest. It was clasped between metal prongs that held it safely in place at the end of the long silver chain. "I've seen a stone almost identical to that, just—it was a deep orange—and the chain was gold."

Maeson looked to Elspeth in confusion, but it was Niall who spoke. "Ramil, the High Lord of Benmoor. He wears a similar stone around his neck."

"That's the one I saw. He was wearing it last night, at Lumeri." I felt like I was helping to solve a mystery as everyone glanced at each other.

The corners of Elspeth's mouth tightened, and she looked down at the table between us all, watching the steaming tea waft into the chilled air. "Your memory showed the truth of this."

She *had* squeezed my hand slightly when I recalled seeing the necklace.

Maeson shook her head. "No fae other than an Elder should be in possession of an Alatyr. It must have been a replica."

"The Elder of Benmoor has not been seen or heard from in quite some time . . ." Niall said as he focused on Elspeth's Alatyr, brows pinched in deep thought.

Maeson sat up straighter in her seat. "What do you mean? Do you know something?"

He scrubbed a hand over his face and sighed. "Just what one of my court members has taken note of on his . . . visits. But it's worth looking into."

Elspeth nodded as she spun the stone in her small, pale hand. Her black eyes seemed to travel to a far-off place, looking, searching. A long moment passed before she finally shook her head as if to clear away what she'd seen.

Maeson leaned forward and placed her hand on the Elders. "What's wrong? What did you see?"

"We Elders do not communicate with each other often, but each Alatyr is connected. I reached down the stones link toward Benmoor's. Nothing can be spoken directly that way, but I could have at least felt his presence if he wore it. But . . . nothing. There is only silence."

Maeson shifted on her cushion. "What does it mean?"

"It means things are changing," Elspeth answered, her gaze falling on me with seriousness.

Too much seriousness.

She squared her shoulders to me. "A path has been laid for you my dear. If you are ready for a revelation, there's no better time than now."

I glanced at Niall. "If you're going to tell me that I'm not human, I'm afraid someone beat you to it."

The Elder looked at Niall as well, then cleared her throat. "You were indeed born from a line of humans. But your ancient ancestry contains more than just a human lineage. Many thousands of years ago, there was a god who fell out of balance with the rest. You know of the history, yes?"

I nodded, but those words . . . I knew what they implied.

She folded her hands on the table. "His deeds led to your direct ancestral line."

Niall stiffened at the same time I did.

Across from me, Maeson's mouth hung open as she looked between Elspeth and I, not quite believing what she'd just heard.

"That's not possible," I said, shaking my head. "Are you saying that one of my parents was descended from the child who survived Lyceius's claiming?"

Elspeth nodded. "Your father was the link. Karios and the fates saw to it that the necessary power would not surface until the right individual came along to fulfill the prophecy. Until *you.*"

My blood ran cold.

It was just as Niall had suspected—

No.

They had to be wrong.

"You can't know all this just from the memories I showed you," I said skeptically.

"I looked a bit deeper than that," she admitted, though there was no hint of apology in her tone. She didn't so much as blink. As if this revelation hadn't just ripped a hole in my chest and shredded through my entire existence.

My mind began spiraling. Denial surged up my throat like a maddened beast, ready to spew words of rebuttal—discredit her theory entirely.

Niall took a long gulp of his tea and eyed me over his cup, waiting for my reaction, but I forced myself to remain composed.

The Elder tilted her head as she regarded me. "Those men got a rise out of you, my dear. That's what brought forth the light. It surfaced with the stress you were under. I can feel the strength of it in your blood. The power you carry is not matched anywhere in these realms. Dare I say, not even by you, High Lord." She looked at Niall, and I followed her stare, watching his face as it changed into something like pity.

I let my eyes fall back to the table between us. "Is that why you called me 'Bringer of Light'?"

A slow nod. "It is known that the savior would come upon the realms with the power of a star. You are the one the prophecy spoke of. The display of power only further confirms it."

"Why a star?" I asked.

"Ah," Elspeth said, nodding. "Lyceius's light is akin to that of the sun. But he corrupted that form of light when he rebelled. And what other light source is there that can rival it? When Karios descended, and imbued your bloodline with a kernel of his power, he capitalized on the trace of Lyceius's that already ran in it. It was Karios who shaped your gift into what it is—who manipulated your form of light—making it similar, but not the same."

Similar, but not the same.

I tried to digest the words as best as I could.

The prophecy . . . The savior . . . Concepts that humans refused to acknowledge. How was it that I was suddenly tangled up in all of it?

I couldn't help the scoff that escaped me. The irony of this so-called *revelation.*

The fact that I'd even crossed The Veil was—

A sudden realization struck me.

The king's men must have witnessed me crossing The Veil, which would confirm my mixed lineage to anyone who saw it. And they would certainly tell the King . . .

Shit.

He was already so paranoid after his son was attacked several years ago. If he had been informed, the chances of me returning home . . .

Double shit.

I could feel those chances dwindling away by the second. Even if I was to return, I would surely be hunted, just as I assumed I'd be. Cutting my hair and taking up baking was starting to look like a very real future for me.

My heart began racing. This was all too much—

"Auren? Are you all right?" Maeson leaned forward into my line of sight.

I didn't answer. Too busy tumbling through my own internal panic.

"Who was the man in your memories?" Elspeth asked. "The tall one with the golden hair?"

That snapped me out of it.

"Silas," I answered, lifting my gaze.

"He . . . *yielded* to you." It was more of a statement than a question.

"Yes. But I don't know why. He was a perfectly capable fighter."

"Sounds to me like he knew."

"But it happened after the competition. How would he have known?"

Niall shifted on his cushions, drawing my attention to him as he said, "Only a fae or a Dionach would be able to sense your power."

I looked at him warily. "Do I even want to know what a Dionach is?"

He let out a small laugh. "The Dionachs are an order of guardians that hail from the Neveshir Isles, south of here. Each is born with the sole purpose of protecting a specific being—known to them as their Dionam. Someone chosen for them by the gods and the fates. It's what gives the Dionachs their purpose."

I'd never heard of the Dionachs, and I was pretty sure I hadn't come in contact with any of them either.

"They're descendants of witches," he continued. "And because of their lineage, they can sense power just like the fae can."

Witches. I had definitely heard of *them.*

Impulsive creatures that looked uncannily human. They'd come here thousands of years ago with their goddess, searching for refuge from their own war-torn world. They kept to their own territory—four small isles off the coast of the fae realm. Thankfully, humans never had to worry about them much, except for when merchant ships wandered too close to their shores, curious to catch just a glimpse of the beings that dwelled upon them.

None of those boats ever returned.

"But Silas didn't look like anyone special. I mean, he showed no signs of being anything other than human." I replayed my memory of him, searching for any indication that he was something . . . *other.*

"Dionachs can glamour themselves to look human," Niall explained. "So, you might not have suspected anything if he was using a glamour. His wings and markings would have been hidden."

"Wings?" I glanced at the delicate wisps that adorned Elspeth's back.

"Not like hers," he said. "Theirs are heavy and feathered. Far grander and much more powerful than anything the Ancient Fae ever possessed. And their markings sit along the sides of their temples, framing their eyes." His hand traced an invisible marking around the areas on his own face.

I tried to imagine Silas with huge feathered wings and markings on his face, but I just couldn't picture it.

Then, I remembered a detail from our sword fight. Something odd that I'd tucked away in my memory. Something that *did* stand out.

"I managed to cut Silas with my blade—twice. Neither wound produced any blood. Both just healed instantly."

"There you have it," Niall said, leaning back on his hands.

"Just like that? He's a Dionach?"

Niall nodded with certainty. "They don't bleed unless they're dealt a fatal wound. And they can only be killed by piercing their heart with iron, or by decapitation. They're essentially immortal—if no serious harm befalls them. Their healing abilities are something even us fae are envious of."

I stared down at my tea. "That still doesn't explain why he yielded to me though. Or why he was there in the first place—glamoured as a human swordsman."

I swirled the liquid at the bottom of my cup, and it instantly filled itself up. When I looked up, Elspeth was lowering her hand. I nodded to her in thanks before continuing my thought process out loud.

"What if he sensed my power and wanted me to lose control so he could confirm it? Maybe he's working with Lyceius." I worried my lip on the thought that I could have misread Silas from the beginning.

"No." The Elder's voice cut my suspicions short. "The Dionachs are loyal to Karios and their goddess. Not a single one has ever swayed allegiances to Lyceius. And none will. They are inherently good beings—sworn to protect—and dedicated to their cause. To go against that would defy their very nature. They could not survive it."

"So, he must've had a reason. He had to have been there to protect someone . . ." As soon as the words were out of my mouth, I realized who he'd been there for.

"You would be the most likely candidate," she stated.

"But I fled the castle. What happens to him now that I'm here?"

"If he was truly there for you, he will find you eventually. Nothing can keep a Dionach away from their Dionam once they're aware of who that being is."

I stewed on the info. "And what about the man who helped me out of the castle?"

Elspeth pursed her lips, as if recalling what she'd seen in my memories.

"His name was Weston," I offered, if only to explain to Niall and Maeson, who were clueless as to whom I was referring. "He was my guard, and he was desperate to get me to safety once he found out what happened. He could've handed me over to the king, but he didn't."

Maeson traced her finger on the table's rough-hewn edge. "He could have been fae—glamoured—and acting as one of the King's Guard. But if so, the question remains: how did he and Silas know about you in the first place?"

For an awkwardly long minute, we all sat in silent contemplation, until Niall said, "Seems I may have a few questions for my second set of eyes."

At his words, Maeson sat up intently and flushed pink.

31
A NEW REALITY

MAESON SHIFTED ANXIOUSLY ON HER CUSHION WHILE NIALL SMIRKED at her.

"I'm surprised he hasn't already come to find you," he said.

Her eyes lit up. "He's in Elandrew?"

"Did you think I'd come here without him?"

"If you did, I'd be concerned. He's necessary—to keep you in line." Maeson seemed to admire whomever it was they were speaking about.

I gently cleared my throat to remind them that I was still here, and that I had no idea where this conversation had gone.

"My advisor, Aremis," Niall explained. "Maeson's quite obsessed with him."

Maeson launched off her cushion, onto her knees, and smacked the High Lord across his muscular arm. The sound echoed throughout the earthen chamber.

The reaction seemed like something I would have done to my brother when he made a sarcastic joke, and I began to see that Maeson and Niall had a similar relationship to that of siblings.

Niall chuckled again and brushed off the point of contact, like she had left dirt on him. "She's protective of those she loves."

She scoffed. "I do *not* love him."

He raised a knowing brow at her, and she turned away, suppressing a smile.

Then, Niall's eyes went distant for a long moment.

Maeson and Elspeth watched and waited, like he did this quite often.

"Mmm," he muttered. "Might have to resort to other spying eyes. Aremis is a bit busy at the moment."

He must have briefly checked in with this Aremis person with the mind-speaking ability he possessed.

I didn't bother asking if that was the case because my own mind was swirling with all the other information that had just been dumped on me.

And as much as I wanted to just forget what all I had learned and make my way back to The Veil by myself, I knew I couldn't. Elspeth's revelations felt like an anchor grounding me to this realm. Rooting my feet to fae soil.

I had always felt that I was destined for something bigger. I was talented, and good at anything that I put my mind to, but as the years passed, I still felt like I hadn't quite achieved all that I was capable of.

Like I hadn't found my purpose.

I thought I had found it at the king's tournament. But when the moment of victory came, it fell devastatingly flat.

And now, I'd just been told that I had power coursing through my blood. Blood that had been tampered with by both Karios and Lyceius— according to Breck's history lesson.

Not quite the fate I'd had in mind.

The timid part of my soul wanted to deny everything and wrap those kernels of power up to be stowed and locked away forever, but the bolder, more curious side was currently winning that internal struggle.

I came back from my thoughts to find Niall watching me intently.

"What's our plan, Niall?" Maeson asked.

He ran his hand through the dark length of hair on top of his head and rubbed at the back of his neck briefly. "The plan is to get more answers. Ones that require a bit of spying."

"Be careful, High Lord," Elspeth warned. "You play dangerous games."

"I am only seeking what—"

The Elder cut him off. "Until you're sure who is aligned on the right side of this prophecy, you need to be careful with whom you indulge this information. And before you depart, you and I must have a conversation. Privately." She motioned for him to follow her.

They took up a shadowed corner across the room, while Maeson pulled me over to a worn tapestry that was strung along a length of roots jutting out from the dirt wall.

It was a map. Up close, the fabric looked a little worse for wear around the edges, with some fibers having become frayed along the bottom section, but for as old as I imagined it to be, its condition was surprisingly good.

Maeson gestured to the depiction of the large continent that spanned to each corner of the fabric. "This is the entirety of our realms."

My eyes roved over the artwork. Whoever created it had paid close attention to the fine details. Although some spots had faded, the words, and the main territorial features were still visible, rendered in paint and ink that was still withstanding the test of time.

On one side, in dark scrolling letters, "The Realm of Anbrya" was written. On the other side, "The Realm of Belthria," where the human lands were depicted.

I hadn't known the world was this large outside of the small sliver of it that I knew back in Galenagh. An entire grand landmass existed, and I would never have known, had I not ended up on the other side of it.

My eyes roamed the vast expanse of each realm.

Maeson stepped up to my side, offering me a lop-sided smile. "Since you're sort of wrapped up in it now . . ." She pointed to the easternmost fae territory, bordering the human realm. "We are here."

The giant arched wooden doors that Breck and I had entered through were delicately rendered in ink and paint, near the center of Elandrew, and trees dotted the rest of the landscape, leaving hardly any unadorned fabric.

She moved her finger southeast toward the trees and the human realm's border, to where King Broderick's castle was labeled just on the other side of The Veil. "You were found somewhere over here I assume?"

"I think so. I ran directly from the castle, so that would put me out somewhere near . . . here." I touched the fabric in the heart of The Great Wood, and she nodded.

"The terrain here in Elandrew begins to lose its dense trees the further west you go, as the ground gives way to sloping hills." She traced her finger past Elandrew, further west, into the next territory. "This is the Highland Court."

The territory was labeled "Vahrenhall," and in its midst was a sketch of an odd building, with timber frames and roofs that bowed upward to points.

Another wooded area named "The Elderwood" was sketched in the northern part of the territory, spilling over its western border.

"What's that place?" I asked, eyeing the cluster of trees.

"The Elderwood? It's a place to worship the gods. It's quite enchanting. Full of creatures and beasts and magic. Vahrenhall claims the majority of it, but there is a stretch that falls within Calledan's borders."

Her finger drifted, pausing over a cluster of mountain peaks that spanned across the next section of tapestry—across an entire territory.

Calledan.

"This is where Niall hails from," she said. "The Mountain Court."

There was no house, or building, depicted in his territory. Instead, one of the many mountain peaks had a large black smudge of ink across it.

A jeer at the dark power that once resided there.

"The furthest westward territory," Maeson continued, "is the Desert Court of Benmoor. The mountains drop into a harsh landscape of sun-beaten sand that stretches as far as the eye can see. And amidst it all is a thriving city."

Benmoor's courtly home was sketched on the westernmost tip of Anbrya, its main building depicted in the same reddened color as the sands it sat upon, a large dome crowning it.

"And the last of our territories is the Arctic Court in Drastia." Maeson lifted up onto the tips of her toes to point above the Mountain Court, where the mountain ranges from Calledan turned white with snow as they spread northward into Drastia. Again, no building was shown, but a door appeared cut out into the side of a mountain that bordered what looked like a lake.

I scanned the tapestry once more, marveling at the size of the continent. Then, my attention snagged on a few small pieces of land that sat alone off the coast of the highlands. Scrawled alongside them were the words, "The Neveshir Isles."

The place of the witches and Dionachs, I recalled.

The Veil was labeled on the map as well, running northward along the length of the border between Anbrya and Belthria, before splitting east to west, separating our two realms from a vast region that spread north. A region that was nearly as large as the human and fae realms combined. Nothing but mounds of stone and cracked, barren land were drawn there. A drought-stricken expanse, upon which was written, "Salterra, The Wastelands." I stared at the stark contrast of the gray plains against the rest of the map.

Maeson noted where my stare had landed, and frowned. "It's a shame that both our kinds lost such valuable land."

"It's larger than I expected," I said.

Before I could say anything further, Maeson cleared her throat and nudged my arm, nodding toward the other end of the room where Niall and Elspeth were making their way back over to us.

The former's face had drained of color.

He slowly lifted his gaze to me, and I could tell something was different. He beheld me almost as if he was scared of me.

What exactly did Elspeth tell him?

Maeson broke the uncomfortable silence. "Everything is settled then?"

Niall gave her a stiff nod. "My advisor is going to need to do some reconnaissance, so we will have to wait a few days before we meet with him." Another wary glance at me. "I'm expected to be at another meeting with the other High Lords later today. Perhaps you can take Auren to see your workshop during that time? I'll come there afterwards."

She nodded. "Of course."

When he looked back at me, he said, "We should get back before Breck loses his mind."

"Won't he be suspicious as to why we've been gone so long?" I asked.

A hint of amusement crossed his features, and his mouth lifted in a sly smile. "I'll bring him the head of a keres if that helps explain our whereabouts and the elapsed time. Or perhaps I should just let him assume other scenarios as to why you and I disappeared together."

I gave him a pointed look, while simultaneously trying to hide the flutter that his words incited within me.

Elspeth took a shaky step forward to me. "You are always welcome here, Auren. If you ever need assistance, our doors will be open to you.

Your blood will act as a key, allowing passage through our spells and wards."

Upon hearing that, Maeson whipped her head to me and grabbed my arm. "That was how you crossed The Veil, Auren! Your blood! Any being with powers—even a demigod—would be susceptible to our wards, but *you* . . . you have the blood and power of *two* gods within you. That's how you were able to cross The Veil." She looked me over from head to toe. "I bet you can bypass any ward or enchantment with ease."

I chewed on the information. It made sense, but it was still hard to swallow. "Would that explain the exhaustion I felt when I crossed over?"

Niall's deep voice cut in. "I think you exhausted the majority of your power in that episode at the castle, and after being on the run, you had next to nothing left. It may have taken the help of the fates to get you through—given the state you were in."

Elspeth nodded in agreement.

It's you. Those were the words Niall had said to me when he first saw me.

He'd sensed the *power.*

Power, where there should have been none.

"You sensed it on me when you first saw me. You could feel my power." It wasn't a question, because I knew I was right.

Niall's swallow was audible. "Yes . . ." He opened his mouth, then closed it again, deciding not to continue with whatever else he was about to say.

Maeson gave my arm a gentle squeeze. "You and Niall should get back. I will come to collect you later."

I nodded. "I'll be waiting."

We thanked the Elder, and Maeson showed us the way out, back to the world above, closing the door behind us once we emerged from the tree.

I fumbled over the entangled roots, shielding my eyes from the sunlight until they re-adjusted.

Niall led the way through the thicket of trees, quickly setting us back on a trail. He'd been quiet for the entire trek underground, brooding about something ever since he and the Elder had their private conversation.

But I wasn't about to let this time alone go to waste.

"What exactly did Elspeth tell you back there?" I asked. "You've been acting strange ever since."

He glanced at me over his shoulder but made no effort to speak.

"*Niall!*" I grabbed his wrist to pull him to stop.

The thrumming in my chest instantly intensified, and I quickly let go with the jolt of it. He didn't seem bothered by it though. His eyes searched mine, swarming with a hundred things he wasn't saying.

Why wasn't he saying anything?

I shook my head, scoffing. "Sure, when I need to give you information, I have to, but when *you* are called to give *me* information, you can be as silent as the grave." I turned and started walking again.

He ported right into my path, and I strode directly into him, his scent filling my nose as my face collided with his broad chest.

"By the gods!" I yelped.

He reached up to steady me, but I skirted his hand and stomped around him, sniffing back the stinging tang of the impact that now lingered in my nostrils. He chuckled softly and followed, his footsteps lingering half a pace behind mine.

I could feel him watching me.

"Someone once told me it's rude to stare." I made sure my annoyance came across clearly as I tossed the words back at him.

"You would think the daughter of a god would consider it an act of flattery."

There it was. That playful attitude of his.

Unfortunately, for him, I wasn't in the mood for it.

I whirled on him and it was his turn to come up short and bump into me. Except when he did, I wasn't a solid wall. I stumbled back at the collision, but his arms snatched a hold of me.

"I do *not* wish to be called that! Or a demigod. Or a halfling, or whatever else you can think of. I don't even know how to use this power. What makes you think I have—at the very least—even accepted it?"

He was quiet for a moment as he looked down at me, chewing on his bottom lip rather enticingly. "It's something you must learn to accept, Auren."

"I'll accept mine when you accept yours." I pushed away from him. "It seems you're in just as much of a predicament with accepting the powers *you* were given." A low blow—I knew it—but my frustration was building, and his lack of cooperation and handsome face were making my head spin.

His expression turned dark as he stepped up as if to challenge me. "You don't even know what I'm capable of, and the little information you've managed to glean is nothing but dust on the surface." His voice became a growl, and he leaned in so close that I could feel the heat of his breath as he whispered, "I could make you bow to my every whim with a simple thought."

He set to moving around me, circling, like a predator closing in on its prey.

"I'm not afraid of you, remember?"

"Oh, but darling, you should be." He picked up a piece of my hair and let it slowly slip through his fingers as he continued his prowl. "And until you've trained and learned to use and control your power, you're as good as powerless against anyone who can wield theirs. I could teach you how to use it. How to shield yourself from threats, both external and internal." The last of my hair slipped from his fingers as he faced me fully again. "If you'd let me."

I studied him. Something was off. He was doing a good job at trying to maintain his intimidating, slightly arrogant, dark façade, but I could tell something had softened him a bit after that conversation with the Elder.

"Why bother? Why would you even want to help me? You owe me nothing." I truly didn't know why he would offer. This wasn't even his territory. "I'm sure you're going to have to return to your courtly duties in your own territory soon anyway. So why even try?"

He was silent for a moment before answering. "Because I was once in your position. In denial. Coming into a power I didn't know. And it terrified me."

"Having this power doesn't terrify me, Niall."

"It will." He spoke with a deep finality that buried under my skin.

Off in the distance a voice called out my name, and I spun, searching for the direction it came from.

What if it's a search party?

I glanced back at Niall, only to find him looking longingly at me. Like he had so much to say, but couldn't. Like something in that very moment was on the verge of slipping away . . .

The emotion in his face . . . it made me want to—

The voice called out again through the trees.

It was Breck's voice, and it was closer this time.

I shook my head and turned, jogging toward it, unsure if Niall was going to follow.

Breck appeared around a large tree trunk not too far off, covered in sweat and breathing heavily. At the sight of him, I exhaled with relief. He was alone, which meant that hopefully he hadn't alerted anyone as to our disappearance.

"Good gods, *where were you?*" He exhaled as he collided with me and pulled me into a tight embrace. He smelled of the woods with a hint of vetiver and sweat.

"We got attacked by a keres. Niall killed it after it chased us into the forest." I looked back over my shoulder to see Niall slowly approaching. When he beheld Breck holding me, he stiffened, and I swore I saw his hands clench into fists then relax at his sides in a quick movement.

Breck brought my face back to him. "A keres? Are you hurt?" He immediately began inspecting me for cuts or bruises.

"I'm fine. Just a bit tired. There was a second keres not far behind, so we just continued running until we could circle back."

"You two were gone for nearly two hours. I was this close to alerting Killian." He held up his pinched fingers, indicating that he'd almost gotten desperate, then sighed. "I'm glad you're all right."

He looked back at Niall. "Thank you for taking care of her. The keres don't normally come this close to the court's populated areas. I owe you a debt of gratitude." He spoke as if I meant something to him. Or maybe he'd been dreading the consequences he would have faced if he'd returned without me. The relief on his face could've been for either scenario.

Niall, on the other hand, looked like he was going to come unglued at the seams. He stood awkwardly stiff, head slightly tilted down, as if he didn't want to fully look at what was in front of him.

Is he jealous?

"Indeed. We both know Auren is . . . special," he ground out.

"She is." Breck regarded me once more and finally released me, taking a step back and making sure I was truly unscathed. "We should get you back to The Woodland House. I can have some lunch brought to your chambers while you rest. In the meantime, I have a meeting I need to prepare for."

"Is it the High Lords meeting?" I asked.

Breck looked from me to Niall, probably wondering how we had time to share a conversation while we were on our two hour long "escape from the keres."

"It is . . ." he said, his eyes now fixed on Niall.

"You're right," I said, quickly taking Breck's elbow in mine and pulling him away. "I would very much like to go rest for a bit." He turned with ease along with me, donning a content smile.

I heard Niall's footsteps not too far behind us as he followed.

32

THE SEIDR

THERE WAS NO GUARD AT MY DOOR AGAIN. PROBABLY THANKS TO NIALL.

The fact that my chambers were once again left unguarded triggered a few mumbled curses from Breck upon our arrival, and I pretended that I didn't catch Niall's faint smirk as he watched Breck get flustered.

Both of them seemed to have developed their own cares for me, and I didn't quite know what to make of that just yet. But I trusted them more and more with each conversation. What that said about my judgment abilities at this early stage—I wasn't entirely sure. I'd always been too trusting with others.

The two of them entered into a deep, hushed conversation as they left, neither of them seeming happy to go to the meeting in the first place.

I sighed. What I would give to be a fly on the wall wherever they were headed.

I kicked off my boots and walked over to the chairs in front of the fireplace. As I sank into one, my eyes fell on my sword. It still rested in its sheath against the stone hearth across from me. I was just about to reach for it when Sorscha peered around the edge of the other chair.

"Hi." I smiled.

Her lips spread into a successful smile this time, revealing her small, sharp teeth.

She must have been practicing.

She emerged with a tray of freshly baked bread, and a pitcher of water, full of bobbing slices of colorful fruit. After setting it on the small table, she leapt into the open chair, taking a crouched position on the cushion, where she watched me.

"Thank you for this." I plucked a piece of bread and handed it to her, and she leaned back slightly, unsure of the gesture. "It's all right, take it. I don't mind sharing."

She eyed the sliver of bread and reached up for it. Her movements were a bit slower this time, like she was making it a point to operate at a more normal speed. Her small teeth bit off the tiniest piece, and she chewed it quietly.

"My favorite is toasted bread covered in melted butter with cinnamon and sugar sprinkled on top. You would love it."

Sorscha looked up at me keenly, then popped out of sight, leaving the piece of bread to fall onto the chair cushion. I reached to brush it off, but she popped back into the same spot with a plate full of the buttery, cinnamon sugared toast I had described. She'd prepared four pieces, cut diagonally down the center and dripping with gooey goodness.

I let out a surprised laugh as she eagerly handed the plate to me. "You must try one too," I said, setting the plate on my lap and handing her a slice.

The Ancient Fae bit into the crunchy yet soft crust and her eyes fluttered closed as she savored it. She reached for another piece and eyed the bread in awe. Then, she disappeared, taking a few moments longer to return. When she reappeared, a giant tray was balanced in her small arms, stacked full of all types of breads and pastries—all which were smothered in melted butter and cinnamon sugar.

"Sorscha!" I laughed, helping her set the platter on the floor in front of the hearth. She didn't even wait for me before she snatched two pieces of different sugary breads and began gnawing on them excitedly.

With a sudden realization, she popped away and back again, this time with a book in her hands. She set it next to me and patted the top of it. As I reached for it, a blanket fell out of thin air and landed on top of my head. I batted it away and found her snickering at me under a blanket of her own.

I decided that she was an absolute delight.

Wrapping the blanket around myself, I plucked a jam filled pastry that was now covered in the sweet crystalized butter and bit into it.

My fingers grazed the exterior of the book—a well-worn, ash-brown leather. Etched at the top in the center, was the word *Seidr.* It was smaller than a normal sized book, which led me to believe that it belonged to the Ancient Fae. But what it lacked in height and width, it made up for in depth.

On the first page, an image was drawn of a man wearing a crown standing amongst three women holding long staffs.

Karios and the fates.

They appeared as if they were stepping through the clouds on the wind. I traced my finger over the inked lines that formed their likeness, giving me a visual of each deity.

As I flipped to the second page, a folded, worn paper sat tucked into the spine, and I caught it before it slipped out. On it was a delicate scrolling of the prophecy that Breck had spoken earlier.

> *With the coming of the dawn,*
> *the fate of all to the fate of one.*
> *A flame of light, a flame of dark,*
> *a golden shroud brought from a spark.*
> *A piece is lost, and then it's worn,*
> *stars and ash bring forth the storm.*
> *Two great powers to bring the change,*
> *the gods will rise upon a new age.*

I began to think that Sorscha chose this book intentionally. Or perhaps Elspeth had communicated to her to bring this particular one to me.

I read the prophecy back to myself again as Sorscha peered over the platter of sweetened breads, her eyes looking from the page to me in earnest.

"Do you know of this prophecy?" I asked her.

She dipped her chin slowly and flicked her wrist over the pages causing them to fan open to a section further into the book.

The chapter she'd turned to was about Lyceius. It told of his light, and how it was similar to that of the sun's. True light, which was a gift only wielded by him. It was all-powerful, its source—inexhaustible.

I turned the page and another slip of folded paper slid down into my hands. It was small and looked to be the personal note of a scribe. The script was elegant, and there was a delicately pointed star drawn at the top left corner, next to a word I didn't recognize: *Euryphaessa*. Scrawled below it were the words: *The white light of a star, divine and wide-shining. A cold, deadly, kinetic energy.*

I thought back to the first time the light had burst forth from me at the castle, and began to recall the way the air in the chamber had changed. The temperature had fallen greatly in the seconds following my emission of light.

Cold energy.

The two men that had been closest to me . . .

Dead.

I sagged against the chair. If I truly was the *one* the prophecy spoke of, Niall might have been right about training. I had no idea what I was dealing with, and no idea how to go about harnessing this "cold, deadly, kinetic energy."

I wasn't even sure if I *wanted* to. But did I even have a choice?

"Does this book say anything about the talismans of the gods?"

Sorscha perked up and flicked her wrist again above the pages, flipping to a chapter located about midway. Sketches of different objects filled the pages—a small hand with a ring, a larger hand with a cuff around the wrist, a necklace, a dagger, a helm, a crown.

Talismans.

But the one that I was looking for . . .

I turned the page and found my prize. Inked in the center was a man with fair hair wearing a thin horizontal band just above his brow, the ends of which disappeared beneath his hair, just above his ears.

Lyceius.

I traced a finger over his forehead. The band was what gave him the ability to focus his power and channel it in a controlled way, instead of unleashing chaos. I continued scanning the pages, until my eyes snagged on familiar words: *imbuing objects with power.* There were detailed instructions on how to imbue an object, the stipulations that come with the process, and the terms and conditions upon which it was possible. But one sentence stood out above the rest: *an object that is imbued with magic can be brandished by another who is of the same bloodline.*

A mother could pass on her enchanted heirloom for her daughter to use. A father could leave a powerful sword for his battle-ready son. The descendant of a god could wield their talisman with or without written or spoken consent. Which meant that if my ancestry was true, I would not only be able to wear the talisman of Lyceius, but I could use it.

I shut the book and stared ahead at the ashen logs in the stone fireplace.

The relic *must* have been taken on my behalf. Someone who knew this information—knew of *me*—must have done it. Preventative measures didn't seem to warrant such an act. This was intentional. This was planned.

Someone knew.

Niall needed to be informed about this.

I sighed and looked over to Sorscha, who was slumped back against the chair, fast asleep, with sweet bread still in both hands.

I'd barely had time to skim over the history of the Ancient Fae and the gods that seemed ever-more present in this realm than they did in the human one, when a knock sounded on the door, and the handle turned.

Maeson swept through the doorway, her unbound hair shining like the color of the trees in autumn. "I've come to collect you for a tour, my lady."

33

MORE GOOD THAN EVIL

MAESON LINKED HER ARM WITH MINE AS WE LEFT MY CHAMBERS AND walked down the hall. Once again, I found myself glancing back over my shoulder to the other doors, wondering which was Niall's.

I imagined that the High Lords would soon be meeting again about the relic's whereabouts. And with the information I now knew about the talisman of Lyceius, I was itching to know if there had been any luck in locating it.

Maeson chatted about the history of The Woodland House during our entire walk through it. To passersby, it might have seemed as if she was giving me an innocent tour, but it was merely an act, to shake off any suspicions as to where we were headed.

We exited through the entrance Breck had first brought me through, down the sweeping steps, and out into the forest. Around us, woodland homes rose from the earth and entwined with the trees, their vaulted roofs stretching high into the canopy, with pathways and stairs strung throughout the thick branches. It wasn't until we were a decent distance out into the forest that Maeson dropped the act and spoke freely.

"Are you familiarizing yourself with Old Magic?" She grinned like she knew something.

"W-What do you mean?"

Her grin widened. "I know that a certain ancient book was borrowed from our archives earlier today . . . by Sorscha."

My face heated. *Had Sorscha done something treasonous by lending me the book?*

"Don't worry, it's completely fine. Elspeth allowed it," she quickly reassured me. "And Sorscha admires you. I think you've made a friend. And if you are a friend of hers and of Niall's, then you are certainly a friend of mine." She gave my arm a tight squeeze.

I smiled. I never really had a female friend who claimed me as her own. Sure, I had plenty of acquaintances. And then there was my mother —she and I had been very close. But every other girl who I'd grown up with had either deserted me or found some reason to part ways over time. I was always left feeling like I had done something wrong. Like I didn't quite fit in.

I guess it was because of the life I'd chosen. A life with a sword always in my hand. I was different from all the other ladies in Belthria— who preferred raising families and the simple crafts a woman was expected to keep to.

Things that didn't make you break a sweat or someone's skin.

Maeson seemed like someone who had taken a similar path—the one less traveled on. Someone who had a genuine heart and a fierce mind, and didn't abide by society's rules. She would be someone I could align myself with and call friend.

She picked up her step and tugged me along, gesturing to the lush greenery around us. "Each tree and root is filled with magic. Every herb can be utilized in some form for healing, or for destruction. It's the same in every territory. This is what the Ancient Fae honed for millennia. You see, in the beginning, Karios weaved this world into being and gave it purpose. Gave it life. The *Seidr* teaches those purposes, along with the histories and practices of long ago."

"Does every court have a *Seidr*?" I asked.

"They do. Though each copy varies slightly with specifics—which were added in after the land was divided into territories. They tell of how our ancestors used Old Magic for *good.* But Old Magic also has a dark side. Like all magic there's a balance. It can heal, but it can also curse just as well. Create just as easily as it can destroy."

We rounded a cluster of trees, and the path dropped down into a small clearing. Several large root systems mangled together above the ground, forming a basket of roots around the base of a giant oak tree. And mounted partially onto the base of its trunk and the roots that flowed from it, was a small door. A decorative swath of dried herbs tied with twine hung from its center.

"Here we are!" Maeson chimed.

"This is your workshop? It seems a bit . . . secluded."

"Oh, it is. And I like it that way. The further away I am from the bustle of things the better. I usually just port in, but you haven't ported yet, and I don't want to just throw you into something like that. It's quite an experience."

How thoughtful.

As we stepped up to the door, I suddenly became light-headed. When I began to sway, Maeson caught my arm, opening the door with the flick of her wrist and pulling me inside. The dizziness vanished as quickly as it came once we crossed the threshold.

"Uhh, sorry about that," she said, steadying me. "Those are the wards. If you're recognized as a friend, the dizziness fades as soon as you've crossed the threshold."

I shook my head a bit to make sure it felt completely right. "And what would happen to an intruder?"

"Most would die on my doorstep."

I gave her an incredulous look, but she simply shucked off her green cloak, hanging it along the wall inside, not giving the comment a second thought.

Once my eyes adjusted to the dimness, I peered around the room. The walls were covered in paintings, framed in wood and mounted with thick ivory-colored twine along the roots that traversed the packed earth. Candles sat nestled in rough-hewn sconces in absolutely every nook and cranny, with wax trails that cascaded down from each taper and bled onto the surfaces below. Thick woven fabrics in various shades of green and rust lined the stone paved floor.

Against the wall across the room was a long, waist-high wooden table that housed all sorts of bottles and brews, herbs and dried leaf varieties, and the occasional tweezers or tools strewn about. Above the table hung dozens of bundles of dried flowers and vines, some that looked as old as the tree roots we stood under, and some that looked freshly picked—having yet to wither and fade.

A corridor to the right led off to a small room down the hall, and as I stared down it I heard something moving toward me. The quiet pitter-patter of paws grew closer, and out of the shadows, a red fox launched itself into Maeson's arms.

"Oh, my love, I'm happy to see you too," she cooed at the bundle of fluff that nuzzled into her neck. "Auren, this is Wrynn."

Wrynn threw her head over Maeson's shoulder to look at me, tongue lolling out the side of her mouth, and tail swishing happily.

"She's beautiful!" I exclaimed.

"She keeps me company. I've never been lonely, but I realized after she found me, that I actually prefer the company of another living thing." She ruffled her fingers through Wrynn's fur for emphasis.

"*She* found *you?*"

"Yes. One night, several years ago, when a storm was raging through the forest, I heard her crying outside my door between bouts of thunder. She was just a kit, alone in this world and soaked to the bone. Whether she was abandoned by her pack or had just gotten lost—I can't say for certain. But I like to think that perhaps she was forsaken like me, and the fates brought her to my doorstep. From that night forward, she's never left my side."

My thoughts snagged on a particular word in her story. "Forsaken?"

"Oh yes, that. My parents thought I was born without magic. All younglings show signs of their power and abilities within a few years of birth. I didn't. My mother was an extremely skilled healer, and my father possessed the power of fire. They wanted to create an enigma, a being with a type of power that runs in High Lord's families—beings blessed with *two* gifts. My parents wanted a son or daughter capable of both wielding fire and remedying it. Being the vain creatures that they were, when I showed no sign of those abilities, they discarded me like I was trash, hoping their next youngling would be their crown jewel. One born with the wealth of power that I seemed to lack. It's a rare occurrence—to be abandoned. It's even more rare to be taken in willingly by another.

"But one morning, Elspeth stumbled upon my makeshift den in the roots of a tree. And with her kind heart she took me in and raised me as her own. I've spent more time underground than above it. And I've been here ever since."

She set Wrynn down, and the fox cautiously made her way over to me, sniffing, assessing. When she deemed me worthy she rolled over onto her back at my feet and panted lazily. I knelt down to give her some rubs on her stomach and scratched under her chin gently.

"What of your powers then? Did they surface after all?" I asked.

Maeson smiled. "They did indeed. After Elspeth took me in, she began a series of tests to try and unlock them. She could sense it when she first found me. Much like she sensed your power when she met you. My power was hidden under emotions I'd suppressed. Eventually it surfaced, and I knew then that my parents would rue the day they cast me out." She slung her thick hair back over her shoulder, holding her head high. "They'd created what they longed for after all. It's too bad they'd never know it."

"So, you can wield fire *and* heal?"

"I can. But Elspeth didn't just stop there. She trained me in the ways of Old Magic—straight from the *Seidr*. My healing and fire abilities are brought forth from the Old Ways, which is a far more powerful point of access than just dipping into your raw power. When someone uses their magic—whatever it may be—they draw from the well inside them. If that well is full, they're able to use their gift at full strength. If their well has been drained . . . you get the gist."

"Makes sense," I said, standing and brushing fox fur from the webs of my fingers.

"There's always a give and take. Remember that. The use of one's magic requires payment in the form of power. There must be a balance. Therefore, magic is limited. A fae can use magic, but only until their power is depleted. At that point, they burn out and they'll need to rest to regain their strength. Usually several hours of sleep can replenish one's power reserve. But if they exhaust their power down to absolutely nothing, they risk death."

"So, magic and power are not the same thing then?"

She shook her head and stepped over to the nearest candle sconce on the wall. "*Magic* is a broad set of abilities that all fae are capable of. It could be the mundane daily tasks of opening doors, glamours, lighting candles with a snap—" Her fingers cracked the air, snuffing out the nearest candle flame. Then, she brought it back to life with another click. "Those sorts of things. *Power* is what we draw from to use our special abilities. Each being has a well of it within them. The depth of that well determines the extent at which we can operate. Certain fae are also born with heightened abilities that are more specific, and some can have multiple gifts—like Niall, and like me. And if one can tap into their power using Old Magic . . ."

"It enhances it even more," I finished her sentence.

"Exactly. Old Magic is also what allows the wearer of the Alatyr to call upon the gods for help. If granted an audience with a god, and they intervene, the result could be significant."

"And what deems someone worthy of an audience with them?"

"If the fates do not see that the god's intervention will be of a greater benefit to the realm, they will not allow it. But it's also said that there are ways that one can rob the gods and the fates of their say in the matter. That is the dark magic that I spoke of earlier. It's not a thing to be meddled with. And it does have consequences."

I nodded my understanding, but a question lingered in my mind. "Elspeth said nothing of my gifts—just that I had power. How do I know if I have a specific ability of my own?" I still wasn't sure if I even wanted to have a gift of my own. But the thought did make me curious as to what it would be—if and when it surfaced.

"Well, you're half human. So . . ."

"So, not an option then," I muttered.

"But," Maeson went on, "you do have the blood of two gods in your veins. So all bets are off. You've only just discovered your power. We know you're gifted with Lyceius's light—"

"The uncorrupted kind," I cut in.

"Yes." She laughed lightly. "Once you begin your training, any other gift should show itself—if you have one. It can take time though, as mine did. Now." She changed the subject. "Let me show you around." She gestured to the table across the room, and I followed her to it. "This is where I spend most of my time. I like to create and experiment. Mostly healing salves and tonics."

I marveled at each tiny vial—some clear as water, others inky and thick. A few of them shimmered under the candlelight. There had to have been a hundred tinctures, stacked in jars, suspended in metal clamps, all part of the organized chaos that was the tabletop.

We started down the adjacent corridor and Wrynn pranced past us, slipping into the shadows up ahead.

"There's not much to this place as far as size goes, but I've always preferred a cozy den," Maeson explained as we entered a rounded room with a rather large bed and a trunk overflowing with clothes. "I am a bit of a comfort snob though." She ran her hand along the plush bed before reaching to shove the billowing clothes back into the trunk.

"A comfort snob in need of more storage space," I said as she grunted.

"I have more sweaters than I can count. What I would give for a proper armoire." She sighed dramatically and plopped down on the edge of the mattress.

A large cushioned hammock hung above the bed from a thick root that cut through the earthen wall. Wrynn's head popped up from inside it.

Maeson giggled at the fox. "She tucks herself away in there like a hermit."

I took a seat on the edge of the bed and folded my hands in my lap. "This is a lovely place to live, Maeson."

She let out a smooth laugh as she slumped back completely. "The home, yes. The court, not so much."

"What do you mean?"

"This court—a pathetic excuse for one if you ask me—is the epitome of what Killian has made it into. A joke. A mask. A court that would rather spend its time dancing around decorated patios drinking wine and gossiping. Killian is such a young High Lord. The opposite of what this territory needs. Plus, he spends half his time off gallivanting, or whatever he does. For centuries now, Killian's family has dug this court into a hole. We were once highly regarded. Now, the only court that seems to have any constant communication with us is the Desert Court. And their High Lord is just as brash."

I began fiddling with the tassels woven into the bedding. "Killian hasn't made a good impression on me thus far, to say the least."

Maeson tossed her head toward me theatrically. "Did he compel you? He does it to everyone."

"He did. At Lumeri," I replied.

"That prick." She slapped her hands against the bed and fisted the blankets. Above us, Wrynn's ears perked up at the sound, and her tail flopped out of the hammock and swung back and forth casually.

"My words exactly," I muttered.

"He's so immature," Maeson grumbled. "His father sought out Elspeth's knowledge for years. He even threatened to expel all the employed house-fae from The Woodland House if she wouldn't teach him a thing or two about compulsion. My theory is that's why Killian is so good at it. But if he knew the power *you're* capable of, he would've never attempted anything on you. And—if you haven't already figured it out for yourself—who you are is information that should be kept from Killian at all costs. He's a snake. Him and Ramil."

I nodded, thoroughly agreeing with her. "But what good is compulsion when someone knows you're doing it to them?"

"Sometimes it's not that easy to tell. Compulsion can be obvious, like if I commanded you to drink a poison that I created, and you did so, even though you knew it was wrong. Other times, words can be woven into spells in the mind and spoken so that the person hears something else entirely. Something enticing. I could tell you that the poison is nothing but wine, and hand it to you with a smile. You would hear those words and believe me, but in my mind, I would be weaving a spell that dictated you take the drink without refusal. It would seem to you as if you were doing it of your own free will, but in reality, you weren't."

I knew that feeling. Killian had shown me firsthand last night when he'd manipulated my emotions.

"Sometimes, after something has happened, one will recall feeling slightly odd during a situation. But there's no way to prove a compulsion truly happened. The only beings that can sense those types of spells are witches."

"So that makes everyone susceptible?"

Maeson shrugged. "Unfortunately. But there is more good in this world than evil. At least, that's what I like to think."

"I like to think the same. But given everything I've just recently learned about the past . . . I'm not so sure."

She repositioned herself and gave me a knowing look. "If you're referring to yourself, you have nothing to worry about. Elspeth is particularly attuned to things. When she looked into your mind, she looked further back than what you showed her. Just because you have a direct link back to Lyceius's bloodline doesn't mean his evil dwells in you. You are also the daughter of Karios. He chose *you* to fulfill the prophecy in the first place."

That last fact struck me differently.

How did he *know?*

"But I wasn't even born yet, Maeson. How could he have picked me? And, if I'm considered a daughter of Karios, how am I not considered a daughter of Lyceius as well?"

She blew out a long sigh. "Oh Auren, your human mind has a lot of catching up to do. No offense."

"None taken . . . I think."

She laughed. "Where you're confused is with the *intention* behind your existence. Lyceius laid with many human women with the intent of creating a plethora of beings that were loyal to him. His intentions weren't specific. Karios laid with one human woman, with the *sole intent* of creating a savior for our realms, and he does not do things on a whim. His power surfaced in *you,* as it was destined. Yes, there were others who came before you in the same bloodline, but *you* were his *intended,* his trueborn offspring, created for a greater purpose."

Maeson was right. I had always wanted to serve a purpose beyond just being good at my small talents. Perhaps that was why I'd always felt like I was destined for something more. Because I actually *was.* A great deal more—it seemed.

A flicker of worry crept into my mind. "What if I can't live up to what everyone expects of me?"

Maeson sat up and put a gentle hand on my knee. Her green eyes sparkled in the candlelight. "Auren, listen to me. You are not alone in this. I will help you all that I can. And so will Niall. He has experience with things like this. He went through it personally with his own power. And you need not worry, nothing is going to come of this today. Nor tomorrow or the next. This has been unraveling for centuries. Right now, we just need to make sure no one else knows what you are."

"And how do we make sure?"

"Niall has Aremis for that. You'll meet him soon."

I watched her face slip off into a memory. "You're . . . close with Aremis?"

Her smile rose and then fell. "I've known him for many years, but always from afar."

"You have feelings for him," I guessed, but it wasn't a question. I could see the longing in her eyes as she spoke of him.

She sighed. "It's obvious, and you haven't even seen us in the same room yet. Gods spare me."

"Why not tell him, then?"

"Auren do you know nothing of love? I must pine after him until he realizes my feelings, and then—*if* he reciprocates them—I must push him away and make him chase me, before I give in and succumb to my heart's greatest desires." She flourished her hand in the air dramatically, then let it fall to her forehead.

We both remained quiet for a moment before launching into a laughing fit.

"Are you sure *you* know anything about love?" I asked.

She rolled over onto her stomach and propped her hands under her chin with another sigh. "I know nothing except what I feel when he's around. You'll see eventually. I'm a mess around him."

A mess.

That's what I was. A confused, conflicted mess. How was it that I could resent something, yet be curious about it at the same time?

"Any advice?" Maeson asked, snapping me back from my fleeting thought. "On love?"

I shook my head. "Sadly, no. Haven't had the best of luck in that area."

"Ahh." She sectioned off a lock of hair and began twirling it around her finger.

The room grew quiet, both of us stewing on our issues, until I spoke again. "I've been meaning to ask, how did you and Niall meet?"

"Oh, that's a funny story actually. It was during the battle of Gabbath. I was tasked with helping the healers of this territory send aid to our wounded forces up on the front lines. Since my abilities grant me the power of healing *and* wielding fire, I was the only one capable of delivering the supply loads and protecting myself in the process. We'd lost several shipments and some of our best healers to ambushes, and all our hard work was being undone.

"So, I began porting all supplies and healers into northern Calledan myself. On one of my runs, I came across a group of Calledan's warriors who'd fallen back to help protect a small village that didn't have time to evacuate. But the creatures they faced kept pouring in, and the warriors were quickly becoming overrun. I didn't even think twice. I sent my fire upon the creatures and saved the fae from having to use their power—which was still needed on the battlefield—and probably spared them from being seriously injured.

"Two of the warriors approached me immediately afterward, eager to thank me and to know my name and where I came from. It was Niall and Aremis. That's when we met. After that, I continued to travel north to help the wounded, and that's how I got to know Aremis a bit more. It was always in quick conversations and passing glances, but it was enough. Until it wasn't. The more I saw him, the more interested I became, and when Niall figured it out, he never let me live it down.

"My friendship with Niall continued over the years as he kept in touch for certain salves and tonics for some of his warriors. Sadly, there are many who still need continuous treatment for the lasting effects of the last war that left their minds scarred." She sighed, taking to fiddling with the tassels on the comforter just as I had. "He's always said that there's a place for me in Calledan as a healer—or whatever I wish to be—should I ever want to leave the Woodland Court. I often dream of leaving this place and seeing the rest of the world. But I have Elspeth and Wrynn . . ." She looked up to her bushy-tailed fox, lounging in her hammock.

We were silent for a moment.

"I can't believe you actually saved them," I said with a grin.

She laughed. "Neither can I. And I still like to remind Niall about it every now and then." She winked. "Speaking of Niall, he should've been here by now."

"Maybe the meeting took longer than expected."

"It's possible." She drummed her fingers against her upper lip. "Well, let me show you a few basic salves. They're easy to make and the ingredients are common all over the realm. It'll pass the time until he arrives."

I followed her back into the workspace, and she prepared some cured meats and cheeses, and freshly picked apples, setting them out onto a plain wooden board for us.

We ate and talked, learning more about each other while we ground up plants and mixed salves and smooth balms.

An hour passed. Then two.

Niall never did come.

34
TEMPTATION

I DIDN'T KNOW WHY MY MOOD TURNED SOUR AFTER WAITING FOR NIALL and realizing he wasn't going to show. Perhaps I was looking forward to spending more time with him than I realized.

Maeson walked me back to my chambers and bid me goodnight, saying that she would find me again for some more lessons in the next few days. I thought about protesting that I might not be here in a few days, but strangely, the words evaporated off my lips, and I remained silent. The thought or hope of returning home was becoming a more distant thing as time passed, and I wasn't sure how I felt about that.

After a warm bath, I put on my silken night clothes and made myself a palette of blankets and pillows in front of the fireplace. I sat with the *Seidr* in my lap and unsheathed my sword to examine it.

My father taught me the importance of taking care of a weapon. He used to say that all objects had a core, and with it an inkling of feeling. If we treated them with respect, we would get the same in return. Part of me always wondered what made him think that, but as I got older and began to appreciate the smallest things and the few items I could call my own, I understood. It wasn't that the objects themselves were animated things, but it was more of a way to remind us that we should be grateful for what we have.

There wasn't much I could do to care for my sword without a

whetstone or some oil, but I examined it nonetheless, making sure it was in good condition.

A few moments later, I sensed a presence behind me. I shot up, leaving the *Seidr* to fall to the floor with a heavy thud as I swung my sword around only to stop-short of Niall's tanned neck. Shadows wafted up from his shoulders at the sight of my blade so near to his skin.

His honey-golden eyes sparked with amusement and the corner of his mouth turned up. "You ruined my surprise," he said amusedly.

Despite his light reaction, I steadied my blade, bringing only my body closer as I held my arm in position. "Where were you earlier?" I asked, trying not to sound pained with the disappointment of his absence.

He gestured to my sword at his neck. "In worse company than this I assure you."

I raised a brow at him. "And you still chose that rather than coming to collect me as you said you would?"

He tilted his head forward, flexing his neck over the edge of my sword. I flinched as his skin kissed the blade. "Is someone jealous?" He smirked. "Trust me, I would much rather have been at the tip of your blade than the company I was with."

I tightened my grip on the hilt.

He eyed the blade with amusement then pushed it away with a single finger and walked by me. "There were a few unforeseen matters I needed to take care of. I do apologize for my absence."

I rolled my eyes and sheathed my sword as he knelt down and picked up the *Seidr.*

"Doing a little late-night reading?" he asked, eyeing the book. "This is a sizable tome. Learn anything good?"

He handed it to me and I took it, unfolding the two pages that had become creased during the book's tumble. "More than *you've* been able to teach me."

"I don't see anyone else stepping up to the task." He gestured to the space around us.

"I'll have you know that Maeson taught me how to make a healing salve for wounds—and one for pain. And I'm sure Breck will continue my archery lessons and possibly more when he's filled in on what we've learned."

"He cannot help you the way that I can."

"And why's that?"

"He doesn't understand your power like I do, Auren." He moved around me, brushing his arm against mine as he took a seat on my array of blankets.

I gave him a long, assessing look before slowly lowering myself back down to the floor. "My power is none of your concern, and I don't need your help." I flipped open the book to find the spot I'd left off at.

A low rumble came from his throat as he turned a hand back and forth in front of the fire. "You can deny it all you want, but you need me."

I stopped short on flipping through the pages and looked over at him. He was still concentrating on warming a hand to the flames. He took his time swinging his gaze over to meet mine.

The room suddenly felt too warm, and Niall looked too perfect with his dark hair—so brown it was nearly black—and stubbled cheeks bathed in firelight.

"Why would I need you?"

He angled his body to face mine, drawing up a knee and resting his elbow upon it. "I can help you access your power and channel it properly." He flicked his eyes up and down over me, and I suddenly remembered I was in nothing but my silken night clothes. His voice became low and sultry. "It needs a proper . . . outlet."

I swallowed hard, my cheeks heating at what seemed like a hidden implication.

"If you don't expel that energy properly," he continued, "it will gradually eat away at you." He drew his lower lip in between his teeth, and I watched the movement with baited breath.

Suddenly his shadows grasped my knees and slid me across the floor to him in one quick movement, bunching the blankets up in between us. Without them, I would have practically been in his lap. His eyes were fixed on mine as he said, "In addition to learning to hone your power, you need to learn to cast a shield."

"Why?" My voice was no more than a whisper.

He settled closer to me and pushed my hair back from my face. "Because, it can stop you from being compelled."

His finger-tips ran over the shell of my ear, and he dropped his hand down to run the backs of his knuckles over the point of my shoulder. The gentleness of his touch sent a chill through me, and my silken camisole betrayed me as my skin prickled, my breasts pebbling beneath the fabric. His eyes flicked down and then back up to mine, newly heated with a simmering glow.

I wanted to look away and cover myself, but I was frozen. Not by any means of magic—just of my own existence. In such close proximity, I couldn't help but take in the details of his face. I noted the single, dark freckle just below his right eye, near his temple, then I continued over the bridge of his nose, briefly studying each of his features, until my gaze fell onto his lips. The flickering light moved tantalizingly over them, and my own lips parted ever so slightly.

"Want a taste?" he murmured.

Whether he was speaking of magic, or of himself, I wasn't sure. His deep voice was lined with a temptation that made my breathing hitch, and I caught myself leaning further toward him. "Are you compelling me?" I whispered.

"Not in the slightest, darling."

We lingered where we were.

My heart was a wildly beating backdrop against the ever-present thrumming that took root in my chest whenever he was near.

I *did* want to taste. The thrumming insisted that I *act on the feeling*. I knew this wasn't a compulsion. It was of my own inclination—

A loud pop crackled from the fireplace, startling me into a jolt and snapping the line of tension that had gone taught between us.

I leaned back, reeling myself in, and the corner of Niall's mouth lifted in a faint grin as I cleared my throat.

"Auren . . ." The way he spoke my name sent a wash of shivers down my body again. "I'm serious about your training. I wouldn't want you falling prey to someone else."

I fumbled my fingers on the blankets that were wadded up between us. "You should probably go," I said reluctantly. It was far from what I wanted, but too many thoughts swirled in my head to think straight. "You can start teaching me a thing or two tomorrow, when I can . . . concentrate better."

He grinned fully this time. "But I like when you struggle to concentrate."

Gods, that damned grin was going to get me in trouble.

He made slow work of standing and straightening out his shirt. "Tomorrow it is then. I'll come snag you before anyone else does," he said with a wink.

Then, he vanished into nothing, leaving a kiss of shadowy smoke in his wake, and my heart a little more vulnerable than it had been.

35
A SOFT SPOT

THE NEXT MORNING, I WOKE TO THE SMELL OF MORE CINNAMON SUGARED bread.

I rolled over, smiling at the thought of Sorscha bringing me the warm toasty delight. My smile quickly disappeared when I saw Niall sitting in a chair before the smoldering fire, one ankle over a knee, sipping from a steaming cup.

Thoughts of the morning after Lumeri jumped to the forefront of my mind, and I quickly double checked myself, making sure that I was fully dressed.

"Good morning." He smiled, raising his cup at me like it was no big deal that he had been here while I slept.

He was clad in an outfit of all black and looked terribly good for it being so early in the morning.

I sat up on my elbows, blustering with disbelief. "Excuse me?"

I had to admit that a part of me was a little giddy at seeing him in my bedchamber again, but the other part of me was struggling with being caught off guard.

How long has he been here?

He sipped loudly and stared at me over the cup's rim with raised brows.

"You're in my chambers. *Again,*" I said pointedly.

"I thought you were starting to like my little surprise visits," he mused, lowering the mug. "Although, it is nice to not be greeted with a sword at my throat this time."

I scoffed and threw the blankets off of me. "You're lucky you got here before I woke up," I said as I passed by him, making an obvious glance at my sword before heading straight for the bathing chamber.

I closed the door behind me, realizing all too late that my day clothes were still out where *he* was. When I opened the door again he stood directly on the other side.

"Good gods!" I jumped back, startled.

"Looking for these?" He held up the neatly folded pile.

I snatched the clothes from him and shut the door. His quiet laughter echoed after me.

After dressing and washing my face, I pulled my hair back into a long braid and emerged into the main room again to find Niall helping himself to my favorite toasted bread. His brows were pinched as he tasted it. Sorscha had apparently shown up while I was getting ready, and she sat beside him, nibbling on the bread as well.

Niall turned the toast back and forth, curiously observing it. "What is this creation?"

"Let me guess, you've never had it either?"

"Obviously not. It's delicious though," he said.

"It's my favorite, actually." I made my way over to see what was left. "Evidently, it's going to be my every meal from now on." I gave Sorscha a sly grin and winked at her. She beamed and turned to Niall, waving her toast at him.

He threw his head back and laughed. "What have you done to her?"

"Made a friend, apparently."

He licked the sugar crystals off of his lips—the motion sending a flutter through me. "So it seems," he said, watching me from under raised brows.

"Don't get any ideas," I said, snatching the last triangular cut piece of bread from the plate.

"Am I not your friend?"

"No. You're a High Lord, who happens to sneak into my bedchamber while I'm sleeping and steal my breakfast."

His expression turned smug. "I also saved your life, and now, I'm offering to help you. Purely out of the goodness of my heart."

I rolled my eyes. "The goodness of your heart remains to be seen."

"Always with the quick conclusions." He grinned, adjusting his shirt around his neck, the shadowy wisps of his shroud peeking up from beneath the tapered collar.

Then, he stood, offering me his arm. "Shall we head out for your first lesson?"

"All right then." I dusted the sugar off my hands and accepted the arm he offered me, linking my elbow in his.

The space outside my chamber door was empty, yet again, and I swung my look of suspicion over to Niall.

A grin spread across his face, but he kept his eyes forward. "It seems that every guard assigned to this post somehow finds themselves standing watch over the wine cellar." He then made a show of looking terribly confused. "It's the strangest thing."

"Uh-huh . . ." I drew out the word, staring sidelong at him for a few more paces.

I wasn't going to complain about the absent guard though. It cleared a path for an easy escape—should the desire come nipping at me again. For now, it felt like that urge to flee had been squashed. Suffocated and drowned with all the life-changing information that had been heaped on me yesterday.

After tossing and turning last night, the only thing I could think about was my lineage. How the word *human* didn't even feel right on my tongue, knowing what I descended from.

There was a chill lingering in the air as we neared the main entry of The Woodland House.

I looked back over my shoulder as we passed another house-fae—this one carrying a stack of bright white linens. None of them had even looked in our direction or taken notice of us during the entirety of our walk.

Strange.

"We're glamoured," Niall murmured into my ear as we descended the stairs.

"What? Why?" I asked. I didn't feel any different and wouldn't have known I was glamoured if he hadn't said anything.

"Don't worry. It's just a sensory glamour. It makes us invisible to the eye. No one knows we're here."

My mouth fell open. "How does it work?"

"So many questions," he tutted.

"Well, you're the teacher here, so you'd better start explaining some of these things."

"We're not starting with glamours. We're starting with shielding. Then you'll practice honing your power. I had to use the glamour so that no one saw me leaving with you. There would be questions and word would spread to Killian if we were seen together. And he's already rather fussy about not having seen you yesterday."

Killian. I'd almost forgotten about the High Lord whose home I was currently staying in. "Did he say something?"

"Just that he felt like a terrible host for having to spend his time in meetings and not tending to your every whim."

I jerked my shoulder into his side at his sarcasm, coaxing out a chuckle.

"He *will* come calling for you today, and when he does, I want you to have already practiced shielding yourself so that you can use it if you need to."

I nodded. He was right. After everything Maeson had informed me of yesterday, there was a good chance Killian might try to spin his words into compulsion again, and I didn't want to find myself tripping over his falsehoods while we were in private. If I had to endure him, I would rather do it with the ability to shield myself.

I looked around, noticing we were headed in the opposite direction of where Maeson had taken me yesterday. "Where exactly are we going?"

"North."

"North," I repeated and waited. When he remained silent, I sighed out of my nose. "And what's north?"

"A secret."

This male.

As if he hadn't just left me hanging on that last response, he switched to casual conversation. "So, tell me, love, what other things do you like besides that sugary bread?"

"Complete, elaborative answers," I smarted back at him.

And since when did he call me "love"?

He grinned. "Duly noted. And?"

This time, I took a moment to think. I hadn't thought about those things in a long time. Ever since my parents passed away, there was so little time to indulge in what I truly enjoyed—aside from sword fighting. I'd either worked or fought in tournaments for winnings just to help keep my brother and I afloat.

My mind wandered to Liam and his welfare. *Had word spread that I'd gone missing? By now, I might be presumed dead and he would be planning for a—*

I stopped myself from spiraling down that road. Finally, I said, "I enjoy things that I can do alone." Niall looked over at me with genuine interest in his eyes, so I elaborated. "I've never had many friends to call my own. And it's just been my brother and I ever since our parents died." I could practically feel Niall wince at the dark path my response had taken, but I couldn't help it. It was the truth, and the event had only served to solidify my way of life even further.

More words began spilling from my mouth like a tap that wouldn't turn off. "When my brother's gone working—which is all the time—it's just me. I've always been pushed aside by others, or taken advantage of for my kindness. People who don't know me keep away because of my reputation for sword fighting. So, I've just gone through the years as my own friend. My own company. The only person I can truly rely on."

The loner.

When Niall didn't say anything back, I peered up at him. He was watching me intently.

"I understand that completely," he said. "And I'm sorry for your loss. I too have lost my parents."

"So you know the grief of it, then."

"Very much so." He sighed.

We walked a few more paces and then he spoke again. "When I was younger, my father was hard on me. I always felt that I had to perform the best—out-wit everyone around me. It put a competitive nature in me that drove everyone else out. Others saw me as intimidating, fearing what I was capable of. It didn't help that my ancestor had given my family a bad name. I was skilled in combat, but gaining friends was not my strong suit. I didn't gain any of value until I was quite a bit older. And even those friendships began on rocky foundations. But today, they're my family— the only family I have. Yet, I still find myself just like you, opting to do everything alone. It's often easier that way."

Something inside me softened toward him. His words . . . they hit me like a spitting image of my own reality.

"It is," I said.

I wouldn't have guessed that we would have such a thing like that in common.

"So, is there a lucky man back home pining over your absence?"

His question caught me completely off guard, and I stuttered at first. "Uh, um—no. There's my brother of course, but no other man. No love interest whatsoever."

Love interest? Gods, why would I say that?

I silently cursed at myself and cleared my throat.

Niall peered over at me. "Have you ever *been* in love?"

I snorted at the idea. What I thought I knew of love didn't seem all that great in hindsight. "I thought I was in love once. But I don't think it was right. As usual I came out of that alone as well." I paused, thinking back on that time. "Tell me something, can you love someone who doesn't truly love you back?"

Niall contemplated the question for a long moment before finally answering. "I think love is a shared feeling between two beings. If one loves, and the other does not, then the fates have not destined them for each other. So it can't be real."

"I guess I never thought of it that way." I stared down, watching the thick patches of clover pass beneath us, cushioning our feet as we walked.

My thoughts drifted back to last night . . . the way he'd acted . . . what he'd said . . .

Want a taste? He'd spoken the words like a suggestion rather than a question . . .

I stole a glance at him. "I'm sure you have beauties lining up for you in the mountains, though."

He let out a throaty laugh. "Not in the least."
My brows hiked up. *What does* that *mean?*
"So, *you've* never been in love then?" I asked.
A grin spread across his face, but he remained silent.

36
MENTAL SHIELDS

THE REST OF THE TREK WAS CALM AND SILENT—SAVE FOR BIRDSONG AND the trickling of a stream nearby.

I stewed over the information Niall had given me about himself, assuming he was doing the same. Every so often I would sense him looking sidelong at me. It took us catching each other staring several times before I finally forced myself to focus on the path ahead.

He was truly nothing like Breck had made him out to be.

And his face was such a pretty distraction . . .

"Ah, here we are," he said.

A crumbling structure came into view through the trees. "*This* is your secret spot?" I looked at the cracked steps leading up to a bleached white stone slab surrounded by broken pillars. The trees and vines had long since begun to reclaim the structure, overwhelming the white stone with their greedy grasps. But they seemed to be holding most of the remaining columns in place— despite the cracks.

"It is. No one actually knows who this temple was dedicated to. It's been abandoned for as far back as any Ancient Fae can remember. Hardly anyone comes out here to it."

"So, how do *you* know about it then?"

"Like I said, *hardly* anyone comes out here to it. Don't worry, I have sources that I trust."

I wasn't worried. I'd already decided that I trusted him. But he didn't need to know that just yet, so I kept my expression unimpressed.

When he saw my scowl, he laughed lightly. "Okay, okay. I charm beings with my good looks to gain information."

That answer was no better.

I rolled my eyes and made my way up the steps, while he took them two at a time behind me with his long strides.

"Apparently, that doesn't seem to work on you though," he added sweetly, baiting me as he passed.

"Hmm. I wonder why?"

I made my way to the center of the structure and turned in a circle upon what appeared to have once been a dais. The tree canopy above was peeled back, offering a generous view of the sky, a swirl of early morning pastels waiting to embrace the golden sun.

"Why indeed." He lifted a playful brow at me. "Do you have a shield up that I'm not aware of?"

"I would need to have a decent teacher for something like that to happen," I said.

"Well, ask and you shall receive." He flourished his hand and began a slow walk around the edge of the platform. "First lesson of shielding: There are two types of shields, mental and physical. A physical shield can be cast for yourself and for anyone you deem necessary. Like what I did for you with the keres. A *mental* shield is used solely for yourself."

I nodded in understanding.

"It's important to have a physical shield, but a mental shield is essential, especially when you're around certain fae like Ramil or Killian. Both High Lords have an affinity for tricks, compulsion, and Old Magic. While they won't always use it, sometimes you can't tell between a trick and the truth. It's best to always be on guard."

"So, if I have a mental shield up, will they be able to tell?"

"Only if they attempt something and you don't fall for it. The only issue we currently have is that right now they both think you're human, or at least we *hope* they still think that. If they were to try something and run into your mental shield, they will automatically know that you're much more. But we can worry about that later. The important thing is for you to not fall prey to anyone's musings."

Like when someone had tried to pry into my mind at Lumeri.

But they didn't just try—they nearly succeeded. And I didn't want to feel that type of violation ever again.

"Now, a mental shield is the hardest to produce and requires a good deal of mental strength to hold for long periods of time. Thankfully it doesn't pull from your power as much as a physical shield will. Also, thankfully, you most likely have a vast wealth of power in that body of yours." He crossed in front of me, scanning my entire body with his eyes. "So, we don't have to worry about you running out once you build up your tolerance." When he met my stare again, he winked.

I shifted my stance and crossed my arms, a flush of pink brushing over my cheeks.

"I want you to imagine a wall of stone," he instructed, and I closed my eyes. "No, no. Eyes open. You can't take the time to shield with your eyes closed. You have to be fully aware and ready to do it at a moment's notice."

I pressed my lips into a thin line.

Fine.

I tried to focus, but my skin was heating under his golden stare. "I can't do it while you're watching me."

"Yes, you can." He didn't look away.

I sighed with annoyance and focused straight ahead at a partially crumbling pillar, pretending Niall was one as well. Then, I envisioned a wall made of white stone just like the ones around us, fortified and strong, running the length of my minds-eye. "Okay, I think I've got it."

"Now *feel* that wall. Let it be a presence in your mind. Let it take root there and become a permanent fixture around your thoughts and emotions. A castle rampart—if you will. Everything inside is precious and untouchable as long as that wall holds."

The wall rooted itself to the ground in my mind, and I imagined it boxing everything up, closing all doors and pathways to the outside world.

"Does it feel strong?" Niall asked.

"I think so," I replied, fairly sure that what I was creating in my mind was a stable thing.

"Good. Now, I'm afraid I have to do something you're not used to," he said, approaching me.

My focus instantly broke when I looked at him. "What do you mean?"

"I'm going to mind-walk. In *your* mind."

I instantly recoiled. "Why?"

"Because, I need to check your shield. Ramil almost got into your head at Lumeri. And it would have been all too easy for him to do it."

My mouth parted. *The strange presence . . . the red mist . . . That* was *Ramil.*

"H-How did you know what he was trying to do?"

"I was keeping an eye on him." Irritation lined his voice. "He shouldn't have been meddling. Especially not with you."

I thought back to how the presence had vacated my mind the moment a pulse of energy shook the pavilion.

"So, I'm assuming it was you who sent out that pulse of power? To stop him?"

"It was."

We held each other's stare for a long moment.

"Thank you," I said.

He nodded once, then continued on. "This is the ultimate test. If you can stand against mind-walking, everything else will be easy."

"So, you're starting with the most difficult thing? Thanks."

"You're perfectly capable, darling."

I tossed him a smile that didn't meet my eyes.

"Don't be afraid. I would never hurt you." His voice was smooth and steady. "It's just going to feel like my essence entering your mind. I won't do anything more than enter and check the strength of your shield. I promise."

I opened my mouth, then closed it, figuring questions would only help to a certain extent. I would have to find out through first-hand experience if I wanted to make progress. And I would rather find out with him than with someone else.

I've trusted him this far . . .

"Okay." My voice was shaky, my nerves fired up with anticipation.

"Don't break your focus when you feel me. Just concentrate on the wall. Nothing else."

I bobbed my head a few times and focused my eyes on his, imagining the wall I'd built.

Without blinking, he reached out. Not with his hands, but with his mind. A smattering of inky darkness and shadowy tendrils of smoke broke across my consciousness and swarmed toward the wall, reaching in long, hungry pulls. Grasping for purchase.

I balked at the sensation, but I kept my eyes steadily on his, not entirely seeing him in front of me as I held my focus inward on my mind.

The darkness caressed the stone wall, searching for cracks. It felt like Niall—somewhat familiar—only darker, and more primal.

I shivered.

Then, the tendrils peeled back and slammed into my wall with a force I didn't expect. My focus faltered, and a crack split up the stone, the darkness driving forward as soon as it sensed the weakness.

All at once the wall crumbled, and like a dam breaking, I felt him flood into my mind. Panic washed over me as I mentally scrambled to push him back out, but nothing was working. It became abundantly clear that if he wanted to—if he were a more sinister being—he could latch onto my thoughts, my very consciousness, and I would be nothing but a husk to do his bidding.

I stumbled back, flinging my arms out in front of me, grasping for anything to tether me in place.

In a blink Niall's essence vacated my mind, and he was there catching hold of me in his arms. My knees wobbled, but he held me steadfast against him.

A cold sweat broke out across my forehead as I found my footing.

"Easy now. I've got you." His voice was a soothing balm against the defeat I felt in my mind. "Are you all right?" His eyes searched mine urgently as he steadied me.

"I'm okay. It just caught me off guard." I took a deep breath and pushed it out to calm my mind. "That was so strange." I rubbed at the sides of my head as if it would ease the weird prickling sensation that lingered deep inside.

"That was me giving you a *fraction* of my force." He gently removed his hands from me once he knew I was steady enough. "Now, you see how easy it is to slip up. Once that wall weakens, there's no keeping anyone or any outside influence out."

"Yeah." I blinked rapidly to get my thoughts straight. "Let's go again."

Niall raised a brow. "Already?"

"I want to master keeping you out." I gave him a little side-smile. He squinted and the corner of his mouth turned up.

I quickly dove back into my mind and fortified the wall, knowing he could sweep in at any moment. Just as I locked it all away again, the darkness plunged in, pounding against the wall in a torrent of shadowed waves. It was stronger this time, but I held my focus, willing the stone structure to stand firm.

I heard Niall speak in front of me. "Push back," he commanded.

I did as he said and the darkness recoiled.

A small sliver of surprise flickered through me.

His power dove forward again, and I pushed against it. Then, everything went quiet, and the tendrils of darkness dissipated into nothing. I shifted my focus to Niall's physical presence thinking he was finished. But it was a trap. Blackness gathered in a frenzy. It scaled the wall and plunged into the courtyard of my mind.

I cried out as I went down onto my knees at the defeat.

Niall dropped to a squat in front of me as I sank back against my heels in frustration. "Second lesson of shielding is to never assume someone has retreated." He placed a finger under my chin and lifted it gently. "You're doing well."

I blew out a breath.

"It's not as easy as it seems, but with practice you'll get better, and your shield will strengthen. The trick is to be able to hold it in place while also going about your daily activities. Holding a mental-shield while holding a conversation is difficult at first, but the more you train your mind to operate with a constant shield, the more easily it will come."

He stood and offered me a hand. I took it, gratefully, and he lifted me to my feet.

"Again," I said.

Inclining his head to me, he took a casual stance, slipping his hands into his pockets and leveling his eyes to mine.

His grin came at the same time the darkness did. But this attempt was different. It was hungrier, more anxious, pacing back and forth in front of my stone wall.

I decided to try a different approach as well, envisioning—what I assumed was—my power. The ball of energy that I felt in the core of my chest . . . the force that had formed in the midst of my panic at the king's castle . . . I imagined it in my mind and reached for it.

Something sparked to life. It felt old and ancient—yet new and unchallenged. Like a presence that had long since been tucked away, sleeping.

And I had just woken it up.

It stirred.

An entire essence of my own. *My* power.

I channeled it. Coaxed it to do as I willed. It felt natural, like a waltz. A give and a take. A question and an answer.

Before his essence had the chance to make a move, I zeroed in on it and lashed out. My own essence rose up and took form as a stream of white light, burning colder than anything I'd ever felt. And as it barreled forward, the darkness scattered into smoke.

I reserved some of my essence for the wall itself—infusing it into the crevices like an impenetrable mortar. And then, the light regrouped outside the wall, lying in wait for another threat like a predator ready to strike at its prey.

In front of me, Niall shook his head in disbelief and reached out to grab my shoulder. But I waited this time before pulling my focus away from the shield.

"Auren," he spoke. "Come back to me."

At his words I instantly shifted my focus back to him, and a huge smile spread across my face. A laugh escaped me next because he looked absolutely bewildered.

"How did you . . ." His voice trailed off.

"I just reached for it, and it answered." I couldn't wipe the stupid smile off my face.

Deep inside my chest I felt my power's presence. It was awake and alive.

Waiting.

I hadn't wanted it when I first found out that I had it inside me. But now that I'd called it forth freely, I knew there would be no sending it back.

Niall was trying to form words. "It's . . . powerful," he said a bit warily while rubbing the back of his neck with his hand. "What does it feel like to you?"

"Like an unfathomable amount of energy."

"It obeys you . . . right?" I heard the concern in his voice this time.

"Yes. I don't feel any indication of it wanting to act of its own will," I reassured him.

Reassured *myself* too.

Niall studied me for a long moment, then took a couple of slow steps back before saying, "I want to try something."

Expecting the dark tendrils to rapidly spring forth, I dipped back into my power, reinforcing my mental shield. But to my surprise, his essence calmly gathered in a single, solid form just outside of my stone wall instead. The shadow gently whirled amongst itself, leaking out inky black wisps, then coiling them back in. It looked curious, as if it was feeling for something. Like it was observing of its own accord.

Like it was . . . *sentient.*

Now that his essence was calm and collected, mine rose to greet it, gently pulsating, almost as if in recognition.

Pitch black tendrils reached out in undulating wisps, stretching toward my light, and my mouth fell open as I watched the darkness inch closer in my mind.

Three paces away.

Two paces.

One.

The tip of a tendril neared, and a ray of my light stretched out to meet it.

And then, they touched.

37
LIGHT AND DARK

My chest was bursting. Not with pain, but with a vibration. A thrumming—like the previous version I had felt—intensified a hundredfold as our essences stood before each other, connected by a touch.

I could feel his power. It wrapped around mine like a cocoon, protecting it, caressing it, claiming it as his to defend. Mine sang in approval, emitting a softer glow that seemed to wash over his with peaceful ease.

As I looked inward, watching our two forms embrace, I became aware of something touching my hand.

Not something. Someone.

Niall.

He had crossed the distance between us and was now holding my outstretched hand. I had physically reached out for him just as my essence had in my mind. His fingers were wrapped around mine, and my focus shifted to the physical contact.

His jaw was slack with awe.

My cheeks turned pink as I felt our connection with my hand and in my mind simultaneously. The light and darkness were still embracing, still holding on. Neither of us had called them back. Nor had they vacated of their own accord. Then, I realized I was very well aware of the present, while also holding my shield.

A corner of Niall's mouth lifted, and his eyes lit into a golden glow as a soft glow of my own began radiating off of me. "Auren," he said.

At the sound of my name on his lips, I stepped forward and tilted my head back to look up at him.

He lowered his head down toward mine, while his free hand gently pushed back a stray piece of hair that had come loose across my cheek, tucking it back over my ear and letting his fingers linger there.

In my mind, our essences were moving, whirling around each other, learning each other's presence. Committing themselves to memory. Attaching themselves to one another.

I took in a small gasp of air at the feeling that ignited in my chest. Not the thrumming this time, but my power. It pulsed through me. Flowing through my veins in a cool current.

His essence was affecting me.

It was a sensual stirring. A sensory message. A carnal pull toward him.

His name was on the edge of my lips when the ground beneath us suddenly shook. Small stones and dust rattled free from the already crumbling pillars around us. The trees quivered, branches hissing as they rattled.

Niall's hand tightened around mine, while his other pulled me in close. The pulsing power of his shield flared and settled around us as we both scanned the forest.

The shaking stopped as quickly as it came, leaving only the hushed flutter of leaves that shimmied to the ground.

"What was that?" I whispered, afraid to speak too loudly after what felt like an incoming threat.

"I'm not sure," he said, shield retracting as he turned to scan the forest once more. "Third lesson of shielding: if you feel threatened, don't ever second-guess it."

Duly noted.

"And what was that . . . *other* thing?"

The connection.

He looked down at me. "*That* . . . was interesting."

The heat of the previous moment had fled from both of us, but there was a hint of something there in his eyes. Lingering. Longing.

"Has your power ever acted like that before?"

"No, it's never behaved that way with anyone. To tell you the truth, I didn't know what it would do, but I didn't expect for *that* to happen."

"What does it mean?"

His thumbs settled into rubbing smooth lines on the backside of my hand, which he still held. "It means, we have more questions than answers, and I'd like to remedy that."

A question jumped to the forefront of my mind. One that had puzzled me since I'd met him. And since we were on the topic of things that we weren't sure of . . . "There's this feeling in my chest. I've felt it ever since I first saw you, after I crossed The Veil. What does it—"

Another sudden jolt rocked the dais once more, causing a pillar to topple over the edge and shatter to pieces on the ground below.

I wobbled and grasped onto Niall's arms, instincts honing in on the possibility that something was terribly wrong. "That . . . doesn't seem good."

"No, it doesn't." He shifted me into his arms like he was preparing to lift me off the ground. "Do you get nauseous easily?"

"Uh—no, I don't think so . . ."

"Good. Because I'm going to have to port us back."

My eyes widened. "Port? But I've never ported before."

"Exactly." He tossed me an apologetic smile.

"Wait, wait, wait." I pumped my hands in front of me as he secured me in his grip. "What exactly is going to happen?"

"I'm going to port us to the outskirts of The Woodland House. We can't port directly inside from an outside location, so that's as close as I can go, but it'll be quicker than trying to run the distance back. It'll be like moving down a tunnel, quick as a blink."

"O-Okay. Just don't drop me." I felt ridiculous saying it, but I was legitimately concerned about the concept of porting.

His solid arms cradled me to him, as he murmured, "Never, darling." And without hesitation we launched.

What we launched into—I wasn't entirely sure. A blur? A void? Everything and nothing at the same time?

Light and sound and space obscured around us as we flew through it. I felt whole and torn apart all at once. My physical existence protested against the feeling of collapsing into essentially nothing. All I knew was

Niall's presence against me, and I curled into him for a brief moment before everything ceased. Then, I felt the fabric of my being stitching itself together again as we materialized.

I bent over my knees, catching my hands on them as I whooshed out a breath. "That was *not* 'quick as a blink'!"

He laughed quietly beside me, rubbing a hand against my back in soothing circles. "I'm impressed. Most pass out their first time."

I lifted my head to glare at him. "You don't say."

His smile threatened to knock the air out of me again.

Slowly I stood up and willed the dizziness in my head to settle. We were still in the forest, but we had materialized near the pavilion where we'd danced at Lumeri. I could hear a few males shouting back and forth in the distance.

Niall kept his hand on the small of my back as we strode for the pavement. "Come on, just a bit further."

I had just evened out my breathing again when, without warning, he swooped me back up, and we were gone into everything and nothing again before I could protest. His quiet laughter echoed in my ears as the world around us roared by.

38
HALF-LIES

W<small>E MATERIALIZED NEXT TO MY BED, AND</small> N<small>IALL GENTLY LOWERED ME</small> onto it. I instantly rolled over and buried my head in the pillow to keep from heaving my guts up.

"Why?!" I groaned.

Niall laughed and leaned against the bed post. "I had to get you somewhere safe."

I tossed my head up dramatically and looked back at him, cutting my eyes in a slash.

He chuckled. "Don't give me that look unless you can back it up."

I sighed and turned over onto my back, throwing my arm over my eyes. "I can't do *anything* at the moment."

"Apologies for having to do it twice. But I wanted to get you here before I go see what's going on. I don't want anyone knowing we were gone, or together, for that matter."

I mumbled a few words at him under my breath.

He leaned in and placed his hands on either side of me. "What was that, love?"

I peeked out from underneath my arm to find him hovering above me, a handsome grin spread across his face.

My jaw quivered as I fought back a grin of my own. "I said, let me know when you know something." Trying to seem irritated was impossible when all I wanted to do was look at him now that he was up close again.

"Mmm." His voice rumbled in his throat. "Of course." He lingered over me for a moment and then stepped away. "Don't leave while I'm gone. I won't be long."

Without waiting for my reply, he vanished, leaving wisps of smoke in his wake. They seemed to stretch out to me before evaporating into the air.

I rolled over to sit up and caught myself with my hand on the mattress. "Oof. I've got to get used to that." My head still spun, my essence a whirl within it, coming down from the encounter with Niall's.

Sorscha was nowhere to be found and the room was quiet, so I decided that a cool bath might help level me out.

After submerging myself and scrubbing, I stood and stared at myself in the mirror. The face that stared back was the same, yet something about it was different. My complexion seemed a bit brighter, as if it had been renewed by a small kiss from a star. And my eyes . . . the irises weren't as dull as before.

The daughter of a god.

Bringer of Light.

The words swirled in my head. But all I saw was a petite swordfighter from Galenagh, even if it felt like that life was slowly getting left behind hour by hour.

I wanted to learn more about this power and this prophecy, but part of me clung to the hope of going home. I was waging an internal war with myself, and today's entire experience had just complicated it even further.

As I walked into the main room to get dressed, Breck suddenly materialized in front of me. I screeched, clutching my towel against my otherwise naked body. His face reddened as he beheld me, but before he could speak, I threw my free arm up into the air. "You too, huh?"

He looked at me in confusion, mouth opening and closing repeatedly. I didn't wait for an answer as I gathered up my clothes, and stomped back into the bathing chamber to get dressed. When I heard him start to follow, I jabbed a finger back at him. "Wait out here!" I commanded, slamming the door behind me.

Once I was dressed and had combed my hair, I opened the door and found him pacing back and forth.

Relief washed over him when he saw me. "Thank the gods you're all right."

I tried to walk around him, but he caught my arm gently, and I canted sideways against his chest. His other hand found my lower back and steadied me.

"Auren, what's wrong?"

I lifted my head to look at him, and watched his throat work on a swallow as he stood there, waiting for my answer. His skin felt warm and damp where his shirt clung to his tapered waist, his bronze hair a bit more mussed than usual.

What had he been doing?

"I'm fine. Just a little tired of everyone porting in here on a whim and startling me." I tossed my wet hair over my shoulder.

Breck frowned. "Who's *everyone?*"

Shit.

"You and Sorscha. She ports in and out constantly so it just seems like a lot." A half-lie. I bit the inside of my cheek hoping he wouldn't dig further. He still looked a bit skeptical.

Then, he noticed the *Seidr* on the small table, and his frown intensified. "Auren, listen to me. You shouldn't let anyone else in here. Don't answer the door for anyone. Now is not a good time."

"Why? What's happened? I was in the bath when I felt everything shake . . ." Another half-lie.

"What you felt was Vanir's power. The keres attempted to break through the wards. He scared them off."

"*That* was Vanir's power?"

"Why is that the only part of the sentence that you heard?" He looked at me like I was insane for not giving a second thought about the keres.

When I didn't respond, he gently took my hand and led us over to the chairs. "We were alerted to movement along the outskirts of the court. That's where Killian found a group of the keres attempting to get past the wards. Some came dangerously close to succeeding, so Vanir stepped in and fortified what magic was there with his shield. He sent a few ripples of it out into the surrounding forest to deter any more creatures who might have been contemplating a breach."

"But why would the keres be trying to get through?"

"We don't know. They usually keep well away from here. But they're drawn to power. They feed off of it. What we don't understand though, is what could have enticed them, or why they would come so close again. The wards that Killian has in place act as a shield to the inner court. No one outside should be able to see or feel what goes on here. Anyone inside should be able to use their power and not ever have to worry that it would be a siren song for those vile creatures. Not to mention no one uses their power in great enough strength to even warrant something to come sniffing around in the first place. Even so, the wards would have been strong enough to snuff out any hint of it."

"That's strange." I instantly thought of my use of power in the ruined temple with Niall, and a pit formed in my gut.

Could that have drawn the keres in again?

Breck stared at the blackened hearth and the pile of ash from last night's fire. The one Niall and I had sat in front of. Where he'd pulled me close, and I'd wanted to—

"What's really strange," Breck said, interrupting my thoughts, "is that it wasn't just a couple of them. It was a dozen or so."

"*A dozen?*"

He nodded. "Killian is furious. He ordered everyone on lockdown again. And," he hesitated before adding, "he wants to speak with you. Alone."

I winced. The last thing I wanted to do right now was talk with Killian.

I began to wonder if he was starting to suspect something.

My power stirred within me, and I straightened as the familiar, steady thrum began along with it.

Behind us, Niall appeared, perfectly composed as he took in the scene, eyes landing on me with an undeniable intensity.

Something must have clicked into place in Breck's mind because he looked back and forth between Niall and I skeptically. I hoped he hadn't realized I'd sensed Niall's arrival before he ported in, or that the High Lord was the other *someone* invading my personal space. But I could tell that one or perhaps both of those things crossed his mind as his jaw flexed.

"Morning," Niall greeted him with no major enthusiasm.

"Niall," he said dryly.

The tension was palpable as they stood at odds with each other.

In an attempt to ease the awkwardness, I asked Niall, "Did you bring anything with you to eat? I'm starving."

Both males looked at me and blinked.

Guess that wasn't the right thing to say at the moment.

Niall stepped forward. "I did not, but I can certainly take you to get whatever you'd like." He reached a hand out to me.

He had always offered me his elbow when Breck was present, and I realized then that the gesture had previously been out of respect. Now, he seemed to disregard any feelings or opinions Breck might harbor.

Breck took a step towards me as well. "Auren, Killian wants to speak with you. He won't want to be kept waiting. I can make sure food is brought here when you're finished." He lifted a hand. "I'll escort you."

I looked between the males and their outstretched hands, each one of them vying for mine. I blinked, trying to suppress my grin, then stepped past both of them. "Thank you. But I think I'll just see myself out to meet with Killian." I paused mid-step and spun on my heel. "Where is it exactly?"

Both of them lowered their hands in defeat, and Breck spoke. "I'm afraid he's in his private quarters." He looked over at Niall, who stiffened at the words.

I had no idea where Killian's private quarters were or how to get there in this polished stone maze, so I opted for the only option I could think of. "All right then. Breck, lead the way." He lifted his chin, savoring the small win, but his face quickly fell when I continued, saying, "And Niall will join us for extra protection. Apparently, there are some ruthless keres lurking nearby."

I crossed the room, stopping by the door to allow them to exit first. Breck kept his eyes down as he walked past Niall. The High Lord bit his bottom lip—holding in what I'm sure would have been a bold grin—as he followed. He lifted his brows as we briefly locked eyes.

I tossed my head back and looked up to the ceiling, saying a silent prayer to Carina—the goddess of patience and grace—to grant me exactly those two things when it came to these males.

Patience and grace.

39
DECEPTION

THE WALK TO KILLIAN'S PRIVATE QUARTERS WAS A LONG AND QUIET ONE. Both Niall and Breck were tense and brooding. And I was the common denominator between them.

Secretly I was quite content with having the two of them worrying about my well-being and continuously vying for my attention. It was rather comical to see them flustered when my regard swayed to one more than the other.

I grinned to myself at the thought.

Killian's pointed arch door stood at the end of a wide hallway, framed with climbing vines of evening primrose, their blooms slowly closing back up beneath the now mid-morning light.

We halted several paces from the entry, and Breck gave me a stern nod. "We'll wait for you here."

Niall tapped a finger to his temple twice as I passed by him. A reminder to make sure my mental shield was intact. I reinforced the stone wall in my mind just as he'd taught me, watching the doors swing open upon my approach.

Once inside, I took in the space. It was grand and open, with ivory stone pillars bolstering an arched ceiling. Dark green and gold rugs accented the ornate alder wood sofas and armchairs. Though it was mid-morning, the chambers were still darkened by the long fabrics that no one had bothered to pull back from the windows.

A plush, four poster bed three times the size of the one in my chambers sat against the left wall with sheer ivory curtains draping down from the top of its canopy. Off to the right was a tall table, and atop it were at least a dozen bottles of what looked to be fae wine and other colorful liqueurs. I eyed the variety of bottles from where I stood until the door next to the table swung open.

Killian was dressed in a midnight blue long coat with golden stitching along the cusps of his wrists and lapels. His hair looked a bit tousled, but it was back to its sleek white-blonde color with dark roots peeking through. This time, a sword was strapped to his hip in a black leather scabbard. It jostled with his long strides as he entered the room.

"My lovely guest. I apologize that I've kept you waiting these past couple of days. I'm sure my cousin informed you—I've been rather busy. Please, sit." There was nothing welcoming in his tone. He had all the pleasant nature of a stag with its horns lowered to strike.

He strode to the liquor table and selected a decanter, pouring two glasses and handing me one as he joined me on the sofa. I sniffed at the light pink liquid, picking up on floral notes with a hint of peach.

"My favorite wine," he said, taking a rather large sip. As a polite gesture, I sipped once from mine as well, then set it on the table in front of us.

He reclined beside me, tossing an arm over the back of the sofa. Crystalline blue eyes bore into mine, assessing. "So, tell me. What have you been up to the past few days?"

I knew I hadn't done anything wrong, but he made me feel like I had. I definitely didn't want him knowing who I had been spending my time with, or what we had learned, so I acted like the demure human he thought I was. "I've toured much of your court and I've—"

"Don't lie to me Auren," he abruptly cut me off.

I blinked. *Did he know something?*

I checked my mental shield.

Intact.

"Well, I did have a small archery lesson." I lowered my chin in a play of innocence.

His expression settled into mild satisfaction at the admission. "Archery. Why archery?"

"I was intrigued. And truth be told I've never shot a bow until yesterday. It was quite thrilling."

He swirled the liquid around his glass and watched it spin. "Did my cousin offer you his expertise on the matter?"

"He did."

"Mmm." He sipped. "And what of the High Lord of Calledan?"

My heartbeat stuttered. "What of him?"

"He is staying as a guest of my court, and yet he's been notably absent as of late."

Shit.

"I wasn't aware that the other High Lords were all still here, until earlier. And anyway, I was told to keep my distance from him at Lumeri."

"And have you?" He lifted his eyes to mine again.

My body went still as his question fell upon me like an accusation. I checked my mental shield again.

What did he know?

"You couldn't even keep your distance at Lumeri, and that *display* you put on with him . . ." He scoffed and threw back another gulp of wine. "Do you deny it?"

I willed myself to keep my composure. "It was not a *display.* It was a simple dance."

He harrumphed, draining his glass this time. "One that you freely accepted?"

"It was the polite thing to do, was it not? I conceded to a dance with you, didn't I?"

In an instant, he was over me, pressing me back into the arm of the sofa. "You must be either incredibly dumb or extremely ignorant. You don't know this realm or our ways. What each of us is capable of doing to someone like you."

He acted as if he was angrier with me than was necessary.

Like he held some ridiculous grudge.

I wanted to push back at him, but he was so close I would head-butt him if I did. The thought was tempting. I gritted my teeth. "I'm more than capable of protecting myself."

"Oh, yes. What's this I hear about you being skilled with a sword?" His eyes roved over my face and snagged on my lips.

I hesitated to reply, because I hadn't recalled telling him about my sword skills—aside from my passing mention of it at Lumeri with the High Lord of Benmoor, Ramil.

"Yes, sweetheart. My cousin speaks of all your little talents. Swords, arrows . . . I hear you're quite dangerous with pointy things."

Swords and arrows. He said nothing of my power. Breck must have kept that part to himself—I hoped.

When I didn't reply, Killian pushed up from the sofa and walked over to refill his glass. This time he slammed it back in one swallow. I stood as well, not feeling like getting cornered on the sofa again.

To my surprise, he crossed the room to a shadowed alcove and pulled a sword off the wall. As he turned and stalked toward me, I edged around the furniture and began backing up, unsure of what he was doing.

I really wished Niall had gotten to the *physical* shielding part of our lessons.

In a blink, Killian had closed the distance and had my back flush against the wall. A breath of his magic had my wrists pinned at my sides. I yanked to wrench them free, but the magical restraints only tightened.

He ran his free hand up my left arm, dragging his fingertips across my exposed collarbone. "Funny . . . you seem like such a delicate thing . . ."

I bristled at his words, skin crawling under his touch.

"Are you a great deceiver, Auren?" His voice started to take on a tone that made me nervous. The last time he spoke this way, I almost—

The thought shattered as he shoved the sword against my chest. "Show me," he bit out.

My restraints gave way, allowing me to grasp the weapon, and he stepped back, unsheathing his blade from the scabbard at his hip.

As much as I didn't want to partake in this, I knew it was probably the best thing to keep him from attempting any mind-tricks. Especially when I felt like he had just come close to trying it again.

I found my grip on the sword's hilt, and rolled my wrist, cutting the blade through the air, savoring the whistle it sang. It was a familiar, heavy weight, much like my own sword, and something condemning flickered in Killian's eyes when he saw how easily I handled it.

He brought his sword down hard from above. A sloppy move—one to test my strength. The fae were significantly stronger than any human opponent, that was glaringly apparent.

My power stirred in my chest, begging to come forth, but I willed it back down and grunted, heaving his sword off of mine with a solid push of my own physical strength. His eyes widened and he lunged again. The clash of metal echoed off the walls as our swords collided.

Clang.

Clang.

The door behind us burst open. I whipped my head around as both Niall and Breck stormed inside, furiously assessing the situation—ready to defend me.

Shit, shit, shit. Why couldn't they just stay outside?

Killian lowered his arm and clicked his tongue. "Deceived in more ways than one, it seems."

I kept the sword out in front of me—just in case the situation descended into chaos—and stepped toward the two males I trusted.

"What is this?" Breck demanded. His voice was deep and laced with anger at seeing Killian bearing a sword in my presence. "Are you all right, Auren?"

"I was proving a point." I pressed my lips into a hard line and looked at Niall. His eyes were aglow, churning a brilliant molten gold.

"Easy now, High Lord." Killian snickered as a smug smile spread across his face. "She was just showing me some of her skills before we indulged in . . . other matters."

Both males started, but Killian tutted them back, raising his blade. "It seems I have a lot to catch up on." He glanced between the three of us. "Maybe we'll get to that at dinner this evening. You're all required to attend." He slid his sword back into its scabbard. "Now, get out."

40
HERE GOES NOTHING

"BRECK, YOU SAID THE KERES CAME UP FROM THE SOUTH . . . MAYBE they felt my power when we were training, north of here."

Breck nodded, still deep in thought. "If they couldn't determine where it came from, they very well could have just made their way up to the first place they suspected—the place that was most populated."

"That sounds like the most plausible answer," Niall said as he ran his hand through his hair.

After the mess we had found ourselves in with Killian, the three of us had returned to my chambers to have a discussion. I decided it was important that we told Breck the truth of what had happened in the forest when Niall and I had gone missing, and about our visit with the Elder. Niall disagreed at first, but relented when I explained that Breck had done well to throw Killian's suspicion off by talking up my sword-fighting. And since he had yet to divulge any other information to Killian, I deemed him trustworthy enough. Plus, we needed someone who had Killian's ear and access to everything he knew.

Breck had leaned against the wall in silence, staring at Niall as he brought him up to speed. Disdain swirled in his eyes the longer the High Lord spoke, and I'd watched his expression flicker from hurt, to anger, before finally shifting to something akin to acceptance.

Then, a thousand questions came spewing from him.

Ever since then, we had been piecing together what we knew.

"So, what's our next move?" Breck asked, arms crossed as he leaned against the hearth.

Niall sighed from where he stood staring out the small window. "Dinner this evening is going to be interesting."

"And we're *required* to attend," I added, flicking a speck off the arm of the chair I sat in.

"It's going to be an interrogation," Breck muttered. "And the worst part is, the other High Lords will be there to witness it. Killian won't make any brash moves though. Not with all the others still here."

"If any of us are questioned, Auren's powers must remain a secret," Niall warned. "And Auren, darling, don't draw attention to yourself."

I frowned, but nodded.

"We'll reconvene back here afterwards."

Breck and I agreed.

Killian had sent a dress to my chambers for the occasion; a green heap of gossamer, with layers that cinched up at the tops of the shoulders and fell down the backside in long, trailing swaths of fabric.

I'd taken one look at it and declined.

Sorscha scrambled to find me an alternative—leggings and a linen tunic—as I'd instructed, but Niall insisted that I wear the dress to appease Killian. Let him gloat on the small win and keep his suspicions to a minimum. So I'd stowed away the pants outfit for another time and bitterly donned the dress.

When it was time to make our way to dinner, Breck arrived to escort me. He had chosen a forest green tunic with a matching surcoat, embellished with deep gold leaves across the shoulders and chest—his signature colors—it seemed. A male of the woodlands through and through.

He wore a sword at his hip this time, and had brought a smaller dagger —which he insisted I wear in case something went awry. I strapped it to my right thigh, where it was perfectly concealed beneath the swaths of fabric.

We were told to arrive at dinner just after sundown, but the room was already full of chatter when we entered. It appeared that everyone else had been given an earlier arrival time. Thankfully, we had anticipated as much.

The audience of heads all turned from where they were seated at the decorated table, as Breck and I entered the room. Killian watched us with disdain, his expression flaring with annoyance that I didn't enter with Niall as he had expected. The other High Lords all acknowledged us with a nod or a tight smile as we claimed two seats that were side by side near the head of the table.

A palpable tension hung in the air. I took note that every fae now donned a weapon at their hip, and guards stood watch in all four corners of the room.

Niall entered several minutes later, clad in all black, from his finely tailored jacket to his leather boots. He always looked perfectly put together.

Hewn from stone.

Dangerously handsome.

And not a weapon on him. He'd never carried one—not that I'd seen. Perhaps that's what made him even more intimidating. After all, he could shatter someone's body from the inside out, in more ways than one.

He went to the empty seat down at the far end of the table and pulled out the chair, dragging the legs noisily across the floor. He took his time scooting it into place until it was just right, then he cast out a mocking smile as he settled into place, shifting his hips, until he'd found the perfect angle with which to recline and scrutinize everyone at the table.

I quickly smoothed out the grin that tugged at my lips and looked around. There were others in attendance aside from the High Lords. Nobles or part of Killian's court, I assumed. The only one I didn't see was Senna, Laurent's mate. In fact, the only other female at the table was the same one that had stared me down in the throne room when I'd first arrived. She now sat at Killian's left, shoulders back, head high, her kohl-lined eyes pinning me in my chair.

She wore a midnight blue dress that matched Killian's outfit, with a plunging neckline that showed off her assets. A thin golden circlet encrusted with sapphires adorned her forehead, framed by her long, dark brown hair.

Seated next to her was Ramil, and I couldn't help but see a resemblance between them. They had the same lightly tanned skin and high cheekbones, but where Ramil's eyes were hazel, hers were a deep brown, the color of freshly churned earth.

I shifted in my seat, feeling like every eye was trained on me, and worrying that this was somehow going to go south very quickly.

Killian finally spoke. "How nice of you three to join us. I was just beginning to fill everyone in on the intel I received earlier."

Ramil straightened in his chair.

"About the keres?" Breck asked.

"Yes," Killian replied, his frown somehow deepening even further. "A scout of mine reported a group of them taking particular interest in the temple ruins north of here several hours ago."

Breck stiffened. "That wasn't long after Vanir reinforced our wards."

"That's correct, Cousin," Killian confirmed. Then he directed a question down the table. "That wouldn't have been you, would it, Niall?"

Every head turned.

Niall sat casually in silent grace, tracing his finger in a swirling motion on the polished marble tabletop. "What need would I have with the temple ruins?" he asked, sounding bored.

"You tell me. None of us recall seeing you since the previous High Lords meeting. Perhaps you've found something here that interests you more?" The implication of either the relic, or me was not lost on anyone here. But I couldn't tell which one he spoke of.

Niall tilted his head. "You seem to have forgotten that I prefer my personal space."

"Not when my relic has been stolen and my court threatened with a breach," Killian ground out.

"Thankfully, Vanir was here to reinforce your wards then," Niall taunted, glancing over at the High Lord whom he mentioned.

I looked over at Vanir as well. His long dark-blond hair was unbraided and fell past his shoulders in soft waves. He hadn't bothered to dress up for the occasion. He sat stoically, seeming uninterested in the conversation, but at Niall's comment, the corner of his bearded mouth twitched upward ever so slightly.

Killian's fist came down on the table. "Need I remind you that you have no grounds to slander *my* power, when that relic was sent here for safe-keeping because *your* ancestor couldn't keep a leash on *his.*"

Breck shifted toward me, moving his hand down to his hip near the pommel of his sword.

Niall's finger stilled on the table.

A tense silence fell.

No one moved.

"Excuse me, but, what is a keres?" My voice was quiet—as I intended for it to be. I knew very well what a keres was, but Killian didn't know that. No one else was aware that I knew—besides Breck and Niall. But I would play the part of a naive human as long as I needed to; a demure doe in a room full of wolves.

Niall lifted his eyes to me and shifted his head to the side, ever so slightly. *Careful darling,* his voice echoed clear as day in my mind.

I startled, chills cascading down my spine at his deep timbre. His voice sounded so clear, as if he was . . .

Mind-walking.

I fought the urge to look at him—convinced that Killian was monitoring my every glance. It took nearly all of my will-power not to react.

The room remained quiet for far too long, the silence screaming at me to recover my composure. So, I schooled my face into neutrality and swung my attention back to Killian, smiling politely as I awaited his answer.

He pursed his lips. "Ah. I forget that our special guest has no knowledge of the terrors in this realm." He shot a pointed, insinuating glare back at Niall. "The keres are creatures that stalk our lands. Filthy leeches that prey on our power."

"Is that why I was advised to not go venturing off into the forest?" I looked to Breck in earnest, hoping he would play along.

"Yes . . ." Breck agreed, catching on. "There are creatures beyond our wards that are not kind to the fae, or to humans."

Well played.

Killian swirled the wine in his glass. "Yes, you should be glad that you were here and not out there when it happened." He obviously had no idea I'd even left the grounds today.

I watched as he speared a piece of meat off the table and scraped it onto his plate. Then another. Everyone else took it as their cue to do the same, and some of the tension eased as plates were filled and the guests began eating.

Killian continued watching me, so I kept my eyes on the food and reinforced my mental shield as I let Breck serve me my plate.

Laurent spoke up this time, his voice like a soft song. "Perhaps I can send some scouts out across the border of Drastia. There's been some movement on Salterra's plains as of late, and I don't find the emergence of the keres to be a mere coincidence, given everything that has happened recently."

Killian didn't look up. "If you think it's appropriate."

"I think it's wise that we *all* take necessary precautions," Ramil said, dabbing his chin with his cloth napkin. "Perhaps, whoever took this relic journeyed to the temple ruins with it. *It* could have summoned the keres if they sensed it being outside of your wards."

Laurent countered, "The power of a talisman would have been felt across all the territories if it had been used. This was nothing of the sort."

Niall let out a short, dry laugh down the table, and everyone swung their stares to him. "You're all forgetting that a talisman can only be wielded by the god to whom it belongs." His statement stopped the room. "So, unless Killian is harboring Lyceius, that's out of the question." He rubbed his thumb and forefinger together as if rolling a grain of sand between them. The look he threw Killian's way said he had half the thought to think the High Lord capable.

"How dare you make such insinuations," Breck growled in Killian's defense. Either he was showing his true loyalties, or he was stringing a ruse to get himself back in Killian's good graces.

I placed my bet on the latter.

Ramil set his wine glass down with a thud. "He knows not what he speaks."

No one else dared say anything as the High Lord of Benmoor and the High Lord of Calledan shot daggers at each other with their eyes.

Finally, Vanir spoke, his words a gruff voice of reason. "The relic was taken during Lumeri. Fae come from near and far in this court and beyond —in ridiculous attire that might as well be a disguise. It's possible that someone was here who should not have been. Someone who could be working for Lyceius himself."

The room grew still.

"Have you seen something?" Killian asked.

"No," Vanir answered. "I was just pointing out the obvious."

Down the table, Niall's mouth lifted at the corner, but he kept his eyes down.

It suddenly occurred to me that there was some sort of understanding between the two of them. Allies, perhaps. And Vanir—like Niall—looked like he would rather be receiving a lashing than sitting at Killian's dinner table.

Killian continued. "How do you suggest they bypassed my wards then Vanir? The relic has been well guarded for over a millennia. No one can just walk in to claim it freely. Not to mention that its location is not public knowledge."

"Perhaps it was Old Magic." Vanir shrugged.

A few hushed comments passed amongst the table as several fae murmured their own speculations to each other.

Ramil reached up and twisted the stone that hung around his neck. My attention snagged on the move. When he caught me watching him, he slowly let it fall back against his chest and reached for his wine instead.

Killian leaned in, resting his elbows on the table. "Old Magic is not so easily accessed . . ."

"And Old Magic cannot simply be blamed for everything that goes awry in this realm," Ramil said. He waved his arm across the table casually, but his tone seemed a bit defensive.

I dared a peek at Niall and saw that he had moved on to fiddling with his napkin, entirely uninterested in the conversation.

Out of nowhere, the dark-haired female spoke, her voice a soft and smoky timbre. "Have none of you given thought to how a human is sitting at this very table? Or have you all forgotten?"

The room fell quiet again, and I instantly felt on edge. She had drawn all attention back to me, and I needed a quick way to deflect. I didn't need anyone else figuring out that I wasn't fully human. Better to throw them off and place the blame of my crossing on something that would be completely out of my control.

I quickly pulled something together to take the speculation off me. "Perhaps something bigger might be going on between the realms."

Ramil narrowed his eyes on me.

"What do you know of such things?" Killian asked, cocking his head with sudden interest.

Shit. Here goes nothing.

"Nothing but speculation," I said. "Before I crossed over, I was competing in the king's annual tournament, something he has hosted for years now." Killian's eyes squinted ever so slightly, like he'd just gained some sort of confirmation. Something that would condemn me of an unknown act. I shook it off and continued. "The winners gain a prestigious place as part of his guard. There was always suspicion as to why he's so eager to reinforce his guard in the first place. Many think he's preparing for something."

Killian shifted in his seat. *What do you know,* his eyes seemed to say.

Niall's voice swirled in my head like he was sitting next to me. *Are you doing what I think you're doing?*

I knew better than to look down the table at him, so I kept my eyes freely roaming, focusing on no one in particular.

Get out of my head! I thought back. His deep throaty laugh echoed in response, and I pressed my lips into a hard line and made a fist under the table.

But I quite like it here. Being in your mind is far more intriguing than this conversation we're all having.

I squeezed my fist harder. *I can't hold a private conversation with you and have a real one with them at the same time, so shut up!*

I would definitely be having some particularly incisive words with him about choosing this exact moment to use his mind-walking, err—*talking*—on me.

Think of this as a training lesson. All it takes is a little concentration. I could hear the smirk in his voice, but his face betrayed nothing when I finally shot him a look that promised payback.

Killian was mumbling something about the king as I tuned back into the conversation around me. A male down the table whom I didn't know called out, "What if he has loyalists from our side—working for him?"

Another asked, "Could they have forged an alliance with our enemies that we aren't aware of?"

Chaos broke out across the table.

Niall's deep, sultry voice caressed my mind again. *Look at what you started.*

I sucked on my bottom lip to avoid wanting to look at him. *Stop. It. Make. Me.*

Killian and the dark headed female took up a conversation of their own. Breck was hollering at Ramil about something. Everyone else was speaking over each other and pointing fingers.

I dared another look at Niall. He'd slouched to one side of his chair, fist on his chin, a vision of someone who could care less about being in this room.

We can talk later, I said flatly in my mind.

Oh, but darling, right now I'm enjoying this too much. Tell me something about yourself.

My eyes widened. *Now is not the time!*

Now's the perfect time. You're training. Tell me something.

Killian was still speaking with the female, but he was looking at me now.

Shit.

Sweat broke out across my forehead. I couldn't listen to them *and* Niall at the same time. There was no way. I thought of something quick to get Niall off my back.

I'm a bad liar, I thought—*said*—or however this mind-to-mind conversation was happening.

That damn throaty laugh again. *Are you? Seems like the lie you just told them was a success.*

Indeed. Everyone's focus was no longer on me.

Except for Killian's.

"Human kings have always had their own agenda," I heard someone say.

"They haven't trusted us since the second war!" another snapped.

Niall's voice dropped to a very low and throaty pitch in my head. *I think I need to test this claim for myself.*

Before I could protest, he spoke again, but this time a sensation came with it. His essence pressed up against mine in an intimate caress, and his words were nothing more than a whisper in my mind as he said, *Can you feel that?*

I shuddered as the feeling overwhelmed me.

Tell me Auren, can you feel me?

Something about his voice and that all-encompassing feeling of his essence against mine sent a wave of heat licking down low in my core.

I let out a shallow breath and shifted in my seat. *Barely,* I thought back. Whatever he just did, I did not want to give him any confirmation that it affected me.

Gods, you really are a bad liar, aren't you? Because I can feel you—

A tingling sensation began between my thighs, and I stood up abruptly, pushing my seat back with a bit of vigor.

"Lord Killian." I choked on my words over everyone else's voices, and all conversations paused. "I would like to continue our conversation somewhere a bit more . . . private." I forced myself to smile as I moved around my chair.

Killian's face flashed with surprise and intrigue, catching my implication. "Of course," he said. As he stood, I caught sight of the female's hand falling away from his thigh from under the table, and next to her, Ramil was looking less than pleased.

Killian took me by the hand, leading me toward the doors. "Right this way."

Niall's voice in my head was silent now. And when I glanced back, both his and Breck's jaws had gone slack.

41
CLOSE CALL

KILLIAN FLICKED HIS WRIST, AND THE LARGE DOORS SWUNG OPEN TO A meeting room down the hall. Just like earlier, he went straight to pouring two rather large servings of an odd colored liquid.

"This is a specialty in my court," he said as he handed a glass to me.

I sniffed the dark purple drink. Berries, a hint of cinnamon, and a floral note that I couldn't quite place overwhelmed my nose. It was a perfect blend of tart and sweet on my tongue, and the tension eased from my shoulders the moment I swallowed a sip.

Killian's eyes danced with mischief in the light of the orbs that bobbed around the dark room. "It's made from the elderberries of the forest. And a few other ingredients of course." He took a seat on the small sofa, sipping his drink and settling into the cushions, while I remained standing. "I'm happy that you wanted to speak with me alone. Sometimes I don't trust the other High Lords to have my best interests in mind. Everyone's out for themselves."

I nodded, gripping the glass with both hands as I watched him get comfortable.

"And I do hope you understand my reasoning for being so brash earlier today. Niall's presence is not one I tolerate so well in my court." He eyed me over the rim of his glass as he drank again. "So, tell me more about this king of yours and this competition."

I turned the glass in my hands as I spoke. "Well, the most skilled fighters of our realm go against each other for the chance to become one of the king's guards. This year, I became one of them."

Killian's face remained neutral, but his eyes reflected a thousand questions racing through his mind. "Go on," he urged, nudging his chin at me.

There would be no lying my way out of this. If he suspected I wasn't telling the truth, I had no doubt that he'd try to pry into my mind. And if he did, and sensed my shield . . .

"I was elected to duel with the prince. And I won."

"And how did you best the prince?" His voice was pitched low as he swirled his drink.

"I sliced open his leg."

Killian worked his jaw like the thought bothered him and excited him at the same time. Then he frowned. "None of that explains why you were able to cross The Veil, Auren."

"The prince's guards . . ." The words died on my tongue. I was caught between not wanting to give him any more information, and fearing that if I didn't, he would take it from me anyway. "They wanted revenge. I fled and was chased to The Veil."

"You fled?" he asked with such a dry tone that I bristled at his lack of empathy.

"Yes, I fled. The prince sent his men to—" I paused, not wanting to say it. "It was a misunderstanding."

He lifted his eyes to me. "You harmed the prince. Seems only natural that he would want justice."

"Justice in the form of—" I shut my mouth. I was not going to argue the need for justice with someone who clearly didn't care to understand. "Injuring the prince was an accident. I didn't intend for it to happen." *Lie.* I took another drink, letting it soothe my nerves. "And crossing The Veil was an accident too. Someone must have—"

"Yes, yes, we've been through the part where you claim someone must have manipulated The Veil. What I want to know is why you think the king had anything to do with it."

I suddenly wished I was better at spinning lies than swinging swords. My fingers fiddled with the stem of my glass. "I'm afraid I don't know the specifics."

"That can't be right," he said, examining his glass as he held it up to the light. "You seemed so eager to pull me aside and spill all your little secrets. The king, his guards . . . the people's *suspicions* . . ."

A rush of anxiety flooded my gut as his eyes met mine again, but I remained silent.

"We can do this the easy way or the hard way," he casually threatened, tossing back the remnants of his drink.

Think, Auren. Something—anything will suffice. It's not like he's going to go and confirm it with the king himself.

"All I know is, the king . . . well, ever since his son was attacked, he's been strengthening his guard at a rapid pace. The people . . . some think he's paranoid. Others think he's up to something. But no one knows what." Gods, I was rambling. "I only suspect his involvement because I was pushed across The Veil by his men. And no human can cross—everyone knows that. So the only other option would be that someone tampered with The Veil. Maybe he's working with someone here in this realm. Maybe—"

"You can stop lying to me, Auren."

My breath caught in my throat. "Excuse me?"

Killian's sly smirk appeared. "This is no simple happenstance. And I don't think you're the delicate little thing you play at being. I know there's something different about you. I can sense it."

My heartbeat sped up. I checked my mental shield, my hand drifting down to the slit in my dress, ready to snatch the dagger—should I need it. "I assure you I don't know what you mean—"

"Are you a spy, Auren?" Killian's glare cut like a serrated dagger. "Or are you a fae? A glamoured traitor, perhaps? Working for the king?"

The accusation hit me hard. This was *not* what I wanted him to be thinking. "N-No! I'm not fae! I'm human! I promise you that I arrived here against my will, and I—"

He held up a hand, silencing me with a small pulse of his power. "Come. Sit."

Then I felt it—the ripple against my mental shield, telling me that he'd just tried to compel me. It rolled off the barrier like water on a well-oiled surface. The moment I saw his brows pinch in confusion, I quickly moved at my own will, making him think the magic had worked, and if anything, it had only lagged. Thankfully, his expression smoothed back out. My heart pounded dents into my chest cavity as I approached him, hoping he wouldn't question it.

He set his empty glass on the side table, and reached for me—snatching me by the hips as I lowered, and pulling me down onto his lap instead. With the sudden movement, I noticed that my body felt both heavy and lighter at the same time. When I shifted uncomfortably, he winced—as if he had a sore leg muscle—and re-positioned me further up his thigh.

One hand came to rest low on my waist, while his other hand lifted to the base of my glass. With his finger, he tilted it upward until the liquid flowed down my throat. "Tell me what you felt when you bested the prince."

His request was at complete odds with everything he had just implied, and it threw me off. Of all the things he would want to know . . .

I tried to stiffen my back, but my muscles were too relaxed for the movement to pull me away from him like I wanted.

"I . . . enjoyed it." A piece of me internally cringed at the tone in which I said the words. They fell too easily off my tingling tongue.

His hand slid further up my waist just under my breast, squeezing slightly, and I could feel it all too well through the thin gossamer that hugged my frame. He leaned in close. "Did you enjoy seeing him bleed?"

His breath slid against my neck as he breathed in my scent, and exhaled. I felt his lips brush over my pulse, but no heat swept over me like it had with Niall.

Did I tell him what I did to the prince? I couldn't recall. Perhaps the drink was stronger than I thought . . .

All I managed was a nod.

His fingers trekked across my ribs, and I got the sense that if I lingered here too long he would get too curious. Dig too deep.

Someone behind us cleared their throat.

I slowly turned to see the female from dinner standing several feet from us, her face a picture of disgust. I hadn't heard her open the door or step inside.

Killian was in no rush to move away from me. Instead, he leaned around me and glared at the female. "Something wrong, Morah?"

"No, my lord." She dipped her head. "But, my father would like a word."

Killian harrumphed and turned back around.

"I'm afraid it can't wait," she bit out.

"Mmm." He waved his hand at her.

She frowned and returned to the door, nearly slamming it behind her as she left.

"Unfortunately, duty calls." His crystal blue eyes met mine. "I hope you'll join me again tomorrow evening. Or perhaps I'll come collect you before then and give you a more personal tour. Maybe then you'll indulge me with a few more details of your curious journey here."

I forced a smile. "I look forward to it."

When I stood, my legs wobbled slightly. Killian didn't seem to notice as he finished his drink and straightened his jacket.

"I'll send my cousin for you," he said as he disappeared into nothing.

42
THE LIBRARY

Breck cast several anxious glances at me as he escorted me back to my chambers, but I was more focused on keeping my feet steadied beneath me. The elderberry liqueur was a pretty potent thing.

"How did your discussion with Killian go? Did he say anything?"

It took me a moment to collect my thoughts. "It was . . . strange. He wanted to know what I did to the prince, and if I enjoyed making him bleed." I frowned, thinking back on the odd encounter. Thankfully that other fae, Morah, interrupted before Killian could get any more curious.

"My cousin has always been intrigued with the macabre," Breck said, a tone of disgust lining his words.

From what I'd seen of Killian, that seemed fitting. But why would he even care about that? What good was the information to him?

I quickly recalled how he'd tried to compel me again. How the attempt had slid off my mental shield and he'd been so close to questioning it. Should I mention it to Breck? I would definitely need to tell Niall—

"Where is Niall?" I blurted out.

Breck's answer was in no way enthusiastic. "He's having a few words with Vanir. He'll meet us after they're finished."

I nodded, but the motion sent my head into a slight spin.

We approached a very large doorway that hadn't been open on our way to dinner. Slowing my steps, I peered into the room.

"That's the library," Breck informed me.

Without acknowledging him, I started toward it and entered.

A beautiful glass dome stretched overhead, where the stars were winking into existence in the now moonlit sky above. Intricately carved wood ladders sat motionless where the library's patrons had last left them, scaling massive rows of shelves that reached all the way up to meet the glass.

I walked out onto the entry mezzanine and peered down over the railing. Two levels wound down below, all lined with more shelves of books and the occasional creamy stone wall in between, followed by a third level, on which I could see a fountain in the center surrounded by a small pool of water. Something down there beckoned to me. It pulled at my essence like it longed for me to come and see.

Breck came up to my side. "Beautiful," he said quietly.

"It is," I agreed, taking it all in. But when I faced him, his eyes were fixed on me, not the library around us.

"Can we go down there?" I asked, leaning back over the railing.

"Sure." He held his arm out toward the spiraling staircase to our right.

I took each step slowly—partially because I wanted to soak in every detail of the place as we wound down through it, and also because my legs were starting to feel less and less stable.

"What else did you and Killian discuss?" he asked.

"He accused me of being a spy." I heard Breck's steps stall on the stairwell behind me. "Then he presumed to get closer with me. Thankfully that female he was with at dinner interrupted and called him elsewhere."

Breck's voice went low. "Did he attempt to compel you again?"

"No. But he definitely wasn't shy this time."

"If he put his hands on you—"

"Breck, I'm fine. I was trying to distract him, remember?"

He didn't respond, but his steps pounded heavier as we wound down another turn.

It was colder on the lowest level, and the moonlight that stretched down from above illuminated the water flowing from the scalloped edges of the fountain. The pool surrounding it was glittering and swirling, a dark pearlescent blue, like it was full of stardust. Water lilies—turned gray in the moonlight—spun amidst the tumbling drops.

Surrounding the fountain were stone pillars like the ones at the temple ruins, all claimed by vines and opening to small alcoves around the room which were hidden in shadow.

I approached the fountain, intrigued by its iridescence. "What is this place?" I asked, running my hand through the trickling water. It beaded and rolled over my skin like oil.

"It's called the Spring of Sephta. It existed long before these walls did. The Ancient Fae say that upon Gaia's creation, Sephta herself came down and blessed it. That's what gives the water its unique appearance. The Woodland House was actually built around it. There's a spring in every territory, protected by each court and sacred to the Ancient Fae. Every year the Woodland Court dedicates offerings to the fountain and asks for good fortune for the year to come. All fae are welcome to each of the springs."

I looked up at Breck. "And do *you* ask for good fortune?"

His shadowed face became illuminated as he stepped into the moonlight. "I do."

I scooped more of the strange, cold water in the palm of my hand and let it dribble out, picturing fae gathered around the edge of the fountain, laying flowers on the water's surface, or casting pebbles into it—whatever it was they did when they made an offering.

Breck spoke quietly as he held a finger out to catch a droplet of water. "I don't like the way Killian and Niall look at you."

"They're just being typical males. Human men are the same way back in my realm. Well, not so much with me actually. It's a rare day when a man pays me any attention."

He let out a short huff of air. "That's not possible."

"Oh, it is. I'm known for my sword skills and willingness to get a little dirt on me, not my ladylike mannerisms. Most men are too intimidated to even approach me, let alone get to know me. They look at me—sure—but no one wants a woman who wields a sword better than them. I'm quite used to it."

Breck took my arms and gently turned me toward him. "Then they are sadly mistaken." His soft curls slid down over his forehead, casting his face in shadow again. "You're special Auren. And not just because you're the one the prophecy spoke of. You have a strength that I admire. You're not afraid to speak your mind, or ask a million questions, or stick up for yourself. You have courage. Something that I find hard to muster up for myself sometimes." He moved closer. "I've never met another like you. You wield your mind like you wield your sword." His hand came up to cup my cheek, lifting my face further towards his. "You're beautiful."

His shadowed eyes searched mine. Then, he leaned in and placed the softest kiss on my lips. It was delicate and sweet. Like he was testing or asking for permission.

My mind became a jumble of emotions, muddled with the elderberry drink Killian had served me. I wasn't sure why part of me was allowing this when the other part of me wanted to shy away. But when I lingered too long on my thoughts and didn't turn from him, he pressed in further.

His lips swept over mine completely, and I opened for him. Both of his hands cradled my face, holding me close as he kissed me.

It was a lovely thing, to feel wanted. To feel seen, and beautiful. To be admired by someone who saw parts of me that others didn't always see. But something about the kiss didn't feel quite right. Breck was a handsome male, I couldn't deny that, but something inside my chest told me to wait.

I could feel his heartbeat pounding as I pressed my hand against his chest and gently pushed away, breaking the kiss. He put his forehead to mine and I teetered back, bumping into the stone pillar.

His brows bunched up as he searched my face. "Is everything all right?"

I blinked a few times. "I think so."

"You taste like . . . elderberries . . ." His eyes widened. "Auren, are you drunk?"

"What? No!" I replied. I shook my head, but the slight movement sent it spinning, and I wobbled.

He stepped back, holding me at arms-length again, surveying me.

I willed my mind to clear a bit. "Clearly, I'm not drunk. I've held a conversation with you just fine."

"What did Killian serve you?"

"A specialty of some sort." I straightened my posture, making sure I embodied my claim of sobriety.

"Was it elderberry liqueur?"

I bit down on my bottom lip as I nodded.

"You didn't drink all of what he gave you, did you?"

"Just, maybe . . . almost," I said, a bit of anxiety starting to spark. My blood seemed to slow in my veins, yet my heart beat faster.

"Shit, Auren. I'm sorry. If I would have known—I . . . I shouldn't have kissed you."

I gripped his hands with mine. "It's okay. Really. I'm just . . . I'm actually worried about how the climb back up the stairs is going to go."

Breck ran a hand through his hair. "Elderberries have a relaxing effect at first. But it's something you have to get accustomed to in small doses. The drink takes a while to get fully into your system. But once it does, it's like four times as strong as our wine."

"Oh." As if his words summoned the elderberries' effects, a wave of drowsiness washed over me, and my knees wobbled.

He caught me as I tilted forward. "Okay, sunshine. Let's get you to bed."

I had no objections.

He swept me up into his arms and carried me up the stairs and all the way back to my chambers . . . where Niall was conveniently already waiting.

The High Lord was in front of us in an instant. The motion made me queasy just witnessing it. "Where were—What happened?"

"Took a detour to the library," Breck said. "She wanted to see the fountain. And she just informed me that Killian gave her some of our famous *liqueur*. It took its full effect on our way back."

Niall cursed under his breath.

"Trust me, I'm going to give Killian a piece of my fucking mind about this," Breck said as he carried me over to the bed.

"No . . . Issnnot—a—biggdeal" My words came out all slurred this time.

Damnit.

Breck set me down softly and gathered the fabric of my dress, piling it up around me. Niall pulled the blanket up to just below my neck and brushed the hair away from my face. If I wasn't so out of it, I probably would have made a snide comment about the two of them doting on me.

Satisfied that I was tucked in and relatively safe for now, Breck stepped back. "I'm going to track Killian down and make sure this doesn't happen again."

Niall nodded. "I'll stay here tonight and watch her. If she lied about how much she had, she could very well be sick in a few hours, and Sorscha is already gone for the night."

"Ididdn't—liee," I groaned, but neither of them seemed to hear me.

Breck hesitated but finally relented, nodding to Niall. "Take care of her," he ordered.

"You don't have to tell me twice," Niall responded. But there was no sarcasm in his voice. Only concern.

As the door snicked shut, the room began to tilt.

43
DAMN ELDERBERRIES

I GROANED AS THE BED SPUN BENEATH ME. A MALE IN DARK CLOTHES WAS instantly beside me, brushing my hair out of my face.

The room was dark, save for a small fire flickering in the fireplace.

How late is it?

I forced my vision to focus as Niall sank into the mattress at my side. "You're in for a rough night, I'm afraid." There was pity in his voice.

"Why'd—Idrrrinkthat—ssttuff?" I groaned again.

"Because you didn't know any better, and Killian's a bastard."

A surge of heat flushed over my body, and I broke out into a sweat. "Isit—hotinnherre?" I tried to fan my face with my hand, but my arm flopped lazily back to the bed.

Niall let out a soft chuckle. "Here, let's get this blanket off of you."

Even with the blanket removed, the sweat came in droves, coating my skin anew as soon as it dried from the last bout.

Niall got up and poured me a tall glass of water.

"Iff—I—tryto—situpp—I won't . . ." My voice trailed off as another wave of heat washed over me.

Niall gently lifted my head and held the glass to my lips. "Nice, easy sips," he said softly.

I sipped once.

Twice.

Hiccup.

"Oh *noooo*," I moaned.

Hiccup.

Niall chuckled a little harder this time, and I tried my hardest to smack his arm, but mine wouldn't move an inch off the bed.

Damn elderberries.

He placed his hand on my upper chest, and a soft pulse left his palm, radiating into me. The hiccups ceased.

"Wha—how'dyou—"

"Magic." He wiggled his fingers at me.

"Cannyou do that—withhmy head too?"

"I'm afraid there's no magic to help with that. The drink will have to wear off on its own, unfortunately."

When he made to stand up again, my fingertips caught onto his other wrist, and he stilled.

What came out of my mouth next was a complete surprise to me. "Willyou—help meout—of this dress?" Niall raised a brow. "It'sss *hot*," I added, trying not to sound desperate.

He set the water on the bedside table. "Do you want it done the easy way or the hard way?"

I had no idea what that meant. Did the easy way involve magic? Or was magic the hard way? Magic was a good thing, right?

Apparently my decision-making skills were more impaired than anything else thanks to that stupid drink, so I settled on, "Yuurchhoice."

He grinned and leaned back over me. Even though my vision was a bit blurry he was still perfectly gorgeous. His fingers were warm and gentle as they slid underneath the gathered fabric atop my right shoulder and began dragging it down my arm.

I decided that looking him in the eyes while he undressed me was a bit more awkward than I could stand, so I closed my eyes and just let myself feel.

He lifted my arm and the fabric slid down further until my wrist was through it. Then he moved to my other arm, his hands working together in smooth movements. He moved to the bodice of my dress next, reaching under and behind me to pull the tie free and loosen the cinched waist. I let out a long exhale at the new-found space to breathe normally again.

Thankfully I was wearing a low-cut chemise underneath, saving me from baring absolutely everything to him. At the same time, I found myself not caring too much if it was him that saw me. Whether or not that was the elderberries meddling with my judgment—I didn't want to know.

He slipped the bodice down over my breasts and passed my waist to where it bunched around my hips. Gently, he tugged the dress down until it snagged on Breck's dagger that was strapped to my right thigh. "Well, that's intriguing," he murmured, easing the material around the blade.

I cracked one eye open, then both, only to find him focused intently on my legs as he slowly lifted them one by one out of the wads of fabric. His fingers grazed my skin along the backside of each thigh, and my eyes fluttered closed again.

That felt intentional.

My head tilted back deeper into the pillows.

Once the dress was a pile of green fluff on the floor, he trailed his fingers up the backside of my calf. I shuddered at the touch, chills blooming along my skin.

Next, he found the buckles on the strap to the sheath and undid them. The leather came away, and he set it aside, only to return his hand to where the dagger had been. He began rubbing at the lines that the holster left on my thigh, seeming carried away with the feel of my skin against his fingertips.

A new sort of heat crept over me. My power stirred and settled, leaving me tingling beneath a fresh sheen of sweat, my chemise clinging to the dampness that washed over my body, outlining the gentle lines of my figure.

I reached out for him, finding his hand again, and when I tugged him closer he obeyed. His weight shifted over me, and I wondered if he would try to kiss me too. Something inside me wanted him to. The thrumming in my chest purred deeply.

He slowly interlaced his fingers with mine, his callouses pressing into my palm.

"Stay with me," I whispered. The words came out clearly, even though sleep was only seconds away from claiming me.

"Always," he whispered back.

Outside in the distance, I heard the desperate howl of a wolf, just before I winked out like a candle in the wind.

44
CONFRONTATION

I WOKE UP WITH A RAGING HEADACHE.

Somehow, I'd managed to have three physical encounters with three fae males in one night—two of which were not of my own accord. And the one I actually enjoyed was the one that consisted of hazy memories.

I peeled my dry tongue from the roof of my mouth, tasting the lingering hint of mint. Patchy memories of spending a significant amount of time in my bathing chamber replayed in my mind. I recalled crouching over the latrine, heaving until my eyes watered. Someone holding my hair back, and wiping my embarrassed tears away. Then being handed some mint leaves to chew on as I was carried back to bed by—

My heart plummeted.

Niall.

I looked over to where the High Lord dozed in the chair by the fireplace. The *Seidr* was open on the table next to him as if he had been reading throughout the night.

He had taken care of me.

I began to remember the details as I laid there watching him. I combed further back through my memories, to the image of him slowly undressing me. Taking his time.

He'd held my hand, and I'd asked him to stay. I wasn't ashamed of that though. Somehow, I had already known he would. And there he sat, sleeping peacefully, still dressed in his all black ensemble from the night before.

Which meant he'd doted.

On me.

All night.

A grin slid across my lips at the thought.

Then there was Breck. He had kissed me in the library, and I didn't entirely know how to feel about it.

Breck was my first friend here. Someone I trusted and felt safe with. There was no denying that he was attractive and sweet, but there was something missing. A thrill, perhaps.

That thrill jolted through me as Niall stirred.

He lifted his head and instantly looked in my direction. I tried my best to give him a decent smile despite my throbbing headache, and the tension in his brows eased at the sight. He rose and came to sit beside me on the bed, smoothing a hand over the blanket that now covered me. "I already know how you're feeling," he said as his nose wrinkled up. "It'll fade once you get some food in your stomach and some fresh air."

"That's good to hear. Remind me never to drink that stuff again." I rubbed at my forehead with my thumb and forefinger.

"I told Sorscha to take the day for herself, and that I would take care of you. I knew you wouldn't mind." He tossed a sly grin my way, and damnit if I didn't want to melt at the sight of it.

"Did you, now? Wait—how were you so sure that I wouldn't mind?"

"Because, I know what you were feeling last night, when I was in your head at dinner." His grin turned into a smirk.

I cut my eyes at him. "About that . . . You do realize you chose the most inopportune moment to mind-walk, right? And just how were you able to *feel* me anyway?"

"I thought it was the perfect time, seeing as we were so far away from each other at the table." He gave me a pout, and I bit my tongue to keep a grin from surfacing. I wouldn't let him win that easily. And I wasn't about to let him know that I'd actually enjoyed the whole mind-walking thing. "As far as the *feeling* goes," he continued, "I have a theory for that."

"Do tell," I groaned, turning my body to face him.

"When we were training and the essences of both our powers . . . embraced, I think that formed some sort of connection."

"You've never *embraced* someone else's mind before?"

"No. When I enter someone's mind it's only ever to convey a message, or you know, turn whatever's in there to ash."

"That's good to know," I said. The act felt intimate. A part of me was relieved to hear he didn't have that same experience with everyone else.

I paused on the thought. Where was *that* coming from?

"I've never shared my essence with anyone else like that before. Actually, I don't even think it was something I intended to do. It just sort of happened."

I hadn't intended for my essence or my power to reach out for him either. It had done that of its own free will.

"Mine acted the same way," I said.

We stared at each other for a moment, each of us in our own heads about it.

"So, did you mean to make me feel that way at dinner?" I asked.

He smirked. "You mean all hot and bothered?"

"I was *flustered.*"

"Oh, I know," he replied. I rolled my eyes, and a deep rumble left his throat. "I like seeing you flustered," he added.

A small noise chimed from over by the fireplace, drawing our attention. Sorscha stepped forward with a plate of cinnamon sugared toast and fresh fruit and placed it on the chair.

"I thought I told you to take the day off?" Niall said to her playfully.

She smiled—this time a perfect version of it. Then, with a small wave, she popped away into nothing.

"That little one sure does care about you," Niall said, shaking his head as he stood and offered to help me rise from the bed.

It was then that I realized I was only wearing my chemise. Though Niall had already seen me in it—while in a much rougher state of consciousness—I still found myself hesitating to crawl out from under the covers.

As if I'd spoken the thought, a bundle of dark blue fabric dropped down out of thin air onto the bed.

I gave Niall a pointed look, but he shook his head holding up both his hands in a plea of innocence. "Sorscha," he said.

I snatched up the fabric and unfolded it. It was a soft, lightweight robe, and I smiled at the gesture, sending a thought of thanks to the sweet house-fae as I slipped it on and slid out of bed.

A new sense of calm settled between Niall and I as we ate—until the memory of Breck crept back into my mind. I debated whether or not I should tell Niall about it. But the thought of ruining the peaceful moment made my head throb again. I decided I would tell him later—after the elderberries finally left my system.

"What's on the agenda for today?" I asked through a mouthful of toast that I prayed soaked up every last trace of that vile elderberry drink.

"Training. A physical shield this time." He dusted his hands off and leaned back. "I have to get back to my court soon. It's not good for me to be away for extended periods of time. But today we'll focus on this, and then figure out where to go from here."

The thought of him leaving sent my stomach sinking into a pit. "What happens when you leave? What am I supposed to do?"

"We'll figure something out," he assured me.

"I don't want to stay here," I said quietly, surprised that I found myself not really desperate to go home to my own realm yet either.

He studied me.

"I want to go where you're going."

Where this newfound sense of confidence came from, I didn't know, but what I did know was that I wouldn't stay here—not alone. The look on his face told me that he agreed.

"I'll sort that out," he said, mouth lifting in a grin. "Now get dressed, and let's go see what we're working with."

Thankfully I had an entire outfit ready to go thanks to Sorscha's efforts from yesterday evening. I finished strapping my sword at my hip, and we were on our way into the forest again.

Niall glamoured us through The Woodland House until we were out near the pavilion. It looked so different in the daytime, empty, lying dormant until the next celebration required it. I remembered Niall explaining how it sat on the outskirts of the wards, so it was easy to port from once we walked a little bit past it into the forest beyond.

I had been mentally preparing myself for porting again, figuring I needed to get used to it for obvious reasons. And given the fact that my head wasn't in the ideal condition to be making quick movements, I was praying to any god who would listen that I didn't heave up my toast onto Niall's perfectly crisp black tunic if he decided we were porting anywhere for this lesson.

To our surprise, Breck was waiting on the pavilion when we arrived, and the look on Niall's face told me that he hadn't extended the invite to anyone else.

Breck looked a bit wary. Like he hadn't gotten much sleep. His clothes were far too casual—wrinkled even—and his hair was limp.

"Rough night?" Niall greeted him.

Breck eyed the two of us before answering. "I waited up for Killian to finish with his . . . musings."

"And?" Niall pushed.

"And then I gave him a piece of my mind." He crossed his arms over his chest. "Where are the two of you going?"

I waited for Niall to speak, not liking the way Breck was presenting himself.

"For a quiet stroll," Niall said casually.

Breck noticed the sword hanging from my hip. "Strolls require weapons?" The tone of his voice was different, almost accusatory.

I shifted on my feet. "After last night, I don't want to be without it."

He was acting like we were doing something wrong.

Something didn't feel right.

Breck looked between us again. "Killian has ordered that you not leave the premises. I'm to escort you back to your chambers, Auren." When he unfolded his arms and took a step forward I took one back away from him.

"What exactly did he say to you?" Niall asked, positioning his body in front of mine.

The stance made Breck's eyes flare. His voice rose exponentially. "You mean after I yelled at him for disrespecting Auren and threatened him not to try anything else on her again? He reminded me of my place. Made me sit and watch as he did explicit things to another female that I'm sure he would have done to Auren if given the chance. And then he assigned me the pleasure of making sure the two of you stay away from each other."

Underneath his obvious ire, there was a hint of something more vulnerable. A sentiment he was keeping to himself.

Niall slid his hands into his pockets. "You care for her," he said, picking up on the emotion that laced Breck's words.

Silence.

"Oh." Niall snickered. "This is good. Killian realized it too and sentenced you to be her jailer."

The line of tension went taut between them. I could feel the strain, feel the thread of decency quickly unraveling.

I squared my shoulders behind Niall. "I don't need a jailer. I've done nothing wrong."

Breck took another step. "Auren, it'll be okay. Let's just get you back to your room, and we will figure this all out."

"I don't think so," Niall warned.

"This doesn't need to get complicated. I'm just following orders." Breck looked at me. "Killian is going to be expecting you this evening, and I don't want to see his wrath set on you if you're not where you're supposed to be."

"I'm where I'm supposed to be right now," I said defiantly.

Breck breathed out harshly through his nose. "Auren . . ." His voice was foreign now. Commanding. The gentle male that I'd met in the woods, who had helped me get accustomed to things and told me he admired me, was gone. Killian had locked that version of him away. And I would be damned if I let myself get locked away along with him.

His stride was determined as he approached, and I clutched onto the back of Niall's tunic.

I didn't want to have to do this. I cared for Breck, but he wasn't himself. He was under the influence of Killian. Obeying orders. Maybe even a compulsion. And as much as it was going to pain me to do this to him, I knew I had to . . .

"He kissed me," I blurted out.

Breck halted mid-step, and Niall went utterly still under my grip.

The look in Breck's eyes was pain and regret and shame all at once.

Niall, on the other hand, began simmering with rage. "*Who* kissed you?" he growled.

I slowly nodded toward Breck. "*He* did."

A deep rumble rolled through Niall's chest, and his eyes lit like burning pits of gold.

Breck began stepping forward again, and Niall's lip curled back in a snarl.

"Calm down, Niall. I can explain," Breck said as he inched forward cautiously. "Let me just get Auren back to her chambers, and then you and I can talk."

"You're not coming anywhere near her," Niall seethed as his arm reached back, protectively staking his claim. Shadowy wisps of black flame began leaking out from behind his shoulders, their sights trained on the perceived threat.

Breck paused, eyeing the shadows before looking at me. "Auren, I'm sorry. I didn't mean for . . . I care for you. You know that."

The shadowfire pulsed in response, ready to act on Niall's command.

"Just let us go, Breck. I will be at the meeting with Killian later. Just let me figure this out."

"You don't get it," he said. "Killian will have my head if I disobey him."

"He's your cousin," I countered. "I'm sure the two of you can come to an understanding."

"You don't know him, Auren. He threatened to compel me. I cannot refuse. This is Killian being gracious by sending me instead of apprehending you himself."

"Then find a way to stand up for yourself, Breck. You told me that's what you admired about me. So, find a way. Fight it." I slowly backed away towards the edge of the pavilion, pulling Niall backwards by his shirt.

Breck stepped toward us once more, arms out to his sides. "Auren, please." He shook his head. "Don't do this." Don't do this *to us.*

But for me, there was no *us.* There was no *me and him.* The feelings

314

were one-sided. I just couldn't bring myself to speak the words and break his heart even further.

He quickened his step, but the shadows snatched his wrists and restrained him. Grunting in desperate frustration, he yanked against them, but they only hauled him further back. "*Auren,*" he pleaded.

I winced, quickly realizing that porting was going to be a necessity after all—before Niall's shadowfire was forced to do any damage.

Once I neared the edge of the pavilion I called out, "I'm sorry," and when my feet hit the dirt, I turned and bolted off into the forest. It only took a couple of seconds for Niall to swoop me up mid-run and port us away, just as I'd hoped he would.

45
NEW TERRITORY

Upon landing, I kept my eyes shut and bent over my knees as my favorite toast threatened to come back up my throat. My head was spinning again, confirming that the elderberries were still lingering in my bloodstream.

"I'm glad you caught onto my plan," I said, opening my eyes and turning to Niall. But he remained quiet as he scanned the area we stood in.

I expected to see the abandoned temple, or at least another spot deep in the forest, but what I saw was nothing of the sort.

We stood on grass that was such a brilliant shade of green, I had to blink down at it twice. And when I looked up, two hulking slabs of stone stood before us, with a third laying across the top of them, creating a primitive doorway to the land beyond. The header had strange markings carved into it, but I didn't have time to commit them to memory as Niall pressed a hand against my back and ushered me through the entrance alongside him.

As we moved between the stones, a gentle breeze picked up my hair, running through the long strands like invisible fingers. Niall watched protectively as it swirled around my body as if it was inspecting me. Then, it moved to circle him in a quick gust before it vanished.

"What was *that?*" I breathed out.

"*That* was Vanir," Niall said, straightening out his shirt from where I had clung to it.

Panic set in as I surveyed the land again. "Where are we Niall?"

"The Highland Court."

A dozen reasons why I should *not* be in the highlands raced through my mind. "But—what about my meeting with Killian?"

"I'll have it handled," was his only response.

Before I could argue, his hand—which was still poised on my lower back—gripped my waist, and he ported us again.

This time when we emerged, I staggered forward, fighting a bout of nausea as it rushed over me. Niall's hand found the small of my back and steadied me, briefly, before he stalked off.

Once my head leveled out, I focused on our surroundings once more. There was no stone doorway. Instead, a dozen or so towering gray stones were positioned into a perfect circle around us.

In the distance, a rocky, grass covered landscape formed plateaus that rose up in jagged formations in all directions. The sky above us swirled in a mass of gray and brown storm clouds, shutting out the sun.

Niall pointed to the center of the stone circle. "Stand over here."

I stared at him, not fully certain what was going on, or why he was being so short with me all of a sudden.

"Stand over here so we can start your lesson," he said. When I didn't move his eyes began to simmer with their glow. "Auren, please," he said through clenched teeth. "I'm trying my best not to port back there and strangle Breck with my bare hands."

Oh.

I finally strode over to the center of the stone circle where he had indicated. "Breck didn't mean any harm. He just cares about me."

Niall faced the rocky peaks off in the distance, sliding his hands into his pockets as a rumble of thunder rolled through the sky. "And do you care about him?"

"He's just a friend. I don't see him as anything more. He has my best interest at heart—I know it. And we trust him in all of this, remember?"

Reminding him of that last part probably wasn't helping. I was pretty sure that after this, Niall wouldn't be so trusting of him.

He stood in silence for a moment before replying. "He was acting on Killian's command, and for that, I can relent in my anger a bit. But he kissed you of his own free will. Furthermore, he did so while you were drunk on elderberry liqueur and not in the state of mind to think straight. That, I cannot let go of so easily."

"Why, Niall?"

He pressed his lips into a thin line, obviously feeling some strong emotions, because the golden glow in his eyes remained steady.

His presence entered my mind and brushed up against my mental shield. Dark tendrils of inky flame wafted up around the wall, like his essence was asking for mine to come out and greet it. My light was instantly there, answering the call, and I noticed his shoulders relax a bit.

But he still wasn't answering my question.

I scuffed my boot through the grass, waiting. When I realized he wasn't going to answer, I sighed, long and heavy. "On with it then. Train me."

Niall blinked. "That's it? You're just going to blow over it all?"

I shrugged my shoulders. "At least I'm not locked up in my chambers. I'm with you. I'm safe."

His voice softened as he said, "You're always safe with me."

"I know." There was now a small muddy hole where I'd ground the grass into a pulp with my boot. "So, teach me."

Leaving his hands in his pockets, he faced me fully and studied me. When it seemed like he had seen enough to calm his emotions, he finally spoke. "I brought you to the highlands because it's somewhere Breck or Killian wouldn't expect me to bring you. And Vanir keeps the wards over his territory impeccable."

"You and Vanir are allies then?" I'd guessed as much at last night's dinner, judging by their subtle nuances.

Niall nodded. "Him and I share similar values, and our two courts have always been trusted allies of one another since the formation of the separate territories."

"Did he know we were coming?"

"No, but his territory is always open to me should I ever need it. And vice versa. But I still have to enter at a designated point of entry, just like everyone else does."

"That's what the stone doorway was? The entry to Vahrenhall?"

Another nod.

I thought back to the arched wooden doors carved between the trees in Elandrew through which Breck had taken me.

"This stone circle is protected, warded with Vanir's shields to glamour any use of magic and power from being detected by the outside world. We're safe to train here without any unwanted visitors like the keres paying us a visit."

That was a relief. I scanned the area, thinking that at least if there were any keres lurking around, we would be able to see them from a good distance away.

"All right. So . . . what's first?"

Niall glanced up at the sky, monitoring the darkening clouds as they gathered and bulged. "I want you to start by exploring the well of power within you," he said. "We need to know what you're working with before you channel it in a physical form. Focus on your power and call it forward like you did when you fortified your mental shield."

I closed my eyes and began the descent, summoning the core of energy in the center of my chest. A gentle coaxing just like before.

My power hummed underneath my skin, breathing again as if for the first time. It was like an ancient being, but one that I recognized something of myself in. It belonged to me. And I willed it to obey my command. The energy coursed through my veins, cooling my blood as it pulsed through me.

When I opened my eyes, a faint white light had settled around me like an aura.

Niall looked fascinated, and he rubbed at his jawline as he stepped closer. "Good," he said, nodding in approval. "By calling it forward, you're asserting control. You must train it to obey your command. If it's as strong as I think it is, you'll need to have a firm grip on it and learn to expel it in a healthy and controlled way. It will learn your triggers, your strengths, and weaknesses, as well as your nature and tendencies. I'll teach you the methods that worked best for me when we get to that point."

My triggers. My strengths and weaknesses. I wasn't even sure I knew what all of those were.

Death of a loved one . . .

Trigger.

Persevering when learning a new skill . . .

Strength.

My focus became ruffled as I watched the wind whip at Niall's hair, lifting the longer strands and dropping them onto his forehead. My fingertips twitched with the sudden urge to push back the errant strands, and I blinked rapidly and clenched my fists, realizing my distraction.

Weakness.

Shit.

"Everything all right?" he asked.

I nodded a bit excessively, using the motion to shake myself back into focus. "Just, uh, getting my head straight."

A quick flash of light bolted through the sky and thunder tumbled after it, resetting the scene.

Niall took a step toward me. "Good. Physical shielding requires some concentration. When your body feels threatened or senses danger your natural fight-or-flight instincts kick in and so does your power. You can channel it to produce a shield for yourself or for others, or both. Right now, I want you to focus on manifesting one for yourself. It's a simple command, but one you must feel. Imagine pushing your power out as a forcefield that encases your body."

I concentrated my gaze on the muddy, shredded grass that my boot had scuffed into mush. As my focus shifted from summoning my power, to wielding it, the glow faded from my skin, absorbing back into me only to be pushed out again in the form of a shield. A strong pulse of energy radiated from deep within my chest, and I commanded it just as Niall had instructed, envisioning a bubble around me similar to the one he'd manifested. The shield flickered to life around me and settled into a steady barrier that hovered near my skin.

Feeling triumphant, I lifted my head, only to catch a glimpse of Niall's black flame just as he struck. It lashed against my shield only to be repelled. As it slunk back toward him, I smirked.

Then, I pushed out a pulse of power. It hurdled into Niall and sent him careening backward unsteadily before he regained his footing.

"Auren," he growled.

"What?" I held my hands up, suppressing a smile.

The corner of his mouth lifted, and this time I saw a flicker of black flame move from behind his shoulders.

My shield held, thwarting his efforts, and I pushed my power out again —a bit more forcefully. The wave slammed into him, sending him lunging backward, his boots digging harsh lines several feet long through the once perfect grass. He snapped his head up and glared at me when he finally came to a halt.

"Come on *High Lord,* I'm just an amateur after all," I said, letting my shield fall away and taunting him with my tone as if it was no effort to throw him off.

In a blink, I was staring at empty space as he snatched me from behind. His right arm came up around my throat, fitting the crevice of his elbow against my neck in one quick movement, while his left hand twisted mine around my back.

Normally, I would have panicked at the fact that my neck was completely enclosed; that my breath could be snipped off with one brutal squeeze. But my senses didn't react as if I was in danger. My power didn't even stir within me. It was as if something deep inside me knew he wouldn't hurt me.

His breath warmed my neck as he pressed into my ear and said, "You know, it only takes a second for me to incinerate someone from the inside out." He shifted his stance against me, tucking me tighter to his body. "You threw away your advantage by getting cocky. I'd advise against that."

I patted his right hip with my free hand. "And *you've* made a fatal mistake. Had you been wearing a blade, it would be mine now, and you'd be bleeding out from a severed artery . . . right about here." I tapped the inside of his thigh to indicate just where my reach would have dealt the killing slice. He pressed his lower body further up against my backside, as if drawn to my touch.

Lightning splintered through the clouds and thunder cracked around us.

"Careful with that hand, Bringer of Light, or you'll bring something else upon yourself."

I found myself leaning back into his arms. He was solid as stone from head to toe, every muscle taut and hewn from the mountains he hailed from. Not only was I enjoying the feel of him being so close, but I was finding a new sort of thrill in showing him what I was capable of.

My chest thrummed at a heightened pace. "You have no other physical weaponry that I'm aware of," I quipped.

"Ah, but that's where you're wrong." He loosened my hand from behind my back, letting it fall to my side and allowing him to be fully against me. I blushed at his new positioning, and at *all* of him that I now felt; thick and heavy and situated against my backside. "Want to amend your statement?" he purred against my neck.

Another flash of lightning sent a more menacing rumble through the sky. The air smelled of dirt and rain as the wind kicked up around us in a faint howl, but Niall continued to hold me tightly against him.

"Are you this brash with everyone else?" I said breathily, wiggling slightly against his hold.

He shifted his weight, and a growl rolled through his chest like the thunder around us. "Just you it seems." His lips grazed my ear as he released my neck.

I turned around to face him, beholding his smirk.

The cool wind was now whipping our hair as the scent of rain grew closer.

"Lesson number one of physical shielding: always be quicker than your opponent. Lesson two: never assume they can't get past your shield. Always be on the defensive, regardless."

He was right. I'd dropped my guard for a split second when I had the upper-hand, and he'd pounced, just like he had during our mind-shielding lesson.

Raindrops began pelting the ground around us. I raised my hand to shield my face from the onslaught, but the moment I lost my view of him, I knew I'd made a mistake.

He seized the opportunity and lunged, snagging me around the waist and porting me to yet another unknown destination.

46

VAHRENHALL

W<small>HEN WE MATERIALIZED, I WAS INSTANTLY PELTED IN THE FACE WITH</small> rain.

I quickly pushed my power out to form my shield when I noticed Niall staring down at me, his face still taking the assault from the large raindrops. His eyes glinted with a silent challenge that seemed to say *what about me?*

Never one to back down from a challenge, I willed my power to shield him as well. It took a bit more force, but the raindrops ceased as the invisible barrier encapsulated him.

He lingered a moment to see if the effort held, then he grinned. "If you insist." He eased me forward with a gentle hand against my lower back. "If you falter now, we're going to be very cold and very wet."

Great, no pressure.

I concentrated on holding the shield as best I could as we moved along the cobbled street.

We had materialized in a much more populated area this time.

A city—by the looks of it.

This one was a stark contrast to the Woodland Court and the human realm. Clusters of buildings lined the street we were on, each one made of darkened timber, with grand wooden beams that curved upward towards the sky at the ends, and steep, sloped roofs—some made of thatch and others made of thick, blackened shingles.

We maneuvered around several fae who were sloshing through the water as shops closed their windows and merchants pulled coverings over their vendor carts, tucking them under nearby awnings.

It was a market. Axes and spears, hides and wools, bottles and crates —I caught a glimpse of each before they were covered.

The rain was coming down in heavy droves now, blowing sideways with each gust of wind, cascading off the thatched roofs, and rushing in streams down the sides of the dark stone street.

"Why don't they just shield themselves?" I asked Niall as I watched the locals scramble.

"Takes too much effort. All fae have a well of power in them, but most would exhaust themselves holding a shield for a long period of time. It's easier for them to just find shelter and save their power for the magic they use in their daily tasks."

Under a covered entryway to our left, a female gave her head a rough shake, and her sopping hair was instantly dried. She then waved a hand down her body, and the water evaporated from her dress. She fluffed out the pleated skirt and went inside to wait out the storm.

Niall nodded toward what we'd both just witnessed. "Believe it or not, that actually uses up less power than a shield."

"Huh," I mused. "And you couldn't just do that for us?"

He chuckled lightly. "Where's the fun in that? You're training, remember? And I never take the easy way out."

Figures.

Up ahead, there was an immense structure that stood taller than any other nearby. Four levels stretched into the sky, each shrinking in width as they stacked atop one another. I peered up at the vaulted roof peaks. The wood beams ended in carved depictions of what looked like wild serpent beasts with spiked heads and scaled skin, their wooden tongues frozen in a flailing motion between their open maws. Double doors made of thick, weather-worn wood, that bore countless marks and gouges, greeted us at ground level.

"Your sword, Auren," Niall said as we approached.

I gave him a wary look. "What for?"

He gestured toward the door. "It's tradition for new travelers to leave their mark before entering The Great Hall. If you wish to enter, you must make the mark with your blade."

I unsheathed my sword, and he stepped aside allowing me plenty of room to strike.

It took me a moment to focus on maintaining the shield around us while swinging my sword, but I managed. In one clean movement I sliced a gash in the left half of the door. The mark flared briefly with a white light before fading out, and with a loud clang, the doors unlatched and slowly swung inward.

Niall's essence brushed up against my mental shield, checking it. He gave me a bemused look. "You've held both shields intact this entire time?"

"You act like it's challenging, *High Lord*."

I stepped forward through the doors, dropping the physical shield behind me a bit early and letting a splash of water fall from the eave right onto his forehead. He stalked after me, slicking back his newly wet locks of hair and shaking his fingers out at his side, his throaty laugh promising sweet retribution at the next available opportunity.

The smell of wood burning fires and something like sweet ale mingled in the damp air inside The Great Hall. The ceiling vaulted the span of all four tiers I'd seen on the outside, narrowing as it rose, and coming to a point high above. Smoke danced amongst the rafters and curled around the thick wood beams where huge, rounded fixtures were suspended, each one stacked high with hundreds of flaming candles.

There were several wooden pillars lining each side of the grand space, separating a center area with an impressively long wooden table from the sections that housed smaller tables along the outskirts of the room. Cracked, battle worn shields with scrolling symbols etched along the edges hung on each pillar.

And at the far end of the hall, under a giant antlered skull, sat a large wooden throne upon a bed of furs and hides. Two sizable copper basins of fire framed each end of the dais on which the rustic throne sat.

The details suddenly faded to the background as the room's occupants became the forefront of my focus. Several tables were full of fae eating hearty plates of meat, drinking from mugs the size of my face, and conversing in good company. None seemed to pay us any mind aside from a few lingering glances.

Vanir's tall, broad frame rose up from a small table on the right side of the room. His long dark-blond hair was braided back down the center of his scalp once more and freshly shaven on the sides, accenting the points of his ears. The fur pelt that lay over his shoulders emphasized his breadth and managed to make him look even more hulking. His woven, sleeveless tunic showed off his muscular arms that ended in leather cuffs around both his wrists. Around his waist was a leather belt from which an axe hung, and his pants tucked into his calf-high, worn leather boots.

A warrior bred for battle.

I didn't recall him looking so rugged at Lumeri.

He strode right up to Niall, and they clasped each other's forearms with a loud clap. The warm greeting of two friends. He braced his other hand on Niall's shoulder, his own shoulders shaking as he let out a breathy laugh. "Do I need to be on the lookout for anyone chasing you this time?"

Niall smiled. "You know I hate depriving you of a good fight, but unfortunately not this time, old friend."

Vanir grunted and turned his attention to me. "Welcome to Vahrenhall, Auren. Your blade left a fine cut. The gods will be pleased."

"Thank you. This place is unlike anything I've ever seen." I glanced back up at the ceiling high above.

Vanir lifted his eyes as well. "It's been kept as it was since my great ancestors lived and ate and drank within these walls. You'll find that we are a bit more traditional here in this territory." He looked toward Niall. "This one, on the other hand, enjoys his comforts and the pleasures of a more contemporary lifestyle."

Niall made a show of looking around the room. "Yes, well, that's the one area where our standards do differ."

Vanir grinned. "Come. You're just in time for some fresh meat and ale. That storm is going to be raging for a while anyway. No sense training in it." He turned and led us to a long table, where several fae males gathered their mugs and vacated their spots for the three of us.

I whispered to Niall, "How did he know we were training out there?"

Niall grinned and tapped his temple with his finger.

Right. Mind-walking.

"So, he knows? About me? About my . . ."

"Mmm-hmm," Niall hummed as we followed Vanir through the room.

Breck had mentioned that Niall had gone to have a chat with Vanir back in Elandrew. He must have filled him in then.

We sat, and a female immediately brought us heaping plates of roasted chicken and potatoes, along with three large mugs.

My stomach let out a loud growl.

"Ale for my oldest friend, and cider for my newest," Vanir said, raising his mug to both of us. Niall toasted and happily took a long swig of his, while I cautiously sniffed at mine.

Vanir's brows furrowed in confusion.

"She just came off a rough night with Killian's elderberry liqueur," Niall informed him.

The High Lord of the Highland Court leaned forward, shaking his head. "Fuck. That stuff is brutal. This drink is nothing of the sort. It might actually help any lingering fog in your head from those damn elderberries. You don't need to worry." He gave me a heavy pat on my shoulder—his attempt at reassurance.

He seemed sincere enough, so I dared a sip.

It was a mild ale with a taste of clean, crisp apples and a hint of sweetness that lingered on my tongue. Pleasantly refreshing.

"I won't go near that elderberry shit," Vanir continued, frowning into his mug. "Had one of the worst hangovers of my life after Lumeri in the Woodland Court when I was younger. Never again."

Niall pointed a finger at him over his ale. "I remember that night." A snarky grin spread across his face. "I walked in on you in *my* bedchamber with three females, a house-fae, and a whole lot of empty bottles."

I swung my head toward Vanir, wide-eyed and waiting to hear more.

He cracked a smile of his own. "That was a fucking good time— something all Lumeri celebrations are known to provoke." He threw me a wink.

"Don't get any ideas, Van," Niall teased.

Vanir simply chuckled in reply and drained his mug in one final gulp. "Please, eat," he said.

I wasted no time devouring the delicious food. When I looked up,

Vanir was watching me with a raised brow, and I grinned a bit sheepishly through my mouthful of chicken.

"When was the last time you ate anything?" he asked.

"This morning. But my meals have mainly been sugared bread and some fruit."

Vanir looked at Niall, who said, "You know how little Killian cares about ensuring his guests are taken care of."

"And it didn't cross your mind to sneak some meat and cheese from his kitchens for her?"

Niall reclined in his chair. "I had to keep a low profile. Snatching food from the kitchens wouldn't have aided in that, now would it?"

I pictured Niall doing just that: tip-toeing around the kitchens late at night, sneaking meats and cheeses and whatever else he could find into a little basket for me. The thought made me laugh, and I coughed, trying not to choke on my food.

"Not a statement I thought I'd hear from the Lord of Glamours," Vanir said with a rough chuckle.

I raised a brow at Niall. "Lord of Glamours, huh?"

"Vanir is just easily impressed."

"And rightfully so," Vanir said. "Never met someone as profound at glamours as him."

Niall lifted his mug and stared into it. "The skill is something I owe to my mother. She had a particular knack for it." He took a long swig, not elaborating further.

"So, what's your plan from here?" Vanir asked, seeing the shift in Niall's demeanor and changing the subject.

"Killian expects her back this evening," Niall said. "And I need to have a word with Breck." He met my eyes with a very serious expression. "But you will not be attending another meeting with Killian."

Relief washed over me.

"Do you think it's wise for the two of you to go back after you've already left?" Vanir questioned.

Niall sipped his ale. "Actually, Van, I was going to suggest that Auren stay here with you for the brief time that I'm gone."

My eyes widened, words of protest building on my tongue. While I was sure Vanir was a decent male, I didn't want to be left alone in another territory that I knew nothing about, and a strange pit opened up in my gut at the thought of being apart from Niall.

"But I want to go with you," I objected before Vanir could get a word in.

Niall met my wide-eyed stare. "Auren, it's safest if you stay out of the Woodland Court. If Killian were to get his hands on you—"

"You said I'm safest with *you,* remember?"

Silence stretched between us. Vanir flicked his eyes back and forth from Niall to me, waiting. Finally, Niall's resolve crumbled, and he nodded. "You're right." He set his mug down on the table and traced the rim with his forefinger. "But you'll have to stay in your chambers when we get there, while I talk with Breck."

"I will."

Then, a thought crossed my mind. "But won't Killian know when we arrive? We have to pass back through the gate—" I cut my words short when Niall lifted a scheming brow at me. "You're going to glamour us aren't you?" His answering grin was all the confirmation I needed.

Vanir leaned forward over the table. "Are you sure you can trust Breck? He's the High Lord's cousin. There's got to be at least some ambition there."

The fact that Breck was Killian's cousin had always perplexed me. The two were nothing alike. They looked far from related, and their lives couldn't be more opposite. Breck enjoyed the forest. By all accounts he was made for it. Killian seemed out of place. He didn't quite fit.

"Breck doesn't seem like the type," I said. "He's always spoken with respect toward Killian."

"Just because he speaks respectfully, does not mean he's incapable of being disrespectful," Niall clipped.

"All I'm saying is that I trust him. He led me to safety and took care of me when I first crossed The Veil. He taught me a lot about this realm, actually. If not for him, I don't think I'd be as at ease with everything that has transpired."

Niall speared his chicken and conceded. "I agree . . . that we can trust him. He's always been trustworthy in the many years that I've known him. But I will speak to him about how that last situation was handled, and I can't guarantee that it'll be pleasant."

"What happens after?" I asked.

"We go home," Niall said smoothly.

Vanir raised his brows at his friend. "So soon?"

"I have a few matters that need to be taken care of." He held Vanir's stare like there was more he wasn't saying out loud.

Vanir gave a subtle nod. I searched his expression, but his face didn't betray his thoughts—nor did it give away any hint of what Niall had said to him in his head. He reached for his ale, raising it between the three of us once more. "To your endeavors."

Niall and I raised ours in response.

"The gate is always open, should you need to pass through here again this evening. It's time for *our* Lumeri after all. We'll be having the bonfire out near the foothills. Auren might enjoy it. Surely you can spare a night." He gave Niall a particularly mischievous look.

My eyes lit up at the thought of another Lumeri. I began trying to imagine what would take place, given that this territory was vastly different from Elandrew.

"In the meantime," Vanir continued, "feel free to show her around once this rain lets up. I'll have the guest house prepared and outfitted, just in case."

"Thank you, my friend." Niall bowed his head in gratitude.

With that, Vanir stood up and clasped Niall on the shoulder before offering me a smile. "Excuse me while I go make my rounds."

I watched him weave through the room toward a group of what looked like huntsmen that just entered the hall. "He's actually very pleasant."

"He may look like a brute in every way, but he's a big softie. He reserves that side of himself only for a select few though, so you should feel honored."

I recalled the night that I met him. "Laurent wouldn't let him speak to me at Lumeri out of fear that he would scare me off."

"He's always a bit on edge when he's in other territories. It's probably best that you didn't strike up a conversation with him then. You might have come in here thinking differently."

Niall tipped his ale back and finished it.

I finished my cider too and licked my lips, reaching for the new mug as it appeared on the table. "I could grow to really like this stuff. I can't even feel the effects of it." Surprisingly, the lingering effects of the elderberry had vanished as well.

Niall laughed. "It's a watered-down version. They reserve the stout stuff for nights like tonight. And just wait until you try one of *my* court's specialties. With your affinity for sweet things, I know you'll be begging me for more of it once you get a taste."

The insinuation in his words wasn't lost on me. I eyed him, trying to see if he truly spoke of a particular drink or of something else entirely. When his grin turned mischievous, I had to turn away to keep from blushing at the implication.

"For now," he said as he stood, "if you feel up for a little more shielding practice, I can give you a tour before we need to head back to Elandrew. Bring your drink with you—an incentive to keep the shield up."

He plucked his new mug from the table and gestured toward the door. I stood, grabbing my cider, and stuck my tongue out at him as I walked past him.

Before we reached the door, he gently snagged my arm and murmured playfully in my ear, "I will have you know that if you get water in my ale like you did on my hair, I will have no choice but to reprimand you."

I fought back a grin as I pushed out my physical shield to encompass both of us.

Good girl, he purred into my mind.

His words sparked an ember in my core. I whipped my head back around to him with an incredulous look on my face. "Do you have to say stuff like *that?*"

"Sensitive to certain phrases?" he simpered.

I feigned a sound of disgust and turned my back to him, hearing him chuckle deeply behind me. "Careful or my shield might just slip," I called back over my shoulder as he reached around me to pull open the door.

His eyes flashed golden, and I heard his voice in my head say, *I dare you.*

The rain had eased slightly, but it was still coming down enough for me to be thankful for my shield, which held—for now. As long as I remained focused.

Niall kept casting distracting side-glances at me while we walked. I swore he was fighting back that damned grin as he told me about

Vahrenhall. I knew he was curious as to how long I'd be able to hold both shields *and* concentrate on what he was saying.

When I attempted to ask a question, my mental shield faltered. I recovered it quickly—only to fumble with the physical one. And in the midst of the error, Niall stopped and peered down into his mug, assessing if a raindrop had found its way into it during the brief lapse. I watched him, half thinking he was joking about the comment he'd made, and half wondering what his version of reprimanding consisted of.

"So close," he said as he walked past me.

I didn't know whether or not that meant I'd been quick enough, but I decided that if I didn't ask, he might forget about it. There was also the fact that if I *did* ask again, I'd probably lose one of the shields a second time.

We finished off our drinks as we walked, and the mugs vanished from our hands.

Around us, a few vendors had begun reopening as the rain lessened. To our left, the worn door of a shop was propped open, and Niall grabbed my hand and pulled me inside.

We were greeted by an older male whose thick gray hair was braided similarly to Vanir's and whose full beard covered his neck down to his collarbone. He dusted off his stained apron and removed his long leather gloves. "How can I be of service to you two today?"

The man was a trapper. All manner of animal hides, skins, and pelts hung from the rafters and were stuffed into cubbies.

My attention snagged on a basket that sat on a small wooden stool just inside the entry, and I ran my hand through the soft black and white furs that were spilling over the edge.

"Shopping for a nice, warm cloak for the lady," Niall said.

I looked up realizing he was referring to me. "Niall, I—"

He cut me off by holding up a hand.

"Certainly, my lord." The older male bowed. "Let me take a look at you, my dear." His well-worn and calloused hands gently patted my shoulders before he spun me around slowly. Wrinkled, gray-blue eyes assessed me for a long moment before his head bobbed with a confirming nod. "I believe I have just the thing for you." He held up a finger as he turned around and disappeared into a back room through a small doorway in the corner.

In his absence, I turned to Niall. "I don't have—"

"Relax. Let me take care of this. It gets much cooler here in the evenings than in Elandrew, and you'll need it for the mountains as well."

I bit my lip and didn't argue. The small bundles of fur pulled at my attention again, and I admired them as we waited.

Moments later, the trapper returned with a mound of black wool in his arms. "Try this on." He unfolded it, revealing a long cloak with a thick pelt of peppered, black and white fur around the collar. He placed it around my shoulders and stepped back, admiring the fit. "Yes, yes, the perfect size I think."

It was just long enough to graze the backs of my knees, offering plenty of warmth for my body.

"This was woven by my mate." He ran his shaky fingers along the hemline as his gaze drifted off on a memory. "She made it for herself but was never able to wear it. It seems, I have finally found someone who can." He dusted off the shoulders. "The fur is of a silver highland fox. The prettiest in the land."

My fingertips reached up to graze the fine pelage.

I'd never owned a cloak of such high quality. I imagined the trapper's mate stitching every thread in the back corner of this stone-gray room. Knitting every inch with love. "It is truly beautiful. Are you sure you're willing to part with it?"

He smiled gently. "The time to let it go is long overdue. She was fond of those foxes—the silver ones. The ones you went to when you walked in." He gestured toward the basket I'd been pawing through. "It would please me if you would wear it."

My eyes burned, and I blinked away the sting of tears as I mustered a smile.

"What can I give you for this?" Niall spoke softly.

The old trapper shook his head and hands simultaneously. "No need for that, my lord. It is a gift."

I looked around the small shop. It was in desperate need of repairs, and the rafters could use some reinforcing. The chair behind his work table had definitely seen better days. I wanted to protest that we would pay him regardless, but I wasn't in the position to do so, since I had no coin to pay for it myself.

Niall reached out a hand to the trapper who clasped it and nodded.

"Now, go on," the trapper said, shoeing us out the door. "Lumeri is tonight, and I'm sure you have preparations to make."

I thanked him as we stepped out into the spitting rain, and he waved us goodbye from the threshold.

As the door closed and we started walking, I heard a large thud back inside the shop, followed by a whooping cry of astonishment and glee. The door behind us yanked open, and the trapper called out to us, but Niall just grinned and waved his hand over his shoulder as we continued walking.

I looked back, and upon seeing the tears in the trapper's eyes, the pinch of his brow, and the astonishment that bracketed his mouth, I knew that Niall had paid him far more than just enough for the cloak.

47
FRIEND OR FOE?

An hour later, we stood at the edge of the city on a rocky outcrop that overlooked the rain-soaked landscape.

Vahrenhall—for all its vast, untamed expanse—felt like a peaceful glen, hidden from the world. Farms and homesteads dotted the hills as far as I could see. Smoke rose from chimneys, and horses grazed freely over the plush, highland grass. It was a peaceful sight, similar to the farms in the far reaches of Galenagh.

The mountains to the west loomed, standing watch along the horizon, and I knew it was only a matter of time before I'd journey there too.

At least, I *hoped* to.

Niall had mentioned it in conversation with Vanir, which, in turn, had spurred something in me. Some strange feeling of yearning. An urge to get closer to those mountains and what lay within them. I glanced over to where the High Lord of those very mountains stood next to me, staring out across the highlands.

His rugged features ensnared me like they always did. My eyes traced the profile of his face, and I watched as the damp breeze ruffled the stray strands of hair that fluttered across his forehead.

The corner of his mouth lifted when he felt my lingering stare. "You held both shields in the trapper's shop," he said.

I blinked, letting the words sink in before realizing he was right.

"*And* you engaged in a conversation while doing so. I'm thoroughly impressed."

I smiled down at myself. "I did, didn't I? I wasn't even thinking about it."

"If I had to bet, I'd say you were thinking too hard about it before and not trusting your power."

"You're probably right," I agreed.

In the distance, a few horses brayed, drawing our attention back out to where they'd taken to romping wildly through the glistening countryside.

"Tonight's celebration is a sight to see," he said. "The Woodland Court may boast about their outfits and finery at their Lumeri, but here in Vahrenhall, it's just as enchanting—without all the pomp. The pyre will burn into the early morning hours—if not longer. But it's best to see it when it's first lit."

"Will we make it back in time?" I asked.

"I'll make sure that we do."

"What exactly is the plan when we get back to Elandrew?"

I wasn't excited to be returning, but the thought of being away from Niall was worse. It chafed at my insides and made my heart a little more anxious. The feeling made no sense to me, but I couldn't ignore it.

I was also slightly worried that Killian would somehow sniff me out and summon me, so I needed to know that there was a failsafe. Getting stuck in the Woodland Court and being Killian's prisoner was not an ending I would accept.

Niall faced me. "I'll port you to your chambers, and then I'll take care of my business with Breck. If anyone else comes to collect you, do not answer the door. Keep your shields up at all times. I'll be back for you as soon as I'm finished."

"Leaving me alone to shield myself, huh? I must be getting pretty good," I said playfully.

He let out a light-hearted chuckle. "For someone who's only practiced for half a day, your skills are exceptional."

"Guess I have a pretty decent teacher." I grinned up at him.

"I'm glad to hear that you approve." The smile that stretched across his face sent my heart fluttering. He stepped closer and reached both his hands out toward me, closing his fingers around mine when I placed them in his grasp. "We should get going before it gets too late."

"Are you going to glamour us now?"

"It's already done," he said.

I looked down at myself. "I don't feel any different."

"That's because I'm so good at it."

A laugh burst from my throat. "What happened to your advice of not being cocky?"

"Sometimes it's necessary." He winked.

I rolled my eyes and fought back my grin. "Hypocrite."

"Call me a hypocrite all you want," he said, pulling me closer, "but my hypocrisy is what's going to get us past the gate without Killian knowing it's you and me."

"And just how is that possible?"

"When he senses our arrival, it'll seem like two commoners. No hint or trace of our actual selves. I could make it to where we're invisible all together—like I've done before—but then he would know something was amiss, because the physical presence would be detected by the wards regardless. Unfortunately, there's no glamour that can trick the territorial wards into not sensing a presence."

I nodded, wondering who he'd glamoured me to look like.

"Are you ready?"

"To port? Ready as I can be." I tightened my grip.

"They say the fifth time's a charm."

"Do they actually say that?" I asked skeptically.

He pulled me into his arms. "Let's find out."

Before I could protest or prepare, we vanished.

Niall was mostly right. Or the cider had helped a lot more than I imagined it would. This round of porting was indeed easier.

My bedchamber was exactly as I had left it. After checking the area and both of my shields, Niall departed, assuring me he would hurry back.

I strolled over to the armoire, and opened it, finding only the handful of items I knew were there—a few ill-fitting beige tunics, a pair of leggings, and Breck's dagger that I'd worn under my dress the night of Killian's little dinner party. I eyed the weapon, before taking it off the shelf and walking over to the bed with it.

The sheath was well-worn, and it could use a new buckle. I turned it over in my hands, recalling how Breck had handed it to me with such pride. Like it was a piece of him that would be there to protect me if need be.

He was a good male. He cared for me and wanted to protect me. But he was going to have to let me go.

I placed the blade at the edge of the bed and laid a hand on it. He'd find it here, I had no doubt.

Perhaps if I left a note . . . to thank him . . .

Yes, I needed to thank him. But how?

My eyes scanned the space, finally falling upon the *Seidr.* It sat on the side table near the chair Niall had slept in, next to the folded robe that Sorscha had given me. As I eyed the book, a thought popped into my head. There were handwritten notes on slips of paper that had been stuck between some of the pages. If I could just tear a blank piece off one of the scribe's notes and write a small word of thanks on it—

Suddenly the air in the room changed, a shift in the atmosphere that I could feel, and just as I registered it, my shield rippled behind me. An object ricocheted off the invisible barrier, the sound echoing in my mind like a muffled clang.

When I turned, I saw the dark-haired female from Killian's dinner standing with a dagger raised in her fist.

Morah.

Muscle memory slid into place, and I unsheathed my sword while stepping into the openness of the room.

She tried to kill me!

I hadn't heard her come in, same as the first time when she'd slipped into Killian's meeting room without a sound.

The reality that I would have been bleeding out alone in my chambers if Niall hadn't shown me how to shield myself hit me as I stood there, waiting for Morah to move.

Her face was contorted with disbelief. Clearly, her intentions were thwarted by the shield she didn't expect me to have. She seemed caught between whether to stay or flee. But I blocked her line of exit.

Unless she could port . . .

If she could port, she could attack from any angle.

I double checked my shields again. Both were intact.

Another round of holding two shields and a conversation wasn't on my list of plans today. And I was also a little wary of how well they'd hold up if I was engaged in a sword fight, but I'd have to try my best, and trust in my power, if it came down to that.

I took in Morah's presence as she continued to stand there. She was about my height, and thin, but more blessed in the chest than I was. Her arms were slender and toned, like mine. Her long dark brown hair hung loosely down to her lower back, and her form-fitting teal dress accentuated her hips. She looked to be about my age, but her pointed ears meant she might very well be hundreds of years old.

After a long, awkward moment of us staring across the room at each other, she finally lowered her blade. Her full lips parted. "You have a shield," was all she said, surveying me like I was a wild animal.

"I do," I replied.

She shifted uneasily, palming the small blade in her right hand.

"You're Morah," I said, recalling her name from the other night when she had interrupted Killian.

She ignored my statement. "How are you being shielded?"

I decided to ignore her question too. "How did you get in my chambers?"

More awkward silence.

A pin-pricking sensation skittered over my entire body. "You're not glamoured . . ." she assessed.

Was that what that feeling was? Being checked for a glamour?

I raised a brow at her. "So, you were just going to come in here and try to kill me?"

"I wasn't going to kill you. Just threaten you and have you answer some questions."

"By holding a blade to my throat?" I took a step and angled my sword down at her, taking the dominating position.

She stood her ground, but I caught the slightest flinch in her legs as she studied my movement. Judging by her stance and awareness, I could tell she was good at predicting someone's next move. Her shoulder lifted in an arrogant shrug. "Creature of habit, I'm afraid. And yes, my name is Morah."

We stared each other down, and I reinforced the angle of my blade at her chest.

"You don't fear me?" she questioned, seeming a bit puzzled.

"No," I said sternly. "Why are you here, Morah?"

She watched my blade. "Like I said, to ask you some questions. You can start by telling me how you're being shielded, human? Who is casting it?"

I said nothing.

A cruel smile tugged on the corners of her mouth. "You're not human at all, are you?"

I tightened the grip on my sword. "You're mistaken."

Now would be a great time for Niall to show up.

"Don't lie to me. You are no more human than I am." Her voice grew more condescending with each word. "The moment I saw you enter this place at Breck's side, I knew something about you was different."

"Then apparently you're pretty bad at making observations." I wasn't sure how much further I could deny it. One attempt to tap into my mind and she would see that I was shielded there too and know that it was of my own doing.

"You may have all the High Lords fooled, but you don't fool me. Who, and what, are you?"

"I am Auren, daughter of Thiago and Maris, I—"

"Your name is already known. Spare me the unnecessary details." She twirled her blade in her palm as she waited.

"I'm just a human."

Despite the ease of claiming to be human, I had a hard time believing the words as they came out this time. A part of me seemed to have changed since I'd willingly tapped into my power. Saying that I was human no longer even sounded right.

What was worse now, was that it didn't *feel* right either.

"Then what interest do you have with Killian?" she asked defensively.

I gave a gruff laugh. "I have zero interest in Killian, I can assure you."

"Then stay away from him," she warned, halting her blade twirling for a brief moment before resuming.

"Trust me, I'm doing my best."

"Didn't look that way the other night."

Oh, she's jealous.

"What did it look like then?"

Morah's face darkened. "It looked like someone who needed to be put in her place." She switched the blade to her other hand, quick as a blink.

"And who is he to *you?*" I asked.

She was quiet for a moment, like she was mulling over something she didn't quite want to admit. "He is my betrothed."

Betrothed?

I began lowering my sword. "Good luck with that," I said, feeling a bit sorry for her.

She stared at her blade now. "It's not by choice."

I waited for her to look back up at me, but she continued focusing on her dagger.

"Your father is Ramil?" I had only guessed it at dinner, but seeing the resemblance and hearing her speak, I was almost certain I was right.

This time, her eyes met mine. "How did you know?"

"You two have similar features."

She went back to examining her blade.

"You don't approve of the match between you and Killian?" I pressed.

"Did I say that?" she snapped. When I didn't reply, she sighed deeply, a bit of that condescending façade cracking. "Anyone in their right mind would stay far away from Killian. But my father's court is in a very tight alliance with him."

"And you must do as he says?"

She pushed her shoulders back. "My father isn't one to take 'no' for an answer."

I would think not. Ramil seemed like someone who always got what he wanted. And if she was his daughter . . . "Are you like your father then?"

She snickered brashly. "What, sitting around waiting on others to do my dirty work? No. I have my own set of skills and I put them to good use. Besides, this court needs some restructuring. Killian belittles it more and more with every year that passes." She tapped her blade against her opposite palm before sliding it into a hidden pocket at her hip. "I don't even know why I'm telling you this."

"Because you know I'm not a threat," I answered simply, hoping she'd agree.

Her deep brown eyes scanned over me, not totally trusting, but her expression did lean more toward favor than not. "Why are you here Auren? In our realm?"

Just as I was about to reply, a knock sounded at the door.

Shit.

If it was Niall, he wouldn't like the looks of this. But knowing him, he would have just ported straight in, unannounced . . .

So definitely not him then.

Fuck.

A second knock came. Morah's frantic expression told me she didn't want to be caught in here or in the middle of what was about to happen, so I did the only thing I could . . .

"Who is it?" I called out.

"It's me," a smooth, silvery voice called back.

Relief washed over me. "Come in, Maeson."

Upon hearing the name, Morah's eyes widened.

The door swung open and Maeson's delightful smile immediately turned sour as she beheld Morah and I. She quickly shut the door behind her. "What's going on here?"

"A misunderstanding," I replied, looking at Morah, who nodded slowly in return.

Maeson came to stand by my side, warily eyeing the intruder. "Sneaking into places you shouldn't be, Morah?"

Morah snorted.

"You two know each other?" I asked.

"In a manner of speaking, yes," Maeson answered.

"She knows *of* me," Morah corrected her.

Maeson rolled her eyes.

"Morah snuck in and nearly held a blade to my throat. We were—"

"*Nearly?*" Maeson cut in.

Morah crossed her arms. "Your friend here has a shield up. I couldn't touch her."

Maeson looked over at me with shock. "How?"

I gave my friend a look to remind her that we weren't alone in this conversation, and I wasn't sure if the information should be openly shared, especially with someone who had Killian's ear.

She caught on. "Right . . ." She drew out the word.

"Yes, I'm still here," Morah said, clearly annoyed.

"You shouldn't be though." Maeson cut her a look. "Why were you sneaking in here anyway? Auren has done nothing wrong to you."

Morah leaned against the chair closest to her. "I wasn't going to hurt her. I just wanted to set some boundaries."

I looked at Maeson. "Like I said, a misunderstanding."

Morah continued. "What I don't understand though, is how she has a shield. If someone is casting it for her they must have a damn good reason. And if she's doing it herself, well then, there are some things I truly don't know yet."

Maeson and I swapped glances, each trying to read the other.

Then a thought popped into my head. Niall had created the bridge between us in order for him to mind-walk. I wasn't exactly sure how it worked, but maybe that bridge always stayed open . . .

I looked into my mind—where our essences always met—and anxiously called out to him. *Where are you?*

No response. He must be busy. Or maybe the mind-walking, err —*talking*—didn't reach across certain distances. Or didn't work from my end after all. I was stupid to think it would.

Maeson faced me. "I only know three things about Morah, and of those things I'm certain about all of them."

"Oh, do tell," Morah butted in sarcastically.

Maeson continued as if Morah wasn't there. "She is known for her deadly skill with daggers, she moves as silently as a wraith, and . . . she is not her father."

Morah appeared surprised by the words. "Well, on those things, we can agree."

The tension seemed to ease.

"When she says you're not your father, what does she mean?" I asked.

"Tell her," Maeson commanded.

Morah glared at her. "It's no secret that my father has his own agenda. He has for many years. Not even I know all of his plans, but part of them includes marrying me off to Killian. It will solidify the alliance between our courts."

Maeson frowned. "And you truly trust that all he wants is to strengthen the dynamic of our courts?"

"Did I say that I trusted him?" Morah snapped. "Regardless, I cannot question him. I do what I'm told. I have to."

I watched her closely. "Did he threaten you?"

"Not in so many words. My father deals in . . . other things." She looked to Maeson and inclined her head. "You know what I speak of."

Maeson stiffened. "That was something I'd only assumed but never confirmed."

"Well, take it from me, he has an arsenal at his disposal."

Maeson chewed the inside of her cheek, taking Morah's words into account.

Niall's voice suddenly danced across my mind. *Are you about ready, darling?*

I released a breath. *Yes. Very much so.*

He chuckled deeply. *Missing me already?*

Don't get cocky. I could use some help—

Before I could even finish the thought, Niall ported in, amassed in a cloud of shadows. My chest thrummed at his arrival as he smiled down at me. Behind him, Morah slowly stepped around the chair, putting it between them. When he noted my off-kilter smile, the sword in my hand, and the hesitant wave Maeson offered, he whirled around. His attention landed on Morah, and she shrank under his stare.

"You shouldn't be here," he growled.

"I know that," she said, holding her ground the best she could.

A beat of silence passed.

"Then why are you still here?" Niall warned.

"Wait." I held up my hands. "Don't send her away yet. We were just getting somewhere."

Niall turned back to me, brows raised in question.

I considered telling him that she came at me with her blade drawn, but

I really didn't want to ruin whatever progress the three of us had just been making.

"Do you know who this is, Auren?" Niall asked.

"Ramil's daughter, Morah," I answered.

"Exactly. Ramil's daughter." He turned back to her and spoke. "Give me one good reason why I should let you linger a moment longer in this chamber, let alone trust anything that comes out of your mouth."

Morah tried her best to straighten her shoulders in defiance. "As Maeson said just a moment ago, I am not my father."

"So I've been told. But that's something I have yet to discover for myself," Niall countered. "Why are you in Auren's chambers in the first place?" He looked amongst the three of us. When none of us offered an explanation, he huffed a laugh. "Okay, I'll take my best guess here. Morah entered unnoticed, threatened Auren and didn't expect her to put up a fight, then Maeson arrived and has been trying to diffuse the tension but has only made it worse. How far off am I?"

"Mostly correct," I said.

"I have not made it worse." Maeson crossed her arms.

"Your little non-human has a shield around her," Morah stated flatly.

The room quieted again as Niall swung his head to her. His voice was pitched low as he said, "So, you *did* threaten her."

"I tried," she replied truthfully.

Gods. Did she have a death wish?

Niall's eyes cast out a glow as he took a step toward her, yet she continued. "If you're the one protecting her you're a fool."

She had to have a death wish.

"And you're not the heir of Benmoor, so I'd suggest you watch your tongue when you speak to me." Niall's threat made her go stiff.

I would hate to be on the receiving end of those threats.

I wondered what he meant when he said she wasn't the heir of Benmoor. If she wasn't, then who was?

Morah cut her eyes at him. "You should trust me when I say that I am not my father. For starters, I just told you the truth instead of trying to act like I was here to play nice."

He lifted a brow. "Should I thank you for that?"

She didn't respond, seeming half afraid to.

Niall assessed her for a painfully long moment. So long, that I could almost swear he was having an entirely different conversation in his mind with someone who was not in the room. Then he spoke. "Auren's shield is of her own doing." Whatever he had gleaned from whomever he'd just privately spoken with must have been enough for him to decide to let Morah in on this.

She leaned around him to look at me, her eyes widening with realization. "She's really not human then?"

Niall shook his head slowly. "As you already suspected. But you didn't ever voice your concerns to Killian. Why?"

Her jaw was slackened as she focused back on him. "I have a goal to achieve here in this court, and I don't want the focus shifting when I'm making progress. How did you know that I knew?"

"My advisor has followed you for some time now."

She scoffed. "That sneaky bastard."

"You have no room to talk on that front," Niall pointed out.

Morah sighed deeply. "She was distracting Killian. I had to come and have a word with her. You don't know what my father will do if I fail at this."

"At seducing the High Lord of the Woodland Court? I think you've pretty much got that part down, from what I hear."

I immediately thought back to what Breck had said. *He made me sit and watch as he did explicit things to another female.*

He must have meant Morah.

Part of me wondered if she really even enjoyed it or if it was all a ploy. She did have a seductive look about her—dark eyes, full lips and breasts, smooth, lightly tanned skin. Any male would probably find her alluring.

Her expression soured. "If Aremis gave you *that* information, I'll be speaking with him personally about violating my privacy."

Niall tilted his head. "I'm afraid that information came from a bit closer to Killian's home than yours or mine."

It took Morah a moment before she realized Niall was talking about Breck. She threw her hands up and turned toward the fireplace. "So, you have everyone working for you now, is that it?"

Niall smirked. "I have eyes and ears everywhere, Morah, you know this."

346

"Well, fuck. Look, I had my reasons for coming here. Just like I have my reasons for not telling Killian about your little not-human pet. I don't know what you two are playing at, but keep it out of this court!"

"She's not my pet," he growled.

Morah shifted on her feet but didn't take back her words.

Niall pushed out a harsh breath, trying to calm his irritation. "You know of the prophecy?"

"Yeah, I know of it. Who doesn't?" Morah snipped.

He cut his eyes at her, then looked at me. *Show her your glow,* he spoke into my mind.

What? How? I'm not emotional right now.

He grinned. *Just think about me. That should do the trick.*

He was insufferable.

Fighting back a grin of my own, I returned my sword to its scabbard. My eyes closed just as his essence entered my mind to help, and my power instantly awakened to greet it, dancing and pulsing around his.

I heard Morah gasp.

When I opened my eyes, the glow was pulsing from me in time with my heartbeat.

Morah stared in disbelief, connecting the dots, and upon her realization, she immediately dropped to one knee and bowed her head. "Euryphaessa," she said under her breath in reverence.

"The one who is to come." Maeson nodded, holding her head in a lowered position for a long moment.

Niall looked at me with pride.

As my glow faded out, Morah lifted her head and rose back up slowly. "I apologize. I had no idea you were . . ." The shame in her voice was a full reversal of the defiance she tried to uphold before.

"It's all right. You couldn't have known," I said.

"But now that you do"—Niall leveled a look at her—"you will treat her with respect."

She nodded.

"Morah," Niall pressed, "Killian can't know. You're well aware of what both he and your father would do if either of them found out."

"Then why are you telling her?" Maeson questioned.

"Because, I'm afraid we might need her help. And I've just been assured by my source that she harbors no true mal-intent."

I assumed he was speaking about Aremis, because Maeson chewed on her lip and didn't argue further.

"How am I supposed to help?" Morah asked. "I mean, I will gladly be of service to you," she said to me. "But how?"

We spent the next few minutes gathered close in discussion.

Morah would keep quiet about what she'd learned. She would seek out Breck for information first, and then continue her path forward with Killian and report to Niall with any new info. Her task was to keep us informed of both Killian's and her father's movements. Aremis apparently had intel that suggested Ramil had been in recent contact with emissaries from The Wastelands. Which—I was told—was not a good thing.

No sooner than we finished our discussion, a harsh knock sounded on my door. Unease slid amongst the four of us as we silently looked around at each other. Niall gave Morah a nod and she bowed her head in return, bringing her hand up to her chest in a fisted salute toward all of us. Then, she backed into the wall with fluid grace, fading into the stone and disappearing.

I blinked rapidly in disbelief. No wonder I hadn't heard her arrive in my chambers earlier—or the other night with Killian. She could walk through the damn walls.

The knock sounded again, harder this time. I nervously glanced around the room, and my heart stuttered as my eyes landed on the *Seidr.* I didn't want anyone to find the book here and become suspicious.

In a split-second decision, I tiptoed over and snatched it and my robe off the table, wrapping the book in the material to conceal it.

I returned to Niall's side just as a deep, foreign voice spoke from the hallway. "Lady Auren, you have been summoned to the High Lord's chambers and must come at once."

None of us said a word out loud, but Niall spoke to both Maeson and I in our minds. *Auren and I are leaving and won't be coming back. Say the word and I'll take you with us.*

Maeson's eyes lit up with hope, then fell flat again on a second thought.

I know you have a life here, Maeson. You have Elspeth. But we could really use you. You're wasted in this court. Come with us. You know you've always had a place in Calledan.

The pounding on the door resumed.

"Last call, Lady Auren, or I'll be forced to enter."

Maeson finally nodded.

I need to hear you say it, Niall said into our minds.

"Yes," she whispered aloud, lifting her chin higher.

We all vanished just as the door came crashing down.

48
BROKEN THINGS

Time and space distorted around us, then the lush green grass of the highlands was back beneath my feet.

Maeson spun and looked around, taking in the stone archway we stood before. "Uh . . . where are we?"

"The Highland Court," I replied proudly.

"But I thought we were going to Calledan?"

Niall chuckled at the bewildered expression on her face. "Soon enough. But for now . . ."

He ushered us through the arch, and a gust of wind spun up around us, whipping at Maeson's hair before it vanished.

"And that was Vanir's welcome party," I explained.

"Oh."

Niall put his hand on Maeson's shoulder. "I'm sorry to have thrown this upon you so quickly. I know it was a big decision."

She looked up at him. "Don't be sorry. I saved you once, and now, you've saved me."

He gave her a soft, knowing smile, but when his attention turned back to me, that smile fell. "Is that . . ." He paused, staring at what I held in my arms. "The *Seidr*?"

I glanced down to where the edges of the leather tome peeked out from under the confines of my robe.

Maeson's eyes widened.

It took me a moment to realize that I'd removed the ancient book from the court that it belonged to . . . which probably broke some fae law I wasn't aware of.

Whoops.

"I . . . didn't even think about that when I grabbed it," I said regretfully. "I just didn't want anyone else to find it."

Niall let out a short laugh and shook his head. "Seems we need to make one more stop." He lifted his arms for us to grab onto.

The world tumbled by in ribbons of green and gray, until we materialized in the same stone circle Niall had brought me to before. The sky still looked like it would open up at any moment and unleash a torrent of rain like it had done earlier, but for now, it held.

"I'll need the two of you to wait here while I return that." Niall nodded to the *Seidr,* reaching his open palm out toward me. "May I?"

I placed the bundled book in his hand and winced, giving him a lop-sided grin.

"It's no trouble, darling." He chuckled. "Be back shortly." Wisps of black smoke and shadows took his place as he vanished.

Maeson gave me a cheeky look. *"Darling?"* She raised a brow, emphasizing the word.

I shrugged. "He's always called me that."

"He *never* calls anyone that," she said pointedly. "He's starting to dote on you."

"He is not. He's just . . . sweet." I caught myself grinning just thinking about it.

"You two are cute." She smirked.

"That's not—we're not—"

"Whatever you say." She cut me off with a wave of her hand as she went to take a seat on one of the stones near the center of the circle.

"Maeson, he's a High Lord. And I'm just . . . well I'm not really sure what I am, currently."

She leaned over and re-laced her knee-high boots from under the long skirts she was wearing. "You two are more alike than you think."

I didn't entirely know what to say.

I couldn't explain or deny the pull toward Niall. The one I'd felt since the day I saw him in the forest. Something about him thrilled me, and the thrumming that was an ever-present hum every time he was near was almost like a second heartbeat now. I only seemed to really take notice of it when it flared more than usual.

"I let him into my mind yesterday." The words left my mouth before I could stop them. "And not just for conversation. This was . . . different."

Maeson halted her boot lacing and looked up at me.

I adjusted my sword on my hip and took up a seat across from her on the grass, spreading out my cloak behind me. "We were training, and he was teaching me how to hold a mental shield, and our essences just . . . embraced each other. It was odd, but it felt right. Like our power had been old friends who finally reunited. Like they recognized each other somehow." I paused and sighed. "It all sounds kind of dumb now that I'm saying it out loud." I plucked up some blades of grass in front of me and tossed them to the breeze.

"Auren, it's not dumb. I feel the same way around Aremis. Gods, I would give anything just to be able to *physically* embrace him."

"Why don't you? I mean, you'll be near him now, in the Mountain Court, right?"

Maeson scuffed the heel of her boot along the gray stone. "If only it were that simple."

"Why isn't it?"

"Well, Aremis doesn't really know that I have feelings for him."

"Oh. Well, that's an issue then," I replied.

"I mean, every time we're near each other, he always makes flirtatious comments, and I catch him stealing looks at me. But what if he doesn't think of me the same way? What if he just sees me as a . . . friend?" Her heel was wearing a white line into the stone beneath it now.

"It sounds like you need to speak to him about it. Or, at the very least be more forward with your intentions and emotions and just see where he stands. You'll have the time to do so now."

"That's the thing." She winced. "Aremis isn't very keen on talking about his feelings. He's rather . . . reserved about everything. He had a very rough life growing up. He doesn't let anyone in really. Not when it comes to emotions. I've only seen him be vulnerable once, that's how I know he's capable of it." She sighed heavily. "I just want him to act on his emotions for once. I want to know how he feels. If all those stolen looks were just curiosity or something more. And I'm afraid that if I put myself out there, he'll just shut down."

"Well now that you'll be near him, you'll have plenty of time to do some digging." I wiggled my eyebrows suggestively, but her replying smile didn't reach her eyes.

Her voice became laced with an estranged sadness. "Calledan is becoming everyone's refuge. A place where broken things go to be mended, I suppose."

"I'm not quite sure what you mean by that," I said.

She crossed her ankles and sighed. "Niall's story isn't a pretty one. He suffered alone and in silence for the majority of his life. His Trium is the only family he has, and even they are just a mix of broken souls leaning on one another."

"Trium?" I questioned.

"The three males he trusts most. Part of his court. They're like his brothers. Sworn to him and bound to serve him and one another through their oaths. Aremis is his advisor and spy. Roirdan is the commander of his armies, and Remic is like the ultimate protector of them all. They're all amazing in their own right. Strong, *very* powerful, and not a single one is from Calledan—except for Niall."

"Wait, so the company that helps run his court isn't even from his own territory?"

"Correct. All of them suffered at one point and—as the fates willed it —their paths crossed with Niall's, and they found a place where they could belong in this world. A place where they can heal and realize their potential. Like I said, where broken things go to be mended."

I could tell she considered herself to be amongst that group.

"Maeson, you're not broken. You're just finding your purpose. You were in a stagnant place, but now, you'll be able to thrive."

When she lifted her head this time, she smiled, and her eyes sparked with hope. "So will you."

Her words struck some deep chord within me.

Hadn't I been searching for that very thing? A purpose? A place to thrive?

Could this really be it?

I was in this realm because of forces beyond my control. And in recent days, I'd only thought of home once or twice. In fact, the more I thought about the human realm, the more foreign it seemed to me.

And the more I didn't feel like returning to it.

49
A GUEST OF VAHRENHALL

Not long after Maeson and I finished our deep conversation, the familiar thrumming ignited within me, and Niall's smooth, deep voice sounded from behind us. "She ports better than the two of you."

We looked back at him to see a bundle of red fur in his arms.

"Wrynn!" Maeson launched off the rock and scooped the fox from Niall's arms. She spun with joy, cradling the animal to her chest as it chattered and flourished its tail.

"Sorry, that took a bit longer than I'd hoped," Niall said, tossing me a wink.

Maeson stopped her spinning and set Wrynn down at her feet. "Niall, thank—wait. What exactly did you do?"

"I returned the *Seidr* to Elspeth and let her know what was happening. She will be in contact with you at the Mountain Court soon. She also blessed your journey."

Maeson's eyes lined with silver. "Thank you. That means a lot."

He bowed his head. "I also made a couple small detours." He reached into a pocket of air and brought out a different leather-bound book, full of colored ribbons and strings that dangled from every corner. "I think this belongs to you."

Maeson gasped so loud I thought she would suck the air out of the entire stone circle. "How did you even know where to find it?"

"Elspeth showed me. She said you'd be missing it."

Maeson threw her arms around Niall's neck, and he chuckled and embraced her as well.

When she pulled away, she handed me the book. "This is full of all my concoctions and experiments. A life's worth of work, really."

I ran my hand over the well-loved edges and along the silken ribbons. There were bookmarks sticking out at all different lengths and angles, and roughly torn pages were folded and slipped back in between others. It looked a bit like organized chaos, but Maeson beamed with pride as I beheld it.

"Can we talk about how you pulled this out of *nowhere?*" I asked Niall as I handed the book back to Maeson.

He shrugged. "A pocket in space. Simple magic."

"Very convenient," I said, wondering if my god-lineage would allow me to do simple magic like that.

"Now, if we're going to make it to tonight's celebration, we should get going." He extended a hand out to each of us, but Maeson hesitated to take it this time.

"Any chance you could take me on ahead to Calledan? Wrynn doesn't do too well in a place she's not already familiar with."

When Niall looked down at the fox, Maeson glanced over at me and grinned like she was up to something. I knew what she was doing: removing herself so that the High Lord and I would have the evening to ourselves.

Well played, Maeson.

"I can take you and Wrynn to The Keep. That will give Auren some time to get ready."

Maeson beamed and scooped up Wrynn. Niall gripped us both, taking me first to the place Vanir had prepared for us, and then making the quick trip to the mountains where Maeson would wait for us at Niall's court home.

When Vanir said he would prepare the guest house, I wasn't expecting it to be part of an entire *estate.*

The sprawling guest house sat on a quiet stretch of land to the west of the heart of Vahrenhall. A peaceful, babbling brook wound through the rolling terrain and sidled right up next to the structure before continuing down the gradually sloping hillside.

Built from the same darkened timber I'd seen in town, and soaked to a dark shade of carbon from all the recent rain, it stood out against the backdrop of green. Curving beams hoisted the structure's lofty roof, boasting more of the same carved heads and necks of a creature's gaping maw at each corner of the eaves.

The property sprawled out on a single level with four private wings. Niall informed me that the northernmost wing was reserved for him and his guests all year round. Given that he and Vanir were such good friends, I understood why he'd been given a permanent quarter.

I stood in the common room of his wing, admiring the cozy sitting area. There was an oversized fireplace and hearth, a small personal library, an entire cask of ale, and a giant floor-to-ceiling window looking out over the hills and mountains in the distance. At opposite edges of the room were four closed doors—the separate bedchambers.

Niall advised me to make myself at home. And so, I began by trying to open a door to a bedchamber—only to find it locked. Same with door two.

Door three opened.

Just out of curiosity, I tried door four.

Locked.

Three it is.

I snickered to myself. Niall would have to get cozy on the settee in the common room.

Inside the bedchamber, everything looked ready to welcome the High Lord of the Mountain Court.

On the wall across the room there was a sizable bed with a thick wooden headboard. The tops of each post were carved into those odd creatures—which was a little off-putting—but the craftsmanship was admirable. The wood floors were polished and lined with soft fur rugs, and candles slowly lit themselves throughout the space as the sun sank lower in the sky.

A soft click sounded behind me, and I turned to see the tall armoire opening on its own. A sword, a worn-out shield, and several pairs of black clothing items—undoubtedly Niall's—hung inside in a neat row.

Then the second door on the cabinet opened, revealing an additional neatly folded pile of clothes on a small stool, with a hand-scrawled tented card atop it that read:

For my new friend.

Ale for my oldest friend, and cider for my newest, Vanir had told us earlier.

I smiled as I picked up the clothes and held them to my body. It appeared that he'd sized me up almost perfectly. He had provided a pair of thick black leggings and a long-sleeved, fitted gray tunic that had beautiful black scrolling designs stitched along the tops of the shoulders and down the center to the hem.

After washing my hands and face in the spacious bathing chamber, I put on the new clothes, stowed my sword in the cabinet, and draped my cloak across the bed until I needed it.

Back in the common area, I walked over to the wall of bookshelves and ran my fingers along the spines of the books as I surveyed them. There were a surprising range of titles.

Ancient Fae History: Volumes One through Four.

Fountains of Folly.

The Warrior and The Wraith—

A familiar feeling washed over me, and I turned to see Niall materializing in the center of the room.

I greeted him with a wicked grin. "Which one of you and your Trium reads romance novels?"

He crossed his arms and cocked his head. "That would be Roirdan. How do you know there are romance novels on that shelf?"

I tapped the spine of *The Warrior and The Wraith.* "We have this book in my realm too. After all, the Warrior *is* human."

"And have *you* read it?" he asked as he sauntered towards me.

"A noble, wounded Warrior, lost in a far-away land after a brutal battle, finds himself in the care of a Water Wraith. Despite all he's heard of the creature, he can't help but to fall for her as she tends to his wounds." I thumbed through the pages. The copy was well-worn, suggesting whoever read it frequented it often. The top corner of each page was thinner and slightly discolored, where fingers had been licked to turn the papers one by one with each re-read. "I never read the ending though," I admitted, sliding the book back into place on the shelf.

Niall was hovering over me now, his voice pitched low. "The Wraith casts a love spell on him, and he succumbs and falls madly in love. So much so, that he forgets his men and the war. Shortly after, she realizes that despite the spell, she has developed a true and deep love for him, and when she lifts it—revealing her intent and also her true feelings—the Warrior is outraged." He paused, running the tips of his fingers through my hair. "But, he learns to forgive her, eventually falling in love of his own free will. He lives out his days with her in contentment, never fighting a battle again."

I turned and looked up at him, my arm grazing his. "So, you've read it as well?"

He shrugged. "It was the only option available at the time."

"Has anyone ever told you that you're a bad liar?"

He leaned a shoulder on the bookshelf and faced me. "No, because I never lie."

"That's a lie right there," I said, jabbing a finger at his chest.

He caught it in his hand and pulled me closer. "I don't lie because I don't want anyone to ever question me. So, just know that everything I say to you is true." He smiled fully, showing his gleaming white teeth.

The room fell silent as he held my hand against his chest. The angles of his face were cast in the shadow of the candlelight. And that smile . . . I didn't want to look away.

My heartbeat suddenly became too pronounced, so I cleared my throat and gently pulled my hand out of his, taking a step back. He let it go, leaving his own hand to linger against his chest where I'd left it.

The fireplace across the room flared to life, causing me to jump.

"Food is next," Niall said, still leaning against the shelf.

"What?"

Not a second later two plates and mugs arrived on the table nearest to me with a thud. I jumped again clutching at my racing heart.

Niall chuckled. "Told you."

"That wasn't much of a warning," I scolded.

The food smelled delicious—a dark roasted chunk of meat, smothered in sauce, with a heaping pile of vegetables and bread on each plate. I immediately moved to the table.

"Vanir treats his guests properly. Dinner is always served on time, regardless of if you're hungry," Niall explained. "Don't wait on me. It's getting late. I'm going to wash up and change while you eat, then we need to make our way down to the foothills for the lighting of the pyre." He pushed off the shelf and went into the other room.

I sent a silent thanks to Vanir as I scarfed everything down.

With a full stomach and my cloak wrapped around my shoulders, I watched as Niall approached me with a small brown box.

"What's this?" I asked, accepting it as he handed it over.

"Open it."

I lifted the lid, and inside was a pair of black leather gloves, lined with the same matching fox fur that adorned my cloak. My mouth fell open as I lifted them out and turned them over in my hands. The fur felt like silk in my fingers. "You . . . how did you—"

"I paid another visit to our trapper friend." He grinned. "They're to go with your cloak. You might not need them tonight, but you will need them later on in my court. And Vahrenhall's trappers always have the best quality leathers and furs."

"They're lovely, Niall. Thank you."

He stepped forward with the open box, and I placed the gloves back inside, one at a time. "Ready for another Lumeri?" he asked.

I nodded, letting a wide grin slide across my face as I tucked my arm into his.

Instead of porting, we walked out into the chilled night air and down the sloping hill. In the distance, lit torches were flickering in the night, where a large gathering of fae had already begun.

50
LUMERI IN THE HIGHLANDS

THE FOOTHILLS WERE ALIVE WITH FIRE AND FAE.

But where Elandrew's celebration was all fancy outfits, wings, and wine, Vahrenhall's was much more . . . primal.

The highland fae were all dressed in gray or black. Dark hoods and cloaks swayed about to the beating of the drums that echoed off the nearby mountains. Almost every face was painted white, and black symbols were drawn onto foreheads and cheeks, across eyes and down lips. Some fae wore headpieces made of antlers and bones. Others had woven their hair in such intricately braided styles that each one seemed like a headpiece of their own.

Tall wooden torches were staked into the ground throughout the area, with flames dancing atop them like wild spirits. The firelight cast shadows upon all who weaved in and out beneath it, and smoke wafted high into the chilled night air.

In the center of the growing crowd was a great wooden pyre at least twenty feet wide and more than twice as tall as any structure in the surrounding area. It towered over us all, unburnt and waiting to be sacrificed.

Vanir spotted us and summoned two mugs as he made his way over. "Just in time," he greeted us, handing us each a drink. "You two look the part. Which is no surprise from you." He jerked his chin at Niall, who was always dressed in black.

The High Lord of Vahrenhall's face was painted white like the others, though the paste was already beginning to flake in places, making him look even more rugged than before. A thick black smear cut across both his eyes and over the bridge of his nose from temple to temple. Three black finger marks tracked down both his cheeks.

A crown of spiked antler and bleached bone sat atop his head, accentuating his pointed ears, and his large cloak was rimmed along the shoulders with thick, black, crinkled fur from an animal I wasn't familiar with.

He bumped his mug against mine and drank, eyeing my new cloak. "Seems you found a nice piece to keep you warm."

I ran my hands along the fur around my neck. "Thanks to this one." I elbowed Niall gently, then dipped my head to Vanir. "And thank *you* for the outfit."

"I'm happy you like it. The style suits you well."

Niall glared at Vanir over the rim of his mug.

"C'mon brother. Mine was simply a gift of hospitality. Yours, on the other hand . . ." He smirked and clapped Niall on the shoulder, causing ale to slosh over the side of his mug.

Niall shook the spilled drops off his free hand. "If you keep treating Auren with such great hospitality, *brother,* she's never going to want to leave with me tomorrow."

"Of course I will," I assured him.

"Mmm-hmm." Niall looked out over the crowd with a close-lipped smile.

I followed his gaze. "Why is everyone dressed so . . ."

"Macabre?" Vanir finished my question. "It's part of the ceremony. While we celebrate the light and usher it in, we also believe in banishing the evil spirits, along with the dark. The attire aids in that aspect." He gestured to his face and dark clothing. "It's a rather spooky ancient tradition—scaring away that which shouldn't linger."

The drums faded out, and after a beat of silence they returned in a slow, single, repetitive rhythm.

"It's time." Vanir peeled off toward the pyre.

Niall motioned for me to follow him, and we made our way toward a small table surrounded by torches. Several bowls sat atop it, all of which had been full of white paste, but were thoroughly used up. He dipped his fingers into the only remaining bowl of black paste and scraped a bit onto his fingertips. Then he turned toward me, stepping so close I could feel his warm breath. "May I?"

I nodded, lifting my face up to him.

He brought his forefinger and middle finger up to my right temple and gently drew two lines along the curve of my cheekbone, underneath my eye. Then he moved to the other side, making the same motion across my other cheek. The paste was cold, but it was his touch that made me shiver as his fingers settled on my bottom lip. I watched his eyes burn like molten gold as he pressed down lightly, slowly dragging the black paste down my chin.

The drums were a steady beat in the background, pounding like my heart. I swallowed hard as he lingered above me.

His golden eyes found mine, and his mouth opened slightly as we drifted a step closer to each other.

I felt like I was about to start glowing, so I quickly turned, reaching for the black paste and dipping my fingers into it. "My turn."

Niall lowered his head so that I could easily reach him.

"Close your eyes," I instructed.

I wasn't quite sure what marks to make, so I copied what I had seen on other guests' faces. I placed two fingers on his brow and smoothly dragged them down over a closed eyelid, then his cheek, ending the markings just before his jawline. I repeated the same motion to the other side, letting my fingers pause a moment longer than necessary on his other cheek.

When he opened his eyes again, my breathing hitched. The orange firelight dancing across his face, the golden glow of his irises, the black streaks . . . He almost looked otherworldly. Like a predator in the night, or a warrior about to battle darkness itself. His gorgeous smile sent a rush of heat and flutters through me, and I found myself smiling back.

"You look mischievous," I said tilting my head.

"And you look—"

Behind us, the drums suddenly transitioned into a demanding rhythm and began increasing in tempo, growing bolder. I swung my attention around just in time to see Vanir approaching the pyre with a large torch.

Niall's gaze remained on me a moment longer, before he stepped to my side and peered out over the crowd to where the High Lord of Vahrenhall stood.

Vanir cried out in a deep baritone, "Laetus Lumeri," as he reached out to touch the flame to the pyre. The hundreds of painted fae that had gathered echoed the statement, and in a rush of heat and light, the pyre became a fiery temple. Flames licked up its mass until it was fully engulfed, stretching toward the stars and illuminating the entirety of the foothills around us.

It was a beacon for the gods.

And it was the biggest fire I had ever seen.

The fae began an entrancing dance of wild motions, timed to the steady drums. They unleashed primal cries as they let their bodies sway freely amidst the roaring inferno.

I watched in awe.

Niall was right—this was a sight to see. And Vanir's court was completely different from the last.

The human realm began to feel small and alarmingly stagnant compared to all of this. Not only were the territories in this realm vastly different, but each culture was unique.

I'd spent my whole life thinking that humans were the only truly civilized beings, and that the fae were just ruthless, lawless heathens with magic. Creatures to avoid at all costs. Had it not been for this odd twist of fate and Karios's divine intervention, I would have lived on in blind naivety, stuck in the lies we'd all been taught.

But the fates had directed my path and led me here, and I was . . . grateful.

I could feel Niall watching me, but I didn't move. I watched the pyre burn brighter. Climb higher. Felt the pounding of the drum beats as they reverberated through my body. The ever-present thrumming in my chest settled into a deep bass in the background as I soaked up the sounds, the feelings, and Niall's all-encompassing stare.

"What are you thinking about?" he asked.

I grinned, but kept my eyes pinned on the blaze. "That you're being a hypocrite again."

"Oh? How so?"

"By once again going against what you told me in Elandrew; that it's rude to—" I cut off my own words the moment I turned and looked at him. I had forgotten about the black marks on his face.

Now illuminated in the blazing firelight, he looked like some ancient, primal being, born from the inky depths of the mountains, finally emerging into the light.

"Stare," I finished.

"Hard not to," he replied, tilting his head at me—further solidifying that primal image.

I fiddled with the fur around my cloak, almost nervously. If he only knew that I could very easily find myself staring at him too if I wasn't careful . . . "What were *you* thinking about?" I said, trying to take the focus off me.

"You," he said plainly, thwarting my effort.

Everything I say to you is true.

I lifted my mug to take a drink. Or rather, to hide my blushing face behind it. I gulped down what was left and the mug instantly became heavier in my hand as it filled itself back up.

I shook my head. "That's dangerous."

"That's the Highland Court." Niall chuckled, finishing his and watching it refill.

The fae moved all around us, dancing, swaying, and drinking. They looked like spirits of the night, chasing away a common enemy. Some danced upon each other, while others twirled with their hands held high in the air. A few couples even chased each other off into the darkness beyond the pyre.

Upon seeing several more do the same, I asked, "Where are they going?"

Niall leaned in and lowered his voice. "There's a superstition that by performing certain acts with someone, you help usher in the new light of the dawn."

"Certain acts?" I asked, sipping more cider.

The corners of his mouth turned up. "Sexual acts."

I nearly choked on my swallow. When I turned to look at him, he was fully grinning. "Wait . . . You're serious?"

He threw his head back and laughed. "Is the Daughter of Karios chaste?"

"Don't call me that! There are others nearby!"

"What are you referring to? Being called 'chaste'? Or Daughter of—"

I moved to clamp my hand over his mouth, but he dodged it—chuckling deeply—so I stuck my finger in his face instead. "Don't expect me to talk about my sex life with you in public either."

"So, you'll tell me in private then?" He smirked.

Fates, this male!

A female came stumbling by us, hauling a male by the hand behind her. Both of them were laughing and smiling from ear to ear, and both nodded to us as they passed. I nodded back, giving them a half smile and watching them fade into the shadows beyond.

"And the answer is no," I finally said.

Niall raised a brow. "No—as in—you're not experienced?"

"Gods, Niall. *No*—as in—I'm not chaste."

He moved closer to me. "Good. Because taking part in such acts on Lumeri is said to bring good luck."

"And how would it do that?"

"Well, you do know how the gods and the fates work right? They oversee *everything* that goes on. Which means, they're always watching."

I rolled my eyes. "They don't watch those types of things."

"What makes you so sure? I'd wager it's entertaining for them. Don't you think?"

I did *not* want to think about that.

"No, I think that's absurd."

Now, the thought would probably haunt me.

He laughed again, drinking deeply from his mug. "Well, the stories of old say that it brings good luck to those that partake. I'm just teaching you what I know." He shrugged, staring off at the burning pyre.

I half laughed. "Am I supposed to be thankful for that information?"

"Do with it what you will." He grinned from behind his mug.

I shifted my focus back to the ensuing event, but quickly found my mind wandering. I let out a sigh of annoyance. "Thanks, now that's all I can think about."

He squeezed his eyes shut as he let out a deeper laugh, causing several creases to form at the corners of his eyes. My heart leapt a bit at the sight.

The drums shifted into a faster pace, and everyone began linking arms, forming several rings circling the pyre. Before I knew it, I was snagged by my elbow and pulled into the fray. Niall caught up to me and took my other arm in his as others continued to link on.

The circles moved back and forth, side to side, and the crowd chanted a foreign song with voices that rose and fell in a chaotic, half-drunken melody. Everyone was smiling. Some were laughing as they were yanked this way and that. I had no idea what was happening, and my cider sloshed all around and out of the mug, but I smiled all the same. I caught Niall smiling too.

The dance went on, and the chanting rose higher until everyone burst out into a powerful yell that filled me with excitement. A drunken fae fell into Niall's side, causing him to bump into me, which sent me out into the mob of others who were now freely spinning and falling away into celebratory stupor. And for some reason, I let myself fall into it too.

I chugged what was left of my cider and let it drip freely down my chin as I held my arms out and spun around in wild circles. My cloak lifted from my sides and floated behind me. I felt the cool wind touch my face, then the heat from the still blazing pyre, then the chill, the heat, over and over as I whirled.

And then I was laughing and yelling and releasing all the energy that was pent up inside me. I felt tears bead up in the corners of my eyes as I squeezed them shut and danced. All the revelations and the weight that had fallen on my shoulders over the past few days faded away as I immersed myself in the moment.

My power stirred inside me, but I willed it to calm.

I didn't glow.

I didn't lose control.

I just danced.

51
A SHOW FOR THE GODS

A<small>FTER SEVERAL MORE DANCES WITH PAINTED FAE STRANGERS</small>, I <small>WAS</small> thoroughly out of breath, but absolutely elated. My power was rushing warmly and pleasantly through my veins, but not enough to surface and give me away.

Thankfully, the cider was nothing like the elderberry liqueur. Its relaxing effects had already begun to fade after I had broken a good sweat. Perhaps that was the gods-blood I had coursing through my veins alongside it, keeping me from feeling its full effects. What that said about the elderberry liqueur . . . I didn't want to think about that.

I smiled over at Niall who was standing off to the side of all the revelry, talking and laughing with Vanir. He had watched me the entire time, fighting a grin, with a glimmer—similar to longing—in those honeyed eyes of his.

As we said goodnight to Vanir, I asked if he would send a cask of the cider up to the mountains for me, and he bellowed a laugh, promising he would.

I rambled the entire walk back to the guest quarters. I talked about how human holidays and celebrations were so very dull compared to what I'd experienced here, and asked a dozen random questions, but Niall didn't seem bothered by it at all. Rather, he listened intently, like he was soaking up everything I said and committing it to memory.

Inside the common area of Niall's wing, the fire appeared freshly stoked, and a pitcher of water and some small crackers and cheese were waiting for us on the table.

Vanir truly was a thoughtful host.

Niall took my cloak and hung it in the armoire next to his, then leaned back out of the bedchamber and pointed at the snack. "Soak up some of that cider. I'll draw you a bath." He disappeared into the bathing chamber before I could reply, and I stood there, listening to the water starting and him fiddling around with a few things.

Maeson was right, he *was* doting on me.

I grinned as I ate.

After washing up and drying my hair as best as I could, I slipped into the silky shift that had been left for me to sleep in and curled into the bed. From where I was lying, I could see straight out to the fireplace in the common room.

The sounds of Niall washing and rinsing, and the crackling of the fireplace were a soothing chorus, and I snuggled down further under the plush blanket.

I thought back over everything from the evening. It had been so long since I'd enjoyed myself that much. But what exactly did that say about my life back in the human realm?

Before I could even start down that train of thought, Niall exited the bathing chamber, and I did a double take at the sight of him. A towel that looked two sizes too small was slung low around his waist, leaving his thick abs and the deep grooves at the front of his hips on full display. The sides of his wet hair feathered back, glistening in the candlelight, and the longer top length dripped down his back.

I studied the markings of the shroud on his upper chest from afar, seeing them fully for the first time. The design was surprisingly elegant. Given that it was earned from deeds done in battle, I half expected something harsher, or a bit more unrefined. But the inked lines looked just like his shadowfire.

Tendrils of black flame crept across his collarbone, spreading outward, and a smattering of thicker wisps draped over his shoulders, disappearing down his back. Each one seemed to fade into his skin at the tip, streaming out across his muscles like ink bleeding into water.

A lick of heat curled low in my core.

He snatched a piece of clothing from the set of drawers next to the armoire, and I watched him go back into the bathing chamber. A moment later, he returned wearing nothing but a pair of undershorts.

What is he doing? He's not coming over to the bed, is he?

Oh shit.

"Hope you don't mind, I don't like feeling restricted by a bunch of fabric when I sleep." He motioned toward his half naked body, and I had to look away and work on a swallow.

He lifted the covers on the other side of the bed and slid underneath them.

"Um, excuse me?" I sat up and stared at him.

"Yes?" He drew out the word.

"What do you think you're doing?"

He made a show of looking around the bed. "Getting into bed. Is there a problem?"

"I've clearly already claimed this one. There's a perfectly good settee out there." I pointed to the common room.

"Technically, *this* is *my* bed. And I am *not* sleeping out on that settee. It's not as comfortable as it looks." He leaned back and settled into the pillows, tossing a casual arm behind his head.

"Well, can't you just go unlock one of those other bedchambers or something?"

"Afraid not. Vanir has them under his wards. It's court protocol."

"Court protocol?" I scoffed. "I highly doubt that."

"Go check for yourself." He flourished his free hand.

"I already did. Earlier." I crossed my arms in the hope that they'd somehow tame the sudden giddy flutter in the pit of my gut.

"Relax, it's not like you've never been in the same bed with a male before. I can put a shirt on if it makes you feel better."

I rolled my eyes, but I didn't want him to cover himself up. So, I continued to sit in silent protest, trying to ignore the lick of excitement that rushed through me at the fact that he was half-naked.

"You *have* been in the same bed as a male before, right?"

I gave him the middle finger, but he reached up with lightning fast speed and caught my hand in his, pulling me back against the bed and positioning himself halfway over me in the process. A playful smirk pulled at his lips. "After all the nice things I've done for you today, that seems like a pretty rude gesture."

I moved to defiantly give him the same vulgar gesture with my free hand, but he caught that one too before I could even try. Both of my hands were now pinned alongside my head, and his body was fully above mine.

"By the way, you owe me for getting my hair wet earlier at The Great Hall. *And,* a drop did get into my mug." His grin was smoldering now.

"Did not," I scoffed.

He didn't relent.

I pushed back against his grip, but it only made him lean in closer, reinforcing his firm hold without hurting me in the slightest.

"So, if I allow you to sleep in this bed next to me, will that make up for those mishaps?"

"It's a start," he said, but he didn't move to unpin me. Instead, his eyes searched mine.

I could see his mind churning behind his golden-brown irises, the faint glow pulsing around the edges like a fiery ring. I could get lost in the heat of those eyes and never return.

Deep in my chest, beneath the thrumming, there was an internal pull towards him. Like my body was aching for the closeness. Like the closer we were, the more whole I would feel. As we held each other's stares, I wondered if he felt it too.

His gaze dipped down to my lips. "You missed a spot."

His grip on my hands loosened, but I didn't move to retaliate. I sucked in a shallow breath, holding it in as he slowly wiped his thumb across the lingering splotch of paint under my bottom lip.

He continued to trail his fingers across the line of my chin, along my jaw, and I found myself inclining my head at his touch.

The longer his eyes traced my features, the more intense his expression became.

"What are you thinking about?" I breathed out.

He settled himself down on an elbow, placing his face even closer to mine as his fingers began a slow descent down my neck. Chills skittered down my arms as he mapped the length of my collarbone, then grazed the edge of my silken shift, just above my breasts.

"I'm thinking about how you should let me sleep in the comfort of this bed with you, out of the goodness of your heart." The words were a murmur, his voice deep and sensual.

My stomach gave a small tumble. "You haven't asked me nice—"

"And your lips," he continued, cutting me off. "When I painted them earlier, all I could think about was how badly I wanted to taste them."

I was suddenly hanging on his every word, attune to all the places where our bodies were touching.

"I'm thinking about how I've wanted to taste you ever since you let me into your mind the first time." His gaze snagged on my lips again before lifting back up to my eyes. Orbs of golden fire, heated with a new level of desire, pinned me to the spot beneath him. "Something tells me you feel the same way."

Indeed, my entire body hummed from within, and a smooth wave of heat swept through my core.

He lowered his lips to my neck and placed a gentle kiss along my pulse. "I feel the way your heart speeds up when you're near me." Another delicate kiss, slightly higher. "I feel the way your essence calls out to mine." Another, just under my chin. "And if you didn't want the same thing, you'd have told me to stop by now." He brought his face up to mine again, searching my eyes for confirmation.

"We shouldn't," I said.

"We should," he whispered.

I stared back at him, and the longer I did, the more I could feel my resolve slipping away.

I had been warned about the High Lord of Calledan. That he was wicked and malevolent. But the male before me—the one I'd come to know—was not any of those things. And I trusted him. Had grown fonder of him as the days passed.

I didn't know why I was holding back. Maybe I was afraid to let that last bit of my reserve go, fearing that if I gave in to my desire, I'd be confirming a reality that I still fought against in my mind. But something deep in my soul told me that I didn't need to worry. That I was right where I was supposed to be. That I was safe with him. And that whatever had been brewing deep within me, whatever this sense of longing was, I wouldn't be able to resist it much longer.

The intensity in his eyes mirrored the rhythm of my pounding heart, and as he dipped his head toward mine, my resolve crumbled.

He was right.

I did feel the same way. I did want to kiss him.

His lips hovered above mine, our breath mingling as he waited to hear me say it. To say that I wanted it too . . .

We were circling it like moths to a flame. Closer with every shared breath.

And I was ready to burn with him.

"Niall . . ." His name slid off my tongue in a breathy plea, and his lips were instantly on mine.

My mouth opened for him, and his tongue swept in, tasting me with broad, greedy strokes. One of his hands dug into my hair, angling my head to take the kiss deeper, while he steadied himself above me.

The thrumming in my chest surged as a rush rippled through me.

His kiss was hot and heavy and steeped with desire. It claimed me, like a brand upon my lips, and it felt as if he couldn't get enough of me. I had never been kissed in such a way. And I never wanted it to end.

A burning need pulsed low in my core, and liquid heat pooled between my thighs. A soft moan escaped my throat. I wrapped my arms around his muscled back, bringing him deliciously close to me. He let out a deep groan, grinding his powerful hips against mine. My silky nightclothes and the fabric of his undershorts were the only things between us, and they betrayed us both.

I felt *all* of him.

The evidence of his desire, and the movement of his hips sent a jolt through me. I sucked in a breath, breaking our kiss and tossing my head back.

His mouth quickly found purchase on my neck again, kissing his way along my jaw. "Gods, I've wanted to kiss you for what seems like an eternity," he murmured against my skin.

I let out a soft, breathy laugh. "It's only been a few days."

He lifted his head to look at me again. "It feels like a lifetime."

I melted at those words.

My power danced along my veins, and suddenly, my essence reached out for his. Shadows manifested in my mind, swirling and wrapping themselves around my light as if they wanted to bottle it up and keep it as a treasure. The contact sent a physical thrill through me, a pulsing need.

Niall let his head fall forward again, and the sound he made while exhaling into the crook of my neck was that of a male trying to keep a leash on himself.

I reached out again in my mind, unable to control the urge. A strand of light caressed his shadows rather intimately, and I watched his physical reaction.

His hips twitched upon mine, a guttural groan crawling up his throat as he tilted his head to the side and closed his eyes. "Stop doing that," he growled into my ear.

But my hips pushed back against his like an ebb to a tide.

I didn't want to stop. The sounds he was making, and the mere thought of him desiring me, threatened to be my undoing. I wanted to kiss him again. I wanted *more*.

As if he could read my mind, his eyes snapped open. A fierce fire was burning within them. "Do you know what you're doing to me, darling? Every time you move like that, you make me want—" His words were cut short when I pulled his face back to mine and kissed him again. The move was surprising—even to me—but I needed his lips on mine. And in response, he took me into his arms and devoured me.

Large, calloused hands roved over my curves, and I drew my leg up, bending it at the knee, spreading my legs to feel him against me. His fingers gripped the flesh at my backside and lifted my hips. The press of his manhood against my core had my back arching off the bed, my pulse pounding as an ache grew between my thighs.

He tore his lips from mine, only to plant them beneath my ear, nipping gently at the sensitive skin. "Tell me what you want," he said, peppering kisses along my neck.

Vocalizing my sexual desires wasn't my strong suit. But something about the way he commanded me to speak of them loosened my tongue. "I want more," I said, pressing my body into him. It wasn't the most specific of statements, but it was enough.

His fingers gripped the bottom of my shift and slowly lifted it until it settled past my hips. My leg relaxed, falling to the side, granting him further access, and his hand moved to cup my most private part. A whole new wave of desire washed over me, pooling right where he held me, and the sound he made told me he was thoroughly pleased at what he'd found.

"Gods." He breathed. "Auren . . ." He swiped his fingers through my slickness and drew slow, languid circles along the sensitive center while his mouth claimed mine once more, moving hungrily against my lips like I was his life's-breath.

When his finger pushed inside me, I moaned into his mouth, shuddering beneath him, feeling time and space slow around me, my focus narrowing on every nerve ending between my legs. He plunged deeper with each re-entry, then added a second finger, stretching me further, stoking my fire.

I kissed him desperately, tugging at his hair as he pumped into me at a luscious pace, curling his fingertips along some deliciously sensitive spot deep within me that had me aching as my rapture built.

Thoughts swam through my head as he pleasured me—thoughts of how this was even happening . . .

How right it felt.

How my body sang beneath him.

My muscles coiled around his fingertips as he coaxed my release. I lifted my hips and relished it. I let myself surrender to the feeling of him, to his lips on mine. To his breathing as he watched my body writhe with pleasure underneath him. To the ache that built up so strongly that when it shattered through me, I was digging my head back into the pillows and my nails into Niall's arms as he watched me with a red-hot stare.

As the sensation eased and my breathing slowed, I opened my eyes to see Niall's face illuminated by the white glow that had settled over my skin, pulsing with my heartbeat.

He shifted his weight, propping himself on his arm and gently smoothing down the hair around my face. "So lovely," he murmured, taking in my features. "You have a power over me, you know."

I wriggled under his arm and faced him more fully. "I'm afraid you do too. Obviously." I gestured to the last bit of my lingering glow before it winked out from my body.

The room darkened again. The fire in the common area had dimmed significantly since we'd been here, and the shadows were deepening with every passing minute. In the dimness, Niall's features seemed more pronounced. Like he *himself* was some form of darkness, absorbing it, enhanced and magnified by it the longer he remained in its midst.

My essence stirred, but I remained still, taking in what had just happened. *Who* it had just happened with.

"Why does everyone have an entirely different image of who you actually are?" I asked quietly.

"Because I've made it that way." He traced a line up and down my arm. "I can't have everyone knowing I'm wickedly good in bed and an absolute delight in person, now can I?"

I gave him an eye roll and suppressed a grin.

"Very few get to see these sides of me you know. And you might be the only one who has seen both."

I narrowed my eyes at him skeptically. "Are you lying?"

"I told you, Auren, I don't lie."

"Why wouldn't you want others to know your qualities? Your *actual* qualities—not the sexual ones."

"But, as you've just learned, the sexual ones are something I'm proud of."

"Niall," I chided him.

The bed shook with his silent chuckle. "All joking aside . . . it's complicated."

"Uncomplicate it for me," I said, yawning.

"Another time." He lifted the blankets to cover us. "We should get some sleep. We have a busy day tomorrow, and I need my beauty rest."

I smiled at his light humor.

The mattress shifted as he situated his body up against mine, draping his arm over me and holding me close. "May I stay?" he whispered onto my neck.

Yes. The word was on my lips and ready to soar, but I didn't want to seem desperate.

"Only if you promise to keep me warm," I said, pressing back into his body and closing my eyes.

His breath tickled the shell of my ear as he whispered, "It would be my pleasure."

52

WELCOME HOME

MY EYES FLUTTERED OPEN, AND THE WISPS OF BLACK INK FROM NIALL'S shroud stared back at me.

I was wrapped up in his arms, cradled to his chest, breathing in his scent. His tan skin was smooth against my face, the ink flawless, curving and swirling around his muscles like a lover's touch. I slowly reached up and traced a finger along a wisp of black that dipped below his collarbone.

A deep sound rumbled in his throat. "That tickles."

I retracted my fingers and grinned. "Just admiring your shroud."

"How'd you sleep?" he asked, his voice husky.

I shifted my head onto his arm so that I could see him. "I feel more rested than I have in quite some time."

"You're welcome," he whispered as he leaned down and took my face in his hand, kissing me. The move thrilled me. Another web of desire spun within me as he slid his tongue between my lips, taking the kiss deeper, like he'd been deprived of it during sleep and couldn't wait any longer.

When he finally pulled away, I panted for breath, and he smiled down at me through sleepy eyes. "Good morning." He grinned.

"Indeed it is." I smiled back, blushing.

Can you just stay here and kiss me like that all day?

I was half-tempted to ask the question out loud, but he spoke again before I could decide if I was bold enough to be that straightforward.

"By the way, I'd say last night qualifies as earning our good luck for the year."

I drew back to look at him, confused as to what he meant. Then I recalled what he had told me last night at Lumeri: the sexual acts, the gods watching . . .

I snorted a laugh. "I'd really prefer not to imagine the gods watching that."

He chuckled in response and pressed his lips to my forehead before rolling over and standing to stretch. The muscles across his back rippled and pulled taut, and I quickly looked away before I reached out to drag him back into bed.

Vanir had sent breakfast—magically of course—with a note wishing us safe travels and that he would see Niall and I tomorrow night for Calledan's celebration.

Today, Niall would be taking me to his court's territory. I probably should have felt nervous, but strangely, I felt . . . excited.

Neither of us spoke any further about what had happened last night, even though it felt like we were both on the brink of casually mentioning it.

After a quick and rather quiet breakfast—with several stolen glances on both of our parts—Niall ported us to the edge of his territory.

Behind us, the lush green highlands quickly gave way to the rocky foothills, where darkened stone jutted up from the earth. And before us, the precipice of the mountains of Calledan loomed. I sucked in a sharp breath as I took in their stark façade and staggering height, which had me feeling like a flea in a wheatfield.

A narrow gap cut through the cliff face, creating an entrance to the territory. But it was what stood on either side of the gap that astounded me.

Flanking the opening were two colossal statues of fae warriors, carved into the stone face of the mountains. One wore a helm over his face and held a sword by his side in his left hand. His other hand held a short blade horizontally in front of his forehead.

The second warrior's hands were positioned in front of his chest, one hovering above the other as if summoning a mass of energy between his palms. Both were in a stance that made them appear as if they would step right out of the mountainside. Giants, poised to defend their precious territory.

Beyond them, staggering peaks disappeared into the gray clouds.

"Who are they?" I asked, straining my neck to gaze up at them.

"They're modeled after the two founders of Calledan. Brothers. Both of them formed this court and laid the foundations for its strength and prosperity. They're the reason for our territory's fierce reputation, and why our army is next to none in combat."

"They're very intimidating," I said.

Niall nodded. "This is just one of Calledan's entry points—or gates— as we like to call them. From here, travelers from other territories are allowed to port to their intended destination, same as it is in each court."

I brought my eyes back down to focus on what lay beyond the statues. "How many gates are there to your territory?"

"There are three in mine, and two in Vanir's, since we're bordered on all sides by different courts. Benmoor, Drastia and Elandrew each have one."

"And you're alerted when someone arrives or passes through them?"

"Yes. Each gate is connected to its High Lord through our magic. Come." He held out his hand for me, and as we approached the narrow passage, a rush of shadows spiraled up from my feet to my head before disappearing into nothing.

"Don't worry, I've deemed you worthy of passage," he said, looking back at me with a wink.

"I'd certainly hope so." I half laughed. "What happens to those that are found not worthy?"

"They're held at the gate indefinitely, until they leave or are forced to. The Brothers—whose statues are carved at each gate—fortified this court so well that its wards haven't been breached for thousands of years. Their original wards still stand. Of course, each new High Lord can strengthen them with his own, but theirs were woven with Old Magic and have stood the test of time. Only the clout of a very powerful being would be able to change that."

The wind sang along the stone as we passed through a few hundred feet of the mountain's narrow gap. High above us the walls opened up to the clouded skies. And then, the walkway widened, leading out to an open stone ledge that overlooked the most stunning landscape I had ever seen.

The mountains, in all their glory, stretched before us, rising up like thrones from the dense valley below. Their rugged, dark peaks, laced with the deep greens of the forest, stretched as far as I could see. Some even reached so high they were half hidden in the thick cloud cover that drifted above.

At the bottom of the deep valley, a rushing river with white capped rapids wound its way through the terrain.

It was breathtaking. Wild and untamed.

Niall smiled proudly. "Welcome to Calledan."

As if the gods smiled down as well, a ray of morning sunlight slipped through the clouds and beamed onto the valley below, illuminating the tall, dark pines and the even darker stone from which they rooted themselves.

A strange familiarity settled over me, like a peace I hadn't known in a very long time. I breathed in the fresh mountain air and let my power wash over me. It pushed up against my skin as if to take a peek at what I saw.

This feeling, this place, it felt like . . . home. Not a home I'd ever been to, but one that called to me. Like a parent crying out in joy at their long-lost child's return.

I was at a loss for words.

Niall stood at my side, watching me. "If you think this is something special, just wait until tomorrow night."

"Lumeri?" I asked.

"Yes. It will top Vanir's, I promise you that."

I couldn't imagine anything outshining that enormous fire, but I guess I would find out soon enough.

To our right and left, the path veered off into two sets of stairs that lined the mountainside, leading to different areas that I couldn't see.

"Where is the city?"

From where we stood, there was no sign of life at all. No fae, no towns, no homes. It was like nothing existed except for trees and stone and rushing waters.

"Hidden here and there. Mostly strategically tucked away between several of our largest peaks. I'll give you a tour when we have some time."

He slid his arm around my waist from behind me. "Let's get you home first."

"Home?" I asked, looking over my shoulder at him.

He chuckled, cinching himself up against my backside. "Well, *my* home."

I had a feeling he wanted to add, *and maybe yours.*

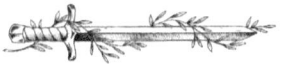

We ported right onto a large, semicircular patio that jutted out from a cliffside, and I blinked in awe at what loomed before us.

Perhaps I'd expected a cabin, or a modest, humble structure with a worn—but sturdy—build. Something similar to what I'd seen in Vahrenhall.

But this . . .

This was refined and opulent and *massive.*

Cast in the shadow of the mountain from which it was built, was a beautiful multi-level edifice that wound around the cliffside. Each level boasted solid floor to ceiling arched windows and eaves that were accented with thick wooden beams, lending a touch of rustic charm to the mass of stone it stood against. Large lanterns with flickering flames bracketed the grand windows, their golden light lapping against the blackened stone. And straight ahead, giant glass double doors awaited us.

Niall placed a hand on my lower back and began ushering me across the patio, but I halted mid-step, turning my head at the sound of rushing water. It sounded so close, as if it was flowing from right underneath our feet. I looked around, trying to find the source.

"Is that . . . water?" I asked.

"It is," Niall answered, and turned to walk me to the edge of the waist-high stone wall that encompassed the patio.

I leaned over and peered down. Indeed, a waterfall charged forth from under us, plunging to the depths. Its pounding roar echoed through the valley, chased by the swaths of mist in its wake.

To the left of the falls, cut into the face of the mountain, was a long, winding stairway that led up to an entrance at the far end of the patio on which we stood.

"This is . . ." Words failed me.

Niall grinned and took my hand, gently guiding me back toward the glass doors. "Not what you expected, I take it?"

I shook my head, gawking upward at the sleek façade as we approached.

The doors swung open into a cavernous room, and the smell of woodsmoke and leather with a hint of vanilla caressed my senses. The walls were the same raw, blackened stone of the mountain, and the polished black marble floors gleamed beneath an assortment of patterned rugs. Furs and plush blankets decorated the oversized, tufted leather sofas and armchairs that formed multiple seating areas throughout the space, and dark emerald green velvet curtains pooled onto the ground around every grand window pane that lined the patio.

Golden orbs that were far bigger than the ones I had seen in the Woodland Court drifted about the space, casting a warm glow upon every surface that wasn't already touched by the natural light coming in from the windows at our backs.

The textures, the aesthetic, the coziness, all of it embodied the mountains; the comfort of their somber strength.

This place was intimate, even in its vastness. It sang to me, tugging at a baser instinct that had me longing to dig my feet in and plant roots.

"Home," Niall hummed, stepping forward and turning a circle.

Home. I could almost picture it.

"We call it The Keep," he said, following me as I perused the space and took in each detail.

My hand grazed over the soft fur pelt along the back of the nearest leather sofa. "It's stunning."

Everything was perfectly curated, and the quality was impeccable. Vanir was right when he said that Niall preferred certain comforts. But I wasn't complaining. In fact, I felt strangely welcomed. Like I belonged.

Niall's gaze went distant, briefly relaying a message to someone on the other end of his mental connection, before he sauntered up to me.

"We have a meeting to attend," he said with a smirk.

"What sort of meeting?"

"The kind where a trio of males might bombard you with endless questions to ease their curiosities."

I looked at him quizzically.

"My Trium," he said. "They've been anxious to meet you ever since Elandrew's Lumeri."

"But, that was—"

"I know. Aremis has a big mouth." He smiled and offered me his hand.

Maeson had mentioned the males that made up Niall's group of confidants.

The Trium.

They sounded intimidating.

Niall led me down a wide hallway just across from the main area. When we came to a large door that had been left ajar, he eased it open, and entered first.

The room had no windows, as it was completely tucked into the mountain. Its walls and floors were the same as the common area, and more orbs floated freely through the air. Stately black banners with Calledan's sigil of a war helm over two mountains hung from golden rods along the sides of the room. And in the midst of the space, a large stone table sat, centered under a grand chandelier that housed several hundred lit candles.

Niall ushered me forward alongside him toward the far end of the room, where three male figures were gathered, laughing in conversation. One was seated on the tabletop with his leg drawn up onto a chair, his elbow resting on his knee. Another stood with his arms crossed and feet spread wide. The third leaned with his back against the wall, his body covered mostly in shadow.

Their conversation paused, and their stares fixated on me as we approached.

"This"—Niall gestured toward the group of males—"is my Trium."

The strangers studied me for a long, intense moment, curiosity glinting in their eyes.

Niall placed a hand on my shoulder, and a grin played at the corner of his mouth as he said to the males, "Don't get any ideas. She's mine."

53
THE TRIUM

THE MALE WHO HAD BEEN SITTING ON THE TABLE SLID OFF IN ONE SMOOTH movement and stepped toward me, his boots moving soundlessly along the marble floor.

His thick, dark brown hair hung fairly straight, just grazing his shoulders, and his facial hair was trimmed close, outlining his mouth and strong jawline. His olive skin appeared sun-kissed even though it was hidden under his very fitted black fighting leathers. Eyes the color of chocolate danced with amusement as he reached up for my hand and gave me a slight bow.

"You make it seem like we're a bunch of savages," he said, donning a grin of his own as he looked from Niall to me. "It's nice to finally meet you, Auren. I'm Aremis." His voice was smooth and polished, like velvet.

"I've heard a lot about you," I said, smiling.

"I can certainly say the same." He inclined his head, then tossed a casual smirk at Niall.

It wasn't hard to see why Maeson was attracted to this male. He was handsome.

And . . . I recognized him from somewhere.

"I've seen you before . . ." I paused, rummaging through my memory until I landed on the instance I was looking for. "You were at Elandrew's Lumeri. You pulled Breck aside for a private conversation."

"Ah, yes. Though that was more of a distraction on Niall's behalf."

Niall leaned in to add, "Otherwise Breck wouldn't have let me whisk you onto the dance floor." He clapped Aremis on the shoulder.

The second male took that as his invitation and strode over with a wicked grin on his face.

I could tell he commanded any space he was in. He had all the outward appearance of a striking warrior, and his muscular chest practically tore at his shirt's open collar. His skin was gently tanned, and his brown hair was bathed in scattered gold tones, as if he spent a good deal of time outside under the sun. Half of it was pulled up into a knot at the back of his head, while the rest fell down in waves to just past his shoulders. His strong facial features were still apparent beneath a slightly thicker beard.

He was rugged, attractive.

Still bearing that mischievous grin, he stopped in front of me and crossed his arms, light green eyes glinting under the orb's light. "So, you're the one Niall won't shut up about."

The male seemed to tower over me more than Niall did—even though they were about the same height. But where Niall was hewn from mountain stone, this male embodied an entirely different breed of fae.

He reminded me of Vanir—burly, and rough around the edges.

Niall shook his head and grinned. "Auren, this is Roirdan. Commander of my armies and a pain in my ass."

Roirdan laughed loudly, his shoulders shaking with the sound. "Don't let him fool you, I'm his favorite. And I *am* a savage." He winked.

"Looks like you're the second favorite now," Aremis cut in, nodding in my direction.

"Shit, I guess you're right." Roirdan unhooked his arms and pulled me in for a hug. I stumbled forward, not expecting the gesture. "I won't hold it against you." He patted me on the back, which rocked me even more, thanks to his strength.

"Careful, Roir," Niall cautioned him.

"You're too strong for your own good," Aremis added.

Roirdan pulled away. "Sorry, little one." His grin shifted to one side as he stepped back.

All three males fell silent, and turned toward the fourth, waiting for him to step out of the shadows.

When he pushed off the wall and slowly came forward, I gasped.

He was *beautiful.*

The light illuminated his long silver-white hair and fair skin. The elegant planes of his face and square chin were cast in the shadow of his strong cheekbones, which framed his gray eyes.

As he moved, the light above crested upon a pair of enormous, feathered wings the color of ash. They were tucked in tightly against his back, but I knew without a doubt that they would be wondrous to behold when he stretched them out completely. The ends of each wing dragged the floor behind him as he approached.

He wore fitted, black leathers—just like Aremis, but his collar differed, reaching up his entire neck to his jawline. A sizable dagger was strapped at each of his thighs, and a silver sword pommel gleamed above his head, fastened between his wings.

He stopped a few feet away, his expression remaining stoic as he took me in.

"And this is Remic," Niall said.

I stared into Remic's gray eyes. They were haunted; with pain or longing or perhaps grief. The way he regarded me made me feel as if those very eyes were peeling back each layer of my soul, trying to see what I was made of.

A strange wave of calmness washed over me, like an invisible force had laid reassuring hands upon my shoulders and told me good news. As if he also experienced the feeling, Remic tilted his head ever so slightly, and the apprehension that I saw on his face quickly flashed to something like a silent realization, or recognition, there and then gone again as he blinked.

"The Dionach," I practically whispered, taking in his wings once more.

"One of many," Aremis stated.

Remic finally spoke. "You know of us?" His voice was equally as stunning as he was. Like water running across smooth stones—sleek and crisp, and as primeval as he appeared.

"I know very little, but yes, I've been told of your kind." I tried my best to keep my eyes on his, instead of staring at his wings, but the task was proving difficult. I'd never seen anyone like him. "It's a pleasure to meet you," I added.

He dipped his head slightly, and as he did, I noticed faint gray markings at each of his temples, framing the sides of his eyes. "The pleasure is mine," he replied in a low tone.

He stepped back into the shadows again, all too quickly.

Not one for many words, then.

Niall pulled out a chair and offered it to me, but I declined, so he sat, throwing a casual arm out on the table. He patted his thigh with his other hand, offering *himself* as a seat, hoping to entice me. My face heated, and I shifted my weight on my feet. I liked that option much more, but instead, I said, "I'll stand for now, thank you."

He grinned and shrugged, casually crossing an ankle over his knee and flourishing his hand at the Trium. "This is my family. Well, as close to a family as we can get. Aremis is my advisor, my second in command, and —for all intents and purposes—my second set of eyes and ears. Roirdan handles the armies, and Remic—"

"Keeps us all in line," Roirdan cut in, as he too tugged on a chair and sat.

I looked at the Dionach, but he remained silent against the wall— completely content to just listen and observe.

Niall continued. "Remic guards us and anyone we deem necessary, as is the Dionach way. He's also our gate-keeper. Should there ever be anyone at our gates that shouldn't be there, he sees to it that they are . . . removed."

Roirdan scoffed at Niall. "What he means is that Remic makes a display of their mutilated bodies to warn others not to fuck with us. Please tell me you aren't sensitive to blood and gore, Auren?"

"Not at all, actually." I smiled.

Niall shot a look at Roirdan, but the commander ignored it, leaning forward in his chair with his elbows on his knees. His eyes narrowed on me, and the corner of his mouth turned up. "Have you ever killed anyone?"

"Roirdan!" Aremis outright scolded him.

I thought back to the two men at the castle, lying motionless on the floor after my power had decided to surface for the first time. I didn't know if they had died that night, or just been knocked out, but something told me the blow had been fatal to the both of them. "I have," I admitted with no hint of shame.

Roirdan simply laughed and said, "Fuck yeah."

Niall was now looking at me like I was an entirely different person.

"So you can fight?" Roirdan continued.

"I can. I'm skilled with my fists and a blade. Before I came here, I had just been named a member of the King's Guard, after winning a competition and besting the prince."

Roirdan sat back in his chair with a broad smile, completely content with what he'd learned. "You and I are going to get along just fine."

"She's not your new battle-buddy," Aremis said.

I scanned all their faces. "I can hold my own."

Niall grinned in approval.

I looked over through the darkness to Remic, who was still studying me. His face didn't betray what he was thinking in the slightest, but something told me he was more curious than skeptical, and that the scrutiny was typical of his kind.

Roirdan leaned in over the table once more, narrowing his eyes at me with a playful smirk on his lips. "What's your favorite weapon?"

I opened my mouth to reply, but Niall cut in abruptly. "Don't answer that. He'll hide it from you during training."

"Hey," Roirdan chided, chuckling. "When have I ever done that?"

Aremis raised his hand off the table slightly, and lifted a finger. "You did it to one of the newly appointed captains last week, during their midnight muster."

Everyone was silent for a moment, and I caught Remic fighting back a grin as he shook his head.

"Ah, shit. I forgot about that," Roirdan said. Then, he let out a deep laugh. "That bastard's probably still searching for his sword."

I couldn't help but grin.

"There will be plenty of time for you two to connect over weapons later," Niall said. "Right now"—he jerked his chin at the commander—"you and I have some business to take care of that can't be put off any longer."

Roirdan gave him a nod and stood, tossing me a smile.

Niall stood as well. "Auren, darling, if it's all right with you, Aremis will show you to your chambers. I'll return for you soon."

I wasn't exactly in a place to say no, so I nodded, and Niall tossed me a wink as he, Roirdan, and Remic filed out, leaving Aremis and I standing there, alone.

PART TWO

THE BONDS OF FATE

54

A STRANGE GIFT

Roirdan, Remic, Aremis.

I repeated the names of Niall's Trium in my head over and over—committing them to memory.

Roirdan, Remic, Aremis.

They were nothing like I'd expected. So different from one another, yet somehow, they fit together.

Roirdan—the commander of Niall's armies—seemed to be the most talkative of the bunch. His sense of humor and interest in weapons made me feel instantly at ease.

Remic—the Dionach—was a mystery with wings. He'd been quiet during our introduction, watching me with a certain look that I couldn't pinpoint the meaning of. I'd piqued his curiosity, just as he'd piqued mine.

Niall had departed with both males just moments ago to take care of some urgent business. Which left me with Aremis, Niall's advisor and second in command.

He was handsome. Although, each of them were, in their own way, I supposed. And he seemed pleasant. I half expected a group of brutes with no personality or regard for respect—given the way Breck had described Niall's court as a "band of traitors to their own territories."

Aremis's smooth voice cut through my thoughts. "I had hoped to get to meet you in Elandrew after you met with the Elder, but Niall had me checking up on a few things."

I whipped my head over to where he was standing.

How does he—

"Niall filled me in on just about everything," he said, chuckling as he tapped his temple twice.

"Right." I recognized the gesture.

Mind-walking.

It made sense that he would be privy to everything Niall knew—being his advisor.

Niall had also told Morah that she'd been followed, and didn't deny when she'd accused Aremis of being the one to do it. How was he able to do so much for Niall without being seen? How could he follow someone and never get caught?

I looked up at him again. "Can I ask you something?"

"By all means," he said.

"How come I never saw you again in Elandrew after Lumeri?"

He gave me a casual smirk, then suddenly, the space around him pulsed. The outline of his body became like a force field, palpitating with a faintly iridescent distortion that blurred the edges of his being. He looked as if he were going to fade out and vanish at any moment. Like he was an image that didn't truly exist in a corporeal form.

Like a mirage.

The pulsing force hovered around him as if it were an entity all of its own. "I am what's called Cheshm Zadan. This"—he gestured to himself—"is my gift."

I studied the distortion, my fingers itching to reach out and touch it. To see if he was still truly there. "What is it, exactly?" I asked.

"A second set of eyes and ears, capable of seeing and hearing things that other gifted beings cannot. We refer to it as the Aura."

"So, are you fae? Or . . ."

"Yes, I am fae. But this gift sets me apart." He tilted his head to the side and gauged my reaction as I stared at the Aura.

It looked as if it should emit a sound—something akin to a humming, but it was utterly silent. If it *did* have a sound, it was one that I wasn't able to hear.

"It's mesmerizing," I said. "It reminds me of the boundary around The Veil."

Aremis considered my statement. "An interesting comparison. It's thought that the Cheshm Zadan are a result of the mingling of witches and the fae in the ancient past, but no one is certain of our lineage. The gift has presented itself amongst so few, and at such random intervals, that it's difficult to trace back. The last fae with this ability existed several hundred years ago. Then, I came along. The power only manifests in certain offspring, but no one knows why. Because of our rarity, my kind is highly coveted by all the courts, and that means my gift puts the court my allegiance is tied to at a great advantage, and a great risk."

"And how does it work, may I ask?"

"It allows me to be in two places at once. I'm here, but I can project my Aura out beyond myself to gather intel. Two beings in one, essentially. The Aura has its own consciousness—an essence, if you will. I simply sync my willpower to it and instruct it. It listens, watches, and reports. I am simply the vessel it's attached to."

On a silent command, the Aura seeped back into his skin, returning to wherever it was housed inside him, leaving his body to appear normal again.

"What you might find most intriguing is that my physical form can also fade into the Aura and disappear completely. But the effort is taxing, and I do not do it often. Not many know what I am and what I can do, and it's not knowledge that I want everyone to know."

Powers like his and Niall's were far beyond the mundane magic I'd imagined the fae having. Both of their gifts seemed as if they had come from somewhere else. *Something* else.

Something . . . *other.*

Then again, all forms and calibers of magic were as foreign to me as they were astonishing.

"And you've had this power since birth?" I asked.

"Yes. The power itself manifests rather quickly. Cheshm Zadan live very difficult lives as younglings, having not yet learned to master it. When not controlled, it sounds like a thousand voices speaking at once and a thousand images playing across your mind's eye."

I winced at the thought. "That sounds . . . terrifying."

Aremis nodded. "Most who are born with the gift do not survive past a few years of age. They're often driven mad by it. Most are not mentally strong enough to overcome what they do not yet know. But for those who do . . . it is a blessing. And a curse."

"And how did you learn to control it?"

"It requires a mind that can embrace the chaos and remain unfazed. I had to center myself and force my mind to be at the forefront. The power is there, yes, but so is the entity within me. I had to show it that *I* am the true being with existential power. That *I* hold the control. I'm not sure how I was able to compartmentalize that as a youngling. One of the lucky ones, I guess." He lifted his face to the black banner that hung on the wall and regarded it for a long, silent moment.

I watched him curiously, trying to work out the enigma that he was. The struggle he must have endured. Who he had to become in order to embrace the chaos he held within him.

"But enough about me," he said, leaning against the table and resting his palms on the edge. "Niall mentioned that your power is very strong, and that you've been successful at calling it forth. Did it come naturally for you?"

I nodded. "Much easier than I expected. But I know I have a lot to learn. I'm still so new to all of this."

He met my stare and held it. "Given all that you know, are you still reluctant, or have you started to consider that your fate truly lies within this realm?"

It was a loaded question, and one that I wasn't sure how to answer yet.

"If I'm being honest, I'm still not quite sure."

A beat of silence passed.

"Good." He tapped his open palm on the table, then pushed off it and walked by me. "Come."

I turned to follow. "*Good?* How is that good?"

He tossed me a grin as I caught up to him. "You went from thinking you're simply human, to finding out you're actually a being of immense power. If you had come to terms with that within a matter of days, I would think you were corrupt or reckless. But I sense you're neither of those things, and your answer proves it." My confusion must have shown on my face, because his grin only widened. "It means you're not power-hungry. And that's a good thing."

"Oh. Um, thank you?" I would have to take that as a compliment.

He dipped his chin as he opened the door. "Acceptance will come with time, Auren. For now, let me show you to your chambers."

Aremis seemed older than he was. The way he spoke, the way he carried himself felt like he was wise beyond his years. It made sense that he was Niall's advisor and second.

He matched my stride, giving me a quick briefing of the rooms as we passed them, indicating where different hallways led. The Keep was a network of spaces built into the mountain, and each area was just as dark and cozy and beautiful as the last.

On the level above the meeting room we'd been in, a quiet hallway sat with only a handful of doors, spaced out far enough from each other that I knew each of the chambers must be generous in size.

"Remic and Roirdan's quarters are just there." Aremis pointed to our left as we passed a few doors. "Mine's here, across from yours. It's safest to keep everyone closer together in a vast place like this."

Just as he finished explaining, a door down the hall opened and a head full of tumbling red hair leaned out.

"Auren!" Maeson yelled as she locked eyes with me and raced down the hallway. "I thought I heard someone talking!"

As soon as she threw her arms around my neck to hug me, she stiffened.

"Maeson? What's . . ." I pulled back, following her gaze to Aremis.

She cleared her throat as lady-like as she could and quickly straightened her skirts, wobbling slightly.

"Hi," she said to him.

"Hi," he replied, shyly.

"I see you've met Auren," she said, clasping her hands in front of her.

"I have." He was suddenly all awkward facial expressions and no voice. Completely at odds with how talkative he had just been with me. He began to clear his own throat, but fumbled on it. "H-How are you?"

"I'm well, thank you." Excitement rang through her voice, but when Aremis didn't continue the conversation, her face fell.

She focused back on me as she gripped my hand, quickly recovering her composure. "Looks like we'll be next to each other now."

"Yes . . . It seems *everyone's* rooms are close by." I flared my eyes purposefully at her, hoping she would catch my hidden message.

At first, the words washed right over her, but then, she caught on. Her gaze swung back to Aremis. "Oh . . ."

He'd suddenly found his own chamber door far more interesting than it should have been.

Well this is awkward.

I cleared my throat and offered the only reprieve I could think of. "Thank you, Aremis. I think I'll tour my chambers with Maeson while I wait for Niall to return."

He nodded and stepped away quite inelegantly.

A mix of emotions washed over Maeson's face, but I didn't let her linger. I grabbed her by the arm and hauled her inside my new chambers. She walked straight over to the small leather sofa facing the fireplace on the far wall and plopped down on it.

I leaned my back against the door and shook off the second-hand embarrassment that had sprouted in my gut for Aremis. Maeson had mentioned that he was reserved. Now I understood what she meant.

When I finally focused on the room I stood in, my eyes went straight to the floor-to-ceiling windows that bracketed both sides of a black stone hearth, framing a wondrous view of Calledan's mountains. Black velvet curtains pooled onto the ground at each end, drenching the room in Niall's favorite color.

In the corner to my left, several golden orbs hovered, casting a buttery light on the spacious bed that was set within an alcove. A small stack of books sat atop a fur pelt on the single nightstand, and several cozy blankets were folded neatly on the bench at the foot of the bed. To my right, an armoire stood near the bathing chamber door, as well as a small golden table with a set of drinking glasses and a carafe of water.

I crossed the space to the windows and drank in the sights. The chamber faced the same direction the patio did, overlooking the stairs that wound up the mountainside, and out beyond to the staggering cliffs that rose in every direction.

The view was breathtaking.

"Does your bedchamber have windows like this?" I asked Maeson.

"Yes," she replied quietly.

I turned back and found her staring ahead at the fireplace.

She snapped out of her daze and met my stare. "Mine only has one window though."

The interaction with Aremis was bothering her—that much was clear.

I took a seat next to her on the sofa. "Did Aremis know you were here?"

She sighed and fixed her eyes on the mountains beyond The Keep. "No. I haven't left my chamber. I've been resting since I got here."

I slowly nodded. "And I take it Niall didn't mention that anyone else's bedchambers were on this hall?"

She shook her head.

A long, quiet moment stretched between us, and then, to my surprise, she perked up, shifting to face me further. "But, I've been thinking about what you said. That I should talk to him. See if there's actually something there." She fiddled with the hem of her sweater. "So, I guess now that I know he's close-by . . . that makes it easier."

"Exactly." I tossed her a smile.

"As long as he doesn't shut down again, like he just did," she added, chewing on her bottom lip.

"I think the fact that you were here just caught him off guard."

She thought about that for a moment, then smirked. "I'm glad it surprised him."

"Why is that?"

"Because if I know Aremis, he'll run straight to Niall and ask for an explanation. And if I know Niall, he'll tell Aremis to ask me himself. So Aremis will *have* to bring it up at some point."

"See"—I flourished my hand between us—"that's a start. And I'll be here too. You know, in case you need someone to make up excuses to get you some alone time." I wiggled my brows at her, recalling how she had used Wrynn's social anxiety as a means to skip out on Vahrenhall's Lumeri.

She caught onto the implication and grinned. "By the way, how'd that go?"

I chewed my bottom lip, debating what to tell her.

"Oh, don't you go quiet on me now. I need details." She tucked her feet up on the sofa and leaned forward, ready to devour any information I was going to give her.

I described Vahrenhall's Lumeri, painting as vivid a picture of the celebration as I could for her. As for what happened afterward . . . I kept the details to a minimum. She squealed when I told her that Niall and I had kissed, and grumbled when I refused to give her the explicit details.

We spent a good while sharing gossip and trading stories and giggling like two adolescent girls. And just after promising that I'd accompany her on a shopping errand so that she could fill her new armoire with dozens of sweaters, I felt Niall's presence. The thrumming within me spiked before his knock sounded at the door. I turned right as it opened, and smiled as he strode in.

He lifted a playful brow by way of greeting. "Gossiping about a High Lord in his own home could be considered treasonous."

"Depends on the gossip," I replied.

A grin spread across his lips. "Let's hope it was the good kind. Find everything to your liking?"

"It's lovely," I mused, glancing around the room again. "And the view—"

"Is entirely unfair," Maeson butted in, feigning a jealous tantrum. "I demand a room with more windows."

Niall laughed. "For someone who loves the underground, I'm surprised you're not begging for a room deeper in the mountain."

Maeson smirked. "I'll take one of those too."

I couldn't help but laugh as I watched her level a look at him.

"Anything else?" Niall crooned. He'd probably see to it that whatever was requested was done, regardless of if it was a playful jest.

She tapped her finger to her chin, then settled back into the sofa contentedly. "That'll be all for now."

"And you?" Niall asked, eyes fixed on me again. "Anything *you're* in need of?"

I swallowed hard as thoughts of the other night flooded my mind and rushed to the tip of my tongue.

A kiss. Your hands on my body.

"Not that I can think of at the moment," I answered.

His eyes flickered ever so slightly, like he knew what I was thinking. "Well, I have something for you that I think you'll be quite happy about."

A small figure popped into existence next to him. Black eyes, and a mouth full of small, sharp teeth smiled up at me.

"Sorscha!" I stood to go to her, but she closed the distance in a blink and leapt to embrace me. I squeezed her and laughed, looking at Niall in question. "How?"

"I snagged her when I went back to return the *Seidr*. She's helped me make sure everything was prepared for your arrival."

I set her down and she beamed, smoothing out her hair in quick strokes, like a cat would smooth its fur.

"Thank you for bringing her here," I said.

Niall inclined his head and came forward, offering me his hand. "I hate to break up this little reunion, but I'd like to get a bit of training in with you this afternoon. So, if you'll join me . . ."

I took his hand and looked back at Maeson, who was giving me a cheeky grin. "We'll continue our gossip later."

"We'd better," she said.

"Mmm. So, you *were* talking about me?" Niall hummed in my ear.

"The real question is, did I speak well or ill of you?"

His smirk widened just before we vanished.

55
PORTING LESSONS

Porting. That's what today's lesson was going to be.

Niall had brought me to the base of the mountains, to a place called The Elderwood, where the oldest temple in Anbrya stood. Black stone steps jutted from the forest floor and crept up the sloping terrain, leading to a structure, which towered amongst the trees.

"This is a place for worshiping many gods, and where special ceremonies and rites are held," Niall explained quietly as we ascended the steps.

A colonnade of intricate arches stood at the face of the temple, which was built from the dark mountain stone, and polished smooth, not looking nearly as old as I imagined it was. I could see large basins of fire within, and a multitude of flickering candle flames—the only light inside the otherwise dark space. The rest of the temple's interior remained a mystery. The gentle chant of female voices, and the hollow lull of a deep bell echoed out of the darkness.

"Can we go in?" I asked.

"Another time, perhaps. The priestesses are in prayer." His hand at my waist gently guided me to the right, but my stare lingered as I tried to peer inside.

We continued past the temple, where similar, smaller structures sat tucked away in the pines, all connected by a paved pathway that wound through the forest.

Patrons quietly went about their business, paying no attention to us as we strolled by. Some carried small urns or bundles of flowers. Others carried with them only a solemn expression and dampened eyes.

I slowed my pace as I watched a fae female and what looked to be her young daughter, walk out of the nearest temple. The youngling's eyes were wet with tears, and her mother lifted her gently, speaking soft, comforting words in her ear.

"What are they doing?" I whispered to Niall.

"Some temples are for worship and celebration. Some are for prayer. And some"—he nodded toward the female and her daughter—"are for remembrance and mourning."

The female locked eyes with Niall and gave him a sad smile, briefly inclining her head as she passed by.

Niall did the same.

No words were spoken. None were needed.

And the fact that there wasn't so much as a hint of urgency for her to bow or address her High Lord upon seeing him, baffled me.

We kept quiet as we wound down the path, until we came upon a stream that skirted a large stone slab. The area was tranquil, secluded; the trickle of water and the whispering wind in the trees being the only sounds other than our footsteps.

Ancient pines, birch, and elms stood around us like statues of giants, silently watching as we stepped onto the open foundation. Judging by its size, I assumed it had once been the base for another temple. One that never saw its completion.

I scanned the trees, but it seemed we had wandered down a path no one else was interested in taking.

We were alone.

Niall watched me as I turned circles on the pavement. "Ready to learn the inner workings of your favorite method of transportation?"

He seemed particularly eager to see this come to fruition, and I'd be lying if I said I wasn't also trying to keep a lid on the jar of butterflies that were writhing like wild beasts inside my stomach.

"I think so," I said, taking in the space, purposefully dulling my enthusiasm so that if I failed at this, I wouldn't be too embarrassed. "I've gotten a better handle on the motion sickness part, so that's a start."

"When you port yourself, you're less likely to feel nauseous."

"Perfect. How hard can the rest be?"

He grinned. "For starters, it's best to practice in an area without any obstacles. And I definitely don't want you doing this at higher altitudes yet, so that's why we're here. Just be mindful of the trees."

"What's wrong with higher altitudes?"

"If you miss your target area, you could go tumbling right off the edge of a cliff. Or you might just port into thin air between mountain peaks."

"Oh." I hadn't thought about that.

I shifted back and forth on my feet.

Is porting really that hard?

"Unless, you'd rather give it a try up there first?" He pointed up toward one of the towering peaks and smirked.

"No, this will do," I said, glancing around and taking note of the close proximity of the trees around us.

My gaze returned to him, snagging on his lips. Lingering on them.

He stared back. "If you keep looking at me like that, we won't get anywhere with this lesson."

I cleared my throat, pushing back thoughts of last night that tried to surface in my memory again.

He narrowed his eyes and gave me a sideways grin like he knew exactly where my mind had gone. "How about if you manage to port successfully, I'll reward you." His gaze dipped to my lips. "With whatever you desire."

The way he said *desire* sent a rush of heat through me.

"Anything in particular come to mind?" he simpered.

I smiled, doing my best to keep my composure. "We can decide on that later."

He inclined his head. "Fair enough."

It was an effort to peel my eyes from him and turn toward the center of the stone clearing, but I managed.

He stalked away toward the edge and took up a position there. "Porting is a simple act in itself. It's visualizing your place of reappearance that gets complicated. Think of it like mental shielding, you need to visualize it to be successful. Now, I want you to clear your mind."

Easier said than done.

The look that I gave him said as much.

I lowered my eyes and breathed, inhaling the heavy scent of the trees and the crisp mountain air, and exhaling, expelling every lingering thought that danced into my consciousness.

"You'll need to shift your perspective from what's nearest to you now, to what would be nearest to you if you moved to where you want to be. That's why you can only port to places you've been to. You have to picture where it is that you want to go. Make sense?"

"Yes."

"Now, pick a corner of the pavilion and envision yourself standing there. Picture the distance of the trees around you from that spot, compared to where you currently stand. That will tell your minds-eye where you want to go. Once you're focused on seeing the space around you, call to your power, and will it to move your body there."

I lifted my eyes and settled them on a light-barked birch tree that stood an inch or two off the pavilion's edge across from me. I shifted my perspective from where I stood, to what I would see if I were right in front of the tree's trunk.

Here goes nothing.

I shut my eyes and tugged on my power, willing it to move my body in that direction.

After a few seconds, I popped an eye open, but I was no closer to the tree than I had been. I kept my eyes open and tried again.

Visualize. Tug. Nothing.

My hands clenched into fists.

I glanced over at Niall, who watched me with a faint grin on his lips from where he leaned against a thick tree, arms crossed in amusement.

I sighed, trying to work out the logistics of it in my head. There had to be something I was missing.

The first time I had ported with Niall, it had felt like my body had been pushed through a void. Like I'd been both whole and torn apart on the journey, and knit together again at the destination. That concept seemed relevant enough, and applicable, so I honed in on the tactic and tugged once more, telling my power what I wanted from it. In a rush of air, my body moved through space and time from where I had just stood, to the spot I envisioned myself at.

A brief moment of glee began—and then died suddenly as I materialized and my face slammed into the tree trunk. Pain roared across my nose, and I stumbled back.

Niall was instantly there to catch me, but he couldn't hold back his laugh. "Well that's one way to do it."

A flurry of embarrassment and resolve flooded my veins.

I grasped at my nose, catching the dribbling blood in the palms of my hands. "Damnit," I muttered.

"Are you all right?" he asked, turning me to him.

I sniffed, wiping at the blood with the back of my wrist. "I'm fine."

My nose began tingling—healing—I realized. The broken blood vessels were using the power that now flowed freely within me. Before I knew it, the coppery tang of blood disappeared.

"You'll learn to gauge the amount of power you need for each port. Long distances require more power. Shorter distances like this don't need as much. Try not to focus so hard next time."

He swept the locks of hair out of my eyes before stepping away again to the edge of the platform.

I strode to my original spot and tried to reset my focus, but I could feel him watching me. "Maybe if you weren't staring, I'd have better success," I called out over my shoulder.

A deep chuckle echoed across the pavilion, but when I turned toward where he had been standing, he'd vanished.

I looked around. No sign of him.

Good. Maybe I won't make such a fool of myself this time.

A jagged tree stump on the opposite end of the pavilion was my next target. I visualized myself near it—but not close enough to touch it—and called on my power.

Nothing.

I grunted in frustration and cleared my mind, picturing only the details of the stump, the serrated surface, its dried bark cracking and peeling away from its core. I envisioned myself staring down upon it.

Space whooshed around me, and I came up about four feet short of the stump, teetering on my toes with the forward momentum I arrived with.

A thrill went through me, and I looked back over my shoulder. But I was still alone.

I bit the inside of my cheek and searched for another spot to focus on, giddy with excitement. The stream alongside the pavilion; I pictured myself on the other side of it, boots digging into the river rock—

Whoosh.

Leaves and pebbles crunched under my boots as I landed just at the water's edge. My heels dipped into it slightly as I balanced myself out.

The large stone boulder beneath the trees to my right—

Whoosh.

Within an arms-length.

The center of the pavilion again—

Whoosh.

Two feet to the right.

My heart raced as I whirled and hunted for my next destination. Through the trees I spotted a small cave opening with a ledge about ten feet up from the ground.

Niall had warned me of heights, but my self-confidence was insatiable.

The moment I ported I knew I'd made a mistake. Where I expected my feet to meet stone, they met air instead, as I missed the ledge by two feet.

A yelp burst from my throat as I began free-falling, grasping at air, anticipating the crack of my bones as the ground rose to greet me.

Then, Niall was there, snatching me out of the air and porting us back to the ledge I'd been aiming for. I clung to him, trying to catch my breath as adrenaline coursed through my body.

"And this is why we don't practice with heights," he said once we'd materialized on solid ground.

I leaned around him and looked over the ledge. It seemed higher than it had from the ground. High enough to cause significant pain, and definitely some broken bones.

"Thanks for that," I said sheepishly.

He studied me as he held me in his arms. "You really are fearless, aren't you?"

"Apparently so." I looked back up at him. "I thought you'd left?"

He grinned and arched a brow at me. "I would never leave you by yourself on day one of porting, for this exact reason. I sensed you'd be a bit reckless."

I scoffed. "I'm not reckless."

"What do you call this then?" He gestured to the ledge we stood on.

"Okay, fine. No more porting to high places."

A laugh rumbled in his chest.

"Where did you go anyway?"

He nodded out toward the trees. "I was watching from the shadows."

"Creep," I said playfully.

His laugh echoed in the cave this time. "And just so you know, if you port somewhere and immediately find yourself needing to get out, you can port again instantaneously, all you have to do is think it."

"Well, that knowledge would have been helpful moments ago," I quipped.

"Yes, but first you need to master porting to the direct spot you're envisioning." He straightened my collar, his fingers gently grazing my neck.

"Working on it," I grumbled.

His eyes settled on my lips, and his hands slid up from my collar and cupped my face, gently lifting it to his.

He kissed me, slowly, lazily, deeply, as if we had all the time in the world, and my body melted in his arms. When he finally pulled away, the corner of his lips tilted up in the most perfect grin. "Did I guess correctly? Was that what you desired?" His voice was nothing more than a purr, and gods it had me wanting to capture his mouth again.

I leaned back in his arms, smiling. "Wouldn't you like to know?"

He chuckled and pulled me back into him, returning us to the stone slab below.

I practiced for a while longer, focusing on the placement and stability of my landings. The target area was a leaf the size of my hand, and the damned thing maddened me each time I missed it. I could have sworn it was moving on a phantom wind during the split second it took me to port to it.

Or perhaps that was Niall, moving the leaf with his magic just to get a rise out of me.

After four failed attempts to land on the designated target, and some simpering from Niall that had me convinced it was all his doing, I managed to land on top of it. Unfortunately, I also wobbled and stepped out to catch myself.

A grumble worked its way up my throat. The goal was to stick each landing without faltering—in case I ever had to port onto a narrow ledge or anything similar.

On the next try, I held my footing.

When Niall walked up to check my placement, and tried to make the case that I wasn't perfectly centered over the target, I flicked him on the shoulder, earning a laugh from him that confirmed he'd been meddling with the leaf, just as I'd thought.

A few more successful landings later, my power sputtered. My arms grew heavy, and it became increasingly more difficult to focus on my destination.

Niall ported us back to The Keep, but instead of arriving inside my bedchambers, we materialized just outside my door. Down the hall, Maeson and Aremis stood alone in conversation. Both of them glanced our way.

I lifted my hand and waved to them.

"One last test," Niall whispered in my ear. "Passing through physical objects."

My eyes widened as I whipped my head to him.

He patted the door with one hand before sliding both into his pockets and stepping aside. "All you have to do is picture your bed."

I hesitated and eyed the door. "There's nothing else to it? No resistance, or"—I flicked my eyes to him—"funny business?"

His answering smile did nothing to reassure me.

"Fine." I squared my shoulders and pushed a breath out through my nose.

Certain that Maeson and Aremis were still watching, I rallied my power one last time. I pictured the open space next to the bed—and with that image in mind, I tugged on my power and disappeared from the hallway.

Once inside, however, I slammed into the footboard of the wooden bed frame and let out such a sharp yelp that I was sure everyone in the hallway heard.

Niall appeared behind me with that damned grin on his face as he beheld where I ported to.

"Don't even start," I said, pointing at him as I rubbed my aching knee.

"Wasn't going to say a word." He bit back a full smile as he strode toward the seating area.

I followed him and sank onto the sofa, yawning deeply, while he claimed a spot near the window and watched me.

A heaping plate of cheeses, breads, fruits and cured meats appeared on the low table between me and the hearth. My stomach growled. I snatched up some cheese and popped it into my mouth, waiting for Niall to make some sort of comment about my poor depth perception, but he remained suspiciously quiet.

I examined a piece of melon in my fingers next, while weighing the silence between us. "There's no difference in porting through open space, or solid walls, is there?"

"None whatsoever." He grinned. "But I did enjoy seeing your effort."

The melon drenched my taste buds in sugar as I sank my teeth into it and glared up at him. I hardly had the energy to do anything more than that.

He said something else, a mumbled sentiment that sounded further away with each word, but my ability to focus had waned. My eyelids were growing heavier by the second. I fought to lift them as I swallowed the last of the fruit.

The world winked in and out as the curtains were drawn.

Then, strong arms were carrying me to bed, tucking me underneath the plush blankets, and smoothing strands of hair away from my face as my head sank further into the pillows.

Officially exhausted from training, my body relinquished its last bit of consciousness as the door snicked shut.

Everything went quiet.

And so, I slept.

56

FIREFALL

When I woke, I wasn't sure what time it was, thanks to the thick velvet curtains that smothered any inkling of light from the windows.

I had been in such a deep sleep—thanks to the drain on my power from porting practice—that it took me a moment to gather my surroundings.

The room was quiet, the candlelight casting soft, docile shadows along the dark stone walls. The sight would have lulled me back to sleep, but Sorscha poked her head up from the foot of the bed, her wings flitting excitedly behind her.

I could feel Niall's presence before he appeared, materializing just inside the door. The atmosphere changed, just like it always did when he entered a space, causing a smile to tug at my lips.

"Why even have doors if you just port past them every time?" I asked, reaching above my head to stretch out the last bit of stiffness from my arms.

"I like surprising you," he answered, stepping closer.

He had changed clothes and was wearing a fine black doublet, cut close to his chest and waist, with a sleek neckline and intricate stitchwork that lined the lapels and stretched down the center to the hem. Tapered black pants hugged his muscular thighs. A regal look. More refined and sleek than I'd seen him wear.

I lifted a brow. "Going somewhere?"

"I am. And so are you."

I looked at him with confusion.

"Calledan's Lumeri is tonight. I came to wake you so you can get ready."

Wait . . .

"Lumeri was supposed to be—"

"Tomorrow? Yes. That's today."

I looked around, but with the curtains drawn, I was disoriented. "How long did I sleep for?"

Niall chuckled. "Since yesterday afternoon."

"What?" I sat up in a panic. "I didn't mean to—"

"No need to apologize. It's natural to need to sleep after using your power in large amounts. That was the first time you'd used a good deal of it. You'll get more tolerant the more you train."

Sorscha was now perched on the bench at the foot of the bed watching me anxiously.

"Why are you looking at me like that?" I asked her.

She turned to Niall, as if she was requesting his permission for something. He gave her a nod, and in a flash, she moved to the armoire and returned with a long dress, laying it on the bed before me.

Niall lifted the hem. "I had a very special tailor make this for you."

"Gareth?"

He nodded.

I stared in awe, then reached out and ran my fingers over the exquisitely crafted details. "How did he make this in time? And how did it even get here when he's in the Woodland Court?"

Niall leaned in. "If you have to know every little detail, it takes the fun out of the gift." The corner of his lips lifted.

I grinned up at him. "It's gorgeous. Thank you."

"You're most welcome," he said, backing away. "I tried to let you sleep as long as I could, but we're cutting it close. We have about an hour until we need to port to the foothills of the mountains. I'm sure Sorscha will help you get ready."

The house-fae bobbed eagerly at the edge of the bed, waiting.

"All right, all right. I'm up," I said, laughing.

She quickly darted off into the bathing chamber, and I immediately heard the tub filling.

"See you soon," Niall promised as he slipped out the door with a wink.

I ventured into the adjoining chamber and halted at the sight.

In the center of the space, an extra-large, copper clawfoot tub awaited, steam wafting from its basin like bleached wisps of Niall's shadowfire. The dark ceiling above it reflected the water, seeming to come alive, dancing like glittering, liquid night.

The black stone walls were sparkling under the orbs that circled the perimeter, and a multitude of pillar candles were lit along several alcoves. It had all the ambiance of a temple, hidden deep within the earth, and I wanted nothing more than to sink into the tub and stay awhile.

Sorscha was nowhere to be found, so I stripped.

I sank to my collarbone in the water and exhaled, feeling the tension flee from my muscles.

A small tray with a washing cloth and a few corked glass bottles of soaps and shampoos sat on a skinny table near the edge of the tub. I uncapped the first delicate bottle to take a sniff. My eyes fluttered closed. Vanilla and chestnut.

The scent of . . . *Niall.*

A small, giddy rush danced along my spine as the fragrance clung to my senses.

I slathered the cloth with the soap and worked it into a frothy heap, then pressed it against my skin. The steam, and his scent, wrapped around me like an embrace. If I closed my eyes, I could picture him sitting across the tub, his intoxicating grin threatening to undo me; his heated stare, dripping with the same desire he'd had two nights ago, gaze drifting from my eyes, to my lips, then past where the water lapped at the swells of my breasts. His hands, reaching under the water, touching my inner thigh, moving higher—

My eyes snapped open, and I jerked up, not realizing I'd slumped so far down into the water that it was rippling against my chin.

I shouldn't have let my mind wander like that. Not when we were short on time. Not when I wasn't even sure where these thoughts were coming from in the first place.

I finished bathing and washing my hair, then sat in my robe while

Sorscha worked her magic. She dusted my eyelids a sultry, smoky gray, and painted a deep burgundy balm across my lips. With a simple wave of her hand, my hair was dry and full of luscious curls that hung down around my shoulders and back. A pair of small, jeweled earrings appeared in her hand, and she threaded them through my ears with a grin.

This kind of attention and primping was still so foreign to me that it took me a moment to relax and let her work. But when she was finished, I stood in front of the large, gilded, gold mirror that was mounted on the wall in the bedchamber, smiling at what I saw.

Niall had designed a spectacular dress, and Gareth had executed it perfectly. The gray fabric was sheer across my chest and arms, the neckline dipping into a deep vee between my breasts, which were covered with a sea of gold and gray beads and jewels that wrapped around the entire bodice. The beading even crowned the tops of each shoulder, trickling down the sheer fabric that encased my arms and ending with a band of jewels around my wrists. A layer of thicker, cream-colored fabric lined the dress from the waist down, and long layers of dark gray gossamer cascaded down from both sides. Gold and gray beads peppered the skirts and twisted in swirling patterns along the hemline.

It embodied the elegance of the Mountain Court.

I was in the midst of turning to admire the backside of it when my door opened. I whirled to see Maeson standing in the doorway with her jaw hanging open.

She was dressed in a deep, plum-colored gown, so dark it was almost black, and the dark gray cloak that was clipped around her neck flowed behind her as she entered.

"You look stunning," she said with wide eyes as she shut the door behind her.

"As do you," I replied, gesturing toward her outfit. The neckline and cinched bodice accentuated her subtle curves, and the sleeves opened up at the elbows into long sections of flowing fabric. "Gareth even added Wrynn to your dress." I pointed toward the dark purple crystals that were stitched into the bodice of her gown, taking the form of a fox that wrapped its way down around her waist, glistening in the golden light.

She smiled down at the rendering, then frowned as she asked, "Who is Gareth?"

"Niall's new favorite tailor, it seems," I mused, sliding my feet into a pair of soled slippers that matched my dress.

A knock sounded on the door, and it opened slightly, allowing a deep voice to rumble through. "Auren, if you're ready, I—" Roirdan stopped short as he pushed the door fully open and beheld me. He cleared his throat and tried again. "I'm here to escort you to the festivities."

My heart sank a bit at the sight of the commander at my door instead of the High Lord.

"Don't worry," he quickly added, "Niall simply needed to see to a couple of things beforehand. He'll meet us at the foothills." He offered me his arm, then looked over at Maeson. "Aremis will be here momentarily to escort you as well. You both look lovely this evening, by the way."

"Thank you, Roirdan," I said, taking his arm.

He had changed into a heavier black tunic with an embroidered section of leather across his chest. Nothing like the finery Maeson and I were wearing. When he caught me eyeing his choice of attire, he smirked and said, "I'm bred for war, not parties."

Something I could relate to.

I wouldn't go as far as saying *war*—since I'd never seen it myself—but a sword and scabbard around my hips always tended to suit me better than a bustled gown.

That was, until I'd seen the types of gowns the fae realm produced. "Normally, I'd agree with you, but I must say, these are starting to grow on me." I ruffled the skirts of my dress for emphasis.

"I get the feeling you're the type to hide a blade somewhere under there, no matter what the occasion." He smirked down at me.

"On the contrary. I'd rather strap it to my hip, over my dress, for all to see."

"Even better." He laughed. "I always say, 'intimidation is the best form of flattery.'"

I snorted a laugh. "Pretty sure the word is *imitation.*"

His nose wrinkled with disapproval. "But that's nowhere near as fun as seeing an enemy think twice about challenging you. That's always more rewarding."

I liked Roirdan. He was easygoing and seemed like someone who would always have my back and my best interest in mind. I could easily see him and I being friends.

"Now, if you're ready, I do believe if I keep you here any longer, Niall will have unpleasant words for me."

"Ready when you are."

I turned back to Maeson, who was admiring her dress in the mirror. She waved to my reflection, and then, I was gone.

We moved effortlessly through wind and space. But compared to Niall's porting technique, Roirdan's was full of brute force, and I had to smooth the hair that whipped loose around my face as soon as we materialized again.

The grassy clearing in the foothills where we emerged sat at the base of a breathtaking waterfall. The tree line ended far behind us, as if it knew not to creep any closer to the monstrous falls that cascaded from the peak high above.

Further across the clearing, the fae of the Mountain Court were gathered, dressed in classic, elegant finery, and tasteful outfits befitting the evening. No costumes, elaborate face paint, or wings. Just beautiful fae.

Niall stood at the edge of the crowd, hands folded calmly behind his back. His golden eyes pierced the space between us. They glimmered in the fading light as they roved over my body and found my own eyes once more.

A thick, single-shouldered, black cloak was slung over his right shoulder and clasped around his left. The top was adorned with a crinkled black fur pelt—the same kind I had seen Vanir wear.

He started our way, along with Remic, who flanked him at his right, and Vanir, who had arrived from Vahrenhall, following closely behind.

"Here's the true vision that I'll be in awe of this evening," he said, taking my hand and pressing a kiss to my knuckles, his eyes never leaving mine. "You look exquisite."

I instantly smiled.

Remic approached and dipped his head toward me. He looked different in the outdoor evening light. His long hair was flowing gently behind his shoulders, and his gray eyes were an even darker shade of ash under the slowly sinking sun. He was dressed in a finer version of the black leathers he had been in earlier, and I concluded that he probably always wore some variation of the same thing—given his nature and purpose.

The daggers were still strapped to his thighs, the sword still at his back.

Behind us, Aremis and Maeson appeared, porting in from The Keep.

Aremis was also in an all-black ensemble, including a fine tunic and cloak of his own. Clearly, he and Niall were the two that didn't mind donning a bit of courtly finery.

Maeson's expression was caught between excitement and anxiousness, and Aremis looked a bit awkward as he walked stiff-backed with her at his side. It did seem like he was trying though. After all, he'd made the effort to escort her himself.

We all gathered in a small circle, and Niall addressed Maeson and I. "Since neither of you have seen tonight's event, I wanted to make sure you had the best seats in the house." He gestured to the spread of fur blankets that were laid out across a few large boulders behind us.

The thoughtfulness made me smile.

"What exactly are we going to be witnessing?" I asked.

Niall helped me up onto one of the stones. "It's called Firefall. Each year, on this day, the sun sets at precisely the right angle above the Artemian Peak—that one there," he said, pointing to the mountain towering behind me. "When the light is just right, the waterfall becomes lit, as if it was on fire."

He gracefully shimmied up onto the rock next to me, wrapping my cloak around my shoulders a bit tighter.

More doting.

I could feel Maeson grinning from where she sat by Aremis. I didn't dare look at her, because I had no doubt she was itching to make a comment about it.

Aremis chimed in. "Those that gather tonight will cast out enchantments to enhance the water's natural glow. It's believed that it helps ward off the evil spirits that roam the land."

Niall leaned in closer to me. "After the sun sets, and the water flows normally again, there will be a feast and dancing closer to the base of the falls."

"Is that where you've been? Getting everything ready?" I asked.

"For the most part. I enjoy helping out those who work hard to put it all together. And I know my court appreciates me taking the time to do so."

He looked back down the clearing, and I followed his gaze.

The grass ended where a spacious stone slab began near the water. There, a multitude of elegant tables sat waiting for guests, and strings of lights flickered above them.

The fact that he wanted to be a part of the logistics of the celebration, to help decorate, or prepare, or whatever it was that he had the urge to tend to, made my heart soften toward him even more. It still puzzled me that he didn't want that side of him known to those outside of his court.

Nearby, Roirdan and Remic struck up their own conversation with Vanir about an outpost of some sort, and Maeson was chattering about Lumeri in the Woodland Court while Aremis listened tentatively, briefly lifting his eyes to her every few seconds.

I noted how each of the males all kept their attention divided between the conversations they were in and their surroundings.

Always on alert.

A few minutes later, Roirdan leaned back against the rock on the other side of Niall, and Remic took up the spot closest to me. Vanir stood close by as well, gazing out over the crowd.

All of our attention focused back on the falls as an eerie quiet fell over the clearing. It was as if the mountains waited in silence too. Only the falling waters echoed their roar into the distance.

I turned and glanced behind me, to where the sun was now no more than a sliver above the Artemian Peak, and I caught myself holding my breath as it slipped out of sight.

I whipped my head around just in time. In a cascading rush, the water tumbling over the edge of the cliff lit molten orange, licking like streams of fire toward the pooling water hundreds of feet below, illuminating the mountainside like a flickering flame. The mist that drifted in its wake rose through the air like golden dust.

A soft chorus of awe echoed throughout the valley as the fae marveled at the sight.

It was the most beautiful thing I had ever witnessed. Vahrenhall's tower of fire paled in comparison.

As the water tumbled down, the Mountain Court fae lifted their hands and chanted a soft-spoken verse, in a language that was foreign to me.

Niall leaned in again and whispered, "They are blessing the light and welcoming it."

The falls pulsed brighter, casting light across the entire clearing, until every face was kissed by its brilliance. I watched it drift over everything like an answered prayer, and then turned to see that Niall hadn't even bothered to watch the waters turn molten.

He was fixated on me.

"You're missing the show," I said with a shy smile, pointing at the spectacle.

He cocked his head, then the corner of his mouth lifted. "Why would I watch something I've seen hundreds of times, when something more beautiful is sitting right before me?"

Over his shoulder, I spotted Roirdan slowly turning to look at us with a sly grin plastered to his face.

My cheeks drenched pink, but I couldn't contain my own grin as it surfaced.

Remic shifted beside me, straightening his posture and clearing his throat—the only tell that he'd also overheard the High Lord's flirting.

Out of the six of us, he was the most stoic and stern, barely leaning back on the rock, hands casually resting near the daggers at his sides.

Niall finally looked out at the falls just as the glow was fading. When the waters ran clear once again, a quiet cheer went up from the clearing as the fae celebrated and offered what looked like blessings to those with whom they embraced, linking arms with one another across their chests and touching foreheads. It was the most endearing form of camaraderie I'd witnessed amongst the fae courts so far. And to see it coming from the court that I had been warned about . . .

Aremis's voice speared my attention as he called out loudly, "Laetus Lumeri." The rest of the crowd echoed in unison. I even found myself saying it quietly as I watched the fae begin to migrate toward the base of the falls.

Rich aromas of breads and spices floated on the breeze, up to the rock we were perched on.

As if answering the summons, Niall slid down in a smooth movement and reached out a hand, beckoning me to join him. "Shall we, darling?"

57

THE EDGE OF DESIRE

The air grew cooler as we crossed the field and neared the water. The large stone patio that sat at the base of the falls was made from the same black mountain stone, smoothed and polished from millennia of natural weathering.

An invisible barrier held back the mist and overspray from the pounding waterfall, keeping the area where the fae were gathered completely dry. Another enchantment worked to muffle the sound, quieting its roar into a soft hum.

Polished wood tables decorated with elegant garlands of greenery and stacked full of all sorts of edible delicacies lined the perimeter. Wine was being poured and passed. And somewhere nearby a quiet melody of music was starting.

The sun was well beneath the mountain peaks now, casting the sky into a wash of purples and blues and the world beneath it into a dim darkness. Twinkling string lights glittered above the patio, reaching across from one wooden post to another, while numerous orbs bobbed and floated high above, lighting the spaces in between.

Niall snagged two glasses of wine, handing me one.

The Trium stepped up to our side along with Vanir, and together, they surveyed the area, making sure everything was as it should be—and probably assessing for threats. Remic definitely looked like he was gauging the crowd and marking anything suspicious.

Maeson grabbed my arm and squealed as she pulled me to the edge of the gathering fae and began marveling.

Everyone was dressed in elegant evening attire. Glasses clinked, laughs floated along the wind, and I soaked up every joyful sound.

Several fae approached Niall, shaking his hand and bowing gently. I couldn't help but watch him as he carried on conversations with a genuine interest and casual smile.

He couldn't keep from glancing my way either.

"Hello? Auren?" Maeson waved her hand in front of my face.

I suddenly realized I had completely tuned her out. "Oh, I'm so sorry, Maeson. What did you say?"

She giggled and twirled her glass in her hand. "I'm just obsessing over this entire night. Just like how Niall is obsessing over *you*." She threw her elbow into mine.

I rubbed at my arm, fighting a grin. I knew she would bring it up at some point. "Stop it. I'm sure he's just curious. He's seen Firefall hundreds of times anyway, so why watch it again?"

But I knew better.

Maeson gave me a look that said she knew better too. "Why do you keep denying it? He's interested in you." She took a swig of her wine. "I think he may even be falling for you."

"He is *not* falling for me. I think he's just . . . I don't know. He's helping me figure this whole prophecy thing out." I drank from my own glass, needing something to distract me.

She scoffed. "You and I both know it's more than that, Auren. I've always been able to sense these things."

"What things?"

"Emotions," she clarified between sips.

I looked over at Aremis. "Uh huh . . . And you still can't get a read on that one?" I nudged my chin toward him.

"*That* one's tricky. Which makes me even crazier for him." She sighed and let her head loll to the side as she stared across the distance between them.

Aremis sensed her eyeing him and looked over in our direction. Both of us quickly made it a point to take interest in the nearest objects we could find . . . our wine.

"We've had good conversation," Maeson said. "Mostly just catching up on the time that's passed. But he's coming around. He complimented me when he saw me back at The Keep. And when we ported, he held onto my hand a bit longer than necessary."

I grinned, hearing the giddiness in her voice as she fawned over the smallest details of their interactions.

When I glanced at him and caught him eyeing Maeson, he quickly hid his interest and turned to feign conversation with Remic.

My grin widened.

"You two are a mess," I said to her.

We both let out a laugh and sipped our wine.

"Speaking of emotions and all that—" I started to say.

Shit. How do I ask this without sounding awkward?

"Um, do you happen to know how to make a particular tincture that . . . prevents . . . certain consequences of certain actions?"

Maeson's brows furrowed, then quickly straightened as she realized what I was asking. She shifted her stance and lifted a brow at me with a knowing grin.

Fates, was she going to make me say it?

"I just mean in case things get . . ."

She sipped her wine, waiting for me to get all the words out.

". . . Physical between us—not that it will." My cheeks flushed an embarrassing shade of pink. "And not that it has," I quickly added. Hopefully she couldn't tell that I was lying about the last part.

Her grin spread. "I knew you two were—"

"It hasn't gone that far," I said, quickly cutting her off, face burning under the weight of her knowing smirk. I let out a sigh. "I just mean that it might. Or it could. Just—can you?"

Gods, I should have had more wine before tackling this conversation.

"Happy to. I'll have it for you tomorrow. If you can hold out that long." She waggled her brows at me.

My mouth fell open, and I let out an incredulous scoff, then the both of us launched into a laughing fit.

If Niall cornered me again, kissed me, so much as *looked* at me the way he did in Vahrenhall, there was no guarantee I'd be able to hold back.

"Thank you," I said after catching my breath. "I used to take a preventative back at home, but now that I'm here . . ."

"Say no more." She clinked her glass against mine, then tossed the rest of the wine back in one gulp. I did the same, suddenly feeling the need to soothe my nerves.

The music kicked up and so did the chatter. Some took to dancing, while the rest of the crowd dispersed to the edges of the pavement.

Across the way, I recognized Laurent, the High Lord of Drastia, as he stepped out of the throng of revelers toward Niall, followed by Senna close on his heels. He was tastefully dressed in a light blue doublet and cloak lined with pale gray furs. She complimented him with a matching dress and a long cape that hung in shorter swaths across her chest, draping back over her right shoulder to a pool of furs that dragged the ground.

No sign of the remaining High Lords—Killian and Ramil— which wasn't surprising.

Niall pointed in my direction, and Laurent's gaze landed on me. He gave me a gentle smile and inclined his head in respect.

I did the same.

"What do you think they're all talking about?" I asked Maeson as we watched the group fall into conversation.

"Probably politics. It's always politics with those males." She tipped her empty glass at me. "I'm going to go find more of this."

"Would you take my glass too?" I asked, handing it to her.

She nodded. "Don't go far."

Seeing Maeson walking in the other direction, Aremis broke from the group of males he was with and walked toward me.

"You just missed her," I said, pointing to Maeson through the crowd.

"Purposefully," he replied, trailing her with his gaze for only a moment before he turned back to me. "I'd like to ask you for a dance."

"Wouldn't you rather dance with her?"

"I would actually like to dance with *you*. And"—he bit his lip, seemingly a little embarrassed—"possibly ask you for some advice while we do so?"

A smile tugged at my lips, and I placed my hand in his. "Of course."

"I must warn you though, I may be a bit rusty with the steps." He gave me an apologetic smile as he turned us into the crowd and fell into rhythm with the beat.

"You seem pretty good, in my opinion," I said, noting the natural grace to his movements. He danced almost effortlessly. There was no way he was "rusty." He was probably just being polite.

"Glad you think so," he said. "What did you think of Firefall?"

"Definitely the most magical thing I've ever witnessed." I looked around as we danced. "Your court is definitely not what I expected . . ." My voice faded out as my eyes landed on Niall.

"Ah, yes," Aremis said, noting my stare. "And how are you liking *him?*"

I blushed from head to toe.

Does he think there's something between us? Had Niall told him we'd done something physical?

"I—we—" I fumbled over my words.

Aremis chuckled innocently. "I wasn't assuming anything other than the interest I see he has in you. I'm only wondering if you return the sentiment."

I looked back at the High Lord of Calledan.

I do return the sentiment. I am interested.

The words crowded the tip of my tongue, toeing the line, testing the edge. But they remained there.

Aremis tilted his head to the side as he watched me. "Your eyes speak for you."

I blinked and looked away, pretending to be enamored with the crowd instead.

"There's nothing to be ashamed of. I can sense something between you two. I haven't sensed anything like it in a long time."

If only he knew about the thrumming, and that it felt like an entity was coming to life within me whenever Niall was around. Or the fact that I seemed to lose all focus when his golden eyes stared into mine like he was reading my soul.

I wanted to ask what he meant about *sensing things,* but part of me was hesitant for confirmation.

"I could say the same for you and Maeson."

He stiffened slightly at her name.

"Do *you* return any sentiments toward her?"

It was his turn to blush, but he hid it well. "About that . . ."

He scanned the crowd before he spoke again. "What has she said about me?"

I reined in my grin.

Progress.

"She admires you."

Interest piqued on his face, and he cleared his throat. "In what way? Romantically?" He suddenly didn't know where to look, and his eyes darted around the dance floor.

Adorable.

"It's not my place to say. But if I know anything about romantic interest, I suggest you go make yours known to her—if you have any." I gave him a quick wink when his eyes flitted to mine.

This time, he couldn't hide the color that flushed his cheeks.

"Perhaps I will," he said, seeming to stand a little taller. "Thank you."

"No need to thank me. Just don't let that slip away."

He nodded, knowing what I meant. He knew Maeson liked him. He was just too unsure of himself to act on it or pursue it.

"There's nothing we regret more in life than chances not taken." I paused at my own words as they came out. Here I was telling Aremis to take a chance on Maeson, and *I* was the one toeing the line with whatever Niall and I had between us, afraid of what it was—if it was anything at all.

As if summoned by my thoughts, the High Lord sauntered through the crowd of dancers, making a direct line for us. A beautiful grin graced his face, and his eyes twinkled under the string lights.

His voice was smooth as glass and fell on my ears like velvet as he said, "I came to advise my advisor that a certain red-headed damsel is in distress over by the wine barrels." He directed our line of sight with his.

Sure enough, Maeson was surrounded by a group of fae males who looked all too interested in what was beneath her dress, their faces laced with feral grins, eyes glinting with mischief.

Aremis threw me an anxious smile. "If you'll excuse me." He passed me to Niall before storming across the dance floor to stake his claim.

I shook my head and giggled as I watched him plant a step between Maeson and the blond-haired fae who stood entirely too close to her.

"I think it's safe to say Aremis and I are officially friends now. I didn't think I'd be advising *your advisor* on romance tactics."

Niall chuckled and took a drink from his glass. "And what of me then? Am I your friend too?"

I paused.

What is he? What is this thing between us? Friends don't kiss each other the way he kissed me. Nor do they elicit arousal and put their fingers—

I stopped myself before those heated memories fully surfaced.

Choosing my words carefully, I answered, "You're helping me. So, I guess that makes you my friend."

He raised his glass, then polished off the remnants of the drink. I watched his throat work as he swallowed, and my own mouth instantly dried out.

"Well then," he said, his empty glass disappearing from his hand, "if we're friends, would you dance with me as well?"

I sucked in a shallow breath. The last dance with him had been an event all in itself, and worry started to creep up about the possibility of glowing again in front of another crowd.

"I'll try not to get you all hot and bothered this time." He smirked.

"I—that was . . ."

Shit.

His smirk widened. "Like I said, I'll *try.*"

"What happens if I *do* glow again?"

"I'll cast us into shadow. No one will notice."

"Great, so we'll just be a big blob of shadows dancing across the floor?"

"Precisely." He took my cloak off my shoulders and tucked it into a pocket in space, making it disappear entirely.

"I really need to learn that trick next."

He chuckled. "It's not a trick, remember? It's magic. And it's *very much* real." The emphasis he put on the last part of that sentence made my stomach flutter as he stared into my eyes.

Maybe I was reading too far into his words—something I seemed to be doing a lot of lately. But his eyes spoke volumes as they roved over me and my dress.

Just friends?

I didn't think so.

"Where do the items go?" I asked, suddenly needing to change the subject before my thoughts took over.

"The cloak is hanging, the glass is on a table," he replied, taking my hand and twirling me further onto the dance floor.

"Specifics would be nice," I said as he pulled me back into his arms.

"Later. Just enjoy this dance with me."

I half expected him to introduce me to the crowd, like Killian had, but his eyes never left mine as he held me close to him. This wasn't a spectacle for the High Lord, nor was it a chance for him to show me off. It was just me and him and this dance.

The music ushered us along in a waltz, much like the one we'd first shared. But unlike that first dance, his grip was more familiar this time, his body pulling me into him like gravity.

"What are you thinking?" he asked quietly.

"I was thinking about our first dance."

"Reminiscing?"

I rolled my eyes. "It wasn't *that* memorable."

He leaned back, briefly holding me at arms-length while he gave me a pointed look. "Is that so? Well, we can't have that be the case. I'll have to make sure this dance leaves an impression on you." His arms tightened around me, cinching me up against his broad chest.

We spun a tight circle, staring at each other as we moved, and for some reason I couldn't find any more words to fill the silence. After a long minute under his intense stare, I caved and looked away, surveying the dance floor around us, only to find every fae in attendance watching us on bated breath. Even those that were dancing around us kept their heads on swivels.

"Um, Niall, why is everyone watching us," I whispered.

"Probably because I've never openly danced with a female at a public event."

"Never?"

"Never. I'm usually busy tending to other matters. Very seldom do I stay and revel in the celebrations."

I glanced around again, suddenly feeling like a burden. "Oh, you don't need to stay for me if you don't have the time. I can enjoy the night and find my way back to my chambers later. I'm sure Maeson—"

"I'm making the time," he cut me off, guiding me into a spin.

Several quiet gasps echoed around me as I twirled on the tips of my toes, my dress flaring out in all directions.

He reeled me back in with his hand and his devastating smile, catching my waist with heartbreaking tenderness as I spun into him.

"Please, don't fuss over me. You're a High Lord, I'm sure you have more important things to do than dancing."

"Thankfully, being a High Lord also means I can determine what's important, and what's not." His hand tightened around mine, and he leaned down a bit closer to my neck. "If I'm being honest, I'm quite glad everyone is watching us."

"Why is that?"

"Because, training under pressure is the best way to learn."

"We're not training, we're dancing," I corrected him.

"Ah, but you're keeping your mental shield intact, aren't you?"

There was no time to answer before his essence slipped into my mind and reached out toward the stone wall that I had left completely neglected. It gave way and crumbled under a single tendril of smoky shadow, and all at once I was at his mercy.

He lingered at the edge, waiting.

This could go one of two ways.

He could let his essence loose, or vacate as quickly as he'd entered. One move would be all it took to undo me in so many ways.

I stared into his eyes, anticipation burning a hole in my gut.

The shadow held its ground at the threshold, contemplating or waiting for permission—I didn't know. But I suddenly found myself wanting him to command me. To bend me to his will—see what he would do with a small snippet of control.

My essence took form, pulsing like a beacon, as if it was luring him in, urging him to lose himself with me.

His body shuddered, and his eyes flared into a golden glow in such a quick movement, it was as if he was losing all control over himself.

The hunger in his stare swallowed up the space between us.

Then, in my mind, his essence lunged, colliding with mine. They swirled in their own dance, pulling at one another until his commanded mine and bent it to his will.

I pressed into his hard body as if by reflex, my skin heating underneath my dress. My mouth watered for him. My fingers ached to grip him tighter, clinging to the back of his tunic.

We were like magnets being drawn together by a force that was greater than ourselves.

Our steps faltered, but we kept dancing.

Spinning.

Niall's mouth parted and his brows knit together. He wanted more, just as I did. The emotions on his face made me want to crush my lips onto his. I could feel him through his pants, straining with desire as he pressed further into me.

It was too much. It was taking over us.

We spun faster.

A gasp escaped my throat as the leash on my emotions slipped, and I felt the glowing light radiate from my body.

Quicker than I could have anticipated, Niall wrapped us in shadow, and then his lips were on mine. He claimed me like I was an oasis of water in the desert, kissing me so deeply and furiously that I never wanted it to stop. I wanted to stay wrapped in his shadows and kiss him for days. Hours. Months.

His hand slid around my neck, pulling my head back to make me open wider for him.

As his tongue swept in deeper, I remembered the fae around us, and I pulled back from him and panted frantically.

"Niall—"

Before I could finish, the air whooshed around us, and the shadows swirled in our wake as we vanished.

58

NO SELF CONTROL

THE CANDLES FLARED TO LIFE ALONG WITH THE FIREPLACE, BUT IT WAS the luminescence of my body that cut through the darkness of my chambers where we materialized.

Still in his arms, my back was thrust up against the wall as his lips found mine in another crushing kiss.

He was ravenous, and so was I.

I tore at the clasps on his doublet—not sure how it was fastened together —desperate to get my fingers on his skin. When the fabric separated, I worked at the buttons of his shirt underneath, flinging it open. My hands landed on his bare chest, and I didn't hesitate to run them along the sculpted muscle there before winding them up around his neck and plunging them into his hair.

Our lips moved in perfect sync, and I drank him in as I willed my power to calm, my light winking out as it settled.

The room sank back under the confines of flickering flames, and Niall's teeth bit into my bottom lip playfully as he reached down and lifted my dress. Gripping me by the back of my thighs, he situated my hips in line with his, pressing firmly to hold me up as his hands continued roaming.

I arched off the wall, and he reached for the clasps at the back of my dress, working at them frantically until they came apart enough for him to tug the fabric down my arms, exposing my breasts. He hoisted me higher and took one into his mouth. I moaned, leaning back into the dark stone wall, my chest thrumming underneath his lips as he sucked and licked and kissed his way from one peaked tip to the other.

My body ached for him. The heat between my thighs needed sating. And as if he heard my silent plea, his fingers moved from my thigh and slid my undergarment aside, revealing the slickness that was waiting for him.

He growled as he swiped a finger along my center. "Are you craving me as much as I'm craving you?"

"Obviously," I whispered playfully, shifting my hips, chasing his teasing touch.

But that wasn't the answer he was looking for.

Out of the darkness, his shadows appeared. At first, they delicately pulled my wrists from the sleeve cuffs, but once my hands were free, they grasped both and pinned them to the wall above my head.

"I want to hear you say it," he commanded as he continued circling my center, taunting me.

I gasped as he rubbed his thumb over my most sensitive spot, then pulled his hand away again.

"I crave you," I said breathlessly, needing his touch.

Upon hearing my words, he wasted no time plunging in. With two fingers, he entered me, while his shadows held my wrists firmly in place against the wall.

"You're exquisite," he breathed as he pumped his fingers in and out, watching my expression change with the movements. "I've thought about touching you like this all day."

My thighs gripped his waist tighter, and I arched my back against his touch, urging him toward the sensitive bud at my center, chasing that feeling of pleasure as it wound up inside me, begging to come undone.

Then, his shadows released my hands and he swept me from the wall, spinning us toward the bed. The moment my back hit the sheets the shadows returned, and both my arms were pinned above me again as he straddled me.

My dress became a pile of fabric gathered around my waist as he lifted my leg and hooked it around his hips.

His fingers dove in and out of me at a slow, tantalizing pace, and I writhed against him as he worked me steadily.

In my mind, our essences were still tangled up in one another, exploring in their own way, just as he was exploring me. The dueling sensations pushed me to the edge. I called out his name in my head, a plea and a prayer. And like a leash being snapped, his shadows burst out in my mind, flooding my vision and overwhelming every one of my senses.

I cried out as I came, hard and fast, each delicious wave of ecstasy spurred on with the curling and pumping of his fingers.

My power kissed along my veins, sparks of light fizzing at the synapses as I gathered my breaths and calmed my racing heart.

"That was . . ." I panted, losing my train of thought. "I didn't have my shield up."

I shivered as he removed his fingers, feeling his groan of satisfaction vibrating through me.

He grinned, dropping down onto his elbow beside my face, his hair falling onto my forehead. "I noticed."

"So, your bright idea was to provoke me? In the middle of a public event?"

"That wasn't my full intention," he admitted. "But I couldn't stop." He nipped at my bottom lip.

Bathed in steady candlelight from the wall sconces that framed the bed, his features were even more devastating.

"This was different from last time," I said. "Our essences were connected."

"Was it such a bad thing?" he asked, trailing his fingers across my collarbone as I lay beneath him.

"It just took me by surprise, that's all."

His gaze roved over my face before he answered. "It did to me as well."

"It was like they were feeding off our emotions. Is that normal?"

"I'm not entirely sure."

I let my eyes drift down his neck, then his chest, to where the marks of his shroud stood out in stark contrast to his skin. I wanted to reach up and trace over each wisp of inked shadow, but instead, my hands drifted down his abdomen.

I couldn't fight my desire. And I wanted him to feel the same pleasure he'd given me.

He shifted his hips just out of reach, and gave a breathy laugh. "Worry about me another time, darling. Just enjoy this moment with me."

I smiled gently up at him. Then, the burning need to know the answer to a question I had asked myself over and over, surfaced. "The thrumming in my chest, can you hear it? Or feel it?"

In the silence, he stilled above me, and my stomach hollowed out.

My mind began racing.

Did I say something wrong? Is the thrumming . . . bad?

"You feel a thrumming in your chest?" he asked quietly.

Too quietly.

I tried to read the emotions on his face, my thumping heartbeat growing heavier again, pounding harder the more I tried to decipher his reaction, making me painfully aware that I was becoming too invested in this.

"Yes, but I'm not quite sure what it is," I said carefully. "I've felt it every time you're near. The first time was when you caught me in the forest. I thought it was just a reaction to your power, or your magic. That's what I've chalked it up to this entire time. I never really got the chance to ask. Perhaps I was afraid to."

I could feel him holding his breath, and those seconds ticked by agonizingly slow, itching at my patience.

Finally, he said, "I think we should have a visit with the Elder of my court tomorrow. She might have some answers."

Before I could reply, a very particular knock came at the door. Niall gently swung a blanket over me and rose to answer it. "It's Remic," he said over his shoulder as he strolled across the room, shirt and doublet still unfastened.

I sank a little further under the covers as he cracked the door open to have words with the Dionach. They spoke low, and I heard Niall chuckle before he nodded and closed the door again.

"He was just checking on us."

I winced. "Did we cause a scene?"

"Seems like everyone was a bit curious as to our little spectacle, but the Trium kept the wine flowing, in hopes that no one would think too deeply about it."

"Oh. Good."

Another close call.

Wrapping the blanket around me, I stood and headed for the bathing chamber, too many thoughts swirling in my head.

Niall caught me as I passed him.

"Auren, thank you for going to Firefall with me."

I stared up at him. "Thank you for taking me."

"Is there something you need—"

"No, I'm fine. I just want to clean up a bit." I gestured at my half-fastened dress, my mussed hair, and the remnants of every ounce of bliss he pulled from me, wrapped up under the blanket.

He nodded, then flicked his wrist toward the other room. "I've summoned some fresh clothes for you to change into."

"Always so thoughtful." I smiled as I slipped behind the door.

Once I was alone, I shook my head out and blinked at what had just happened. My power was humming along my skin, stirred awake by the intensity of my emotions.

Emotions that our essences were entangled with.

How is that even possible?

And what is this thing between us?

I had more questions than answers, but I couldn't get my mind to focus. It was still strung out, sated from Niall's lips and talented fingers.

After freshening up, and dressing in the lined leggings and cozy sweater that Niall had summoned for me, I emerged to find him lounging across the sofa, feet kicked up in casual elegance. My cloak had been brought back from the magical beyond, and was draped across his knee.

"Better?" He grinned.

"Better."

"I had a thought," he said, standing. "It's still rather early, and the Elder is a bit of a night-owl. How about we make the trip tonight? The mountains under the night sky are quite the sight."

He approached and draped the cloak around my shoulders, as if knowing I'd say yes.

The idea sounded perfect. I wasn't the least bit tired since I'd slept for a day and a half. Plus, I still had things that I needed to talk to him about, and more questions to ask.

"Lead the way, High Lord."

Wrapping me in his arms, we dissolved, our existence thrust through the chilled night air, climbing in altitude.

The mountaintop upon which we landed seemed to be at the center of the Mountain Court. The surrounding rocky peaks rose up as far as I could see in every direction. A black and blue night sky stretched out overhead, peppered with twinkling stars. Streaks of constellations threaded through the tapestry of darkness like iridescent ribbons.

"Slight detour," Niall said. "I wanted to bring you here first." He gestured to the cleared space we stood in.

There was a small stone bench behind us that looked well-worn from either age or weather. Probably both. We took a seat, and I tipped my head back to view the entirety of the sky.

"This is called The Lookout," he said. "It's warded to recognize the High Lord of this court. Only myself, and those who I bring with me, are allowed access. No one else can port to it."

"It's beautiful up here," I said as I scanned the mountains around us and the sky above. "Thank you for bringing me."

"Every time I've come here, I've always been alone. It's the only place I'm able to find true peace."

A crisp breeze whistled around us, carrying with it the scent of woodsmoke and the sharp pinch of pine needles. In the distance, I could hear the very faint melody of music from the ongoing celebration of Firefall as it wound through the peaks.

I tucked my hair back behind my ear, recalling a small slice of this world that I had once called mine. "I had a place back home where I could go for the same thing."

"Tell me about it," he said gently.

I sighed. "It was just a hidden glen in the forest near our house. The trees there grew in a perfect circle that was open to the night sky."

Such strange trees. I'd always wondered where they had come from, with their smooth, white bark that felt like it had been glazed in a firing kiln, and their paper-thin leaves—black as a raven, whispering foreign words on the wind.

"I kept it clean from any fallen branches and leaves. Sometimes I'd even take a blanket out to lay on while I stared up at the sky and counted falling stars. It always brought me peace—especially if I'd spent a day fighting or competing. It helped clear my head."

Niall nodded slowly, understanding me fully. "I always end up here when I find myself having to make hard decisions. Can't tell you the amount of times I've come here just to remind myself of who I am and what I stand for—what all I have to fight for and protect." He let out a long sigh. "If I'm being brutally honest, I've also spent many nights on this bench cursing the gods."

I glanced over at him, but he kept his stare fixed straight ahead.

"Up here feels like the closest I can get to them. So I always thought that maybe they'd hear me. Be more inclined to listen, at least. But it ends up the same way every time. I speak my mind, just to be met with silence."

My heart stuttered. I knew the feeling so well—when the weight of the world was falling hard on your shoulders and you'd met your wit's end. That weight had been a familiar friend since my parents died. And I'd carried it with me. Laid in that glen with it. Curled into myself in the center of those monochrome trees like a damned bullseye for the sky above, praying for the gods to just send me a sign. Show me a path. Give me a purpose.

And here I was, in another realm, harboring a power I hadn't known existed within me. And I had the blood of the gods running in my veins.

Perhaps there had been a plan all along. A true purpose, waiting for me where I'd least expected it. And the weight that I'd felt—that *he'd* felt as well, the pressure we'd put on ourselves—perhaps it was all out of our hands from the beginning. Something we mortal beings tried desperately to grasp the concept of, tried to bend and shape and form to *our* plans. *Our* ideal fate. But our fate was never for us to decide.

I turned my head to Niall again, gazing at him in reverence. My heart swelled with all the common ground that he and I seemed to share.

Two beings of separate realms, yet . . .

"I know exactly how you feel," I said softly.

I'd never related to someone more. I saw a piece of myself in those honeyed eyes. Something I hadn't ever recognized in anyone else.

I placed my hand on his and squeezed it gently. I didn't care how he interpreted it. It just felt right. And that was all I needed. He gripped mine back, and something sparked in his eyes.

He shifted his body toward me, and I leaned back into his chest, allowing him to wrap his other arm around me. We sat in silence for a long while, watching stars shoot overhead, just being content in each other's quiet company, until a thought came to mind.

"I learned something from the *Seidr* that I thought might interest you," I said quietly.

"I'm listening."

"There was a chapter solely devoted to talismans, and it said an object that is imbued with power or magic can be used by someone of the same bloodline. So, I'm guessing that answers our question on whether or not I would be able to wield the band of Lyceius."

Niall tensed behind me. "I was afraid of that."

I sat up and turned to look at him. "Why would you be afraid?"

"Because that's a burden you shouldn't have to bear. Not alone. The talisman is no fickle thing. It belongs to its wielder. It—" He paused. "It crowns a god."

It crowns a god.

The heaviness of that statement settled in my mind.

I had no desire to be a god.

We fell quiet again, the silence only broken every minute or so by fleeting voices chanting far off at the base of the falls. When Niall pointed his finger out across the vast range, I shifted my head against his chest to follow it.

There, nestled high between two peaks, was a tiny orange light that I hadn't noticed.

"That's where we're going. That's where the Elder lives."

The speck of light was barely visible, and I squinted to try to bring it into better focus.

"Her name is Amarna, and she's never steered me wrong in all the times I've gone to her for advice. I think she will be of some help."

"Do you seek her out often?" I asked, silently wishing we didn't have to leave just yet. That we could sit here a while longer so I could soak up these feelings, these revelations, *all* of it.

"Probably more than most. But I believe those that have come before us have a lot to teach us."

Thoughts of my parents flickered in my mind, and a sad smile worked its way across my lips.

Wise words.

I gave his hand another gentle squeeze. "Then let's go see her."

59

THE ELDER OF
CALLEDAN

AMARNA'S CABIN WAS BUILT ON A SOLITARY BOULDER THAT HAD FALLEN
and wedged itself in a crevasse between the mountains. And I had never
been more terrified of the ground giving out from underneath me.

Niall ported us onto the very small doorstep, which was barely deep
enough for both of us to stand on without risking a fall into the chasm
below.

"Now can you see why porting to an exact place and having your
balance is important?" he whispered into my ear.

I nodded a bit excessively. I understood *very* well.

The door creaked open, and a welcoming female voice called out,
"You may enter."

We stepped in, and the smell of freshly baked pies instantly filled my
nose. What looked like a tiny cabin from the outside was easily three times
that size inside. Apparently, magic could allow that to be possible.

There was a steady fire roaring in the fireplace, and all along the wood
walls hung various tapestries, maps, and satchels full of scrolls and
parchment. Two cozy settees that were well-worn with age, sat in the main
area, ready to receive guests.

Amarna leaned around the kitchen wall to our left, wiping hands that
looked to be covered in smashed berries on her apron. "Come in. You're
just in time for pie."

She was small—like Sorscha and Elspeth—but her pale skin took on a warmer hue in the firelight. Her wings draped delicately from her back, and her hair was pulled into a neat, solid white bun at the top of her head. She appeared aged, but didn't yet have the deep creases embedded into her skin as Elspeth had. She looked rather spritely for someone who was thousands of years old.

Niall pulled out a chair for me at the wooden table, where a dozen small pies rested and cooled—fresh out of the oven.

It wasn't lost on me that the chairs and table were built for a normal sized being. In fact, all the furniture was.

"I come here quite a bit," Niall explained. "Hence the larger furniture."

"Had to have the entire place refurbished to accommodate this one and his Trium of oafs," Amarna said with a snicker.

Niall chuckled. "Careful with whom you're calling an oaf," he said playfully.

"That Dionach is the only civilized one in your lot," Amarna said, looking up at him from under her brows while she wafted the pies.

He waved her off. "Yes, so you continue to remind me. You only favor him because he's quiet."

"You're absolutely correct. It's a nice change."

Her sarcasm made me grin.

Niall leaned over to me. "She's a bit cranky this evening."

"Don't start with me, boy." She gave him a snarky smile as she moved around the table.

Her long necklace swayed as she moved, catching my attention.

It was an Alatyr. Smoky quartz on a silver chain.

She lifted a brow. "So, are you going to introduce me to the beautiful one you've brought with you? She feels . . . different."

Niall obliged. "Amarna, this is Auren. Auren, meet Amarna."

The Elder inclined her head to me, and I returned the gesture. She wiped remnants of pie onto her apron and reached her hand out toward me, palm side up. "But why has the High Lord brought—" Her words ended abruptly, and her black eyes went distant the moment I placed my hand in hers.

She tugged herself closer, eyes darting back and forth, assessing, questioning. I was startled when she suddenly placed a hand just above my breastbone and held it there for a brief moment before whipping her head to Niall. Something crossed her delicate face that I couldn't quite read as she said, "High Lord, you keep too many secrets."

He shifted uneasily at her words.

She turned her head back to me and sank into a low bow. "And you . . . you have finally come. A child born not just of human blood . . ." Her eyes scanned over my face as if she didn't believe what she was seeing. "Euryphaessa."

"We've spoken with Elspeth of Elandrew," Niall informed her. "She answered some questions, but there are still gaps in what we know."

Amarna looked back and forth between Niall and I. "There are gaps in what *one* of you knows. There is a thread between the two of you that one of you does not yet see."

"Please, no riddles. You know how much I hate those," Niall said dryly.

She swung her head back to him and scowled. "You know of what I speak, boy. I should leave that conversation to *you*. You should have had it already."

"What conversation?" I asked. "What thread?"

"You've felt a pull to him from the first day, have you not?"

I straightened. A pull?

Did she mean the thrumming?

"A thrumming, yes," she said, echoing my thought.

I glanced at Niall, who looked frozen between protesting the entire conversation, and fleeing the room.

"Yes . . . I've felt the thrumming since the day that . . ." My voice trailed off at the realization. The thrumming *was* connected to Niall. But perhaps not in the way I originally thought.

"Since you met this High Lord in the forest," she finished my statement. "I saw your encounter just now, as I held your hand. I felt what you felt. You feel it even at this very moment. It strengthens when the two of you are near, does it not?"

I nodded, but I couldn't find my voice anymore.

She looked at me like she could see every thought and emotion that was crawling up my throat and sinking in my stomach. "For our kind, the thrumming is a sign."

My breath caught. I suddenly knew that whatever revelation she was about to speak was going to be significant.

Life altering.

But it was Niall who said the word in such a low tone that I barely heard him. "Mates." The word was no more than a whisper off his lips, and yet it stole the breath from my lungs.

Mates.

But how could I be mated to one of the fae . . . to a High Lord?

The Elder had to be mistaken.

But when I let the word sink in, when I thought about the way our essences embraced each other, and how it affected our emotions and powers . . . it didn't feel entirely wrong.

The thrumming that I thought was tied to me being near his magic, was actually tied to *him*.

Amarna nodded toward Niall. "You knew this."

Her words made my entire body stiffen.

I slowly turned back toward him, narrowing my gaze. "You *knew?*"

Amarna bit her bottom lip and leaned back from the table, avoiding the High Lord's stare as he weighed his next words carefully.

He winced. "Auren, listen to me. I—"

"You knew, and you didn't tell me?" My voice shook.

He shot another look of frustration at Amarna, then returned his eyes to mine. "I didn't want to scare you off. It all happened so fast and—"

"When did you realize this?" I said in a harsh whisper.

He hesitated. "I felt it when I found you in the woodlands. I sensed what you were to me then. And after our first dance in Elandrew, there was no denying it." He paused. "Elspeth confirmed it."

My jaw tightened.

"I was going to tell you sooner, but I thought that if I did, it would seem desperate, and you'd think I was trying to manipulate you. I have never lied to you. I told you, I do not lie—"

"But you kept it from me."

I stared down at the pies. I wanted to take one and shove it into Niall's face.

As soon as the thought crossed my mind, Amarna let out a raucous laugh. "You have a fiery spirit, Euryphaessa. I wouldn't blame you if you did."

Niall looked at me in question, and I shook my head to clear my thoughts, forgetting that the Ancient Fae had an affinity for reading minds.

Amarna cleared her throat and spoke again. "Auren, you must understand the High Lord's hesitations. He has a lot riding on his shoulders as well—the entirety of the realms does. But he is truthful in his words. He does not lie." She turned to him. "Still, my boy, you should have told her sooner."

"Auren," Niall tried.

I held up my hand. "I'd like to speak with Amarna. Alone." My tone was clipped, but I couldn't help my emotions.

I didn't feel betrayed, but I felt like I had lost a foothold on myself. It was all too much, just as Niall was afraid it was going to be.

I'd grown up never wanting anything to do with the fae.

Keep away from the forest and The Veil.

The fae are the enemy. They are to be avoided at all costs.

Those were the things that were ingrained into our minds as children.

All my life I lived in fear of this realm. And now, I was completely entangled in it, with so much of it riding on my shoulders that I began questioning everything I had ever known.

How can I be a human, the daughter of a god, and *be fated to a fae?*

The utter insanity of it swarmed my thoughts. I could feel my emotions taking over, and my power tingled underneath my skin as it surfaced. A faint glow radiated from my body. I didn't even bother hiding it. I simply let it roll off of me in waves.

Hopefully there wasn't a raging mountain troll or some monstrous creature lurking nearby to notice.

Amarna read my thoughts and chuckled to herself. "There are no trolls dear. But nonetheless, your power is safe here. Take the time you need."

She ushered Niall into the other room and briefly stood in front of him, with what I could only assume were a few words of mind-to-mind reassurance—or perhaps scolding—before she returned to the kitchen alone.

With delicate fingers, she plucked a pie and set it in front of me with a spoon. "Eat. You'll feel better."

I stared at the golden crusted treat, but didn't move to consume it. My power continued rolling off me in waves as I stewed on all the information.

"Any words of advice?" I asked. "Niall says you're full of that." I couldn't help my dry tone. But I got the feeling she understood where I was coming from.

She studied me curiously, watching how I handled my power. "You are mates," she said. "That is a fact. And you are the daughter of Karios. That makes anything possible. Humans cannot be mated to the fae, but you are not fully human. With the seed of Karios, you are far from that. Far from a fae as well. But that does not nullify the possibility of the two of you being a mated pair. The fates work in mysterious ways. You will have time to accept it and come to terms later."

When I didn't reply she tilted her head. "Your power is unrivaled. I can feel it. It needs form and discipline. You do not fully have a grasp of it yet. Nor do you know what you are truly capable of. The High Lord can help you with this."

Still, I didn't respond. No part of me felt like accepting Niall's help at the moment.

I stabbed the pie with the spoon and watched as steaming berries oozed out of the flaky crust.

Amarna sighed. "The burden is heavy, my dear, but the fates have blessed you with someone to help carry that weight." She cast a glance into the other room, where Niall sat hunched over on the settee, deep in thought—and possibly regret.

Her words washed over me and settled, and I numbly took a bite of the pie.

I understood what she meant about having someone to help bear the weight of it all. Maybe it was just the thought of who Niall was before I came into the picture—a fae High Lord—that made me push against the notion that we were destined to be together. But I couldn't deny the way I felt whenever he was near, and *that* complicated my feelings even more.

And on top of everything, there was still the matter of figuring out the extent of the power that Karios seemed so eager to *bless* me with.

"I knew someone who was like you once," Amarna said, quietly. "He too was thrown into something he did not fully understand. History remembers him as 'The Dark One' but I remember him by his real name. Evander."

The Dark One.

I'd heard the same reference the day of my archery lesson with Niall and Breck.

I finally looked up at her.

She seemed to be weighing something in her mind. Then, she reached into a pocket in space and pulled out a leather book, bound with thin straps that wrapped around it several times. As she set it down in front of me, I snapped out of my stupor.

"This has been in my possession for a long time," she said. "Not even the High Lord has read it—nor has he wanted to. Perhaps you can read it with him when the time is right."

"What is it?" I asked.

"The personal journal of the High Lord Evander. He was Niall's ancestor, his great, great grandfather. As I said, history knows him as 'The Dark One.'"

"The keres called Niall by that name when it cornered us."

Amarna chewed on her lip. "The keres can sense power. They feed off of it. It would make sense that it sensed Niall's ancestral power when it came in contact with him."

She slowly released the journal to me. "I myself have not even read this in its entirety. It holds Evander's private record of what he suffered through when his power . . . turned on him. I have kept it safely tucked away knowing that it would be of some benefit at some point.

"Evander's house-fae—who has long since passed on—continued recording in it after the High Lord finally fell victim to his power. He hoped that if the same power were to manifest further down Evander's bloodline, the journal might help that fae learn to avoid the same fate. Thankfully, that house-fae was still alive when Niall was born, and he taught Niall everything first hand. And to everyone's surprise, Niall succeeded where his ancestor could not.

"I think whatever is in this journal will lend insight into what a power like yours is capable of if not properly honed, and how important it is that someone be there to guide you."

"But my power isn't like Evander's or Niall's," I said.

"That is true, but it is still unprecedented. The Dark One earned his name because of what his power *did to him*, not for what it was. He simply could not control it. It was too great a burden."

"And Niall knows of this journal?" I glanced over to the other room where the High Lord now stared out the window.

"He knows of it, yes, but has never wished to read it. He was not ready to face what's inside." We stared down at the bound book between us that seemed to have a presence of its own. "Now, I'm afraid, it's necessary. For both your sakes."

"I thought you said you hadn't read much of it?" I questioned.

Her face turned sad. "I was very close to the house-fae who wrote it. Devoted to Evander, he was. I'm well aware of what this journal contains without having to read it. The one who does must be ready to deal with its contents on a personal level. Niall has grown into his power and accepted it—mastered it even. Something Evander could not manage to do. It's time the young High Lord's eyes were opened to the extent of it, because a power like his, and like yours, will always tend to be unpredictable."

Part of me wanted to say that I wasn't totally sure Niall had accepted his power in the way Amarna thought. That there was still self-doubt in his mind on some level. But I wasn't petty enough to throw him under her scrutiny when there were greater issues to face. Perhaps it was because my damn feelings for him were growing, despite the frustration I currently felt toward him.

I placed a hand on the journal. "And you believe *I'm* ready to read what's inside? I only just learned of my power."

Her eyes met mine and softened as she offered me a kind smile. "You *must* be ready."

I rubbed my fingers along the journal's edge. "I'll read it with Niall. Eventually."

When I'm not so aggravated with him.

Amarna bowed her head. "The realm depends on it."

The words made me squirm a little.

"But what's the extent of all this? I mean—to what end?" I asked. It felt like an insurmountable load of responsibility had suddenly been dumped at my feet.

The Elder took my hands in hers. "This journey is yours and the High

Lord's. No one knows how the events of the prophecy will unravel, or what they will reveal. But one thing is certain, Lyceius is preparing his armies. He has been building a force that somehow evades even our most skilled scouts. The Wastelands are alive again, and they are restless. So, you must be ready."

"He wants to finish what he started . . ." I thought aloud.

"He will try." Niall's deep voice filled the room from where he now stood, leaning against the doorframe to the kitchen.

It was an effort to keep my eyes lowered so as to not look up at him. Part of me wanted to, and the other part felt chaffed about this entire situation.

Now that he had rejoined us, Amarna spoke to us both. "I suggest that the two of you keep your mate status to yourselves for now. And keep a distance from each other until she can better understand her power. Both of you can be influenced by your emotions, and we don't need her losing control before she even learns it."

I nodded.

Keep my distance. Not a problem.

Amarna gave me a look like she was calling my bluff. "While you will not be able to fully fight the pull toward each other, it would be easier on you if you tried, at least until you've trained. If others discover you too soon, word may reach Lyceius before you're ready. We must avoid that at all costs. No one should know, aside from your Trium."

"I'm afraid that's a problem," Niall mumbled.

Amarna cut her black eyes across the room at him. "And why is that?"

"There are four others—outside of your favorite little Trium—that know." He slid his hands into his pockets, a casual stance, which only angered Amarna.

"This is serious, boy. Who else knows?"

"Make that six others," he amended.

She blew a harsh breath out of her nose.

"First there's Breck—Killian's cousin. He was the one who found Auren after she crossed The Veil into our realm. Then there's Maeson, a woodland fae who is now residing here in Calledan. We go back a very long—"

"That matters not!" Amarna spat.

Niall looked up at the ceiling as he continued to recall the others. "The Elder of Elandrew . . . Sorscha, a house-fae who is also now residing in Calledan . . ." Amarna's face contorted at the odd group of beings that he was rattling off. "Vanir, and . . . Morah—Ramil's daughter."

The Elder was now enraged. "How did the snake's daughter come to know of this?"

She wasn't the first to call Ramil a snake, and she probably wouldn't be the last. His own daughter had said as much.

"She tried to kill Auren."

"She didn't try to *kill* me," I corrected. "She was going to catch me off guard to question me . . . with a dagger to my throat." I winced as I tacked on the last part.

"Fool!" Amarna shouted. "Did it cross your mind that Ramil could have slithered his way into his daughter's head? That he might be guiding her every move? That wretched High Lord has already betrayed my kind by going against our sacred laws, and now, with the possible murder of the Elder of Benmoor—"

"It's been confirmed?" Niall cut her off, his face brimming with shock.

"I received correspondence from Benmoor's Ancients days ago. They have not heard from their Elder in quite some time. So if this is true, it might very well be that Ramil has acquired something of great value, and there is no doubt in my mind that he will use it to his full ability. Sacrificing his daughter as a means to an end gives him no pause. And you were a fool to trust her."

"I have it on good authority that she can be trusted," Niall said.

"On whose authority? Your spy?" She scoffed. "You're going to get that male killed with all the espionage he does for you in his home court." She shook her finger in his face. "I know you are not foolish enough to ignore the price that some would pay for his head, or his loyalty. That entire household would kill to have Aremis back in their possession. Or perhaps you are a fool, since you put your faith in Morah."

I became utterly confused. "Wait. Aremis used to work for Ramil?"

Niall pushed off the wall and came closer. "Yes, but not of his own free will. I met Aremis after the Battle of Gabbath, when my father sent me to Benmoor to spy on Ramil. We had just fought off a legion of Lyceius's armies, a battle in which Ramil and his forces were nowhere to be found. He had promised us his loyalty to the fae cause, and then kept to his desert while we bled ourselves dry. My father wanted to know what had happened, but with tensions so high and the threat of Lyceius still looming, he couldn't leave Calledan. He sent me into Benmoor, undercover. I got caught on day one. The only fortunate thing was that it was Aremis who caught me."

Amarna snorted. "Served you right, sneaking around another's home." I could feel her rage cooling down a bit.

He ignored her and continued. "Aremis and I were both young. I was freshly shrouded, and newly tried in battle. I knew how important a good spy would be for our territory—and for my future court. When he caught me, I hadn't even known he was there. He'd followed me from the moment I entered his territory, to the minute I stepped foot inside the palace. No one knew who I was because I hadn't given my name. But Aremis knew. He'd done his share of spying in every court by the time he was two hundred and fifty years old, and he knew very well who I was. He didn't alert anyone though. He just watched me with his Aura from afar, and waited until the time was right to apprehend me.

"He later snuck into my cell and questioned me. He only did so because he knew I was a High Lord's son. He risked a lot to do it. But for three nights, he visited. We talked, and shared stories and information, and I told him of my intentions, my father's suspicions, and of the threat of war that was bound to return.

"I learned of his kind—the Cheshm Zadan, and how he was living as a hostage inside his own court's palace, doing the bidding of his High Lord, spying for days on end with no rest, killing at Ramil's command like it was sport. He wanted out. And I needed a spy.

"We spoke of our ambitions, and of how when I came to power, things would change. His values aligned with mine, and next thing I knew, he was smuggling us both out of Benmoor. I got stabbed along the way and nearly died, but he saved me then too."

"You got stabbed?" I asked, finally lifting my eyes to his. I saw a bit of tension leave his shoulders at the fact that I was acknowledging him. But how was he just going to skip over getting stabbed so nonchalantly?

"I did," he confirmed.

A twinge of anxiety sprouted in my gut at the thought of Niall getting injured. Mate or no, I quickly reminded myself that I was a tad irritated with him at the moment.

Amarna must have gotten a read on the thought, because she clicked her tongue. "He's fine. Didn't learn a damn thing from it though." This time, her smirk was on the playful side.

Niall huffed a laugh.

The Elder smoothed out her apron. "I'm not saying that Aremis misjudged Morah. But she could have played him falsely to begin with."

"I understand your concern." Niall ran his hand through his hair. "And it's been noted. But there's nothing I can do about it now. She knows, and has sworn us her loyalty and secrecy."

"For now," Amarna quipped. "In the meantime, no one else is to know. It's also unknown whether or not Killian's cousin will end up betraying you with the information—"

"He wouldn't," I cut in. "Breck took care of me. He was concerned for my well-being and always did his best to steer me clear of anyone he thought was a threat." I could feel Niall stiffen as I spoke of Breck, but I pretended not to notice.

"Be that as it may, Euryphaessa, you must be careful at all times. Regardless of whether or not someone says they are your friend, they can just as quickly become your foe. High Lord, you know this. I would expect nothing but your utmost protection for her, especially while you train her."

"She has all that I have to give. I'll have the Trium guarding her at all times."

Being guarded at all hours of the day and night was the last thing I wanted. "I'm perfectly capable of taking care of myself," I quipped, clutching the journal as I stood.

Amarna stood as well, ignoring my proclamation. "I will consult with Elspeth about the previous meeting between you all." She turned to Niall. "I mean it, High Lord, it is best if she is trained before you two . . . act on anything."

"So we keep our distance . . . for how long?" Niall asked while glancing at me. I could already tell he was going to struggle with the task.

Fortunately, my current emotions had me convinced I would have no issues keeping my distance from him for a while.

The Elder worked her jaw a moment. "You'll know when the time is right."

Niall nodded and gave her a bow. "Thank you for seeing us. You have my gratitude, as always."

I started to thank her as well, but she held up a gentle hand and closed her eyes. "You need not thank me Euryphaessa. I am here to serve, and am always available for assistance, if you should need it. You have a house-fae in your midst now as I understand it?"

"Yes. Sorscha. She came from Elandrew with me."

"I will be in contact with her. Should you ever need me on a whim, you can speak with her, and she will summon me."

"Thank you," I said, offering her a smile.

With one last look at Niall she said, "Stay out of your own head, High Lord." And with that, she departed into the other room.

Niall reached out for me, ready to take me into his arms to port us back to The Keep.

But to his surprise, I stepped backward, and disappeared into nothing.

60

TENSIONS

THE WIND HOWLED AROUND ME AS I CLUTCHED ONTO THE JOURNAL WITH all my might and envisioned the patio leading to The Keep.

There was no stopping now. I was committed.

I pictured myself in the center of it, so as not to risk landing on the edge or—gods forbid—miss the patio all together.

I could feel Niall's panic barreling down our mental connection. And in that moment, I realized why that connection had manifested in the first place.

It was because we were mates.

That bridge between us was becoming more pronounced as time went on. It began with me sensing his familiar presence before he ported in from somewhere. And now, I could feel his emotions.

His anxiety was practically flowing into me. I blocked it out with the wall in my mind and clenched my teeth, envisioning the patio.

The ground arrived much sooner than I anticipated, and I crashed onto my knees with the sudden impact. The journal flew out of my hands, landing a few feet in front of me. The sound of rushing water told me I had made it—not as gracefully as I wanted, but I'd done it.

Niall slammed into the stone in front of me not a second later and whirled, finding me rising up from my knees. "Are you hurt? Why did you—"

"I'm fine," I clipped as I snatched up the journal and walked around him into The Keep.

I had half a thought to port again into my bedchambers, but I decided against it and strode quickly and quietly up to the second floor, the way that Roirdan had taken me. Thankfully, The Keep was laid out much more simply than The Woodland House, and I could easily recognize the turns I needed to take.

Niall didn't say another word as he followed, but I could feel his unease.

My door opened on his command before I reached it, and I strode through with him right on my heels. Once inside, I turned and looked at him, beholding the worry that was written all over his face. I quickly averted my eyes elsewhere, not wanting to witness any of his pain.

A tense silence wrapped around us.

Part of me ached to embrace him and assure him that I was fine, but the stubborn half of me remained where I was, keen on giving him the cold shoulder for a while.

I couldn't think straight. I needed some time to myself, to figure all this out or just come to terms with it.

He took slow steps toward me. "Auren, may I please explain?" He paused, waiting for me to object or tell him to stop, but I remained silent, clutching the thick journal against my chest. "You had just learned the truth about your lineage and were told that you were born of a god. I didn't want to add more on top of that."

He finally came within touching distance, and my hands ached to reach out to him. If this was what being mates consisted of, he was probably feeling the same way.

"Auren, I would never lie to you or keep anything from you. I just . . . I didn't want to scare you off. Please, just look at me."

I closed my eyes and took a deep breath before opening them and finding his. The glow was absent, nothing but longing and apprehension left beneath his furrowed brows.

"I don't know what to do with all this," I finally said.

He slowly reached up and brushed the hair away from my face. His touch was like a chord being strung, igniting the thrumming in my chest once again.

"What would you like for me to do?" he asked softly.

"I'm not sure." The journal now felt like a lead weight in my arms. "This is probably a good place to start." I lifted it between us and he dropped his hand.

"What is that?"

I turned the book over. "It's a journal. Amarna said it might help me. It belonged to your great, great grandfather."

He stiffened and took a step back. "*Evander's* journal? She . . . she gave that to you?"

"Pulled it right out of one of those magical hidden pockets."

I told Amarna that I would read it with him . . . eventually. When I was level-headed, and not reeling from all the revelations and my new *mate*.

I set the journal down gently on the table by the sofa. When I rose back up, I swore Niall was closer than he had been seconds ago. The candlelight cast his face in dancing shadows, highlighting his strong jaw and the hint of stubble along his cheeks and around his mouth, which I always felt when he kissed me. My power stirred beneath my skin but I quickly shut it down, willing my essence to stay quiet and keep to itself.

Now is not the time to feel things for him.

Ever since he said the word *mates* back in Amarna's cabin, I felt the connection pull taut between us. Invisible, but still a very real presence to my minds-eye.

And now, the tension along that connection was palpable.

The silence strained the space between us, and I no longer knew what to do with myself.

I turned to walk away, but he caught my arm and pulled himself to me.

"I cannot deny you, Auren. One thing you should know about mates is that it's going to be impossible for us to keep ourselves away from each other for too long, now that the connection has been recognized. It would drive us mad to deny it, and I don't want there to be a rift between us."

"And do I get to choose if I want to be your mate?"

The words fell like boulders into a gaping chasm.

He froze. Then his fingers let go of my arm in one cold movement. "You . . . would reject the bond?"

I immediately wanted to take back my words after seeing the hurt in his expression. It was only a question, yet it looked as if I had just wrecked his world.

It wasn't that I wouldn't accept him, I just needed time to come to terms with it. There was no denying my feelings for him, but whatever human part of me was left needed a moment to catch up to this new reality.

"I didn't mean that I wouldn't accept whatever this is. I'm just overwhelmed. I need time to think. I need to sort things out and wrap my head around this."

He nodded, but his face still harbored a tinge of fear.

"I'll . . . sleep on it," I said as light-heartedly as I could, hoping it would give him a bit more reassurance and allow myself some time to calm my nerves.

His eyes searched mine for a moment longer before he spoke again. "Tomorrow is Drastia's Lumeri. Theirs falls only a day apart from ours since their territory is aligned to our north. I would like to return the favor of attending, since Laurent was kind enough to attend mine." He hesitated, then asked, "Would you be willing to go with me?"

I made a show of acting like I was thinking about it, when I already knew my answer was yes.

Don't seem desperate.

After a few moments, I settled on, "Okay."

He dipped his chin in a nod, and a small hint of relief washed over his face. "I'll see you tomorrow then," he said, dipping his head once more as he turned toward the door.

I yielded a step toward him. "Niall? Wait."

He spun so eagerly, I thought he would come rushing to me.

"Where are your bedchambers?" I asked.

He raised a brow at me.

"I mean . . . you know . . . in case I need anything."

Good job at not seeming desperate.

He pointed upwards. "I'm just a few levels up, tucked further into the mountain. I prefer a very quiet and secluded space."

"Oh. I see."

He took a step back toward me. "I could stay here if you'd rather—"

"I need to be alone with my thoughts," I said.

Resigned to accept that this was going to take time, he nodded. "Just promise me you won't go porting about The Keep?"

"Why?"

"Because I don't want to be up all night worrying about you falling off the edge of a cliff on accident."

I chewed the inside of my cheek before answering. "I won't port." He raised the same brow again, which told me he didn't believe a word I said. "Besides, I'm actually rather tired." I tried for a yawn, but couldn't coax it out.

"I'm sure you are," he said, giving me a slight laugh. "Sweet dreams, darling."

I missed him the moment he stepped past the threshold.

The door shut, and I was finally alone with my thoughts.

I paced, not knowing what to think or do.

Mate. Mate. Mate.

The simple word packed a life-altering blow, and it rang in my head alongside a swirling torrent of feelings. Churning over and over again.

Mate. Mate. Mate.

Looking over at my bed, I tried to coax myself to get in and relax.

A few seconds passed, and I glanced back at the door.

I wasn't ready to go to sleep just yet.

61

MIDNIGHT VENTURES

I DIDN'T KNOW WHERE I WAS GOING TO GO, BUT I LEFT MY CHAMBERS.

Niall didn't make me promise I wouldn't wander around The Keep. Just that I wouldn't port.

A late-night venture would surely help ease my mind.

With no access to windows or moonlight the hallway was incredibly dark, save for a single, dimly lit orb that hovered in place at each end.

The orb closest the stairs wiggled to life, flickering brighter as I passed by. It began following me, lighting the way as I descended into the main area of The Keep, then ducking off to a corner to hover and wait.

The curtains that framed the floor to ceiling windows on the far side of the room remained open, letting the bright white beams of the full moon wash over the furniture and flood the space with an ethereal atmosphere.

The fireplace crackled quietly, near fizzling out.

It was so quiet and still. So much so that I could hear the faint sound of the water rushing beneath the stone floors and plummeting down the mountainside. It was soothing. Like the mountain was also awake, pushing back against slumber to bathe in the moon's light.

I entered the vast space, running my hands along the leather and furs, searching for the perfect spot to curl up and just relax and think, when a gleaming light caught my eye outside the windows.

Out on the patio, near the same ledge I'd peered over when I first arrived here, a set of enormous feathered wings framed the hilt of a silver sword which flashed brightly in the moonlight.

It was Remic. He stood tall with an elegant grace as he looked out over the mountain range. The peaks beyond him appeared crusted in silver under the moon, a stark contrast to the blackened night sky.

I walked up to the windows, keeping enough distance to stay in what little shadows remained. I wondered what he was doing out there. Whether sleep eluded him too, or if he was watching—perhaps waiting—for something.

As soon as the thought crossed my mind, he turned. I flinched when his eyes pinned me where I stood. But he didn't make a move. He simply noted my presence and turned back toward the silver peaks.

How could he even see me in the shadows?

I blew out a breath. There was no sense in staying hidden now. He would probably only find me again when he came inside.

So, I went out.

The air was crisp and cool. I was thankful that I had stayed in my leggings and sweater instead of venturing out in my nightclothes.

In the distance I could still hear the faint sound of music and revelry. It had to be well past midnight now but the fae seemed to still be celebrating at the falls.

As I drew closer to the Dionach, I shuffled my feet so as to alert him that I was approaching—even if he probably already knew. He seemed like the type to react intensely to anything that startled him, so I'd rather be considerate.

I strode up to the ledge beside him, and placed my hands on the stone, leaning over slightly to gaze down into the depths below. "How late will they celebrate?" I asked quietly, lifting my gaze out toward the echoing music.

"Some will stay until dawn," he replied, equally as quiet. His smooth voice had a slight accent that I hadn't noticed before.

I glanced sidelong at him. "Can't sleep either?"

"It's rare that I sleep."

I nodded. He was short with his responses, but I didn't get the feeling that he was doing it to be rude. He seemed genuine—just not inclined to elaborate.

"You sensed me when I was inside?" I was curious as to how he had known exactly where I'd been standing.

"All Dionachs have a hyperawareness. It is what sets us apart as guardians."

"So I guess there's no sneaking up on you then?"

The corner of his mouth lifted ever-so slightly. "No."

I peered down the cliffside and out into the vast chasm between the staggering peaks once more. "It's beautiful out here."

He followed my line of sight out across the landscape. "Are there mountains where you are from?"

I didn't expect the question from him, but welcomed his attempt at conversation. "Nothing like this—that I know of. The best we have is probably a miniature version, but I've only heard stories from travelers."

"You do not travel much?"

"No. Never really had the chance to. But, if I were afforded the opportunity, I would." I glanced at him again. His eyes were cast low, listening. "It's always been my dream to travel. To see places that merchants speak of when they come back from trading. I'd love to see the sea someday."

"Where I come from, the sea rages under near-endless storms. It is quite remarkable."

"The Neveshir Isles, right? I've only ever seen it on a map." They were the four small dots off the coast that I'd noted when Maeson had shown me the map of our world.

A world I hadn't known the extent of.

"Yes. Though, I haven't been back in quite some time." His wings rustled behind us and I couldn't help but look back at them.

"Do you fly much?"

He glanced over at me. "All the time."

What a stupid question.

"What I meant was, do you ever fly for . . . fun?"

His brows gathered together at my question. "I have not flown for 'fun' since I was young."

"That couldn't have been too long ago though—" I stopped myself. I assumed he was still fairly young. Even with his silver-white hair, he looked around my age, perhaps only a year or two older.

A few seconds passed before he turned his head and looked over at me fully. "It has been over two thousand years."

I stared at him, my jaw slack. But he held his composure.

Oh, he's serious?

I saw it then. The age. It wasn't visible in his face, or his skin, or his posture. It was in his eyes. The depths of millennia were set into them like stones at the bottom of a deep lake, heavy with times come and gone and all that he must have witnessed.

"I wouldn't have guessed you were that . . ."

"Old?" he finished for me. A breeze swirled around the patio, lifting the long strands of his hair. "No one ever does."

"Is that normal for your kind?"

When he didn't answer right away I feared I might have crossed a line. "I'm sorry, I didn't mean to offend you. I just don't know much about Dionachs."

He reached up and brushed his hair behind his shoulders. His face softened as he said, "You did not offend me. We are blessed with long lives like the fae. We are bred from the witches of Neveshir, therefore our lineage allows for many unique qualities. A long life can seem like a blessing to some. Others find it difficult if they suffer hardships or have known loss."

From the way he spoke, he must have had personal experience with one or both of those things, and that made my heart hurt for him.

To my surprise, he continued. "Every Dionach is bred for a purpose. The fates assign each one of us a charge, or what we call a Dionam— someone we are fated to protect. Our job is to keep them from harm. Until the day we receive our assignment, we will live out our lives, protecting and serving at will."

"So, is Niall your Dionam, then?"

Remic looked down at the waist-high stone wall that kept us from toppling over the edge of the cliffside. His tone became stern, tinged with pain. "No. My Dionam is not yet known to me."

The words echoed in my head, and I was instantly overcome with the need to take away his pain.My chest ached at what he must be feeling. I didn't know much about the Dionachs, but from the way he described their life's purpose—to not yet find the one he was meant to protect after thousands of years—that would be a soul-crushing blow.

"Remic, I'm sorry, I shouldn't have asked—"

"You do not need to be sorry. It is no one's fault but mine. I have searched for many years to no avail. But I still have hope that I will one day find who I am meant to protect. I will find my purpose."

"How will you know?" I asked quietly.

"Some say that it is a feeling you get when you first come in contact with your Dionam—or how you react at the sight of them being threatened. Others say it will be a pulling—a need to comfort or protect that we will feel deep inside. More than just a command given by someone else." He lifted his eyes to mine, studying me intently, like there was something he was trying to glean or confirm for himself.

I broke our eye contact and smoothed my hands out along the stone wall, tracing the lines of mortar. "Strangely, I understand your longing. A longing for a purpose that you know you're meant for but haven't found."

I was nearing a mere thirty years of age, and trying to find my purpose had already begun to weigh heavy on me in the years prior. If I'd lived as long as he had and not yet found it . . .

His eyes remained on me as I elaborated. "I was struggling with the same thing back home in the human lands. I fought to earn an income because I was good with my fists and my sword. I loved it—yes—but I knew that there was something more for me out there. I just didn't know what. Now, I guess I know." I sighed and looked out across the night sky. "Turns out I'm not even truly human." I said it more to myself than to him. "My purpose has been here, in this realm, all along. It just took me a while to make my way to it."

I looked up at Remic again and gave him a small smile. "Perhaps you're still making your way to your purpose, too."

His eyes lightened and a faint smile lifted the corners of his mouth. "Thank you, Auren. Your kind words mean a great deal to me."

We stood in comfortable silence for a while longer, taking in the night sky before I decided it was time for me to let him have his space again.

"It was a pleasure speaking with you," he said politely as I bid him goodnight.

"We should do it more often," I said, smiling.

He dipped his head in a bow and watched as I retreated back through the doors into The Keep.

Once inside, I shivered as the warmth of the room seeped into me. I hadn't realized how cool the breeze had truly been.

Out of the corner of my eye, I thought I saw movement in a shadowy alcove far across the room. Footsteps scuffled about and I instinctively reached for my sword, only to find my bare hip. I silently cursed. Being caught without a weapon was something I never liked.

Then I remembered my shield and quickly threw it up around me, reinforcing my mind as well—just in case.

The moonlight touched every surface in the room except for the back wall where the noise had come from. When I tried to peer into the darkness there, it just stared right back at me, revealing nothing.

Off to my right, I heard more footsteps and laughter followed by a shushing noise before whoever was there disappeared. I sighed, realizing it was probably a couple of fae sneaking around with each other. After all, it was Lumeri and *the gods were watching.*

I made my way back toward the stairs promising myself that one night soon, I would come find a cozy sofa and curl up with a book. Perhaps the journal—if I was in the right mood for the solemn accounts it held.

At the foot of the stairs, the same orb that had led me here rushed to greet me. Maybe I was finally getting tired or delirious, but I had half a mind to want to speak to it, wondering if it was being bothered to light my way, or if it was always up this late.

Oh, why not?

"Sorry if I'm keeping you up," I muttered.

To my surprise, the orb paused for a moment and gently pulsed back at me, spinning softly before it continued moving along.

I huffed a laugh and shook my head. "So, you understand me, then?"

The orb dipped once, hovered, and then resumed its lead.

Sentient orbs. I would have to scold Niall for not informing me of that little detail.

Once I reached the familiar hallway, I noted that every door was dark underneath, except for mine and the one directly across the hall from it. I couldn't remember to whom it belonged, but I tip-toed closer out of curiosity. I could hear shuffling noises, but nothing that gave away who was still awake. Whoever it was, they sounded like they were having trouble.

The orb hovered nearby, seemingly just as curious as I was.

"Don't suppose you can tell me whose chamber this is?" I whispered. But the orb just bobbed in silence. "I figured."

Then, something fell with a loud thud behind the door, and I jumped. There was too much commotion inside to be normal, so I leaned my ear up against the wood hoping to glean if whoever was on the other side was all right.

Suddenly, the door opened, and I gasped as I stumbled inside, falling against a large, muscular, half-naked male body.

Roirdan let out a startled noise as my cheek hit his sweaty chest. "What the—" He fumbled with me as I peeled myself off of him, then he smacked his hand over his bare chest and let out a breath. "Gods, Auren! You scared the *shit* out of me!"

I flushed red, but couldn't help my laugh as I stared at him. He was tangled up in his pants which were down around his ankles. His hair was unbound and tousled in knots, and his lips looked kiss-swollen.

I peered around the space.

There was a seating area immediately inside, with several chairs that were all a bit misplaced, fur pelts lining their seats and backrests—all a bit off-kilter. Pillows had been tossed about, and the remaining pieces of his clothes were strewn all around the floor and on the rumpled bed. Empty bottles and too many wine glasses for just one person littered the tables.

I quickly realized what I'd intruded on and backed up to the door, rummaging behind me for the handle. "Roirdan, I am *so* sorry. I heard something that sounded like a struggle and thought perhaps you might be in trouble." I squeezed my eyes shut, silently cursing at myself.

He calmed his breathing and tossed his hair out of his face. "No trouble here, just . . . uhh, one second . . ." He reached down and tried to pull his pants back up, but failed miserably and careened back onto the nearest armchair. "Fucking leathers," he muttered, opting to tug his pants off completely. He flung them across the chamber, and I watched them hit the tapestry on the wall and fall to the floor with a heavy thud.

I continued to avert my eyes from him. Thankfully he was wearing a set of undershorts, but I still felt like it was a sight I shouldn't be witnessing.

There were definitely others here—or there *had* been—judging by the state of the place.

"Roirdan, what exactly happened here?"

I regretted asking as a cocky grin slid across his face.

He righted himself on his two feet. "Oh, you know, just a little after-party. You didn't happen to see a couple of females out in the hallway, did you?"

That explained the giggling and scurrying downstairs.

"I think they went downstairs," I answered.

"Ah, shit," he said. He proceeded to stumble to his bedside table where a large decanter of wine sat. "Wine?" He offered. The glass wobbled in his hand as he attempted to fill it.

"No, thanks. An after-party huh?"

"C'mon little one, it's Lumeri. It brings good luck if—"

I interrupted by clearing my throat. "No need to tell me, I know about the good luck thing."

"Do you now?" He raised a brow and grinned mischievously at me.

"Niall . . . explained it to me in Vahrenhall."

He sipped from his glass, spilling more outside of his mouth than he managed to swallow. "Uh huh. I'm sure he did." He winked. "Laetus Lumeri."

I gave him an awkward smile. "Uh, well, sorry again for the intrusion. Have a good . . . whatever this is," I said, half-laughing as I pulled the door open and stepped out. I heard him chuckle as I crossed the hall to my own chambers.

The orb sped up to follow me and nudged at my door, as if it were asking permission to go inside. I opened the door and waved my arm for it to enter, and it drifted in and spun, much like someone taking in a new space would. I grinned as I watched it move, exploring every nook and cranny.

Sorscha's head perked up from the sofa, her sleepy eyes blinking through the shadows. She smiled, and then noted the orb as it floated around the room. When she looked back at me anxiously, I nodded, assuring her that it was okay.

She yawned and sank back down into the plush blankets that surrounded her, while I plucked the nightclothes from the armoire and changed.

I slid into bed, and the orb took up a place next to the door and dimmed to a soothing glow.

"Looks like you're in here for the night," I said to it as I yawned again.

It pulsed lightly and dimmed further this time, as if to say, *thank you, now sleep.*

62

JOIN ME FOR BREAKFAST

THE WIND WHIPPED FURIOUSLY AT MY HAIR AS I STOOD IN THE MIDST OF A *barren, gray land. Dust blew by, stinging my face and tinkling against the sword hanging at my side.*

Cling.

Cling. Cling.

I could feel a sinister presence growing closer, but there was nothing to see for miles. Nothing but a dead wasteland full of crumbling hills and boulders.

I could sense it, though. Whatever it was, it was hunting.

Hunting me.

Suddenly the ground beneath me shook, and a searing pain shot across my head. A terrible screeching noise pierced the air, so loud that I clasped my hands over my ears as blood began dribbling out of them—the warmth spilling between my fingers and down my neck.

My mental shield shook. The wall of white stone that I'd built up and armored with everything that I had shuddered and cracked.

Then, I saw them. Clawed, black tipped fingers appeared from thin air and slithered their way up the wall in my mind, scratching and tapping on every crack and crevice. More and more of them came, climbing higher, swarming the wall, pulling and scraping for purchase.

I pushed my power into the stone, reinforcing it with all my might. But

one by one, pieces fell, until like an avalanche, the wall crumbled, and
darkness swept in.

I jerked awake in a cold sweat, gasping for breath.

The room was quiet.

Sorscha still dozed peacefully on the sofa, surrounded by her mound of
blankets.

I pressed my head back into the pillows and tried to calm my racing
heart. I hadn't had a nightmare in years, and even then, it was nowhere
near as disturbing as this one was.

This one felt *real*. It felt *personal*.

I checked my mental shield.

The wall of white stone stood tall and pristine, just the way I always
left it. No hint of black claws, or cracks, or any of it.

Once the irksome feeling finally vacated my bones, I fell back asleep,
and this time, I did not dream.

Morning came when the sentient orb bobbed next to my bedside, gently
coaxing me to wake with its warm light.

It must have been aware of the moon and sun's positioning, alerting
those inside the mountain to the proper time of day.

I rose and stretched, rubbing the sleep from my eyes.

Sorscha was gone. She'd probably woken hours ago—the busybody.

As I looked around, I noticed a note tacked to the post at the end of my
bed. I crawled across the mattress and snatched it up.

Join me for breakfast?

I knew this could only be from Niall, and I grinned down at his
penmanship and the invitation.

The orb bobbed in my line of sight, and I waved the paper toward it
and smiled. "An invitation to breakfast, it seems."

It pulsed quickly and hurried over to the door, anxiously waiting.

"All right, all right. Give me a second to get ready then."

I slid out of bed and freshened my face, combing my hair and opting to leave it down. In the armoire, I found an impressive array of clothing options. I swore, Niall must have had Gareth making clothes by the hour and porting them to Calledan upon completion. An entire selection of different tunics, several long, cozy sweaters, and some leggings and leathers all lined the shelves. Nothing frilly or gaudy, as if he knew those types of things repulsed me.

His thoughtfulness tugged on my heartstrings.

I selected a fur trimmed tunic and matching belt, with a pair of lightweight leggings and boots and quickly got dressed.

The orb sped off down the hall the moment I opened the door, double backing a few times as it waited for me to catch up. Soon, I was in an entirely new wing of The Keep, following its light through the winding corridors as it led me to my destination.

As I walked, I began thinking about last night and the entire conversation with Niall about *mates* that had left me parting ways with him rather awkwardly. I'd been overwhelmed—as he feared I would be— and I hoped he wasn't still worried about rejection. I wasn't quite sure how he was going to act today, given that I had basically shunned him after leaving Amarna's cabin.

I wasn't even sure how *I* would feel when I saw him this morning.

As badly as I wanted to stew in bitterness about the fact that he had hidden life-altering information from me, I couldn't help but feel giddy at his breakfast invitation.

The dark halls curved back toward the exterior of the mountain face, and another set of tall windows came into view overlooking a quaint patio below.

The breakfast area was situated on a small terrace built out onto the side of the cliffs. Planters overflowing with vines swung from the banisters lining the stairway down to the seating area, where a large stone fire pit flared in the center of the cozy space. A table was set for two on the right side of it.

The morning sun was still rising on the far side of the mountain, leaving the shadows and cool air to linger.

As I descended the stairs, I spotted Niall standing against the railing overlooking the valley below. The sight of him made the thrumming in my chest kick up in tempo, and I knew instantly that I would forgive him without a second thought.

He turned when he sensed my arrival, and his eyes followed me down the steps.

"Sleep well?" He greeted me with a smile.

"Well, no, actually." I half-smiled back, knowing that was not the answer he'd probably expected. "But this looks lovely." I eyed the table and the mounds of fresh bacon and sausage, breads and fruits.

He pulled my chair out for me with the flick of his wrist, and draped the lightweight blanket over my lap as I sat.

"Thank you," I said, trying not to fawn too hard over his mannerisms.

"Tell me about your night," he said, pouring me a cup of steeping, hot tea.

"Well, I wasn't tired, so I wandered around briefly, and ended up having a nice conversation with Remic outside the main area of The Keep."

He lifted a brow at me as he listened and served us breakfast.

"Then, I went to Roirdan's chambers, where he was basically naked—"

The serving fork tumbled loudly out of Niall's hand onto the plate, and his eyes shot up to mine.

"It's not as bad as it sounds," I quickly reassured him. "I heard lots of noise coming from behind his door—like he was struggling or something —and I thought maybe he was in trouble. So I tried to listen. Then he opened the door, and I sort of fell into him."

Niall's eyes were wide, and I could see the questions stacking up in his mind.

"He was apparently having an intimate little after-party with a few females. He was perfectly fine." I speared some cantaloupe with my fork. "Then I—"

"There's more?" Niall raised both brows.

I nodded. "I found out that the orbs are sentient. Why didn't you tell me?"

Niall shook his head in confusion. "Orbs?"

"Yes, the orbs. They can understand us?"

The look on his face said that he didn't know why the conversation had taken this strange turn. "Yes . . ." he drew out. "They're aware of our comings and goings. Obviously, they can't communicate, but they understand. What does that have to do with last night?"

I grinned. "Well I wouldn't have been able to find my way around if I hadn't had help."

He squinted. "Did you make another friend?"

"As a matter of fact, I did. It stayed in my chambers last night and woke me this morning. It even led me here." I looked back over my shoulder to see if the orb was still hovering by the top of the stairs. Sure enough, I could see its faint glow from inside the windows.

Niall followed my gaze, seemingly both confused and amused. "Uh huh . . . Anything else?"

I paused for a moment before answering. "I had a nightmare."

He turned back to me, searching my eyes. "Are you all right?"

"I'm fine."

"Do you want to tell me what happened?"

I could tell he was concerned and trying to not seem too anxious or press me for too much information, probably thinking I would shut down too easily after what had happened last night. But this was something I actually wanted to discuss.

I tasted the fruit, savoring the sweetness before I explained. "I was in a wasteland, alone, but something was searching for me. I got this intense pain in my head, and there was a loud screeching in my ears. It broke into my mind, and all I saw were black, clawed hands. First there was just one pair, then there were so many I couldn't count them. And then my wall came crumbling down, and I woke up."

His face went pale as he mulled over my words.

"Niall?" I reached out for him without thinking.

He looked at where my hand had grasped his, and slowly wrapped his fingers around mine. "Did you see anyone in the dream? Was anyone there with you?"

"Not a physical being. But there was a presence, and I didn't like the way it made me feel." I shuddered as I recalled it. "What do you think it means?"

He studied our hands as he smoothed his thumb back and forth over my knuckles. "I'm not sure, but it has me worried. There's been movement in Salterra—out on The Wastelands. Aremis has been looking into it."

"Is it Lyceius?"

Someone cleared their throat at the top of the stairs, and Niall quickly let go of my hand and picked up his fork, as if there was nothing to see between us.

Right. Distance. No public displays of affection.

Best to start now.

I pulled my empty hand back and made a show of smoothing the blanket out across my lap, while Niall speared a piece of fruit.

Aremis was leaning casually over the rail looking down at us, his eyes sparkling with amusement. "Laurent sends his thanks and says that he'll see you both this evening in Drastia." His eyes flicked between us, a grin wavering on the edge of his lips as he noted our awkwardness. "Also, I received an update from the border patrols. We'll need to call a meeting before you leave today. It's something you'll definitely want to find time to discuss with Laurent tonight."

Niall nodded, thanking Aremis for the update, and the advisor slipped back inside, leaving us to continue our private breakfast.

"Well that doesn't sound too good," I surmised.

"Nothing good ever comes from the border," Niall replied. "I'd rather not receive any news than receive an update. But the patrols and their scouts are paramount when it comes to keeping an eye on our enemies."

"Do you mean Lyceius?"

"Him and his armies."

My eyes widened. "Armies? As in, plural?"

"Yes. The last time we fought against his legions, it was a bloodbath. I think we only lived to see the end of that battle because he went easy on us. Feeling out our power. He's been relatively quiet the last several years, which makes us all uneasy. But we know his forces are ever-growing. Our patrols steadily bring word of new legions, or a new breed of creature that strays too close to our borders. Over the last year, sightings have ramped up. More disturbances have been happening in our realm, and in yours."

I looked down and poked at my food, thinking back on the attacks that had plagued the human lands.

"Do you remember the keres? They're the spawn of Lyceius. Centuries ago, he experimented and created them from the products of his human mingling."

"They used to be *human?*" I nearly choked.

Niall nodded grimly. "Yes."

My heart sank. I thought that something about the creature looked human when it cornered us in the forest cave. Its form had become so unnatural and distorted because it had been tampered with.

Knowing that the keres were once human made me internally condemn Lyceius all the more.

"The keres are just one of his many abominations. See, Karios is the god of creation, not Lyceius. Anything Lyceius creates is corrupted, wrong. It was not meant to be. Yet somehow, he's found a way to do it. And since they've found a way to get through The Veil, the keres in particular are scattered all throughout both realms."

"That's what's been wreaking havoc in the human lands," I deduced.

Niall nodded again. "Their main purpose is to hunt for any sign of heightened power. Here in the fae realm, power is abundant, that's why we have wards up to seal the creatures out, otherwise they'd be breaching our cities right and left. Your power drew them out in Elandrew, and I suspect that after your display back at the castle, it wasn't long before a swarm of whatever keres were lurking in that forest overtook the grounds, looking for the source."

"Do you think they could have alerted Lyceius?"

"That I don't know, but I would assume so. They're loyal to him. His power gives them life, so denying him information would be detrimental to them. That's why it's important that you're here and kept under fae wards. Your power is too sensitive. They sensed you once. Twice . . . that might prompt Lyceius to send his other cronies to investigate. Not to mention that the fae realm has its own creatures that lurk in the wilds. They're not of Lyceius's making, but they're just as foul and deadly as the keres."

I swallowed hard and pushed the bacon around on my plate. "Would more of his creatures be able to get past The Veil?"

Niall shook his head with uncertainty. "I don't know. Things are changing. The Veil used to be impenetrable. We have no idea why the keres were able to make it across in the first place."

"So, why did they only come searching for me when I was in Elandrew? I've lit up and used my power in Vanir's territory and in this one, and nothing's tried to come after me since."

"My theory is that if they were already looking for you near the castle, and some had crossed into Elandrew, then they were conveniently close. Which would make it easy for them to pick up on the use of power and track you. That, or Elandrew's wards are weak because Killian doesn't care to re-enforce them the way Vanir and I do with ours. The wards in Vanir's court and in mine won't falter. You don't need to worry about that."

It made sense. But I still didn't like the fact that my power was a beacon to such sinister creatures. I sighed. "I need to train. I need to learn to wield my power so I can help with whatever's to come."

Niall scanned my face like he was wondering when I'd become so determined to hone my power. But he didn't question it. "I have a plan for that. Aremis and I discussed it a bit last night."

"*That's* what you were all discussing during Lumeri?"

Niall leaned back in his chair and laughed. "No, darling. That's what we discussed after I left your chambers."

"Oh."

Wait.

"So that means you were—"

"Awake and aware of your little exploration? Of course, I was."

I crossed my arms. "You were spying on me?"

"No, I was just aware that you had left your room. In no way did I spy on you."

I raised a brow at him. "But you knew where I was?"

"I knew you didn't leave The Keep, which was all I needed to know. What you do here is your own business. I was mainly concerned that you would try to port somewhere, and I would need to go and catch you." He smirked as he wiped the corners of his mouth with his napkin.

"Well just so you know, my goal is to not need your assistance again when porting. Then maybe you won't be such a snoop."

"I'm not a snoop," he challenged. "But I care about you, and I want you to be safe."

Hearing him say that he cared about me made my stomach flutter again. But last night's emotions were still a bit raw, and I wasn't quite sure how to go forward knowing that we were *mates*.

I wasn't sure how to handle that at all actually. And trying to suppress the intense longing wasn't doing me any favors. I settled on giving him a polite smile and he seemed content with that.

"So, how are we going to move forward with training?" I asked, taking a bite of my food.

"This morning, I want Maeson to teach you some old remedies to a few things you might readily encounter in this realm. Especially since we're traveling to Benmoor in a couple of days."

My brows hiked up. "Ramil's territory?"

Niall let out a long sigh. "Yes, unfortunately. I don't usually attend his Lumeri events, but by doing so this time, Aremis can go *snooping*—as you prefer to call it."

I rolled my eyes playfully.

"I seriously considered having you stay here with Roirdan, but I would rather have you close to me. I don't care that Amarna told us to distance ourselves."

"Oh. Well . . . good." I didn't want to stay by myself.

I wanted to be near him.

Chafing mating bond be damned.

And this conversation had suddenly become too serious. I needed his banter. Craved his playful sentiments and snarky remarks. I tossed him a challenging look, enticing him with my words. "If you were to leave me here, who knows where I might decide to port off to."

He waved his fork at me, taking the bait. "You're forgetting that you can only port to places you've seen or know."

"Perhaps I'll port back to Vahrenhall and spend some time with sweet Vanir," I teased. "I'm sure he wouldn't mind looking after me while you're in Benmoor."

Niall's nostrils flared, jealousy glinting in his eyes. He tried to cover it by taking a stiff sip of his now cold tea. "I'm sure he wouldn't mind one bit," he ground out. "However, the closer you are to me, the better I can watch over you, and the more relaxed I'll feel."

Although I agreed with his logic, it still wasn't the playful banter I'd sought. I speared some meat with my fork and tried once more. "Remic seems like he would give his life to protect someone. Would *you*—" I cut my words short at the sight of his expression.

He stared at me over his cup, his face a picture of smoldering intensity as he said, "I would tear the world apart for you and give my life a thousand times over if it meant you were safe and unharmed."

My lips parted at his words.

I hadn't expected that answer. Nor had I wanted any more of this serious talk. But there it was. His true feelings. And he'd just laid them out across the table like a flayed open heart.

I knew he cared for me—he'd admitted it minutes ago. But the extent to which he described made me want to bury myself in his embrace and never let him go.

"Niall . . ." I murmured.

"It's the truth. You will always be safer with me than anywhere else." His grip on his tea cup threatened to shatter the porcelain if he squeezed any harder. But his knuckles gradually eased, regaining their color, and he set the drink down, wiping his palms against his thighs under the table. "If you wish to accompany me to Benmoor, then you shall. Remic and Aremis are going as well."

I nodded, giving him a delicate smile. "I'll go with you."

He nodded back, the tension easing from his features. "Good. But first, concentrate on learning a few things from Maeson today. She's itching to be of some use around here. I had a few of my house-fae set up a small workshop for her nearby. It's just a temporary place, but it'll do for now."

He stood and offered me his hand.

I hesitated to grab it. "Aren't you worried someone will see?" I half-joked.

"What, with all the spectators around?" He gestured to the empty patio we occupied, a bit of familiar sarcasm finally lacing his words. "I'm only porting you to where you need to go, which *requires* physical contact." He winked.

I knew this was more than just him keeping his distance because Amarna told us to. He was giving me the space I needed, and that made me grow even more fond of him.

I bit my lip and placed my hand in his, happy to feel the contact again. As he whisked me away, he pressed a reverent kiss to my temple, and something inside me eased.

The next thing I knew, we were taking form outside a small cottage tucked into a grove of thick pines alongside a quiet stream. The cottage was cast in complete shadow—thanks to the surrounding mountains. It hardly looked like it ever saw any sunlight in all its seclusion. The perfect place for someone to hide away for a few hours, face deep in tonics and salves.

I could already hear Wrynn's cackling fox-chatter inside as Maeson spoke to her.

Niall gently knocked on the door that had been left ajar. Wrynn poked her head out and commenced into running circles around our feet excitedly.

"Come in!" Maeson waved, welcoming us. As we stepped inside, she beamed, gesturing around the space. "Niall, this is perfect. I can't thank you enough."

"It's only temporary, until I can find you a better location and a bigger space," he replied, trying not to step on Wrynn's tail as she scampered beneath us.

"Oh, no, please. I would gladly live here. It's absolutely perfect. It feels like home." She looked around, smiling.

Two wooden tables lined the center of the main room with bottles and decanters full of just about everything that I remembered seeing in her old home. And she'd taken to lighting dozens of candles. Stacks of them lined the shelves and window sills and decorated every nook and cranny.

She wrapped me in a pleasant hug, still speaking to Niall over her shoulder. "Your house-fae are delightful by the way. They even found me some of the rarer herbs that it took me months to collect back in Elandrew. Auren and I can brew up some good stuff today."

"Glad to hear it. Teach her some basics. We'll be heading to Benmoor in a few days, and I want her to be knowledgeable."

Maeson nodded and patted her leather book with all the ribbons and strings dangling from it. "I've got it covered."

"I'll see you this afternoon, and we'll head to Drastia before dark."

I nodded.

He turned and gave Wrynn a little pat on her head and a scratch under her chin, and she swung her tail happily. "Behave yourselves, ladies," he said as he winked and ported away.

I turned to Maeson. "Where do we begin?"

63
NEW INSIGHT

HOURS WENT BY IN A BLINK, AND WE BARELY MADE A DENT IN MAESON'S well-loved book, which not only kept all her notes on the different plants that can be harvested from each court, but also held the recipes and specific instructions on how to prepare them. Most species were common and easy to find, while others were so rare, they only flowered once every year. My head spun with all the ways that something as simple as a leaf could be used.

We mixed what was called an Elder Leaf Salve, using dried leaves from the Elderwood trees, which flowed rich with the magic that dwelled deep in the land. After steeping them in oil, they were strained and ground to a pulp, and some beeswax was added to create a balm. It could be used to treat wounds that were taking a bit longer to heal, or to staunch bleeding. If one's magic became hindered, or their power depleted by the kiss of iron, the balm could be the difference between life and death.

I learned that wild seeds were a common ingredient used by the Ancient Fae to either enhance one's power, or render it completely useless. The Moon Hedge plant was a species in the fern family—commonly found in the woodlands. Its small, pale, white seeds—no larger than grains of salt—can temporarily enhance one's ability to shield themselves and make their innate magic stronger.

The burning of the black seeds, from the flowering Zaldora plant, can stop a Cheshm Zadan from casting eyes and ears over the area. The chemical properties emitted into the air when the seeds are burned will temporarily blind their Aura. It smelled briny when burned, which Maeson explained is normal—given that Zaldora is exclusively found near the sea along the coast.

Foxroot was something that seemed to grow everywhere. The plant produces small white flowers that lie low to the ground, and their roots are the color of a red fox, with lots of tiny tendrils that resemble fur. When the root is ground up, its properties change. If inhaled, it can temporarily stun an enemy and cause intense systemic pain. If the roots are brewed, they can induce hallucinations and lead to temporary memory loss in larger doses. The flowers, however, can be ground up and brewed as a tea which can help with fevers.

It amazed me how different parts of the same plant can be both the cause of pain, and the remedy for it. I began to see why Maeson was so fascinated by it all. With all her knowledge, she truly held the ability to save lives, or take them on a whim.

I plucked a rather dull looking vial off the shelf. It was clear, and looked like plain water from the nearby stream. I uncorked the top to smell it and see if it was indeed water, or something else. I drew back immediately at the potent smell of licorice. "What's this one?"

Maeson looked over and quickly snatched the vile away. "The Proper Death."

"The *what?*" I asked, blinking at the name.

"You heard me. It's a poison. It can be easily masked when added to certain drinks such as wine, and no one would ever know. But if you know what to look for, that distinct hint of licorice gives it away. When left out to dry, the poison dwindles down into a fine powder, which can be mixed and burned. If inhaled in significant amounts . . ."

"I'm assuming it kills you?"

"It can. Eventually. It paralyzes you first—stifles your power and all magic. Death could follow in minutes, hours, days, it depends on the individual and how much was administered. But there is a remedy."

She moved to the lower shelf and fingered through a few bundles of dried herbs until she found a woven satchel. From it, she pulled out a long, purple flower petal. "The remedy—oddly enough—is poisonous as well. But they work to cancel each other out." She handed me the petal to feel. "The Bitter Lily. Chewing a couple of these petals will save your life—should you be poisoned by The Proper Death. The problem is finding them. They are very rare and only grow in a hot climate—as they thrive in the heat. The other problem is that once you've been poisoned by The Proper Death, it's almost impossible to move. So, the idea of finding and ingesting the flower in time . . ."

"That's inconvenient." I frowned.

The purple petal was at least four inches long, and smooth as silk. The color was so vibrant, that I was pretty sure I would know it if I ever saw it again.

I handed it back to her.

"Very inconvenient. But, it never hurts to know." She shrugged, sliding the petal back in the satchel. "The good thing is, The Proper Death is very tricky to brew, and it requires knowledge of practices of Old Magic, which include certain spells that must be spoken while brewing. Hardly anyone knows those spells anymore, so it's very unlikely that the poison would ever be used." She tucked the satchel back in its spot on the shelf then leaned in close to me. "I've heard stories back in Elandrew that Killian's father used to have his devoted house-fae test all his drinks first, and had a healer nearby with a pocket full of Bitter Lily petals on his person at all times. Talk about paranoia."

"Sounds like he had a lot of enemies."

"Indeed," she replied. "Oh, and I almost forgot." She leaned over to a small cabinet and plucked out a small, corked, glass bottle with a dropper. Smiling, she placed it in my hand. "The tincture you requested."

I tried not to blush as I examined the pale yellow liquid inside.

"Take a couple drops by mouth once a week. It should last you quite a while."

"Thank you," I said, slipping it into my pocket.

She gave me a wink and went back to her concoctions.

When we'd exhausted all her empty bottles and bowls, I stepped outside to get some fresh air, while she remained in the cabin and tidied up the aftermath of our creations.

I wandered down to the trickling stream nearby and took a seat, propping myself against a tree.

The cool air that lingered in the shadow of the mountains kissed my skin, bringing with it the crisp smell of pine and a hint of woodsy musk that I'd only ever smelled in this territory.

Evander's journal pressed into my side, tucked into the waistband of my pants. I lifted up my tunic and pulled it forth, laying it on my lap. Until Niall could teach me how to stow it away in a magical pocket of space, my waistband was the next best thing.

I brushed my fingers over the cover of the journal, which was empty of words, the leather worn smooth by years of handling. I unwound the straps and took a deep breath, knowing that once I opened it, there was no turning back.

The cover folded open with the ease of a page turned thousands of times, and inside, written on the first page, were the words:

To die to yourself is to truly live.

The hand-written script was impressively neat, and the ink was still dark, as if the pages hadn't seen the light of day since it was last shut and wrapped up tightly.

Or, it was the last thing to have been written. A final statement, to sum up a life's worth of deeds.

A legacy.

The paper was slightly yellowed, but nothing that seemed remotely close to what thousands of years old should have looked like.

Perhaps an enchantment kept it in its excellent condition.

The following page was left blank. The one after held the same graceful script:

Today, I decided that I can no longer keep these unfortunate occurrences to myself. I will begin by saying that what is happening to me has been going on for quite some time. Now, I am afraid that it can no longer be avoided and thus needs documentation. I fear that what I am experiencing will greatly affect those around me, and I want it to be known that I am doing everything in my power to control it. But I am hopeful that it will not get to that point. Thus, my words will stand as testament, to see me through this.

I am five hundred and sixty-seven years of age and my power is continuing to change. My power should have matured a few hundred years ago, but as of late, it only seems to be growing stronger.

Late last winter, I suffered a terrible dream.

I dreamt of a battlefield. Dead fae and our enemies alike covered the ground in mounds. The battle raged around me, and I was witness to the greatest horrors of it. In the midst of the carnage, I heard a deep battle cry. I turned and saw a young male swinging his sword like he was in a dance. He sliced through the creatures like they were air. He moved beautifully. I saw a bit of myself in him, in the golden fire raging in his eyes from under his helm.

In the distance I witnessed our armies being overpowered by a legion that swept in from the east. Our forces began to fall at twice the rate they already were. The young male saw it too. He turned and scanned the battlefield, and I could tell by his expression that he was desperately trying to form a plan. He let his sword fall to the ground and looked down at his hands as shadows ignited into black flames above them. It was shadowfire. The same gift I bear. Only, this male looked much too young to be wielding it in the manor he was considering.

I knew this power. It was so deadly, so unpredictable,

that if he were to unleash it here, the consequences would be unmatched.

I pushed against the bodies as they crashed into me. I tried desperately to get to him in time. To stop him from making a mistake. But his eyes grew frantic. Tears lined them just as they lined mine. He scanned the battlefield once more, the shadowfire growing in a fury around him.

Then his eyes landed upon mine. With a silent plea of forgiveness, he held my stare as he unleashed his power. I yelled and reached out for him, but it was no use. I was blown back by the shockwave and awoke suddenly. I knew then that I had to do whatever I needed to in order to prevent this burden from ever falling upon another.

I am still haunted by the look in that fae's eyes. The fear that I saw there is the same that I feel now.

For this type of power does not tread lightly.

It consumes.

The entry ended, and tears lined my eyes as I looked up from the page. Evander had seen Niall.

In his dream, he had seen his great, great grandson on the battlefield. This vision must have been what spurred Evander to want to discover a permanent fix. To find a way to tame it. There was no way to know whether or not another fae down his bloodline would inherit his power, but it had bothered him enough to record it. To try to find a cure.

I sensed Niall before he appeared. Chestnut and vanilla swirled along the breeze as he approached.

"Seems you've found the perfect place to rest. You and Maeson must have—" He stopped short when he rounded the tree and saw what was in my lap. "Is that . . ."

I nodded. "Come sit with me. I think you need to read this."

He stared at the journal like it was coming to life. "I'm not sure if that's a good idea."

"I've just read the first page and trust me when I say, you need to read this, Niall."

He hesitated and rubbed at the back of his neck, but he finally bent down and took a seat, stretching his boots out until they almost reached the water's edge. "What have you learned so far?"

I could hear the hesitation in his voice, but I didn't want him to fear this journal. If anything, I wanted him to appreciate it. Evander hadn't just kept this journal for himself. He'd kept it for the benefit of those who came after him.

I didn't reply, I just leaned into Niall and held the book between us, turning back to the inside cover.

To die to yourself is to truly live.

Niall stared at the sentence, re-reading it several times before nodding.
"I think it means—"

"It means"—he interrupted—"that he knew the sacrifice he would have to make, long before it was necessary."

I looked up at him.

"Go on," he said, nudging his chin toward the journal.

I turned the page.

Today, I decided that I can no longer keep these unfortunate occurrences to myself . . .

I let him read about the nightmare, glancing sidelong at him every few seconds to see his reaction. I only knew when he finished reading by his continuous stare at the end of the page. He didn't blink. He just stared.

"Niall . . ."

"He saw *me*," he whispered.

Upon hearing his words, the pain in the way he whispered them, tears welled up in my eyes.

"And that was the first thing he wrote about."

One tear dropped down my cheek and landed on Niall's arm, bringing his thoughts back to the present. He lifted his hand to my face to wipe the next few away before they fell.

"There was a house-fae that helped my ancestor," he said, solemnly. "His name was Verdi. He helped train me when I came into my power as a youngling. Without him, I don't know what would have happened to me."

"Verdi," I repeated the name. "Then I am thankful for Verdi. That he helped you when no one else would."

Niall looked back down at the ink and closed his eyes. "When my father saw the power his grandfather had possessed, surfacing in me, he panicked. The only way he knew to deal with it was to shut me out and push me away. He thought I would be unpredictable. Verdi took over as my caretaker. He was old to me back then, but now I realize just how ancient he truly was. Having served four generations in my household, I'm surprised he had the capacity and the will to continue with me. But he did.

"I had suffered my power alone as a youngling until Verdi helped me hone it. He tried to persuade my father, even kept progress notes every time we trained to convince him that I wasn't a threat. But my father still refused to acknowledge it, or me. He thought Verdi was just as delirious in his old age as my ancestor was when he lost control."

He fiddled with the corner of the page, needing something to do with his hands as he spoke. "My father denied me many things growing up. I had to take it upon myself to secretly sit in on court meetings just to get the basic rundown of how to run the territory. I trained with our forces whenever I could. Verdi even hired one of the best swordsmen from our infantry to train me personally after nightfall. I learned to make a blade an extension of myself, and made sure that I would be as deadly with a sword as I would be with my shadowfire—if I ever saw battle. Verdi helped ensure that I was prepared on all fronts because he knew that—whether my father wanted it or not—I would one day rule. He was counting on it. Because his training *would* work. It had to.

"When our territory was on the brink of war, my father finally decided it was time to clue me in. Thankfully, I had my ways of gleaning information here and there, so I wasn't going in completely blind. I tried my best to show him that I was worthy of being his son. That I was responsible and had a grip on my power. He was still more than a bit wary of me and kept me at a distance, but at least he was finally trying.

"When we received word that Lyceius had moved his armies to our borders, my father had no other choice. I was thrown into command like I'd been groomed for it, expected to know what I was doing. It always baffled me that my father just assumed I would survive and thrive in whatever he threw me into. But I did. I made sure that I did. I wouldn't be the one to let him down, nor would I see disappointment from anyone when it came to my operations. But none of the soldiers knew me. No one really even trusted me because of my lack of presence in court, but I stood tall and commanded them. I entered battle as a stranger, and emerged shrouded, with an army of loyal warriors at my back, and my father's blessing as his heir.

"I met Aremis shortly after and began building my court. It took years to gain the trust of those around me, and to convince the court that I was no threat. The armies backed me, but the skeptical males that made up my father's council were still unsure. And every time I added another male to my trusted Trium, there was talk and question of my intentions. None of them are from here, so naturally, their loyalties were questioned, and therefore, mine was too. But my father knew each of the males that I'd surrounded myself with and had come to trust them, so the court eventually had no choice.

"Before he died, my father blessed my ascension, but never once did he say he was proud of me. I don't even think he took the time to wonder how I wasn't a clueless idiot when he thrust me into court politics like I was born for it."

Suddenly, I saw past Niall's unwavering exterior.

The High Lord that sat next to me was forged from the broken pieces he'd managed to gather, scraps of whatever he was given. As he lifted his head and stared out across the stream, I saw all the vulnerability in him, all the struggles he had overcome. The face he normally wore was an iron-forged mask. The male underneath was conflicted. Strong, but sensitive. And I wanted nothing more than to curl into him and soothe all the edges of his past that still haunted him.

I watched as he stared off in memory, like he was picturing his father —silently speaking to him across the void of death that separated them.

His voice dropped to a low pitch. "Just once, I would have liked to hear him say he was proud of me. For all that I endured. All that I had to glean on my own. All the personal trials and the late-night training sessions under cover of dark, and teaching myself the histories and workings of our realm. Countless hours spent in that damn library, alone. Wondering if I'd ever be enough. If the knowledge of just one more book might make me worthy of being the perfect heir."

He lowered his gaze back to the journal. "If my ancestor could see how far I've come, that his efforts weren't in vain . . . If my father could see that I didn't let it overcome me . . . I wonder now, if they would finally be at peace?"

64
DRASTIA

Niall and I stayed by the stream for hours. I eventually dozed off on his shoulder, while he combed his fingers through my hair. Then I woke to a gentle kiss on the edge of my temple, and the smooth, deep timbre of his voice.

"Time to head back and start getting ready for tonight," he said.

I sat up, a bit stiff from the hard ground beneath us. My eyes met his, and I searched their depths, gauging his emotions.

He knew the question I wanted to ask before I spoke. "I'm okay," he reassured me. "This has taken a weight off of my shoulders that I never knew was there. Thank you for listening."

"I may not always have the right things to say, but I'll always listen."

He brought his hand up and cupped one side of my face. "The fates knew I needed you, Auren."

Warmth enveloped my heart. "Why do you say that?"

"Ask anyone. I do not openly express my emotions or talk about my personal history. Yet, with you, I have done nothing but that since we met." He leaned his forehead against mine. "You do something to me that I can't explain."

Back at The Keep, I stood in the center of my chambers, staring at the fireplace.

Niall's words—the recollection of his youth, the struggles he'd faced, the way he'd touched me and told me he needed me . . .

You do something to me that I can't explain.

Replaying the words in my head made that warm feeling inside me swirl and settle, nestling up against my heart once more. I stood in contemplation, trying to decipher the feeling as the fire crackled.

A moment later, I heard a gentle click and turned to see the armoire doors opening, reminding me that I needed to get ready. My eyes fell upon the new dress that hung at the forefront, the black fabric seeming to gobble up the light. I stepped up to it and traced my fingers along the bodice. The fabric was thicker than I was used to, made for a colder climate, with long sleeves and a high collar. I admired the intricate, swirling, gold embroidery that crowned the shoulders, and the two solid gold decorative brooches that adorned what would be the points of my collarbone once it was on my body. They were connected by a delicately braided gold rope. Two more sets of brooches and ropes lined their way down the chest of the dress; a simple decoration, one that seemed to convey status, seemed to signify someone of the Mountain Court.

I immediately caught the implication.

My lips tilted up in a smile.

I stripped, tossing my clothes into a pile by the foot of the bed, then pulled the dress off the hanger and slipped into it. As expected, it fit me like a glove. The heavy fabric brushed the floor with a thick whisper as I moved.

Sorscha appeared and hurried over to tend to me. I knelt down to allow her to close the long zipper up the back of the dress, and when I stood again, she beamed with pride. A pair of insulated black dress boots appeared in her hand, and she moved to set them down next to my fur cloak and gloves, which had been magically summoned and were now laying across the foot of the bed.

I followed her into the bathing chamber where she fashioned my hair in a low bun with a braided crown, and ensured that my complexion was exactly how it looked on the night of Firefall. She'd even threaded dangling gold earrings through my lobes; a set of delicate pendants that matched the brooches across the front of the dress.

I turned a circle and stared at myself in the mirror.

The other dresses I'd worn to the past two events had been drizzled with jewels and spun from delicate, elegant fabric. They were beautiful and had turned every head. But this one . . . this one was . . . regal.

It exuded authority.

I was fully covered, yet my presence was somehow more commanding. I shifted my shoulders back and held my head high, favoring this look above all the others.

My power stirred in agreement.

I knew that Niall approved as well by the look he gave me upon entering my chambers.

His eyes lit in an instant. "That has to be my favorite color on you," he said, eyeing my curves as if the dress wasn't separating him from my bare skin.

"It's black," I replied. "Of course, it's your favorite."

A deep rumble rolled through his chest as he strode up to me.

His finely cut jacket had the same gold designs stitched on it . . . in the exact same locations across his chest and shoulders.

"Shouldn't 'not-mates' not be matching?" I asked, looking back and forth between the obvious similarity in our outfits.

"Let them think what they want. If anyone dares to say something, I'll put them in their place."

"Niall," I warned.

"Politely," he added, brushing off the sleeves of his jacket before summoning a thick cloak of his own. He swung it around his shoulders.

I watched his fingers fasten the clasp into place across his chest, and a thought crossed my mind. "Will Killian be there? Or Breck?"

"I don't expect them to be. There was some tension between Laurent and Killian in Elandrew, and Aremis says they're not on the best of terms at the moment. But don't worry, if either of them are there, I won't let anything happen to you."

"I know," I said. "Anything else I need to know about Drastia before we get there?"

He reached out and grabbed my waist, cinching it up to his. I gasped at the sudden movement and the feel of his hard body against mine. As our bodies began to fade from existence, I heard him say, "Don't be afraid of the wolves."

We landed on a thick patch of ice, surrounded by placid, glacial water on all sides. The forest on the mainland in front and behind us was covered in thick, fluffy, white snow, but there was no land bridging our small piece of ice to it.

The bitter wind gusted, nipping at my cheeks and ears, and I wrapped my cloak tighter around me as Niall tucked me into his side.

And then I heard them.

The growling started behind us, and when I turned to look, I froze. Standing not ten feet from us were the largest white wolves I'd ever seen. I stumbled a step back, and another growl had me whirling. They had surrounded us, appearing from thin air.

They stood nearly as tall as my shoulders, circling us, sizing us up. I stared, wide-eyed, wanting to convince myself that they were just an enchanted mirage to ward off trespassers, but as the wind sped past and their fur whipped against their backs with it, I knew they were very much real.

"Uhh, Niall . . ." I stepped closer to him, pushing out my shield in a panic.

"You don't need that here," he said, rubbing my arm through my cloak. "They won't hurt you. They know me."

I latched onto his arm, certain that he was mistaken. "Are you sure about that?"

The six wolves drew closer, their claws scraping against the ice with each step. Then, upon picking up a familiar scent, their growls turned to curious sniffs, and they backed away calmly.

Relief washed over me and I dropped my shield.

"Keep your mental one intact," Niall murmured.

Ahead of us the water crackled as it froze over, knitting itself together to bridge the icy piece that we stood on with the mainland ahead. Niall's arm was a steady brace as he escorted me across, toward the hard-packed snow. The wolves trotted past us on either side, tongues now lolling out of their mouths, tails swishing happily. I steadied myself and watched as they set into a slow trot down the pathway, leading us into the frosted forest.

The wind ceased as we ventured deeper into the trees, and the crunching sound of the snow beneath our boots filled my ears.

Just when I began to think to myself that Laurent shouldn't make his guests walk an entire frozen forest to attend his event, we arrived at a large clearing full of sleighs.

"No, we don't have to walk the entire way," Niall said, seeming to read my mind. "I thought that too—the first time I came here for Lumeri. Thankfully, Laurent and Senna take particular care of their guests."

We approached a sleigh and stepped up, taking a seat on the thick, white, fur-lined benches. There was no driver and nothing to pull it. Instead, it moved on a magical command, a phantom wind, and the next sleigh approached to take up the empty space, awaiting another arrival.

Niall leaned in, his breath warm against my ear as he said, "Laurent has the power to control the elements. You won't feel the harsh arctic wind for too long—unless he deems it so."

"He prefers to keep the cold?" I asked, suppressing a slight shiver, despite my cloak, gloves, and thick dress.

"It's the nature of the Arctic Court. But the chill will lessen as we get closer to the main city. There is only so much tamping down a High Lord can do on the natural climate."

"Glad I have these," I said, rubbing my gloved hands together.

"Yes, whoever got those for you must be a real gentleman. So thoughtful. So—"

I yanked off a glove and smacked him on the arm with it, and a laugh rumbled through his chest, warming my heart with the sound.

I settled into his side as we passed through the wild, wintery forest. The firs and pines bowed under heavy dollops of snow. Thick, powdered drifts lay smooth and untouched underneath sweeping branches. Icicles hung heavy from the boughs above, twinkling in the twilight sky that was turning a blushing shade of pink, casting a candied light upon the frosted landscape.

The temperature rose a few degrees the further we traveled; still cold but not unbearable. Then, the trail curved, and once we rounded the bend, it opened to a view of a sprawling white valley.

The city was nestled within, draping across the expanse like a blanket, warming the frozen ground with its pleasant glow. It stretched all the way to the foot of the mountains in the distance. There, a magnificent glacier jutted out of a mountainside, a mass of jagged cerulean blue ice from which a castle façade was carved.

"The ice castle of Drastia," Niall said, pointing directly where my eyes were fixated. "We can either port in from here, or take the scenic route."

"I'd love the scenic route, if there's time."

"I thought you'd say that." He grinned.

The sleigh moved along with our will, descending the trail, taking us down through the winding streets of Drastia's charming city. All was quiet, peaceful. More sleighs toted their passengers down the snow dusted streets, all headed in the same direction: toward the glacier that sat like a beacon overlooking the city below.

The white buildings were nestled up against each other along the quaint streets. Varying roof styles leant a bit of cozy character to every home and storefront. Gathered bundles of pine branches hung in swaths across doors and along lampposts, tied with light blue and silver ribbons.

Vendor carts lined the walkways. One was still open, serving mugs of steaming beverages that smelled of roasted nuts and cinnamon. Another shop had a customer trying on an array of fur hats. A few younglings raced down the snow-shoveled path alongside our sleigh, waving ribbons on sticks—similar to the ones I'd seen in Elandrew.

The city was splendid. And even though it was covered in snow, the territory clearly thrived; completely at odds with how humans had to *endure* a few months of winter each year.

Here, the fae embraced it.

As we neared the glacier Niall slid his arm from around me and put some distance between us on the bench. I disliked the idea of it but understood his reasoning. We needed to appear as non-mate-like as possible. And I couldn't risk glowing again in public.

The castle façade quickly stole my focus as we approached. It was breathtaking, a striking contrast of crystal blue ice against the dark face of the adjoining mountain. Its slick surface glimmered in the dancing light of the torches that lined the pathway up the hill to its doorstep.

Fae were exiting sleighs and strolling up the entry, all bundled in elegant attire in varying shades of white, gray, and blue.

"I still think the matching outfits were a bad idea," I muttered as our sleigh came to a halt. Wearing solid black, the two of us stuck out like sore thumbs amidst an entire city covered in white.

Niall merely grinned at the remark.

Knowing him, he probably *wanted* to make a statement, make it known what court we hailed from; his way of laying claim to me without having to lay a finger on me at all.

I side-eyed him, considering his tactics as two fae males dressed in white and gold finery approached our sleigh. One of the strangers offered a gloved hand to help me down onto the snow-dusted ground. I accepted the gesture and stepped out, my boots giving a muffled crunch as they met the snow.

Niall followed and stepped up to my side, watching me as I tilted my head back to gaze up at the set of grand, icy doors that stood before us. They swung open without a sound, and we entered into a sprawling space made of pure magic.

The entire castle was carved from the glacial ice, with crystalline walls the color of cerulean and slate, and floors that looked like cracked diamonds. Giant icicle chandeliers hung down at staggering lengths across the tall rough-hewn ceiling, white fur rugs lined the walkways, and an imperial staircase climbed up on each side of the room, carved along the icy walls. Everything remained perfectly frozen and utterly gorgeous.

Another fae male dressed in uniform pointed us in the direction of the courtyard across the entry.

Niall leaned in to murmur in my ear. "Laurent and Senna delight in perfectionism."

"I can certainly see that."

I observed every little detail as we strode through the arctic estate, following the procession of guests. Each tabletop was made of pristine white marble adorned with the most stunning greenery arrangements flowing from crystal vases. Groups of iridescent orbs floated freely in the air, lighting the alcoves and hallways that led further into the depths of the mountain. Everything was delicate, sophisticated. And despite the multitude of lights and the warmth of the bodies that congregated within the icy walls, nothing melted.

Enchantments.

Another set of doors opened before us and music and conversations filtered through. The courtyard beyond was exposed to the sky, where darkness stained its way overhead, chased on its heel by the first winks of the night's stars.

A grand fountain carved from ice sat in the center of the space, trickling with the clearest water I'd ever seen. Around it, elegantly dressed fae were sipping on wine and mingling under the light of the drifting orbs and the occasional decorative lamp post, carved straight from the ice.

A pleasant tune of stringed instruments wove through the air, carried on a gentle breeze.

We approached the top of the steps leading down to the throng of Arctic Court fae, and every head seemed to turn toward us at once.

I glanced at Niall. His head was held high as he offered his elbow to escort me.

We descended the steps and those nearest us cautiously stepped back, clearing a path for the High Lord of the Mountain Court. When their wide eyes peeled away from him, they landed on me. Heads turned to whisper. Brows pinched and raised in surprise.

I could feel the tension and the hushed questions floating in the air, thickening with each step we took. Apprehension, uncertainty, surprise, all of it circled us as we cut through the gathering.

We were a splash of ink, bleeding through a stack of pure white parchment.

But strangely, I didn't feel deterred by the stares and the feelings of unease radiating off the crowd.

I felt . . . empowered.

Niall kept my arm tucked in his, linked at the elbow, but the gesture might as well have been an oathing stone between us, joining us together for all to see. In the guests' minds, I was tied to him—our matching outfits surely sending the subliminal message he'd intended.

Ahead of us, light golden hair and a familiar square face smiled at me the moment I made eye contact with her. Senna tapped Laurent on the shoulder, and upon turning to see us as well, he shook hands with the male he'd been conversing with and the couple strode forward to greet us. They were a vision in pale gray and steel blue, adorned with white fur around the collars of their respective outfits.

"My friend." Laurent eagerly clasped Niall's hand. "Thank you for coming."

"Glad you were able to witness another Firefall as well."

"Ah, yes, we enjoyed it very much. It's always a stunning sight, and you are ever the generous host. You know, your Trium is always welcome here as well. Those males are quite the group, but I am glad to see that you've at least brought Auren." He turned to me, taking my hand and bowing slightly. "Welcome to our home."

Senna placed a warm hand on my shoulder. "So glad you could make it, Auren."

"Thank you both. Your home is divine."

They both smiled.

It didn't take long for Laurent to notice our matching black outfits, and his brows knitted together when he did. "A bold color choice for the *two* of you." He observed.

Niall didn't seem phased. He scanned the crowd, waving a hand, as he said, "Everything I own is in this color. And everything in my guest's quarters is coincidentally the same. Thankfully, Auren didn't mind."

I tried to give a convincing smile as the High Lord and Lady of Drastia surveyed the similarities between my dress and Niall's jacket.

"And how much longer will you be staying in Anbrya, Auren?" Laurent asked, lifting a curious, but innocent brow.

I stiffened slightly, internally scrambling for a simple answer that wouldn't trigger a million other curious questions. "Niall has kindly offered to host me for the time being, so I am at his mercy."

"Well, with the hospitality his court provides, you must be in no hurry to return to Belthria."

My heart stuttered, searching for any hidden weight to his comment, any suspicion it might be laced with.

"Oh she must be reveling in it. Our stay last night was delightful," Senna chimed in, washing away the unspoken question in Laurent's statement. "And Niall, I must inquire as to how I can procure some of that lovely cream liqueur that was served in our guest chambers. I'm afraid it might be my new obsession."

Laurent laughed lightly, all questions fleeting from his eyes. "Yes, she was quite taken with the taste. She would've finished the entire bottle herself if I hadn't asked for a glass."

Niall smiled and flicked his wrist, summoning a dark bottle in his grasp. He handed it to Senna. "A gift, then."

Senna squealed with delight and summoned a crystal glass, immediately uncapping the bottle and pouring herself a heavy serving. She tipped it to Niall in thanks.

Laurent smiled and shook his head. "If you spoil her like that, she'll start expecting it."

A laugh rumbled through Niall's throat. "I'll have to stock your personal stores with plenty of it then, so you can offer her a treat whenever she likes. After all, what good is a mate, if not to spoil her incessantly?"

My breath caught in my throat.

Senna grinned, and Laurent's brows lifted ever so slightly, his gaze flicking to me.

Niall knew what he was doing with that statement. But before any of us could respond, he leaned in close to Laurent, lowering his voice so that only the four of us were privy to what he was about to say. With all the wary, wandering stares still being cast in our direction, he kept a faint grin in place, so as not to seem like he was whispering threats. "I need to have a word with you in private sometime this evening. We have movement on the front."

Senna lowered her glass, eyes bouncing between the two High Lords with a hint of worry before she schooled her face into passiveness again.

Laurent played it off as nothing as well, giving an inconspicuous nod and donning his own innocent smile. "I shall find you later then. In the meantime, please, do enjoy yourselves. And I hope you came hungry. Senna has outdone herself putting together the menu for tonight." He planted a gentle kiss on his mate's cheek.

Witnessing their affection made me long to do the same with Niall. But I reminded myself of the ruse we had to play at, and instead opted to chew the inside of my cheek raw.

Drastia's High Lord and Lady resumed their mingling amongst their guests, and I tucked my hand into the crook of Niall's arm as he led me through the courtyard.

The sun had officially disappeared behind the mountain, and the ice upon which we stood took on an eerily dark blue hue.

We crossed the space, nearing another set of steps where the ground dropped down into the second tier of the courtyard. From there it opened into a snow-covered field that led to what looked like a frozen lake, surrounded by more lit torches.

Just before we came to the steps a shadow moved on our right. The figure stepped into the light of a nearby lamp post, and a pretty face with sultry, kohl-rimmed eyes greeted us.

Morah.

65
LUMERI IN THE ARCTIC

MORAH SCOFFED, LOOKING POINTEDLY AT MY DRESS, THEN TO NIALL'S outfit. "Did he force you to match him, or did you freely choose to?"

I swung my head in Niall's direction. "See, literally everyone is taking notice."

Niall looked down his nose at our newest ally. "You're feisty this evening."

Morah surveyed the crowd behind us, seeming a bit on edge. "My escort was getting on my nerves."

"Who's your escort?" I asked.

She rolled her eyes. "The High Lord's cousin."

"*Breck?*"

"Yes, Breck. Who else would it be? Now, lower your voice."

Niall narrowed his eyes at her commanding tone, but I looked right past it. "Not Killian? I mean—wait . . . Why aren't you here with Killian?"

"I had to get information to you somehow, and I couldn't do that with Killian at my side, now could I?" Her smile was a bit more sarcastic than she probably meant for it to be. Or maybe I was just giving her the benefit of the doubt.

Niall, however, was not having it. He leaned in over her and let out a low-toned threat that sent chills over my skin. "You will speak to Auren with the respect she deserves, or I will see to it that you do not speak again."

Morah didn't move an inch, but the slight pursing of her lips told me that she hated being reprimanded. "My apologies," she bit out. "It's been quite an ordeal lately." She spoke through clenched teeth, and I could sense her frustration. She knew what she was risking by meeting with us, yet here she was, being true to her word.

"We weren't aware that you would be trying to meet with us, or I'm sure Niall would have made things a bit easier," I said, trying to diffuse the tension.

Despite what Niall might think of her, there was something about Morah that I liked. She might have tried to stab me first and ask questions later, but I'd always been one for giving second chances.

"No, I wanted it this way," she said. "Killian has been in an outrage since you disappeared without his permission. Of course, his blame went straight to you." She looked at Niall. "I've had my hands full trying to keep him otherwise occupied and not set on hunting the both of you down. After you left, I sought Breck out. I had to let him know that I'd been clued in, and I needed his help. Killian grows more paranoid by the hour. There's only so much we can do to keep him from lashing out. And after Breck failed to apprehend you the last time . . . We're all walking a fine line from one day to the next."

"So, how is it then that he's still in Elandrew and you're here with his advisor?" Niall asked.

Morah cut him a look as if to say *I was getting to that.* "I created a diversion near The Veil. Used a bit of my power in rapid spurts outside of the wards and drew some keres in. Breck and his scouts 'found' the disturbance and relayed the message to Killian. He himself went to investigate. It's keeping him occupied, for now. I offered to attend this event tonight in his stead, and luckily, he agreed. Then he decided to send Breck with me for good measure." She looked out over the crowd again, searching—I assumed—for the High Lord's cousin. "Which is just lovely, because all he's done since you left—including the entire trip here—is ask if I've heard from you, Auren."

I winced. "How is he?"

Something like pity crossed her eyes. "He's fine. Just ashamed. In more ways than one, I'm guessing. He wouldn't go into detail, but he keeps saying he needs to make things right with you. Whatever that means."

Niall's jaw tensed, and Morah lowered her eyes. But his tension had nothing to do with her tone. It had everything to do with the fact that Breck was here, and most likely wanted time with *me*.

Around us, the crowd slowly began filing down the courtyard tiers and out toward the lake, but Morah continued, lowering her voice to a low murmur. "After the High Lords returned to their courts, Killian commissioned Breck to lead daily scouting details and stationed patrols at the border nearest to where you crossed. When they spotted King Broderick's men lingering near The Veil, they made contact. Apparently, the king's men have been patrolling their side, desperate to locate either you or the weakness in The Veil that allowed you to cross.

"When the king heard of what happened the night of the champions dinner, he assumed that you were a fae spy and that you were there to harm the prince. He ordered that you be hunted down. But when he was finally able to communicate his concerns with Killian, he was informed that he was wrong. That you're not fae. When Killian found out about the events at the castle, what you did and why you fled, he was beside himself. Said he'd sensed something different about you from the start. He was outraged that you were within his grasp and he didn't act on it. You're lucky he was so preoccupied with other things. We should all be thanking the fates, because if he would have kept you there—"

"She would've *never* been his prisoner," Niall cut her off with a tone of steel. "Nor will she ever be anyone else's. I'll make sure of that." His glittering golden eyes pierced through the moonlit night with a look that promised retribution to anyone who dared challenge him.

"As I was saying," Morah continued, earning an irritated look from Niall, "Breck sat in on as many meetings as he could since then. He even got criticized pretty harshly for not sensing something was different about you, and for not alerting Killian sooner."

I chewed on the inside of my cheek, feeling sorry that Breck had taken the brunt of Killian's anger when he was only trying to protect me.

"There was talk of 'continuing the search' and something about raids in the human realm, and then my father got involved. Once Killian told him what the king said, he became entirely convinced you have something to do with the prophecy. He said as much at their meeting yesterday."

"But what would either of them want from me?" I asked.

Morah exchanged a look with Niall. "I've suspected for some time now that my father has been in negotiations with Lyceius. For what—I'm not sure. But if he thinks you're connected to the prophecy in any sort of way, I would assume you'd be a bargaining chip."

I stiffened.

It made sense. And that would explain why both him and Killian found me so *interesting.*

"Breck and I think Killian and my father are more interested in getting their hands on you to have some sort of sway over Lyceius. But we're not even sure if Lyceius knows about you yet. No one has heard of any movement on that front."

"I have," Niall said, frowning.

Morah and I looked at him.

He surveyed the crowd, keeping his voice low. "Earlier, Aremis called a meeting. Our patrols came back with sightings of new legions breaching their previously established perimeter. They seemed to be breaking out into smaller groups, some disappearing completely overnight, and others moving several miles west. We don't know exactly where the smaller groups went off to, but I have a feeling Lyceius is a bit more informed than we think he is."

Morah shifted her weight back and forth on her heels, weighing the information. "I can try to sit in on more of Killian's court meetings, I'm sure if he knows of anything he'll—"

"No need," Niall said in full confidence.

"What do you mean?" she asked.

"Your father will be hosting Lumeri in two days."

Morah folded her arms. "And?"

"And, we will be attending. Aremis won't be too happy about it, but perhaps he can gain some insight. Besides, people are always inclined to talk and gossip at parties, are they not?"

Morah shook her head. "You shouldn't attend. I can't guarantee that Killian won't be there."

We fell into silence as a couple of fae walked by, giving us all a long stare before hurrying off to follow the crowd.

Niall placed a hand on my back. "We better rejoin the party, or this conversation will start to look suspicious."

Sure enough, we were one of the last small groups yet to make our way toward the lake.

Morah glowered at Niall for longer than necessary, then peeled away and sauntered off into the crowd, blending into it within a blink. A moment later, we followed.

Down at the water's edge, house-fae were passing out colored paper lanterns and small taper candles. Niall accepted two of each.

"How does this work?" I asked, watching as everyone in the crowd assembled theirs.

"First you shape the lantern, and then, these candles fit into the small holder at the bottom. Like this." He set his candle down on the ground and took mine, gently pressing open the paper contraption. I watched as he smoothed out all the sides and set the candle in between the prongs.

He settled in behind me and placed the lantern in my hands. "Once everyone is ready, they will light with flame, and then the *magic* happens."

"It's like you use magic for everything," I teased.

"Speaking of magic . . . That little pocket in space that you love so much is quite simple to manifest."

My eyes lit up. "Oh?"

"It's as simple as holding an object and picturing a gap in space that you create in your minds-eye. For example, I picture a very specific armoire. When I picture it and slide the object inside, that's where it stays, until I retrieve it."

"That's it? You just think up a fake space and send stuff to it?"

He chuckled softly. "That's the gist of it. But the place has to exist in real life. You're basically just accessing it with your mind."

I eyed the extra lantern and candle lying at my feet. "Interesting."

Suddenly, the crowd quieted. Up along the banks of the water, Laurent stood, stretching his arms up to the sky.

"Laetus Lumeri," he called out. The crowd echoed in unison, and he followed with two claps, igniting every candle across the snow-covered field.

"Are you ready?" Niall asked.

I nodded in anticipation, bracing my lantern between my hands.

Laurent smoothly waved his arms as if to summon a current of wind, and as commanded a gentle breeze swept up from the ground.

"Let go," Niall whispered into my ear.

"What?"

He lifted my hands in his, repeating, "Let go."

I did as he said, and the lantern floated upward on the wind.

All around us, the colored contraptions lifted into the night, rising higher and higher as they made their way out over the lake. The sky looked as if it were strung with glowing gems. Blue, purple, pink, and orange littered the darkness, their paths winding around each other as they drifted on Laurent's magical current. It was enchanting, and I caught myself leaning back into Niall's chest as I watched.

Within a few seconds, I realized what I had unconsciously done.

I forced myself to step away from him, and the chilled air instantly swarmed the space between us. A bitter sense of wrongness nipped at me alongside the frosty air. The pull between us seemed to demand that I return to his arms. I wanted nothing more than to obey and lean back into him, but with the risk of getting carried away in our emotions like we did at Firefall . . .

I could feel Niall's stare, and I looked over at him.

He smiled gently. "Enjoy this moment, Auren."

"I am," I said as I turned my face back to the night sky. "You should be too."

"I am," he murmured.

His eyes remained on me.

66
ALMOST MENDED

AFTER THE LANTERNS HAD DRIFTED SO HIGH THEY LOOKED LIKE GLINTING stars ready to be swallowed up by the night, we returned to the courtyard area, where tables of beautifully curated food displays had been arranged along the edge of the open patio.

Senna had chosen the most delectable foods—small servings of flaky fish that were fanned onto toasted bread cut into the shape of half-moons, crackers dressed with spreads and crumbled cheeses, skewers of meats, dripping with sauces and spiced oils, flaky pastry cups filled with baked fruit compotes and drizzled in a thin, white glaze, and apples covered in gooey toffee and dusted with thick sugar crystals.

The tables stretched the entire length of the courtyard, and we grazed upon each of them, marveling at the presentation before sampling, our noses filled with the warm scents of rosemary and cinnamon. More of the lovely string music echoed through the night, inviting dancers to twirl under the arctic sky.

Several large copper fire pits flickered with flames, giving off some heat and adding to the luxurious atmosphere. Despite the fire's warmth, the ice stayed perfectly frozen.

Morah found me again, and when Niall and Laurent disappeared for their private conversation, she and I had taken up a corner near the dance floor, passing the time by watching the elegant couples sweep around the space in a choreographed dance.

"Are you shielded right now?" Morah asked, keeping a watchful eye on the guests around us.

"Are you thinking about stabbing me?" I replied, doing the same.

She flicked her eyes over to me and her mouth quirked up. "No, Euryphaessa. Just making sure you're safe." She looked back out, then patted her hip. "I do have my daggers on me though, just in case. Anyone stupid enough to try something wouldn't make it very far."

I grinned. "Perhaps I should hire you as my personal guard."

She immediately whipped her head back to me, then proceeded to study me for a long moment.

"It wouldn't be offensive to ask of you, would it?"

"No. It would be an honor," she said, though disappointment laced her voice and her eyes darkened with a shadow. "The thing is, it would mean abandoning my current post."

Given that her father had betrothed her to the High Lord, who—from the sound of it—was currently my newest enemy, I knew it wasn't something she could easily get out of, nor would I want her to take the risk.

"Well, if the time is ever right, and the fates align, perhaps then it could be possible."

She stared at me in awe, then tilted her head as if she was working out a difficult puzzle. "You know, I thought that since you're the daughter of a god, you'd be demanding, or arrogant. I assumed that you, like the gods, would be . . . fickle. But you're none of those things."

"I will never be those things." I spoke the words like a promise. Because they were. If I fully accepted and embraced this hand that the fates had dealt me, my humanity—who I was at my core—would remain unchanged. I would hold myself to that standard indefinitely.

"You will make a great ruler someday," she said quietly.

The words fell on me with a weight I didn't expect, and I couldn't help but snort through my nose. "Ruler? What makes you say that?"

She huffed a laugh. "See, you don't even aspire to rule or even assume the title that is yours by right."

"What title?"

"Your purpose is to defeat Lyceius, is it not?"

I nodded, not quite following.

Her eyes sparked with hope. "Upon Lyceius's defeat, a new god must ascend. And you are the only one with a gift of light akin to Lyceius's—powered and blessed by Karios. You will be the new goddess of light."

The dancers still twirled, and the music still played, but that all faded away, and only one word echoed in my head . . .

Goddess.

Morah looked at me, wincing when she beheld my shock. "You didn't know?"

Breck had mentioned something along those lines in his lesson about the prophecy, but in all my information overload, I must have glanced over it.

"It was mentioned, but I didn't consider the reality of it."

When one god no longer existed in that form, another must take their place. And if that was true . . .

Fear crept into my gut.

I wasn't ready for that.

My heart shoved against my ribs, threatening to pound through them if left unchecked. Then, a familiar voice called out my name behind me and the pounding ceased as my heart *plummeted.*

I turned and found Breck standing a few feet away. He looked sleep deprived, apprehension and regret weighing heavily on his face as he took me in. My heart resumed its shoving as I struggled to find words to say to fill the hollow space between us.

He softly cleared his throat. "I'm glad to see you're all right."

I straightened my shoulders, pushing back thoughts of being a *goddess* along with them. "I'm doing well."

Morah stood utterly still, gauging the tension between us.

Breck glanced at her, then back. "I, um . . . I would very much like the opportunity to apologize and make things right between us."

"So would I," I said quietly.

Morah began slowly taking her leave. As we made eye contact she glanced off to the left, indicating where she would be keeping watch from.

I nodded.

Breck fiddled with his hands but didn't make a move to come any closer. It struck me then that the last time he had moved toward me, I'd retreated, and fled. I internally cringed, remembering the hurt on his face. Much of it was still there now.

I stepped toward him, closing the distance between us. "I'm not going to run off this time." As I said it, I wanted to punch myself in the gut.

He continued nervously wringing his hands together as he watched me.

"Breck, this doesn't have to be complicated—"

"But it is." He cut me off. "Auren, I'm so sorry. I'm sorry for misreading everything and for kissing you in the library. Especially when I hadn't known you'd been served elderberries. And I'm more ashamed of my actions after that. I should have never threatened to lock you in that place. I was jealous of Niall and mad at Killian, and it just all became too much. And now I fear that it cost me our friendship. And I value that more than anything."

That sounded like the Breck I knew. But the male who stood before me seemed to be a broken version of him. If my forgiveness was what would help piece back together his dignity, then I wanted that.

"I forgive you, Breck. And I want to apologize too."

"You have nothing to be sorry for, Auren—"

"Yes, I do. I wronged you by outing you to Niall like I did. I let my emotions get the best of me too. Seeing you acting under Killian's command made me sick, and I hated that you gave in to him so easily. But I shouldn't have done that. And now, I fear that I may have ruined whatever friendship there could have been between you and Niall."

He nodded slowly. "I understand your actions. I deserved them. And I do wish to mend things with Niall too, at some point."

I gave him a slight smile, feeling my nerves settle as the tension eased between us.

His voice was almost shy as he spoke again. "Would it be too much to ask for a dance?"

I recalled my first Lumeri in the woodlands when I danced with Niall and feared that Breck would see. Now, here I was being presented with the reversal of the same situation. But as much as I knew it would annoy Niall if he saw Breck and I dancing, I also knew that it would help to keep talk about my attendance with the High Lord of Calledan to a minimum. Niall would just have to trust me and understand that it wasn't personal.

"One dance," I consented.

A few curious fae watched us as we joined the dance floor.

Breck was light on his feet and moved with precision. He held me at a respectable distance, but I could still feel a hint of longing in his embrace.

"So, you're truly well?" he asked, looking down at me.

"I am. Between all these Lumeri celebrations, I've learned quite a bit. I'm also making progress in my training."

A hint of his handsome smile peeked through. "That's good to hear."

I wanted to launch into telling him about my power, but I needed to ease into this.

He gently cleared his throat. "I, uhh, found my dagger on your bed. That's how I knew you weren't coming back."

Damn. So much for easing into this.

I lowered my gaze to the details on his dress coat. "I meant to leave a note. I never got to thank you for letting me borrow it."

He dipped his head into my view, drawing my eyes up to his. "You could have kept it, you know."

I gave him a light smile, but shook my head. "No, I couldn't have." And I also couldn't move forward with this conversation when there was still information I hadn't told him. "I have a lot to fill you in on, Breck. But first, there's something you still don't know about when I crossed The Veil."

Any progress we had just made sputtered out before my eyes as his smile fell. "Auren, I hate that you felt you had to keep things from me. You can trust me. I'll always remain loyal to you. I'll spend my life proving it. This entire thing is bigger than any of us. And I was the one who found you when you crossed over into this realm. It should be me who stays by your side to see everything through."

I winced. *Gods, he does still have feelings for me.*

Was he holding onto some hope that I'd forgive him and he could try again? Could he not sense that my fate was entwined with another?

"I do trust you Breck, it's just . . ."

"Just what?"

"You asked if I saw anyone else in the forest after I crossed The Veil. Well, I did. I saw a male, dressed in all black . . ."

Breck instantly knew of whom I spoke, and his face contorted into confusion, then disbelief. "You told me that you didn't see any other fae—"

"I lied." More than once he'd asked if I'd seen anyone else before him, and I'd lied each time. "Niall found me just before you did."

His arms stiffened, but he continued leading me around the dance floor. "I knew I smelled his scent out there that day."

"He had only just found me when he heard you approaching, so he—"

"So he did nothing? *Nothing* to help you?"

"He couldn't, Breck! What would you or Killian have done if you had caught him out near The Veil? How would he have explained it?"

He looked at me warily. "Explained *what?*"

If I told him the reason, if I told him what Niall and I were, he wouldn't take it lightly. And on top of that, no one else was supposed to know.

The words balanced on the tip of my tongue as I worked up the courage to let them spill.

Breck's brows furrowed in confusion. Then he closed his eyes and let out a sigh. "Look, Auren, I don't know what Niall told you about me, but I can assure you everything I've done was to keep you safe and keep you away from Killian—"

"Breck?" I tried to cut in—

"And that night in the library, I kissed you because I—"

"*Breck!*"

He closed his mouth and stared at me.

I could still see that spark of hope in his eyes that told me he wasn't done trying, and the fact that he still hoped—still cared in that way . . . I needed to snip that bud before it bloomed.

"He was there because something called to him. He was there because he felt . . . *me.*" The next words felt so foreign—yet so right—as I finally acknowledged it aloud. "He's my mate."

Breck's arms went slack and his steps halted so suddenly, that the other dancing couples stumbled around us.

"Breck, come on," I said, lifting his arms back into position and pulling him into motion again. He moved but his feet were heavy and careless.

"You are mistaken," he said in a clipped tone.

"No. I'm not," I clipped back, noting the ire and hurt behind his eyes.

I'd wanted to ease into this conversation for this exact reason. To avoid the sting. But there was no delicate way to break someone's heart.

"I felt it the moment I saw him. There was a thrumming in my chest. I thought it was from some remnant of power that latched onto me from The Veil when I crossed, or that it had come from his power when he found me. I couldn't explain it. And every time he's ever been near, it strengthens. It's a pull that I feel deep within me. And he feels it too."

Breck shook his head in denial. "He's lying to you. He could be compelling you, Auren."

"He's not. Two Elders have confirmed it."

His steps faltered again. "What did you just say?"

"The Elder of Elandrew and the Elder of Calledan both confirmed it."

This was something he simply did not want to believe, I could see it in his eyes. And I suddenly found myself with the urge to defend Niall, to explain that everything Breck thought he knew about him was wrong. "You think you know who Niall is, but he is *not* that male. He is so much more than what everyone makes him out to be. He cares about his court and his people. His power is next to none, but he has worked his entire life to make sure that he wouldn't be anything like his ancestor."

Breck was staring off above me now, averting his eyes from mine. He knew I was right. He just didn't want to admit that Niall wasn't the enemy. And he definitely didn't want to admit that he had fallen for someone else's mate.

"Why do you cling to the notion that Niall is so wicked?"

He sighed through his nose, finally falling somewhat in step with the beat of the music. "It's all I've ever known of him. I know it's no excuse, but it's the only thing I've got. Every time he attends a High Lords meeting, he's arrogant. Condescending to everyone around him. I only know what I've seen and what I'm told, Auren. And everything I've witnessed has only supported this claim."

"That's a poor excuse. You don't understand him. And Killian has always been at odds with him, so he planted that seed in you as well. Niall is one way in public and another in private. His reputation proceeds him, yes, but he keeps it that way for a reason. If you'd give him a chance, you would quickly see . . ." My voice faded out as I realized Breck was going to remain stubborn no matter what evidence I offered.

His eyes finally met mine, catching sight of my building frustration. "I want to believe you, Auren."

I let out a sigh of my own. "But?"

"But, I just don't trust that one moment you appear in our realm, and then suddenly you're his mate."

"I didn't believe it at first either," I admitted.

I'd assumed that Niall was everything Breck had warned me about, until I was shown otherwise. And if this thrumming and aching need wasn't gnawing at me every waking moment, I wouldn't have believed we were mates either.

As if speaking of him drew his attention, I felt Niall's eyes on me from across the courtyard.

I turned my head to see him standing near Morah. His face was a portrait of calm, but I could feel his jealousy creeping down our connection in my mind. Morah was speaking to him, but his focus remained on Breck and I, tracking us across the floor with a lethal stare.

Shadows swirled to life in my mind as his essence took form and hovered near mine, looming like a grumpy chaperone as he growled my name. *Auren . . .*

I dared a look in his direction again as I sent a thought back. *Don't get me riled up right now, I don't want to cause a scene.*

And just how do you think I'm feeling?

I glanced over at him again.

This time Breck noticed. "Is he mad that we're dancing?"

Why are the two of you dancing? Niall growled.

I faked a smile at Breck. "He's perfectly fine with it."

We can talk about this later, I shot back at Niall. The connection went silent, but it still pulsed with his raw irritation.

Breck and I finished out the dance, and I tried to lighten the mood with a brief summary of my training before the song ended. He was happy to hear that I could at least shield myself properly, and port if I needed to. When the music lulled to a snail's pace, he gave me a gentle bow, but there was a sadness still lining his features as he met my eyes again.

He escorted me back to the side of the courtyard where Niall and

Morah were waiting. Niall met him a few steps out and took me beneath his arm, no longer caring if anyone noticed.

"Thank you for allowing me a dance," Breck said, his voice so low one would have thought he was ashamed.

I discreetly nudged Niall in the side, urging him to say something back. "That looked a little long to be just *one* dance," was his reply.

Damnit, Niall.

Not helping.

"Breck has sincerely apologized for everything, and extends his apology to you as well." I stared up at Niall, hoping he would catch my hint at peacemaking.

He straightened his shoulders and slowly removed his arm from around me, finally realizing it had been a possessive move, and we were still in public.

"I've been informed by Morah that you've done a great deal to keep Killian occupied since we left," he said.

Breck nodded once.

"You have my gratitude."

Breck dipped his head again, acknowledging Niall's thanks.

When neither of them said anything further, Morah split the silence. "Well then, it's about time I go do my duty and play nice with the other dignitaries." She latched onto Breck's arm and tugged. "Come along, Breck—for your own good."

He hesitated, but followed.

Morah was right. This was no place for mending relationships. As badly as I wanted for it to be.

The two of them stalked towards the entrance where Laurent was conversing with a few others—including Vanir—who raised a glass toward Niall and I.

"When did Vanir get here?" I asked.

"He arrived late," Niall clipped, his tone immediately garnering my attention. "Follow me." Without waiting, he strode off through the crowd. I had no option but to follow.

67

SHADOWS IN THE NIGHT

I FOLLOWED NIALL DOWN A SERIES OF LONG GLACIAL HALLWAYS, TRYING to keep up as he rounded corner after corner. Beautiful domed caverns packed full of icicles that were larger than me glittered under orb lights as we passed by, but I couldn't even pause a moment to get a good look at them. "Where are we going?" I called after him.

No reply.

As soon as we turned another corner he stopped short, grabbing my hand and flicking his other wrist at a closed door nearby. It opened violently and he hauled me into the room.

Candles were lit and orbs bobbed in the corners of what appeared to be a guest chamber. Once we were both inside, he dropped my hand and began pacing, taking long, deep breaths in and out through his nose.

"What's wrong?" I asked.

"Do you truly not know?" His eyes lit gold as he stared at me. "Of course, you don't."

I bristled. "I know that you're being a prick right now."

He spoke his next words through clenched teeth. "I leave you for a few gods damned minutes and *he* swoops in. Do you have any idea how hard it was for me to watch you dance with him?"

"Niall, he didn't mean anything by it. He even kept his distance until I gave him permission to come near me."

"It doesn't matter if he was five feet from you or five miles, the thought of him caring for you sets me on edge."

"Niall it was just a—"

"*Just a dance*. I know. But you're my *mate,* Auren. That means I feel *everything* when it comes to you. The longer I'm around you, the stronger this connection becomes. It's a territorial instinct that kicks in, and males get the brunt of it. I thought I was jealous and protective of you before all this, but once I knew for a fact that you were my mate, that all changed. It heightened. Just seeing Laurent take your hand when he welcomed you here had me on edge. And watching Breck—a male that I have no doubt still harbors feelings for you—spin you around that dance floor . . . it took every ounce of my willpower not to intervene."

Oh.

He could have fooled me. "It looked like you were handling it quite well," I said, thinking back to his perfectly calm façade.

A bitter, harsh laugh escaped him. "Well trust me, I wasn't." His eyes were simmering, their glow an indication of just how frazzled his emotions were, how deeply he felt . . .

The bond; this tether between us that I couldn't deny even if I was forced to. He'd been carrying the weight of it all on his own, without knowing how I felt; thinking there was a chance I wasn't going to accept it.

The thought chipped away at my heart.

"Auren, if he—"

"I told him that you're my mate," I said, hoping to put his worries at ease.

He halted mid step and looked at me, brows drawn together in disbelief as he held my stare from across the room.

"I didn't want him going on thinking there would ever be anything between me and him."

Niall shifted on his feet. "Does that mean . . . you . . ."

I slowly closed the distance to him. "I wish you had told me right when you found out, but that doesn't matter now. The point is I can't deny that we're mates any more than you can. I still don't know how it's possible, but that doesn't mean I don't feel the truth of it."

The tension eased from his face. "While I feel very relieved to hear you say that, no one else was supposed to know."

I stepped up to him and took his hand, aligning our fingers before folding mine in between his. "I know, but I had to say something."

There was a moment of silence, then his grip tightened around mine, drawing my eyes back up to his. A hunger hung heavy in his stare, and he lowered his gaze to my lips, desire dancing on the tip of his tongue as he opened his mouth to speak. "All I've wanted to do is be near you. Gods, I've wanted to kiss you so fucking badly since last night—"

"Then kiss me."

He angled his head like the words were a trap I'd laid between us. "Auren, I—"

"Kiss me, Niall," I commanded.

The hand that held mine pulled me to him, and my chest sang with the all too familiar vibration as our bodies collided. His lips met mine and his tongue swept in, claiming my mouth in a luscious kiss.

Gods it felt so good to kiss him.

Then, his hands were roaming, one finding purchase on the back of my neck, fingers curling into my hair, the other gripping my hips. His hard length pressed against my abdomen, and I arched into him, needing to feel every fiber of his being against me.

Our kisses turned desperate, and I reached down between us, palming him, wanting to free him from his restraint and take what my body desired.

"As badly as I fucking want to," he growled against my mouth, shifting his hips just out of my reach. "If we take this any further, I'll be in an entirely different state of mind."

"What do you mean?" I said, breathing heavily.

"Once the mating bond is sexually acted upon to a certain extent, the possessiveness takes over. It's known to last a couple of days, but each male handles it differently, and there's no telling what my reaction will be. If you think I'm ravenous now . . ."

"Oh," I said, blushing at the thought.

"All I know is that I do *not* want to be in another's territory, surrounded by countless other males when it happens."

I looked up at him playfully. "*When* it happens?"

"Oh darling, it'll happen. Now that you've accepted it, there's no escaping me." He gripped my backside and squeezed, flashing the grin that continuously had me falling over and over for him.

I snaked my arms around his neck and looked up at the ceiling as I asked myself out loud, "Hmm, is that *really* what I want?"

He smiled, taking the bait, and his essence broke across my mind, snatching mine up in shadows. I swooned without a second thought, a rush of liquid heat pooling between my legs.

"Go ahead, tell me you don't want it," he murmured, knowing he was right. His strong hands slid up my waist. "Tell me that you don't want me," he teased again in my ear. I opened my mouth, but words failed me. "You can't," he said under his breath as he nipped at my neck.

Chills blossomed down my arms and across my chest. "Should I pretend that I don't?"

"You can try," he whispered.

There was no denying what I felt for him—the need that I couldn't quench. I bit down on my bottom lip and ran my fingers along the collar of his jacket, down the lapels, tracing the gold embroidery. Then I let my hand trail lower, running the length of his torso.

I flicked my eyes up to his and tilted my head back, luring him in for another kiss. But just as he leaned down, I let go and turned toward the door. His mouth opened in disbelief as he followed me.

"You cruel thing," he purred over my shoulder as we exited the room. My inner-struggle must have shown on my face because he gave me a knowing grin. "Harder than it looks, isn't it?"

"I don't know what you mean," I said, peering down the hallway as if I wasn't full of carnal need.

He chuckled and straightened his collar. "Well, if you feel up for staying, Laurent and Senna have prepared rooms for us." He glanced over his shoulder at the one we'd vacated moments ago. "That wasn't one of them."

I gave him a look. "All right. Which ones are ours then?"

No sooner than the question left my lips, Vanir breezed by in the adjoining hall and halted when he saw us.

He smirked, turning toward us, his presence filling the open hallway. "I'm not interrupting, am I?"

"Not at all," I chimed back. "I was just a bit tired and was on my way to find my room."

Vanir's smirk remained. "Well, I think I can be of some help with that matter." He clasped an arm around Niall's shoulders, and directed him to a door on the opposite side of the hall from where we just were. "Your room, my friend, is here. And yours . . ." He walked over to me and began ushering me down the hall, making sure to speak loudly enough for Niall to hear as he said, "Is down here. By mine."

When I looked over my shoulder to find Niall staring daggers through Vanir's hand on my back, it took everything that I had to not laugh. Thankfully the two were friends, which was probably why Vanir was getting away with provoking him.

"Don't worry," he called out to Niall. "If I hear anything down at this end, I'll make sure she's safe and sound."

Niall stumbled half a step at the sight of Vanir opening my door, and the leash on my laugh finally snapped. The last thing I saw before I slipped inside the door was Niall giving Vanir the coldest look I'd ever seen while rolling the tension out of his shoulders.

Vanir chuckled deeply as he bid me goodnight and closed the door behind me. I leaned against the inside of it, and surveyed the room.

The candles were aglow, illuminating yet another room carved from ice. The temperature still remained pleasantly warm despite the surroundings; an endless enchantment of some sort that I was grateful for. The bedframe and headboard were carved from white birch wood, the four posters at the corners spiraling up toward the ceiling in an intricate twisting pattern. Plush bedding as white as Drastia's snow and trimmed with gold stitching lay perfectly across the mattress, and a pearl white clawfoot tub sat in the corner next to an elegant dresser and a small entryway to a chamber that I assumed held the latrine.

The space was quaint, and impeccably decorated with delicate touches; fresh flowers in a crystal vase, an ornately detailed hand mirror, and a personal tea kettle with several satchels of herbal tea made the room even more inviting. There was even a blue flannel nightgown folded and tied with a white ribbon on the pillow. Senna had a flare for personal touches.

I changed, and shimmied under the blankets, settling in and staring up at the dark blue, icy ceiling. The flickering candlelight reflected off its surface, making it look alive, lulling me into sleep.

Just as I was about to doze off, my power stirred within me. My eyes flew open and all my senses went on high alert.

There was a presence nearby.

No, not nearby . . . *in* my bedchamber.

I started to push out my shield, but the presence became familiar, and the moment I saw it, I knew what it was.

Shadows gathered inside my door. Niall's shadows. The spitting image of his essence given physical form. They swarmed amongst themselves just as they did when they came to me in my mind, only these were real and very much tangible.

They crossed the small space, settling at the end of the bed, leaving an impression in the comforter where they perched, watching me.

I watched them back, a smile creeping across my face. "Is that you?" I asked, as if I was speaking to Niall.

In answer, the shadows sank down across the bed and spread out, covering me like a blanket.

"You just couldn't stay away, could you?"

The shadows fluttered calmly in reply, then gently lifted the corner of the blanket, and paused. When I didn't object, a few tendrils broke off and moved underneath, slinking right up against my skin. I sucked in a breath as one glided down my side, caressing my bare thigh. It was surprisingly cool to the touch and sent a shiver down my body.

The one that still hovered above me lifted a tendril and touched my cheek—just as carefully as Niall would—then it drifted down and pressed lightly against my neck like a hand.

Back underneath the blanket, the shadow moved further up my thigh in soft swirling motions.

I didn't move to stop either of them.

Then, I felt *him* in my mind.

His voice was deep and sultry as he said, *Do you know how badly I want to be under those sheets with you right now?*

A low laugh rumbled in my throat. *All because Vanir—*

I don't want to hear another male's name on your lips, he cut me off sharply. The shadow against my neck tightened, while the one on my thigh moved tantalizingly higher, sending a thrill through me.

Jealous? I teased.

It'll be my name on your lips tonight, he growled. *Only mine, Auren.*

Another sliver of shadows separated and tugged the blanket down. It moved like Niall's fingertips across my breasts, squeezing just enough that I let out a small whimpering sound at the sensation.

His throaty laugh echoed down the connection between us.

How is this even possible? I asked in my mind.

Need I remind you of how powerful I am, darling? My shadows do my bidding. And that includes pleasuring my mate.

The shadows shifted, two more tendrils breaking off, wrapping around my wrists on his command, putting me fully under his control. I pulled at them to check their restraint, but they only tightened their grip as the ones between my legs moved higher, pushing my gown up as they went.

"Niall," I whispered aloud. But there was no reply. Nevertheless, he was watching. Feeling. He was here just as much as his shadows were.

The moment his shadows brushed over my center I let out a moan. They stroked me the way his fingers would, entering me in one smooth push, then setting a tantalizing pace.

I closed my eyes, picturing him above me with that wicked, sexy grin as he watched my ascent. The visual was met with his deep voice, coaxing me to the precipice.

That's it, he said.

His shadows thickened inside me, and I succumbed to their decadent ministrations, letting them wind me up. They worked me just as *he* would if he were here, tendrils flicking at my peaked breasts in rhythm with the ones between my thighs, until I plummeted over the edge into ecstasy, grasping at the bedsheets as I whimpered and moaned his name.

His talented shadows rang every last drop of satisfaction from me. They lingered for a few moments longer, tenderly caressing me as I basked in the aftermath. Then, as quietly as they came, they slipped away.

When I opened my eyes, I was alone, but I heard his voice roll like thunder through my mind as he let out a breathy groan. Heat washed over my cheeks at the sound—at what it sounded like he was doing.

I wanted to say something, but instead, I listened, hoping to hear another noise, or a confirmation that he was indeed enjoying himself just as I had.

When he spoke my name again, I jolted.

Auren . . . he purred deeply, his voice confirming his satisfaction.

Yes? I waited with baited breath.

My shadows were gentler than I would have been, he said, sounding slightly out of breath. *The things that* I *would have done to you . . .*

I shivered at his words.

His gentle, throaty laugh echoed into my mind, then he whispered, *I plan on showing you those things, very soon. Goodnight, my darling.*

68

LETHAL OPPONENTS

I HAD AWOKEN WITH THE FRESH MEMORY OF NIALL'S SHADOWS BETWEEN my legs, and his promise to show me certain *things*—the thought of which stole my focus all morning long.

We then shared a very sexually tense breakfast amongst Laurent's court, and I'd never felt so distracted, yet completely enamored.

Niall looked to be handling it about the same as I was.

Vanir had given both of us a knowing look and continued smirking throughout the entire meal.

Now, I stood in front of Roirdan at the ruins of the temple of Eryx— god of the sky and the night, high up in the mountains of Calledan. After enduring all that I had last night and this morning, I needed to get some of the emotional energy out of me.

Clear my head.

Swing a sword and sweat a little.

Or a lot.

With Niall's restraint at an all-time low, I was surprised he was okay with leaving me alone with another male for training. Though, I had a feeling he wouldn't stay away for long.

The space we stood in looked as though it had once been a lovely temple. The stone was a stark contrast of white alabaster against the dark rock of Calledan's mountains. Although it was in partial ruin, most of the pillars still remained standing, forming the perfect area to train.

Roirdan told me he preferred this place for its solitude and strategic location. Training at a higher altitude would benefit our stamina and allow us to fight at a much stronger capacity down at sea level.

As we sorted through our weapons, I studied what was left of the towering pillars. The tops of the white stone looked charred where some of the pieces had broken off.

"What exactly happened here?" I asked, lifting a hand toward the battered and damaged areas.

Roirdan gazed up to where I was pointing. "Dreki. Damn things don't know how to leave anything standing." He opened another bag of blades and began rummaging through them.

"What are Dreki?"

"Oh. Right. Forgot you've probably never seen one. They're huge beasts, five times the size of a horse. They have four legs with deadly sharp claws, and scales covering their entire body down to their long tails —which are covered in spikes. Both males and females have wings and can breathe fire, but the females usually aren't as large. They have nasty tempers though and aren't afraid to scorch something just for the hell of it."

He looked back up to the tops of the remaining pillars. "Males did that when they were defending this place. The brutes don't know their own size or strength."

"Kind of like you, then," I said.

Roirdan chuckled and shrugged. "Can't help it."

I shook my head and grinned. "They sound deadly, though—the Dreki."

"Oh, they are. Vanir breeds them—the crazy bastard."

I fumbled with my sword. "Vanir *breeds* them?"

Roirdan nodded. "They hail from Vahrenhall, deep in the highland hills. Vanir's ancestors have been breeding them for millennia."

An image flashed in my mind of carved creatures with open maws, flailing tongues, and serrated teeth.

"I saw depictions of them while I was in Vahrenhall," I mused, remembering how they'd adorned the points and eaves of rooftops and the bed posts in the guest wing.

"That would be them." He pulled a longsword from its sheath and examined the blade, setting it aside as his weapon of choice. "Just wait until you see one in person."

My imagination ran wild at the thought as we moved to stretch and warm up, but I forced myself to focus on the task at hand, not the giant beasts that roamed the Highland Court.

I didn't think Roirdan really knew what to expect from me, so I used that to my advantage as we readied for our first round of swordplay with one another.

He sunk into a stance and extended his arms out at his sides. "Show me what you've got."

I held my sword behind my back and began slowly circling him. He lifted a brow at me as he watched me move. I made a complete lap around him before approaching, sword still behind me, a mirror to my spine.

Just as I got within striking distance of him I dipped forward, spinning, and swiping the blade for his chest as I glanced by him. The move caught him completely off guard, and I didn't give him any time to recover. I swung low, and his sword barely reached out to meet mine as he skirted me to my left.

"You're quick," he observed, following my movements with his eyes, anticipating my tactics before he lunged. His size and strength were reflected in the force of his swing—which rattled my bones as my sword collided with his.

I pushed off a small ledge to my right, putting my own body weight behind the thrust I dealt back at him. He leaned just out of my reach and brought his sword down hard—a power move that I'd seen a hundred times.

I dodged his strike and swung my blade from the ground up before thrusting in a series of small movements, showcasing my speed and precision.

"*And* you're efficient," he added. "Impressive."

I smiled and wiped a bead of sweat off my forehead.

The sun steadily climbed higher over the exposed temple ruins while I demonstrated my skills, pocketing each nod of approval and surprised brow hike that Roirdan threw my way.

Eventually, I rolled the sweat-soaked sleeves of my tunic up as far as they would go, and Roirdan took off his shirt and tied his sun-kissed brown hair in a low bun. His muscled skin was glistening with sweat, his shroud draping over his shoulders like a badge of honor. If Niall showed up anytime soon, his mating-male ego would surely be tested.

I noted how Roirdan's markings were different from Niall's. They were harsh lines and symbols that reminded me of those I'd seen on the shields in the Great Hall. I admired them for what they were: a battle-tested triumph, a testimony of deeds done.

As we trained, it began to make perfect sense why he was the commander. His knack for teaching and leading was an innate part of him. Built into his very being. He valued every minute of practice, every opportunity to lend insight. And his authority was impossible to ignore—one I'd look to on the battlefield, if I were ever facing down an enemy alongside him.

He showed me a better grip for my sword, which greatly reduced the strain on my forearm when blocking certain moves. He also tidied up my footwork and taught me a few new maneuvers that I hadn't seen before.

One of his signature moves was to keep his favorite dagger hidden away in one of those magical pockets of thin air. When he surprised me by reaching into nothing and pulling the dagger out in the midst of the fight, I immediately wanted to adopt the move.

We continued practicing with daggers until I was drenched in sweat, and had somehow managed to land a successful slice along the back of his wrist. It was a tiny thing, and it healed almost instantly, but I felt triumphant.

"You're easily one of the best female fighters I've trained with," Roirdan said, finally signaling for us to rest.

A swell of pride filled my chest as I caught my breath. It wasn't often that I was praised for my skill. Back in Belthria, when a man was bested by a woman, the loss was usually brushed off as bad luck on his part.

For a fae warrior to say he was impressed, it meant a great deal to me.

Roirdan was a brutal fighter. He was taking it easy on me, but I could tell that in a real fight, he was a force to be reckoned with. His movements were tactful. Practiced thousands of times and with such efficacy that a battlefield would seem like a ballroom against his skill.

"Are there many female fighters here?" I asked.

He huffed a laugh. "Of course. There are thousands across the realm."

My mouth parted in disbelief. "Thousands? And they're trained just as the males are?"

"Why wouldn't they be?"

I looked down at my sword and squeezed the pommel tightly, suddenly realizing how inferior I'd felt in the human realm. "In Belthria, it's so uncommon, that . . . I'm the only female that I know of who can wield a sword the way I do."

Roirdan tilted his head. "Are you serious?"

I nodded.

"Then how did you learn?"

"My father taught me. Where I'm from, it's practically unheard of for women to take up arms. None are ever really given the chance to learn, even if they have the heart for it. But somehow he knew that I would need the skill." I stared at my blade like I could see my father in its reflection, smiling back at me with pride.

Boots scuffed against stone, and when I looked up, Roirdan was only a few steps away. He nodded his head several times as he regarded me then placed a hand on my shoulder. "Your father should be proud."

"I like to think he is," I said, smiling gently as I watched the sunlight dance off the sharpened edge of my blade.

Roirdan seemed to pick up on the hint of sadness in my voice and didn't press further. He simply tapped his blade against mine, drawing my attention back up. "I meant what I said. Easily one of the best."

I gave him a soft smile. "Thank you." *For not underestimating me.*

I'd spent years honing my craft in a realm that would never appreciate it. But here, my skills were respected and valued, and Roirdan's words were something I didn't realize I'd needed to hear.

An hour later, we were enjoying a break after a round of hand-to-hand combat, when Niall arrived with Aremis and Remic in tow.

I smirked. Just as I'd thought, he couldn't stay away.

All three of them were dressed for training, carrying their weapons and donning fresh faces, ready for sun, sweat, and swordplay.

Niall strolled toward us, unbuttoning his shirt, and throwing an obvious glare at Roirdan's already shirtless torso before cutting his territorial eyes back to me. He peeled away the fabric, exposing his shroud and the tanned skin and muscles beneath it. My mouth instantly watered at the sight.

"Hopefully you still have some energy left for me," he said, the corner of his mouth lifting.

"If you came to show off, Auren has already been thoroughly impressed," Roirdan chimed from where he was perched on a broken temple pillar. "Anything you show her will pale in comparison."

Niall summoned a thick black sword in his outstretched hand, and cut the impressive blade through the air with an arrogant grin. "Is that so?" He eyed Roirdan, as if he was still assessing whether or not his commander being shirtless around me was a threat.

Remic took up a viewing spot at the edge of the temple, silent and stoic as always.

Roirdan stood as Aremis walked over to him, and they clanged their swords in greeting.

"We've come to get a little bit of practice time for ourselves," Aremis said, nodding in my direction. "Want to show us what you've been working on?"

"Two against one?" Roirdan said, striding over to my side and nudging my arm, pitting us against Niall.

The High Lord shrugged. "Whatever it takes."

Roirdan moved first, and I watched the dynamic that he set. Niall maneuvered with ease around each move, as if he'd seen them a thousand times.

I entered the match just as Niall parried, but he whirled his blade in the air to his other hand, and swiped at me with it. When I leapt out of reach, he moved as quick as a shadow and was behind Roirdan in an instant, pointing his blade at the commander's spine.

"Tiring so soon, Roir?" he teased.

Roirdan let out a growl and twisted, knocking away Niall's blade in one quick move. He tossed his own blade to the side, and launched forward with balled fists. Each punch and block cracked the air again and again in quick succession as they sparred, not moving more than a few feet forward and backward from where they'd abandoned their weapons.

Then, Roirdan thrust an open palm toward Niall, and a jolt of power pulsed outward from it, rimmed at the edges with sparks of lightning. But

Niall's shadows reacted. The pulse was met with a wall of shadowfire, deflecting the electric charge to the pillars that stood watch around us.

"What was that?" I yelled.

"Petty, is what that was," Niall tutted.

"Just trying to spice things up." Roirdan snickered, dipping down and swiping his blade back up in his grasp.

Niall lifted a brow, and with a silent command his shadows wafted out from his shoulders and encircled the commander, whipping out like black flames.

Roirdan answered my question while he defended himself against each lashing shadow. "I can"—his blade sang as it sliced—"summon"—the shadows evaporated, only to appear in another spot, poised to strike—"lightning," he breathed out, leveling his eyes to Niall again.

When one of the shadows nipped at his forearm, he snatched his arm back and watched the blood form a scarlet bead on his sun-kissed skin before it disappeared. "Bastard," he spat, though he had a grin plastered on his face.

He backed off, inclining his head to Niall, the victor, and took a seat next to Aremis.

And then, all eyes went to me.

Niall stalked toward me with his mouth set into a cunning smirk. I had barely enough time to see him move before our swords crossed. In one quick motion he slid his blade down mine, catching it by the hilt, and with the flick of his wrist my sword was flung from my grasp, landing several feet away on the pavement.

Victory dripped from his winning smile.

But I wasn't finished. And he didn't expect my next move.

Without missing a beat, I spun, and as I did I reached into my own pocket of space and brought forth one of Roirdan's daggers, cutting upward with a reverse grip. Niall's eyes went wide and he jumped back—but not quick enough. The tip of my blade grazed his ribs, drawing a thin bead of blood that swiftly disappeared. The look on his face was shock and awe as he watched the blood retract before he whipped his head up at me.

Roirdan threw his head back and roared with laughter at the sight. "Never fucking thought I'd see the day!"

Aremis clapped in approval from the sideline, and across the temple, a faint grin was set on Remic's face.

I flipped the dagger over in my palm, ready to continue.

"How did you do that?" Niall asked, running his fingertips over the spot where I had nicked him.

I nodded my head toward Roirdan. "Your commander taught me a thing or two."

Roirdan's smile dripped with pure male pride. "She's a quick learner. She's actually very impressive. Even managed to draw blood from me too." He rubbed his wrist, as if tending to a phantom pain where the cut had been.

Niall raised a brow at me.

"What? Oh, come on, you didn't really doubt that I had skills, did you?"

His face softened and he replied, "I never once doubted you, darling. You just continue to impress me."

"None of that sappy shit," Roirdan whined. "We're here to draw blood."

"Who's next to bleed, then?" I called out, taking a seat next to the commander. He handed me a large flask of water and clapped me on my back, rattling my ribs, but I smiled nonetheless.

Aremis stood and grinned. "Let me show you how a Cheshm Zadan moves, Auren."

He was dressed much more casually today in a simple tan tunic and black leather pants. The ornately decorated scabbard that hung low on his hips came free with a single clasp, and he drew a short sword from it, placing the empty casing on the stone behind him. He twirled the sword in his hand like a baton, the gemstones embedded in the pommel glittering in the sunlight.

Niall took a ready stance across the pavilion, but Aremis continued twirling his weapon, not deigning to make the first move.

Suddenly, Niall spun, and swords clanged.

I did a double take to where Aremis had just been standing beside me, and gasped as I watched what appeared to be a ghost of his physical form evaporate.

He *had* made the first move.

I stared out to where he was now fully materialized in combat with Niall. They parried once, twice, then Aremis moved, his previous location fading as soon as he appeared again to strike.

His movements were so quiet, wickedly fast. It was as if he was pulsing through existence, cheating time. The way he moved was entirely different from porting.

I was in awe, desperate to decipher his technique.

He forced Niall's back to the nearest pillar within a few steps. But Niall's shadows whipped back in defense, giving him a chance to move out into the open again.

Aremis glided, blade in hand. His entire body moved fluidly, and he looked as if he could continue all day and never tire. His technique was entirely different from any I had ever seen—wide, low stances, and leaps and spins that had me getting dizzy just from watching.

Niall's head was on a continuous swivel—anticipating his opponent's next move. His shadows defended against any advances that Aremis's Aura made.

Both males were stunningly lethal fighters in their own right, and by the end of their match, both had managed to make each other bleed.

I handed them water as they took up spots nearby on the crumbling wall.

Roirdan stood and motioned for Remic to meet him next.

The Dionach bowed his head and slowly unsheathed his sword from between his wings as they flexed and opened, revealing their grandeur.

My mouth gaped at the sheer size of his wingspan. How he wasn't in constant pain from supporting such things was a complete wonder to me. They had to span at least ten feet wide. In the sunlight, their gray color appeared almost silver.

The collar of his black leathers rose up his neck—covering its entirety and adding to his threatening presence. I wondered if he ever wore anything different, or what purpose the fashion truly served—if any.

It was then that I noticed him in comparison to the others. He stood taller than each of them, and even though they were all intimidating in their own right, there was something uniquely different about the Dionach. The lack of emotion on his face was enough to intimidate any enemy, but the way he carried himself was even more distinctive.

Where Roirdan was the embodiment of battlefield rage, and Aremis was precision and stealth, and Niall was full of cunning and wrath . . . Remic was death wielding a blade.

"It's been a bit since we've had the chance to spar," Roirdan said, holding both a short sword and an axe.

Remic briefly examined his blade. "Long overdue."

The commander clanged his weapons together and took a fighting stance. "Let's fix that."

Roirdan moved, and Remic followed, the perfect mirror to his opponent. So perfect, in fact, that it was almost eerie.

Remic's steps and turns were sure and precise. Each block—each strike he dealt—was punctuated with such force that Roirdan's weapons shook with the impact. And when the commander decided to take it up a notch, the Dionach rose to the challenge.

Roirdan grunted with the force he was putting behind each attack. Yet still, Remic remained silent and composed. This was child's play for the Dionach. I could see it in his eyes. There was an otherworldly force driving him. A force that made him lethal to anyone he was up against. He would bring a reckoning upon his enemies—that I knew with certainty.

"Is that all you've got?" Roirdan taunted, despite his heavy breathing.

Remic's eyes narrowed. In one smooth movement, he sheathed his longsword and drew both blades from where they were strapped at his thighs.

Then, he was upon Roirdan in a fury. His movements were so swift I could have sworn Roirdan took multiple cuts all across his chest and arms as he frantically attempted to block each attack. It wasn't until the pommel of one of Remic's blades caught the commander in the chin, that he halted his pursuit and stepped back, returning both blades to their sheaths.

His perfect composure slid back into place.

Roirdan spit out a mouthful of blood, giving the Dionach a wicked grin. "Fuck yeah. That's what I'm talking about."

Niall snorted.

"I think I need training sessions with each of you," I marveled. "You're all a force to be reckoned with."

Niall leaned over and planted a swift kiss on my forehead as Aremis spoke. "We are more than happy to train with you. A mind that is willing to learn should never be left wanting or neglected."

Excitement skittered through me. If it were possible to learn to fight with each of their techniques combined, I wanted to be the one to do it.

The next day, I worked with each of Niall's Trium. Aremis, Roirdan, and I trained in a quiet chamber in The Keep using daggers and short swords. Aremis introduced me to the intricate stances and spins that were crucial to his technique, while Roirdan focused on tidying up my footwork and how I handled each blade. My leg muscles were barking in protest halfway through our session, but I savored the feeling of progress. The pain that came with mastering new skills was always one that I welcomed.

Remic and I trained in The Elderwood, where Niall had first taught me to port. He showed me how to imbue my movements with a touch of my power, which would help reinforce my blocks and attacks when I came up against stronger opponents. After a grueling afternoon of failed attempts, I successfully managed to rattle a few trees with a pulse of my light, and Remic seemed pleased.

I still didn't know what special ability I was capable of—if something like that was even possible for me—but I was assured that with time, I would find out.

Niall and I spent the evening together reading entries in Evander's journal, most of which told of the High Lord's comings and goings, with a few that were full of complaints of headaches and strange dreams. But I had a sinking feeling that we would uncover information of a much greater importance the further we read.

The following morning, Roirdan surprised me at breakfast with a small, slender, red box. Niall looked at him in question as I opened it.

"Thought you deserved one of your own," Roirdan said as I lifted the lid and beheld something wrapped in green velvet.

I pulled back the cloth and the rounded hilt of a dagger greeted me. The blade was similar to the one Roirdan had let me use for training— slightly curved, with an intricate design etched along the spine. But this one had a smaller handle to fit my smaller hand. At the end of the blackened hilt, a polished black gemstone was set into the pommel. It glittered like the inky night sky over Calledan.

"The hilt and the stone are hewn from the mountains. I had it modeled after the one you liked so much. This one's yours." He handed me a matching black leather sheath and smiled.

I turned and threw my arms around his neck. "Thank you, Roirdan."

He let out a deep laugh and hugged me back just as fiercely. "Use it well, little one."

Niall clapped his commander on the shoulder.

"Just try not to cut me with it," Roirdan joked, gesturing to the tip of the blade. "That thing's sharper than all the weapons in The Keep. Even yours, Aremis."

I laughed and shook my head. "No promises."

Aremis curiously reached for the blade. "May I?"

"Of course," I said, handing it over to him.

He examined it, nodding approvingly. "This is fine work. Very light." He scraped the tip over his palm, drawing blood with the slightest bit of pressure. His brow hiked up. "Very sharp indeed."

"My bladesmith never skimps on quality," Roirdan replied proudly.

I fit the sheath to my belt and slipped the dagger inside. "It's perfect."

Aremis stepped forward and placed his hand on the pommel. "Make sure you have it with you when we go to Benmoor today," he said. "And pray you don't need it."

69

BENMOOR

THE RED SANDS STRETCHED AS FAR AS MY EYES COULD SEE, AND DRIFTED over the stone platform we stood on, which rose up alone from the endless desert.

Niall, Aremis, Remic, and I had ported to Benmoor's gate after having a thorough briefing and making sure we were all on the same page about our attendance of this Lumeri.

Roirdan stayed behind in Calledan as a precaution, and because it was always best to have at least one of the Trium in the Mountain Court when the High Lord was away. Niall would be in communication with him if necessary.

The air was thick and parched, with no relief of a breeze. Even the sky couldn't escape the desert. It loomed above, tinted a reddish-orange hue from the sand's reflection.

Suddenly, the ground pulsed and walls of sand rose up around each side of the platform, encasing us in a room of red. The grains moved and churned on themselves like the walls were alive. The sound grated on my ears like sandpaper on stone, and I clapped my hands over them to block it out.

This was the arrival assessment, just as I had experienced at the other courts.

But this one *irked* me.

"That's . . . disturbing," I practically yelled, watching the moving walls, half expecting them to leap onto us and drown us under their hot, heavy weight.

Seconds later they slumped back into the rest of the desert, leaving a few fine, sparkling grains to drift in the air.

"I've never liked coming here," Remic growled, shaking dust off of his polished black boots. "Shit gets everywhere."

He had glamoured his wings and faint facial markings. He looked—for all intents and purposes—like a fae, his normally rounded ears now arching to points beneath his long hair.

Still, I couldn't help but see phantom wings behind his broad shoulders and slim waist. Even without them, his presence alone screamed that he was *other*.

Aremis sighed heavily, pulling my attention away from Remic. "Let's get this over with."

Niall turned toward him. "I owe you for coming along. I know you want to keep out of this court as much as possible, but we need to make a statement."

Aremis's jaw flexed, but he offered Niall a small smile. "For the benefit of the realm and for our court, I would do anything, brother."

Niall nodded his thanks and spoke to all of us. "Let's have some fun, shall we?"

Benmoor proper was a bustling city that overwhelmed my senses.

The buildings were built of sandstone, but the color had dulled to a soft beige, faded from time under the harsh sun. The paved streets were crowded with market carts and tents teaming with goods and merchandise. Woven baskets were stacked taller than most of the fae on top of rickety barrows, while fine silks and linens in the brightest pinks and oranges, and the deepest purples and blues, fluttered from storefront trellises. Tapestries of every size hung from wooden clips along thick twine, and the aroma of decadent spices crept up my nose; cinnamon, saffron, turmeric and cardamom. Tables of baskets, filled to the brim with fresh pomegranates, persimmons, peaches, and grapes, sat in contrast with the slabs of heavily seasoned meat that hung from strings, ready to be carved off at the buyer's request.

Flowers blossomed from vines and branches, cascading over balconies and framing doorsteps, bringing life to a world otherwise covered in sand.

Above us, fae leaned out their windows and snapped clothing and linens against the open air before hanging them to dry along ropes that strung from building to building.

A melody of sitars and foreign flutes wound their way through the streets and alleyways as we made our way forward.

I was amazed at the culture, but Remic and Aremis looked like they were one step away from porting back home out of disgust.

As we passed by a cart overflowing with more fresh fruit, Niall tossed a couple of coins to the vendor and selected a small bundle of plump red grapes. The male bowed earnestly in thanks and gave us a happy smile as Niall handed the fruit to me.

I grinned and popped a small globe in my mouth. A moan escaped my lips as the sweet burst of flavor washed over my tongue. "These are the best grapes I've ever tasted."

Aremis looked over his shoulder from where he was leading the way, and his slight smile told me he would probably agree.

Niall plucked one for himself and tossed it up, catching it in his mouth.

"Hey! These are mine," I said, snatching the fruit out of reach.

He laughed, holding up his hands in playful surrender.

The street narrowed, and Niall reached up to hold back a swath of cloth that hung down into the pathway, letting me pass underneath first.

The scenery that lay beyond was different, and smells of incense and spices began to burn my nostrils. Some fae were lounging in dark corners, smoking from long, golden pipes. Others were offering deals on small bags of herbs, shaking them in my face as I passed by.

A dazed male with bloodshot eyes stumbled into my path and collided with my shoulder, nearly taking me down to the carpeted stone floor.

Remic was immediately at my side, towering over the stranger, hands poised on his daggers. "Watch it," he threatened, momentarily letting his glamour fall.

At the sight of the wings towering over the Dionach's shoulders, the male instantly sobered up and fled in the opposite direction.

Remic's glamour snapped back into place, and he turned around, studying our surroundings suspiciously.

Niall followed suit, as we all halted.

"It seems I might have made a wrong turn," Aremis said warily.

"Come." Niall motioned to us all. I grabbed hold of his shirt, while he placed hands on both his advisor's and the Dionach's shoulders, and we ported.

"Apologies," Aremis muttered as we collected ourselves. "It's been quite some time since I've ventured into the city proper, and it's changed a lot since then."

Niall didn't fault him.

Remic on the other hand gave Aremis a pointed look before turning to me. "Are you all right?" he asked sternly.

"I'm fine. The man was clearly just drunk, or perhaps high," I said, thinking back to the scene.

"Why did we have to go through the damn city in the first place?" Remic growled at Aremis.

Niall hushed us all as he straightened his shirt out and stared ahead. "There are many eyes and ears here. Remember that. And I wanted Auren to see a bit of the territory. That's why."

That did nothing to quell Remic's obvious annoyance.

I turned and peered up at what Niall was looking at.

Ramil's palace.

A set of grand, wide steps led up to a building made of red desert sandstone. The façade boasted a series of arched colonnades that framed both sides of a giant, pointed-arched entry. Its wooden double doors were open, flanked by two male guards dressed in knee-length tunics over matching loose-fitting pants. The fabric of their uniforms was such a dark purple it was almost black. Gold sashes belted their waist, giving form to their physique. Long, curved swords hung at their sides.

As we ascended the steps and approached the guards, I noted the suspicion in their kohl-rimmed eyes. Both of them shifted their weight uneasily as we passed by, but neither of them moved to block our entry.

Through the doors, we entered into a large courtyard that was dripping with color. Plants, vines, and florals of many varieties were decorating each corner, thriving amidst the heat. They spilled over the edges of the clay pottery that housed them, adorning each step and bannister with a splash of life.

Intricately woven rugs lined the floors, and silken swaths of fabric curtains fluttered in the breeze from the beams that stretched above.

In the center of the courtyard was a square pool, lined in dark blue tiles, which tinted the water a deep cerulean. A few finely dressed courtiers chatted nearby, puffing from slender golden pipes, while several fae females with dark hair, and eyes rimmed in kohl, lounged on either side of the pool, dipping their feet and hands into the water, and sipping from fine chalices. They wore sheer, gauzy fabrics, and their feet were sandaled; a style I'd never seen, or even knew existed.

As we entered the space, we were greeted by an olive-skinned male with a long black beard, wearing floor-length black robes and a gold cummerbund. His pointed ears framed a gold brocaded hat that covered his thick black curls, which were tied back low at his nape.

I recognized him. It was the same male from Lumeri in the Woodland Court. The one that Ramil dismissed when he and I had entered into a discussion. He gave a bow to us and then his eyes went directly to Aremis. "The prodigal son returns," he sneered. His voice was grating, and his accent was heavy.

I instantly loathed him.

Aremis shook the hair back from his face and clasped his hands behind his back, standing a little taller. "No, Ferhan. You know very well that I will never return in that sense. I'm only accompanying my High Lord for the special occasion this evening."

His High Lord.

Meaning Niall. Not Ramil.

Ferhan finally dragged his amused gaze over to Niall. "Ramil is pleased to welcome you all as his guests," he said, though his tone was the complete opposite of welcoming.

When his attention fell on me next, Remic stepped closer to my side.

"And, Auren, is it? A pleasure to see you again." His dark eyes assessed me like I was a prized mare that had just pranced into his stables.

Niall's voice was hard as stone as he placed his hand on my shoulder possessively. "She is under my protection."

Ferhan flicked his eyes from Niall's hand, to his face, back to me. "Ah, accounts seem to differ on that. But nevertheless, she is most certainly welcome in our court." A corrupted grin tugged at the corners of his mouth before he turned on his heel. "Come. Enjoy some refreshments. Ramil will be with you shortly." His words echoed after him as he led us across the courtyard and down a long hallway to a seating area.

We waited on cushioned benches surrounding a golden table as a small house-fae with skin the shade of burnt umber, poured us each a goblet of a slightly green liquid. When she looked up to hand me my glass, I noticed her eyes were a strange shade of copper. She moved along, handing a glass to each of us. But when she beheld Remic, she retreated, setting the glass on the table and scurrying away.

Instead of sitting like the rest of us, the Dionach stood watch, too on edge to be stationary for even a moment.

"What is this?" I sniffed my goblet. It smelled like mint, but I didn't trust it.

"A traditional drink," Aremis answered. "It's supposed to be refreshing, but I never did like the taste of it."

Remic stepped in quietly and took the glass from my hands. "Let me." He didn't hesitate to lift it to his lips and take a drink.

I gasped, realizing what he was doing, and wanting to call out for him to wait, but Niall placed his hand on my knee. "It's fine. Remember, he is not easily killed," he whispered with a wink.

"Then how would he know if it was poisoned?"

"His senses will alert him if something is wrong with anything he ingests. But it will not affect him."

We all watched him drink and waited for a long moment after, until he nodded sternly and handed the glass back to me. With that, Niall sipped from his, and I decided to as well.

The crisp tang of vinegar, the freshness of sugared cucumber, and a medley of honey and mint swirled on my tongue. It was odd, and I sipped once more in assessment, but found that, like Aremis, I didn't care too much for it.

A fountain trickled nearby, filling the silence as we waited for Ramil.

Niall's voice entered my mind like a smooth caress. *I already know Ramil will be anxious that you're here. His advisor no doubt alerted him.*

Ferhan is his advisor?

Yes, and a conniving one at that. Do not trust him.

I figured as much.

Look at me, Auren.

I lifted my eyes to him.

Remember what we talked about. Keep your mental shield up at all times. Let me worry about the physical one.

I nodded.

The house-fae reappeared at the entrance to the hall and cleared her throat, motioning for us to follow her.

Aremis led, Niall and I followed, and Remic trailed behind—just like before.

There was something about having three deadly males surrounding me that made me feel invincible. No matter that I had enough power coursing through my veins that I could probably level the building . . . if only I knew how to hone it properly.

The polished, red granite floors gleamed up at me, and the pillars that we walked through all shone like they were freshly wet. Smoke wafted through the corridor, the air heavy with the scent of saffron.

The High Lord of Benmoor was seated in the center of his throne room in a hand carved wooden chair that was inlaid with gold, atop a bed of layered, tasseled rugs. Ferhan stood to his right, wearing the same sneer on his face as before.

Ramil looked indifferent, almost as if he was lost in his own train of thought. But when he saw me, he reeled himself back to the present.

Rising, he straightened his lapels and clasped his hands in front of him, inclining his head toward us. "My guests from the Mountain Court." His tone was laced with venom as he looked at each of the males that stood before him. "And from the land of Belthria," he added, eyes narrowing on me. "I wondered where you'd slipped off to." When I said nothing in reply, he flashed me a false smile. "I'm honored that you chose to join us for our Lumeri. But the company with which you came . . . perplexes me. Last I saw, you were in the hands of Lord Killian. It appears I was not made aware of the exchange."

He was playing dumb. We all knew it.

None of us took the bait.

Taking the silence for the insult that it was, Ramil ground his jaw. But he didn't linger on it.

He moved his stare along to Niall. "It has been quite some time since you've stepped foot into my lands." He then glanced over to Aremis. "Some time indeed."

Aremis said nothing.

Niall slipped his hands into his pockets and tipped his chin back slightly. Finally, he said, "Call it progress."

Ramil paused and considered Niall, eventually nodding slowly. "Progress."

He summoned a house-fae with the clap of his hands and ordered that four guest chambers be made up—one for each of us. Niall didn't object to the number, and neither did I. We still needed to make it appear that we were simply acquaintances attending an event. Nothing more. But I could tell just by looking at Ramil that he suspected something.

As the males conversed, I remained quiet, assessing the area. Sheer fabrics hung in swaths, framing the section in which we stood. The architecture itself was stunning enough that it needed no decoration, yet still, richly colored rugs stretched along the floor, tall gold candelabras adorned the corners, and vases of purple, long-petaled flowers sat on either side of Ramil's chair and in every corner of the room.

It amazed me that flowers of any kind could thrive so well in such a harsh climate.

My attention snagged on the talisman dangling below Ramil's diaphragm, but no sooner than I noticed it, the High Lord's hand wrapped around it, as if to shield it from view.

He turned, leading us from the room, and Remic's steady hand pressed against my back, guiding me along as Niall and Aremis followed.

A warm breeze circulated throughout the palace. The temperature was pleasant—something that must have been upheld by magic because it was nothing like the thick air of the open desert or even the city streets. Porticos jutted out every so often, revealing elaborate fountains and seating areas just beyond. Court members wandered through the halls, but none bid us any sort of welcome as we passed.

My guest chambers were decorated with plush, jewel-toned furniture, delicate tapestries, and large vases displaying a variety of palms and flowering plants. Sheer curtains swayed along the entry to a private patio just beyond a quaint seating area. A house-fae delivered a tray of meats and cheeses without speaking a word, and as soon as she popped away, Niall ported in.

He laid a bundle of sheer amethyst fabric on my bed and stepped back with a wicked grin.

"Why are you looking at me like that?" I asked, glancing over to the strange cloth he'd deposited.

He folded his arms and leaned back against the wall with one foot bent up against it. "Because, the attire here is something I can't wait to see on you."

I strode over to the bed and lifted the material with a single finger. It was so light that it fluttered back to the sheets. Turning back to him, I crossed my arms. "How does that even count as clothing?"

"The females here like to show off their curves. It's always been a bit risqué." His eyes flicked up and down my body. "I must admit, I've been imagining you in it for days." He slid his tongue along his bottom lip, suggestively.

I lifted a brow. "And have you thought about just how many other males will also be privy to me in this outfit?"

Silence.

He hadn't.

He worked his jaw as he looked back at the fabric, second guessing his plan.

When he pushed off the wall I threw my hand out and snatched the fabric up in my arms. "On second thought, I think this will suit me just fine. The color is so feminine," I said, rather enthusiastically. "It'll bring out my eyes, don't you think?" I held the material against my body and twirled around.

"Auren, maybe you—"

"I rather enjoy dressing the part," I cut him off, paying his attempted argument no mind. "Especially when it's such a unique culture." I slipped off my shoes one by one and began unlacing my tunic. "You should probably be getting ready yourself. If I heard Ramil correctly, our escort will be arriving fairly soon."

My tunic slipped down over one shoulder, and Niall stiffened. In an instant he was in front of me, but he didn't touch me. Instead, his lips lingered over mine. "You'd better be on your best behavior tonight," he growled. "No teasing."

I tossed him a cheeky grin. "Or what?"

A sound rumbled deep in his throat. "Or I'll have to teach you what the consequences of your actions are."

Before I could retort, he backed away into nothing, leaving a wisp of shadow that brushed my exposed collarbone before fading away.

I grinned, then frowned as I looked down at the sheer material in my arms.

This will be interesting.

The dress was much harder to put on than I anticipated. After I had wasted most of my time struggling with which drape went over which body part, I finally figured out the layout and situated it around my body. Thankfully, the material covering my most intimate parts consisted of multiple layers so that it wasn't *completely* transparent.

I turned, admiring my reflection in the mirror by the bed. The wide, sheer straps fell over my shoulders, covering my breasts and meeting in a deep vee that came together below my navel. From there, it hung straight down to the floor. The backside was the same. My ribs were open to the air on both sides, and the slits that ran the length of my legs revealed the small curve of my hips and my lean, toned thighs.

A belted sash, encrusted with gold medallions, citrine and topaz gemstones, and purple tassels, held everything in its place around my hips, but one light breeze, and I would be baring everything to anyone who was looking.

I tugged the material around my backside to cover myself as best as I could, frowning when I could only move the fabric so far. Modesty didn't seem to be in the Desert Court's interest when it came to fashion.

Niall really didn't think this one through.

Thankfully I could hide the dagger that Roirdan had given me in my magical pocket of space. There would have been no concealing it under this damned fabric—or lack thereof.

I was in the middle of fashioning my hair into a braided circlet around the base of my head when I heard music begin somewhere out past my patio. The foreign tang of a string instrument I'd never heard before drifted in through the curtains, followed by the steady tempo of a drum. The celebration was starting.

I quickly secured my braid in place with the hair pins I'd found in the vanity, and swiped some kohl around my eyes like I'd seen Morah and the other fae of this territory wear. I shoved the small jar and brush back into the drawer and pulled on the thin slippers that Niall had left with the dress.

The house-fae returned without a moment to spare, beckoning me harshly toward the door.

Outside, Niall and Aremis stood waiting, sipping from tall thin flutes, while Remic watched the hallway. When I stepped out, each of them turned toward me, and Niall choked on his swallow. Aremis shook his head and grinned to himself as the High Lord wiped his chin with the back of his hand and cleared his throat. Remic's mouth twitched up at the sound.

"Just remember, you dressed me in this." I winked at Niall as I walked past him, knowing he was losing his mind at the sight of the dress fluttering open at my hips as I moved.

Behind me, I heard Aremis chuckle, followed by the clinking of glass.

70

LUMERI IN THE DESERT

Aᴌᴛʜᴏᴜɢʜ ʜᴇ ᴡᴀʟᴋᴇᴅ ǫᴜɪᴇᴛʟʏ ᴀɴᴅ ᴋᴇᴘᴛ ʜɪs ᴄᴏᴍᴘᴏsᴜʀᴇ, I ᴄᴏᴜʟᴅ ꜰᴇᴇʟ Niall simmering with anger at any male that looked at me. And there had been quite a few as we walked the halls of Benmoor's palace. His tension bled into my mind along with his shadows, seeking a way to mark me as his.

I smiled to myself as I caught him trying to blink away the wisps of golden color that sparked to life in his eyes each time a balmy breeze lifted the sheer panels of fabric.

We didn't make it far before a familiar face stepped out of the dark hallway to our right and brought us to an abrupt halt.

Morah stood in our way, looking striking in a gown almost identical to mine, but in a shade of deep magenta. Her eyes sparkled beneath her dark lashes, and her hair was swept over one shoulder, tumbling down her chest like waves of burnt molasses. A stack of golden cuffed bracelets lined her forearm, and intricately jeweled earrings dangled from her ears, sweeping the tops of her shoulders.

"Welcome to my home," she said with a saccharine smile.

She looked down at our small escort and hissed, and the house-fae quickly disappeared. "Nosy, conniving little things. They listen to every whisper, and are just as quick with tricks." She folded her arms over her chest and her smile quickly faded. "Now, just what are you all doing here?"

It was Aremis who spoke up. "Pleasure to see you again, Morah. It's been—"

"Too long. Yes, I'm aware. I'll ask you again. What are you doing?"

"We were headed to Lumeri," I said, glancing at the males at my side.

"Do you know how stupid of an idea that is?" She looked at Niall. "I warned you about this. Why would you bring her near my father? And furthermore, why would you even come when you knew Killian would be here?"

Niall was quiet as he considered her question, then a look crossed his face that I hadn't seen before.

"Didn't think that through, did you?" Morah asked.

Maybe Niall's mind was truly muddled with the mating bond.

She rolled her eyes. "You males really do get lost in that feral need of yours."

I whipped my head back to her.

We didn't tell—

"Relax. Breck told me," she clarified before I could even ask.

Aremis stepped closer. "What would you have us do? Your father has already welcomed us."

Morah looked me over once more. "I'll tell him you fell ill—something you ate while in your chambers. If he asks anything further, I'll cover for you." She paused, then gave me a sly grin. "You would have broken some hearts tonight in that outfit, Auren."

And probably would have sent Niall into a territorial frenzy.

Niall shifted uneasily beside me, and I stifled my grin.

"Now go find some place to lay low for the evening. My father will expect to see you before you depart tomorrow. I'll be in touch later." She prowled off, snagging a fluted beverage off a house-fae's serving tray as he crossed her path.

I turned around to the others. "Well, now what?"

Aremis bit his lip. "I think I have an idea. But first, we'll need another drink." He held up a finger, then briefly disappeared.

When he reappeared, he was holding a rather large bottle of what looked like sparkling white wine. Then, he ported the four of us to a lonely, dilapidated building that sat in silence in the middle of the desert.

Remic spun around slowly, assessing, then swept the grounds for threats while I looked up to the exposed sky above.

The building had either lost its roof long ago, or it never had one to begin with. And we were surrounded by nothing but sand for miles in all directions.

"Is this one of your secret hideouts?" Niall asked Aremis, dragging a fingertip along the edge of a waist-high sandstone wall.

"Yes and no. I used to come here when I needed to quiet my mind."

Remic returned to my side. "So, why bring us here now?"

Aremis shrugged and strolled along the cracked pavement, pausing over a damaged mosaic rendering of a god pointing a spear towards a sky strewn with constellations. He uncorked the bottle and let it breathe. "Because, no one ever comes here. As it is with all the ruined temples." He looked up at me. "This was a temple to Eryx, god of the sky and night. As a youngling, I couldn't sleep much, so when I failed to clear my mind or get the voices to stop whispering, I would come here and watch the stars shoot out across the desert. And my head would finally fall silent. I always felt that Eryx knew my struggle. Heard my pleas and offered me a bit of solace in return."

He took a long swig from the bottle. "I was the only one who ever visited—even when I was younger, so trust me, it's all ours." He scuffed his boot over the tip of the mosaic spear before lifting his gaze toward the bruised sky.

"Why is it in ruins?" I asked.

"It was simply abandoned due to its old age. The harsh desert sand and sun have no regard for nice things. The ruined temples in the other courts are all a result of Lyceius's wrath. His creatures destroyed many of them during Parradiom—the first war. They did it out of spite against the gods who didn't side with their cause. Loyal patrons tried repairing them, but morale was low then. Many just resorted to seeking out the gods in private, in fear that Lyceius would hunt them down personally if they were caught praying for his demise."

I frowned. "That's actually really sad."

Aremis passed me the bottle and nodded. "Benmoor was spared the brunt of the physical damages of each war because it lies the furthest from The Wastelands. But war takes its toll in other ways."

Thankfully I hadn't seen war in my short lifetime. The thought of living through any battle—especially one against Lyceius and his creatures was daunting enough.

I looked at the three males, each of them solemn-faced, as they either recalled memories, or were actively suppressing them. They had certainly seen more than I could ever imagine.

I sipped from the bottle. The slightly carbonated liquid fizzed in my mouth and tickled my taste buds. And because fae wine didn't affect me as it should, I savored another gulp.

The final moments of dusk crept over the shifting sands, and were quickly chased away by the night and its dark. The rising moon dusted the tops of the rolling dunes in a coat of dull, silver light.

Aremis pointed ahead toward an unknown location. "Make yourself comfortable, and keep an eye out in that general direction."

"What are we watching for, exactly?" I asked, peering off into the ever-growing darkness.

"You'll see," he said with a slight grin. He pushed his dark hair back and claimed a seat against a worn, broken pillar, like he had probably done hundreds of times in the past.

Niall took a seat on a waist-high stone wall and patted the area next to him as he looked over his shoulder at me.

I handed the bottle over to him and adjusted my dress carefully as I sat. "At least you won't have to worry about me in this ridiculous dress out in the public eye," I jested.

Niall frowned. "Shame. I was looking forward to incinerating at least a few males for laying their eyes on you."

I gasped. "You wouldn't!"

The corner of his mouth lifted up as he pressed the bottle to his lips and took a drink.

I elbowed him in the arm. "Choose my outfits more carefully next time then. No one needs to die for your lust-addled decisions."

He glanced sidelong at me before smiling fully, licking the wine off his lips. The motion sent flutters through my stomach, and made me want to lean over and take his tongue into my mouth. See if the sparkling wine tasted even sweeter from there than the bottle.

It didn't help that ever since I'd seen him outside my door dressed in his fine black and silver high-necked tunic, and pants that clung to every curve of muscle along his impressive thighs, I'd been thinking of taking it all off of him, piece by piece.

I rubbed my thighs together at the thought.

He noted the movement and continued smiling as he said into my mind, *Whose thoughts are lust-addled now?*

Don't even start, I thought back.

C'mon, tell me what you're thinking, he crooned.

I shot him a look, then narrowed my eyes, noting how his mouth had settled into a smug grin.

Two could play this game.

I glanced down and began rolling the gems and tassels on my belt between my fingers, the movement drawing his attention. *If you really must know, I was thinking about this dress. It's not really that ridiculous. It's actually kind of . . . elegant.*

My fingers drifted to the plunging neckline that bared the delicate space between my breasts, brushing along the slight swell of them. *The fabric is so light, it feels like I'm wearing nothing at all.* My internal voice became heady as I baited him with both my words and my hands. His eyes followed, darkening as he watched. *And*—I traced a line down my chest, then spread my hand across my thigh—*it's strategically designed.*

I slid my hand into the opening at my hip and slowly crept toward my center. *It helps with . . . all this heat.* I watched Niall's mouth part slightly, and knew my pun had landed perfectly as planned, because when he lifted his eyes to mine, they were smoldering.

His voice rumbled in my head. *Don't be a tease.*

I glanced back over my shoulder, ensuring that Remic and Aremis were still focused on the sky, then moved my fingers a bit further between my thighs. *Seems to me like you're enjoying it. What if I just . . .*

The moment my fingertips grazed my center, he reached out—quicker than a blink—and snatched my hand away. His voice rasped against my neck as he leaned in and said, "Darling, don't test my resolve, because I'm walking a very thin line."

I grinned and let out a quiet laugh. "I see what you meant when you said you like seeing me flustered. It *is* rather enjoyable."

He laughed and shook his head, then his face turned serious as he looked down at where he held my hand in his. "I apologize for you having to witness Lumeri out here, and not there." He nudged his chin out toward the desert, where the lights flickered like hundreds of small fires on the horizon. "I should have considered Killian's attendance. It's not like me to be so distracted."

"You don't need to apologize. Everyone makes mistakes."

His voice dropped low. "I don't."

"That's impossible."

He traced small circles on my palm with his finger, sending shivers up my arm. "I don't make mistakes because I refuse to be a High Lord who messes up or miscalculates. I have to plan for any possibility. I have to know moves before they're made. It only takes one mishap and an entire court can suffer for it."

I closed my fingers around his. "Niall, you're setting impossible standards for yourself."

He was quiet, but he didn't object.

I knew this wasn't about tactics and foresight. This was deeper. It was about his power, and his fear that if he wasn't ten steps ahead of everyone else, something would catch him off guard, and he would lose control. It was the control that he sought. Not of territories or courts, but of himself.

He sighed and spread his hand out to encompass mine, entwining our fingers. "Auren, there's still so much about me that you don't know. There's a side of me, of my power, that I'm reluctant to ever let you see. It's not because of who I am when I use it, it's because of what I feel when I do."

I studied him closely, glimpsing the apprehension in his expression as he continued staring down. "What do you feel when you use it?"

His lips parted ever so slightly, like the words were there—about to slip off the edge of his tongue, but his jaw tightened instead, and he swallowed whatever he'd been about to say.

"Niall?"

"You don't need to worry yourself with that," he finally said. "I have control over my power. I always have. My biggest fear now is that I could very easily lose control if something were to happen to you. The way you make me feel . . . my power would be irrepressible if it ever came to enacting vengeance for you."

I smiled softly. "Mmm, romantic."

"I'm serious." His hand came up to cup my cheek. "You are my awakening and my sweet destruction."

His eyes sparkled like golden moons over midnight waters as I met his stare. My face heated under his touch, and just as I leaned in to press my lips against his, a loud *pop* echoed across the desert and Niall's face lit up in bright green light.

I whipped my head around and looked up to see thousands of falling green sparks, twinkling on their descent to the ground. Then, a red fireball shot up into the air. I watched as it climbed higher and burst into a giant wheel of scarlet glitter, spilling down from the heavens like ruby jewels. The punctuating *pop* echoed across the sands with it.

I gasped in awe. "What are they?"

"They're fireworks," Niall said, watching me just as he did during Lumeri in Drastia.

Another light soared up, whirling in a stream of purple. Then several launched all at once, each bursting with glittering white light that fractured the blackened sky and rained down like falling stars.

I had never seen anything like fireworks. They were the embodiment of magic, and I smiled, committing each one to memory and basking in their dazzling light as more and more erupted.

Streams of golden yellow soared skyward, then burst, but this time, the sparks gathered into a formation and flew on the wind in the shape of an enormous raven.

More creatures made of sparks descended from the fireworks one by one, illuminating the desert in a stream of color as they danced among the stars, cracking the atmosphere as they came and went.

Niall's hand stayed steady in mine, his thumb rubbing lines back and forth across my wrist.

I stole a quick look over my shoulder at Remic and Aremis, who were silently watching the spectacle, their faces alight with each flash of color.

Not a second after I turned back, another stream of sparks blazed into the night. They ruptured, then coalesced, and the faces and bodies of two creatures with scaled skin, long spiked tails, and giant wings roared across the sky.

The Dreki. They twisted through the night before spreading their wings out and descending toward the sand, disappearing into it.

A trio of serpents followed, sparkling a brilliant shade of blue as they twined their way into the heavens then faded away on the breeze.

Then all went quiet.

I scanned the darkness, waiting . . .

Waiting . . .

A great *boom* shook the sands as an entire mass of fireworks launched all at once.

The finale, Niall said into my mind.

My eyes widened as the night *exploded* with color.

Hundreds upon hundreds of starbursts and swirling wheels of light lit the desert below. It was a beautiful mayhem, echoed by deep booms and trills that packed a punch in the air like a pulse.

As the spectacle reached its end, and the remnants of the last fireworks trickled down toward the sand, cheers echoed across the landscape. Smoke drifted on the breeze, rippling in gray waves through the atmosphere and peppering my nostrils with its astringent aroma.

Music began off in the distance, and I knew the revelry and celebrations were only just beginning. I looked at Niall, then back at Remic and Aremis, who actually seemed more content to be here, instead of out amongst everyone else.

"Best seat in the house, if I do say so myself," Aremis said, smiling through the silver light of the moon. "Did you enjoy it, Auren?"

"I loved every second. And this happens every year?"

Aremis nodded but looked at Niall a bit sadly. I followed his gaze to meet the High Lord's.

"Auren, this court and ours are not on good terms—to say the least," Niall said. "In my lifetime, I can count on one hand how many Lumeri events I've attended in Benmoor."

The previous joy died out in my throat. "Oh. Right."

Glad I committed those fireworks to memory then.

Aremis rose and walked over to us. "We don't come here often. But, if you want fireworks, Auren, we will bring fireworks to Calledan for you." He snagged the wine from Niall and took several long drinks, handing it off to Remic when he'd had his fill. "Now, if you'll excuse me, I believe I have a job to do." He took a bow at the waist.

"What are you going to do?" I asked.

He looked up, as if searching for Eryx. As if all the answers he'd ever sought were draped amongst the stars. Just out of reach.

His Aura flickered to life around him like a second skin, glimmering faintly in the moonlight, and the corner of his mouth tilted up as he answered. "What I'm best at. Espionage."

71

THE REVOLUTIONARY

BACK AT THE PALACE, I STAYED CONFINED TO MY CHAMBERS—AS ONE suffering from a supposed bout of food illness should be. If pressed for specifics, I'd blame it on that strange "customary drink" I'd barely sipped on when we arrived.

Remic stood guard outside, refusing to leave despite my insisting that he go relax or at least take a break and enjoy the celebration. Neither him nor Niall would leave me alone for more than a moment knowing Killian was somewhere on the palace grounds. And since Niall was making an appearance at the celebration so that Ramil wouldn't ask too many questions, and Aremis was still out dabbling in his "espionage," that meant Remic wasn't budging.

I had to admit, it was nice knowing he was just outside and that he wouldn't let anything happen to me.

I sat on the plush chair just inside from the patio, partially hidden behind the curtains, watching what looked to be fae nobles and courtiers as they stumbled throughout the lantern-lit courtyard below, laughing and sloshing their drinks.

When the door opened behind me, I twisted in my seat, expecting to find Niall, but it was Morah who swept into the room with a grin.

"Did Remic let you in?" I asked, surprised she didn't opt to just walk through a wall instead.

"He did. He's a handsome one."

I raised my brows at her.

"What? I like his hair."

I snorted a laugh. "His *hair?* I would have thought you'd say his wings."

"The wings are nice too." She slid into the chair across from me and pulled her long hair over her shoulder and began weaving it into a loose braid. "Did you enjoy the show?"

I stiffened, unsure if I should mention that I'd left the palace grounds after she'd told me not to. But when she lifted a knowing brow, I huffed a laugh and answered. "It was stunning. I wasn't expecting anything like that."

"I knew Aremis would take you to see it some way or another. He's always had a kind soul." Strangely, her voice sounded bitter as she said it, or maybe that was a tinge of regret.

"Are you two not on good terms?"

She picked at the hem of her dress. "We grew up together. Me—the daughter of the High Lord—and Aremis, his trusted *pet.* I used to call him a *pet* because that's how we treated him. I didn't know any better when I was young. I only did what my father told me. Acted how he taught me to act. Liked who I was told to like. My father used Aremis, ran him into the ground for his spying abilities. I didn't see it until later on in my years . . . when my father had my older brother taken away. I began seeing things in a whole new light then."

"You had a brother?"

"His name is Fallon."

Is.

"He's . . . still alive?"

"Yes. Though, no one speaks of him. Many have already forgotten he exists, either out of fear of my father's wrath or out of neglect."

"Oh."

A brief silence fell between us, leaving me feeling as if I might have journeyed into forbidden territory.

But then Morah lifted her eyes to the world beyond the patio, and explained. "When Fallon was barely in his third century, he began to lose his eyesight. The healers called it some kind of 'mystery disease'—a magical blight that took his eyes and stifled his magical abilities. Our father, of course, saw it as a weakness. But the healers were not entirely correct in their assessment. While his eyesight waned and eventually faded, his magic never disappeared, it *changed.* It grew into something stronger. The loss of his vision not only enhanced his other senses, it gained him new abilities. He began seeing things that his eyes could not."

"What do you mean?"

She shifted in her seat and looked at me. "He became a seer. Someone who sees far more than just what's in plain sight. It didn't happen all at once though. It started with elaborate dreams that spurred him into confiding in our father. When what Fallon saw in his dreams began coming to fruition, our father ordered the healers to study him further. Then the Elder got involved. Soon, the premonitions weren't just coming to him while he slept, they began to plague him while he was awake as well. He would rattle on warnings about things to come—no matter how great or small they might have been. And pretty soon others started to take notice.

"When he accurately foretold the end of the last war and the death of Killian's family, our father was suddenly rivaled for power. Who wouldn't want a High Lord that could see things to come? We would be a formidable court. A truly successful court. But our father was—and still is —too greedy to let the power pass to anyone else.

"Our court petitioned to have Fallon seated as co-regent alongside our father, so that we could benefit from his magic. But all our father saw was a threat to his throne. Funny thing is, my brother never wanted the throne." She grew quiet and began fiddling with her bracelets.

A hint of sorrow crossed her face before her voice grew cold and hateful. "My father poisoned my brother and locked him away. He keeps him under constant poisoning, just enough to subdue and sedate him, but not enough to kill him. Instead, the monster uses my brother's power, siphons it for himself. He uses it to fuel his own magic, giving the illusion that he's still powerful enough to retain his status. In truth, he holds most of his power through the fear he instills in those around him.

"But he can't have everything. While he can continue to siphon Fallon's power, he cannot gain any insight from him or use his magical ability to see things that are to come. The poison renders that ability useless. The only way our father could see *anything* other than what's right in front of him was through the Elders." She gave me a look, silently prompting me to connect the dots.

"Benmoor's Elder has long been missing . . ."

She nodded slowly, her eyes going dark. "My father used Fallon's power and stole the Alatyr from our Elder. With the Alatyr in his possession, my father has access to Old Magic without restraint. That's how he's been so successful in his endeavors.

"Aremis was the one who found Fallon many years ago on one of his spying missions for Niall. He's known where my brother is being kept and has checked up on him religiously." She lowered her eyes to the ground, suddenly looking more vulnerable than I'd ever seen her. "I will forever be in his debt for it. If it weren't for Aremis, I would have never known what happened to my brother. And if my father had his way, he'd make sure Fallon stayed dead to the world. Dead to me. The only thing that keeps my rage somewhat in check is that he's not awake or aware of any of it. He's not suffering, he's just in a suspended state. But I hope that will all change soon."

"Are you planning something?" I asked quietly.

A fierceness burned in her eyes as she met my stare, but her voice matched that of a murmur. "I may seem like the submissive daughter who goes along with my father's demands, but I'm actually far from that. There are many in this court who have not forgotten what he's done, and their allegiances lie silently with Fallon. I've been working carefully to seek each of them out. There's an alliance of those who would see my father cast out and Fallon reinstated as the rightful High Lord of Benmoor—as is his right. The problem is getting my father away from the Alatyr for long enough."

"What does the Alatyr have to do with it?"

"Whoever possesses the Alatyr is granted near-immortality."

"*Near?*"

"The wearer still ages, and will eventually die, but the stone extends life. That is why it's always passed on to an *Elder* and not someone in their prime. It's too tempting for someone to use it for the wrong reasons and reap the benefits while living out a long and full life. While it's in my father's possession, he could essentially live for thousands of years longer than he could without it. A tyrant's dream." She scoffed harshly, pressing her lips into a thin line. "All while my brother rots away in a cell, breathing in fumes."

"How long has he been kept that way?"

She was quiet for a moment before answering. "Eighty-eight years."

My throat constricted.

Eighty-eight years was more than a standard human lifetime.

"Morah, I'm so sorry. If there's anything I can do to help, please let me know." I wasn't sure what sort of help I could offer, but if it was my brother—if I was in her position . . .

My heart clenched at how she must feel; desperate for his liberation, but bound by patience and restraint in order to successfully see it through.

As much an internal war as it was external.

The curtains stirred on the breeze, and she followed the movement with her eyes, caught in her thoughts and her gathering fury. "Can I ask you something?"

"Of course."

"How often do you pray to the gods for help, and none comes?"

Realization suddenly dawned on me that the gods had been just as silent to her as they had to me, but she didn't give me the time to answer before she continued.

"I've begged and pleaded to the gods for help more times than I can count, and none have answered. Yet here you sit, and you willingly offer your help."

"I'm not a god," I quickly corrected her.

"You have Karios's blood in your veins. You're as close to divine as the gods themselves."

She was always quick to remind me of the bigger picture of my fate— something that tugged at my soul a little more each time she spoke of it. Nevertheless, the word *divine* was still hard to digest.

She reached out and touched my hand. "I'm grateful for the offer, but you're already helping in a far greater way. You're here to fulfill the prophecy and undo a greater evil. For now, let *me* help *you*."

I smiled. "All right."

She gave my hand a squeeze before letting go and sinking back against her chair.

"Thank you for telling me about everything," I said. "For trusting me."

"Don't get all sappy on me now." She smirked.

I let out a laugh. "Right. I forget you're more of the stab first, apologize later type, so I guess that means sentiments are lost on you."

She laughed as well. "Damn right. And just so you know, Aremis and I still have some tensions to work out from our youth. It's hard to let old habits die. We're in a better place now than we were. He just doesn't fully trust me—yet. But when he sees the extent of what I've been able to amass underneath my father's heavy thumb, I think he'll change his mind."

I hoped he would—for all our sakes.

I'd only known Morah for a brief moment in time compared to everyone else, but what I'd come to know of her was that she was devoted, and her will was just as fierce as her heart; something I believed Aremis would hold in high regard.

The courtyard outside fell quiet as courtiers and their lovers found themselves in darkened corners or disappeared to their own secluded chambers.

I turned toward Morah and propped my chin on my fist as I leaned onto the armrest. "I never asked, what exactly does your magic allow you to do—besides sneak up on people and go through walls?"

She shrugged her shoulders. "I guess you could say it's similar to that of a wraith. Not in body or spirit though. I'm fully fae, but my magic manifested in a unique way that allows me to embody a wraith-like existence on command. That's how I'm able to move through physical obstacles. It also grants me incredible speed. Growing up, my trainers said they'd never seen anyone move as fast as me. Not even a Cheshm Zadan."

Now *that* was hard to believe.

"I've seen Aremis in training," I said. "He's wickedly fast."

She smiled, showing her teeth. "I'm faster."

A knock sounded at the door, and Morah had a dagger in her hand quicker than I could glimpse. When she saw my look of surprise, she smirked. "Told you. Faster."

The door opened, and Niall sauntered in like he owned the place. "Hello, beautiful," he said, walking straight toward me. "Miss me?"

Morah answered before I could. "I don't think you leave her side long enough for her to actually miss you." She gave him a playful smile, then tossed me a wink.

I couldn't help but laugh. "Morah and I were just finishing a very deep conversation."

"Were you now?" He eyed the both of us.

Morah nodded, twirling the small blade between her fingers twice before it disappeared from her hand. "Yes. And now that you're here, I have some news for you both. My father announced tonight that he will be hosting a betrothal celebration in honor of Killian and I." She sneered at the words. "It will be in a month's time, but I just wanted you to be prepared. I'm not thrilled, as you may have guessed. And I have a lot of work to do on my end because I have some plans for that Woodland bastard."

Niall nodded. "Thank you for the update." His tone suggested that he was already privy to the information—courtesy of Aremis.

She pursed her lips, catching his implication, then tossed me a smile on her way to the door. "I'll see you soon," she said.

Niall stepped closer as the door closed. I took his hands in mine, and we stood there, facing each other, letting ourselves have a moment.

"Don't try anything, darling, neither of us want to lose control in a place like this."

"I won't try anything. I just want . . ."

I looked down at our hands. I hadn't realized how much I craved them in mine. How the touch of his skin ignited something in me that I had never known before. How my power called to him every waking moment.

I wanted him. Wanted to feel his lips on mine.

I didn't want to resist anymore.

"Those thoughts will get you in trouble," he cautioned me.

"Why?" I said, looking up at him.

"Because"—he stepped closer—"they're an exact mirror to mine." He leaned down to my neck, brushing his lips along my pulse. "But it's risky," he murmured. "If one of us were to lose control . . ."

His hands left mine and slid around my hips to grip my backside.

A small sound escaped my lips—caught between a moan and a gentle laugh, as he squeezed my flesh in his grip and hoisted me up around his waist. I could feel the evidence of his desire as he pressed himself between my legs.

Gods . . .

I wrapped my arms around his neck, plunging my hands into his hair as he crushed his lips onto mine and spun us toward the bed. His knees found the mattress and he laid me down upon it, climbing over me. Strong, calloused hands ran down the length of my body, finding no resistance from the barely-there dress I still wore.

I mindlessly pressed my hips up to his, grinding with need, heat gathering at my core. He growled and pushed back against me, moving his mouth to the sensitive spot under my jaw.

How can he do this and expect me to abstain?

"Stop warning me against doing things that you yourself can't keep from doing," I scolded him, tilting my head back to soak up every smoldering brand he left on my skin.

"Can't help it," he breathed, claiming my lips once more, spreading them open again with his tongue and angling his head to take what he craved.

The heat between us built, but he kept his hands above my waist, leashing himself with one final nip along my bottom lip.

A growl left his throat as he tipped his head back and said, "This is torture."

I glanced down between us at where he strained over me. "You did this to yourself, I was perfectly well-behaved until you kissed me."

He let out a small chuckle, then fell silent as he stared down at me, his golden eyes brimming with desire and . . . something deeper. More vulnerable.

"Niall?" I asked, searching his face for an indication of what he was thinking.

"You're beautiful," he whispered.

My pulse fluttered, and I couldn't hide the smile that spread across my kiss-swollen lips. I wanted to bask in his gaze and stare into those golden eyes until time stopped.

The planes of his face, the stubble that lined his cheeks and jaw, the way his mouth tipped up at the corner, giving away his emotions . . .

"So are you," I murmured.

I could feel his heart pounding through his chest like it was trying to escape and merge with mine. I'd gladly welcome it. Give it a home within the confines of my own, tuck it safely away next to my soul.

His hand brushed the side of my face, tracing a line along my cheekbone to my jaw with the gentlest touch. "You make me feel alive."

The words landed with a weight I didn't expect.

They *baffled* me.

He'd lived hundreds of years, seen multiple lifetimes worth of all that this world had to offer, and yet *I* made him feel alive?

As if he could sense my unspoken question, the corner of his mouth lifted, and he took my hand, placing it between us against his throbbing heart. "Feel that?"

I nodded, spreading my fingers out to try to encompass the breadth of each heavy beat.

"No one has ever made me feel this way. No one has ever had such a power over me that I lose myself and can't think straight."

I closed my eyes, letting my breaths fall into sync with his, memorizing the feel of his pulse against my palm.

He pressed his forehead to mine. "And despite the fact that I can't think straight"—he let out a light laugh—"you bring me a peace I've never known."

The words tugged deeply at my heartstrings. Because I felt that with him too. "You sure you can't read my mind?" I murmured.

His deep chuckle rumbled through his chest as he lifted himself off of me. I raised a suspicious brow at him when he didn't answer my question, but he distracted me by reaching into his magical pocket of thin air.

I quickly sat up, eager to see what he would bring forth. When he pulled out a folded set of silky night clothes and handed them to me, I smiled. "Always so thoughtful."

He pointed at me, smirking. "No more teasing. Put these on *after* I leave."

I pouted, earning a full laugh from him.

"I'll be here to wake you in the morning. We'll leave at dawn."

"All right," I said.

He strode to the door, but halted just before he reached it. "Auren . . ." He turned back to look at me. "Thank you for coming with me."

As he slipped out, I smiled again, clutching my hand to my chest, the phantom pulse of his heart still beating against my palm.

72
A GIFT FROM THE SEIDR

NIALL'S HEARTFELT WORDS ECHOED IN MY DREAM.

No one has ever made me feel this way.

You bring me a peace I've never known.

I dreamt I was floating among the stars, surrounded by a feeling of overwhelming happiness. Elation was coursing through me, warming me like sunlight on my skin, while ribbons of color danced in my peripheral vision. And there, standing in front of me, was Niall. His piercing eyes of golden honey seemed to gaze into my soul, as if seeing me again for the first time, seeing all the parts of me that were just like him. He stared like I was a treasure that he had lost long ago, and found again at last.

Then he smiled.

I awoke feeling a sense of rightness. And for some reason, I couldn't shake the memory of the dream. It planted itself in my mind like a core memory, and all I could do was replay the way Niall had looked at me and smiled.

After obliging Ramil's summons and enduring a very long and scrutinizing stare from Ferhan, the High Lord of Benmoor offered condolences, wishing me a speedy recovery from the sudden "illness" I'd been plagued with. Whether or not he truly believed our ruse—I didn't care. All I wanted to do was return to the mountains.

Once my boots were back on Calledan stone, I breathed a sigh of relief.

My training session with Roirdan wasn't supposed to start until after mid-day, but I arrived early. I needed to work through some things, and think. Swinging a sword always seemed to help with that.

The sun wasn't even halfway up in the sky when I ventured out to the main patio of The Keep, blade in hand. I practiced my maneuvers and parried against invisible opponents, while sifting through my thoughts one by one, replaying the conversations I'd had with Niall and Morah last night.

Morah was leading a double life in hopes of saving her brother and righting the wrongs of her court, while Niall was waging an internal war with himself.

Both fought their battles silently.

Neither would ever ask for help.

But all of it would be for nothing, so long as the greater threat of Lyceius loomed.

I didn't know how the prophecy would unfold, but I couldn't just stand by in denial. Not when Morah continued to risk more than just her own fate with her endeavors. Not after Niall held my face in his hands and told me I was his source of peace.

I paused, holding my sword in mid-air, listening to the blade hum against the friction of the wind.

Niall's words had taken root alongside my heart and ignited something in me.

And now, a seed was sprouting.

What I'd learned had given me a newfound sense of focus and determination. I was ready to embrace my power and the tasks ahead—even without knowing exactly what they would be.

I would do it for Niall.

For Morah and Maeson. For the Trium.

For Breck.

Because all their hopes and dreams—their very lives—ultimately rested in my hands.

And I would not let evil prevail.

Roirdan arrived to find me drenched in sweat with a smile plastered on my face. His answering grin told me he understood that sometimes the best place to contemplate life decisions was in the throes of training.

We practiced for most of the afternoon while Niall and Aremis conducted meetings. Then, later that evening, we all dined together on the small breakfast patio under the stars.

As I sat back in my chair and looked at everyone around the table, time seemed to stand still. There was conversation, and laughter, and the scraping and clinking of silverware against plates; all the sounds of merriment and . . .

Family.

That's what this was.

And I was the newest addition. Technically, so was Maeson, but she had known these males for years. I would have thought she had always been a permanent part of this group—if I hadn't met her before. She was so at ease here. Thriving, just like I said she would.

But strangely, I was at ease too, considering I hadn't sat for an intimate dinner like this—and felt content about it—since my parents died. In fact, Liam and I never sat at our family table again after that fateful day. We'd take our meals at the low table in front of our small sofa, or outside near his workshop, on top of a splintered table full of saws and chisels. But never again did we sit at that family table. There were too many memories there—my mother trying over and over to teach me how to roll bread dough the correct way, my father cleaning and polishing his sword until it shined like new, the four of us talking over a meal and recounting our days' worth of training and work, and birthdays and holidays, full of pie, and vanilla butter cake, and laughter.

Then there was the image of that table flipped on its side, my parents' lifeless bodies bracketing each end of it.

I allowed myself to glance at that memory one last time, to feel the ache of it . . . and then let it go. Because that torn piece of my heart was being mended. Stitched back together with every laugh and grin I witnessed around the table I now sat at.

I never thought I'd sit for another family meal—let alone enjoy it. But now, I smiled.

This felt like home.

And it further solidified the decision I'd made earlier.

When we were finished, Niall and I wandered off alone and found ourselves in the main area of The Keep. The room was quiet, and beams of silver moonlight shone through the tall windows, swirling with the soft golden glow of the fire and the multitude of sconces that lined the dark stone walls.

We picked a plush leather sofa, and settled into it together. I reached into my magical pocket and pulled out Evander's journal.

"Someone's been practicing," Niall said, watching my movements.

I had indeed. It had taken me multiple tries to figure it out after Niall explained it to me, but eventually, I reached out, and my hand had disappeared into the space I'd envisioned.

Now, it was a secret space that housed the dagger Roirdan gifted me, Evander's journal, a spare change of clothes, and something else that I'd been saving in case I needed it . . .

"We could use more light," I suggested. Niall held up his hand, but I caught it in mine before he could summon anything. "No. Wait." With my other hand, I reached back into the pocket in space and brought forth a small candlestick.

Niall's brows furrowed in confusion. "Where did you get that?"

I giggled to myself. "When you abandoned your lantern at Lumeri in Drastia. I wanted to see if I could master the magical pocket thing."

Niall threw his head back and laughed. "You stowed it away?"

"Not at that moment. But later that night, yes."

"You have a habit of staying up late, don't you?"

"I feel most productive at night," I said proudly, twirling the candle in my hand like I would a dagger. "The first time I figured out I'd been successful I was half worried that it would end up somewhere I'd never find it."

"I'm proud of you." Niall smiled softly. "Now, let me enchant the wax so that it never runs out." He waved a hand over it, springing a flame to life. It flared and burned brightly, but the wax stayed solid with no sign of melting. "There. Now you shall never be without light."

"Like I'm not already a walking candlestick when I get riled up." I laughed. "Not to mention every time you touch me. It takes all that I have not to glow at the slightest—" My breath caught as his hand moved, sliding smoothly under the journal to grope my thigh.

"Want to test that theory?" he said, leaning closer.

I closed my eyes and savored his touch, feeling the heat of his palm through my leggings. Unable to help myself, I reached over and gripped his shirt with both my hands to pull him in for a kiss.

When he went completely still, panic sparked in my gut, and my eyes flew open. "What's wrong?" I asked, but he was looking past me.

I turned to see what he was staring at and saw the candle floating in mid-air behind me. I half laughed. "Are you expecting a *thank you* for enchanting it?"

"No," he drawled. "I enchanted the *wax*. The fact that it's *floating* is not my doing."

My smile fell.

I turned back to the candle then looked down at my hands, realizing his implication. I was obviously no longer holding it, yet it remained in the air. "There's no . . . I can't . . ." I couldn't form words.

"Apparently you can. But how?"

I stared at the candle in disbelief. "I-I don't know. I just let go of it and reached for you. I guess I just had the thought that I wanted it to stay where it was, and then it just . . . stayed."

"So, you just thought it, and it happened?"

"Is something like that even possible?"

He chewed his bottom lip as he studied me, then his eyes sparked with an idea, and he looked down between us. I followed his stare just as he grabbed the journal by its binding and hurled it across the room toward the fireplace.

I let out a gasp and started for it, reaching out, but his arm wrapped around my waist and held me against the sofa. Still, my outstretched hand beckoned, and suddenly, the book halted—less than a foot away from plunging into the fire—and retreated back toward me.

I caught it, and stared in shock.

Niall's hands were suddenly on either side of my face pulling my gaze to his. "You have a gift from the *Seidr*," he said as his eyes darted back and forth between mine.

"The *Seidr* is a book," I replied, confused.

"It is, but the *word Seidr* means Old Magic. This magic is something that's been lost for thousands of years. But somehow, it seems to have re-emerged in you."

A re-emergence of things of old.

"Every fae can do simple acts of small magic. But to influence an object the way you just did? To bend it to your will on a thought? That's the Old Ways." He studied me in awe, thumbs grazing up and down my cheeks. "I bet you could break wards if you wished."

I forced myself to breathe in and out. "But I'm not fae."

"No. But you have Karios's blood."

My stomach knotted with a sudden burst of anxiety. "Maybe we should go see the Elder?"

"We can go see Amarna about it another time. Right now, I just want to look at you."

His words sent my chest aflutter. "Why?"

"Because you never cease to amaze me," he said softly.

The candle flickered behind me, sending shadows dancing across the planes of Niall's remarkably handsome face.

He pulled me into his chest, and I sank into his embrace. We sat that way for several long minutes before he spoke again. "Don't let all of this overwhelm you. We came here to read tonight. We can focus on your newfound ability tomorrow. All right?"

He reached for the journal, and I nodded, struggling to quiet my mind. But he was right. We came here intent on delving deeper into the journal —for both our sakes.

I settled in under his arm and flipped to the entry we'd left off on. At the top of the page was a short memo, written by a different hand. While the penmanship was not as refined as Evander's, it was still legible.

"Verdi's handwriting," Niall confirmed.

The High Lord has fallen ill today.

This marks the second time this week that we have not been able to cure his pains. He complains of a pounding in his head, and pain that shoots throughout his limbs. When the bouts of pain surge, he often falls into a fit of rage. It is as if his power is growing too strong for his body to handle. It baffles me that one day he is fine, and the next he is caught in this torture.

I will update more in a day's time.

The following entry was another update from Verdi. He noted that he had given Evander a sleeping draught to induce a long sleep, in hopes that the High Lord's body would return to normal.

The next entry was dated several days later, and was in Evander's script.

These past few days have been rough. Though, I do not remember the latter part of them. Verdi, gods bless him, concocted a substance that would help me sleep off the bouts of pain. It is not the pain that bothers me so much as the other thing that plagues me. The rage. This incessant feeling of wrath that overtakes me. I feel it deep in my bones. Like my power is surging beyond my capabilities, begging for release. Verdi thinks that I should try to expel some of the built-up tension when I feel it coming on, but I fear what could happen. I am afraid to admit that I do not feel fully in control of myself anymore. It terrifies me that I don't even know what is causing this. I have no explanation other than my magic is manifesting into something else. There is no record of any ancestor of mine experiencing such things.

Thus, I am alone in this. And I am even more afraid to be alone with my own thoughts on the matter.

I looked up at Niall. "Have you ever had any of these pains?"

He scrubbed over the stubble on his chin and cheeks. "I vaguely remember having what Verdi called 'growing pains' when I was young. I would lay in bed and whine about them. Verdi used to smack my arm and tell me to keep my tears in—that little lords don't show weakness. I eventually grew out of them. But I don't remember getting any sort of head pains."

"Hmm." I turned to the next entry. It was dated one month after the last, the greatest stretch of time between them so far.

> *I have begun a new training regimen.*
>
> *Verdi and I agree that the recent experiences have something to do with my power. Where it should be waning in my age, it is ramping back up instead. But it feels different than it has my entire life. It feels uncontrollable. So, Verdi has developed a routine for me to do every day that seems to be helping keep the symptoms that plague me at bay. We do not know what to expect, but trial and error is better than nothing.*
>
> *I begin the day with a form of meditation, where I focus on my heartbeat and hone in on my power. Then twice a day, we port to the dungeons, and I focus on gently expelling a bit of my shadowfire by funneling it into a pyre at the bottom of the pit. It seems to help calm the burning in my veins.*
>
> *I am hopeful that this regimen will be good for me. I do not like having to cut my duties at court short when I feel one of my bouts coming on. But it is necessary.*

Niall spoke first this time. "Verdi would take me to the temple ruins on the other side of Calledan when I was young. He had me focus my shadowfire on the charred pillars there. Told me I was learning 'precision.' Perhaps he was making sure I had a proper outlet as my power grew, so that I didn't run the risk of *it* outgrowing *me.*"

"That would make sense."

"We should stop there," he said. "Tomorrow is going to be a long day now that we have your new ability to focus on."

I yawned as I nodded, closing the journal.

The candle snuffed out on its own as I plucked it from the air, and I was careful to slide it back inside my magical stash to the same spot it had been before.

Niall grinned. "I can't believe you snatched that up in Drastia. What else do you keep hidden away in that pocket of yours?"

"You'll never know," I said, pushing myself up and instantly missing his embrace.

Back in my chambers, I sat in the center of my bed testing everything I could with my newfound ability: the robe on the sofa, the pillows, even Sorscha. Everything was fair game. When I had managed to lift one of Sorscha's feet with a magical thought, she squealed and skittered behind the bathing chamber door.

Niall's voice cut into my mind a split second later. *I knew you wouldn't be able to sleep.*

I don't know what you're talking about, I lied.

You might as well be shouting it across our minds. I know what you're doing. His throaty chuckle echoed in my head. *You should be sleeping. Quit using your magic, or you'll wear yourself out before tomorrow.*

I blew out a breath in annoyance. *How do you expect me to just put this off until then?*

Another deep chuckle. *If you're dragging during training, it'll be your own fault.*

I crossed my arms and fell back against my pillow dramatically. *I can't shut my mind off. How am I supposed to sleep?*

As if summoned, Niall's shadows gathered at the foot of my bed. *I can help with that,* he said, voice deepening, caressing my mind as a smoky tendril reached toward me.

I summoned my newly discovered ability and sent a pillow hurtling into the wispy mass.

His laugh danced through my consciousness. *Get some sleep, feisty little thing.*

I harrumphed and crawled under the blankets, watching the lingering shadows. They moved and lifted the blankets over me, tucking me in, and a tendril reached up and brushed my cheek gently before disappearing.

I smiled to myself and sank into the sheets, hoping sleep would claim me quickly.

It did.

73
THE MESSENGER

THE FOLLOWING DAY, I TRAINED LONG AND HARD, UNTIL SLEEP CLAIMED me once more.

And before I knew it, two weeks had passed.

I'd spent each day in weapons training with the Trium, and then focused on my power and light with Niall each evening. By nightfall, I would crash into bed and sleep like I hadn't in days.

But it felt good. My skills were sharpening, and my gifted ability —*telekinesis*, as Niall called it—was growing, along with the control over my power. I was able to dig a little deeper, and use a little more of it each day, and each morning I woke with more stamina.

The interim moments where Niall and I were together had been much more difficult. I was constantly wanting to put my hands on him, and he was endlessly teasing me through our private mind conversations while out in public.

It was growing harder to rein myself in. There was no doubt that my feelings for him had taken root, and were threatening to bloom for all to see. At one point I even had the nerve to ask him if I could take lessons in controlling my need for *him* instead of controlling my power. That night ended up with both of us almost losing control in the middle of dinner. Thank the gods for his shadows. They had saved our composure more than once.

Niall was somehow managing to stifle his need, but I could see that he

575

was getting closer to unraveling at the seams as the days went on. And I was sure he was also wondering what Amarna had meant when she said, *You'll know when the time is right.*

Today, we were on edge again.

After spending a day out in The Elderwood with Niall, my frustration had peaked. He could feel it too—which made him even more on edge.

But a messenger had arrived mere minutes ago, and Niall had called a meeting. Now, we sat across from each other in The Keep's meeting room, me wringing my hands together in my lap, him staring daggers of desire into my soul.

I shifted in my seat as we waited.

Damn those golden eyes.

The tension abated as the doors opened and the Trium entered, followed by a fae male whom I had not yet met. He was dressed rather inconspicuously, and he only lowered his dark hood once he was seated between Roirdan and Aremis.

A shield fell over the room, keeping all that was spoken within it for our ears only.

Niall nodded to the male. "I'm glad to see you are well, Folquin."

"I am, my lord. The fates have been good to me. However, things in the north . . ." He reached into the folds of his cloak and retrieved a small ink quill, proceeding to twirl it in his fingers as he rested his hand on the tabletop.

I watched the odd move—which must have been a habit of his—then studied him. He had brassy hair, shorter on the sides and a bit longer on top, feathering this way and that, and his face was peppered with a light dusting of facial hair that he kept neatly trimmed. He looked young but spoke like someone much older, his voice steady and sure.

"I'm afraid I come with news that you might not like to hear," he said.

A messenger, then.

Roirdan kicked a leg up on the table. "When have you ever brought us good news, Folq? No offense."

"None taken. I only wish I could bring you something a little more fortunate for once." He looked at me and gave me a friendly smile, so I shared one back.

"What news?" Aremis inquired.

"I'm afraid it concerns the lady," Folquin said, glancing at me again.

Niall frowned. "Figured as much."

"Lord Killian journeyed to Salterra the night before last." The room stiffened. "And Ramil was with him."

"Any sign of the king or the prince?" Niall asked.

"No. The king has kept to his castle, and the prince has been absent for several days. We assume he's either in meetings, or perhaps staying out of the public eye."

Aremis ran his hands through his hair and sat back in his chair.

Folquin continued, but this time, he spoke to me. "Ramil seems to have figured out that you're not who you claim to be, and believes that Niall snatched you away for himself, for your power."

Niall scoffed. "It's not like I'm keeping her here against her will. Am I, darling?"

"I do recall asking *many* times to return to The Veil," I answered, throwing him a wink.

His mouth lifted in a smirk. "It's far too late for that." He sent a lick of shadows into my mind as he spoke, just to get a rise out of me. I bristled, then shot my essence back at him, caressing seductively up against his. He shifted in his seat across the table and tilted his head, giving me a look that warned against testing his desire.

I grinned and pushed a thought back his way. *Serves you right.*

Aremis cleared his throat, suppressing his smile, and I looked up to see that the rest of the room was now staring at our awkward, silent conversation.

Folquin's eyes darted between all of us. "Also, I'm afraid Ramil has brought those suspicions out into the open. And I think we can safely say that both him and Killian are in league with Lyceius. What they stand to gain from it—I'm not sure. I wasn't able to hear the details of their conversation once they slipped behind their shield."

I glanced back and forth at everyone at the table as they took in the news.

"And there's more," Folquin added. "Lyceius hasn't manifested in physical form in quite some time. But for this meeting, he did."

Aremis straightened. "He's gaining strength. How?"

"Time, I'm afraid. He's been using it well, building his armies, reserving his power."

Roirdan—who'd been spinning his dagger between his fingers—looked up and said, "Then it won't be long before he makes another move."

Remic chimed in from next to me. "And we can assume he's now aware of Auren's existence and whereabouts."

Folquin nodded grimly.

Feeling unsettled, I crossed my arms over my chest, and stared at the new male. "How do you know all of this?"

Niall answered before Folquin could. "He's one of my most trusted eyes and ears."

"But how are you able to be in Lyceius's presence without him noticing you?" I pressed, still directing my question at the messenger, squinting at him like I could see inside him if I looked hard enough.

Folquin's quill twirling halted. He hesitated, then answered. "I'm a shifter, my lady." He dipped his head, as if shifters were frowned upon, as if he was ashamed of his ability.

Confused, I looked to Niall, who offered an explanation. "Shifters aren't tolerated very well in certain parts of this realm. Their gift allows them to change shape or species when they want to—oftentimes to more than one type of being or creature. To many, that makes them untrustworthy and unpredictable."

"Oh."

"But he makes a pretty convincing human," Niall added. "He even serves in the castle from time to time—as needed."

I nearly came out of my seat at that bit of information.

"The castle?" I whipped my head to Folquin. "Have you been there *recently?*"

Folquin nodded. "I have."

"Have you heard any word of a man named Weston?"

He perked up. "Weston? Of the Queen's Guard? Yes, he is quite well. In fact, I spoke with him not too long ago."

I was instantly confused. "The *Queen's* Guard?"

"Weston is Queen Corinne's most trusted guard. Been serving her since she was crowned."

I paused and digested that bit of information.

I'd just assumed the King's Guard was meant to protect the *entire* royal family. I hadn't known the queen had her own protectorate aside from that. And the fact that Weston was her most trusted, begged the question: why would she send him to be *my* escort?

And why, then, would he want me to go to The Veil?

Across the table, Aremis looked to be wondering the same thing.

"And have you by chance heard any word about my brother, Liam Everton?" I asked.

Folquin shook his head. "No, I cannot say that I have."

I knew the odds were slim, but it was worth asking. Perhaps it was a good thing. The further away my brother stayed from the king and the prince, the better.

The room grew quiet for a long moment.

Roirdan lifted his foot off the table and leaned forward, laying his dagger on the stone, and steepling his fingers in front of him. "What's our move?"

Niall's focus had gone distant. He was plotting and planning as he always did. Making moves before our enemies had the chance.

"Remic, I want you to check in with our border detail daily. I need updated numbers and intel from our outposts. Folquin, keep an eye on the north, and on Killian. If he so much as lifts a finger in Lyceius's name, I want to hear about it. Roirdan, I want the army put on standby. Nothing to cause panic, but I want them to be prepared to muster—should we receive any other information. I'll continue training with Auren in the meantime."

Roirdan and Remic gave stern nods.

Niall looked at his second in command. "Aremis, I'm sending you to Vahrenhall. Vanir needs to be informed and kept in the know from this point forward. If we're to face a rising threat from Lyceius anytime soon, we'll need the support from both his militias."

"And what of Drastia?" Aremis asked.

"Leave that to Vanir. He'll know what to tell Laurent and what to leave out regarding Auren. I trust Laurent to an extent, but he's too keen on making nice with everyone—including Ramil—and we need to keep this contained for as long as we can."

Aremis leveled his eyes at him. "Word will get to him eventually, and he'll be hurt that he didn't know beforehand."

"I know. But we'll cross that bridge when the time comes."

"What good does it do if Lyceius already knows about me?" I asked.

Niall's piercing stare fell on me. "He may know *about* you, but he knows nothing of what you're capable of. We do. And that's to our advantage."

74
A HINT OF DARKNESS

ANOTHER WEEK PASSED BY, AND I HAD HARDLY SEEN NIALL.

Ever since Folquin had come bearing the inevitable news, Niall had been in and out of meetings with Roirdan and the Mountain Court's army. When he wasn't out speaking with scouts and captains about training and patrols, he was holding small council meetings with some of the court officials who oversaw the inner workings of Calledan.

Between all those meetings, our training sessions were short and sweet, always leaving both of us itching to steal a kiss or get our hands on one another.

I was getting fed up with the separation.

I felt like I had a rather good grasp on my power now that I'd spent time training and controlling it, and I truly believed I wouldn't slip up. But I reined in my feelings and recalled Amarna's words yet again: *You'll know when the time is right.*

But how would we know? Would it be a feeling?

Perhaps I should have asked those questions when I had the chance. Now, all they seemed to do was rattle around in my head like they could shake apart my resolve if they tried hard enough.

You'll just know, I repeated to myself. *And you won't have to question it.*

While Niall was occupied, I practiced my special ability wherever I could. I made sure to test it on a multitude of things that varied in size and weight. Strangely, the bigger, less complicated movements like hurling a small boulder through the air were no problem. But things like lifting a glass of water and bringing it to my hand from across the room without spilling took some practice. Placing a quill back in the inkwell was another particularly challenging feat. The small things required more control.

And control was key.

I often followed Maeson out to her cabin and practiced in the wooded area nearby, lifting rocks and focusing them at certain targets while Wrynn wagged her tail and watched curiously.

As I progressed, I began practicing at the temple ruins with Aremis. He had built padded torsos shaped like men, and mounted them to wooden posts specifically for this part of my training. With just a thought, I sent daggers and spears through the air at them, each one finding their mark.

Growing up, I was trained to inflict damage and defend myself at an arm's distance.

Now, I was becoming proficient in striking targets at least ten feet away without having to even lift a finger. I didn't even need to carry a weapon of my own when every object around me had become one.

And what surprised me even more was how good I was at it. It felt like something I had always been able to do. Like muscle memory. A skill that I hadn't used in a long time, but was easily rekindled when called upon.

I worked with weapons that were laid out along the floor in random placements, some a foot away, others ten feet away.

What I was most proud of though, was when I was able to sneak Aremis's personal blade from the sheath at his hip. Of course, he snatched it out of the air before I had a chance to send it across the pavilion into the heart of a wooden man, but I marveled at my accomplishment nonetheless.

"You're already becoming a little menace," he'd said, laughing.

Today was different though. Instead of being woken by the orb that liked to devote its time to leading me around and alerting me when it was morning, I was woken by a weight that sank onto the bed next to me. Something light and wispy caressed my cheek, and I leaned into its touch. Then, my eyes flew open to see Niall sitting at my side, a tendril of his shadowfire hovering near my face.

My chest kicked up its thrumming.

"There she is." He spoke low, seeming to admire my sleep-crusted eyes as I blinked him into focus and stretched out my legs beneath the covers.

"Here I am." I half-yawned. "What time is it?"

"Time for you to go put on something warm and join me for a morning treat."

I cocked my head on my pillow. "What kind of treat? And you have the time? You've been so busy lately."

He let out a small chuckle. "One I think you'll be very fond of. And I'm making the time. I apologize that my duties have required so much of me lately. Let me make it up to you."

He stood and walked to my armoire and pulled out a thick cowl-necked sweater and a pair of suede leggings, then laid my cloak on top of them at the foot of the bed. "It's rather chilly this morning, so I suggest this." He gestured to the ensemble he had chosen.

I grinned.

More doting.

"What?" he questioned.

"Nothing." I shook my head, letting my grin spread. "You're probably just the most thoughtful male I've ever known."

He lifted a brow at me and stepped back, leaning a casual shoulder on the armoire. "Is that a bad thing?"

"No, not at all. It's refreshing," I replied.

"Good. You deserve nothing less."

I glanced back up at him. His face was serious.

"I mean it, Auren. Anyone who gives you less is not worthy of you."

His way with words always made me feel like I was a queen, when all I had ever been was myself.

He squinted across the room like he knew what I was thinking. "You don't believe you're worthy of that?"

I lifted my shoulder in a half-shrug. "I've just never been shown the difference."

He studied me for a long moment, and I could feel something like awe tip-toeing its way into my mind from his.

I crawled toward the end of the bed and leaned over to grab the clothes, pulling them with me as I sank back onto my heels.

I knew I shouldn't tease him, shouldn't dangle myself in front of him when we were both so sexually tense, but I found myself lifting the hem of the nightgown, ignoring my better judgment. As I shifted my weight to slip the material over my hips and up toward my waist, Niall went incredibly still. Slowly, I raised the delicate fabric higher, past my ribs, and his eyes followed my hands with deadly precision. I continued past my breasts and took my time lifting the gown over my head, letting my long hair spill over my bare shoulders.

His heated gaze tiptoed along my skin, but I didn't flinch. I liked the way he looked at me as if I was the only woman he'd ever seen or ever cared to see. It made a sweet lick of desire curl low in my core.

I reached for the sweater, and Niall strained, as if he was holding his breath.

One at a time, I slid my arms through the openings, waiting for him to object.

A muscle feathered in his jaw.

When he remained still, I lifted the sweater over my head to pull it on, but the moment it briefly covered my face, the air shifted around me. When I emerged, he stood at the side of the bed, eyes like molten honey pinning me in place.

I turned to face him fully and let my arms fall down at my sides, waiting. The tension between us could be released in one of two ways. We would either leash our emotions like we had been, or we'd give in.

Just a little, I hoped.

His hands trembled slightly as he pushed the hair back over my shoulders. It was a gentle touch, but I knew that deep inside his emotions were raging like a storm. He looked as if he wanted to fist my hair and make me submit to his every whim. I would've expected that from a male like him.

The gentle side of him was something that he claimed only *I* had seen. Something he didn't let others know existed. But part of me wanted to see that darker side of him. The side I glimpsed every time he eyed me like he wanted to make me his.

Make me writhe underneath him.

I wanted a taste of that side. Just a glimpse of it.

He must have read my thoughts, or felt them along the bond between our minds, because his head tilted like a predator eyeing its prey.

"How can your body language remain so calm and at ease when you look like you want to ravage me?" I asked.

"That's not really what you're wondering, is it darling?" He lifted a knee onto the bed in front of me and continued running his fingers through the length of my hair.

I swallowed hard and gently shook my head, entranced by his heated stare.

His looks were lethal. Like darkness caged in a fae form.

"Tell me," he urged.

"I was wondering about the . . . other side of you. The one you keep locked up away."

A wicked grin curved his lips. "And how often do you wonder about that side of me?" He traced my jawline ever so slowly, palm spreading across the base of my neck.

I tilted my head back at his touch, my voice a rasp as my vocal chords worked at such a vulnerable angle. "Honestly, it's becoming more frequent as of late."

His teeth scraped along his bottom lip, and desire shot through me, landing between my bare legs like a perfectly aimed arrow.

He bent over me, mouth brushing mine before drifting to my ear. "Do you crave my darkness?"

His deep voice shook me to my core. The words sent a shiver down my spine and undid something in me.

I knew we were now walking a very thin line.

My lips parted as I answered, "Yes."

When he leaned back to look at me, his eyes flashed like golden flames. And then his shadows manifested like a cloak of blackened smoke, blowing behind his shoulders as if he stood amidst a storm.

His hands slid up the length of my thighs and grabbed me by the hips, hauling me to the edge of the bed. As I fell back against the sheets, his shadows surged forward, pinning my arms above me while he grabbed the lace undergarment that I wore and tugged it down my legs.

There was no gentleness to his movements now. He was ready to devour me.

He spread my legs as he dropped to his knees, and his hands went straight for my center, parting me as he dove in with his tongue. My hips bucked off the bed as he licked my most sensitive part, tongue swirling, thrusting, flicking, each move sending sparks dancing down my legs.

When he added his fingers, I nearly lost it.

I cried out his name, dying to reach for him, but his shadows coiled tighter around my wrists.

He pulled his mouth away and pumped his fingers at a decadent pace that had me climbing toward oblivion. "That's it"—he encouraged— "you're so close, I can feel you."

I tugged at my restraints but they held firm.

The look on his face was full of wicked delight as he watched my brows pinch and my eyes flutter shut. I ground my hips against his hand, chasing my release as it wound up and up, ready to shatter through me.

And when his thumb pressed against my center, I came undone. A cry of pleasure escaped my throat as my body shook, and he worked his hand in smooth circles against the bundle of nerves that had stars shooting across my vision, and a glow radiating from my body.

His tongue licked a claiming line up my center, a deep sound of satisfaction rumbling from his throat. I responded with a whimper as I laid there, trying to gather myself back up and reabsorb the light that I was emitting.

I lifted my head to meet his eyes. He still knelt between my legs, the glistening shimmer of my release coating his perfect lips.

Taste.

I wanted to taste him.

Not his lips. No, I wanted to taste a different part of his body.

When he pushed to stand, and the shadows at my wrists finally loosened their hold, I didn't hesitate. I moved so fast that he stumbled back, gripping onto my shoulders as I grasped his pants and began undressing him from the waist down.

I needed to get my hands on him. See him. Feel him. I wanted him to feel pleasure the way he had given it to me each time before.

"Auren . . ." He said my name like a warning, but made no move to stop me, so I worked the clasp until it came free.

I pulled the fabric down, but before I could get it past his knees, his shadows hauled me back onto the bed, and he continued to strip the pants off one leg at a time, never taking his eyes off of mine. Then, he prowled forward and climbed onto the bed all too smoothly, his powerful thigh muscles flexing as he knelt again in front of me.

He lifted the hem of his shirt to reveal just how eager he was, and I took a deep breath at what I saw. To say he was well endowed was an understatement. The gods had truly blessed him. And he watched me with all the confidence of a prized stallion ready to be let loose.

That darkness still stirred behind his eyes as I reached for him. I gripped him with both hands, working him firmly and slow, and he tilted his head back, letting out a deep groan.

A bead of liquid appeared at the tip of him as he thickened, and I lowered myself and licked it away ever so lightly. His hips spasmed, and he twitched in my hands, a clipped exhale escaping his throat.

The taste of him tingled in my mouth. I dipped my head, swirling my tongue around the tip, teasing and exploring, coaxing another droplet to the surface.

When I closed my mouth around him, he growled with pleasure. "Fuck."

I grinned around a mouth full of him.

My High Lord.

I didn't care that I was thinking of him as *mine*. That's what he was at that moment. And I was going to make sure he felt it.

"Your mouth is . . ." He paused as I brought him back out, and then he shuddered as I took him in again, deeper. "Sinful," he said, finally finishing his sentence.

It *was* sinful. Something had come over me. All I knew was that he ignited something in me, and my heart was ready to burn in his dark flames.

I moved my hand along his impressive length, working him as he watched me swirl my tongue twice around the tip before taking him into my mouth again. My other hand gripped the back of his thigh, steadying my pace.

When I moaned around him, he lost all sense of restraint and reacted, fisting his hand in my hair and guiding my mouth as he began thrusting his hips.

His legs stiffened, and his breathing became heavier. "Auren . . . I should warn you . . ." His voice faded into a deep, rich groan that had me soaked between my legs all over again. His grip tightened, and his hips moved faster, riding my mouth and watching me take him.

"I haven't . . . fuck," he said between his breaths. "It's been awhile . . . since I've . . . done this."

He shouldn't feel ashamed. I didn't care if he finished quickly. I wanted to make him feel as good as he had made me feel. And gods help me, I couldn't stop even if I wanted to.

This thing between us—this *mate* bond—was pulled almost as taut as it could be. Any tighter and I would beg him to enter me where I ached for him most, and ride me into oblivion.

And gods, I wanted that.

I had never been this way with anyone before. Had never been this ravenous.

"Gods, I don't think I can last . . ." His body jolted, and he bucked against my throat. "*Auren*—"

I felt him swell as the blood rushed into his erection. When I glanced up, his brows were pinched in pleasure, his mouth slightly open.

And then, his hand braced the back of my head as he plunged in one final time, hips twitching as he spilled himself down my throat. The sound he made was full of guttural satisfaction, and I savored every last drop he gave as he continued pumping down my throat in powerful spurts.

That incessant need that had been building inside me ignited into something wholly new. Like I had unlocked another level of desire. A heightened sense of *him.*

I took one final swallow and pulled away to look up at him. As soon as our eyes met, he cupped my face and claimed my lips with his, the taste of both of us swirling on our tongues.

When he broke away with a grin, his voice was as rough as gravel. "You shouldn't have done that."

"Why not?" I panted.

"Because now, neither of us will be able to contain our desire."

A smile tugged on the corners of my mouth. "Like we don't struggle with that already? You should have thought about that before you decided to show me your dark side." I traced the lines of his shroud underneath his collarbone.

"That was nothing remotely close to my dark side," he murmured into my hair as he planted a kiss on my temple.

I raised my brows.

It wasn't?

"You could have stopped me if you wanted to," I said.

"But I didn't want to. And now, I'll be thinking about that sinful mouth of yours all day when I'm trying to be a civilized High Lord." He brushed his thumb over my bottom lip.

"Your problem, not mine," I teased.

He chuckled, then straightened the neckline of my sweater, focusing on it longer than was necessary.

I watched his expression flicker before me like some sort of feeling had pushed up against his chest, bubbled up his throat, and now sat behind his reddened lips, fighting to be spilled into the world.

But he kept his mouth shut.

He swallowed hard, reaching back behind him to grab the suede leggings. "Actually, it's your problem too," he said, his knowing smirk sliding back into place. "I'm taking you out, so you're going to have to endure my struggle."

"A front row seat to your struggle sounds quite entertaining," I jested.

"Careful what you wish for," he said, grinning as he slid off the bed with unnerving grace. "Now get dressed. And don't do it so seductively."

I snickered and followed him off the bed, pulling on my leggings as inconspicuously as possible.

"Where are we going?" I asked.

He looked over his shoulder at me and smiled. "Into the city."

75
CALLEDAN

CALLEDAN'S CITY PROPER WAS A PLACE AFTER MY OWN HEART.

Stunning chalets and elegant storefronts built from darkened timber and polished mountain stone, wound through the mountainside along picturesque, sloped, cobblestone streets.

Every entry was swept and tidy, with polished black railing decorating each patio and terrace. Chimneys jutted out through roofs, breathing streams of smoke into the crisp morning air. Opulent lanterns bracketed stately double doors and punctuated each street corner. Some of the buildings even sank into the mountainside, the blackened stone jutting out above them like an awning.

From the sleek silhouette of each pointed eave, to the large crystal-clear windows that graced the storefronts and shops, Calledan was exquisite. Even the foliage was pristinely manicured.

As we walked, I glimpsed small pockets of snow that lingered in the shadows, clinging to the last of the early spring chill.

The sun was a pleasant warmth along my face as it peeked around the edge of the mountains that loomed high above us. I soaked it in like I did the sights of the beautiful city.

Shops were coming to life, with fae tying back curtains and curating their daily displays of goods inside casement windows. But one place seemed to be bustling more than the rest.

A café crowned the street we stood on, with a line of patrons that stretched out the wooden door and down the sloped sidewalk. In front, there was a small gated patio full of couples enjoying steaming cups of deliciously aromatic drinks and flaky pastries.

My mouth began to water as we approached. I didn't think I'd ever get used to everything being heightened in this realm—especially the smells.

Niall ushered me past the guests in line, and when a couple of males saw us approaching, they vacated their seats on the patio, happily inclining their heads toward their High Lord. Niall nodded with a polite smile.

"Does everyone just offer their seat to you when you arrive somewhere?" I asked, watching the males as they waved to a few other patrons in line before heading up the street.

"They do," Niall said as he pulled out my chair.

A tall, thin fae, with golden hair fastened into a sleek bun at the top of her head approached us with a menu.

"Good morning! Can I—" She stopped mid-sentence and dropped to a delicate curtsy. "My Lord, I almost didn't recognize you," she said. "You normally don't come here with . . ." Her eyes slid to me.

He gave her a smile. "Company? You are correct," he said, before turning to me. "See anything you'd like?"

I perused over the menu at all the small sketches of hot drinks drawn in rounded mugs. Flavors of chocolate, vanilla, and hazelnut were listed under local favorites. Then there were several hot ciders, and a steaming honey lavender tea that sounded very tempting. But a specialty drink caught my eye, one brewed with sweetened milk, caramel cream, and medium roasted coffee beans that they called The Calledan Cup—named after the café itself.

Depictions of little baked goods like lemon tarts, pecan clusters, cinnamon apple breakfast cakes, and honeyed toast with fresh fruit lined the other side of the menu.

"I'll take the Calledan Cup and some honeyed toast please," I said quietly.

"And I'll have the usual," Niall added.

The female nodded. "I'll have those right out," she said, hurrying away.

Niall leaned back in his chair and loosened the slightly thicker coat that he had chosen to wear this morning as he watched me. "You have good taste," he said. "The Calledan Cup is my favorite."

It was also the most expensive on the menu—judging from the markings I saw alongside the listing. Five tally marks, whereas most others were only three.

"I can pay you back, whenever I get the chance," I said.

I still had no money to my name and didn't want to come across as if I was taking advantage of his generosity. And I could only assume he now had a very hefty tab with Gareth—with all the dresses and sweaters and other garments he'd been commissioning for me.

"Don't worry yourself over that," he replied, offering me a soft smile.

I opened my mouth, ready to protest, but he raised his brows as if to say, *Don't challenge me on it either.*

Teeth sinking into my lip, I held my tongue and didn't argue. I'd find some way to settle the debt, eventually.

Niall continued to watch me.

"What?" I asked.

"First impressions?" he questioned, gesturing to the city around us.

I had only seen a glimpse of it, but it was by far my favorite territory of the fae realm. The perfect place to want to get lost in for days, weeks— years even. Everything was cultivated with elegance. Tasteful and refined, just as Vanir had said. Even the smallest details, such as the presentation of a morning coffee, were elevated in every way. And that level of pride extended to the fae of Calledan as well—polished leather boots, fur-lined coats and cloaks, even the bakers wore quality leather aprons adorned with shiny silver clasps.

All of it filled me with a comfort I hadn't felt in so long.

It would be a lovely place to have a life.

What would my brother think when I told him about all this? Would he even believe me that it all truly existed? Would *anyone* believe me?

I cleared my throat, realizing I had journeyed off in my own thoughts.

"It's surreal," I said, meeting Niall's gaze, not quite finding the words to bring to life what I was feeling.

He smiled just as a tray of hot beverages and food was placed on our table.

The Calledan Cup was the most delicious thing I'd ever tasted this early in the morning—aside from Niall. It triumphed over the sad excuse of coffee at Galenagh's local spot back home, which tasted bitter, and made me want to take it in one gulp to not have to suffer through it.

We ate and drank and chatted about the town. Niall briefly informed me about its history and how the fae help to ensure it remains cozy and charming—despite its growing population and expansion throughout the valley.

"How far does it stretch through the mountains?" I asked.

"Because of the terrain you'd have a hard time seeing it all in one day. It winds around this peak"—he pointed behind us—"and continues down toward The Elderwood and the river, before wrapping back into that mountainside."

"Quite a large city then," I mused, imagining it.

"The southern portion is the most densely populated. It's nearest to the river, and there's even a view of the falls from the main street. When it snows there, that's a sight worth seeing."

I gazed down the street, then to the mountain peaks beyond. "I would love to see it covered in snow."

"Would you?" Niall asked, staring intently at me again.

I nodded. "I would."

We locked eyes, and the chatter around us seemed to fade away as I imagined snowflakes falling around Niall's handsome silhouette. How they would probably catch in his dark hair, and he'd smooth back that one piece that always fell over his forehead, no matter how hard he tried to keep it in place.

Somehow, I knew deep down that I wasn't going back to Galenagh. To Belthria. That there was a very real chance that I *would* see snow falling upon this very place. And the more time that passed, the more accepting I was of that fate.

But the thought of Liam being left behind still floated to the forefront of my mind quite often.

If I could find a way to get him here, to let him see—

I looked to my left, down the street. "I wish my brother could see this."

"I hope that someday he will."

A shield slipped into place around us, not for protection, but for containing our conversation. As it sealed us within it, all the sound around us became muffled.

"The Veil is only necessary because of Lyceius," he said. "Once you defeat him and the prophecy is fulfilled, technically, the boundary will no longer be needed."

"We," I corrected him.

He looked puzzled. "I'm sorry?"

"When *we* defeat Lyceius. You and I are in this together, remember? Amarna said so."

The corner of his mouth hitched up.

"What?"

"I like the sound of that." He stirred his coffee, half smiling as he stared at the swirling liquid, like he was replaying the words over in his mind.

We.

You and I.

Together.

I grinned, letting the words drift around in my mind too, allowing them to find a cozy place to settle.

Niall finished his drink. "Once Lyceius is gone, I believe there will come a time when humans and fae will coexist in peace again. And perhaps you will be the one to show them that's possible."

I met his eyes. "I hope for that too."

The shield around us fell away, and I could once again hear the bustling noise of the crowded streetside. More fae had arrived, and the line now wrapped around the corner of the building.

Niall reached out for my hand as he stood. I took it, and he pushed in my chair for me as I moved aside. The small contact was nothing more than the quick gesture of a gentleman, and my hand ached for his the moment he let it go.

We stepped out onto the street and only made it a few yards before a group of fae stopped to chat with their High Lord.

When I shifted my hair over my shoulders to try and hide my rounded ears, I caught sight of Niall's fingers twitching at his sides as if he were working his magic. I waited for that prickling sensation to wash over me like it did when a glamour was put into place, but it didn't come.

Curious, I slid my hand back into my hair to check, but my ears were still rounded. I frowned, trying to figure out what he'd done.

The fae glanced my way—confirming that they could indeed still see me—but they didn't linger in their perusal. If anyone sensed anything odd about me, they didn't let on. No sizing me up to see what noble stock I came from. No questions or comments. Niall introduced me as "Auren," with no other elaborations or explanations, and no one pried further. They simply bowed or curtsied, inclining their heads in respect, and smiling brightly.

They probably think I'm just the new female on his arm. How often did he have a female on his arm? The thought sent a sudden pang of jealousy through me. But then I remembered the fae at the café and her comment that he didn't come with guests. *And* hadn't he said that he'd always been a loner?

I found myself preferring to think that he chose to do everything alone, without the company of some pretty fae female on his arm.

Gods. Am I really jealous about that?

More passersby quickly changed their direction to walk with the High Lord for a few minutes and ask their questions or voice their opinions. I kept quiet and listened to their conversations, observing how their dynamic worked.

What I found most intriguing was how oddly casual the conversation was between Niall and these fae.

If King Broderick ever ventured out into the city proper, he always did so on the most regal of his horses, flanked with an entire battalion of his personal guard—all dressed in the royal colors and bearing his banners. It was considered beneath him to even entertain one of his subject's needs outside of court hearings. If anyone were to approach the king, they'd surely be stopped several paces away.

But Niall strolled alongside his subjects in casual conversation, without a weapon or guard in sight. He would put on a helm and go to war for his court, or walk beside them as a friend. Whichever male they needed him to be, he would be it. He had worked to make sure his court viewed him as he is, and not as his ancestor was. And his hard work was evident. They regarded him as their protector and their leader, but also as a friend. Someone they were in harmony with.

The notion was baffling to me, just like it had been when that fae female at the mourning temple had passed by us, and only offered her High Lord a sad smile. It was all she had to give at the time. And it was enough.

When we finally managed to break free of all the conversations, Niall took me to a long street perched higher on the mountainside, full of specialty shops and tasty delicacies. We spent hours walking in and out of shops full of clothes and fine-tailored boots, linens and beautifully woven tapestries, and a candle shop that was tucked into the mountain, stocked with candles that smelled so delicious, I could have eaten them.

Another shop boasted aged bottles of fae wine, and a specialty liqueur that Niall claimed would "steal my heart."

I wanted to tell him that *he* was the one stealing my heart. That with every look, every kiss, every new situation I saw him in, I was falling for him more and more. But I held my tongue and the moment passed, leaving the words marinating in my mouth, waiting to be spoken another time.

He purchased a bottle and stowed it away in his magical pocket of space for later, and ushered me on, seemingly unaware of the thoughts that were clawing at my mind and dancing on the tip of my tongue.

We talked and laughed, and his grin grew wider as the day went on.

When I sampled a local delicacy from a vendor cart, he—ever so intimately—dabbed at the jam that dripped down my chin, locking eyes with me in a heated stare. Our bodies had drifted toward one another, but the moment he'd felt it, he cleared his throat and turned away.

I was beginning to loathe the public, wishing we could just be alone.

I'd wanted to kiss him in the tailor's shop, when he'd given me a sultry look after I held a dress up to myself and spun suggestively. Wanted him to pull me close when I accidentally stumbled into his side while climbing a steep sidewalk. Just the feel of his hand steadying my elbow had my chest thrumming so intensely, that I'd thought the bond between us was going to snap into place on its own accord and *make* us give in to it.

This. Was. Torture.

But we continued on, winding back to a market street that was packed with a late morning rush of shoppers.

A blacksmith with leathery skin and salt and pepper hair flagged us down the moment we entered his line of sight. He was eager to show Niall his latest work, so we followed.

His forge was tucked into the mountain, lit by several burning hearths, earthen fire pits, and a multitude of rough-hewn wall sconces. The scent of smelt metal and charred wood tickled my nose.

Niall proceeded to remove his jacket to test a few new blades that were spread upon a wooden table next to a quenching tub. He selected one and turned it in his hand to admire it, the orange glow of the forge flickering over his face like a breath of fire.

I couldn't keep my eyes away from him as he swung the weapon, muscles flexing and straining against his skin-tight shirt. He moved with such grace, yet each movement radiated power.

To distract myself and keep from ogling him incessantly, I asked if I could try a blade as well. The blacksmith beamed and handed me a longsword that he had just forged a week prior. It was intricately carved, and the weight was well balanced. I adjusted my grip to what Roirdan had shown me and swung the blade. It cut through the air with a sweet hum.

I practiced a few movements, testing the blade and its ease of use. The craftsmanship was excellent. I silently wondered if this was the same blacksmith Roirdan had commissioned to make my dagger.

"Impressive," I said, handing the sword back to its maker.

"Thank you, my lady," he said with a pleased smile.

When I glanced at Niall, he was no longer testing the weapon in his hand. Instead, he was observing me, eyes glowing molten gold.

I suppressed my grin and clasped my hands behind my back, pretending to peruse the rest of the smith's den. I could hear Niall exchanging soft-spoken words with the male, swapping swords and flicking his fingers over their sharpened edges, all while stealing a glance at me every few seconds. That sweet tension was building up again, thickening the space between us in the already stifling air.

There was something about seeing him with a blade in hand that gave me chills in all the right places. And judging by the way he was looking at me, he must have felt the same.

But how could he know what I was feeling? I hadn't told him.

Not really.

Earlier, I used the word *we,* and he'd cradled it like a treasure. But what more had I given him, besides that and a fleeting acknowledgement of our mate bond in Drastia? Each time a whisper of those sentiments perched on the tip of my tongue, I held them hostage.

Why was I holding back?

Why was *he?*

There had been several times when it seemed like he had been on the verge of saying something too, but didn't.

Was it truly that Amarna had cautioned us to wait until the time was right? Was that what we were doing? Or were we in our own heads about it, giving it too much thought when we should really just say and do what felt right?

Whatever this was, it felt wrong to continue to fight it. And as I walked around the forge, examining blades and running my fingers along polished steel and raw leathers, I watched him.

Lately, I'd taken note of how his hands always moved when he spoke, especially when it was a topic of discussion that interested him. It was the perfect contrast to how they always found their way into his pockets during confrontations.

I noted the way his voice would rise every time he mentioned something he enjoyed, and the creases that would form along the corners of his eyes when he genuinely smiled. The same lock of hair that fell in a smooth wave across his forehead—that he always brushed back. The brow he favored to raise each time he found something I said intriguing. The shadow along his strong jawline. Even the freckle just below the edge of his right eye, near his temple . . . All things that I loved about him.

Wait—

A sudden realization hit me.

It hit me like a ton of bricks.

My chest thrummed like a riot, and my fingers halted their trail down a blade as I stared at Niall across the blacksmith's forge.

Love?

It couldn't be . . . could it?

I thought I'd been in love once. But it had been a mostly one-sided thing, and it hadn't felt a fraction like what I was feeling now.

This feeling was intense, and overwhelming, and it threatened to take over me and fill my heart so full it could burst.

There was no denying that my heart belonged with the High Lord who stood across the room from me like a perfectly formed shadow in the firelight. And each time I pulled myself away, or tried to deny what he was to me, my feelings only grew stronger.

Amarna said the pull between mates was undeniable—that we couldn't fight it.

And it was now threatening to overwhelm me.

When Niall's eyes found mine again, I could tell his senses had alerted him that something was off. That my heart was about to burst with emotion.

I couldn't form the right words. Couldn't make my jaw work. And it suddenly felt like there wasn't enough air in the room. "Please excuse me," I managed to croak, dashing for the entrance and the open street beyond.

I stumbled into the cool mountain air, pulling in deep, long breaths, and shaking my cloak out to move the air under my arms and cool myself down.

It didn't take long for Niall to come to my side.

His deep voice was full of concern as he leaned in to bring my eyes to him. "Are you all right?"

"I'm fine, just needed some fresh air," I said shakily, tossing my hair back over my shoulders.

Why am I sweating so much?

I started down the street, desperate to do something besides stand there in my internal meltdown. Niall followed, but the awkward silence yawned between us like a gaping chasm.

Both of us attempted to say something at the same time, then fumbled over our words.

Niall managed to form a cohesive sentence first. "Are you ready to head back?"

My eyes darted around the street as I pulled in another deep breath. "No. I just need to walk for a while."

He nodded and forced a swallow.

The street wound on, and I kept moving, feeling Niall's presence like a beacon at my side, calling me to him.

Calling me home.

"Thank you for today," he said, taking my hand and bringing it to his lips.

To onlookers it might have appeared simple enough, but I could feel the emotion behind it as he pressed a kiss to my knuckles. He closed his eyes and lingered there a moment, before lowering our hands. But he didn't let go. He squeezed tightly.

Does he know what I'm feeling?

Is this supposed to be a consolation? Damnit if it is. It's not enough.

I wanted so badly to continue holding his hand, but we were back in the public eye, and I was one small finger-graze away from igniting like a star.

I slipped my fingers from his and continued forward, tucking my arms into my cloak instead. I'd gained a good grip on my power in these weeks of training, despite every playful jest that we gave each other, and every stolen moment that only fueled the fire of our feelings. But I suddenly felt like I couldn't trust myself to be in control.

This was the culmination of everything I'd been suppressing, every action I'd been holding back, all of it coming to a head in the middle of Calledan's busiest street.

Perfect. Timing.

I closed my eyes tightly as my thoughts became maddening. I didn't know how much longer I could take it. Seeing Niall's home—the city and those who he worked so hard to keep safe—kindled that fire I felt for him.

Over the past few weeks, something had changed. The desire was there—in full force, but underneath it all, there was a fondness, an admiration.

I had learned so much more about Niall. And every quirk, every habit, every trait, made my heart swell.

I couldn't keep pretending that he meant nothing to me. Not when I had developed such strong feelings for him.

He had told me that keeping away from your mate was like torture, and I now felt the full weight of those words. Tears began to well up and slip down my cheeks, and I quickly bit the backside of my hand to keep from sobbing.

I could feel him looking at me. Could practically feel the worry radiating off of him.

I had to get a grip on my composure.

But I didn't *want* to.

I wanted to claim him. I wanted to act on every thought and feeling that sped through my mind. This wasn't just passion, or lust, or longing to feel his skin on mine. This was a feeling so deep it hurt. It was an aching in my heart to always have him near me. A desire greater than any I could ever fathom.

I love him.

In a series of events that I never could have conjured up in my wildest dreams, I had fallen in love with Niall.

And I could resist it no longer.

Whether I was projecting my feelings through our mental connection or not, I didn't care anymore. I wanted to feel it all, and I needed him to know.

I opened my mouth to *finally* say something, when he grabbed my forearm and directed me to the left, abruptly cutting across the pathway of half a dozen pedestrians.

We turned down a small alleyway, and there, in a dark alcove, sat a wooden door, forgotten to the world and out of the public eye, framed with worn, wooden crates piled up at each side. Without glancing back, Niall proceeded to walk straight through it, pulling me behind him.

I gasped as we crossed into complete darkness.

76
BLISS

My eyes struggled to adjust to the lack of light. The fact that we had just walked through a closed door was the furthest thing from my mind when I couldn't see my hand in front of my face.

A few small candles sprang to life once our presence was recognized, illuminating Niall as he stood in front of me amidst the swirling dust.

His voice was pitched low as he breathed out, "What was that? You were losing it out there. What's wrong?"

The leash I'd kept myself under completely snapped as my emotions overwhelmed me.

"*What's wrong?*" Light crackled along my skin. "What's wrong is that I can't pretend anymore, Niall! I can't pretend like there's nothing between us! Like I'm somehow fooling the whole world by keeping my distance. I'm only fooling myself, and I can't stand it! And every stolen moment that we have together makes it so much harder when all I want to do is give in and give you everything." My voice broke, and tears threatened, but I willed them to stay down.

He stood in awe, leaning against a bare wooden table at the center of the room, eyes glittering in the flickering light.

When the silence became straining, I threw my hands up. "I can't pretend that I don't love you!" The words came out half hysterical as I shook my head.

Before I could say anything else, he launched off the table and had me in his arms within an instant. The next second, my back was against the stone wall, and his lips crashed onto mine in a fierce claiming. His hands moved to gather up every inch of my body all at once.

He kissed me like he was desperate. As desperate as I was. Passionately. Without restraint.

When he pulled away for a breath, he gripped my face and stared deep into my eyes. "There's no more pretending," he proclaimed. "I knew you were mine the moment you stumbled into this realm. I've loved you ever since Elandrew, Auren."

My heart stuttered

He loves me.

"I think of you every moment of every day," he said. "Every time I get a taste but can never fully have you, it drives me mad. I don't want to go another day without telling you I love you. This is fate and denying each other any longer is just going to wreck us both."

Tears began streaming down my face and his thumbs swiped them away.

"It's always been you, Auren. It *will always* be you."

His lips claimed mine again, and I plunged my hands into his hair, gripping his dark locks as I soaked in the taste of him.

I could feel his heart pounding beneath his chest as he lifted me up under my thighs and turned to place me on top of the table.

Our hands moved in a frenzy, desperately trying to bring our bodies closer to one another.

It felt so good to no longer be bound by restraint. To take what we wanted. What we needed.

To finally give in to the bond.

He suddenly pulled away, leaving me panting for air.

I searched his glowing, golden eyes. "Niall, what's—"

"I've thought of this moment more times than I can count, and never once did it occur in my safehouse."

Confusion lined my face, but he continued, his voice dropping to a rasped whisper as he said, "And my mate doesn't deserve a quick bedding on a dusty table." His eyes combed over me hungrily. "No, my darling. You deserve far more." His tone grew deeper as he leaned in to graze my neck with his breath. "And I'm going to worship you until dawn."

Just as the chills from his words crept over me, his strong arms wrapped me up tightly, anchoring me to him as he ported us.

The wind and the world whipped by, but all of it seemed calm compared to the torrent of emotions swirling inside me.

A moment later, everything came back into focus, and Niall's shadows fell away like fog scattering at our feet. The polished black marble floors of The Keep shone up at us. Candles were lit along the glistening black walls, and a fire was roaring in the fireplace across the spacious bedchamber he'd brought me to.

His bedchamber.

He strode toward his bed with me in his arms, unclasping my cloak along the way and letting it fall atop the sleek fur rugs that lined the floor. With the flick of his wrist, the blankets and dark sheets turned down, and he gently laid me at the edge of the bed, leaning in with his hands on either side of my head. "Now, where were we?"

His mouth met my neck, trailing a line of sensual kisses down it, stoking the heat that curled low in my core. I lifted my chin, arching into each luscious swipe of his tongue as it met my skin.

He slowed his pace, savoring the moments as they came.

But I was needy.

My hands fumbled blindly against his clothes, only to be torn away as he stood.

"What's your rush, darling?" His grin was predatory. "I told you I was going to worship you until dawn. And I do consider myself a male of my word."

He took his time removing his coat, never breaking my stare. One by one the buttons on his shirt came apart, and he peeled the fabric from his body and tossed it to the floor.

My eyes mapped his physique, admiring each muscle. Centuries of training had toned every inch of him. I sat up and traced the lines of ink draped across his collarbones and shoulders. The shroud. An ever-present reminder of who stood before me.

I could feel the power radiating from him, just as I could sense his fierce desire.

He unfastened his pants and they slid down his thickly muscled legs, freeing his impressive manhood, heavy and thick and ready. My mouth watered at the sight, warmth gathering between my legs.

I lifted my sweater over my head, revealing the bralette that clung to my chest, but before I could reach to unclasp it, Niall fisted the fabric, and it turned to ash around me. I gasped as his lips closed over my breast, claiming another part of me. He nipped at the peaked tip, groaning as I whimpered.

He pressed forward, laying me back against the silken sheets. My body trembled in anticipation under the weight of his stare as he began removing my leggings and the undergarment beneath them. I reveled in the way his eyes lit at what he saw, how they feasted on every inch of me.

"You're exquisite," he said. "And you're *mine.*"

With preternatural grace, he climbed above me, slipping an arm around my waist and lifting me further onto the bed with him. "I've imagined this moment a hundred different ways," he said as he lowered his mouth to press a line of kisses down my stomach. "Fisted myself right here where you're laying, as I thought of you." The stubble on his cheek tickled the apex of my thigh, and I sucked in a breath as his mouth drew closer to my center. "And what you did to me this morning . . . that drove me mad with desire."

He dipped between my legs, growling in approval at what he saw. "Look at how wet you are for me already." He spoke the words right onto me, and my hips jerked as he licked the soft, wet flesh. He groaned as he pressed in further, tasting me, his tongue exploring and seeking more.

I gripped the sheets and ground my hips against his talented tongue, the promise of release coming on all too quickly. With one last flick, every tiny fiber of my being came unraveled at the seams and I cried out. Pleasure pulsed through my body in rapid succession as he lapped up every drop of me like it was his prize.

"I've never tasted anything so divine," he murmured against my tender flesh.

Then, he rose and situated himself over me.

I grasped his face—kissing him hard and fast—and moved my hand to reach for him, to guide him to where I needed him most.

All of those stolen moments before had built up to this. All of the tension and teasing, all of the tasting and never fully devouring. It all culminated in this moment.

Niall stilled, perfectly positioned and nudging at my entrance, his golden eyes begging me for more. "Tell me this is what you want," he rumbled deeply as he looked into my eyes. "I need to hear you say it."

I breathed out the words. "I want this. I want all of you, Niall."

His eyes softened for a brief moment, and he placed his hand on the side of my face as he said, "I love you, Auren." And as my name left his lips, he pushed in.

Liquid heat rushed to my core, my body stretching to accommodate the size of him, and I whimpered as he pulled out and then slid back in, a little further this time.

He worked his way in and out, giving me time to prepare for the fullness of him, and watching me as he did so. And then, in one smooth thrust, he seated himself to the hilt. I moaned, relishing the size of him, how good it felt to have him inside me. The sound he made in response was so deep and heavy with satisfaction, that I was dripping all over again from where we joined.

My hands tightened on his waist. I needed him deeper, harder, faster.

He tipped his head back to look at me. "If you want something darling, tell me. Tell me what you desire."

Something ignited in me the way it had this morning, and I didn't even recognize my own voice as I spoke. "Take me, Asher, and make me yours."

I had only guessed that the use of his battle name would be the trigger he needed to break the hold on his restraint.

And I was right.

The words fell off my tongue like a command, and he obeyed.

His eyes flared like kindling had been added to the flames within them, and a muscle ticked in his neck as he tilted his chin like a predator. He growled, low and wicked, and a seriousness spread across his face.

Within an instant, there was no remnant of the male who took his time savoring.

The Asher unleashed himself.

He thrust into me so deeply that I cried out.

I dug my fingers into his back, feeling his muscles contract with every movement he made. Every roll and plunge of his hips had me seeing stars. I would never be able to get enough of him.

He groaned into my neck as he drove into me, holding my body to his, marking me from within. His hand snuck between us to squeeze at my breast, eliciting a whimpering moan from me when he ran his thumb over the tip. Then, in one smooth movement he flipped me onto my stomach and was dragging my hips up to meet his as he knelt behind me.

I looked back over my shoulder at him. His eyes pulsed with their otherworldly golden glow, brighter than I had ever seen. And the face that looked down at me was his, but not. It had an edge to it that I hadn't witnessed before, and it drove me wild.

He nudged at my entrance once again and slid into me with one smooth movement. My knees lifted off the bed as he gripped my hips, bringing me further up toward him, guiding me where he wanted for each plunge.

I cried out his name, fully at his mercy, feeling every glorious inch of him as he claimed me.

The High Lord. The Asher. My Mate.

I was his and he was mine.

My eyes rolled back as he filled me up, pumping in and out at a decadent pace, hitting every sensitive spot and coaxing forth another release.

This was *bliss.*

He leaned forward and growled into my ear from behind, "You're *mine.*" It was Niall, and yet it wasn't. The bond between us was taking over, and his power pulsed through his voice, unraveling something in me.

The thrumming in my chest became more pronounced, as if it was merging with my heartbeat, becoming one driving force within me, forever linked to his.

In my mind, our essences were swirling in their own intense hunger for each other, tangling in a whirl of light and shadow as if they could somehow blend into one. I could feel the mating bond solidifying between us, and I let out a breathy moan as it electrified me from within.

"That's it. Come for me," he commanded, digging his fingers into the flesh of my hips. His voice was still caught between the one I knew and the one that was something deeper, darker. And it guided me toward oblivion.

My body tensed, my release coiling tighter and tighter within my core with each thrust of his hips. A rapturous rush of sparks ignited down my spine, and Niall's name surged from my lips as I was torn from my reality and brought back again, writhing with a pleasure so intense, I swore I'd been remade. My power flooded my veins, gushing from somewhere deep, cooling my skin like liquid night as it barreled through me. Light burst forth from me in all directions, rattling the walls as I continued crashing through wave after wave of pulsating bliss.

Shadows surged from Niall as well, and he let out a roar, spilling himself inside me as his body shuddered.

Together, the light and shadow swirled like the creation of the cosmos, engulfing the room in what was now a physical manifestation of what we saw in our minds.

I dangled on the verge of reality, like a falling star—free from any anchors—as I tumbled through a universe of raw ecstasy.

I could feel him dripping down my thighs, the swell of him throbbing deep inside me. It filled me with a primal satisfaction, punctuated by a final euphoric groan that he rumbled onto the top of my spine.

As the light and shadows faded away, we collapsed onto the bed.

We laid there and caught our breaths together. His forehead glistened with small beads of sweat, and my favorite thing—his eyes—stared back at me with a newfound admiration. The intensity of The Asher had slipped back under the surface, and a look of reverence settled into place over his features.

"My beautiful mate," he said, smoothing my hair away from my face.

I smiled.

The thrumming in my chest was low and steady. A constant backdrop that now blended into my heartbeat. And when his essence manifested in the white void of my mind, mine rose to greet it.

But this time, they were wholly different. They burned like two flames, one made of darkness and one of light. Two souls, intertwined and anchored together by the bonds of fate. They hummed in contentment, like they were finally given what they longed for.

A lone tear glided down my cheek.

Niall was instantly there to gently kiss it away. "What's wrong, my love?" he asked.

"I just didn't imagine the mating bond would feel like this," I said.

It felt like a life-giving breath.

Like I was incomplete before, and he had made me whole.

He tucked another stray lock of my hair behind my ear. "It's a force to be reckoned with. It's funny though, I was beginning to think I wasn't meant to have a mate, until you came and took me by surprise."

"Well, five hundred years without any sign of one would lead me to think the same thing."

"Excuse you. I believe four hundred and sixty years is still quite far from five hundred," he corrected me with a sly grin.

"My apologies, High Lord. I didn't mean to offend such an ancient creature as yourself."

In a blink, he hauled me up onto his lap, his arms completely encompassing my waist. "Disrespecting a High Lord comes with consequences."

I giggled as he nipped at my neck. "I don't imagine anything could top the intense claiming session you just gave me."

He planted a teasing kiss under my jawline. "And, now that I *have* claimed you, I plan on doing it thoroughly and often, in as many other locations and ways as physically possible."

My cheeks warmed at his words. "I like the sound of that."

The golden glow in his eyes flared, then settled to a simmer.

"Speaking of other locations, where exactly were we when you walked us through that door earlier?"

"It's a safehouse. One of many, actually. I have them placed strategically throughout the realm with access allowed to only a trusted few. It's best to always have a place to hide if need be." He kissed my neck lazily, kindling new sparks at the apex of my thighs, making my thoughts blur in and out of focus.

"But the door was in plain sight—" I sucked in a breath as he nipped at my skin once more, then kissed away the sweet sting. "Someone could have spotted us."

"Magic, darling," he murmured. "You do remember that I'm capable of very powerful magic, don't you?"

I tugged on a strand of his hair, eliciting a playful laugh from him.

"To the common passerby, that alley doesn't exist. It's just another stone wall. Only myself, and those I allow, can see it. What everyone else saw was two people getting lost in the crowd." He nuzzled into me. "No one will come looking."

I didn't think I would ever get used to magic in all its entirety, or the feeling of Niall's breath against my neck as he rested against me.

He inhaled deeply, then hummed wickedly against my skin. "Now, enough talk. I promised you pleasure until dawn and I—" He cut his words short, stilling. Then, he jerked his head up, and his eyes went distant.

"What's wrong?" I asked.

His gaze pierced through the wall behind me, then widened at whatever he saw. "Something is approaching from The Wastelands."

I held my breath.

Some . . . thing?

I leaned back and watched his face as he used whatever ability he had as a High Lord to tune into the wards and sense the oncoming threat.

When he had the information he needed, he slid from the bed in one smooth movement.

A fresh set of clothes appeared in his hand and he began dressing. "I've summoned Remic. He's outside the door, and he will make sure no one enters. You'll be safe here."

I scrambled off the bed after him and gathered up my clothes as quickly as I could. "I want to go with you."

"Auren, until I know what's going on, I need you to stay here," he said as he secured the last button on his fitted black tunic. His preternatural fae speed even extended to how fast he could get dressed, and I grunted as I struggled to pull my leggings on against my dampened skin.

He stopped me, taking my face into his hands—firmly, but yet so gently, and kissed me deeply.

When he pulled back, I tried to argue against staying. "But what if—"

"Stay here," he cut me off with a direct order.

But as his fingertips slipped off my arms and he ported, I reached out and grabbed onto his forearm not a moment too late, and was sucked into the whirlwind of space and time behind him, gripping onto his arm with all my might.

77

COME WHAT MAY

WHEN WE MATERIALIZED, NIALL WAS INSTANTLY OVER ME, TAKING ME into his grasp. His face was a mix of fury and fret as he held me steady.

"Fates, Auren! Why would you do that?" Fear unraveled in his voice. "We could have ported into a threat!"

Thankfully, we hadn't. We were standing at The Lookout, high above the rest of the mountain range.

I surveyed everything ahead of me, but nothing appeared out of the ordinary. Just mountains, and the sky dotted with fluffy white clouds that looked close enough to touch.

"I-I wanted to see what was happening," I said, leaning to look around him.

His body stiffened, hands tightening their grip on my arms. But when I looked up at his face, he was focused on something in the distance behind me.

The wind that had been tugging at my clothes suddenly died out, as if all of its current was snipped off at a moment's notice. It seemed to *retract,* like the gods drew it back on a sharp inhale.

The air grew deathly still.

Then, I felt a presence gathering. Like a spider creeping up my spine, it sent my skin crawling, and something inside me snarled in defense, rearing its head as I slowly turned around.

There, spreading out over the horizon of the barren expanse of

Salterra, was a mass of shadows, churning in the air like a nasty storm. A dark phantom against the milky plumes that scattered through the sky as the mass grew, and grew, seeming to creep closer to Calledan.

"What is it?" I whispered.

"I'm not sure," Niall answered. "I've never seen anything like it."

A twinge of his uneasiness crept along the bond between us, and the world seemed to pause, listening, watching—just as we were.

As quick as it came, the ominous shadow shrank back into itself until it was nothing more than a small dot on the horizon. When it winked out of sight, Niall's hands loosened their protective hold.

"That can't be good, can it?" I asked.

"No," was his only reply.

He turned me toward him and gently lifted my chin with his finger, bridging our line of sight. "If I tell you to stay, please listen. At least until I know what sort of threat we're facing."

I nodded. "I just don't want to be without you."

His sigh was heavy with understanding as he moved his hand to cradle my cheek in his palm. "And I can't bear the thought of something happening to you."

A gentle grin tugged at my lips. "Likewise."

He returned a small smile.

"I have power of my own. I can handle myself."

"I know," he said. "But as your mate, I will always put your safety before mine or anyone else's."

I took his hand in mine and looked back out over the barren expanse to the north.

That mass . . . it didn't feel right. It felt *sinister.* Even though it was gone from sight, it was as if something was still there. Like a stain that hadn't quite been removed and had only been pushed deeper into the fibers of existence.

Lingering somewhere beyond.

I shuddered, and my essence stirred, pacing the wall in my mind like it was on edge.

Niall followed my stare. "Let's get back to The Keep. I need to alert the others. And Remic is probably losing his mind since you disappeared."

His grip tightened on mine, and he pulled me to his chest as we ported.

The meeting room was empty when we materialized in it, and Niall's gaze went distant again, communicating with the Trium—I assumed, while I took a seat at the long table. A moment later, the others arrived with questions in their eyes, scanning both of us to ensure we hadn't been harmed.

Remic bypassed Niall and walked straight over to me, his eyes roving intensely, assessing my well-being. When he circled around to my backside, Niall growled from across the room and took a harsh step forward. The Dionach's head shot up, and his wings flared slightly.

"Niall," Aremis said cautiously, holding his arm out as if it would stop the High Lord from launching himself at Remic. "He's just making sure she's okay . . ." He cast a quick, nervous glance over to Roirdan, then back at Niall. "Are . . . *you* okay?"

Niall straightened his shoulders and breathed out through his nose. "I'm fine," he ground out.

Roirdan and Aremis shared another look as they walked around the table and took their seats, while Niall remained in the doorway, grinding his teeth together.

When Remic brought his stool and placed it directly next to mine, Niall stormed forward. He grabbed my chair by the seat, and lifted it with me in it. Then, he proceeded to carry me to the other end of the table, furthest away from everyone.

The Trium watched him with obvious concern, but it was Roirdan who recognized it for what it was. "You two fucked, didn't you?"

I whipped my head around to him, my cheeks heating with embarrassment.

When neither Niall or I responded, Roirdan threw his head back and roared with laughter. "Oh shit!" He slammed his palm on the table. "You did. It's about gods damned time."

A slight grin surfaced on Remic's face upon hearing Roirdan's words.

Aremis shook his head, fighting back a smile of his own. "Well that explains it."

Niall kept his eyes lowered as he sat, adjusting the lapels of his shirt. "Remic, I apologize for that."

He'd momentarily considered him a threat . . .

All of that territorial nonsense had been true after all.

Remic stretched out his wings behind him. "I understand."

"She's my mate," Niall continued. "If any of you haven't already put the pieces together."

Hearing him say it out loud to the others made my heart swell.

"I think we all had that one figured out," Aremis said, looking between the two of us.

"I'm fine, by the way," I said to Remic, reassuring him. "Thank you for checking."

He smiled gently at me and nodded.

I could see where Morah would take an interest in the Dionach. He was beautiful even when he was expressionless. But when he grinned, it leant him an edge that he hadn't possessed before. Something delicate and enrapturing to contrast his unyielding nature.

I didn't dare let that thought linger long enough for Niall to catch wind of it. He would surely go into a frenzy.

Aremis, ever the advisor, was anxious to hear of what we'd seen, eager to assess every detail. The busybody immediately went to work hunting for answers after Niall explained.

Whatever it was, something was happening in the north, and after Folquin's recent message, we were all even more on edge.

The rest of the day and night, Niall wouldn't let me leave his chambers. But it wasn't out of fear of the strange mass of shadows that manifested and disappeared into The Wastelands. It was because all our worries fell by the wayside as the mating bond completely took over.

As much as we wanted to investigate the anomaly ourselves, our desire left little room for anything else. The mating bond was no fickle thing. It was truly temporarily altering our brain chemistry, leaving us solely focused on each other.

Niall made good on his promise to "worship me until dawn." He explored every corner of my body and left a kiss on every inch of my skin. I memorized the planes of his muscles as he moved. We embraced the bond. Lost ourselves to it. Until there was no telling where one of us ended and the other began.

The mirror across the room stood watch over it all. I often found myself staring into it. Seeing Niall take me from behind, pumping in and out of me, head tipped back, brows pinched in pleasure, was my undoing.

He coaxed my release from me again and again, and left me dripping with the aftermath of our passions. After each bout, he kissed me long and slow, taking his time and bringing us back down from the intensity of it all.

In between our explorations, he would slip into the foyer to mentally check in with the Trium, who were ensuring the court ran smoothly during his temporary absence.

Upon his return, we became ravenous once more.

The hours blurred together beneath the haze of the bond. Every kiss, every tender touch, every rapturous moment we spent in each other's arms made me feel alive—more whole than I'd ever felt. But it was more than that. Our souls were tethered, anchored together by the intangible thing that burned between us, stronger with every heartbeat and every shared breath . . .

Love.

A couple of days passed, and nothing out of the ordinary occurred.

No threats. No unwanted visitors. No mass of shadows.

It seemed we were all waiting on bated breath for something to approach from the north. But as the days went by . . . nothing happened.

Then, a letter arrived—as Morah had said it would. The engagement celebration that Ramil had been planning for his daughter and Killian was set to take place in only two days-time.

"Quite the last-minute invitation," Aremis said as he read the scrolled paper and passed it to Roirdan. "If not meant to keep us from planning anything."

We all sat on the private patio where Niall and I had shared our first breakfast together. Maeson joined us too. She'd been busy stocking up extra stores of medicines and healing salves in preparation for whatever was to come our way in the near future.

It was good to see her bright smile.

Morah, on the other hand, had been silent.

Perhaps she was just caught up in all the preparations for the event. Even though we would see her soon enough, I doubted we would be able to steal a moment for conversation in the midst of her father's court. After all, "enemies" didn't have private conversations and exchange valuable information.

Roirdan passed the invitation back to Niall, who rolled it up tightly.

"We will attend. Regardless of Ramil and his loyalties," my mate stated.

Aremis began, "Are you—"

"Yes. I'm sure."

The advisor closed his mouth.

Niall sighed. "We will stay well away from Ramil, does that help?"

"It's not only him that I worry about. It's the entirety of his court."

Niall looked at me. "If we don't attend, he'll see it as a sign of weakness."

"We can't have that," I said, dropping a bit of sarcasm in my tone, which made my mate grin.

None of us felt like it was the smartest thing to do, but to cower behind our wards was also no way to live. Life had to go on, even if it did suddenly consist of watching our backs at every turn.

Thanks to Folquin's information, we knew that Killian and Ramil were both part of Lyceius's dark agenda in some capacity, which meant we needed to keep them close and keep an eye on them.

I reminded myself once again, that this would all happen regardless. Lyceius would find out about me, and he would try to stop me. Or capture me. Or whatever it was he wanted to do with me to keep me from getting to *him* first.

But I was stronger now, and my power was coming into its own day by day. I wouldn't hide behind wards and inside mountains.

I would do what needed to be done. Come what may.

78
THE CLIMB

"Are you ready?" Niall's question hung on the crisp morning air the following day as we stood at the base of the mountain, staring up at the beginnings of the stone stairway that snaked all the way up to The Keep.

From the perspective of the patio, the stairs seemed impressive in their design, dizzying if you tried to visually trace their winding path from such a high angle.

Standing at the foot of them was an entirely different experience.

Daunting is what they were. At their threshold, The Keep seemed a world away, perched somewhere high above.

The founders of Calledan built the stairs as a strategic advantage, carving them into the mountain and setting wards against porting directly to The Keep—an effort that forced every would-be visitor to make the climb, therefore weeding out anyone with ill-intent. Enemies would see it as an obstacle.

But I was not an enemy.

For me, this was an opportunity. Because I was to be the Mountain Court's newest member. One of Niall's chosen—just like the Trium. I would sit in on meetings, give council, and hold status above other dignitaries. As Niall's mate, I would also be given a seat at his right hand —if and when the time came for us to bind ourselves together in ceremony. But in order for any of that to happen, an appointment to Niall's council was the first step.

It was the Mountain Court's tradition that anyone who was to become an influential member of the court must make the climb and swear the oath. The task signified one's commitment to Calledan and all she stood for.

I could tell just by looking that the ascent would be strenuous. Anyone who thought they could tackle this with ease would probably find themselves heaving, exhausted, and seriously considering their actions about a third of the way up. Which was the point. Scaling these stairs was a reminder of the struggles one might face when given such a seat of authority. A reminder of the oath taken. That a court member's decisions affected more than just themselves; they affected the entirety of the territory and everyone in it.

Niall had presented the option to me yesterday after the meeting with the Trium. Aremis had immediately agreed, stating that not only did he think I would be an invaluable asset, but since the prophecy revolved around me, it was in my best interest. Regardless of the blood that ran rich through my veins, I was technically still a human, which meant there was guaranteed to be pushback from the court's other council members. But if I made the climb and swore the oath—as tradition demanded—it might help to smooth out the rough edges when Niall presented me to the others.

I hadn't hesitated to say yes. I knew my answer before Niall had even finished asking the question. But as I laid in bed last night, tucked under his arm, trying to sleep, I couldn't stop my mind from fumbling over the implications.

Doing this—making the climb—meant more than just joining Niall's council. It was solidifying my place here. And that was like taking a permanent step away from everything I'd ever known. From Belthria. From Galenagh.

From my brother . . .

That was the ache that panged at my heart the most.

My place was here. I knew that without a doubt. But it still didn't ease the hurt that the only other person who shared my blood wasn't by my side.

I wanted to know that he was safe. *Needed* to know.

Before Folquin had returned to the king's castle, Niall instructed him to find Liam and get word to him any way that he could. So I'd written a letter, briefly explaining what had happened, and where I had gone. I didn't mention anything about who I truly was, the prophecy, or what I was capable of, in case someone were to intercept Folquin and get their hands on my missive. All I needed Liam to know was that I was safe, and that I would find a way to reunite with him.

Folquin promised he would track Liam down, deliver my message, and then bring me word of his whereabouts and well-being.

Despite the reassurance, I still felt like I was losing Liam by taking this next step.

I needed him to know that I hadn't abandoned or forgotten him. That I'd made it into the King's Guard, and then was forced to flee. All because of fate. All because of something greater than any of us. And by doing this, I was helping both realms. Helping *him*.

I wanted to share all of it in my letter and explain why I wasn't coming straight home, but I couldn't risk it. The vague bits I had given him would have to be enough for now.

I strained to see through the dense fog that blanketed the mountain. The steps carved a winding path, dipping behind boulders and slicing between sections of stone that protruded from the cliffside.

My heart tugged against my ribs like it was desperate for me to begin.

"I'm ready," I answered.

Thunder rumbled in the distance, its deep undulations tumbling through the peaks around us. If it rained, the challenging trek would become an even more difficult and *dangerous* one.

I scuffed my boot along the stone beneath me.

Smoother than it should be.

Add water, and it would become slick as ice.

The wind ruffled Niall's long, black cloak behind him as he reached for the sword at his hip.

"There must be a weight in your arms while you climb—a symbol of your willingness to not falter underneath the burden you bear." He withdrew his weapon, the blade hissing along the casing and singing with a hum as he extended it to me.

My muscles strained at the weight as I took it into my grasp, bringing it in front of me to study its make. It was much heavier than it looked—possibly the heaviest I'd ever handled. The blade was dark as ash, but polished to a shine that made it reflect like a mirror made of obsidian. The hilt was infinitely darker—a void within itself. It rested in my palm like a rift between stars, gobbling up the light around it and making my skin look eerily pale in comparison. There were no adornments or jewels on the pommel, or special details decorating the grip. Only a set of thick, pointed cross guards at the base of the blade.

It was a fierce weapon, fashioned for death.

"It is called Death's Whisper," Niall explained as I surveyed the blade. "It was given to Evander upon his enthronement as High Lord, and has been passed down through our family."

"I've never seen any weapon like it," I said curiously.

"No one knows where it came from or who created it. It was found deep in a cave in the northeastern parts of the mountains by Evander's father, Gavrin. To this day, its make still vexes the most skilled blacksmiths. All of our metalworkers leave their individual trademark on their work. This . . . has no such indication. It's seemingly indestructible though. And it always strikes true. Fitting for this challenge, I think."

I nodded in wonder, tipping the sword back and forth, pondering the manner in which I was going to carry it.

The wind rustled again, swirling up the steps, dispersing the fog and bringing with it the earthy smell of rain.

I needed to get moving.

Niall grunted at the weather, then reached into nothing and pulled out a thick swath of material, motioning with his hand for the sword again. "May I?"

He set to wrapping the hilt, leaving the two long ends of fabric hanging loose as he nudged his chin for me to turn around. He then brought the pieces over my shoulders and looped them under my armpits like he was strapping a pack onto my back. The sword sat flush between my shoulder blades, and he crossed the pieces of fabric over the base— where the hilt met the blade, before bringing them back around to my front and tying them off just beneath my breasts.

"Is that all right?" he asked, tugging gently to ensure the makeshift scabbard held properly.

"Solves my dilemma," I replied with a light smile. "Thank you."

621

He leaned in and planted a warm kiss on my brow, then pulled my body to his. "Promise me you'll be careful."

"I promise."

His arms tightened around me. "I'm forbidden to interfere if something happens, but I'll break that rule for you if I need to."

I grinned against his chest. "I'll be fine."

"I'm already tense as it is every time we're apart, and this—"

"Niall." I leaned back and lifted a brow at him.

He closed his eyes and sighed, offering me a slight smile. "I know you can do this. I just always want to make sure you're safe."

"You're adorable."

A warm laugh rumbled in his chest. "Don't tell anyone else that. I'll lose the dark, ominous façade I've worked so hard to maintain all these years."

I rolled my eyes and huffed a laugh of my own.

His embrace relented, and he glanced up at the sky. "You had best get going. That storm will be here before we know it."

I nodded, shifting the straps around my shoulders. "See you at the top?"

"I'll be waiting." He grinned. "And Auren? Whatever happens, don't give in to your fears."

Without giving me time to reply, he vanished.

Alone at the base of the stairway, I breathed in deep and listened to the whisper of the wind that was now pushing against my back, guiding me forward.

Don't give in to my fears?

Surely he meant "don't give up."

He didn't need to worry about that. The words *give up* were not in my vocabulary.

Steeling my spine, I lifted my foot and took a step, then another, and as I wound up around the first curve, thunder pulsed through the atmosphere, growing ever closer.

The sword was a steady weight at my back, a symbol of the duty I would be bound to uphold. It thudded against my spine with each step as I climbed and climbed.

A few hundred steps up—not even a dent in my conquest—and my thighs were burning. The patio loomed high above, still so far away. It fell out of sight as the stairway briefly cut through a piece of the mountain. When I emerged on the other side, a gust of wind jousted me sideways, slamming my shoulder into the stone to my left.

The storm was approaching.

The sun was hidden behind the gloom of thick, gray storm clouds that had been building. I frowned up at them, taking a moment to gather the stray strands of hair from my face and tuck them behind my ears as the lofty winds picked up and howled.

I continued upward, planting each foot with care and remaining focused. My thighs pulsed as I pressed on up the seemingly endless steps. Lightning splintered the sky above me, and I flinched, feeling overly exposed and vulnerable.

Move.

A rush of adrenaline rocketed through me, and I climbed quicker, but only for a brief moment before—

Splat.

Splat. Splat. Plink.

Thick, heavy raindrops peppered the stone and chimed against the hilt of Niall's sword that stretched above the back of my head.

Move. Faster.

I hissed as an onslaught of rain lashed against my face with the next gust. Squinting, I looked out to my right, where sheets of rain pummeled the valley, moving in my direction.

The weight on my back grew heavier with each passing minute, but I welcomed the burden. That was the whole point of this process. It tested one's will, one's commitment. It gave ample time to consider, and to reconsider.

The gods just so happened to add a storm to the challenge.

Lucky me.

Being Niall's mate, I could have just been given a seat on his council without having to make the climb. But I had opted to abide by tradition. I wanted to gain favor with the rest of his court, not ruffle feathers. Besides, I'd never been one to shy away from an honorable challenge. Perhaps that was why the storm was nipping at me like an ill-tempered beast. Testing my limits—poking at my determination with a sharpened stick.

"Test me, then. I won't falter," I gritted out loud through my teeth. My words were lost in the storm, but I was certain the gods heard them when a bolt of lightning pierced the air between the mountain I was ascending and the peak next to it. The resounding boom was immediate, and it rattled my bones as I planted another step and hauled myself up and up, grinning wickedly at what felt like an unspoken challenge.

A few hundred more steps came and went. The tip of the patio peeked out at me, then fell back behind the cliff face as I wobbled and wound, back and forth. Just when it seemed like I was getting closer to it, the next angle from which I saw it made it appear further away.

A sudden forceful gale ripped at my clothes, yanking me to the side. My heel slid out from under me on the slick stone, and I threw my arm out to catch myself. My palm met the jagged wall to my left. I hissed in pain as the stone sliced into my flesh. I steadied my feet and leaned into the wall, taking a breath and calming my pounding heart. The blood welled, then dispersed into my palm, diluted by the fat raindrops that splattered onto the quickly-closing wound.

Probably shouldn't have challenged the gods.

I slicked my sodden hair back from my face and straightened, planting my boots firmly on the steps again, when a voice whisked past me on the wind.

I whipped my head up, scanning my surroundings, searching for the source of the voice. My gaze traveled further up the mountainside, but there was nothing but stone, stairs, and—

Lightning flashed, and my eyes snagged on a tight corridor that was cut through the mountain. And there, on the left, a darkened doorway sat within.

Thunder crackled around me, sending me into motion.

I had to be at least halfway to the top. The patio loomed, so close, yet so far. But the doorway . . . it was much closer.

I pressed on, keeping one eye on the slick steps—careful to avoid the water that now cascaded down them—and one eye on the mysterious entrance.

Niall hadn't mentioned anything about a doorway, which made me even more curious as to why it was there.

Lightning flashed, illuminating the passage as I approached it. There was no actual door, only what looked to be a dark tunnel leading into the depths of the mountain. I halted in front of it, peering through the heavy rain to try and glean what might be inside.

The wind whispered again as it blew past, the words so fleeting I couldn't make out what was being said. Couldn't tell if the voice was male or female, or if the words were an invitation, or a warning.

Another flash, but the entry yielded none of its interior.

I propped myself against the wall across from it, gathering my wits, resting my legs, reassessing this last stretch of the climb.

Why would there be an entryway into the mountain here? Why not put it at the bottom of the stairs? Was it a passage that would bypass the remainder of the climb? A reprieve for those who might be injured or too exhausted to continue?

"Step inside," the whisper seemed to say as it drifted by again. Or did it? I couldn't tell if it had truly spoken, or if I was forming something out of nothing. My heartbeat was a pulse in my ears, my leg muscles so swollen and full of blood, they could double as water-soaked logs. In this state, I wouldn't be surprised if I'd imagined the words or the voice altogether.

The darkness pressed against the stone's opening, almost as if it was daring me to investigate. As if something was alive within, poised just beyond the threshold.

The world seemed to fall quiet, the pelting rain fading into a muffled drone as I stared at the entrance.

An entry into *what?*

If this had been something worthy of my attention, surely Niall would have mentioned it.

Why *wouldn't* he mention it?

I was wasting time, but something about the doorway intrigued me. I pushed off the wall and stepped closer. No sound, no light, just darkness and . . .

That smell . . .

It was *Niall's* scent. Vanilla and chestnut—faint, but unmistakable. The warm aroma of a fire followed on its heel, wafting out of the abyss.

Is this a shortcut to The Keep?

I drew up to the threshold and swiped a hand at the shadows just beyond. The air within was cool and dry. Tempting.

Too tempting.

The rain pelted my face as I glanced up the stairs. The Keep was close. I shouldn't be lingering and considering this strange doorway.

Just as I turned and placed a foot on the next step, I heard Niall's deep baritone calling my name from the opening. I whipped my head back toward the darkness. His voice sounded far away, like he was deep within the mountain. And there was an air of panic in it, almost as if he were desperate. It sent my senses on edge. Chills prickled down my back and arms, and I shuddered, suddenly feeling the bite of the rain and wind around me.

Was I supposed to venture into the entrance? My mind warred against itself as I shifted my weight on the steps, debating what to do.

The wind gusted against me like an invisible hand, but I turned and ascended another step. The moment I did, Niall's voice speared out of the doorway, *yelling* my name.

This time, his voice sounded *pained.*

My spine went rigid and my fingers were instantly moving to the knot of fabric beneath my breasts. I unbound the ties and yanked the straps, pulling the sword and its makeshift sheath from my back. The soaked cloth fell from the blade, and sword in hand, I stepped through the doorway.

79
THE ENTITY

MY SKIN TINGLED AS THE OPENING DISAPPEARED BEHIND ME, LEAVING ME to stagger forward through the darkness.

It was deathly quiet.

I stepped slowly, lightly, moving the sword from side to side in front of me to gauge my surroundings. But the area I swung it into was empty.

I was alone.

Niall's voice sounded again. "Auren?" A siren's song. Fleeting. Even further away now that I was inside.

But where was it coming from?

I shifted the sword to my dominant hand, and lifted my empty hand before me, drawing on my power. A glowing kernel swirled to life in my palm and grew into a luminous ball of white light upon my silent command. I turned in place, arm extended, but the darkness was too thick. It seemed to soak up all the luster, forbidding me to see anything beyond the confines of the span of my arms.

"Auren . . ."

I jerked to the right—where the voice seemed to have come from— and began walking. I hesitated on each stride, not knowing what I might stumble upon. Whatever this place was, why would he be in it? I started to get the feeling that I should have just kept climbing. But the way he had yelled my name sounded like he'd needed me.

"Auren . . ." His voice was fading.

I quickened my step, chasing the sound, willing the light at my hand to pulse brighter. But there was *nothing.*

"Niall?" I called out. My own voice was instantly gobbled up by the dense darkness. "Niall!"

A hiss bit through the shadows somewhere behind me, and I spun, swinging Death's Whisper in defense. My shoulder protested at the weight of the blade, and my grip wobbled. I needed two hands to wield it.

Just as I had done with the candlestick back in The Keep, I released the orb of light from my hand, and willed it to float in the air in front of me. With both hands, I gripped the sword firmly and set into a stance, still scanning through the inky space for *something. Anything.*

The orb of light turned with me as I stepped in a slow circle, waiting, listening, thinking. "Niall?" I called out, quieter than before.

A low, bitter laugh trickled through the darkness, but it was not Niall's laugh. Whoever it belonged to sounded ancient.

What Niall had told me before I began the climb was starting to make sense now.

Don't give in to your fears.

I steeled my spine and raised my weapon. "Who's there?"

Silence.

"Don't be a coward. Come forth."

The ancient laugh came again, more amused this time. "Coward? I've been called many names, but that is something no one has ever dared to call me."

I braced my grip on Niall's sword. "Care to show yourself then?"

"I have no form here. I exist in the shadows. I am everywhere, and nowhere. Time and space have no hold on me."

"I don't believe you," I said, sending my orb of light to sweep through the space.

"You will find nothing, try as you might. But by all means, search."

Even with the light, there was utterly nothing to reflect off of. The floor beneath my feet might as well have been the night sky that bound the moon; the space around me—the inky black mass that strung up the stars.

"What kind of game is this?" I asked, feeling the prickle of panic nipping at the confines of my throat.

"Not a game, Young One. A test."

Shit.

I knew I should have stuck to the stairs.

"But you didn't," the voice said. "You are here. Where fate has allowed you to venture."

"And where is *here?*" I wasn't even going to bother asking how it knew what I was thinking.

"A fracture in time. A beat between breaths." The voice circled me, humming as if in observation. "You are not like the others. You . . . produced this light."

I called the orb back to me, and it perched above my head, casting me in a halo of luminescence. "What of it?"

The entity spoke again, but it was closer. Like it had followed the light and was now standing right in front of me. "There is a prophecy in this world. I have heard it whispered for millennia . . ." It paused, weighing its words. "Your blood—"

"My blood is none of your concern." I lifted the sword, angling it in warning, pretending the voice belonged to a body that stood only a few feet away. Hating that I felt like an idiot, poised to strike at nothing but a whisper. "Why did I hear my mate's voice? Where is he?"

As non-physical as this entity was, I could have sworn it drew back and sank away to another corner of the blackened space as I stepped forward.

"You are in no place to make demands here, regardless of the weapon you possess." There was an edge of apprehension in its voice, as if it wasn't entirely sure I *didn't* pose a threat.

I straightened, but didn't move to lower my weapon. "You lured me in using his voice . . ."

"The voice of the one who is most precious to you is often the very thing that will drive you to take reckless action."

I wanted to scoff, but the more I thought about it, the more I knew the entity was right. Had it been anyone else's voice, I would have been more suspicious. But with it being Niall's, all logic had fallen by the wayside.

I clenched my teeth together, knowing I would need to play along at whatever game this *thing* was about to introduce. "Then make your demand of me and release me back to the stairway."

The air stirred, as if the entity was moving again. It took a long moment before it spoke. "What is your name?"

I hesitated. Why did it need my name? What would it do with the information?

"Who do you answer to?" I countered. I needed to know that I could trust its loyalties before I spoke any further.

"No one," it stated, and I swore I heard it smile as it said the words. "I was offered this task long ago by one of the founding brothers of this court, Aleris."

Offered . . .

Offers meant bargains. And bargains benefitted agendas.

"And what do you get in return for doing your duty?" I asked.

A sharp hiss punctuated the air. "I am not some subservient thing to be told to do a bidding. It is not duty that keeps me here. It is simply that I am provided what I seek, in exchange for my form of . . . interrogation."

I paused, deciphering everything the entity wasn't saying. "So, whatever you do, you do it on behalf of the High Lord of Calledan?"

"In a sense," it crooned. "But the High Lord does not control me. Not yet. I have been my own master for many ages. One day that will change again. For now, I am content with being here. I prefer to be attached to a single plane of existence, rather than drifting, but I am not bound by anyone, nor to any place. Not now."

I shuddered, wondering what exactly it meant by that. "And what is it that you seek?"

Its voice deepened. "So many questions." It circled me once more, flitting through the dark. "I am here for *you*. Just as I am for every other person who makes this climb. What I seek . . . knowledge. Information. Something no one else knows."

Something no one else knows . . . Interrogation . . .

The words crept through my mind, stilling and sinking in. If it was here for everyone that climbed—

I suddenly came to the realization.

"You . . . you're here to test my intentions . . . to make sure I'm fit for this position in the court—"

A deep throaty laugh floated by, silencing me. "So very wise. I'm impressed. Most are too frightened to think straight."

I huffed a laugh, turning the blade in my palm, not deigning to lower it —in case this was some sort of trick I still wasn't fully processing. "I've endured much worse than a dark room."

"Oh?" The word was laced with curiosity.

"I've seen darkness embodied in a physical form before," I offered. The entity remained silent, listening. "I've stared evil in the face after it killed my parents. So, no, I'm not frightened."

A pause. "Do you think *I'm* evil?" it asked.

"Not the kind of evil that kills recklessly." *I hope.*

"Mmm. And do you associate darkness with evil?"

I opened my mouth, then closed it again, thinking. Was it a trick question?

"Sounds to me like you do. And that blade still pointed at my face confirms it."

I bristled at the thought of its *face* so close to me. "I thought you didn't have a form?"

"Not one that you can see here, but I can still perceive you, which means, visible or not, I still have a face."

I came to terms with its statement in my mind and slowly lowered my weapon, though I kept a tight grip on it—just in case. "My mate, Niall, his power is a form of darkness."

The entity drew closer, its presence more palpable than it had been, taking advantage of the fact that Death's Whisper was now pointed at the ground. "Fated to the High Lord. I should have known. You bear his sword, after all. But you do not fear him?"

"No."

"If the darkness ever came calling and you had the means to eradicate it, would you?"

It was testing me. Perhaps this was what it wanted. "Yes," I answered.

"Interesting," it said, shifting around me. "While this information is a gracious offer, it is still not what I seek."

Damn.

"Your name?" it pressed.

I pushed a breath out through my nose, debating whether or not to say it.

"Have I not gained an inkling of your trust?"

I blinked hard, hoping my eyes would eventually adjust. "I'm wary of trusting something I cannot see."

"Clever," it said, moving away again.

Finally, with no feeling of impending doom rattling my gut, I gave my name. "Auren."

"Auren," it echoed amusedly.

"And what do I call you?"

The air stilled, and the entity stuttered, as if struck dumb by the question. "N-No one—aside from the previous High Lords—has asked for my name in thousands of years."

I suddenly felt sorry for the thing. When it remained quiet, I tried to ease the tension. "It sounds like you should keep better company."

"I should," the voice said, sounding as if it were grinning. "You shall know me by the same name as Aleris did. As your mate does. As Eathril."

"Eathril," I repeated. "Thank you—"

"Do not thank me, Auren. You have not yet endured the test."

My breathing hitched. I had begun to think that this slight progress in conversation might have been enough to tip the scales in my favor, and that he might give me an alternative option. This "test" he spoke of didn't sound like it would be an enjoyable one.

"There is no avoiding it," Eathril said, solidifying my unspoken disappointment.

I shifted on my feet. "What must I do?"

"Do? Nothing. It is what you must *see*."

80

THE TEST

Being told to *see* in the midst of total darkness seemed like a cruel trick. My orb of light pulsed above me as I willed more power into it, trying to get a deeper glimpse into the inky abyss.

"You will not see with your eyes, Young One. This type of sight is meant for your mind. Hence the dark confines of this room," Eathril said.

A room, then. Not a portal to my demise.

A room required a door . . . which meant I could easily get out if I played my cards right.

Before I could ask another question, or begin to plot my escape, I was struck with a sight that was not my own. My eyes remained open, but they were seeing something beyond the space I stood in. A vision played out before me, as real as the sword in my hand. I was standing in the corner of another dark room, one with visible walls and furniture. In the center was a large, round table, and around it stood fae, none of whom I recognized.

The doors swung open and in walked . . . *me*. Niall was at my side, Aremis, Remic, and Roirdan trailing closely behind us. The other fae bowed as we approached.

When Eathril said I would "see," I didn't expect to see *myself.*

I stepped forward out of the shadows, sword still in hand, but no one in the vision noticed me. Conversation ensued, but all the words were mumbled, like a veil was pulled over them. A map was spread out upon the table with haste. A few of the fully armored males pointed at the parchment while others weighed in. All the while, I watched from my corner.

I focused on the version of me standing tall and regal at Niall's side. There was a warm coloring to my face, like I'd spent a good deal of time outdoors. My sword hung at my side in its scabbard, my dagger at the other. I looked—for the most part—the same, but something about me was different. An air of authority perhaps.

Just when I was beginning to question why I was being shown this vision in the first place, the room shook. Rocks crumbled from the ceiling as everyone braced themselves, and I watched in horror as the other me began to push out a shield over everyone in the room, just as the stone came crashing down.

A scream died in my throat as my vision blurred, and I was suddenly standing at the base of a jagged stone mound. At first glance, the blackened stone looked like that of Calledan's mountains, but the atmosphere, the sky, the lack of trees . . . all of it was wrong. The clouds swirled in an angry torrent above, and numerous sparks and embers were floating on the wind, as if there were fires burning somewhere off in the distance.

My attention honed in on the top of the stony hill before me, and the urge to *climb* hit me in full force. I stepped with precision, digging my feet into the grooves and notches in the rock. When I came to the top, I grappled at the edge and peered up at a glistening, black, stone altar. It was a beast of a structure, starkly smooth atop the harsh, rugged mound it sat upon.

I hauled myself up onto the summit, and stood, only to freeze when I saw a stranger standing on the other side of the altar. A male—by the looks of his build. His back was facing me, his black cloak whipping in the wind, his head concealed beneath the large hood.

The wind suddenly changed direction, gusting against my back—toward the stranger, and like a predator scenting its prey, he whipped his head up and spun to face me. The hood was thrust away with another gust, and I stumbled backwards at the sight of *Niall.*

Aghast, I stared at the face that was his . . . but *not.* Black, inky webs bled from the corners of his eyes into his skin, trailing down over his cheekbones, and his pupils were blown so wide, they were a solid orb of black with only a sliver of gold left at the rim.

He was breathing heavily, as if he was in a rage.

But what unnerved me the most was that he was staring right back at me. Unlike the last vision, there was no *other* me. I was the only one who stood before him, and he was very well aware of my presence.

My power ignited along my veins, my essence flaring in desperation at the sight of him. His name fell so quietly off my lips as I tried to gauge what was happening. "Niall . . ."

When I took a step around the altar, his lips peeled back in a snarl. Then, he was shaking his head back and forth, squeezing his eyes shut. When they snapped open again, the gold had beaten back the black just enough. For a brief moment, he looked at me with pleading eyes, before the ring of gold winked out completely, and his expression shifted into something menacing once more.

In one sudden movement, he slammed his fists down upon the stone slab between us with such force that a crack skittered across its massive surface.

I was startled, but I stood my ground. "Niall, what are—"

"You should be running for your life," he warned with a voice that sounded so full of wrath, so otherworldly, that I shuddered. "Or do you value it so little?"

I flinched at his brashness. "I can help you with whatever this is. Just tell me what you need from me." My hand reached out for him as I took a step forward.

He watched the movement with deadly precision, then slowly shook his head. "No."

Something was wrong with him. He didn't look the same, and he definitely didn't *feel* the same. The bond between us was there, but it was pulled taut, straining, like something was dragging him away from everything he knew and was.

"Tell me what to do," I urged.

"Leave," he rumbled.

"*Never.*"

His fist rose again to slam down against the stone, but I thrust my palm out and sent a jolt of light toward him before he could make contact. I watched his eyes lift to mine the moment the light struck his chest. Saw the darkness leech from his irises and the tension in his brows release, right before I was pulled from the vision.

I collapsed to my knees in the dark confines of the room within the mountain. The orb of light that had been above me had gone out, and a strangled sob wrenched free from my throat, the only sound in the deafening quiet that was now almost maddening.

"*Where is he?*" I demanded. "*Where's Niall?*"

The air stirred as Eathril moved. He answered from directly in front of me, like he had also fallen to his knees only a few feet away. His words were measured as he said, "He is waiting for you, on the patio of The Keep."

I palmed the hilt of the sword in my hand, letting the words sink in.

He's safe at The Keep. He's waiting for me.

"So, the visions . . . weren't real?" I needed to hear Eathril say it.

"No, they were not real. But your encounter was . . . different."

Of course it was. I'm *different. It's only fitting.*

"How so?"

I could feel his stare through the darkness. He was studying me. As if *he* were the one with questions, and *I* had the answers.

"You were given *two* visions," he finally said.

"I know—wait . . . You saw them as well?"

"I did." He was frowning. I could hear it in his voice. "But there is only ever *one* vision, Auren."

When he didn't continue, worry sprouted in my gut.

He didn't know where the second vision had come from.

"What does it mean, that I saw two of them?"

"I am not certain. I have the power to elicit a vision and open a gateway in the mind of others to see a glimpse of what is yet to come—but only a glimpse. It is neither the most crucial, nor complete in its presentation, because foresight is not something that is freely given. But it offers enough for me to gather an assessment of one's character and how they would react in times of trial. I brought about your first vision. The second, however, was not of my doing."

"If it wasn't your doing, then whose was it?" *I* certainly couldn't conjure visions.

"I am wondering that as well," Eathril replied, his voice once again moving through the dark.

I remained where I was on the floor, thinking. The first vision was troublesome. But the second one . . . that one bothered me the most. Seeing Niall's eyes, his struggle—whatever that was, unsettled me. It felt too real. Too personal. And I had no explanation as to why I would have seen anything like that at all. "Eathril, are you sure that's the only purpose these visions serve?"

His tone turned suspicious. "Are you accusing me of something, Young One?"

"No," I quickly answered. "I was thinking more along the lines of something else using *you.*"

"Mmm," was all he said.

"What if the second vision was a warning? Something given to me by the fates somehow? Is such a thing even possible?"

As if my questions were equally concerning to him, he hummed in thought. "The fates operate by their own law, so there is no telling what is truly possible. I do not determine what someone sees. That is beyond my control."

"What *do* you control?" *Please don't say the future.* What I had just seen was something I never wanted to see again.

"When I swore my oath to Aleris, I was granted the authority to judge over all who enter this room. If someone is making the climb to be appointed to the court's council, the vision they see is of a particular turning point in their future—if they were to be given that position. If what I see in your vision benefits this court, the current High Lord will be notified of my blessing. If what I see is not in the court's best interest, I will alert him all the same, and you will be his to do with as he sees fit. You would be surprised to know how many are revealed to be a fraud, a coward, or a traitor."

I worked through the information in my head while fiddling with Niall's sword, mindlessly skimming the pad of my thumb against the edge of the blade. It caught on the ridges of my fingerprint with each movement, the sound a pleasant *scraaaape*; a rasped intonation to fill the silent void as I began to wonder what Niall did to those who were found "not worthy."

Then, my thoughts backtracked to the other bit of information Eathril mentioned, and I steadied my voice as I asked, "If the vision is a turning point in one's future, does that mean what I saw will happen?"

"Like I said, it is neither the most crucial, nor complete in its presentation." A cryptic, anxiety-inducing answer, but I could tell by his voice that he was either not willing to elaborate further, or he simply couldn't offer me more information than that.

"But what if—"

"You passed. That is all you need to know." There was sympathy in the way he said it, but the words did nothing to quell my rising concern.

The blade wobbled in my grip, and I didn't even feel its bite against my thumb until warm blood trickled down my finger.

"No!" Eathril hissed, darting closer. "That blood is ancient! Precious!" It felt as if he were gripping my hand, enclosing his incorporeal fingers around it to staunch the bleeding.

I set the sword down and willed another orb of light into my empty hand to survey the damage, but all I saw was a small slice that was already mending itself, and the smear of blood along my palm.

I lifted my eyes to the space around me. There was still no visible sign of Eathril.

"You will not find evidence of my existence," he reminded me. "Not here."

"Where then?" I asked, lifting my eyes to the room beyond.

"Somewhere I hope you never go," he said quietly.

A prickling sensation walked up my spine, and I turned to see the entryway revealing itself once more behind me. I was closer to it than I thought I would be, considering I'd chased after Niall's voice upon entering. Or perhaps the space had just been an illusion, and Eathril could manipulate it as he saw fit.

I retrieved Death's Whisper and stood, blinking at the gray light of the world beyond.

"I have enjoyed our conversation, Auren," Eathril said, his voice coming up next to me, as if he'd walk beside me and see me out.

Pushing back all the anxiety that was writhing in my gut, I mustered up a grin. "Have I made another friend?"

Even without a form, his pause was notable. His presence stilled as he weighed my question. "I do not have the pleasure of keeping friends."

I picked up on a hint of sadness in his voice. "I shall consider you one of *mine,* then." I liked to think that he tilted his head in admiration when he heard my words.

"You are kind. But I would not want to disappoint you. I cannot give you the friendship you seek."

"An ally, then." A being with his particular capabilities would be an asset. And, considering I was the High Lord's mate, and bound to this place, we would most certainly cross paths again. "No need for the pleasantries and upkeep in between. Just good faith."

He was quiet a moment longer. "You are a very powerful ally to have. I would be a fool to decline."

My thoughts exactly.

"Allies," he said softly in agreement.

I nodded through the dark. "Another question, if I may?"

"Go on," he urged.

"What exactly do you know of my power?"

"Ah, yes. The light in the darkness. You are the one the prophecy tells of. Though I did not expect to meet you myself." He remained next to me, facing the doorway—I supposed, staring out into the storm, as I was. "I do not know the specifics of your power, but I can sense the wealth of it that you possess. What you wield now is a weak form of what you are truly capable of—if my senses are correct." He paused. "I have known others who were capable of great power, who used it to further their own evil ambitions, or let it overcome them completely."

I angled my head toward where I imagined him standing. "I'm not—"

"I know. You are unlike the rest. The power you possess would turn a fae heart sour with greed, and drive them mad with an insatiable hunger to rule. But your heart, Auren, is pure and unselfish. You will right many wrongs with what you've been given."

I glanced down at my palm, where the small orb of light gleamed. "I never wanted this power. When I learned the truth of my lineage, I fought against it." Turning my hand over, I watched the luminous ball tumble over my knuckles as I willed it, before I scooped it back up in my palm. "It doesn't seem to have an effect on the darkness here though."

"That is because you have not yet learned to use it to its full potential. If this was just some dark room within The Keep, your light would illuminate it like a beacon in the night. But as it is, you cannot penetrate this particular darkness because I am currently occupying it and am hidden within. Had you already mastered your power, you could cast me out at your will. When you *do* master it, I suspect there will not be a shadow you won't eradicate."

There was so much more he wasn't saying.

I half-laughed. "Are you some sort of god that I'm not aware of?"

"No. Not a god. I am much like you though. Something that might not exist if it weren't for someone else's greed and ambitions. Because of my creation, I am tied to the gods, therefore I share a sense of discernment, though my power is limited. But that is another story for another time. For now, you must leave this place and finish the climb."

I frowned, but he was right. The task wasn't complete until I stepped foot on the patio of The Keep.

"A word of advice," he offered. "Use your shield against the rain. It will make the remainder of the climb much easier."

Of course. Why hadn't I thought of that?

"Thank you," I said. "Eventually I'll remember that's an option."

He gave the faintest chuckle, so quiet I almost missed it. "In the meantime, promise you will not spill any more unnecessary blood. Whether you think so or not, it *is* of my concern. You are too important."

I offered the shadows a smile. "Because I'm the High Lord's mate? Or because of the prophecy?"

"You are important *regardless*," he answered, his voice fading behind me as if he were retreating deeper into the mountain.

Seeing as he did hold some strange loyalty to this court, it seemed his concern was justified. But for an entity that was cloaked in shadow and could sift through someone's intentions like they were on display in an open book, I didn't picture him having much regard for one's well-being, let alone caring if they lived or died. Which brought about a final question . . .

"Eathril?" I called out, turning back into the darkness.

"Yes, Young One?"

"Are you capable of taking a life?" It was an odd question—one that I knew he wasn't expecting, but somehow, it slipped off my tongue like I had no self-control.

He hummed in amusement, as if I had just offered him a tempting wager. "I am," he replied, smiling—from the sound of it, before the room grew hollow with his absence.

I dipped my chin in acknowledgement, tucking the information away. Then, I let the orb fade out, and turned for the entryway, eager to greet the light and the deluge once more.

81
UNWINDING

WITH MY SHIELD SET INTO PLACE AROUND ME, I STEPPED OUT FROM THE confines of Eathril's room. Up to my left, the patio of The Keep jutted out like the chin of a mountain giant, watching me, waiting for me to ascend to where it was perched high above. The waterfall cascaded from underneath it, its roar drowned out by the storm and the thunder that rumbled overhead.

Minutes felt like hours as I lifted one foot after the other and climbed. The time I'd spent enduring Eathril's "test" had given my legs a small reprieve, allowing them to regain some of their strength, but my thighs still burned with each step. Thankfully, his reminder to use my shield kept me from having to squint through the sheets of rain, making the remainder of the climb a little less taxing.

I tried to imagine what Eathril would tell Niall. Would he tell him what he had seen in my vision? What if he didn't? Was that something *I* should bring up? Given everything that was happening, I didn't want to worry Niall with something as ominous as what I had seen.

I wasn't sure what unnerved me more: the fact that I had two visions—when there was only supposed to be one, or the fact that Eathril didn't know where the second vision had come from. There was no way either of them could mean anything good. Especially the second one.

Chills swept over me at the memory of Niall's face. His eyes . . .

barely a trace of gold left in them. And those inky black webs, bleeding through his skin . . .

I blinked hard, trying my best to erase the image and remind myself that it was not reality. For all I knew, the vision could have been a fluke. Eathril had even said that the visions were not complete in their presentation.

Dwelling on it would only distract me. And now was not the time for that. So I pushed the thought to the back of my mind and focused on the final stretch of the climb.

I could have sworn I felt Eathril keeping to the shadows, flitting from one patch of darkness to another, watching me from each passing recess and shallow fissure in the mountainside. I was content to let him accompany me—if that was indeed what he was doing.

Though he had all the makings of something that *should* be feared, I did not fear him. Instead, I'd stared into the darkness and proposed an alliance. It was strategic, yes, but it was also based on intuition. For some reason, I knew I hadn't seen the last of him.

Just when the wind began to calm, and the rain no longer slanted on its descent, I crested a ridge that gave me a full view of the final stretch to The Keep.

A hundred steps. Maybe less.

Niall was standing at the top, gazing down like a beacon against the silver sky. When our eyes met, a proud smile spread across his face, and I mirrored it, desperate to get to him.

My legs protested for rest, but I pushed onward, clutching Death's Whisper at my side and ignoring the weight of it.

Fifty steps away.

Forty.

My heart was pounding, my breath aflame in my chest, but my determination didn't falter. Instead, it was fed by the pride that shone on Niall's face.

Thirty.

Twenty.

His shadows wafted out around him, stretching down the top of the steps as if they would grab me and haul me up to him faster.

Ten.

Five.

I gasped as my boot hit the last step. Niall's shadows were instantly there, swooping under me as my knees buckled, and guiding me into his strong arms. Both of our shields collapsed as we collided, and I inhaled a ragged breath that was full of his scent.

"I've got you, my love," he breathed into my hair as he dug his fingers into it and held me against his chest. "I've got you."

His shadows continued pressing against me, bracing my legs and taking my weight, allowing me to relax against him.

I lifted his sword, and he took it into his grasp, chuckling as he eyed the weapon, then me. "Do I even want to know why this is no longer strapped to your back?"

"No," I said, exhaling. "You don't."

A deep rumble echoed in his chest as he handed the sword off to someone behind him, then returned his arm to me. "I'm so proud of you."

I smiled, feeling the gentle droplets of rain against my face again, and not caring one bit. In his arms, the rest of the world fell away. I was where I belonged. We could be drowning at sea, battered by waves that promised a suffocating death, but in his arms, I would die happy.

"Let's get you inside and warmed up."

As we turned, I saw Remic holding Niall's sword. He dipped his head low. When he lifted his eyes back to me, I saw the relief on his face. Beyond him stood Roirdan and Aremis, shielded from the rain. They too bowed their heads toward us.

Niall nodded to the three of them, then he gathered me up in his arms and ported me to his bedchamber.

Even though it was still morning, the dark, candle-lit space of his private quarters made it feel like it was always night—which was quite fitting, when all I wanted to do was sink into the heat of the water that I heard filling the tub in the adjacent bathing chamber, and rest.

Niall eased me down onto the bed and proceeded to pull off my boots and socks. He set them on the floor near the fire so that they could dry, then resumed his place over me and gripped the collar of my shirt with both of his hands. Without warning, and with what seemed like an effortless tug, he gently tore my shirt apart from top to bottom, ripping the fabric straight down the center.

I gasped and stared up at him. "Why are you tearing it?"

"You're soaked, and it would take ages to try and peel it off of you. I'll get you a new one."

The last of the hem separated, and he slid his warm hands up my chest, pushing the wet fabric away from my body. He wrapped one arm behind me, lifting me off the bed, while his other hand pulled my sleeves down one by one.

I laughed gently in his ear as he held me to him and freed me from the shirt. "You do know I'm still capable of undressing myself, right? I'm not dead."

"But you're exhausted," he purred back. "Let me do this for you."

I settled back onto the blankets as he moved to unfasten my pants, taking his time pulling them down my legs.

He hooked my undergarment under his finger, lifting it off my hip, and with the flick of a shadow, the fabric turned to ash, evaporating into nothing and leaving me bare before him. His eyes slid to my bralette next. That too turned to ash the moment he touched it.

I gave him a pointed look.

He smiled. "I'll replace those too."

"This could get expensive very quickly."

His eyes roved over my naked body. "Worth it."

I grinned up at him. "Remind me to not get attached to my wardrobe."

He scooped me up once more and carried me to the next room. "Or you could just not wear anything at all. You won't find me objecting."

I laughed into the crook of his neck and pinched his shoulder as he set me down next to the sunken tub—which was more like a small pool, carved into the mountain stone.

The steam that curled in the air above the water's surface broke as I descended the steps into the glittering, black basin and submerged myself up to my neck. I let out a satisfied groan as I churned in the water, letting the warmth engulf me and melt away the aches in my legs. Then, I heard the whisper of fabric hitting the floor behind me. I turned to see Niall's cloak in a pile next to the edge of the pool.

He stripped, baring his chiseled frame, corded thighs, and every delicious detail in between, and stepped into the water to join me. "Come here, love," he said, taking a seat on the stone bench at the edge of the tub and spreading his thighs wide.

I sidled up to him, letting him turn me so that my back was to his chest and my hips rested between his legs. His hands slid down to my aching muscles and began gently massaging.

I let my head fall back against his shoulder and breathed out. "Okay, I've decided that I'm going to need to exhaust myself at least once a week now, because this feels amazing."

"I'm more than happy to make this a routine," he murmured in my ear. "But there is no need to exhaust yourself for it. Just say the word, and I will gladly give you whatever you need." He placed a kiss just under the edge of my jaw, and chills broke out across my skin.

A sudden wave of desire washed over me, completely negating my ability to relax and rest. I smiled and melted further into him, pressing my backside against his hips. He hardened behind me, and both his hands stilled for a moment. I ground myself against him again, feeling an intense need to have *him* between *my* legs.

His fingers resumed their ascent, digging into my muscle and flesh as they slowly wrapped toward the inside of my thighs. "Auren"—he breathed—"you just made the climb—"

"I don't care. I want you." I rolled my hips against his manhood, eliciting a hiss from him in response.

The heat from the water seemed to be doing wonders. The aches were easing faster than I expected. Maybe having a god's blood in my veins also aided in that? Regardless, I was no longer focused on recovery. I wanted Niall's lips on mine. I wanted the thick, rigid, length that was pressed against my spine.

He gripped my hips and spun me in the water, lifting me up to straddle him. Then, his hands were cupping my face, his golden eyes flickering to a simmering glow as he stared into mine. "Have I told you how fucking proud I am that you're mine?"

Heat blazed between my legs at his words, and I reached for him, positioning him at my entrance.

"Yes," I whispered. "Now, show me."

Niall's eyes flared, and he claimed my lips in a searing kiss. I sank down onto him, and he parted me in one smooth thrust, filling me to the brim. Both of our moans collided as his tongue rolled against mine.

He reached beneath my backside and raised me up and down along his shaft in a rhythmic motion. The sound I made echoed through the chamber, and his grip tightened, his enthusiasm spurred on by my pleasure.

The steam lifted around us, wrapping us in a sensual veil of mist as our breaths punctuated our movements.

Niall leaned forward, coming to the edge of the sunken ledge. "Wrap your hands around my neck," he commanded. I did as he said, and he rolled my hips for me, sinking deep inside me with each decadent thrust he made.

I turned to liquid in his grip, all of my worries and aches dissolving away completely. I watched his chest and arms flex and contract as he directed my body. Every glorious inch of him fanned the flame in my core that would soon erupt.

My breasts shimmied under the water's surface, garnering his gaze, and I'd never felt so sure of myself. Every time I witnessed how the sight of my body affected him, it made me feel more beautiful and confident than before.

I loved the way he worshipped my body, and the way he looked at me like I was the only thing he ever cared to see in this world.

He angled me just right, hitting every pleasurable nerve deep inside, and then, his hand was moving. His palm splayed across my abdomen, and his thumb pressed against the sensitive bud at the apex of my thighs, flicking in short bursts of motion that drove me absolutely wild. The stimulation had me clenching against him, soaking him with a wetness that made the water feel lacking in comparison.

His eyes spoke volumes—glowing golden, and fixated at where we were joined.

At the sound of his confirming groan, my eyelids fluttered closed, and I came apart in his arms, my head dipping back into the water as I cried out in ecstasy.

Seconds later, he was thrusting into me so deeply that the water between us thrashed. I lifted my head back up, meeting his stare, and found his brows pinched with the height of pleasure just as he climaxed.

His hips bucked forward, shooting warm ropes of his release inside me as he held my hips to him and let out a fierce groan.

His hand braced my spine, and he brought me to his chest as he sank back onto the submerged bench, panting into my wet hair. We held each other for a long while, until the water had calmed around us again.

I pulled back to look him in the eyes. "I love you, Niall."

"And I, you." He captured my lips again, kissing me deep and slow, and I couldn't help that my sex clenched around him. He began to harden again inside me, and he hummed against my lips, breaking the kiss to lift an eyebrow at me.

"You have an insatiable appetite," I said, grinning.

"Because *you* are so irresistible." He twitched within me, then gently pulled himself out and set me beside him on the bench. "But I'll let you rest. There will be plenty of time for more of this later." His wicked grin promised nothing less.

I pushed my bottom lip out in a pout, earning a deep chuckle from him as he drifted further into the pool. The water eclipsed his head as he sank below the surface. When he rose again, he shook his hair and slicked it back with his hands.

"Do you have to make every move so sensual?" I said, rolling my eyes.

"Hmm?"

"You're tempting me on purpose, aren't you?" I sent a splash of water in his direction.

He laughed, turning his head to let the water droplets pelt his cheek. "I would never." With a wink, he sank back under.

I pulled my knees up to my chest, and without thinking twice of it, I reached for the spot on my thumb where his sword had cut me. The phantom wound itched, as if a scab would have been forming—had it been left to heal at a less rapid speed.

Niall surfaced again, and his eyes went directly to the move. He closed the distance between us in an instant and snatched my hand up from the water. "You were wounded." His eyes simmered a brazen gold as he assessed my skin. "How?"

"A slip of my own hand. It was so dark, I couldn't see your sword very well." I reached up and pointed to the spot on my thumb. The small slice had left a thin white scar, whereas the other cut from the mountain stone hadn't. I bared my other palm to him too. "And this one was cut by a rock during the climb."

He lifted both my hands to his lips and pressed a kiss against each site of the healed wounds, then frowned. "Eathril didn't mention it."

"It's fine, really. And it was my fault. I was . . . too worked up about what I saw."

Niall nodded, then met my eyes, seeming to glimpse that there was more I was dying to say. "Don't," he cautioned me.

"Don't what?"

"Don't tell me. It's not for me to know."

"But what if—"

"I know that you passed, and Eathril spoke very highly of you. And that's all I need to know. The fates do not take kindly to those that know more than they should."

I looked back down at where my hands rested in his, recalling the way he'd spoken in my vision. How he'd refused my help, even though he'd clearly needed it.

"Auren," he said, drawing out my name in gentle warning. "I mean it. No one else is meant to know what you saw. It could jeopardize too much."

Or it could make all the difference . . .

I bit my tongue, trusting that he knew what was best.

An amber bottle appeared in his hand, along with a thick washcloth. He uncorked the soap and worked it into a lather, punctuating the air with his delicious scent. I held his stare and settled onto the sunken bench, awaiting his offer. Sure enough, he drifted forward and brushed the cloth along my collarbone. I hummed with contentment and leaned my head back against the stone ledge behind me, letting my arms float freely at my sides.

He worked his way down my chest, circling my breasts with precision, before halting over my ribcage. I knew what his gaze was caught on just by where he was looking; the thin white scar about two inches long that ran between my ribs on my right flank. He studied it, like he could see the moment it happened playing out before his eyes, and how I'd maneuvered —just so—to avoid a punctured lung.

"That was from the day my parents died," I said, allowing him to assess the visible ghost of my past that would cling to me forever.

The rim around his irises flared to life, reflecting small orbs of gold on the water's surface between us. His voice was low as he said, "That could have been fatal."

"I know." I knew it very well. That man had swiped his sword to gut me where I'd stood. But fate had other plans.

Niall lifted his eyes to mine, resuming the languid strokes of the washcloth as he worked his jaw. "I won't let another blade touch your skin," he promised.

When he brought my body closer to his, I leaned into him and pressed a kiss against his shoulder. "I know," I repeated. "And I'll be more careful myself."

He gave a light laugh, then moved around to my back and worked the cloth along my shoulders, peppering my body with kisses of his own as he went. "After this, I need to call a meeting with the council before we leave for Benmoor. We'll need to schedule a time for a formal ceremony for your induction and oathing once we get back."

"There's a ceremony?"

"Yes. It's part of the protocol in this court. The fae *love* formalities."

I spun toward him and gave him a look.

"Don't worry. The ceremony is more of a chance to . . . show off."

I noted the glint in his eyes and the slightest tug against the corner of his mouth. "Sounds like it's more for *you* to show *me* off," I said, grinning.

"Oh trust me, darling"—he tilted my chin up with his finger—"I plan on doing plenty of that."

82

ENSNARED

The following day was the celebration for Morah and Killian's betrothal.

That afternoon, Niall, Aremis, and I arrived in Benmoor.

The sky was darker than usual, like a storm wanted to sweep across the plains. But the skies refused to open up. That didn't stop the wind from wildly whipping the Desert Court's amber banners against their posts outside the palace. The golden crest of a serpent-wrapped dagger seemed to undulate and thrash on its surface as we ascended the steps.

The fabric of my slate blue skirts beat against my legs, and I had to place a hand over my breasts to keep the fabric of the neckline from blowing open and exposing me to the world. Niall and I were still feeling the effects of being newly accepted mates, so the sight might be just enough to set him off. And I wanted to prevent that. No one else knew what I was to Niall—or what I was at all, so it was crucial to keep a low profile today, and then ravage each other again once we returned to Calledan.

As we entered the open breezeway, all of us glanced around. The last time we arrived, Ferhan greeted us almost immediately. But not this time. The halls were relatively quiet, save for the thrashing of curtains and banners throughout the courtyard. The sheer panels rose with the wind, sagging back to the columns in between gusts.

A fae female finally approached us once we were well inside the estate. "Welcome, honored guests." She bowed forward with a flourish of her hand. "Ramil thanks you for your attendance. The celebration will begin shortly. For now, you are invited to take refreshments in the main hall before I escort you to the event." She turned, expecting us to follow.

We did. But something felt odd.

I checked my mental shield, making sure it was intact and fortified.

There were no house-fae bustling through the halls like before. And despite the faint sound of casual conversation and laughter, there were no guests around the fountains or in the hallways. The fleeting voices sounded like phantoms on the wind.

As we traipsed through the palace, I looked off to my right, beyond the covered patio, and out past the multitude of pillars that separated the space. There, I could see several groups of finely dressed fae, gathered and mingling underneath swaying garlands of fresh flowers. A few long tables were all I could make out between them, before we rounded another corner, and the courtyard fell back out of sight.

Both Niall and Aremis had noted my gaze, and we all exchanged a look.

"Excuse me," I spoke up to our escort, "I think I just glimpsed the event back that way. Shouldn't we—"

"Oh yes," she said quickly. "But first, the host has prepared refreshments for all guests upon their arrival. This way."

We turned down another open hallway, and I glanced back at Aremis. The look he gave me said to be on alert.

Up ahead, the space became familiar. We were being led to Ramil's throne room. The same one Ferhan had brought us to when we arrived for Lumeri.

Upon entering, there was a small table with a tray of glasses filled to the brim with a bubbling pink liquid, adorned with small petals and fresh fruit. The escort plucked the stemmed glasses off the tray and handed one to each of us, with an all too pleasant smile.

None of us dared take a sip.

At the lack of interest in the drinks, the escort shifted on her feet, seeming agitated or offended. She looked around and cleared her throat, like her breath was slightly caught. Her smile faltered as she said, "Your host will be with you shortly." And with that, she was gone.

I set my glass back on the table and wiped my hands against my skirts. Niall and Aremis did the same as we all surveyed the space. Ramil's throne sat in the same place under sheer, draping fabrics, surrounded by a plethora of rugs and large urns full of purple flowers just as before. The incense that burned in all four corners of the room wafted high into the ceiling.

The space hadn't been decorated to receive guests like the other areas had. And it was *quiet.* All too quiet for a celebration to be getting underway.

Aremis's head was on a swivel. "Something's not right," he said quietly.

I looked back up again and watched the faint smoke rise and fall as it floated and swirled on the current of air throughout the room.

Then, I *sniffed.*

The scent seemed a bit overwhelming, and I cleared my throat. Incense had always smelled like burning flesh to me and was significantly off-putting. But this aroma had a slightly sweet smell that I couldn't quite pinpoint.

It smelled . . . for a moment . . . like . . .

Licorice.

By the time I turned and opened my mouth to sound the alarm to Niall and Aremis, my head began to spin. I stumbled to the side and Aremis caught me by the arm, but he wobbled a bit as well, and we canted several feet sideways across the rugs before finding our footing again.

The polished, red granite floors spun beneath me.

I jerked my head up at Niall and tried to open my mouth to speak, but nothing came out. It was as if my voice had been ripped from my throat, leaving nothing but the stubs of my vocal chords.

Niall's eyes flashed, and he tried to take a step toward me, but his legs gave out, and he went down onto his knees gasping.

I checked my shields, but they were gone.

Everything was gone.

I tried to summon my light, my telekinesis, *something,* but I felt hollowed out. Like an empty vessel. Everything had evaporated away.

Anxiety took over. I grasped Aremis's baldric—trying to move around him to get to Niall—but I went down onto my knees too, taking Aremis with me. We fumbled over each other as he tried to help me up, but it was useless. Our mobility was slipping away from us by the second.

Niall was only a few feet away, and yet I couldn't get to him. I tried to yell, but the sound died in my throat.

My body buckled on itself.

Auren . . . Niall's voice spoke one last time into my mind before it faded out completely, like he was retreating down a long corridor away from me.

Then, Ramil strolled through the doors as if on a breeze. He moved with haughty arrogance, and I seethed up at him as my body betrayed me and sank lower to the ground.

I felt like I was being pulled into quicksand.

Niall lurched forward over his knees with one hand bracing himself on the ground as he strained to look up at me.

"Having trouble, are we?" Ramil asked through the cloth that was tied around his nose and mouth. Ferhan and several guards followed behind him, all with their faces covered.

Aremis reached for the blades at his chest, but his arm fell back down clumsily to the rug. He did manage to throw an arm over me, trying to keep me close and protect me as much as he was able.

"I thought you'd put up more of a fight," Ramil taunted Niall, looking down on him as he strolled past. "And to think, you all willingly waltzed into my home, practically offering yourself on a silver platter. I must say, this is a bit anticlimactic, but it served its purpose. I ended up with three of you, when all I hoped for was one." I knew he smiled down at me through the mask that kept the smoke from affecting him. "I sincerely thank you for accepting my invitation."

Niall groaned in frustration and fury as he struggled to fight the poison.

Ramil turned and casually walked back to him. "You . . ." He stood over him with his hands clasped behind his back. "It seems you're never too far apart from *her* these days. That must mean something." Ramil looked back over to me.

I bit down on my tongue until I tasted blood. I would have snarled if my body would have allowed it.

"Oh yes, it means something. That, I am sure of. But look at you now."

He pressed the toe of his golden boot against Niall's side and pushed him over onto the rug. "Not so high and mighty now, are you *High Lord?*"

Niall's body slumped over so easily that anxiety crept up my throat like bile. The poison had drained him of his power. It had drained all of us almost instantly.

Aremis shook with rage beside me at the sight of his High Lord lying prone on the ground.

"Take this one away. I'll find use for him later," Ramil instructed. "I have what I need." He turned back to me as two guards came over and hoisted Niall up.

I struggled against the poison, desperately trying to get to my mate. My groans were mere whispers on my lips as I tried reaching out for him, but my limbs were heavy as lead. His eyes held no glow, but I could see the rage within them. The promise that we would see each other again.

Tears streamed down my face as I watched the guards drag Niall's limp body from the room.

Aremis's grip tightened ever so slightly on me—as much as he could muster.

"Utterly pathetic," the High Lord of Benmoor said as he watched the male he had once kept as a pet try to protect me. "Though it's admirable, it's to no avail." He gestured to the rafters above. "This was a hefty dose of The Proper Death, but it seems the two of you might need a little longer to feel the full effects."

My eyes went wide when hearing the name of the poison. Maeson had *shown* me this poison. Taught me about it. But my head was spinning, and it was hard to think straight.

"It's a shame you didn't just drink the wine. Would have been much quicker." He leaned closer and whispered, "Less suffering."

He quickly straightened himself. "A few more minutes should do. In the meantime, congratulations for my daughter are in order. I'm sure she won't miss the likes of all of you." He turned on his heel and motioned for the others—including Ferhan—to follow him out.

The sound of him barking orders ceased as the doors closed us in.

And with that, Aremis and I were left to our demise.

83
BITTER LILY

I GASPED FOR BREATH, BUT WANTED NOT TO BREATHE AT THE SAME TIME. I didn't know how much longer I had until I was completely unconscious. I could feel it creeping up on me, but I had to fight it.

Focus. What did Maeson say about The Proper Death? In the right doses, it could incapacitate. And it could kill if inhaled or ingested for long enough. My lungs grew tighter at the thought.

But what's the remedy?

I looked at Aremis who was now struggling to breathe. His eyes were bloodshot from straining, and he tried desperately to speak but failed. His hand trembled weakly on my arm, his grip faint. Then my eyes drifted from his face to the giant urn behind him in the corner of the room. It was full of purple flowers. Giant bunches of them, thriving in the hot air.

I'd thought it was strange the first time we came here—that flowers like that could prosper in a desert climate. Something about their long shiny petals seemed familiar, and I willed my mind to focus . . .

Then it hit me. The day that Maeson had shown me poisons in her cabin, she'd handed me a petal, saying, *Chewing a couple of these will save your life.*

The Bitter Lily! That's the antidote!

But the flowers were too far away, I would never make it with my failing consciousness and weakening limbs.

I swung my head around as quickly as I could, but it felt like I was moving underwater. When my eyes focused, I saw them. There, not six feet away, sat two urns—one on either side of the throne . . . where they had always been.

I could make it to one of them. I *had* to.

Without looking back at Aremis, I used what strength I had to dig my elbows into the thick carpets and drag myself inch by inch toward the antidote.

Aremis's hand slipped away from me, and it felt like losing an anchor to this world. My body felt heavier with every movement I made, yet my head felt lighter, as if it would lift right off my body.

White spots dappled my vision, and I clenched my jaw.

No. No. No.

I had to make it to those flowers. I would not let Ramil take me to Lyceius. I would not leave my mate or Aremis behind.

The poison crept along each vein in my body, seizing up what remained of my mobility, freezing up my blood. But I fought against it.

Three feet.

I moved inch by inch, hauling my legs—now heavy as boulders—behind me.

Two feet.

I heard Aremis choking on his breath.

One.

My left arm gave out completely and remained limp alongside my ribs.

Grunting in agony, I hoisted myself up with my right arm. The effort was just enough to reach the petals that draped over the edge of the urn, which seemed to stretch out toward my quivering, failing fingers.

I grazed the tip of the plant and willed the last of my strength to grasp as many petals as I possibly could. I yanked off an entire branch and watched my arm fall to the floor as dead weight.

My body shook in protest as I brought my face up to my limp hand and felt the tip of a petal touch my lips. I flicked out my tongue to capture it and bring it in between my teeth. Then, I bit down. As the petal split, the scant juices spread over my taste buds and zinged against my jaw with a sourness that made my eyes water.

The moment it entered my system, my fingertips began to tingle. I took more petals into my mouth, chewing furiously and coughing at the metallic taste. The tingling spread across my body, slowly fighting back the poison, waking my limbs back up.

A few moments later, I turned and crawled as quickly as I could to Aremis. Tears had streamed down from his eyes—which were still open—but he laid motionless, his gaze distant.

Please don't be dead! Please don't be dead!

My voice had not yet returned, but I screamed the thought in my mind over and over as I took his head in my shaking hands and spread his lips open, pushing multiple petals inside. I worked his jaw open and closed so that the fibers would break, and the juices would flow.

Seconds felt like hours, and then his eyelids fluttered. His gaze narrowed back to me, and he coughed.

I gasped as relief washed over me. *Keep chewing,* I mouthed, moving his jaw in motion to help him.

As the petals began to counteract all the poison coursing through his body, he reached up and grasped my arm. His eyes said a thousand words where his voice could not.

I slowly slid my legs underneath me as the feeling returned to them, and we helped each other sit upright.

The poison had worked from my feet upward, and the antidote had worked from my head down. The perfect counteraction—as Maeson had said. Had I not picked up that satchel that day in her cabin, we would probably be dead. Or I would—at the very least—be incapacitated and on my way to Lyceius.

Aremis shook his hands and rubbed his legs frantically as he finally returned to his full senses. He looked around, noting the mangled branch lying next to me. "The antidote . . ." he said in a rasped whisper. Then his eyes lifted, marking all the urns containing the flowers. "They're everywhere. But how did you know they would work?"

My voice caught, but I managed. "Maeson taught me about them. Ramil must keep them nearby in case he's ever poisoned unexpectedly. Thank the gods for his paranoia."

The fucking bastard. To poison us at his own daughter's engagement celebration? He probably found humor in watching us struggle, knowing the antidote was nearby but just out of reach. His first mistake was assuming none of us knew what the antidote was. He would be very disappointed when he realized one of us was educated on it.

Aremis coughed, then gripped my hand. "We need to get out of here, now."

"*No!*" My barely there voice cracked violently.

His expression turned frantic. "Auren, Ramil just tried to kill us, we cannot—"

"I will not leave my mate!" Even though the words came as a gravelly whisper, I knew he could hear the finality in them.

Aremis gripped my hand tighter. "Listen to me. Ramil is going to come back, and when he finds us, he will take us somewhere where there won't be an antidote nearby to save us. We're lucky he left us here thinking we were both too weak to move from where we fell. He won't make that mistake again. Niall will be okay. Ramil won't kill him. And his exposure ended when they took him from the room. We *will* come back for him, but right now, we *must* get out of here."

I shook my head in denial. I couldn't leave my mate.

Niall! I screamed down the bond as best I could.

Silence.

I had no idea where he was—where Ramil had taken him—and my heart was breaking with all the unknowns.

"Auren, don't let the mating bond cloud your judgment," Aremis pressed. I shot him a warning look, but he moved right past it. "I know you'll do anything to protect your mate, but to act now would be madness. You could harm innocents, or yourself, along the way, and still never find Niall. Ramil has catacombs that wind beneath this entire city. And right now, there's no time."

I shook my head, and tears began welling up in my eyes.

Aremis bit his lip and took both of my hands in his. "You can hate me now, but you'll thank me later."

A scream tore through my mind as he ripped me away.

84
THE FIRES OF VENGEANCE

WE LANDED ON THE PATIO OF THE KEEP, AND I IMMEDIATELY COLLAPSED into Aremis's arms in tears. He brought me down to the ground and held me against his chest as I sobbed in rage and anger and fear.

I wasn't angry at him. I understood his reasoning. But leaving Niall behind had ripped a gaping hole in my heart, and despair was quickly settling in.

I dove into my mind, searching for Niall's essence. Something of his that remained. The tether was there—an invisible strand that I could feel— but his essence was dormant, inaccessible.

We might as well have been worlds apart.

I screamed into Aremis's chest as he cradled me tightly.

Moments later, Roirdan and Remic burst through the doors and ran toward us. Remic was instantly down on his knees at our sides, his wings swept back as he demanded, "What happened?"

Roirdan stopped short, noting Niall's absence.

"We were ambushed," Aremis answered. "Ramil used the party as an opportunity to try to apprehend Auren himself. He set us up." He continued holding me, his grip never loosening even though his body shook from the effects of the poison.

Remic placed a gentle hand on my shoulder, and I turned and found his gray eyes. "Auren, do not forget who Niall is. He is powerful beyond measure. And we will get him back. This I swear to you."

His voice, and the promise that laced it, righted all the wrongs in my head. He was right. Niall wasn't weak. His power was untouchable.

But without his power—with that poison snuffing out his access to it—

No. I couldn't think that way.

He wouldn't want me to go down that dark path.

Remic helped me stand and steadied me as we made our way to The Keep.

Maeson came running from the stairs just as we entered, her eyes darting back and forth from Aremis to me. "Gods! What happened?"

"Poison," Aremis said, sounding out of breath.

I quickly wiped away another tear as I gathered my voice. "Ramil used The Proper Death, Maeson. Aremis and I would be dead, or I'd be on my way to Lyceius right now, if it wasn't for you."

Maeson shook her head in disbelief. "What do you mean?"

"The Bitter Lilies. Ramil's throne room was full of them. My guess is that he keeps them near at all times, in case someone ever tries to use the poison on him. Kind of like how Killian's father kept some close too."

Aremis's eyes swerved to Maeson, seeming to realize she had known something he didn't. He beheld her with surprise, probably wondering what else she knew of Killian's father.

"Maeson . . ." I paused, hating the words that were about to come out of my mouth, dreading them because speaking them only further solidified the rip in my soul. "He took Niall."

To my left, Roirdan seethed.

Maeson paled. "Oh Auren, I'm so sorry." She began shaking her head, then looked at Aremis. "Do you know where he's been taken?"

"The catacombs beneath the palace—most likely," he said, his expression sobering. "My guess is that he's somewhere near where Fallon is being kept."

"Fallon?" Maeson looked confused.

Right. She wasn't aware of Morah's brother—the rightful heir to the Desert Court's throne.

"I'll fill you in later," I told her. "Right now, I need to sit." My head was starting to feel full of pressure.

Remic guided me to the nearest chair, and I sank into it. Aremis slumped into the one next to me.

"You both need something for the aftereffects of the poison," Maeson said. "I'll be right back." She ported away.

Roirdan paced for a moment, hands balled into fists, jaw flexing. Then, needing something to do with his hands so he didn't put his fists through the wall, he gathered chairs for himself and Remic, and took a seat. His voice was low and gravelly as he asked, "So, what's our next move?"

I waited to hear any suggestions, but neither Remic, nor Aremis said anything. Instead, everyone turned to *me*.

"What?" I asked suspiciously.

Remic leaned forward awkwardly in his chair, trying to keep his wings splayed at just the right angle to allow him to even sit in it. "In fae culture, mates pull rank. You are the High Lord's mate. Therefore, you take his place in his absence."

Aremis and Roirdan nodded.

Remic's words slowly sank in. "Wait. You're saying that I . . ." My voice trailed off at the realization.

"You assume his role. Take on his title. And we follow your lead," Aremis confirmed. "Typically, there would be a mating ceremony first—to take vows before the gods and all that—but we know what the two of you mean to each other. We see it."

I worried my lip as I mulled over his words. "But what about the council—"

"Fuck the council," Roirdan spat.

Aremis sat up further in his chair as best he could. "When it comes to matters like this, it is *our* decision, as Niall's Trium. We have the final say."

I looked between them.

Their thoughts all seemed unanimous.

Maeson ported back and stumbled into Aremis's chair—which hadn't been there before she left. She cursed as her knee collided with it.

Aremis reached a hand out to steady her. "Careful," he said.

She looked at where his fingers touched her skin, and the rest of us watched as both their necks flushed with color.

When he let go, she snapped back into focus and turned to me. "Here, eat a few bites of this." She handed me a woven pouch full of dried herbs. "It will bind to the lingering poison and help soak it up. It can take several hours for it to filter out of your system without it. I'm surprised you were able to port back here while still under the poison's effects."

I nodded toward Aremis. "That was all him."

Maeson flickered her eyes to his once more, her gaze lingering on him for a moment before noticing the circle of chairs we now sat in. She glanced between all of us. "What exactly did I miss?"

"I've just been informed that I'm in charge now," I said skeptically, digging my fingers inside the pouch to get a pinch of the herbs, and coughing at their earthy taste as I passed the pouch to Aremis.

Maeson took a seat on the arm of Roirdan's chair. "Of course. You're the High Lord's mate."

"And this is just common knowledge?"

"Well, yes. Mates are everything to the fae. When a High Lord finds his mate, they are treated as equals. And since you have the power of Karios in your blood, you have even more of a right to the claim."

I slowly nodded.

Then, Remic's head jerked toward the mountain range out past the patio.

"What is it?" I asked.

"Someone's at the western gate," he said, standing quickly.

"Go," Aremis told him. "We've got this."

The Dionach ported away, and Roirdan stood, drawing his sword and pushing his shield out to encompass the room as he approached the doors.

Aremis got to his feet and moved Maeson and I behind him. We all watched out the giant windows in silence.

A minute passed, then Remic landed hard on the other side of the patio doors, wings splayed wide. Roirdan lowered his shield, and when the doors opened, we all gaped as Morah rushed in and headed straight toward me.

Her rich teal and gold gown whipped behind her, and the jewels hanging from the circlet she wore on her forehead jostled wildly as she closed the distance, eyes fixated on where I stood.

Roirdan made to stand in her path—not liking the way she was coming at me—but she held up a finger to him. "Don't," she commanded, and to my surprise he halted.

It was Remic that thrust out his arm and snagged her by the waist, hauling her back several steps.

"Let go of me!" she snarled, jerking against his grip.

He was solid as stone, not moving an inch as she squirmed. "State your intentions," he growled. "Now."

Finally, she stilled, and her eyes found mine. There was a plea behind them, creeping past her steeled exterior. "I want nothing to do with my father," she declared. "What he has done is unforgivable. I have no further ties to the Desert Court beyond my loyalty to my brother." She shook the hair from her face, and Remic loosened up on his grip. "And the Woodland Court can find someone else to burn alongside Killian, because it will not be me."

Everyone in the room watched her, waiting for her next words.

"I sensed something was wrong. Then Ferhan told me what my father had done." She paused, swallowing her fury and as it bubbled to the surface. "I've stated my intentions to you before, and I pledge myself formally, now. My allegiance is to you. If you'll have me."

Remic slowly released her, but she made no move to approach me.

Instead, I approached her. "Your father has my mate in chains," I said, slowing to a stop a few feet from her.

She lifted her eyes to me, tears threatening to spill over her lashes. "I know. And I swear before the gods that I will help you get him back."

There was a determination in her eyes, one that I had seen in the guest chamber in Benmoor, when she'd spoken about her plans to unseat her father and instill an uncorrupted leader—her brother—to her court. She knew what it was like to have someone taken and locked away at the hands of her father. The grudge she held against him was no longer just personal. It was on behalf of all of us.

I glanced at Aremis, and he gave me a slight nod. Remic and Roirdan didn't object either, though neither of them looked thrilled.

I lingered in thought a moment longer, before stepping up to her and taking her hands in mine. "It would be an honor to have you by my side."

Relief flooded her face, and to my surprise, she threw her arms around my neck. "Thank you," she breathed out.

I squeezed her tighter and said, "Just promise me you won't go around stabbing the Trium if they get on your bad side."

She let out a laugh. "I'll try my best." When I let her go, she donned a playful smirk. "No promises though."

Across from us, Aremis's mouth tilted up at the corners. Morah noticed and turned to him, her face smoothing into seriousness once more. "I'm glad the both of you made it out. And I'm deeply sorry that Niall didn't."

Before Aremis could reply, I said, "We're going to get him back."

"What are you thinking?" Morah asked.

"We do what we're best at. We fight. And we kill anyone who gets in our way."

Morah nodded in approval, as did Maeson. The Trium straightened at my words, as if being summoned to battle. The same determination flickered in their eyes, igniting the fires of vengeance deep within them.

I lifted my chin as I beheld the five who stood before me. My friends. My newfound family. Each of them cared for me, and I cared for them. I would rise to the challenge and be a strong leader in Niall's absence. It's what they needed. It's what *I* needed.

The reality of it was, we *were* preparing for battle—the likes of which we did not yet know. But I was not afraid. I would fight to the fucking death to get my mate back. With these five by my side, I would tear apart the world.

A glow settled around my skin as my power stirred in my chest and crackled along my veins, burning out the last of the poison, and ready to strike at my will.

I looked into my mind, into the void where Niall's essence usually greeted me, and found my own clutched onto the tether that was left.

I sent a thought to him. An unwavering promise.

I wasn't sure if he could hear it, but I tried anyway.

I'm coming for you, my love. And there's not a thing that can stop me.

ACKNOWLEDGMENTS

To finally have this book out in the world after three years of hard work is such a fulfilling moment. Not a single day has passed where I haven't wanted to be a hermit, locked away with my computer and my snacks, pouring my heart into every sentence I type. Each minute—each hour—that I've spent (and will continue to spend) with this story and these characters brings my heart so much joy. When the idea for this story came to me, I didn't know where it would lead, but I knew that it would take bits of my heart with it. I've always been the type of person to plan every little detail of everything I do, but when it came to writing this book, the characters had plans of their own. What spilled forth on the pages was equal parts "well-planned plot" and "where did this come from?" But I embraced the thrill of the process and surprised myself along the way. Auren's journey is a reflection of my own, in a way. Every aspect contains a little piece of my soul. And this book has reminded me that life has a funny way of getting you where you need to be, even if the path along the way is unexpected.

To my husband, who was the first to read this book and has seen it from its very beginnings—I love you more than words can ever describe. Thank you for all the countless hours of pouring through pages with me and listening to me ramble on about characters, backstories, plots, and concepts, and for telling me it's 2AM and I should probably get some sleep. Your love and excitement for this story fills my heart, and I'm so thankful for your enthusiasm and insight. I'm so blessed to have you by my side, cheering me on. Thank you for loving me truly, deeply, endlessly. Niall is the written embodiment of you.

To my parents, my biggest fans—thank you for your never-ending love and support, and for always encouraging me to chase my dreams. You've shown me that with hard work, perseverance, passion, and faith, anything is possible. Mom, you read books with me every night growing up. We embellished the voices and acted out the scenes like *we* were the characters. And those memories live on with me. It spurred my love for reading and writing. And for that, and much more, I thank you. Dad, you trained me in the Martial Art of Tae Kwon-Do since I was five. You showed me that a girl can be just as tough as the boys—even if I had to wear a padded chest protector when sparring, to keep from getting the air knocked out of me by a particular boy who had a mean left kick (my future husband). I really did live out the part where the book character is a badass who can defend herself with her fists, and a weapon. Thank you for that confidence, and the lifelong skills.

—I love you both to the moon and back.

(For all those who are wondering about what was mentioned above, I met my husband via Tae Kwon-Do when we were children. My father trained us both. Yes, we did spar each other. Repeatedly. Yes, he knocked the air from me more than once. And yes, I eventually punched him back.)

Enemies to lovers indeed.

To my editor Caitlin Lengerich—you're a true gem. When I came to you with over 200,000 words and a million questions, you didn't balk. Thank you for loving this book, the characters, and their story. Your feral excitement and enthusiasm has been so encouraging, and your feedback has meant so much. I'm so grateful for your insight, and your friendship along the way. I can't wait to answer every "WHAT DOES THIS MEANNNN?" you've ever asked.

To Olivia H. and Amber J.—I love and adore you both. Your encouragement and support while I talked about this unnamed, lengthy book I'd been writing for several years means so much. Thank you for taking the time to read it before it went out into the world, and for your priceless feedback. I'm glad you love reading as much as I do, because you're committed now. Get ready!

To all the friends and fellow authors that I've met on Bookstagram along the way—I want to thank each of you for your friendship. This journey has been a long one, and I wouldn't have gotten here without the wise words and advice from those who've traversed this path before me. I'm eternally grateful for you all.

And to you, the reader, thank you for spending your time between these pages. I hope that you found something about this book that you loved, and I hope you're ready for more. Niall and Auren's story is just beginning, and I think you'll be surprised at where I plan for it to go!

See you in the next.

ABOUT THE AUTHOR

Malarie has had a passion for writing since she was young, and has always loved the worlds and realms of fantasy. She also has a particular fascination with ancient history and culture, which she enjoys weaving into her stories. She holds a bachelor's degree in Art from Texas State University, and when she's not writing, she can be found drawing and illustrating in her art room, or reading in her personal library. She lives in the Texas Hill Country with her husband, and the two enjoy traveling abroad whenever possible.

Keep up with her on instagram:

instagram.com/abookshelfofmagic

www.ingramcontent.com/pod-product-compliance
Lightning Source LLC
Chambersburg PA
CBHW021928110726
47901CB00003B/755